THE BLOOD WITCH SAGA

THE COMPLETE SERIES

NATALIE J. CASE

Copyright (C) 2023 Natalie J. Case

Layout design and Copyright (C) 2023 by Next Chapter

Published 2023 by Next Chapter

Cover art by Lordan June Pinote

This book is a work of fiction. Names, characters, places, and incidents are the product of the author's imagination or are used fictitiously. Any resemblance to actual events, locales, or persons, living or dead, is purely coincidental.

All rights reserved. No part of this book may be reproduced or transmitted in any form or by any means, electronic or mechanical, including photocopying, recording, or by any information storage and retrieval system, without the author's permission.

THANÁTOU

NATALIE J. CASE

This book is dedicated to my family, both blood and chosen. You inspire me every day.

And to my beta readers/editors for the incredible feedback.

CHAPTER 1
OF UNKNOWN ORIGIN

My earliest memories are of blood, the hot, sticky taste of it on my tongue, the strange, copper scent of it suffocating me. I had no context for these things. I knew that I was small, and I knew that the stain of it was on my soul, but like so much of my life before I was ten, I could only guess.

That was where my life began, on my tenth birthday.

It began on a bench outside a police station one early Saturday morning. I was found in a semi-catatonic state, sitting with an old beat-up suitcase containing a few changes of clothing, and a backpack with a note inside giving my name, Thána Augusta Celene Alizon Archer, and age, along with a few books and a stuffed dog named Rusty.

I was found during shift change, and my next hours and days were filled with fear and disorientation as I was taken from the police station to the hospital, and from there to a group home. I spent the better part of a year there before they found me a place in foster care. All searches for my parents came up empty. All attempts to figure out where I'd come from came to nothing.

At times, nightmares would soak my dreams with terror, taking me back to that memory. I would wake gasping and rubbing at my skin, trying to clean the blood from it. I was always off-kilter for days when it happened, and it took me until I was nearly seventeen to realize that it always happened on the same night every year. I guessed it was some kind of anniversary.

I was luckier than some, my tour through foster care only saw three homes, and I only left the first one when my foster mother got a job transfer to Texas and the second one because the couple was divorcing. I arrived at my final foster home one week before the start of school my junior year of high school. I graduated near the top of my class, which wasn't hard considering the number of stoners in the class, and I managed to scrape up a few scholarships and grants to apply toward my state college degree. I worked at a bookstore just off campus to supplement my education and allow me to eat. It also served to keep me in books, and even allowed me to indulge my passion for "ye Old English" and the study of the surviving literature from the time. I was wise enough to know that the job prospects were small in such a rarified field, so I graduated with a business degree just generic enough to afford me a chance at almost any kind of job in the corporate world I decided to chase, though I continued to take elective classes to feed my love.

I entered the adult workforce a month after graduation, starting in a mid-sized company that produced small gadgets, at the time it was largely calculators and the like. I started in the quality control group. By the time I was nearing thirty, I had worked my way into middle management. The next year, our company got absorbed into a bigger company, and eventually, I was relocated to El Paso, Texas to work in one of their plants.

I was in a small rental apartment, most of my belongings still in storage back in New York, making do with a bed, armchair, and a bistro table. It wasn't like the place mattered all that much. I knew going in that it was temporary. I was going to be there a year tops before I was sent to Silicon Valley to manage a new product line. I was running late to work one morning in late October, thumbing through a file folder of employee reviews on my way to the car when I heard a man clear his throat. I glanced up and involuntarily took a step back.

The man was disheveled and out of place, his black, dust-covered clothes looking like something from an earlier century, or a black and white movie from the fifties. He had a hat atop his mop of black curls, which hung well below his shoulders, with a ridiculous feather tucked in the band. It alone seemed untouched by dust, or maybe it was sand, its blue and green ruffled by the light breeze. He cleared his throat again and stepped closer. "Thána Alizon?"

I wasn't sure who this man was or why he knew my name, even if he was pronouncing it as if the h wasn't there, but I found myself nodding slowly. "Thána, actually. Like thick. And my last name is Archer. And you are?" Alizon was a part of my name according to the note in my backpack all those years ago, but it had given my last name as Archer. It spooked me a little bit that he knew that part of my name.

"No one of consequence. I came to warn you."

My eyebrow arched of its own accord. "Warn me?"

He nodded urgently, stepping toward me again. "You are in danger here."

"Right." I dismissed him and moved to my car, unlocking the door, and tossing my briefcase and the review file onto the passenger seat. "Look, buddy, Halloween is next week."

"I know, that's what I'm here to warn you about. You must be vigilant."

"Right," I said again, getting into the car. "Go try your line on someone else. Halloween's a pain in the ass, but it isn't anything more. I'm late for work."

"Yes, very late," he said, his eyes lifting to the sky.

"Whatever." I started the car and pulled the door shut, shutting out the weird man and his weird warnings. If I broke the speed limit down Railroad Avenue, I might get to the office in time for the morning stand-up meeting. My assistant met me at the door of the conference room with a cup of coffee and my day started. It was much like any other day. I handled time off requests and sat in on meetings about circuit board quality and RMAs. By the time I left to go home, the strange man and his strange warning were all but forgotten, at least until I saw him again.

I stopped at a grocery store to grab a few things because I was sick of takeout in a town where takeout consisted of pizza and Tex-Mex burritos. I had a few things in my cart, and I was rounding the corner onto the cereal aisle when I saw him. He had his hat in his hands and he seemed nervous, more so than he had been that morning.

"Thána Alizon, you must hear me."

"Dude, are you following me?" I asked, fishing in my pocket for my cell phone. "I could call the cops."

He shook his head almost violently and held out one hand. "The police cannot help you. Let me."

"Look, I don't know what you think is going to happen to me, but I'm a big girl and I can take care of myself. So, get lost."

"You can't handle **this**, not without help."

"I've had enough of your crap. Leave me alone." I pushed past him in a fit of anger, grabbing a box of store-brand granola and throwing it in my cart on my way to the checkout. The man had put me in a foul mood, and I still had to finish employee reviews.

I purchased my meager supplies which mostly consisted of food I could microwave, the granola, and two bottles of wine. Fortunately, my apartment complex was only a few blocks away and I could get home, put away the food and open a bottle of wine. A nice pinot noir would be a good companion to reviews. It wasn't like I'd known any of these people for more than eight months, so my evaluation of them wasn't going to be at full value.

With a bag of microwave popcorn and a glass of pinot, I dropped into the comfort of the plush recliner. Taking a sip of wine, I tucked the popcorn between my thigh and the arm of the chair and reached for the folder. I'd groused that the process wasn't automated and digitized, but I'm fairly sure it fell on deaf ears. Our plant manager was the kind of guy that wanted everything in hard copy, even to the point of making his secretary print out all of his emails.

I worked my way diligently through the folder, and the bottle of wine, until I got to the last few reviews. I'd saved the hardest two for last. Juan Cordova and his buddy Rodrigo Alvaro, the two troublemakers on the line. With a sigh I got up to pour the last of the bottle into my glass, shaking my head as I considered how rough to be on them in the review. They were always the last two to come in for their shift, maybe not late every day, but cutting it close. More than once they'd come back from lunch break with the smell of beer or tequila on their breath. They did good work, most of the time, and Juan's soldering technique was among the best in the plant.

Deciding to come down closer to the middle, I wrote praise for what they both did well and marked them down for attitude and attendance, and called the whole thing done. I was ahead of schedule, which was how I liked it. I could start the one-on-one conversations with them the following week and have them all turned in to my boss before the November first deadline.

I downed the last of the wine, threw the popcorn bag in the trash, and decided to head to bed. It was early, but so was my alarm. I double-checked the door lock, changed into my pajamas, which basically meant a T-shirt and shorts, and climbed into bed. It was a warm night, and I pushed the comforter to the end of the bed and fell into the warm fuzziness of the slight buzz from the wine.

Pounding on my door woke me some hours later, pulling me up from dreams about blood and ash. I stumbled to the door, disoriented. Strong hands pulled me out of the door when I opened it, and that scared me into wakefulness. Sirens swirled in the air around me and the strong arms belonged to the building manager who was shaking even as he let go of me. The building was aflame, residents staring and standing sullen in puddles of water from the hoses trying to quench the flames.

I joined them, watching wordlessly as firefighters tried valiantly to save the building. I blinked and tried to climb out of my wine-soaked brain failure, my vision temporarily obscured by that frustrating and frightening memory. It wasn't coherent, and it changed from time to time, but there was always blood, a lot of it, and sometimes maybe fire. Someone died. Of that I was sure. I pinched the bridge of my nose and pushed the whole thing away. I hadn't figured the dream out in the twenty-two years since waking up on that bench, I wasn't going to figure it out standing there in a puddle of water in my bare feet in the early hours of the morning.

By the time the sun was up, the fire was out, and water dripped from what was left of the building. My apartment still had walls, but the ceiling had been burned away and everything inside was smoke and water logged. One of the firemen brought me some stuff from my dresser, including Rusty the stuffed dog, and my briefcase that had been near the door, and they rescued the folder from the kitchen counter, though that too had been soaked. Everything was dripping wet and stunk of smoke.

There was talk about where we would stay and how it would be arranged, followed by most of us breaking up into small groups. For once I was grateful to have left my cell phone in the car and for the fact that I kept a spare key in a magnetic box hidden under the back bumper. I called into work to let them know I wouldn't be in. My boss was sympathetic and told me to let her know if I needed anything. I sort of laughed and told her I needed just about everything.

That was when I saw him again, the strange man. His suit was clean and unwrinkled, his hair practically shined in the morning sun. His green eyes were watching me as I got out of the car and started toward the property manager. I detoured toward the man. "Did you do this?" I asked when I got close enough, my voice pitched a bit higher than normal.

"Of course not. I warned you."

"No, you were a cryptic creep. Is this what you were warning me about?"

"I told you it isn't safe. They know where you are."

"Who?" I asked, crossing my arms. It probably looked ridiculous in my shorts, T-shirt, and bare feet, but I knew that when properly suited for work, it had a withering effect on anyone I leveled the look at.

"I could explain it all if you would just come with me."

I shook my head. "I'm not going anywhere with you. Explain now or I'll tell the fire marshal that you were acting strange and following me."

He shook his head and tried to take my hand to lead me away. "Please, it isn't safe. They weren't sure which apartment you were in, but now you're exposed. They are probably watching us right now."

"Wait, are you saying that whoever started this fire was looking for me?"

"It fits their way. They would kill an entire building of people just to flush you out so that they could get to you."

I don't know if it was the fire, the old memory dancing in the back of my mind or what, but somehow his words chilled me. "Who would want me dead?" I asked, glancing around us. "I'm nobody special."

"It isn't so much you specifically, and they're trying to kidnap you…so that they can kill you later. Come with me, I will keep you safe."

"I'm not going anywhere with you. I don't even know your name."

He took a step back and removed his hat, sort of bowing toward me. "Forgive my manners. I am Finneas Connor. I was a friend of your father's."

That brought me up short. "My father?" I shook my head. "I've never had a father. Or a mother. You clearly have the wrong person."

"How many Thána Alizons do you think exist in this world? I am not mistaken. Neither are they."

"Who are they?" I asked, frustrated now that I'd let him draw me in this far. "You keep saying 'they' but you're not explaining."

"It is a long story, one better told by a warm fire with a glass of brandy. Come."

"I've had enough fire for one day, thanks." I turned away and started back toward my car. I needed to try to get the smell of smoke out of my clothes and find a pair of shoes and sort out what else I needed. I didn't have time for fairy tales.

"Who is that?"

I looked up to find the woman who lived in the apartment beside mine. "Some whack job," I responded. "He says he knew my father." I snorted and looked back at him. "I didn't even know my father, so…" I let the thought trail off before looking back up at her. "Sheila, right? So, what are we doing?"

"Chuck's getting us set up at that motel across the street, at least short-term. Bill has been through this before." She pointed at a man I didn't know. "He lost a house about five years ago. He said he'd help with getting through the Red Cross stuff and whatever. He's collecting information for them."

I nodded, locking my car with its reeking pile of clothes and my briefcase. At least I had that which meant I had my wallet, so I could get money. I followed Sheila to where Chuck, the building manager, was on the phone. All in all, there were about ten of us out of a home, all of us in our thirties and early forties. All of us without spouses or families. We were a sad lot.

By noon, we were checked into the motel and able to shower. Bill had scrounged up clothes for us with the help of the Red Cross. I pulled the track pants on without bothering with the underwear of unknown origin and tugged on the T-shirt over the sports bra they'd given me. The bra barely covered my larger than average breasts but held me in tight. Everything was very clearly secondhand, especially the broken-in sneakers, but I was dressed. That meant I could get food and clothes for work in the morning.

I returned to the bathroom to pull a comb through my hair once the mirror had defogged. My black hair was super curly, except that I visited a salon once a month to get it chemically straightened. Left to its own devices, it would become a mop of frizz. I seldom bothered with makeup, my vaguely olive skin was naturally smooth and evenly colored, and I'd always thought that eye shadow and mascara and the like were just too much work for every day.

My dark-green eyes looked dull and tired, which I suppose was a pretty fair assessment of my state of being at that moment. I wasn't sure how much sleep I'd gotten between the end of that bottle of wine and the fire.

Satisfied that I was presentable enough for hitting the mall, I grabbed my car keys and headed out, though I admit to glancing furtively around me as I went, vaguely afraid some boogeyman was going to jump out to grab me.

CHAPTER 2
WORDS ON A PAGE

My assistant, Jessica Flores, met me at the door with coffee and a frown the next morning. "Why are you here?"

I took the coffee and drank nearly half of it in one go. The motel had miserable coffee. "I work here, last I checked."

"No one expects you to be here."

"You did," I countered, lifting the coffee cup.

"Well, I know you better than the rest. Here are the notes from yesterday, I figured you'd want to see them before the stand-up."

"Thanks." In return, I handed her the now mostly dry file folder with the employee reviews. "I think I saved them. Mostly. Can you go through them and make sure everything is legible?" I took the notes, glancing over the page. "Have we figured out what is causing the excessive solder problem on the wave line?"

She shook her head. "John Padilla is going over the boards from yesterday. He thinks it's a board design issue."

I nodded and turned toward the conference room. "Make sure I get results from him by close of business." We parted ways, and I took a moment to take a big breath and steady myself before facing the assembled line supervisors and product managers. I waded through all of the platitudes and attempts at offering me comfort without actually throwing any punches, which I figured was something I didn't get enough credit for on a day-to-day basis.

By the time the end of the day rolled around, my shoulders were tight, and my head was throbbing, and I wanted to go back to the crappy motel and crawl into its crappy bed and try to sleep more than I had the night before. However, Jessica reminded me that we were supposed to be meeting at the Iron Horse for drinks for one of my inspectors' birthday.

I pulled into the local watering hole, which doubled as a biker bar, and promised myself a single drink and the minimal amount of socializing before I got out of the car. I half expected Finneas whatever his name was to be lurking in the shadows, or maybe his mysterious bad guys. I put him out of my mind and headed inside the Iron Horse Saloon, where I could see a group of my product line was already in full swing. Lupe, who was the birthday girl, was laughing, bent over the table as I came in and approached the bar.

I held up two fingers to the bartender, then indicated Lupe and dropped a twenty on the bar. Best to get my birthday drink out of the way early so I could skip out. Debbie poured two shots of tequila and hung a lime wedge on each glass. I took it to the table as Lupe sat up, wiping her eyes.

"Boss, you made it!" Lupe stood, her smile wide. "You didn't have to, you know?"

I smiled and handed her the shot. "Wouldn't miss it." One of the guys passed the saltshaker and I dutifully mirrored Lupe's movements to down the shot. They all moved seats so I could sit and my lead, Arturo, leaned close enough that I could hear him over the general din. "Hey, don't feel like you need to stay. We all know what you're going through."

I nodded at him. "I got nothing to go home to but an empty motel room with a crappy bed, worse coffee, and a broken hot tub."

He crinkled his nose, then lifted his hand to signal Debbie, then a circle to indicate he was buying a round. "I don't need another," I said.

He chuckled. "Everybody needs another."

"I have to drive home." Nevertheless, I did the shot with the rest of them. Which meant I had to stay and buy a round for the whole group.

Before I knew it, I was four shots in and starting to regret my decision to come in the first place. I got up to go to the bathroom and stopped at the bar on the way through. "One for everyone but me, I need caffeine and food. Peter still in the kitchen?"

Debbie nodded. "Nachos, fries, and some wings?"

"Am I that predictable?"

"Only when you're drinking tequila," Debbie answered. "You should stick to whiskey."

"Tell me about it." I was a little unsteady on my feet as I made my way into the tiny bathroom with two stalls that seemed to shrink every time I came in the place. My head was buzzy, and my stomach reminded me that I hadn't stopped for lunch that day, making that greasy roach-coach breakfast burrito at morning break my only food. I relieved myself and washed up, stopping back at the bar to give Debbie my credit card to run for the round and the food.

I hung around another hour, keeping to my diet coke, and eating until I felt like I was sober enough to walk the three blocks to the motel because I had no delusions about being sober enough to drive. I wished Lupe a happy birthday one last time and made my exit, tucking my keys between my fingers like they'd taught me in my sixth grade PE self-defense class because I had three blocks to walk, and it was close to midnight in a city that had a lot of violence. Not that I had a lot of illusions about fighting off thieves and rapists, but I wasn't afraid to slash and run.

I could walk back and get the car in the morning. Most of the walk was through a residential area, but the last of it was on well-lit and busy streets. I was cutting through the parking lot of the nearly defunct shopping center and could see the door of my motel room when I heard tires squealing and looked behind me to see a car barreling right toward me. I ran toward what I thought was the safety of the building, but it kept coming, picking up speed.

I jumped to the side, falling and rolling on the broken concrete as the car crashed into the brick wall of what had once been a Dillard's department store. Climbing to my feet, I was already cursing, and obviously not thinking clearly as I yanked open the driver's side door. I only had a second to look before hands were grabbing me and pulling me away.

"Are you crazy?"

I blinked into Finneas's eyes, confused as he pressed me into the wall around the corner from the car. "I'm not the one driving like a fucking lunatic." I pushed him away and moved back to the corner. I could have sworn there was no one behind the wheel. Now there was no car, just the impression it had made in the wall. "What the actual fuck is going on?"

"Like I've been trying to tell you, someone is after you. They would prefer to take you alive, but dead works too."

I rounded on him, shoving him against the wall. "For all I know that someone is you. None of this started happening until you showed up here."

He held up both hands in surrender. "No, not me. As I said, I am a friend of your father's. We heard rumors that someone caught your scent, so I came to try to find you before they did." He chewed his lower lip and bobbled his head a little. "I probably led them to you, now that I think on it, so maybe you're not wrong."

"Tell me why I'm not dragging you up the street to the police?"

"They can't protect you," Finneas said.

"And you can?" I asked, less than amused by the turn my whole existence had taken since this man had come into my life.

"Gods, no. I can only help you find help. My gifts are largely passive, tracking and the like."

"So, help me, you had better start making some sense or I'm going to start throwing punches," I growled the words, getting more irritated with the man as the seconds crawled by.

"May I suggest we get off the streets? No telling where your would-be assassins have gotten themselves off to." He gestured toward the motel, shrugging me off, and ducking around me before straightening his suit coat and adjusting his hat. He set off at a brisk pace, leaving me no real choice but to follow.

I unlocked the door and opened it, my eyes searching around the gloomy room. I half expected someone to jump out of the shadows at me.

"Not to worry, I warded the place before I came to find you," Finneas said, as he held a hand to the door and then murmured something I didn't catch. The whole door seemed to shimmer and then he was pushing me in and following. There was a wooden box on the bed, a trunk really, beautifully carved with ornate scrollwork, and a silver clasp. "I've been holding that for you since…well for quite some time."

"Who **are** you?" I asked, half certain that the answer to that question would only raise ten more.

"Just a family friend."

"I have no family," I responded, though the bite in my words was dulled by my distraction with the box.

"You may find you are wrong," Finneas responded, bowing slightly.

I inhaled, tearing my gaze from the trunk to look at him. I was tired, half-drunk, and ready to be done with all of it. "Get out."

"I'll leave you to your business, but I will be near enough to protect you until you are safe." He tipped his hat toward the trunk. "I think you'll find that your transfer to San Francisco will come sooner than you expect. You need to get there soon. You'll be safer there."

I turned to the trunk, fingering the clasp. "What do you mean I'll be safe…" I turned to look, but Finneas was gone, just like the car.

"Fucking tequila," I muttered. I rubbed my head and stared at the trunk, not entirely sure I wanted to know what was inside. For the moment I decided it could wait and I went to the bathroom to get a glass of water. My head was not going to be a fan of me come morning.

Still rubbing at my head as if that could stop the impending headache once I was sober, I sat on the bed, turning the trunk to face me. It was only slightly smaller than my old steamer trunk had been, but much more beautiful. The bulk of the trunk was a pale wood, nearly white, but the scrollwork and accents were in a rich mahogany. The lock was unlike anything I had seen before, and I wasn't sure exactly how I was supposed to open it.

There was something that looked like a button, so I pressed it. For a moment nothing happened.

"Right thumb, please," a voice said.

I looked around, half expecting that Finneas had returned from wherever he had gone, but when the strange man didn't appear, I lifted my right hand to the box and touched my thumb to the lock. There was a whirring sound and then a pop, and the lock opened. For a long moment, I just stared at it, trying to decide if I was drunker than I had thought I was, but really? I had seen a car ram into a brick wall and then just vanish, and a man had disappeared between one word and the next and a strange box had spoken to me.

So, yeah, I decided that it was the tequila and vowed to never let them make me drink it again.

Still, curiosity won me over and I eased open the trunk's lid, shifting closer slowly, half-convinced something was going to jump out of it and eat my face. Instead, I found a neatly ordered trunk filled with what seemed to be family memorabilia from a family I didn't even know. There were baby clothes and a silver rattle, an envelope of baby teeth and as I shifted some of it, my hand found something heavier.

I lifted it slowly. The binding was old leather with an unusual coat of arms etched into the front and it was bigger than a phone book. I sat back against the headboard and let one hand caress the leather reverently. Whoever had crafted this book had been skilled.

I opened the cover, my breath short and escaping from behind my teeth which had clamped down over my lower lip as my heart raced. I don't know exactly what I was expecting, but the first page deflated those expectations.

The words appeared to be in some foreign language that might have been an approximation of Greek or maybe some Cyrillic language, or something like it, but I was only guessing based on some tickling in the back of my brain that I couldn't identify. I couldn't read it, and that was the important bit. With a little less trepidation, I turned a few pages until I came across something I did understand, pictures.

They were old, ancient even, faded and yellowed, the sepia tones bleeding into one another as wizened old faces grinned out of them. Clothing from a century ago or more hung from gaunt frames while toothy grins beamed at the camera. Women wore furs and had hair swept up off graceful necks while men wore suits and hats, not unlike what Finneas wore.

The quality of images improved a few pages in, and I was starting to notice which faces went with which faces, and as I turned another page, I saw a face so similar to mine, I had to look up at the mirror across the room from me to confirm what I was seeing.

She was younger than me, and the picture was sixty or more years old, but those dark eyes that gleamed in a bright afternoon sun were my eyes, and the thick, unruly black hair that hung in curly sheets, all puffed up in the humidity was the image of my own, or mine before I had chopped it to shoulder length and paid a fortune to have it straightened every month.

Her skin was far fairer than mine, however. I baked in the sun like a Thanksgiving Day turkey does in the oven, my skin going from pale olive to a roasted tan that let me blend in with the locals enough that everyone was surprised I didn't actually speak Spanish, other than the little bit I remembered from Ms. Lorenzo's Spanish class in high school.

My finger caressed over her young face, then as I turned a page, an envelope fell from the book, sliding to the floor under my leg. I set the book aside and retrieved the envelope, turning it over to find my name in a beautiful script. It was just my first name, and it was only plain blue ball-point ink, but it struck me hard. I don't know why, but suddenly it was real…or something.

This trunk had belonged to someone before me, someone who knew me. Someone who was family.

I put the envelope down and stood, pacing to the door, then around the bed, and into the bathroom, round and round while I pulled my hands through my hair and shook my head and tried to deny that any of the last week had happened.

My family was gone. I had accepted that fact a long time ago. I had no family. I had filled those empty holes with my work. I didn't need old wounds ripped open by some fucking magical box from some family who had abandoned me on a park bench when I didn't even know who the hell I was.

I wasn't doing this. I shoved the envelope back into the book, put the book in the trunk, and put the trunk on the wobbly table by the window. I slammed down another glass of water and brushed my teeth, double-checked the lock on the door, and turned off the lights.

I was going to forget the whole damn thing.

CHAPTER 3
MERRY MEET

My plan worked, to forget the entire week, to forget Finneas, and not look at the trunk. I got through the weekend, got Rusty and my smoked-out clothes to the laundromat to rid them of the final remnants of that mess, and I even went to a Halloween party that a coworker was hosting at her new McMansion in the new subdivision and stayed for nearly a half-hour before I claimed a headache and took off for the motel.

By the time Monday rolled around I was able to put it behind me, as long as I didn't look at the wooden trunk. To solve that problem, I put it in the trunk of my car. Out of sight, and all of that.

Monday, I was juggling my coffee and briefcase to get my badge out of my pocket, when my boss opened the door for me, grinning like she had a secret. "Either you let your husband back in the bedroom, or you got Jaime to actually study for a test," I joked.

She followed me to my desk. "Remember when you told me you couldn't wait to get out of here?"

I raised an eyebrow. "You mean, the day I landed here? It grows on you." The city would never be home, it was too dry, dusty, and stifling for that, but I had started to get used to the place.

She nodded knowingly. "Yeah, but you're not going to say no to a transfer."

That got my attention. "What?"

She held up a hand. "It's not exactly what was promised, but they have a product line that's struggling, and their manager just walked out. Corporate office wants to send you out early, see if you can get it on its feet again."

"Isn't that what I was supposed to be doing here?" I asked, turning on the computer.

"You have. Your line has improved tremendously. I'm giving it to Alex. It's a step up for him. They want you in San Francisco by the end of the week."

I blinked at her, trying to catch up. At least I didn't have a house to sell, or much in the way of belongings. "Okay…so what's the incentive for me?"

"Pay increase now, and another when you get the move to the new product line, plus a housing benefit for the first three months to give you time to get settled. They have corporate housing. There's a furnished apartment waiting on you."

I sipped my coffee and nodded slowly. "I guess I better get Alex in here and start getting him up to speed." Alex was a good guy, and he had the chops to be a good manager. He'd started out on the lines, moved up to line lead, then to inspector, and from there he had been working under a senior product manager for more than a year while he finished his BA. This would be his first position with the title manager, but he had the skills.

I spent the time from then to the morning meeting getting my things together for him, which was fairly easy, considering I always knew the job there was short-term. I'd expected another six months, in reality, but I wasn't going to argue with the change. I wanted out of El Paso after the week I'd had.

We told the product line later that day and had a brief going away party at lunch on Tuesday. Before the sun was up on Wednesday, I was on the road, headed west. It was October 31st, Halloween. I wasn't a big holiday person. Holidays always made me feel like the interloper I was, lurking in the background of my foster family's happiness.

Halloween was worse than Christmas at times. My costumes were always hand-me-downs from years past, worn by other foster kids before me and trick-or-treating always felt far too close to begging for me to be comfortable. It was just as good to be on the road then. I wouldn't have to deal with trick or treaters or anything.

I got as far as Los Angeles and got a hotel room. I left the mysterious trunk with its mysterious contents in the trunk of the car, but pulled in my suitcase, and grabbed Rusty off the dashboard. Maybe it was silly, a grown woman hauling around a stuffed animal that was so threadbare and worn, patched in multiple places, and goofy looking, but it was the only thing I had left of the time before, and I'd gotten accustomed to always having him near.

I planned on ordering pizza and getting a good night's sleep so I could head out fresh in the morning. It was six and a half hours to the corporate housing place, and I wanted to get there with enough time to check in with my new boss.

Two bites in, there was a knock on my door. I muted the TV, which I'd set to a news station, and went to the door. I looked through the peephole, squinting at the old woman on the other side. "Girl, stop eyeballing me and open this door," the woman demanded, making me step back.

"I don't know you," I responded, frowning at the door.

"Of course you don't, but I aim to fix that. Now, open this door."

I will probably never understand the impulse at that moment to do as she said, but I unlocked the door and opened it. There in the hotel hallway was the most unlikely woman I had ever seen. She was old, in her eighties or nineties maybe; I'm a terrible judge of age. Her hair was an array of white with blue, purple, red, and yellow braids that were arranged in a mess of swoops and loops spilling out from under a precariously perched green top hat with yellow tulle exploding out one side.

The wrinkles around her eyes seemed to make them sharp somehow, and her nose showed signs that it had been broken at some point in her life. Her emerald green dress was like something from a Victorian painting and yet didn't seem out of place in the least. She tut-tutted at me and waved her intricately carved cane in my direction before bustling herself over the threshold and into my room. "Not even a beginner's warding. Really, this simply won't do!" She dropped an old-fashioned handbag onto the bed and turned to look me over. "Close the door, dear. You're letting in the bugs."

I was staring. I knew I was staring. I shook my head and closed the door, confused about what exactly was happening. "Who are you?"

"Ah, yes. Good. You have at least some common sense then. I am Merry Ander-Wheather. Your—" she squinted at me like she was trying to remember something, "Your great-aunt."

"What?" I was still stuck on the sight of her and the way she barged into the room. I looked at her again and realized. "Finneas." I pinched the bridge of my nose and held my breath, wishing the whole mess away.

"The dear boy did say he was having trouble getting through to you. That's why I'm here instead. We felt maybe family would be more—"

Cold rage dumped into my stomach, and I threw the piece of pizza in my hand in the general direction of the box. "I have no family." I ground the words from between my teeth and stepped toward her menacingly. I had nearly a foot of height on her, but she was clearly not intimidated.

She drew herself up to her full height, planting her cane between us like some kind of boundary. "You may not know it yet, Thána Augusta

Celene Alizon, but you do indeed have a vast and varied family who have spent **years** looking for you."

I took a step back. "I'm not that hard to find." I had never heard my full name pronounced that way. Like Finneas, she said Thána with that odd inflection, the h nearly silent. I'd only ever seen the full name written, on that note in my backpack that day. Everyone ignored my middle names. I was just Thána Archer most of the time, though I did have a couple of foster sisters that called me Arch. I turned away from her, hiding the tears that had welled up unexpectedly. "I lived in the same town for years."

She was staring at me; I could feel her. "I mean, the same place where I was left. Twenty-two years ago." The anger stirred again, and I turned back. "You should have started there."

Her black eyes softened, and she nodded sadly. She pulled the only chair in the room closer to her and climbed up on it. She was so short her feet didn't reach the floor. "Oh, mi paidí, I know." Her voice took on an accent of some sort, but I couldn't place it. Maybe Greek, but not really. "If we had known where she took you...but everything was so—" she waved her hands and shook her head. "There is time for that when we are all safe."

"Safe?" I asked. "Safe from what? Disappearing cars?"

"Finneas told us, of course. Their methods are crude." She shook her head. "There is much for you to learn, dearest Thána. So much. For now, let us just call them 'those that wish you dead'."

I closed my eyes and pinched the bridge of my nose again, as if the action could magic me back to before Finneas. It was all too much. My stomach churned with rage, mixed with an age-old desperation for family, and I thought for a moment I might be sick from it all.

"I should have come myself to begin with, but then, I am no tracker like Finneas."

I turned to look at her, and for a moment I was reminded of a woman's face I had seen in that book that was in the trunk Finneas had given me. It was the eyes. Her face was set round with wrinkles and her hair had lost the shiny black of youth, but her picture was in the book. "So, Great-Aunt then?" I asked. "And you're here to...what, exactly? Tell me I'm a fairy princess and whisk me away to a magical land to ride unicorns and drink dewdrop tea?"

She snorted. "Heavens no, child." She shook her head vigorously and laughed so that the entire chair shook. "No royal blood in either of your family lines...well, except that Lord...whatshisname five generations back on your father's side, but his family was disgraced long before we rejected the monarchy as a governing system." Her eyes swept the room. "Where's the trunk?"

I was frowning so hard my face hurt and I tried to force myself to relax the muscles, at least a little. "What?"

"The trunk. Finneas did give you the trunk?"

Right, the one with the magic lock on it. "It's in my car."

"Oh, no, that won't do." She stood up and bustled to the door. "It's not safe out there."

"It's fine," I answered. "It's locked in the trunk."

"Oh, child, you have much to learn. We must bring it inside."

"I don't want it inside," I said abruptly, moving so I was between her and the door. "I don't want it at all, honestly."

Her face clouded over, and she stared at me for a long time like she couldn't believe I had said such a thing. "You can throw away your heritage, Thána, if that is what you desire, but it will not protect you one little bit from those who mean to end you before you've begun. Now, go and get the trunk, and be quick about it."

I grabbed my keys from the dresser, shaking my head as I went out the door and down the stairs to my car. I popped open the trunk and took the ornate box out, setting it on the ground so I could close the trunk again. I had no idea why I was humoring the crazy old woman. If I'd had to guess it was that little girl inside who ached with not knowing her family, latching on to the first semblance of family that presented itself.

When I got back to the room, Merry was busy emptying her handbag on my bed. I shut the door and crossed the room to put the trunk on the table. "What are you doing?" I asked.

Merry didn't answer, just started humming and she took a bag of rocks to the door. I watched her stack them in sets of two. The rocks were nearly perfect cubes and they seemed to catch the light as she moved. When she had four sets of rocks spaced evenly across the front of the door, she sat back, her mouth moving, though I heard no sound.

There was a flash, and something seemed to extend up from the rocks to cover the door. It was see-through, but it shimmered in the light from the nearby lamp. "There now, that's better."

I squinted at the door and moved closer. "What is it?"

"Wards," Merry answered, moving back toward the bed. "A simple sort of wards to guard a door or window."

I ghosted my hand over the shimmering surface. Static electricity filled the gap between my hand and the barrier, prickling my palm with energy. When I turned around, Merry had retaken the chair and was happily munching on a piece of my pizza.

"I'm starting to think this whole thing is just some crazy tequila-fueled nightmare," I muttered, shaking my head. "Maybe if I go to sleep now, I'll wake up back in my apartment and none of this will have been real."

Merry apparently found that funny, her eyes twinkling at me as she chuckled. "Come, Thána, you know in your heart what is real." She tapped the box with her cane. "Open."

"You're awfully bossy for a woman I just met," I muttered, but I dutifully pressed my thumb to the lock and the lock opened. I reached into the box and pulled out the book, opening it where the envelope had been stuck into it.

"You haven't read it yet?" Merry asked, jabbing a finger at the envelope.

"No." I still didn't want to read it. Instead, I pointed to a picture. "Is this you?"

She leaned in, her eyes crinkling as one finger traced over the much younger face. "Ah yes. The woman beside me is your grandmother, my sister. Her name was Celene Edith. Now she was a powerful woman."

I looked back at the picture. Celene Edith stood inches taller than Merry in the image, a rich-looking fur coat drawn around her. She was well-coiffed, her dark hair smoothed and shaped and swept up into a tidy knot while Merry beside her looked like she had crawled out of bed for the picture, her hair a wild mass of black curls.

"You should read the letter."

Merry's voice pulled me back from the picture and her finger poked the envelope closer to me.

"Maybe I don't want to," I responded. "What good could it do? It doesn't change the fact that I was left abandoned with no memory of who I was." The words sounded overly bitter, even in my ears. I was behaving like an adolescent.

I snatched the envelope and paced the room with it. Unopened, it was nothing significant, just some artifact of a long-forgotten past. Once it was opened, everything changed.

"I can tell you only that you were loved, child," Merry said, her words softly hanging in the air between us. "Your mother saw no other recourse to keep you safe."

"My mother?" I had long ago come to grips with the notion that either my parents were dead, victims of some horrific death that was so great I blocked it, and them, from my mind completely, or that they were heinous people who couldn't be bothered with me.

Neither of them gave me great comfort, but it seemed easier than what Merry was saying, what secret this envelope held. "I can't take you the next step on this journey until you've read the words your mother left for you," Merry said.

I sighed and turned the envelope over. I was being silly. Just open it. I slipped a finger under the flap and broke the seal. A folded piece of paper was all the envelope contained. I pulled it out and unfolded it, turning to the light from the window to read it.

CHAPTER 4
REMEMBER ME

My dearest Thána,

My beautiful child, forgive me for what I have done. I was desperate to keep you safe from the men who killed your father. I hoped that by blocking your gifts and hiding us from your memory you might escape their grasp.

The spell I used was powerful magic but has already begun to erode. If you are reading this, a blood tracker was able to find you, and the time has come for the spell to be undone.

The words below will pull the string and allow your gift and memory to unspool. Everything you need is here in this trunk. The house awaits you; the key and deed are here.

If I can, I will come to you there and we can be a family once more. Until then, be safe.

Love,

Alana Alizon, your mother

I WANTED TO CRUMBLE THE PAPER UP AND THROW IT AWAY, BUT MY EYES WERE drawn to the tidy script over and over. At the bottom of the page, there was a series of strange words, foreign and weird. My mouth moved, sounding out the words in a hushed rush. "*Me aftés tis léxeis, anatrépste ti échei gínei.*"

"*Ginei*, the G should sound like a Y..." Merry said as she watched me. "And soften the x in *léxeis*."

I repeated the words with her corrections and held my breath. I don't know what I was expecting, but nothing obvious happened.

Merry, on the other hand, looked thrilled. "Good, good. You should probably sleep now. That spell will take its toll."

"And what about you?" I asked.

"I'll be right here, keeping watch. No matter how open the veil is, no one will find you tonight."

I was certain I wouldn't sleep, not with a strange woman in the room, not with so much happening that seemed impossible. I pulled back the blankets and slid into the bed while Merry moved around the room turning off lights. She hummed softly to herself and settled back into the chair. My mind churned around the words of the letter. My mother and father had once been a part of my life. I had no idea what either of them looked like, what their voices sounded like. No matter how I strained for the memory, all I had was static and blood.

I don't know how long I spun around and around with questions and doubts and that nagging question about my sanity, but eventually, it spun me down and unconscious.

I woke to the smell of coffee and the sweet, yeasty scent of donuts. Merry was sitting in the same chair, feet tucked up under her, a pair of glasses perched at the end of her nose, a powdered donut in one hand, a tattered paperback in the other. On the table in front of her were two steaming cups of coffee and from the smell of it, not the usual motel swill.

I stretched slowly, feeling each joint pull and realign and come back together before I slid out from between the sheets to get to my feet. I eased into the bathroom and shut the door, thinking about the drive ahead and wondering if my newfound relative was planning on riding with me. I did my business and washed my hands before emerging back out into the main room.

Merry looked up from her book and nodded at me. "Better. I got breakfast." She nudged a white paper bag toward me as I came closer. "Chocolate frosted with sprinkles."

I blinked at her, but it was too early for the likely answer to my question about how she knew, so I just accepted it and took the donut and my cup of coffee back toward the bed. I drank half the coffee gone before I went after the donut, and when that was half gone as well, I cleared my throat. "Is it safe to assume that you will be joining me for the ride north?"

"Someone's got to keep you alive," Merry responded. "How's your head?"

I frowned at her. "My head?"

She shrugged. "Figured you might be a bit tender. You did just rip off a twenty-year-old Band-Aid last night."

"I'm fine." I frowned at my donut, trying to figure out what she meant. "A hot shower, then I'm ready to go." I finished my donut, then the coffee, and headed back into the bathroom. A part of me still believed I was going to wake up to find it all a dream.

I showered efficiently, scrubbing my fingers through my hair, and tilting my head back to rinse the shampoo out. I kept my thoughts centered on the drive and what to expect when I got there. I froze as I reached to turn the water off, suddenly remembering words from my mother's note. *"The house awaits you; the key and deed are here."*

I climbed out of the shower and started to towel off, then wrapped a towel around myself, though it was too small to cover me completely, and opened the bathroom door. Merry still sat in the chair, donut, and book in her hands.

"What house?" I asked, pulling my suitcase up onto the bed.

"Your house, of course," Merry said, as if the answer was obvious.

"I have a house?" I was frowning again. I forced myself to stop. An image floated up from the dark recesses of my mind, a blue cottage-style house, with a big, grassy backyard. It felt familiar, though I would have sworn I'd never seen it.

I pulled on pants and a shirt from my suitcase and crossed to the wooden trunk, opening it and looking through the various papers and mementos until I found the deed. It was old, the paper yellowed, and it seemed to be written in Spanish, but the dialect was unlike any I had ever seen. I translated what I could before I looked through the attached pages.

Essentially, the land had been granted to my mother's ancestor, back when California had still been held by Spain. It had included five acres, which eventually was whittled down to one acre as the family sold off lots over the years. On that acre sat a house, and behind it stretched a wilderness area and garden.

I set aside the deed and looked in the box for the key. I found a small velvet bag and opened it to find a set of keys, and stones like Merry had put at the door. I dumped them into my hand and rolled them around. They felt familiar, but the thought was fleeting, and I couldn't hold on to it.

"We should get moving," Merry said. "The blood tracker could already know where you are."

Putting everything back into the trunk, I had another image bubbling in the back of my brain, a woman with dark hair and dark eyes, tears on her face telling me I would be okay, and it was for the best.

I shook my head to clear it. Was it my mother? I had no memory of her to compare the image to. I blinked away tears I didn't want to shed. I had put my thoughts about family away a long time ago. I didn't need them creeping up to cripple me.

"Let's go." I nearly growled the words, though my frustration was only with myself. Merry didn't deserve that. I sat on the bed and pulled on my boots before zipping up my suitcase and closing the trunk.

Merry mumbled some words and picked up her stones, secreting them away into a pocket. She picked up the trunk and nodded. Together, we left the room and went down the stairs to my car. She stood behind it for a long time, her eyes closed.

"They haven't caught up yet, but they can't be too far behind. And who knows how many of them got through while the veil was at its thinnest," Merry declared as I opened the car trunk and put the suitcase in.

I took the trunk from Merry and tucked it in beside the suitcase. "Are you ever going to tell me who 'they' are?" I asked as we climbed in, and I started the engine. "And why they want to kill me?"

She didn't respond until I had us on the freeway headed north. "They are a...religious order, for lack of a better term. Very old-fashioned notions about your kind. They are the reason there are so few of your kind left. They believe you are the kin of Hathus."

"My kind? Hathus?" I asked, sparing a glance at her. She was staring out the windshield, her face unreadable.

"Hathus is the god of the dead. These people call your kind *thánatou*, the death bringer."

"Excuse me?" I managed not to drive us off the road but earned a few angry horns from drivers beside and behind us. "Death bringer?"

She shook her head. "You are a blood witch, Thána. You eat disease and flush it out through your menses. Sometimes that heals the sick. Sometimes it eases them into the next life."

What? What I was hearing simply couldn't be real. That was Hollywood stuff. It was ludicrous. "I don't understand anything you're saying."

"I speak the truth. You will know it soon enough. In the meantime, we need to beat these fanatics to a place that is safer, strongly warded against their trackers."

I shook my head, but the words kept rolling around inside me. Blood Witch. Death Bringer. Sparks of knowledge flared in my mind, but none of them brought any clarity. Splatters of memory, unconnected and unexplained followed words that sounded like a made-up language, maybe. At least they weren't Spanish, German, or Hindi. I was familiar enough with those sounds.

Some part of me kept telling myself that they had the wrong person. I was no witch. I didn't believe in witches or magic or whatever god this woman was talking about. Hell, I didn't even believe in the gods I was familiar with.

I would explain that to the next would-be assassin, I decided. Once they knew that I was just a middle-management corporate lackey, they would leave me alone.

Right. I managed to believe that until we were nearing the turn-off for Los Baños. It was almost one in the afternoon, and I pulled us off to find lunch. Merry stirred from her spot, yawning, and looking around us before nodding.

The truck stop was busy. I pulled up to the pumps and got out to fill the tank while Merry fussed with her shoes and her hair, which had all sort of shifted to one side while she slept in the passenger seat beside me. She shuffled off in the direction of the bathrooms while I pumped.

I was alone then when it happened. Out of nowhere, hands grabbed me and pulled me backward between the pumps and I could feel the sharp edge of a bladed weapon against the skin on my neck. I held up both hands in surrender and stilled my instinct to try to run.

"My wallet is in the car," I said, though part of me was quite sure no thief was brazen enough to strike in broad daylight in full view of the security cameras like that.

"We don't want your money, *Thanátou*." The voice was gruff and even without seeing my assailant, I could tell he was angry.

"Okay, what do you want?"

"To bleed you dry and end your blasphemous life."

That escalated quickly. "Here?" I have no idea why that was my response. He pulled me back, one hand fisting in my hair. We turned, and I could see where he was taking me. This wasn't happening. The corral that hid the station's trash was in front of us. Sure, I thought, that seems a much more likely place to be stabbed.

"Hey!"

Two men were coming toward us, and they started running when my assailant flashed the knife in their direction. "Stay out of this."

"Not today, pal." The first of them was within striking distance and I was whirled to the side, into the fencing of the corral. His hand was firm, pressing my face into the fencing while he brandished his weapon at my would-be saviors. I squirmed, but all it accomplished was the fencing embedding itself in my skin. I heard sirens in the distance and wondered if someone had called the cops.

I would hope so. It was the middle of the day after all. The sound of a punch landing intruded on my thought and the man holding me fell back against me.

"Knife."

"Yeah, I see it."

I tried to turn to see, but all it showed me was the back of the man's head. Then he shuddered, and the knife clattered to the ground. His hand left my head and I pushed off the fence and away from him. I could see police cars now, at least two of them closing on us. My assailant growled and shoved my rescuers off of him before he fled. Several of the arriving officers gave chase. I got a good look as he dodged around a car. He was my age maybe, with a shaved head and dark skin, wearing a black suit.

Somehow, I wasn't surprised when he vanished.

I was trying to catch my breath when the taller of the two men who came to my aid touched my arm. "Are you okay, ma'am?"

"Thanks to you, yes."

He was at least six feet tall and built like a linebacker. His friend was a few inches shorter and wiry, but he was the one who had apparently knocked the knife away. "That's some kind of knife." He squatted next to the blade, keeping his hands away, but giving it a good once over. "You see this, Jerry?"

Jerry was clearly the taller guy who leaned over to see. Before I could learn the name of my second rescuer, police officers were approaching, and we were sectioned off to answer their questions.

The woman who guided me back to my car had a nice face, her red hair pulled into a neat bun at the back of her head. She introduced herself as Officer Simmons and asked me to tell her what happened.

My heart was still racing as I told her the story, my eyes skipping to the spot where I'd been standing when he grabbed me. She stopped me a few times and asked me questions. My hands were mostly done shaking when I was finished. I gave her my cell phone number and thanked her for the quick response.

Merry was coming back to the car now, her eyes wide as she registered the scene. I shook my head at her and went to thank Jerry and his friend once more before I took my turn to go inside and use the bathroom, then grab a couple of sandwiches for us to eat on the road.

As I paid at the register, my eyes swept the faces around me. My heart skipped when I spotted a bald head, but that man's skin was much lighter, and he had a bottle of water in his hands, not a knife. I tried to tell myself to settle down, but when his eyes met mine, I *knew* that he was one of them. Chills ran down my back as I took my sandwiches and burst through the door, all but running for the car. My eye skipped to the rearview mirror as I tossed the sandwiches in Merry's lap and started the car, pulling out quickly as I spotted the man moving toward us, even if he didn't seem like he was in a hurry.

"You okay?" she asked when I pulled us out of the truck stop.

"Yeah, just a little shook up," I responded, still glancing behind us. "It was close. And I think there was another one of them in the store."

"They're getting desperate. They know their window is closing."

"Window?" I got us back out on the freeway, wanting to put as much distance as I could between me and the men who wanted me dead.

"By tomorrow, they have to cross back through whatever portal they forced open or be stuck here until they can capture a permanent portal or until the next time the veil thins. Their next opportunity to cross with a temporary portal will be six months away. A lot can happen in six months."

I shook my head, still not understanding half of what the woman said. She unwrapped my sandwich and handed it to me. I took a bite and firmly determined that once we got to the other end of this drive, I was going to make her sit down and explain everything or tell her to get out and leave me alone.

CHAPTER 5
HOME IS WHERE THE MEMORIES LIVE

It was early evening when we arrived at the address on the deed. The house stood at the end of a cul-de-sac, and while it looked like it could use a paint job and some other work, it mirrored the image in my mind's eye.

On one side of the house was a hulking McMansion that had to have at least five bedrooms. On the other was a more moderate house, with a 1967 Mustang in the driveway. A knee-high, white picket fence ran around the front yard, and cultivated flower beds lined the inside of the fence. Climbing roses filled trellis walls up the front of the porch.

In my mind I could see a woman standing on that porch, calling us in for supper. I turned and saw two girls racing up the street, dressed for summer and gleeful as they fought to be the first one to touch the gate. I shook my head. I couldn't have been but seven or eight in the memory.

I pushed open the gate, holding the keys in my hand. I half expected her to step out of the door, the woman I was assuming was my mother. There was something familiar about walking up that path. The steps creaked a little as I stepped on them, and I could see that some of the wood was sagging in the planks of the porch.

No one had lived in the house since whenever we left, and I still had no idea how old I was when that happened. Still, someone had been taking care of the yard and the flowers. I looked at the keys in my hand, trying to figure out which one of them fit into the lock. It was obviously not the big one. That was an old-fashioned kind of key, and this was a modern lock. I picked wrong the first time but got it right the second and swung open the door.

The door opened on a hallway with a hardwood floor and walls painted bright sunshine yellow. As I stepped through the door, my nerves stilled. I could almost hear the sound of children playing, smell dinner cooking.

I shook it off as Merry joined me. To my right was a staircase and to my left, a large archway opened into a living room. Slipping the keys into my pocket, I followed the hall to find a bathroom, a dining room, and finally a kitchen. Everything was spotless, as if whoever lived here had only just left.

Off the kitchen was a greenhouse of sorts, a porch covered and surrounded by glass and filled with all manner of herbs and other plants. Here too it seemed no time had passed since someone had tended the garden.

As I came back into the kitchen, I found Merry making herself to home. She had found pans and dishes and was busy preparing a meal.

I frowned. "How is the stove working?" There shouldn't have been any gas or electricity functioning. No one had lived in the house in at least twenty years.

"Magic," she said, chuckling lightly. "Go on, explore. Maybe it will help shake those memories loose."

I wasn't sure where she had found food but decided that any answer I got would only lead to more questions. I left her to it and circled back around to the stairs. I ascended slowly, my hand on the rail. There were pictures on the wall, stopping me in my tracks. The largest was a wedding photo, in the middle of the staircase. I recognized the bride as the woman in my slowly returning memory, my mother.

The man who stood beside her was handsome. He was dressed in a dark suit with shiny black shoes. His hair was the lightest shade of red I'd ever seen, with streaks of blond weaved through. I stepped closer, lifting a hand to touch his arm. I had no memory of this man.

Then the memory slammed into me: *Yelling, someone shoving me away, the acrid stink of burning skin, fear flooding me as a familiar voice told me it would be okay, strange words and suddenly everything was quiet...the heat of blood on my skin, metal on my tongue, sirens, then more blood, swallowed down with fear and fury.*

I sat down hard on the step, my hands shaking. I had been small, maybe five. It was the day my father had died. Protecting me.

The blood on my face was his. The man who had come for me, the man who had killed my father...it was his blood in my mouth. I had taken his life. My father had hurt him badly, but I had put my mouth to his and pulled the life out of him.

My stomach heaved, and I ran for the bathroom, dropping to my knees to vomit into the toilet. I dry heaved after emptying the contents of my stomach, until my sides hurt, and the memory blurred some.

I flushed without thinking and got up, wiping my mouth. The memory had never been so visceral, nor as complete. I had watched my father die. Still a little shaky, I left the bathroom and tried the stairs again, keeping my eyes away from the image of my father.

At the top of the stairs, a hall led me first to a child's bedroom. Toddler toys were overflowing an old-looking toy chest, and a basket of dolls and stuffed animals filled one corner. The walls were purple and there was a mural over the twin bed of a unicorn with a rainbow arched over it.

Across the hall was another bedroom and somehow, I knew it had been mine. The walls were a deep crimson, accented with white stars and the bed was covered in a soft blue comforter. There was a desk on one side and there was an open book on it. Math, I knew instinctively. We had fled in the middle of the school year.

There was another bathroom next to my room, and what I knew was my parents' room, but it was the final door that I stopped beside. When we had lived here the room had been off-limits, though I had no recollection why. I lifted my hand to the door hesitantly. My heart raced as I turned the knob, though I don't know what I was expecting, I only know that what was behind that door didn't meet those expectations.

The door opened into a walk-in closet, one side filled with what looked like old pickle jars, empty mason jars, and boxes. The other side was filled with clothes on hangers, winter coats, and formal gowns, plus several garment bags I didn't bother to open. The closet seemed longer and wider than could be possible, the back end of the closet lost in the dark. I stepped into the closet, reaching for the light switch, but not expecting the light to come on.

Nor was I disappointed. There was an urge to know what was back there in the dark. I pressed my lips together pensively, then glanced behind me, half expecting someone to come along and yell at me. Shaking my head at myself, I stepped deeper into the closet, one hand in front of me until I found a wooden door. My eyes slowly adjusted to the lack of light as my hand skimmed over the door in search of a door handle. I eventually found it, and I felt over it before trying to turn the knob.

I wasn't surprised to find it locked. My fingers felt down under the knob to find the keyhole. It was larger than a standard lock, and it reminded me of the big key on the ring I'd found in the wooden trunk. I fished the keys from my pocket and fumbled my way to the lock with the key.

The door opened outward, and I expected to find myself on a balcony or something over the backyard, possibly on top of the greenhouse porch.

The space beyond that door was darker than it should be if it were a balcony, after all, it was still daylight outside.

I noticed too that off in the distance I could see signs of the sun rising, which made no sense at all.

"Oh, my. Hello."

To say I jumped backward would be an understatement, tripping over the door jamb and falling on my ass with a thud and a sudden exhalation of breath.

"I'm so sorry," the voice said, making me look up.

Through the door, I could see…well, I didn't know what I was seeing. It couldn't be real though, that much I was sure of. Because seven-foot-tall men with horns and black skin, dressed in leather and boots just were not a thing that was real. And, let me be clear: when I say black skin, I mean the kind of black that devours light, and when I say horns, I mean **horns**, thick, black horns rising up from his ample head of black hair somewhere above where I expected his ears were and curling back around and down around toward his face.

I crab-walked back further as he reached out a hand to help me up. "What the actual hell…"

He smiled and stepped through the open door. To my shock, as he did so, he transformed. The horns melted away and his skin took on a rich mocha color. Only his eyes remained the same, a startling amber shade that I couldn't take my eyes away from. "I didn't mean to startle you. I wasn't expecting anyone to open the door today."

At least ten questions rushed through my brain in a race to be the first thing out of my mouth, but they were all beaten by, "I'm sorry." I continued staring long after I was sure I should look away. "I…you…" I closed my eyes and shook my head. "Who are you?" I finally managed to sputter as I got back to my feet.

He performed a flourished bow and as he lifted his head, he smiled at me. My knees went a little weak, which had never happened to me before that moment, except that one time I had the flu and a temperature of a hundred and four.

"I am Cambious of Abagh, my friend. Guardian of this Gate."

Like everything about my life since the first time Finneas had shown up in it, I didn't understand what was happening. "Cambious…of…Abagh?" I made the mistake of looking into his eyes again. The pit of my stomach dropped, and I had a sudden need to kiss him, to offer myself to him.

Cambious cleared his throat and stepped away from me. "I'm sorry, it's been a while since I've been in the presence of humans who aren't inoculated for my particular pheromones."

"Your particular what now?" My head buzzed, and my thoughts were fuzzy. I was more sure than I had been before that I had suffered some terrible catastrophe and was lying in some hospital bed, still in El Paso, dreaming up this whole crazy trip.

"Pheromones. I'm an incubus. Well, half incubus. Half succubus. You can call me Cam."

"Right." I was hallucinating, like I did that time with the hundred-and-four-degree fever. Then it was dancing toads and flying mice, but my hallucinations had taken a turn for the decidedly grown-up, if the urge to touch myself was any indication. "I think I should go check on Merry."

"Oh, is she here?" Cambious followed me out of the closet and down the stairs. "I hope everything is okay. I've been keeping an eye on this place while you were gone."

I kept hoping that if I walked fast enough, I would leave the hallucination behind, but he talked about the gardens and the plants on the porch until we reached the kitchen. Merry turned at the sound of our voices and Cambious rushed past me to sweep her into a hug.

My knees were rubbery, so I sat at the small table in the breakfast nook. It seemed obvious that Merry and Cambious had history, though I found their conversation impossible to follow as it slipped from English into something that sounded vaguely Celtic, then dropped back to English.

Of course, my two hallucinations knew one another. I rubbed a hand over my face and tried to tune them out. That was harder to do when Merry put a plate in front of me, filled with a grilled cheese sandwich and a bowl of tomato soup and the two of them sat at the table.

"I knew you were coming, of course," Cambious said. "I just didn't realize it would be today. I thought Finneas was going to keep you safe while the veil was thin."

"Oh, he wanted to," Merry replied. "But this one wouldn't listen to him. Which is why I'm here." I looked from him to her and back again. "Eat, girl. You need your strength."

I blinked and picked up the sandwich, taking a bite tentatively. I chewed and swallowed, then put the sandwich down and looked at her. "Where did the food come from?" I asked, pinning Merry with my eyes. "And how did you cook this when there isn't any electricity or gas? Who is this guy and why was he in that closet?"

It seemed once I started letting questions out, they just kept coming. "How did you find me in Los Angeles? And what is this veil? And how did those men just disappear an entire car?"

Cambious set a hand on my arm, and it brought my demanding questions to an abrupt halt as all of my attention focused directly on the warmth of his skin against mine and how it made me want to melt. He pulled his hand back and I almost reached out for it, wanting to keep touching him, wanting him to keep touching me.

"I filled the pantry and a cooler yesterday," Cam said. "Merry probably used a spell for the cooking, her specialty is kitchen magic. I introduced myself upstairs. I am the Guardian of this gate. I wasn't so much in your closet as I was outside of it...on the other side of it?" He looked to Merry who shrugged. "Technically speaking I was in Spítia."

I didn't know what to say to that. "I'm going crazy. That's the only explanation." I picked up my spoon and pointedly ignored both of them. Maybe if I ignored them long enough, I would wake up and go back to my normal life.

"I should be getting back to the gate. Not that I expect trouble, but it is my job." Cambious stood. "It was lovely to meet you again, Thána. Welcome home."

He was gone before I realized I had never told him my name. I turned to look toward the staircase, but there wasn't even a shadow of him.

"You must be exhausted," Merry said, pulling my attention back. "You finish eating and I'll bring our things inside."

I put my spoon down and stood. "No, I'll do it." There was no way I was letting a ninety-year-old woman haul in my suitcase. I emptied the car, which didn't take long. There was only my suitcase, the trunk, and a couple of other odds and ends. By the time I was done, I was yawning and even though it was early, I was starting to think that sleep sounded good.

I carried my suitcase upstairs where I waffled between my old room and my parent's room. I eventually went into my room and set my suitcase by the dresser. I stripped down into my shorts and T-shirt and crossed to the bed. The sheets were clean and smelled of jasmine as I pulled back the comforter and top sheet. Cambious must have done more than gardening and grocery shopping.

Rubbing a hand over my face, I sat, yawning again. I was just about to turn out the light when Merry appeared at the door. She smiled at me. "I trust you'll be alright now. The veil is closing, and Cambious will guard this gate. I should be heading back. It's a long trip for me."

"Wait, what? I have so many questions."

She nodded, her braids bobbing along. "Read the book, it will help. I'm sure your mother left more information in the trunk too. Get some sleep. We will meet again."

She left me sitting there. I heard Cambious's voice as he welcomed her and talk about transportation, then the door closed, and the house fell silent.

CHAPTER 6
UP FROM THE PAST

I WAS DISORIENTED WHEN I WOKE THE NEXT MORNING, THE UNFAMILIAR ROOM making me panic a little until it all came back to me. I pulled myself out of bed and down to the bathroom for my morning constitutional.

After flushing, and realizing I was going to need to call utilities and such to make the house livable, I paused at the sink, which had no water, and wondered where my wet wipes had ended up. My reflection in the mirror over the sink stopped me.

My hair was a mess, the once neat braid that I'd worn to keep it out of my face for the drive was nearly nonexistent among the strands that had fought their way free. I pulled the hair tie loose, finger-combing through it until I gave up and went looking for my bag with my toiletries and such.

I found it on the bottom stair, behind the wooden trunk that sat on the floor and supposedly held all the answers to all of the questions swirling around in my head. I reached into the bag for my brush and came out with my cell phone instead. I hadn't even thought about my phone since arriving.

At some point, I had turned it off and stuck it in the bag. I thumbed the button to turn it on and set it on the stair as I sat and went back into the bag for my brush. The sound of my voicemail notification sounded, and I picked the phone back up. The number was a San Francisco number. I set the voicemail to play on speaker and started brushing through the mass of knots in my hair.

"Hello, Thána. Bonnie Farva here. I wanted to be the first to welcome you to the San Francisco area. I know you were driving in, so take your time and get settled in, then give me a call. I'd like to see you start on Monday if that's possible."

Monday, so I had a few days. I finished brushing my hair and called Bonnie back, confirming that I would be there on Monday morning. She warned me about the traffic and told me what public transportation options were.

The better part of the morning was spent on the phone, getting the gas and electric and water turned on. With my battery nearly dead, I found a box of cereal in the pantry and a quart of milk in the cooler, so I could eat something. I was still going to need to do something about internet, but that was not as urgent a need.

I figured I would eat, and then I could plug the phone into the car charger while I waited for the water and PG&E guys to show up. I sat on the front porch with my bowl of cereal, my eyes scanning the other yards and houses. It was nearly noon on a Friday, so the street was pretty quiet.

Finishing my cereal, I set the bowl on the rail and stretched. I had a weekend to sort out the insanity that had befallen my life before I would return to something resembling normal.

Not that I knew how to even begin doing that.

I decided that I need to start with the trunk and the book inside. With a heavy sigh, I grabbed the bowl and headed into the house, hefting the trunk up off the floor after putting the bowl on top. I deposited it on the kitchen table and put the bowl in the sink, grabbing a bottle of water from the cooler before I returned to the table.

Trepidation filled me as I pressed my thumb to the locking mechanism and opened the trunk. Since Finneas had given me the damn thing, everything I knew about myself had turned upside down and traumatic memories I had repressed for twenty years were creeping back into my head.

What else would I remember if I dug deeper?

Easing the lid back, I reached in, pulling out the book and the deed to the house and setting them aside. I went back in, pulling out the stacks of papers, the silver rattle, and a small jewelry box.

I sank into the chair holding the jewelry box. There was something vaguely familiar about it. Small, barely four inches by three inches, it was silver and heavy. I opened it before setting it on the table. The inside was lined with red velvet and held a necklace on a silver chain, plus a couple of rings.

The pendant was weighty as I lifted it by the chain, which was long. Antiqued pewter surrounded a large ruby, or what looked like a ruby to me. Around the ruby, there were words etched in that same, strange language that was in the book. I rubbed my thumb over it, my eyes closing as memory bubbled up. I had worn a similar pendant when I was found on that bench, but it had been stolen from me, and I had never known its significance.

I slipped the chain over my head and let the pendant fall against me, it landed below my breasts and lay heavy against my stomach. Somehow it felt…right. I turned my attention to the two rings. One was clearly meant to match the pendant, its heavy silver etched with symbols and holding another ruby. I slipped it onto the middle finger of my left hand.

It fit perfectly and after only a moment, it felt as if I had always worn it. The last ring in the box was black with age, but it had been silver at one time. The stone was faceted like a gemstone but was blacker than any gemstone I had ever seen. I set it back into the jewelry box and made a mental note to pick up some jewelry cleaner when I went out next.

I shifted my attention then to the pile of papers, sifting through them. I found my birth certificate, issued there in California. The name Archer was nowhere to be seen. My mother was listed as Alana Celene Alizon. My father was listed as Patrick Marvin Alizon.

I sat back in the chair, holding the paper, staring at the words. I had turned thirty-two years old a little over a month before, and it was the first time I had ever seen the names of my parents.

For a long moment, I couldn't breathe. I had spent a lot of sad and angry years as a teenager wishing for and hating the parents I couldn't remember. It had taken a lot of counseling and self-determination to come to terms with the fact that, whoever they were, they didn't want me.

Blinking away tears, I set the paper aside. I also found a birth certificate for one Daria Alexis Thea Alizon. She was born three years after I was, in the same hospital. I had a sister. The little girl in that memory of running for the gate.

She would be twenty-nine, somewhere out there. Wondering if my mother would have left any clues to where to start looking, I dug into the rest of the pile.

I had to relinquish my quest when PG&E arrived to check the gas lines, so they could turn everything on, and the same when the man from the water company arrived.

By four o'clock in the afternoon, I had a working house, which meant I could cook myself some dinner. I plugged my phone in and set about getting to know my new kitchen, and what food Cambious had stocked.

I emptied the cooler into the fridge, leaving out the half dozen eggs and pulling some potatoes and a loaf of bread out of the pantry. A few minutes later I had some home-fries cooking and was scrambling a couple of eggs when I heard footsteps.

I froze for a second, then turned toward the sound. I don't know what I was expecting, but I felt let down a little when I realized that Cambious was standing in the archway.

"I hope I'm not intruding," he said softly.

"No. I...wasn't expecting to see you so soon," I replied, turning back to my cooking.

"It's Friday. I tend the greenhouse on Friday," Cambious said, inching toward me. "Unless you would rather do it."

My mouth opened and closed of its own accord. I knew nothing about gardening. I gestured toward the porch greenhouse. "Be my guest."

He smiled, his white teeth gleaming, and my knees got weak. As he got closer, I made myself look away. Something about him made me want to do things I hadn't even thought of in a while. He slipped past me and out onto the porch and I forced myself to focus on my cooking. I poured the eggs into the potatoes and stirred.

I could hear him out there puttering around, humming and singing as he moved through the collection of plants. Curiosity got the better of me, and I moved so I could see him. He had a watering can that looked as old as me, and he was making his way down the long counter, giving each plant attention, watering and singing to them. I found myself drifting toward him, but when he looked up, I pulled myself back to my dinner, which was starting to burn.

I turned off the stove, then plated half of what I'd cooked and took it to the table. I ate while looking through more of the papers, trying to ignore the thoughts in my head about Cambious. I hadn't had such libidinous thoughts since my crush on Muriel Hart in college. She had been a year ahead of me, my roommate's cousin. I had it bad for Muriel and it led to some less than stellar moments in my life, including my first sexual experience, though that wasn't with Muriel.

In fact, it had been with Joseph Myers, which confused me beyond belief. We'd both had a little too much to drink, and I had been desperate to find a way to sate the desire after spending two hours at a party watching Muriel dance with nearly everyone but me. Joseph was happy to oblige my lust.

We dated off and on for a while, despite my confusion. I had been convinced up until that point that I was gay because the only people I seemed attracted to were women, but I discovered that I liked sex with men, so maybe I was wrong about the whole gay thing.

It didn't occur to me then that I was actually bisexual, that took me a few years. But that didn't help me figure out why my head was full of thoughts of Cambious and sex. Distractingly so. I'd just read the page in my hand for the third time when he reappeared.

"I left some food for you, if you're hungry," I offered without looking up and hoping it sounded casual and not like I was begging him to stay.

"Thank you."

I heard him pick up the plate I'd left on the counter and serve up what I'd left behind before he came to join me at the table.

"I see you're settling in."

I nodded and set the page down. I had no idea what it said. I swallowed hard and turned to look at him. "You smell good." I said the words spontaneously, surprising myself.

"Pheromones," he responded, smirking. "We really should get you inoculated if we're going to continue spending time together."

"Are we?" I asked breathlessly. "Spending time together, I mean."

"That's up to you." He took a bite and chewed for a minute. I licked my lips, wanting to follow his fork and press my lips to his.

"The garden..." I managed, trying, and failing to pull my eyes away from his face. "I don't know how."

He frowned at me, as if my words didn't make sense. "To garden?" he asked after a moment.

I nodded. "Do you taste as good as you smell?" What? What the actual hell was wrong with me?

"I think that's my cue to exit." He stood, his chair scraping backward. "I'll see about sourcing some inxbane for you."

"Inxbane?"

"The key ingredient in the inoculation you need." He started for the stairs, but paused, nodding to the papers spread out around the table. "I'm glad you're getting to know your past."

He disappeared, and I turned my attention back to the disjointed story the contents of the trunk told. Everything in the box spoke of my mother, and only the birth certificates told anything of my father.

I pulled the book to me, clearing a space for it in front of me and opening it. The pictures seemed to mean more, now that I knew they were ancestors, family. I examined each face hoping for some flicker of memory. The writing changed languages, the people in the pictures seemed more modern.

Near the middle of the book, I found a page written in English, with pictures of a small house, set back among trees, with a woman who reminded me of Merry standing on the steps with two children.

The note under the picture read: *Celene Edith Abernon with her children Alana and Beauford.*

I looked at the children again, squinting at the girl, trying to decide if this Alana was the same person as my mother, if this woman was my grandmother. I flicked my eyes back to the top of the page.

If it is then the wish of the witch to hide herself from those who would bring her harm, gather these herbs in the dark moon: Wolf's bane, holy thistle, bloodroot, and candlewick and crush them together.

The instructions continued from there, but I was fairly sure that I didn't believe in spells, so I turned the page. The next page was a spell to expel demons, and the next one to hide bad memories. It seemed that the book was not just a family photo album, but the family spellbook as well, and, cookbook, as I came across a recipe for "Stewed Venison Pot Pie, as told to me by Nana Forsight." There was a note in another hand that said that beef could be substituted and taste as good.

The next few pages were back to the strange original language that seemed like so much gibberish, at least to my untrained eyes. There were more pictures, one looking down at a small city from a hill. It seemed it could be nearly any European city, with cramped roadways surrounded by buildings built in varying styles with red clay roofs. It was no place I recognized, however.

Under the picture were the words, "Into *Mágisa*, from the *Vóreion*."

I flipped a few more pages before I found a picture of my mother. She was young, maybe fifteen or sixteen, her dark hair tamed into twin braids that came almost to her waist. She wore a pair of faded jeans and a tank top with a shawl around her shoulders as she stood beside a boy who was taller, but clearly younger. Both of them beamed at the camera as they leaned back against a car. Under it was another picture of her at the same age, sitting with a small child of maybe two in her lap and surrounded by five other small children. The caption was "Alana with her baby sister Anna and brothers Adrian and Christophe, cousins Damen and Josephine, and Astra Linga, daughter of Lissa."

My mother had brothers and sisters...which meant I had aunts and uncles. That was more family than I had ever imagined. I wondered where they were now if they too were being hunted like I was.

A cold chill slithered up my spine as I realized that they might not even be alive anymore. I turned the page, putting that thought behind me. I wasn't ready to mourn family I had never even known, even if I was starting to remember the love my mother had held for me.

Stuck between the next pages was a small cloth bag tied with a ribbon. I lifted the bag, running my fingers over it. Whatever was inside was small, rounded. I held it in my hand and my eyes traced the words written in that strange, nonsensical language on the page. "*Epistrépse se méana aftó pou eíni dikó mou.*" I mouthed the words before moving to the English underneath. "Caraway and mustard seed, to be carried by day and put beneath the pillow at night to return lost memory. Recite the words often. Translation: Return to me that which is mine."

I still didn't believe in spells, but I tucked the cloth bag into the pocket of my jeans. It couldn't hurt, I figured.

The room had gotten dim, and I got up to turn on a light, glancing at the screen of my phone. Somehow it had gone past eight in the evening. I had learned a lot, but nothing to indicate where my sister or my mother might be. I left everything where it was and headed up the stairs. I had meant to shower, but a bath was starting to sound better.

I set the tub to filling and went looking for towels. I had some in the car but didn't want to go back downstairs. I had a vague memory of watching my mother put laundry away and let it lead me to the closet in the hall. Sure enough, there were clean, fluffy towels stacked there. I had to remember to thank Cambius when I saw him again. I didn't know how long he'd cared for the house, but he'd done a great job.

I put the towel on the rack near the tub and stripped down, before stepping into the hot water and sinking down. I hadn't had a proper bath in years. The hot water surrounded me, and steam rose up from the surface. I closed my eyes, leaning back against the back of the tub. The only thing that would have made it better was a glass of wine.

CHAPTER 7
INXBANE

It was there, in the bath, that memory came flooding into me. We were small, Daria and I, playing in the bathtub as our mother watched, laughing. Daria was barely old enough to sit upright on her own and she splashed in the water, giggling as if it were the funniest thing she'd ever done. Daria's skin was pale compared to my olive tones, and the little tuft of hair on her head was a shade of red like our father's.

Mom knelt by the tub, one hand in the water beside Daria in case she needed help. Our father came into the room, leaning down to kiss the top of Mom's head, his eyes sparkling.

The memory was a happy one, happier than I could remember being since. Tears stung my eyes as I sat up, half expecting I could reach through to touch those happy people…but I was alone.

I pulled the plug on the tub and stood, reaching to grab the towel. I dried my legs and wrapped the towel around me, grabbing my clothes as I left the bathroom.

My childhood bedroom seemed to be hung with memories as I sat on the bed. The closet was the magical doorway to some faraway land when I was small. I would go in and close the door and put on my dress-up shoes and dress and emerge a princess. Or sometimes I chose what must have been a cowboy costume that I transformed into a dragon tamer outfit.

I fished the sachet out of my jeans pocket and slipped it under my pillow. So far, all the magic stuff had seemed real, so maybe it wasn't all make-believe.

I dropped the towel and pulled on the T-shirt and shorts I had adopted as my pajamas and turned off the light. Sliding into the bed, my hand reached under the pillow to hold the sachet and I whispered the words again, "Return to me that which is mine."

Sleep was elusive. I tossed and turned, vague snippets of memory chasing me, but nothing solid, nothing I could hold on to. I finally dozed off somewhere after midnight, only to be dropped into my recurring nightmare. It was clearer than before and started earlier in the memory.

A big, warm hand held mine and his voice was telling me we needed to hurry. It was Daria's birthday, and we were bringing her cake. The sun was warm on my skin, and I was wearing my favorite blue dress with white flowers on it.

Daddy suddenly pulled me to the side, behind a car. Our house wasn't far away, I could see it. Daddy was telling me to run for the gate, but I was scared. I could hear my heart in my ears. A man was yelling, magic crackling in the air around him.

"Stay down, Thána. Stay down." He pushed me down and I sat on the pavement, moving under the bumper of the car as Daddy stepped out to face the man. The sound of fighting made me cover my ears, but I could still hear the words the man hurled at my father, telling him that the thánatou child must die.

The smell of smoke and burning flesh, screams as my father took the brunt of the spell, and countered with one of his own. I knew I should run to the safety of my mother, but I couldn't move, not until it was quiet and then I crawled out from under the car. My father lay still on the ground, his face turned toward home.

I crawled to him, tears stinging my eyes. "Daddy?" I turned his face to me, patting his cheek to rouse him. "Daddy?" I leaned in to try to feel his breath on my cheek, my lips brushing his. The air tasted like pennies, flat and ugly and it made me nearly ill.

Daddy's lips opened with my touch, and I opened mine as well. Blood coated his mouth and I sucked in without thought, swallowing as a great breath left him. "Daddy!" I was screaming now, hitting him, begging him to come back. Inside me, a warm feeling was stirring in my tummy, fingers of pain clenching around my small body. My father's eyes were dull, and I somehow knew he was no longer there.

Behind me, the man who attacked us groaned and I turned to him, power burning through me as I grabbed his face in my tiny hands and pulled his mouth open, sucking in until he too was still beneath me.

Blood covered my face and hands, my favorite dress, even my shoes as people began appearing around me. Daria's cake was broken on the ground, pink frosting coating the pavement, my father's hands, and even the side of the car. I curled up with my head on my father's chest, my little hands holding to him, even as my mother came and tried to pull me away.

I woke breathlessly, jumping from the bed and looking around. The dream had been so real, I half expected to be covered in blood. I gulped in air and tried to calm the raging beat of my heart, realizing as I pulled my thoughts back into the here and now that the warm feeling between my thighs was the start of my monthly cycle.

It was early by nearly a week, but then, the only predictable thing about my cycles was that they had never been predictable. I found my toiletries and took care of that situation, dropping my shorts into the pile of clothes I needed to wash and pulling on my backup pair. I was going to need to pick up some new clothes. I had even fewer than I'd had when I'd gotten to El Paso.

I was awake enough that I wasn't going back to sleep, so even though it was only five in the morning, I headed downstairs to make coffee.

That was another thing I was going to need to get out to buy. Cambious had put some in the pantry, but I could tell he wasn't a coffee drinker just by his choice of coffee. I figured I could get out later in the day, find the closest grocery store, and stock up. The clothes would wait until I got an idea of the average dress in the new shop. No point spending money on a bunch of dresses and suits to find out I could get away with jeans and T-shirts.

I sat at the table as the coffee brewed, the dream playing through my mind. That man had been alive before I touched him. His face filled with fear as I leaned over him and he murmured that word...*thánatou*. I was a child, but he feared me. In my dream, he was a dark-skinned bald man, dressed in a black suit, but I couldn't tell whether that was the truth or my subconscious adding the description based on my attacker at the truck stop.

The coffee pot beeped, and I got up to pour myself a cup, thinking about what I had done. I had wanted that man to pay for taking my father from me, and after I kissed him, he died. I had killed him. I wasn't exactly sure how I knew that, or how I did it, but I knew it was true.

I had killed him, and I had taken my father's pain, releasing him to die peacefully. The proof was the way my body reacted. I had become hot in the next hour and my mother had taken me into the forbidden closet, sitting me down on a chair that had a hole like a toilet seat, with a bucket underneath.

I bled. My body cramped as my tiny uterus shed blood like I was a grown woman. Through her tears, my mother tended to me, wrapping me in a makeshift diaper when my exhaustion had me falling out of the chair. We both slept in her bed that night, and for many nights thereafter.

We didn't leave the safety of our property, which was well warded, though at the time I didn't know what that meant. Sometimes we hid in the secret closet. At least once we even went through the door to the other side.

Other men came, their dark suits populating the town around us, searching us out as we tried to live our daily lives. Each time one found us, Mom would do something to change the wards around us and even expanded them to include the whole cul-de-sac. There were spells for us too. Amulets we each wore that were meant to hide us, words we had to say whenever we left the wards.

Eventually, there were too many men, constantly finding us, and we finally ran. I was seven when we left the house.

I sipped at my coffee and considered that memory. It was the day after a man yelled those words at us in a grocery store. Mom piled as many of our things as she could into the car, and we left. She promised we'd come back someday, and that we should see this as an adventure.

The memory ended there. Whatever came after that was still hidden in the dark recesses of my mind. Sitting there, staring back at that moment though, I found myself reexamining my known life.

My menstrual cycle had never been what could be called normal, and it began when I was barely eleven. Of course, this memory made me realize that wasn't entirely true. It was a light flow when I was young, but there were times in my life when it was more like a river pouring out of me.

When I was thirteen, I had a good friend in school who had cancer. I didn't know much about cancer, but I was watching her wither away. My foster mother took me to see her in the hospital. They were saying this was the end, that she wouldn't survive.

I remember crawling up into her bed with her and cradling her close and kissing her to say goodbye. A jolt passed through me, and I jumped from the bed, terrified that I'd somehow caught her disease.

I ran from the room and out to the car. By the time my foster mother got us home, I was cramping and what followed was seven long days of bleeding that was debilitating. I almost ended up in the hospital myself, but when I could finally stand on my own, they were saying that a miracle had happened, and Kate was coming home from the hospital.

My coffee had grown cold as I sat there contemplating what it all meant, so I got up and poured it down the sink and poured a new cup. They called me Death Bringer, but if my memory wasn't lying to me, it wasn't death I'd given Kate. I reached for the book from the wooden trunk and wondered if the answers were somewhere in there.

I had seen the words blood witch under various photos, several of my ancestors had been blood witches, according to the book. I flipped back to the page where my grandmother's face stared out at me, my finger tracing the side of her face. She looked tired. In her hand was a small bunch of leaves of some kind. From there, I moved backward, finding the last noted blood witch before me. She was my great-great-grandmother, Alexis Anagnos. There was only one picture of her, and little more than her name and the notation that she had been a blood witch.

I sat back, sipping at my coffee, looking at her face, and wondering about her life.

I flipped pages, my eyes scanning the words and images, though I wasn't sure what I was looking for. I stopped as my gaze caught on the word "inxbane", and I dragged my eyes up to the top of the page. *"For those who wish to socialize with one of the various creatures who dull the senses, mix a general serum and to it add a drop of blood from the said creature and the proper plant or plants as given below."*

Scanning back to where I'd seen the word inxbane, I found it listed under Incubi, Succubi, and other related lust-inducing creatures. "Yeah, so how do I mix a general serum?" I muttered.

The more I seemed to learn, the more I realized I was in way over my head. With a sigh, I turned the page, skimming through pages of pictures, recipes, and as I found the back of the book, a family tree.

Like the rest of the book, it was focused on my mother's side of the family, going back generations. My name was beside my sister's name, leading to our mother, her mother, and back. Every two or three generations there was an asterisk beside a name, which a note in the bottom right corner indicated meant they were a blood witch.

The page folded out to nearly half the length of the kitchen table. Other markings told of family that were exiled, presumably through a portal like the one upstairs if what I'd learned so far was true. Those who lacked magic ability, certain kinds of criminals, and some blood witches were exiled. Some of the names had titles under their names: Musta Hargrove, Mayor of Cra; Celene Everton, Mistress of Keys for Her Grace, Ella Nore; and others that made little more sense to me.

I finished my cup of coffee and stood up to refill it. The sun was just starting to come up, filling the greenhouse with a gorgeous golden light. I wandered into it with my cup of coffee, glancing over the assembled plants. Some I thought I recognized, but most looked more or less like every other plant to my untrained eye.

I wandered down to the end where there were some miniature trees planted in barrels, the last of the season's fruit on their branches. One was lemon, while the other was orange. I breathed in deep of the scent. It was a mix of rich earth and sun-warmed air, as well as a deep herbal smell that was less any one plant and more the combination of them all.

As I stood there, I could almost see the porch as it had been when I was small, when my mother was tending to the plants. Everything had been lush then, the air scented with mint and jasmine. Like Cambious, my mother had hummed and sang as she worked, and I remembered loving to listen to her.

It was hard to believe so much had changed in the last week. I had been alone in the world until Finneas had found me. Now, if the book was to be believed, I had a family full of aunts and uncles, a sister I was only starting to remember, and a house haunted with memories of a time before I was alone, if only I could remember them.

I drank the last of the coffee in my cup, turning to go back into the house, when my eyes found a row of books along the back of the workbench. They were old, the covers faded. Setting my coffee cup down on the bench, I reached for the first. It was small, the cover a dull red that was worn near to white in places. The writing on the cover and spine had once been gold but was unreadable now with only slivers of gold clinging to the edges of the letters. I opened it, turning past the first few pages.

It seemed to be a recipe book of some sort, though I didn't recognize any of the ingredients, and the instructions were in that strange language I was getting used to seeing, handwritten in an elegant script. I reached for the second, with its blue cover in a similar shape to the red one. Inside the words were English, old English, but readable. Like the red book, it contained recipes with ingredients like mugwort and roots of dandelions and rose thorns. Notes were scribbled in pencil alongside some of them saying things like "substitute thistle pricks to keep depression at bay" and "carry in a pouch to protect from evil eye" and other such odd things. The handwriting was crisp and neat, block letters in black ink.

As I progressed through the books, it seemed I moved through the years, finding near the end a journal that was in a familiar hand I thought was my mother's and filled with her own recipes and notes about plants and spells. The last book was the newest, and it fell open in my hand to the last page with writing on it. I recognized the writing, even if it had yet to develop into the scrawl I knew best.

It was a child's hand, and I had copied from my mother's book, and from the others, small spells to improve memory, to protect from bullies and other similar ones. It wasn't even a quarter filled, but as I paged through, I found a picture, taken on the front porch. We smiled out of the past, my sister and I, our knees and faces dirty, our clothes disheveled, but it was easy to see we were happy.

Under the picture my mother had written, "Thána and Daria, ages 6 and almost 3." My thoughts shifted to the day my father died. This picture had to have come before that, so I was a little older than I had first assumed.

Gathering the books to examine more completely, I headed back into the kitchen, stopping when I found Cambious standing there. In his large hands, there was a small jar. He smiled and my knees got a little weak. Thoughts flashed through my head, thoughts about sex. I pushed them away and deposited my books on the counter.

"I brought you some inxbane," Cambious said, lifting his hands a little.

"That's great," I responded, sighing. "It would be even better if I knew what to do with it."

He chuckled and gestured toward the books with his chin. "To start with, you need to make a simple serum. The instructions should be in the brown book there. Once it's ready, bring it to a boil and drop in a pinch of this and I'll add a drop of my blood. Let it cool and drink it down."

I nodded. "You say that like this is just normal." I reached for the blue book and started paging through it.

"Well, for me it is." Cambious put the jar on the counter. "I'll gather what you need from the greenhouse. You get started in here. You'll find a saucepan in that cupboard by the stove."

"What, no cauldron?" I asked as I squatted down to look in the cupboard. He peeked back from the doorway out into the greenhouse.

"Well, we could, but it's a bit big for what you need."

I closed my eyes and shook my head. "Of course there's a cauldron." With a deep sigh, I banished my thoughts about Cambious and sex, then the ones about how crazy this whole thing was and the wondering when I'd wake up to find myself still in El Paso. I pulled out a saucepan that looked big enough and set it on the stove, pulling the book closer and searching through it until I found a page titled, "Simple Serum, for use in various spells, incantations, and inoculations" and let my eyes scan the page. It seemed simple enough.

I rummaged through cupboards until I found a Pyrex measuring cup and put two cups of water in the pan. I turned the heat up to medium and turned my attention back to the book.

The recipe was written in a neat hand, but the notes in the margins were little more than a scribble and hard to decipher. "There should be jars in the pantry with the liquid ingredients." Cambious's voice floated in from the greenhouse.

I raised an eyebrow at the door before picking up the book and taking it into the spacious pantry beside the refrigerator. Everything in there was neat and tidy, canned goods all lined up with their labels facing outward, boxes lined up along the top shelf. In the back, next to what appeared to be canning jars filled with assorted vegetables, there were old-looking glass bottles that looked like they were made for keeping spices, or maybe lab specimens.

Consulting the book, I needed rose quartz and obsidian waters. I had no idea what that meant, but I read the labels, all lined up in alphabetical order. I located the two I needed and went back to the stove where Cambious was shredding something green and herb-like into my pan of water. He looked up and stepped back, gesturing to the stove. "You look like you're doing just fine," I said, setting my two bottles down.

"Ah, but then you wouldn't learn." His deep voice rumbled through me. I could feel it in my chest, and it sank through me into my groin. My insides trembled with unbidden desire. "I've done the first step. I'll move away until you're ready for my blood."

I nodded absently, shutting my eyes, and breathing in slowly until I felt the urges settle a little. When I opened them, Cambious was not in my line of sight, so I moved back to set the book on the counter.

The water was just starting to boil, the shredded greenery churning in circles and diving down, only to rise again and circle around until the current sucked it back down. It was nearly mesmerizing. I tore my eyes away from it and read through the next step.

I needed to add three drops of each of the two waters, then boil for two minutes before adding the chamomile, which I was at least familiar with. I rummaged in the drawer nearest the stove, somehow knowing that I would find an eyedropper there. First the obsidian. Something tickled the back of my brain about obsidian being protective, a barrier of sorts.

Carefully, I let three drops of the vaguely darkened water drip into the pan, then moved to the rose quartz. That done, I turned to the pile of small flowers on the counter. I'd never seen chamomile fresh like that, only dried for tea. The book said to crush the flowers before adding them to the water, so I set about doing that. I almost forgot Cambious was behind me as I worked until I heard him murmur, "Good, stir it now and take it off the heat."

I was a little startled but grabbed the wooden spoon that looked older than I was and gave the concoction a stir before lifting the pan off the burner and setting it on a cold one. "That's it?" I asked, glancing back at Cambious,

I regretted it almost immediately as my stomach lilted and heat flushed through me. I turned back to the stove to try to control myself.

"Sprinkle a pinch of inxbane over the surface while it is still hot," Cambious instructed.

I could feel him coming toward me and tried to narrow my focus down to my own hands and what I was doing so his closeness wouldn't affect me. It didn't really work, but I pretended that it did. The inxbane was in a frosted glass apothecary jar, the kind that my foster mother kept potpourri in when I was in high school. It was larger than it had looked in Cambious's s giant hands.

With him behind me now, I opened the jar and took a pinch of the dark brown powder. The smell was a bit like cut grass that had been allowed to dry, got rained on, and dried again…not quite moldy, but unpleasant. I sprinkled it into the water and suddenly Cambious reached around me, holding his thumb over the pot. He had already pricked it with something, and he let a drop of blood fall into the liquid in the pan.

The smell that lifted off the potion was a potent mix of that grassy scent of the inxbane and a strange metallic scent that I assumed had come from the blood. "There, now just let it cool before you drink it. Best to swallow as much as you can at once, the taste is awful."

He turned to leave, and I almost reached for him. "You don't have to go," I said, my heart thumping almost painfully against my chest. I licked my lips as my eyes traveled over his leather-clad legs, stopping at his groin for a long time.

He cleared his throat and pulled my attention back up to his face. "If I stay, I fear we may lose control of ourselves. I will come back tomorrow, and we can talk all afternoon if you like."

I was fairly sure he was in no danger of losing control. In fact, he seemed to be the picture of control as he left me standing there in the kitchen. A sudden release of pressure dropped on me when he was no longer within sight and my knees even wobbled a bit.

I reached for the stove and breathed in deep, then realized the dampness in my underwear was probably more than just my arousal. I had somehow managed to forget that I had started my period.

CHAPTER 8
INCUBUS

I stared into the coffee cup, trying to work up the courage to drink my anti-incubus potion. Which was a ridiculous notion if I thought too much about it. Like so much in my life since I first laid eyes on Finneas, I was trying really hard not to think about it too much.

Being me, that meant an endless loop of my brain cycling through thinking about all the ways that this was insane, and I was having a nervous breakdown, to thinking it was some sort of fever dream I was having while lying comatose in some hospital somewhere, to shoving it all down into a dark hole under a manhole cover in my head so that I could function as if it was all perfectly normal.

Finally, after waffling for at least a half-hour, I picked up the mug, took a deep breath, and filled my mouth. Cambious was not wrong about the taste. I almost spit it out and after I'd swallowed, I wasn't sure I wasn't going to just throw it all back up, but a couple of deep breaths seemed to do the trick. At least until I dumped the last swallow into my mouth.

I gagged after getting it down, leaning over the sink just in case. I could taste moldy grass and something musty and oddly dry. I rinsed the cup and filled it with water, chasing the potion down, and hoping it shut the door to regurgitation behind it.

I had books covering most of the surface of the kitchen table, the book from the trunk, the books from the greenhouse porch, and books that I'd found hidden in among more traditional volumes in my parents' old room. There were straight-up spell books, history books that resembled no history I had ever learned in school, and several that were in a language that was not the same language I was becoming used to seeing. If I had to guess I would have said Welsh or Gaelic.

Pushing down the feeling of my stomach attempting to heave itself up through my throat, I went back to the table and my efforts to make sense of the memories that kept bubbling up inside me and the assorted "magic" that was apparently my heritage.

I pulled the black book that had clearly been mine closer and opened it to the beginning. On the first page I had written, *"This book belongs to Thána Augusta Celene Alizon, of the Houses Alizon and Anagnos, Blood Witch."*

The next page was dated September 10, 1990. My seventh birthday. There was a poem of sorts on the page, rhyming couplets that was labeled "A Spell for Patience" and I found myself speaking it out loud.

Patience is a virtue,
This I know is true
Let patience grow inside me
Make me still like a tree

I wasn't sure it made any sense, but then what about my life did at that point? Each page was dated and contained either a poem or a recipe of some kind. There were more blank pages than filled, and the last was dated April 4, 1991.

There was no recipe or spell, only the words, *"Símero, févgoum. Mia méra, tha epistrépsoum."*

Sighing, I reached for one of those that I took for history books, only it bore little resemblance to the history books I'd read in school. It told the early history of when people began migrating from the world on the other side of the door hidden in my closet.

There were portals in many countries around this world, and presumably, they connected to the world that was my parents' homeworld, though I was starting to feel some prickle of knowledge lurking just out of reach about many portals and many worlds. I was giving myself a headache attempting to remember so I relinquished the thought

Families from Spítia, my mother's home country, and others on that world, sent those born with no magic through those portals, at first to protect them from those who believed that the handicap should not be allowed to propagate. Eventually not having magic was outlawed for a while and banishment was the only option to prison or death.

A side note on that chapter said that blood witches were sometimes banished as well, due to the stigma attached to the gifts usually granted to a blood witch. I wondered if that was why I had been born here, on this side of the portal.

From what I could tell skimming through the book, the world on the other side of that door upstairs was divided into eleven countries, who, much like the world I lived in, fought long bloody wars over points of theological and philosophical beliefs, imagined slights against their leaders, border disputes, as well as points of magical contention.

It seemed the more I learned about the past, the more I saw I needed to learn. Setting aside world history, I went back to my family book, turning the pages until I found the picture of my mother when she was younger. I turned several pages without really looking at them, stopping when a feeling of ice creeping up my hand drew my attention down to an image of a fortress of sorts with a caption under it, "Mauno Kourt, home of the *Adelfótit tou Día*." My eyes scanned up the page. The lettering was neat and clean, each stroke even and lined up. "The Brotherhood of God formed first among priests of Jeus who broke off over the belief that *"Aíma mágissa"* or blood witches, sometimes called *thanátou*, were abominations from the god Hathus. This is believed to have itself been a bastardization of the prophecy of *Aímatos*, the gathering of all bloods to fill the river Spítia and purchase another ten thousand years of our lands from Hathus, to whom it belongs."

Under that paragraph was a list of names, ages, and dates. A chill seeped into my bones as I scanned them, all women with the last name Anagnos, which must have been my mother's family name seeing that I had claimed it in my own book. There were twenty or so, the dates separated by everything from fifteen years to nearly one hundred and fifty.

I didn't need words to tell me that these women had died for little more than the fact that they had been born, blood witches all of them. Like me. Had I been born in the same times and places, it might have been me. The youngest had been merely nine years old.

There was nothing to tell me how they were killed, but I **knew** it was gruesome and painful. Closing the book, I left the room, turning off the light as I headed upstairs. It was early, but I felt as though I had just finished that kickboxing class my assistant had thought would be a fun form of stress relief. I made a stop in the upstairs bathroom to deal with the confirmation of my womanhood and the lack of zygote implanted in my womb, then stripped out of my clothes, dropping them on the floor and crawling into bed.

I was dropped almost instantly into dreams of the past. I saw the day we left that house, running past a car attempting to block us into the dead-end street. I saw a tiny cottage house covered in ivy and climbing roses where my mother's smile was sad and my sister played in a sandbox with someone's forgotten army men, calling them her bo-bos.

There were flashes of men with bald heads, or maybe the same man over and over, I couldn't be sure, but I knew each time I saw him or them, we would pick up and leave, usually in the dead of night.

Toward morning the feeling of the dreams shifted, and that same cold burning sensation shook me as I fell down a hill, running madly, bare feet pounding against barren land, stumbling over broken earth.

"*Althea Anagnos, you have been convicted of being thánatou. Your punishment is death by Aimorragía.*" The woman screamed around the leather gag and thrashed in her captor's hands, fighting desperately to break free of the heavy chains around her wrists. She was dragged forward, up some scaffolding to a platform. The shift she wore was ripped from her bruised and bloodied body and a rope was tied around her ankles. The men that surrounded her wore deep red robes and hoods and gloves, the only flesh showing was around their eyes. An order was given, and Althea was lifted feet first from the platform, struggling even then to get free.

Three men stepped up to her, blades in their hands. Silently they stabbed her skin, careful to avoid major arteries until they had opened fifteen wounds. Then they carefully cut open each thigh and her neck to expose the pulsing arteries. Each was carefully pricked with the sharp, curved point of their blades, ensuring her death would be slow and no doubt excruciating.

I could hear the chanting then and that fortress filled my vision, almost as if I were flying toward it. A woman was curled up in the corner of a cold, stone cell, surrounded by men in the same dark red robes, chanting something I couldn't quite understand.

I woke to the sun streaming in the window, shaking a little as the dreams shifted into memories that were my own and those that could never be mine. Something made me wonder if that was part of being a blood witch…something about shared blood, connection, which could transcend the limitations of time.

It was Sunday, and I still hadn't gone to get groceries, so I decided that would be my first course of action. After a quick shower, I threw on the last of my clean clothes and reminded myself I needed to do laundry. I hadn't seen a washing machine in the house, so I bundled all of my dirty clothes into my duffle bag and headed out to find a laundromat as well as the grocery store.

In all, it took nearly three hours, but when I came back to the house, I had clean clothes for a couple of days, and food that would get me through the week.

As I was unloading the car, I had the feeling that someone was watching me, but looking around I couldn't see anyone. It was a little disconcerting, especially knowing that there were people out there who wanted to kill me. The image from my dream sprang to mind, Althea Anagnos hanging from her ankles as her life's blood drained from her body.

I shook it off and juggled my grocery bags and duffle to get the front door open. Hands reached through the door, taking my groceries before it had even registered that someone was there. Cambious grinned and headed to the kitchen with the bags while I closed the front door. I followed behind him, feeling like something was different.

It took a minute for it to dawn on me that the potion must have worked. I could look at him without the overwhelming lust. The feeling, or the lack of feeling, was odd. "Thanks," I muttered when I caught up to him.

"How are you feeling today?" Cambious asked, emptying my bags, and starting to put things away.

"A little anxious about work tomorrow," I said honestly.

He nodded. "First days can be hard." He moved around the kitchen easily, like he owned the place. In some ways it was more his house than mine.

"Can I ask you some questions?" I asked, sitting at the table with all of my spread-out books, most of which only filled me with more questions and very few answers.

"Of course."

I wasn't sure where to start though. I pulled my mother's big book to me and opened it to the page with the fortress. "What can you tell me about this place?" I asked, turning the book toward him. My fingers tingled where they touched the picture.

He raised an eyebrow. "That is the Mauno Kourt. Why do you ask?"

"I saw it in my dreams last night," I said. I scanned the words above the picture. "I saw her too." I pointed to Althea's name. She had died nearly a century before at the age of twenty-six. "I watched her die."

His eyes were filled with concern as he sank into a chair beside me. "Your gifts are awakening."

"I'm not sure nightmares count as a gift," I said. I shook off the apprehension that the dream brought with it. "I saw someone else too. Here." I touched the picture again, the same cold tingle rising up my fingers and into my palm. I pulled my hand away. "She was in a cell. These men were chanting...I don't know what they were saying."

Cambious made a face, like he smelled something rotten. "The Brotherhood."

"Are they the men trying to kill me?"

He nodded. "Most likely. There are a few other sects, but they stick primarily to preaching and trying to legislate their hate. It's only been the last seventy years or so that the laws banishing blood witches have been lifted. There are precious few of you left. The Brotherhood, and others, believe that the gift itself is to be eliminated, that it is anathema to Jeus, which is ludicrous, of course."

I nodded, not fully understanding, but tucking the information away. "And they killed all of these women." My finger dragged down the list, stopping at the nine-year-old.

"They were most active after the laws that banished blood witches because they felt they weren't restrictive enough. The last few centuries they've been mostly a secretive organization, hiding in the shadows and striking at those who, like yourself, were living in exile in the various worlds accessible by portals, like yours. Often, those witches had little to protect them because here their access to the education they would need to wield their powers effectively had been limited."

I looked at the list again, then frowned. "The last few centuries?"

He leaned forward and looked at the list. "The last of your family taken and killed was nearly two thousand ago, here. Agatha."

"That date is only fifty years ago."

Cambious chuckled. "Ah, yes. Right. I forget you don't know the basics. Spítia and the other civilizations in my world are several millennia older than yours. It is currently the thirteenth month of the year 4189 on my side of the portal. Our calendar reset when the Great War was finally over, and new boundaries were drawn for each of the noble families. That was in the year 0, but it was several thousand years after we originally established a calendar."

Once again, the immensity of all there was to learn was overwhelming. My head was spinning, and I wasn't sure I even knew what to ask next. "Tell me about you," I finally said.

"Me?" He seemed amused. "There isn't much to tell, I'm afraid. I am the guardian of this portal, it's my job to make sure that no one uses it if they aren't family."

"Family?"

He nodded. "The land on both sides belongs to your family. Only family is supposed to use the gate without permission. We don't usually have a problem, because the land on the other side is a long distance from any city and not the most convenient to get to. There are almost no roads, and with the forest on the east and the marshlands to the south, most people are going to aim for a portal that's easier access."

"And you guard this portal in the middle of nowhere. All the time?"

He shrugged. "I don't need a lot of sleep, but my brother and I trade shifts. He's young though, he doesn't even know your family. We're… bonded I guess is a good word. Our families, I mean. The story goes that your great-grandfather on your mother's side saved my father's life. Our kind aren't particularly well loved, even in our native lands. My father swore a blood oath and bound our families together. We guard your gate, but there are others, and at certain times of the year, when the veil is thin, portals can be forced open by powerful magic, but they close quickly."

Most of that was hard to follow. It was easy to forget that Cambious didn't actually look like the man sitting next to me. No, he had horns and skin darker than night, and who knew what else that I hadn't caught on that first meeting.

"I meant you," I said after a minute. "Tell me about you."

Cambious narrowed his eyes at me. "Are you sure you're ready for that information?"

"In for a penny," I responded. "At this point, nothing is going to surprise me."

His eyebrow lifted. "Okay, but remember you asked." Cambious shifted in his seat but met my eyes with his. "My parents are a rarity. Most often Incubi and Succubi don't intermarry. Their offspring is usually mixed race. My parents are an exception. I have one brother and one sister, plus a large number of half-siblings. I was born a succubus named Cambia, but I knew from an early age that I was male. I had magical surgery about fifty years ago, once I found a compatible male who wanted to transition to female." He paused. "Still with me?"

As with just about everything since I had met Finneas, his words only created more questions. "Magical surgery? Fifty years ago?"

He nodded. "We age a bit differently than humans. So, yes, fifty years ago. We went together. I got her man bits, she got my female bits, some chanting, a sacrifice to Dianos, and a hefty payment later I was an incubus, and she was…whatever the female is for her race."

I blinked a little bit. "And what is her race?"

He bit his lip as he thought about it. "I think here you call them satyrs? The hooves and legs of a goat, but the torso and up is humanlike?"

"So, you're telling me you have a goat's…organ?" I asked, blushing from my toes up.

He grinned. "It was a good trade."

We talked for hours, well past when I should have been in bed. When I couldn't stop yawning, I reluctantly stood. "I have to get some sleep. Tomorrow is going to be a long day."

"I want you to be careful out there. As long as you are on this property, you are protected, but the Brotherhood could still have operatives here."

I nodded and headed for the stairs. I was sure that a return to something that I knew, something that was familiar would help me put all of this into perspective. What I didn't want was all of this intruding into that normal. I didn't say any of that though as I bid Cambious good night and shut my bedroom door.

CHAPTER 9
ENTER THE DAY JOB

The morning of November third dawned clear and a little bit on the cold side. I showered and dressed in the best of the clothes I had left to me, spent the time to blow dry my hair and I even applied the most basic makeup, because first impressions are important. I was going to need to find a hairdresser before long who could wrangle my unruly curls into something tamer.

Breakfast was a cup of coffee and a piece of toast, and I took the time to clean up the books on the table before I left the house in search of the train station. I wasn't prepared for the standing-room-only train, but I staked out a spot by one of the doors, put my headphones on, and turned on some music, then spent most of the forty-minute ride into the city scrolling through the email accounts I had been ignoring. We were maybe three stops from the one where I had been told I should get out and start the three-block walk when I felt eyes on me.

I looked up from my phone, scanning the crowded car that was only just beginning to thin out as we stopped at stations within San Francisco proper. I froze when I saw him, a bald man near the doors that connected to the next car, his dark eyes staring at me with naked hatred.

He didn't blink, just stared at me. I almost missed my stop because I was staring back. I waited almost too late to jump through the doors onto the platform, hoping it would be enough to keep him from following me.

Moving as fast as my less-than-fit body would allow, I raced up the escalator and to the fare gates, then up the next escalator and out onto the street. It took me a few moments to get my bearings, but once I took in the street signs and the landmarks Bonnie had told me to look for, I set out at a brisk pace, glancing behind me frequently to ensure I wasn't being followed.

I was so worried about the man on the train I didn't think about there being others, at least not until a hand grabbed my elbow and tried to pull me into an alley between buildings. I yelled and pulled away, only to find myself sandwiched between two men who each grabbed an arm. "Settle down, *Thanátou*," one of them growled at me. "Do not make us kill others by drawing attention to us."

That was not the thing to say to me to get me to comply. Instead, I began thrashing, pulling my arms away from them, and taking off at a run…not that I could run all that fast or all that far, but I sure as hell was not making it easy for them if I could help it.

"Hey!" Just as one of the men curled a fist in the back of my shirt, a man stepped up beside me and shoved my attacker away. "Ma'am, is this man trying to hurt you?"

I was panting, turning to put the man between me and the Brotherhood thugs. "They're trying to kill me," I said around my ragged breaths.

The man raised a radio to his lips and talked into it, telling whoever was on the other end of the line to get the police to their address. It was then that I realized he was wearing a security uniform. Before my savior could do anything more, both of my attackers disappeared, either into the crowd or into the ether, who knows which.

"I'm okay," I said, thanking the man.

"The police are on their way to get your statement. We'll wait with you."

I shook my head, pulling a shaking hand through my hair and looking around to figure out where I was. "I need to get to work. It's my first day."

"Frank, police should be here in a minute," a voice said behind me. "Did they get away?"

"Vanished," Frank replied, gesturing off up the street. "Ma'am, let's step inside in case they think about trying again."

I let Frank and his fellow security officer hurry me along into a lobby that I immediately recognized with my company's name over the desk. At least I had found the building. "I'm Thána Archer. I'm supposed to start work here today."

The officer who wasn't Frank slipped back behind the security desk. "Who were you meeting?"

"Bonnie Farva."

Frank offered me a seat and I sank into the chair, suddenly cold all over and shaking. Someone handed me a cup of coffee and after a minute, I realized someone was talking to me. I looked up, surprised to find the lobby was full of people. Frank was talking to two police officers and a woman in her forties was looking at me with concern on her face.

"I'm sorry," I said, shaking my head. The steam from the coffee was comforting and I lifted it closer to my face without drinking from it. "I didn't hear what you said."

She smiled softly and sat in the chair beside mine. "It's okay. I'm Bonnie. Frank said you were mugged?"

It was so much more than a mugging, but I couldn't tell her that. "Two guys. I'm not sure what they wanted; they were dragging me somewhere."

"We've had an increase in crime in this area," Bonnie said.

"Ma'am, if it's okay, we'd like to get your version of events," the female cop said, stepping around Frank. She was pretty, her dark braids pulled back neatly into a tight bun at the back of her head.

"I'm fine," I said reflexively. "Just a little shaken up."

We spent the next hour going over what had happened before Bonnie took me through security and out onto the factory floor. The building itself looked nothing like a factory on the outside. In fact, I would have guessed bank or financial institution before I stepped through those doors.

The rest of the day was filled with normal first day things, getting a computer and badge, introductions to more people than I could even begin to remember, and all the rest. My "office" was a small cubicle along the south wall, at the end of my production line, and waiting on my desk were personnel files on each of the people working the line, along with quality and defect reports for the last six months. It was a lot to go through.

The line's quality had been declining for months, but it wasn't clear if the issue was a matter of training, equipment, or the quality of the materials being used. Based on what I could see from just the reports, I knew that I wanted to tackle it with a three-pronged attack. I wrote up my preliminary recommendation: that we send the entire line up to training to be recertified, a full inspection of all of the equipment as well as a spot check of all of the materials being used on the line.

Once I'd finished that, I glanced up at the clock, surprised to see it had gone past six-thirty. The floor was mostly quiet, the small second shift crew busily about their tasks. I gathered my things and headed for Bonnie's office to drop off my recommendations.

"That was fast," she said after I handed it to her.

"I like to jump in with both feet," I replied. "But it's been a long day and I should head home."

"Let me get someone to take you to the train. We don't want a repeat of this morning."

"I'm sure I'll be fine." As much as a part of me wanted the comfort of having an escort, I knew that I couldn't avoid walking by myself forever.

"I'll see you tomorrow. I'm planning on talking one on one with the entire line tomorrow. Personnel files can't tell me who a person is."

"Sounds good. Be safe."

The security guard at the front desk was neither Frank nor the other guy, whose name I never caught. I did my best to be aware of my surroundings and the people moving through the streets, taking some comfort in the crowded platform and trains, thinking it would make my attackers hesitate. I had no idea if that were true, but I held on to it as if it were.

I was on high alert the whole ride home and the walk to my car in the gathering dark, but there was no sign of the Brotherhood or self-steering cars, even as I pulled onto the street and then into my driveway. There was a man putting something in the trunk of that '67 Mustang next door though and he lifted a hand in greeting. "You must be the new neighbor, I'm Steve Marsh."

I smiled and crossed the yard to shake his outstretched hand. "Sort of. I'm Thána Archer. I lived here when I was a child. I'm just getting back." All of my ID was in the name Archer, and the last name on my birth certificate felt strange in my mouth when I had tried it that morning before leaving for work.

"Well, welcome. My wife will be glad to know someone is finally living here. It's been the only empty on the street for a while, but that guy who's been taking care of the place has done a great job with the yards. If you need names for contractors to help you with the paint job and that sagging porch, let me know. My brother and his friends do great work."

"Thanks, I'm not sure I'm ready for that, but I'll let you know." I waved goodbye and headed into the house, flipping on lights as I dropped my keys onto the table by the door. I was exhausted, wrung out from the chaos of the last weeks, the attempt on my life, and the first day in a new job. Part of me wanted to just have a glass of wine and go to bed, but I also hadn't eaten, so I knew that needed to come first. I found the stuff to make a peanut butter sandwich and opened the screw cap on the cheap bottle of wine I had bought the day before, pouring some into a tumbler I pulled from the cupboard.

I was sitting at the table thinking about just how classy my dinner was when it dawned on me that I hadn't had to look for the glass, and I hadn't even considered reaching for the wine glasses further up, just grabbed a plastic tumbler from the bottom shelf. It was muscle memory or something. I'd done it before…probably a million times before we'd left this house.

As I looked around me, I felt more at home than I had ever felt. I did have to do something about my bedroom though. I hadn't slept in a twin bed since my teens, and the childish decor was not suited to my style. I could move into my parents' room, but somehow that felt like a betrayal. As far as I knew, my mother wasn't dead, and she could come home and want her room back. No, I decided sitting there, I would buy a new bed and paint the walls a nice rust or sage, something that suited my more grown-up palette.

There was more excitement to the idea than I would have thought, but I had never really had a room of my own in a place that I owned, though I supposed technically my mother still owned it. I finished my sandwich and took my glass of wine upstairs with me. Looking around my childhood bedroom, I could almost see how it would look with a queen-sized bed, maybe a set of bookshelves, a bigger desk.

I figured I could start the next weekend, I just had to get through the week at work first. For now, I just wanted to sleep and get a fresh start the next day. I finished my wine and set the tumbler on my nightstand before crawling into the bed. As much as I wanted to sleep, flashes of the attack that morning kept playing through my head. Four times now I'd come close to losing my life for some idealistic crusade that I had never even heard of before Finneas Connor had stepped into my life.

Despite my exhaustion, sleep was not coming easily and after an hour or so I got up, grabbed my tumbler, and headed back downstairs to my collected pile of books. Maybe somewhere in them I would find an answer to why, exactly, a bunch of fanatics I had never met wanted to bleed me.

CHAPTER 10
NESTING

There was a time when I didn't feel as though I needed to keep my head on a swivel just going about my daily business. Of course, that was before I knew who I was and before someone had tried to run me down, burn me out, slash my throat or kidnap me off the streets of San Francisco.

By the time Friday came around, with no further incidents the rest of the week, I was starting to relax. I left work a little early and headed to the local hardware store to pick up some paint, then hit up two of the local furniture stores to test out beds. After ordering a bedroom suite, I headed home.

Cambious was on the greenhouse porch as I came in with my gallons of paint and other odds and ends and he smiled as he came to help me. "You've been busy." He nodded toward the books on the table. I had spent my evenings trying to cram as much knowledge about my new reality into my head as I could. I'd even tried my hand at a few of the spells, including that one protection spell I'd found, though I wasn't sure if I'd used the right herbs, or gathered them at the right time because I wasn't sure exactly when the "dark of the moon" was supposed to be.

"There's a lot to learn," I said, putting my bag on the counter.

"I'm happy to see you working on it," Cambious said. "I found a couple of books I thought you might be interested in. This one is a few years old, but it is the most thorough telling of the Brotherhood's history I've ever read." He pointed to a book beside my pile. It was thick, its cover a slick black with the image of that haunting fortress on it. "And the other is one of the only texts that survived the purges of Blood Witches. It is rudimentary, and not really an instruction book, but should ground you in the basics."

"Thanks." I lifted the first book and paged through it. The printing was small, but it was filled with pictures and quotes and looked like something I would learn from. "I was going to throw together some dinner, if you want to join me."

He nodded. "My brother is on guard duty tonight. I would love to join you."

"Great. Could you take the paint up to my room? That's my weekend's plan, to get that painted. I'll get started on food."

I sorted through the pantry and came out with a can of corned beef hash, double-checked that I had eggs, and set about making breakfast for dinner. When Cambious returned, he leaned on the counter watching. "I understand the Brotherhood found you on Monday." His voice was soft and deep, but it made me stiffen up.

"I'm fine," I responded, cracking an egg into the pan. "And I haven't seen them since."

"They must have left a contingent behind after the veil returned to normal. The next nearest permanent portal is in Los Angeles, the one Merry used to find you. It is not a well-known portal and belongs to a family who does not support the aims of the Brotherhood."

"So, I can expect more of these random attacks?" I asked, flipping the two eggs in my pan over.

"And each time they will get closer to their true purpose," Cambious warned. I could feel his eyes watching me, not with that same intensity that once made my stomach drop with desire, but there was concern.

"I'm not sure what you expect me to do about it," I said after a long silence watching the eggs cook. "I am being careful. I'm always aware of who is around me, but I'm not going to just give up living and hide away in this house."

"I wasn't suggesting that," Cambious replied, handing me a plate. "I've just been thinking about it. They won't want to kill you here unless they have no other choice. They'll need access to a portal to take you back, so unless they've found a way to create a new permanent portal, they're going to either try to use yours or transport you to another one."

"Or wait for the spring when the veil thins again," I added.

He smiled. "You have been learning."

I handed him a plate and opened the drawer for forks. "I figured I needed to." I sighed and took my plate to the table. "I am remembering more, but it's not coming fast enough."

"Go easy," Cambious warned as he sat opposite me. "You cannot learn a lifetime's worth of spell work and history in a few weeks' time."

"Now you tell me." I rolled my eyes and settled in to eat. "There is something…" It had been bothering me that all I had to learn from was what my mother left me from her side of the family and there was little about my father to be found. "You said that your family was bound to mine, to my mother's family."

He nodded. His eyes seemed to intensify as he watched me. "I can't find any information about my father or his family. What do you know about them?"

Cambious put his fork down and leveled his eyes at me. "I can tell you that your father loved your mother and you girls with every fiber of his being. He walked away from a fortune to marry your mother. His mother forbid it and threatened to disown him if he married your mother."

"Why?"

Cambious shrugged. "That is not my story to tell. Perhaps you will have a chance to ask her yourself."

"That's not an answer." I sighed in frustration and rubbed a hand over my face. "I have maybe five clear memories of him, and the strongest of them is when he died. I have no doubt he loved me. I feel that love in that memory. He gave his life to save mine. But I know almost nothing else about him."

"What is it you think you should know?" Cambious asked, returning to his food.

I sighed again. "I don't know. What was he like? What did he do for a living? When did they come here to California? Obviously, it was before I was born."

"Okay, I would say that your father was mostly a happy guy, who loved his family. He and your mother met at university and got married shortly before she graduated. They came here when they found out she was pregnant with you. He would travel back and forth for a while when you were a baby, working as a sort of inter-dimensional postman, delivering messages and packages and such between families that have exiles here."

"So, they came here because of me?" I asked without looking up. "Did they know I'd be…what I am?"

"It is never for certain. The gift is exceedingly rare, but there was precedent on your mother's side for one of her children to be born to the gift, and there was dormant history on your father's side, so the chances increased. Your mother was terrified that an increase in activity among the Brotherhood would make you a target, if only for your family names."

"And she obviously wasn't wrong."

"No, unfortunately, she was not."

"And my father...he had magic too, didn't he? I mean, he fought the guy who tried to kill me when I was six."

At that Cambious grinned. "Ah, he was brilliant! Could have chosen any specialty really, or so my father says. He was gifted. He chose to be a garden witch for the most part, with a particular focus on growing magical ingredients that could be used in regular foods, not just potions and incantations. Most of the powders, spices, and such in the pantry are from his stock." He gestured at the greenhouse porch. "But the fruits out there are all your mother's. She could make fruit trees grow anywhere."

"You seem to have known them well," I observed, suddenly curious about Cambious and how old he had to be. To my eyes, he didn't look much older than me, but between his comment a few days before about having his surgery fifty years ago, and how much time he must have spent with my parents, I had to wonder.

He nodded. "After my transition, I came up to the cabin to recover. I started to relieve my father well before your parents came here. Once they did, I spent a good amount of time with them both." We were quiet for a few minutes, then Cambious gestured at my pile of books. "Tell me, have you experimented at all?"

It was my turn to shrug noncommittally. "Not seriously? I mean, Monday night when I couldn't sleep, I tried this one...but I have no way of knowing if it worked."

"Which one?" Cambious asked, one eyebrow raised.

I fished out the book from the pile and found the spell again, then handed the book over. "And you haven't seen any of the Brotherhood since you did this?"

I rolled my eyes, not willing to be convinced it was that simple. "Mind you, I'm not sure I even got the right plants. I was tired and couldn't sleep."

"It was the right night for it," Cambious said, handing me back the book. "And I know you have all of those plants out on the porch, so if you identified them correctly, you might have managed it. I know you've used it before, after your father died. Your mother thought it might help you feel safer."

"Obviously, it didn't work," I countered. "They still kept finding us."

"Ah, but it isn't a particularly strong or lasting spell. Its purpose is to confound your enemies for a short time in order to make your escape."

"Not a whole lot of good then, is it?"

"It's given you a peaceful week, has it not?" Cambious countered. "But perhaps a better place to begin is with something more basic, something of infinite usage."

"I take it you have a suggestion?"

"I do indeed. There should have been a set of ward stones in the box you were given. Have you figured out how to use them?"

I reached for the trunk on the chair near me, rummaging until I came up with the small bag that had the stones. I dumped them onto the table. There were twelve in all, smaller than most dice, carved of what I took to be obsidian. Their edges and corners had been worn over time.

"They were your mother's when she was a girl," Cambious said.

"I'm not sure what I'm supposed to do with them," I admitted, brushing my hand over them. Automatically, I started sorting them into pairs, each of them feeling slightly different, and yet instinctively I knew which ones went with which.

"At their most basic, they keep out the things you don't want getting in. There are larger, stronger versions of those warding stones at all four corners of this property, which is why the Brotherhood cannot see into this house or cross the property line, not without knocking the wards out first."

"So, like a magical door lock?" I remembered Merry using them at the door to the motel.

"More or less. You can use as few as four stones to secure say a window, or all twelve to secure a camp location or ritual site. There are a number of different ways to activate them, but you should start with the most basic." He stabbed a finger at the small book that had been mine as a child. "You should have that incantation in there. I know your mother was teaching you how to use them before you left here."

"Do you know where she is?" I asked, a sudden melancholy filling me. I had spent so many years angry at her, or her abandonment of me at least, that this increasing sense of longing that had been building inside me all week was disconcerting.

"I'm sorry, I don't. Not for sure. She came through the portal without you about five years after she left here, said she was taking your sister somewhere to be safe, and I know that she visited family in Thelos, and Finneas Connor in Greju, but then she just disappeared. As far as I know, no one has seen her since."

Five years after we left the house, so a few years after she had left me with no memory outside that police station in Rochester, New York. I could only wonder what she and Daria had done after they left me there. I yawned and shook my head. Everything was so exhausting. And I had so much more to learn.

CHAPTER 11
GHOSTS OF THE PAST

I spent my weekend painting my bedroom and working with the ward stones. The first incantation scribbled in my childhood handwriting used only four stones, two pairs, and when properly constructed, the resulting ward could secure a window or small door.

Whenever I wasn't painting, I was attempting to make that incantation work. I don't know why I expected it to be easy, but it wasn't. It was Sunday afternoon before I got more than the four stones stacked in pairs, and then it was little more than a flash of something before the stones toppled.

I was reaching for the stones when I heard my mother's voice softly chiding me. "You're trying too hard. Relax. Let the magic flow through you."

I looked up, nearly certain I'd find her leaning on the door frame as she had in my memory. I'd had this same fight with the cubes before. "I don't know how," I whined in my memory.

"You do, Thána. You can do this."

In my memory, I heard myself speak the words of the incantation and I followed my own lead, touching first one stack of the stones, then the second. "*Prostatéfste kai apothéste aftó to chóro.*" To my surprise, the stones seemed to glow for a moment, then between them stretched a field, like the one Merry had constructed in my hotel room in LA. I sat back, satisfied.

After a moment, I reached for the book again, seeking the incantation to disassemble the field. "*Elefthérosi.*" The field collapsed and the stones on the left tumbled over. I ran through the process several times until I was sure I could put them up at will before I pocketed the stones and went to start cleaning up from the day's painting.

I was surprised when the room spun as I gained my feet and fatigue pulled at my limbs. I felt drained. I staggered to the bed and sat down hard, shaking my head. In the book, my younger self had written the words, "It's harder than you think." I was beginning to understand that.

After a few minutes, I was able to get up and get moving again. I went back to the white trim I had been painting before my break, putting a few finishing touches on the door frame before I called it a night. Cambious had told me that relearning the basics might mean rebuilding a tolerance to the toll magic takes on a user. I wasn't sure I had believed him. Hell, I was still on the fence about the whole idea of magic at all, but so far, Cambious hadn't been wrong about anything.

The potion seemed to have worked, which wasn't to say I wasn't still having random dreams about sex and Cambious, but I wasn't overwhelmed with the lust for him like I was at the beginning. And, as Cambious had pointed out, my "hide me from my enemies" spell seemed to have worked as well, at least for the time being. And now, I'd made the ward stones work, at least on a small scale. Maybe in a few days I'd be ready to try one of the more complicated configurations of the stones. There were several written in my childhood journal/spellbook, and I vaguely recalled seeing more in one of the other books.

My mind was still on that as I cleaned up my painting supplies, taking the pan and brushes downstairs to wash. As I stepped off the stairs and turned for the kitchen, I stopped cold. A man was there, between me and the kitchen. He turned and my heart stopped. His eyes sparkled and his smile was wide as he saw me.

"Dad?" I choked out the word, knowing that was who I was seeing, and knowing that it couldn't be real.

He nodded once, still smiling, but his eyes were sad. His mouth moved, but no sound came. His hand reached out and I stepped forward, trying to reach him, but in the split second between picking up my foot and putting it back down, he was gone.

Emptiness sank into my stomach, and I sank with it, ending up on my ass on the wood floor right where he'd been standing. My whole being reverberated with a sudden and desperate longing for the love I was starting to remember, the family I had lost. I was still sitting there, however long later, with paint drying on my hand and tears streaming down my face when I heard Cambious on the stairs. I struggled to get up before he could find me there, but my legs wouldn't cooperate.

"Thána?"

I wiped the back of the hand holding the brush across my cheeks and tried again to stand. His hands came to steady me, and he followed me into the kitchen, close behind me. I put the pan and brush in the sink and exhaled a breath I wasn't fully aware I was holding.

"Are you…?"

I nodded, sort of messy and not at all convincing. "I saw…honestly, I don't know what I saw."

"Come sit down." Cambious guided me to a chair, and I sat gratefully. "Tell me."

I licked my lips and nodded. "Okay, so…I've been working with the ward stones, like you said. Finally got a basic ward up too. Then, it was like I'd been running in sand for hours. I came down here to clean up, and as I came off the stairs, there he was. Just standing there…like when I'd come home from school." That memory flooded me, running in all excited to show him what I'd learned that day, the way he would beam at me in pride and sweep me into his arms.

"Who?"

"You're going to think I'm crazy."

He gave me a look that was all about the crazy my life had become and shook his head gently.

"My father." I whispered it, barely daring to glance up at him as I did.

He was nodding though. "I'm not surprised."

"You're not?" I asked, my voice high and tight. "I was! He's dead, Cambious."

"And you're a blood witch who helped him pass over. If he's going to appear to anyone, it's going to be you."

I shook my head. "I don't believe in ghosts."

He shrugged his massive shoulders dismissively. "Apparently that does not stop them from being."

I took a deep breath and let it out slowly. "Okay, why now? Why here? Why not all those years ago when I was alone and really could have used a father, even one who was dead?"

Cambious took my hands and held them for a moment, then tilted my chin up so he could look into my eyes. Tears ran unchecked down my face and his finger brushed them away. "He is here because here is where he died, *Mikros*. And now is when you are also here."

"It isn't fair," I muttered, knowing I sounded like that six-year-old me in my memory with the ward stones. "I barely remember him, and mostly I remember him dying."

Cambious didn't respond, just pulled me close and folded his arms around me, paint and all. I let him comfort me for a minute before I sniffed and pulled back. I stood, feeling awkward and emotional, and only one of those two things felt normal for me. I'd always been awkward. I'd learned early to shove my emotions down into a dark hole so others wouldn't be bothered by them. Over the years it had just become who I was.

I went to the sink to wash the paint off my hands and clean my tools, working to shove the sudden loneliness and longing for my family back into its hiding place. Cambious gave me the space and was quiet until I was nearly done.

"Your room looks great," he ventured when I was pressing water out of the brush.

"Thanks."

"I was wondering if you'd be interested in coming through the portal with me? I have food and a lovely bottle of *Erythraó* that I think you'd enjoy, judging on what I've seen of your taste in wine."

I turned, thoughts about ghosts and family momentarily forgotten. "Are you asking me on a date, Cambious?"

He grinned. "Not exactly. I just think it's time you see where you come from. I promise to have you home by bedtime."

I nodded slowly. "Just let me change."

"You look fine," Cambious countered. "There's no one around for miles. It will be just the two of us."

"Sure, okay." He stood, holding out a hand to me. I slipped my hand into his, marveling again at the size of him, then he was leading me back to the stairs and down to the closet where he opened the door and held it for me.

I hesitated at the threshold, peering into the darkness beyond. The only light I could see was the soft glow of some lanterns that held down the corners of a blanket a few yards from the door. I held my breath as I stepped through, though I couldn't tell you why, and I let it out when the ground didn't disappear beneath me. The night air was warm and smelled vaguely of something akin to jasmine. The blanket looked to be hand-woven, spread out on a grassy patch between boulders. I couldn't see much beyond the warm yellow light of the lanterns, so I turned back, wondering what the door looked like from this side.

Oddly enough, it looked like a door, stuck into a rock as tall as a house. Cambious ducked his head as he stepped through the door and I gasped as he reverted to his true form, horns and all. I had nearly forgotten. I tried to cover my surprise, but Cambious just smiled. "I also figured it was time you dealt with me in my regular guise. Sit, sit."

I backpedaled to the blanket, reminding myself that horns or not, he was still Cambious, the same guy I had grown to trust in the short time I'd been in the house…which unbelievably had been less than two whole weeks. I sank down to the blanket, shifting until I found a comfortable position. Cambious joined me, his large feet eating the distance from the door. If it were possible, he was even larger in this form than the giant of a man I had gotten to know. He reached for a basket, opening the side, and pulling out first a bottle of wine, which he passed to me.

In seconds there was some sort of music playing, something that had a vaguely familiar feeling. I looked to see him setting down what I assumed was his world's version of a radio. "Like it?"

"I'm not sure," I answered.

He smiled. "It equates to your world's baroque period. Similar instruments, though entirely our own. This piece in particular is from a Greco composer named Alexi Manoko, from approximately two hundred years ago. His use of string instruments is quite inspired."

I handed him back the bottle to open. "I'll take your word for it. I'm more of a Coldplay and Maroon 5 sort of girl."

"And the wine?"

I shrugged. "I pretty much can tell it's wine," I said with a chuckle.

"Well, we will have to work on your ability to read the language of our fair land. It's a red, not too far afield from your pinot noir, though it is a blend. Shall I pour?"

I gestured for him to continue, and he fished a corkscrew and two glasses out of the basket. When he had handed me a glass and turned his attention to the rest of our meal, I took the opportunity to try to learn more about the world I found myself in. Unfortunately, there wasn't much to be seen in the dark. "What time is it here? I remember that first day, it was midafternoon, but it was dark on this side of the door."

"It is approximately two in the morning," Cambious responded, setting out containers of various kinds of food. There was a collection of what seemed to be vegetables, a meat of some kind, something mashed with what looked like cheese on top, and a pie that smelled delicious. "Our days are a bit shorter than yours, our years a bit longer. Which means there is exactly one day each year when we are more or less in sync. The rest of the time we are constantly ahead of or behind you."

I tucked the knowledge into my brain folder for all things not a part of my life prior to the arrival of Finneas Connor and took the fork and plate that Cambious offered me. I served myself some of each of the dishes, saving the pie for once I'd tasted the rest. I was surprised somehow that the meat and mashed vegetable dishes were piping hot as if just served off the stove. Honestly, I'm not sure how anything surprised me at that point, but it did.

As if guessing my thought process, Cambious chuckled. "Magic," he said, as if that alone would answer all of my questions. To be fair, it probably did.

I tasted the meat dish first. It was pale in color, except where the spices tinted it vaguely orange-red. "Chicken?" I asked as I lifted a forkful to my mouth.

"Similar to," Cambious responded, dishing up his own plate.

The taste was similar too, so I guessed it was some sort of bird. The spices brought out the natural flavor of the meat, without disguising it. Next, I tried the mashed…whatever. Had we been in my own kitchen, I would have guessed potato, but the taste was more turnip than potato. "This is really good," I said around my mouthful. I swallowed around my horror at talking with my mouth full, then reached for the wine. The flavor of the wine exploded across my tongue, and I brought the glass back to my lips to drink more. "This is amazing."

It was clear my praise made Cambious happy, his dark skin all aglow with pleasure. "I hoped you would like it. Wine isn't always my forte. I've been working at improving my wine vocabulary." He rolled his eyes a little to the right. "Also, one of my many, many half-siblings owns the winery where this particular vintage was created. She gifted it to me when I told her why I wanted it."

I was suitably impressed, even if I didn't say so right away. We ate in companionable silence for a while, and I didn't even begin to feel the need to say anything, which for me was odd at least.

CHAPTER 12
NEW FRIENDS

ALL TOLD, WE SPENT ALMOST TWO HOURS THERE ON THAT BLANKET, EATING, finishing off that bottle of wine, and sinking back into our last conversation about the history of a homeland I had never known, but found myself sitting in.

"There," Cambious said, pointing over my shoulder. "Can you see those lights?"

In the distance, a series of golden and white lights danced on the horizon, maybe fifty miles away, more if we were on a mountain. "Yeah. What is it?"

"That is Thelos. Your mother was born there. Merry lives on the outskirts."

"Merry lives there?" I stood, turning to squint in that direction…which was ludicrous. It wasn't like I was going to actually see the crazy old woman.

"Not just her. You have some aunts and uncles there too. Even one of your father's cousins. His family wanted nothing to do with him when he sided with your father."

I turned to study him in the half-light provided by the lanterns. "You seem to know an awful lot about my family."

"Well, our families have been joined for over a hundred years."

"A hundred…I thought you said your father and my…grandfather?" I glanced at the glass of wine in my hand, trying to decide if it was strong enough to absolve my inability to remember the exact details. "How old **are** you?"

Cambious seemed amused by my confusion. "Older than you might imagine…and my father was just a teen himself at the time."

I shook my head, too compromised from the wine to give it too much more thought. Even as I sipped at the remnants in my glass, I was thinking that I needed to consider that I had to go to work in the morning. "So, how do you suggest I go about not getting killed or kidnapped by Brotherhood thugs while I attempt to live my life this week?" I asked as Cambious raised the bottle and topped off my glass with the last of the wine.

"Don't go to work?" Cambious suggested. I couldn't tell whether he was being serious or not.

"That is **not** an option, Cambious," I countered. "Even if I own the house and the land, there are still bills to pay."

"And yet, the house still stands today, even though there hasn't been a member of your family in residence in over twenty years," Cambious responded, his hand dropping onto my shoulder.

"There is food, and water and electricity…" I said, shaking my head.

"Perhaps you require a vacation," Cambious offered. "Time to reconnect to a family you have never known."

I shook my head, starting to feel overwhelmed by it all. "I think what I need, my friend, is to get home and shower, sleep…get ready for my Monday."

"If that is what my lady wishes…" Cambious said with a grand bow and gesture toward the door.

"It is."

He crossed to the door and held it open for me. "Until the next time…"

I smirked and rose up on my tiptoes in an attempt to reach his cheek. I only reached as far as the side of his neck, but I kissed it anyway. "Until next time indeed." I crossed back into my house, the house I had been left by my mother, warm and filled with good feelings. I had enjoyed the dinner and the time spent in the company of someone that my known history should have proved to be impossible. I stripped on my way into the bathroom, tipsy enough to not care about the trail of paint-spattered clothing I left behind me.

My shower was quick, just enough to wash the specks of paint from my skin and hair. A quick check that my alarm was set, and I fell into bed, more content than I could remember being. That, of course, didn't last long. I found myself trapped in bloody dreams, my clothing drenched in it, my skin sticky as it dried. I couldn't tell where the blood was coming from, and I couldn't see in the dark. I woke breathlessly nearly an hour before the alarm.

I was shaking as I sat up. Like the dreams I'd had as a child, there was no detail to them, no definition. And yet, they were just as terrifying.

Pushing the hair out of my face, I put my feet on the floor and stood. There was no point trying to go back to sleep, it would just make getting up again worse. Instead, I got dressed and rescued my discarded clothing from the hallway floor, depositing it in my hamper before I headed downstairs to make coffee.

Once the coffee was started, I diverted into the downstairs bathroom to tame my hair, which had started to curl up when I went to bed without blow drying it out. The coffee machine beeped just as I finished straight ironing it into something that resembled my normal straight style, even if it was puffier than usual. A cup of coffee later and I was sitting at the kitchen table amidst my collection of books filled with arcane knowledge.

I opened the book on the Brotherhood that Cambious had brought me. The history of the Brotherhood was fascinating if disturbing. The book posited that the movement had begun as simply a stricter reading of religious texts by a small group of monks dedicated to Jeus, who I gathered was similar to Zeus mixed with Jesus, except of course that this faith had its roots thousands of years before either.

Before the Brotherhood, people with gifts like mine were called, *kapnastís*, which meant "disease eater" and they were revered and sought after to help heal the kinds of diseases that the medicine of the day could do nothing for. In the religious literature, there was a story about a gathering of *kapnastís* in the dawn of mankind who came together after collecting drops of blood from all the many scattered peoples of the world to give the blood as a gift to Hathus, to calm the cataclysm of earthquakes, volcanic eruptions, and other catastrophes as Hathus tried to expel mankind from his land.

In some versions of the myth, the *kapnastís* ingested the blood, then expelled it through their menses into the earth at a place called *Hathus Koúna*, the Cradle of Hathus. They squatted there for five days and nights, giving this gift to the god of the Underworld and when it was done, the land quieted and the volcanoes ceased their flowing. The story told of a time when the next payment would be due, and it was there that the Brotherhood seemed to cut away from the traditional understanding of what would come.

It started with small disagreements with the established understanding and grew over time until a man named Humile Racklish showed up on the scene. It was Racklish, as he rose through the ranks of the order, who poisoned his brothers with the idea that a blood witch did not cure but kill. There is some evidence that Racklish, as a child, saw his mother die at the hands of a *kapnastís* who had been called in too late to save her. Instead, she had taken away the woman's pain and eased her into the next life, and Racklish had decided that this woman had killed her.

It was a fine line, I supposed. Had the woman been left alone, she would still have died. Whoever that blood witch was, she had probably spared her days of suffering or more. Racklish went on to rise to the rank of *Evlogim Patoras*, essentially in charge of his own chapter of the monks. Under him, they moved further and further away from the original scriptures, turning to other works that supported their reading.

My coffee had gotten cold as I read, and when I realized it, I got up to refill it, but noticed the time and set the coffee down and tucked the book into my briefcase. I headed out the door and to the train station. Finding parking was challenging, especially with the construction of a new garage eating up most of the surface lots. I finally ended up on the fourth floor of the existing garage and parked, scrambling to get to the platform.

Of course, my distraction caused me to miss the train I'd been aiming to get on, so I settled in to wait the ten minutes for the next one. My mind rambled over what I'd read, the eerie parallels to some of the history I knew of the religions in the world around me. I figured it had something to do with human nature. I was still pondering that when someone said, "Good morning."

Startled, I turned to see a woman beside me, zipping up her coat. Her smile was bright, and her eyes sparkled. "Hello," I responded, thrown a little bit. I hadn't adjusted to riding public transportation, but I was fairly certain most folks just put on their headphones and minded their own business.

"Haven't seen you before. New job?" she asked amiably.

"Yeah, normally I take the train before this one. Missed it this morning."

"Well, I hope it won't make you late for work." She held out her hand. "I'm Hannah."

I shook her hand, still a little confused. "Thána," I responded.

"We're a friendly bunch on this line," Hannah said, waving as two older ladies walked past us to another spot down the platform. Hannah herself seemed to be older than me, but not by a lot. She was at least four inches shorter than me. Several others were calling out hellos as they got in line behind Hannah. "Everyone, this is Thána. Thána, this is Amber, Purav, and Josie."

I nodded hello, my eyes sweeping over the group. Amber was younger than me, dressed in blue scrubs with a fluffy winter jacket on over them. Beside her, Purav was tall and thin with graying black hair and dark eyes. He reminded me of one of my techs back in El Paso. Josie brought up the rear, with tired eyes and what looked like a bag heavy with books. I couldn't guess her age, but she looked like someone who had been around the block a couple of times.

They bantered, trying to draw me into the conversation, but I've never been good at small talk. Eventually, they managed to get me to tell them how long I'd been in the area, that I worked in the city, and that I wasn't a fan of public transportation. Purav gave me extensive detail about how much easier it was than driving into the city, except for when there were mechanical issues, or someone jumped onto the tracks. I learned that morning that "medical emergency" was the code for a suicide on the tracks, and that it would snarl up the commute for many hours.

"Your best bet then is to get together with other people coming this way and take an Uber." His accent was subtle, very Americanized, and his voice was a beautiful, soft tenor that I found soothing.

"I'll keep that in mind," I said with a small smile. Conversation stopped as the train pulled in, too loud to try to overcome with our voices. We boarded and to my surprise, there were available seats. I pulled my book out of my briefcase as I sat, determined to get a few chapters read before getting to my stop.

"Whatcha reading?" Hannah asked, sitting next to me.

"It's the history of a cult known as the Brotherhood of God," I responded, flipping open to my marker.

"I've never heard of them," Hannah said.

"They aren't from around here." I put the book in my lap and looked at her. She looked genuinely interested, which I wasn't used to. "Some of my ancestors got tangled up with them, and so I wanted to learn more."

"Cults are spooky." She made a face. "I had a cousin once that got mixed up with the Moonies. Mmmhm." She shook her head. "I'll think for myself, thanks."

I had to chuckle. "Yeah, me too. Still, the history of how they get started is fascinating."

She turned to her phone after that, and I picked my book back up. Now and then I let my eyes sweep the faces around me, looking for any hostile eyes and bald heads. As each of my new friends got off the train, they said goodbye, to both me and Hannah, until Hannah and I were the only ones of the group still on the train. I put my book back in my briefcase and stood as we approached my stop.

"Oh, this is my stop too," Hannah said, standing with me. "Which way are you heading?"

"Just a few blocks down from Mission," I replied, moving with the other commuters on their way to the fare gates.

"I'm heading that way too. We can walk together."

A part of me thought that was the worst idea ever, with people trying to kill me, I didn't want her to get caught in the crossfire. On the other hand, maybe they would be less likely to make a move on me if I had company. Either way, it was fairly obvious that Hannah was the kind of person who, once she decided to be your friend, you were not going to shake her very easily. About a block from where I could already see Frank the security guard out front of our building, Hannah hitched her thumb at a glass and steel skyscraper. "This is me. Nice to meet you, Thána."

"Yeah you too," I said, unsure whether I meant it or not. I never really was what you would call a people person. I preferred the company of animals and books.

Frank held the door for me and tipped his hat as I passed by. As I headed for my office, I put the world outside of work away so I could focus on the job at hand.

CHAPTER 13
RUN

IT WAS NEARLY THANKSGIVING BEFORE ANYTHING INTRUDED INTO THE QUIET life I wanted and was hoping I would get. I'd spent the time working, and when I was at home, I was trying to fast-track a lifetime full of knowledge about all of the things I never knew were real, like witches and ghosts and transgender incubi.

There were no new sightings of Brotherhood men seeking my life, and for that matter, no new sightings of my father's ghost either. I was grateful for both. Work was progressing, my line was already showing improved quality and I found myself actually enjoying the company of my fellow BART riders in the mornings, much to my surprise.

Like most other holidays, Thanksgiving had never been a special day for me. Mostly it reinforced the idea that I wasn't a part of the family I lived with. I was always treated well enough, but it never felt like home. I was, however, looking forward to a four-day weekend, time to spend working my way through my beginner's spellbook and practicing with the ward stones.

Or at least, that's what I had planned.

I let my team leave at noon the Wednesday before, finished up some paperwork, and headed home myself. I gave thought to stopping to pick up groceries, then remembered that it was the day before a holiday, and everyone was out in the stores losing their minds over a can of evaporated milk or a carton of eggnog. I decided to order take-out instead and headed for my car in the BART parking garage.

That was when I caught the first glimpse of them. Three of them, dressed in black suits with bald heads. They were standing around my car.

I shrank back to the cover of the stairwell, peeking through the railing. They stood nearly motionless. Behind them, near the front of my car, there was a shimmer of sorts, like light reflecting on water. My stomach twisted and I eased back down the staircase, nearly knocking Purav over. "Oh, sorry," I said in little more than a whisper.

"Is everything okay?"

I shook my head. "No." I wasn't sure exactly what to say. "It's…could I get a ride home, do you think? My…my ex sent some friends of his…and they're just…I don't want to deal with it right now."

"Yes, no problem. Are you sure you don't want to get the police?"

I shook my head. "No, I'll wait for them to get bored and leave. Come back later for my car." I wasn't sure the cops could handle them, with who knew what kind of magic power between them. Home was safe enough though, warded and all that. Cambious could come back with me. Maybe in the morning.

"Why don't you go downstairs and wait by the garage exit. I'll get my car. It's a white Prius."

I nodded, slinking past him down the stairs, my eyes scanning the first level and the exit for more of them. When Purav pulled up, I jumped in as quickly as I could. "I don't think they saw me," I said in relief as we pulled away from the curb. I gave him my address and tried to control the erratic fury of my heartbeat. "I don't know how to thank you. My ex is…well let's just say we see things very differently."

"Are you going to be okay alone?" Purav asked as we stopped in front of my house.

"I won't be alone. I have a friend staying with me." It wasn't a complete lie. Cambious was just on the other side of a door. "Thank you. I hope you have a wonderful long weekend."

He smiled and touched my hand. "Please be careful."

I nodded and climbed out of the car. He waited as I looked around for trouble, then let myself into the gate in the fence. For the first time, I could feel the wards let me in and close behind me. At least I had **that** going for me. I snorted to myself and fished my keys out of the pocket of my work pants, unlocking the door. I waved to Purav to let him know I was safe, and I watched him pull away.

And that was when I saw the two men in black suits step out of two different yards and turn toward me. Quickly, I closed the door and threw the deadbolt. My heart hammered at my ribs as I turned from the door. I had no idea how the wards would hold or how much trouble I was in.

I turned and nearly screamed as once again my father's ghost was standing in the hallway, arm outstretched to me. Once I caught my breath, I rolled my eyes. "No offense, Dad, but now really isn't a good time."

I dropped my keys on the table and my briefcase on the stairs. As I started to go up the stairs to get Cambious, my father moved, suddenly in front of me on the stairs, pointing at the door. "Yeah, I know," I said, staring up at him. "And there are more of them, at least three more. So, unless you're here to tell me what to do now, I need to go find Cambious."

"Your mother."

I stopped with my foot still on the stair, blinking at him. "Did you just…"

He blinked in and out for a moment, then seemed to solidify. "Go through the portal. Find your mother." And then he was gone.

"That's it?" I asked the empty air. Fear thrummed through me, kicking my sarcastic annoyance into high gear. "Find your mother. Right. Just like that. Sure, why not." I stormed up the stairs and into the closet, wrenching the door open. "Cambious, I—" I stopped when the incubus on the other side of the door turned out to be someone other than Cambious. "Oh, sorry."

He smiled at me, his teeth sharp and white as they stood out in contrast to his black skin. "You must be Thána. I am Durious, Cam's brother."

"Oh." Yes, my witty self was on a roll. "I…there are Brotherhood goons outside."

"That isn't good," Durious said. "How many?"

"Two here, another three at the train station surrounding my car."

"That really isn't good."

"Tell me about it. I'm trapped in here now."

"I'll call Cambious. You should pack a bag. We can get you to your family here."

"What good will that do? Aren't there more of them over there?"

"Yes, but here at least the law is on your side and your family will know how to protect you."

Right. Because they'd done such a good job of that in the past. "Whatever. Just get Cambious here."

I closed the door and headed to my bedroom. I had no idea what I needed to pack to go through the portal. I pulled out an old duffle bag I had found at the back of my parent's closet and put it on the bed. I was pulling out clean underwear when the floor beneath me shook and seconds later a booming sound rattled the window. I circled the new queen-sized bed to pull aside the curtains. All five of the Brotherhood stood on the sidewalk outside, right hands extended, left hands clasped around their right wrists, as if physically pushing against the wards.

"Great." I shoved the underwear into my bag, chased it with a couple of T-shirts and a pair of jeans, then turned to strip out of my work pants, remembering to take my ward stones out of the pocket. I had taken to carrying them as some sort of placebo against my fear. I pulled on a clean pair of jeans and paused to shove my feet into my hiking boots. I had no idea what to expect on the other side, and I wanted to be prepared.

Which led me to shove the bag of ward stones in my pocket and cross to the chest beside my new desk. I pressed my thumb to the lock and pulled out the family book, plus the book on basic Blood Witch magic, my own spellbook, and what I believed to be my mother's spellbook. I wanted the history of the Brotherhood too, but that was in my briefcase. I decided to take the risk and raced down the stairs, grabbing my briefcase and hauling it back to my bedroom, shoving the book into the bag with the rest.

I went back to the dresser for a couple of pairs of socks. One of my foster mothers had been obsessed with keeping your feet dry and warm, and it had rubbed off. I even kept a pair in my briefcase, and there was a bag in my trunk with clean socks and underwear.

There was another quake and boom and I nearly fell on my ass, grabbing at the dresser to keep from falling, just as Cambious crashed against the door frame. "What was that?" he asked.

I hitched a thumb at the window. "Our visitors are knocking on the door."

He crossed to the window, glancing out before turning back to me. "They shouldn't have been able to breach the wards I put up to hide the neighborhood."

"Well, looks like they did."

"We need to go."

"Working on it," I said, tossing the socks in on top of the books.

"Now, Thána. They're almost through." He grabbed the bag in one hand and my arm in the other, just as I was reaching for Rusty to throw in the bag too. His hand propelled me toward the bedroom door and into the hallway.

"Won't they just follow us through?" I asked as we stepped through the door in the closet.

"They can try," Cambious responded through gritted teeth. "Durious?"

"Backup is on the way."

"Good. Thána, come here and give me your hand."

I stepped back toward him as he set his key to the lock and turned it. He murmured words in some language I didn't recognize, then took my left hand, quickly slicing across it with a knife I hadn't seen in his hand.

"Ow!" I tried to pull my hand back, but he kept a hold of it, using his finger to spread the blood across my palm.

"Now set it against the door and repeat after me. *Per meum sanguinem.*"

I pressed my hand to the middle of the door, and stumbled over the words, *"Per meum sanguinem."*

"Hoc ostium: et signantes litteras. Et nemo non per gradus sanguinis mei."

I repeated the words and a sharp pain flared in my palm, then a similar sensation to erecting wards from the stones flowed through me and a vaguely blue energy field grew out from my hand to cover the door, then the rock into which it was set.

"That should hold. And if it doesn't, Durious and friends will cut down anyone that comes through." Durious handed his brother a white handkerchief, which Cambious used to cover my wound. "We'll get you a proper bandage when we get down the to the cabin." He shouldered my bag and then pointed me past the spot where we had enjoyed our picnic. On the horizon, the sun was nearly down, making me pick my steps carefully. So far, I had yet to see this place in proper daylight.

Light flared to my right, and Cambious held a lantern up, casting a circle of light to guide us. The path was well worn, but little more than three-foot-wide, leading down from the hilltop. In the distance, I could see the lights of Thelos, and further to the right, I could just make out the dark line of some mountains. The trail turned to the left and I got the impression of tall grass and the smell of something floral.

"Watch your step through here, we haven't gotten up here to regrade the trail after the rains," Cambious said beside me. As if to prove his point, the toe of my boot hit a rock and I stumbled, recovering myself before I fell on my face.

"Someone should get on that," I said to cover my embarrassment.

"We have someone coming next week," Cambious replied good-naturedly. "We're almost there."

"Almost where?" I asked, just as the trail turned again and I spotted a darker shadow in the shape of a cabin with soft yellow light escaping around curtains in a window and smoke curling up from a chimney.

"Durious and I live here. Keeps us close to the portal." Cambious stepped around me as we got closer, opening the door, and ushering me inside. "We'll spend the night, and in the morning, we'll go the rest of the way down the mountain and take my car down to Thelos."

I stepped into a cabin that was not unlike the one my last foster family kept in the Adirondacks. There was a single room that served as living room, kitchen, and dining room, and off toward the back, a ladder led up to a loft that I assumed held a bedroom. It was cozy, though more what I imagined a bachelor pad to look like than the granny-decorated cabin I remembered. There were no placemats on the table, crocheted or otherwise, and a lack of family photos on the walls.

"Car?" I asked as Cambious's words sank in. "You have cars?"

Cambious chuckled. "Our society is thousands of years older than yours, Thána. Of course we have cars. Ours are far more efficient and no longer run on fossil fuels, but otherwise, they are not so dissimilar."

"Oh." Some part of me was disappointed that I had stepped into a magical realm only to find that their method of transportation was no less magical than ours. "Okay, so what's the plan after that? How do we find my mother?"

He frowned at me. "What?"

Right. I hadn't told him about my father's ghost and what he had said. "My father told me, just before you came to get me that I needed to find my mother."

CHAPTER 14
SUCCUBUS

"It is rare," Cambious said, sitting on the overstuffed couch tucked against the window, "for a spirit to manifest with the will to speak unless they are centuries old."

"Yeah, well, speak he did," I countered. "He told me, 'Go through the portal. Find your mother,' and then he just vanished."

"It probably drained him." Cambious put my bag on the floor.

"Well, it scared the shit out of me," I said, pacing the length of the cabin. The energy of that fear was still driving me with the need to run, even though we'd already run and ended up here. The compact kitchen stuck into the corner was far more modern than I would have expected of a remote cabin. The cabin my foster family had taken me to that summer had still had a wood-burning stove and the water came in from a pump attached to the sink.

This had a stove that didn't look all that different from mine, and the sink had a normal faucet. The small counter space was tidy, with canisters that lined the back. I fiddled with the canisters, turning them so I could see their labels. It brought my attention back to my hand and the bright red that was seeping through the cloth tied over it.

"Ah, yes. Let me get the first aid kit." Cambious lurched up and went to an antique-looking cabinet near the small kitchen table. "Come, sit down." He held out a chair for me and I sat, setting my injured hand on the table where he could reach it. His large hands put a metal box on the table and opened it. From what I could see around his hands it was a fairly standard first aid kit, until he put a small jar of dark ointment on the table. "Let me see."

I pulled back the handkerchief and he nodded before wetting some gauze with what I took to be alcohol. He used it to clean the drying blood off my hand before he lifted the jar and daintily used the nail of his pinky finger to scoop out a small amount. Gently, he rubbed the ointment into the cut. It smelled like a combination of ginger and cinnamon, and I expected it to sting, but it didn't. "Mugwort and blood choke," Cambious said, lifting a roll of gauze from the table. "Promotes healing. I have no idea which ointment base was used, however. Durious restocked our kit last."

"It's okay, I wouldn't have remembered anyway," I murmured, lifting my hand a little to make his work easier. Once he had covered my wound and taped down the gauze, he put everything back into the box. "Are we really just going to sit here? Won't they find us?"

He smiled as he stood. "They won't get through the portal, even if they manage to puncture the wards. We are safe enough for tonight. Now, how about some dinner? Durious made a delicious lasagna last night. It always tastes better the second day." I didn't answer, just watched him move to the fridge and then to the stove. His horns nearly scraped the ceiling as he moved about.

The adrenaline was beginning to fade and with it the energy of our escape. "I didn't call Bonnie," I said suddenly.

Cambious turned to look at me, confused.

"My boss," I said. "I don't know how long we'll be gone."

"If you expect us to find your mother, you can bet it will take a while," Cambious responded cautiously.

"I don't know what I'm expecting, honestly." I sighed and cradled my wounded hand as I sat back against the wall. The chairs had been built for Cambious and his brother, and my feet dangled well off the floor. "Mostly I was just thinking that I would rather not die."

"And so far, you are doing well if that is your goal."

I rolled my eyes. "Not really looking for validation, Cam." I sighed again, picking at the edges of my bandage. In less than a month, my life had gone from sedate, even boring, to running for my life into some magical realm with an incubus.

"May I ask what it is you are looking for?" Cambious asked, coming to sit in the chair at the other end of the table.

"I wish I knew," I said without thinking about it. "And it isn't that I'm not grateful, I am. Just…"

He nodded knowingly. "It is a lot for you to accept, these changes."

"Changes I'm pretty good with, actually," I countered. "Growing up in foster care, you get used to changes. It's more the kinds of changes. A month ago, I would have sworn to you that magic wasn't real, that magic creatures didn't exist, and here I am sitting in a cabin on some alternate world with an incubus having come through a magic door."

He chuckled. "I take your point."

I wasn't sure he really did, but I let it go. My hand was a dull throb, and I was starting to feel the adrenaline crash. I leaned back against the wall and closed my eyes. I could hear Cambious humming to himself as he went about getting dinner ready and it was oddly comforting. I dozed there until Cambious set a plate in front of me. It was beautifully set, with a square of lasagna and a bit of salad and even some green beans… or what I assumed were green beans. It was hard to know for sure since we were in a different world. Who knew what odd plants they grew there?

A taste proved that they were in fact green beans, which both relieved me and disappointed me a little. It wouldn't be the last thing to disappoint me there. We ate in comfortable silence, and before I had finished, I was yawning more than I was eating.

"There is a bed up in the loft," Cambious said softly, taking my dish to the sink.

"I can sleep on the couch," I said, stretching.

"No need. I don't need much sleep. I will be standing watch."

I narrowed my eyes at him, trying to gauge whether or not I needed to worry. "I thought you said we were safe here."

He smiled what I assumed was meant to be a reassuring smile and patted my shoulder with his overly large, and clawed hand. "We are safe. We will be safer if someone keeps watch. Off you go. Tomorrow is a big day."

I gave up the argument and headed for the loft. I couldn't see how either Cambious or Durious could even get up there. The ceiling was low at the center even for me, and I'm barely five foot six, and it sloped down on either side. It was a tidy bedroom though, with a huge bed under a round window. There was a softly glowing lamp on a small table beside the bed and a dresser tucked up under the sloping side near the ladder, with what looked like a handcrafted rug covering a large portion of the wooden floor.

I stripped out of my jeans and pulled back the covers. The bed was soft, and it cradled me as I settled in, pulling the blankets and an old-looking quilt up around me. Some part of me argued that I wouldn't sleep, no matter how exhausted I felt after the adrenaline had drained, but it didn't argue long.

My next aware thought was the smell of bacon cooking and murmuring voices. I sat up, stretching and reaching for my jeans. I pulled them on and stood, turning to find a beautiful sunrise painting the skies orange outside the round window. I moved slowly, cautious until I could see down into the kitchen.

Cambious was at the stove and someone with horns like Cambious and his brother was setting the table. She glanced up at me, smiling warmly. She was breathtakingly gorgeous, her mahogany skin smooth and almost glowing, her dark red hair left loose and flowing down her back. Her horns were similar to Cambious's s but closer in color to her hair and more delicate somehow. Her eyes though, those were the same amber as his.

"I think your guest is awake."

Cambious turned, lifting a fork in hello. "Ah, Thána, I trust you slept well."

"I did, thank you," I responded, climbing down the ladder, and crossing to my bag to dig out my brush. I ran it through my hair before turning to introduce myself. "I'm Thána."

She smiled, her teeth white and perfect. "I am glad to finally meet you, Thána. I am Lutia, Cambious is my son."

"Oh." I'm not sure what I was expecting, but that wasn't it. She looked far too young to be a mother to someone Cambious's age. "I wasn't expecting...well, any of this if I'm honest."

She smiled. "I came along with the rest of the family when Durious sent word last night. Thought you might do with a little feminine company. Coffee?"

"Oh, yes. Coffee is good."

"Come sit down. Cambious, be a dear and bring her a cup." She held a chair for me and took the one beside mine. "And don't worry, I brought it with me, Cambious doesn't drink coffee. If there was any here it would be at least twenty years old." She laughed as Cambious put a steaming mug in front of me. He looked a little embarrassed by her.

"Mother, I'm sure Thána isn't interested in all that. We would have managed."

I lifted the cup, letting the steam rise up to my face and breathing in the rich aroma. The first sip proved to be nearly orgasmic, better than any coffee I'd ever tried. "Oh my god, this is amazing," I said, looking up.

She clapped her hands and her face lit up. "I'm so glad you like it. One of my daughters grows it. She has a farm over in Lahos, on the north side of the island."

"She doesn't know where Lahos is, Mom," Cambious said, returning to the table with a frying pan. He put some bacon and two eggs on my plate. "Make yourself useful and get the toast?"

Lutia patted his arm as she stood and went to the counter, coming back with thick slices of bread that had been toasted and buttered. "Tuck in, dear, don't want it getting cold."

I did as I was told, cutting into the eggs, and focusing on my food.

Cambious joined us at the table, putting food on his plate and his mother's.

"My son tells me that you want to find your mother." Lutia looked concerned.

I nodded. "I mean, I honestly don't know what else to do?" I scooped up eggs onto a piece of toast and popped it into my mouth, chewing thoughtfully. "I can't stop these people from trying to kill me. I clearly can't hide from them. And my father told me to find her."

She looked at Cambious who sighed. "If the dead have commanded you, then it is what you must do," Cambious said softly.

Lutia seemed to agree. "And so you must. Where will you begin?"

"Thelos," Cambious responded. "When I last saw Alana, she was headed to Thelos. Perhaps we can pick up her trail there."

"Ah, then you will be joining her?" Lutia asked, clearly not entirely thrilled with that idea.

"How can I not, Mother? She knows nothing of our world. She needs a guide."

"You will need a more convincing glamor then, if you are traveling into the midst of witches for more than a feeding."

Cambious raised a hand to lift a pendant out of the sweater he was wearing. He tapped a finger to the amber-colored stone and the air around him shimmered. When it stopped, he had been transformed. His skin was a dark brown, his eyes a soft brown. His horns were gone, and his dark hair was slightly curly. Had I not seen the transformation happen, I wouldn't have believed it possible.

Lutia nodded, reaching for his hand. "Most impressive."

He tapped the stone again and was instantly himself. "Don't sound so surprised. Merry's daughter made it specifically for me the last time I visited Thelos."

"Just promise me you won't go into Janu."

"I doubt Alana went to Janu," Cambious said. "Eat, Thána, we should get on the road. I need to finish packing." He rose from the table, leaving his food mostly uneaten. I watched him go, up the ladder into the loft, then turned to Lutia.

"What is Janu?" I asked, feeling very out of my depth.

"It is a city in the south where our kind are most unwelcome and when found there, we are executed," Lutia answered, rising herself. "I should see how the gate fares. It was very nice to meet you, Thána."

She left the cabin, and I was alone for the moment. "What have you gotten yourself into, Thána?" I muttered to myself.

CHAPTER 15
INTO THELOS

The walk from the cabin was quiet, the path was well worn and along its edges bloomed a sort of heather, or what looked like heather, though its leaves were blue-green, and its flowers had shades of orange and red. The morning dew still clung to the leaves as we trudged along.

Cambious was quiet. I got the sense that it had to do with his mother and what she'd said about our journey. It was about a mile down from the cabin to a clear space where there were several vehicles parked. They weren't exactly Chryslers, but recognizable as cars. Cambious pointed to a blue one.

He put our bags in the trunk and slid into what I took for the driver's seat. I climbed into the passenger side, my eyes sweeping over the dash. There was no steering wheel, but a console of switches, gauges, and buttons. I noticed Cambious had changed his appearance again, looking the way he had in my kitchen. Still, his head brushed the roof of the car. He pressed a button, and I could feel the car come to life.

A moment later, we were headed down the mountain on a gravel road that eventually turned to something similar to blacktop, though it was a faded green. "I am sorry about my mother," Cambious said after a while. "I was not expecting her to come with my brothers."

"It's okay, Cam," I responded softly.

"She doesn't approve of the closeness between our families." He sighed and shook his head. "If she had her way, we would abandon the gateway and return to Abagh for good, other than to feed of course."

"Feed?" I asked, fairly certain I didn't want the answer.

He nodded. "We need the psychic energy. At least once a month, we need to feed. More if we are expending a lot of energy. For example, when wearing this glamor, I am steadily using up that energy. When I am wearing the other, I use exponentially more energy. I will need to feed soon."

I swallowed around the fear building in the back of my throat. "How exactly do you feed?"

He smiled, turning us off one road and onto another. "Have you no knowledge of what an incubus is, Thána?"

I blushed, remembering the lust that overcame me when we first met. "So, you…induce someone to have sex and…what…suck their energy?"

"The energy that is built during the sex act is what feeds us." Cambious glanced at me, his eyes glittering. "We absorb it. We take nothing from our partner that isn't going to go to waste anyway. Well, most of us don't. We can, of course, but it is considered rude."

"Rude. Right." I shook my head, trying to file the information away, but stuck on the image of Cambious mid-coitus. It wasn't an unpleasant vision, not by a long shot, but it kept me from moving past it.

"This road will take us to Thelos," Cambious said, pulling me back to the moment. "It is a little over an hour away."

"Okay, then what?"

"Then we will begin our search. We know that your mother went there and that she visited with her family. We know that she left again with your sister. We don't know why or where. So, we start there."

It seemed to make sense. "What about these Brotherhood guys?" I asked after a few minutes. "If they tracked me back home, and realize I came through the portal, won't they expect me to go to family?"

Cambious inhaled deeply, then let it out slowly. "It is possible, yes."

My heart sped up a little. "And won't they start by hunting down whatever family I have then?"

"It is possible, yes."

"And if they find me?"

"We fight," Cambious replied, as if it were just that simple.

"Now, why didn't I think of that?" I muttered, sarcasm dripping off each word. "I'm serious, Cam. I've seen how they kill people like me." I shuddered, the image of poor Althea Anagnos hanging by her ankles as the blood drained from her body. It was not the way I wanted to go. Not that I wanted to go at all. What I wanted was to go back to the life I'd had before Finneas Connor showed up. Back to circuit boards and quality meetings and all the rest. Hell, I'd even go back to El Paso.

"I know," Cambious said quietly. "I promise you this, I will do everything in my power to prevent that from happening."

It felt like the kind of promise you made to a child to stop their crying. I was quiet then, withdrawing into my head, my fingers idly playing with my mother's pendant. If I closed my eyes, my head was filled with images of death and blood, some of it mine, most of it belonging to women in the long line of my family. As we neared Thelos, those images became more intense, words screaming in my head, curses thrown as they died, then in a sudden silence I saw the woman in the cell in the fortress again. Her hair had thinned, and gray was chasing the black away. She wore the marks of torture in her skin, and when she lifted her head, her eyes were sunken and hollow, her face gaunt from starvation, but as our eyes met, I knew.

"Mother." I murmured the word as the car came to a stop. "I can see her." I didn't want to move or blink, lest I lose the vision. "She's a prisoner. She's dying." I could feel Cambious touch my arm, but I didn't move. "She's in the fortress, the Kourt."

Her eyes grew wide, as if she could see me and she shook her head, one thin hand rising to wave me off. Fear filled the emptiness of her eyes and almost physically, I felt her push me away. The vision fled then, and I was left sweating and panting. I opened my eyes to find Merry kneeling beside me, the car door open. Her frail-looking hand was on my arm. "Good gracious, *paidía*. Let's get you inside."

I let Merry help me out of the car, my eyes blurry and the world around me feeling less than real. I stumbled up some stairs and then Merry was pressing me to a seat on something soft. I blinked, trying to clear my eyes, but felt as though they just wanted to close. Sleep was pulling heavy on me, and I wanted to demand to know what had happened but couldn't make my mouth open.

"She shouldn't have been able to do that." I heard Merry say.

"Look what it did to her." That was Cambious. I struggled to open my eyes, but they wouldn't budge.

A hand was on my head, petting over it. "Shh, little one, rest."

It had the weight of a command and within seconds I fell into a restless sleep filled with nightmares. Blood filled my dreams, dripping over my face and down my arms, running down my legs as I ran blindly through a forest of blue-black trees on feet that were being ripped by the rugged ground. The taste of it filled my mouth, flat copper and hot, like the taste of death.

I woke suddenly in a house that had sunk into night while I slept on a soft couch, covered with what looked to be a handmade afghan. There was light drifting from a hallway and soft voices that told me I wasn't alone. The dull ache in my left hand reminded me of the cut and I lifted it to fiddle with the bandage. I had expected more pain, but it felt nearly healed…which should have been impossible.

I rose, pulling the afghan around me for warmth and I shuffled down the hallway, emerging into a tidy little kitchen, with a bay window where a breakfast nook was settled, pale blue cushions on the benches.

Merry and Cambious and someone I didn't know sat at the table, looking up as I came into the room. Merry looked a little less crazy than I remembered her, with her hair down and relatively calm, clad in a house-dress like the ones my foster father's mother used to wear in a soft blue. Cambious stood and came to my side, escorting me to Merry's side of the table as she scooted down toward the middle. "How are you feeling?" Cambious asked as I sat.

"Weird," was the first word out of my mouth. It wasn't inaccurate, but less than informative. I sighed. "Thirsty. Anxious. I had nightmares."

Cambious went to the sink and came back with a glass of water for me. I drank about half of it before I asked, "So, what was that? What happened to me?"

"It is called *makrá vlépinta*," Merry said, her voice more serious than I had heard it before. "It is a rare gift given some blood witches in their later years, after much study and mastery."

I frowned hard enough that the spot between my eyes hurt. "Then why could I do it?"

"That is what we have been discussing," Cambious replied. "A blood witch who develops this gift can see into the distant past, the far future, even long distances away in the present. It is said that a strong witch can make herself seen by those of her own blood."

"Oh, she saw me all right," I said, draining the glass of water. "But I can barely make the ward stones work. I'm no strong witch." The words felt strange in my mouth. I don't think I'd ever actually said the word witch when talking about myself before that moment. Not out loud at least.

"Trauma can sometimes kick start a witch's gifts." I turned to the speaker, a woman somewhere between my age and Merry's, her hair cut in a thick, black bob and wearing a dark suit. She had Merry's eyes, though hers were blue to Merry's black. Her face was thin, her fingers stained with ink of a blue-purple color.

"Ah, Thána, darling, this is my daughter Zo," Merry said, her hand on Zo's shoulder. "She studies the effect of trauma on our gifts."

"Mostly the kind of trauma that blocks them, but there are documented cases where trauma of certain kinds, particularly the sudden near-death sort, can open up a set of gifts it would normally take a lifetime to learn, like *makrá vlépinta*."

I stared at my empty glass for a long time before I got up to refill it. As I came back to the table, my head filled with all of the near-death sorts of trauma of the last months, then back to the day my father died. "So, what if that near-death experience happened when I was five or six?"

I could feel them staring at me. Well, Merry and Zo anyway. Cambious knew the whole story. I would have thought Merry did as well, but for all I know my mother had kept that truth hidden, even from the family. "I don't remember all of it, but I very clearly remember the man trying to kill us, and I know that I used my…gifts then, to ease my father's pain as he died, and to take the life of the man who killed him. Is that the kind of thing you mean?"

"You should not have been able to do that at that age, so I'm going to say that yes, that is probably where it started. And the events of recent days have pushed you past your limits again."

"I wasn't under any particular stress when this happened," I countered, sitting back. "We were relatively safe. I was just sitting in the car."

"We should consider the fact that you have never been in the land of your ancestors before either. That could have been a factor," Cambious said.

"Has it happened before?" Zo asked, her intense blue eyes studying me.

"I've had dreams…there was one about Althea Anagnos, it was very real," I responded, getting up to pace. "I watched her die."

Zo nodded. "From what Cambious tells me, everything since we sent Finneas to you has been stressful for you, even coming home to the house where you were born. And there is familial precedent, several of our ancestors were extremely powerful blood witches. It is rumored, for example, that Althea could actually raise the dead."

"Hogswallop," Merry interjected. "Only necromancers can raise the dead. And then, the dead are never really themselves again. The child was near death, the doctor simply announced her demise before it took place."

"I have heard of others," Cambious said softly. "But it has never been proven."

My head was spinning with the implications, and I shook it in an attempt to clear it. "I know next to nothing. Like I said, I can barely use the stones. How am I supposed to…"? I waved my hands in the air, desperation nipping at my awareness. If my mother was a prisoner of the Brotherhood, how was I supposed to save her?

"Well, we shall just have to get you trained up a bit," Merry said cheerfully, patting my hand. "Come, the library is downstairs."

CHAPTER 16
RELEARNING

MERRY'S LIBRARY, AS IT TURNED OUT, WAS A CAVERNOUS BASEMENT AT THE bottom of a staircase at least two hundred steps down, or so it seemed as we trudged down them in a dank sort of darkness punctuated only with small yellow lights every twenty stairs or so. The walls were lined with bookshelves that were overflowing with ancient tomes on subjects I could only guess.

There was a large table filled with scrolls and notebooks and what looked to be a quill pen with an inkpot. Beyond that was a round fireplace over which hung a huge black cauldron. Smaller versions of the cauldron were stacked on yet another table off to the righthand side. In the two corners in the back, there were shelves lined with jars and bottles.

Now, this is what I had been expecting when I was told about witches and magical portals...and to be honest, since I met Merry. She was humming to herself as she moved over to one of the bookshelves, rubbing her hands along the pale blue of her housecoat as she scanned the shelves. "Ah, yes, this should do." She pulled out a large book and blew dust off its cover before crossing to the table. "Well, get over here. Can't learn anything standing by the stairs," she said over her shoulder as she set the book down on the table. I went to her a little hesitantly, not sure what was about to happen. She pulled a stool out from under the table and patted the seat while she opened the book.

"Most of this you will have learned from your mother when you were young. We just need to get you to remember."

"I've been trying. I found my...journal..." I wasn't ready to say "spellbook" out loud. "But other than the ward stones and that one protection thing in the family book, nothing has worked."

She patted my hand, a smile on her wrinkled face. Her eyes were bright as she pointed to the page. "This book is how I learned when I was a wee one. Most of us did at that time. It is a wonderful primer on magic."

My eyes scanned the page. It contained words and hand-drawn sketches of hands in certain positions. I found my hands making the signs under the table. "Start at the top," Merry said, "and learn the pronunciations and hand signs. I'll go get dinner started."

The first word was *dimiourgió*, and the pronunciation guide under it showed it as de-mi-or-geo. The accompanying hand sign showed two fists with arrows indicating that they should be brought together, left on top of the right. I murmured the word to myself and made my hands come together. Nothing happened, but then, as I told myself, it was just a word.

A word that I had no knowledge of. I searched the page for the translation but didn't find one. I repeated the exercise a few times before moving to the next word. *Ánoixe*, pronounced Ah-nix-a came next, with a hand gesture that seemed to imitate opening a book. I worked my way down the page, learning *irémise* (a finger to the lips), *prostatévo*, (hands crossed at the wrists), *páfsi* (left hand perpendicular to the right), *pigaíno* (both hands moving forward), *ýpnos* (right hand flat, left hand moving in to cover it), and *yperaspízo* (both hands come together as if in prayer, then pull apart and turn to face outward).

I went through the words and gestures until I could do them without looking. The bandage on my left hand was making it difficult, so I paused to pull it off. Under the gauze, the cut was nearly a scar, thin and almost not even visible. I had always healed quickly, but not usually this fast. I rubbed my thumb across it before turning my attention back to the words I was supposed to be studying. I felt a little silly sitting there like that, speaking these words and waving my hands around.

After I was sure I had the words and related gestures down, I got up and walked around the room practicing while I waited for Merry to return. I was just about to head up the long staircase when I heard the door open, so I went back to pacing and practicing.

Merry appeared moments later, slightly out of breath and wearing an apron that looked as ancient as she did. "Good, good. Now I will teach you to use them. Come, sit."

I went back to the stool and sat, and Merry came to stand behind me, her hands on my shoulders. "Close your eyes and take a deep breath, slow in, slow out. Let your attention narrow to my voice and your breath. This is how you center."

I followed her instructions, dragging my attention back each time it wandered until I felt something new. "This is where magic lives, *paidí*. Feel it, let it rise up with your words. Open."

I murmured "*Ánoixe,*" and made the gesture. Around me, I heard pages ruffling and opened my eyes. The books nearest me had all opened and the doors on the shelving unit in the corner had as well. "What…"

Merry tightened her fingers on my shoulders. "Close."

I was pretty sure that word wasn't one of the ones I had just learned, but somewhere in the back of my brain I heard my mother's voice saying, "*Kontá*." I said the word and closed my hands, the opposite of the gesture for open. All around me pages ruffled, and I heard the clasp on the glass doors.

"Yes, remember. Your mother taught you these. Now, pick a book and connect with your magic, Go."

"*Pigaíno,*" I said the word and pushed my hands toward the top book on the stack beside me. It flew away from me.

"Come."

"*Éla.*" The word and the beckoning gesture came as if I knew them already. The book returned, landing in my hand.

"Good, protect."

"*Prostatévo.*" I touched my wrists together and the air around me shimmered.

"There are stronger protective spells, but this will do in a pinch, and should repel most basic attacks. Remember though, it only lasts as long as your attention and energy remain." She patted my shoulder and I blinked, letting the magic release. "Defend is a more aggressive version and can be used to push back against an attack. Let's not try it down here. That can wait until tomorrow when we can go to the yard. Come, you should rest, and dinner should be ready."

I was sweating by the time I reached the top of the stairs and fatigue was pulling on my limbs. Merry and I appeared to be alone. "Where is Cambious?"

Merry went to the oven, pulling out a pan of something that smelled amazing. "He needed to feed, so he went to meet up with a gentleman he's enjoyed time with in the past. They have an arrangement of sorts."

"Oh." I'm not sure why, but I had assumed that Cambious, being an incubus, would tend toward a more heterosexual lifestyle, but what did I know about that sort of thing? My education never did cover the sexual appetites of incubi and succubi.

Merry chuckled as if she could read my thoughts. "Our good friend is pansexual, my dear. He can get what he needs from any gender." She put the pan on the counter and dished up two plates, bringing them to the table, then going back to the counter for utensils. "I hope it's good. I had to throw a bunch of stuff together, I haven't gone shopping yet."

The plate was filled with potatoes and what looked like ground beef or pork, spices, and a tomato-ey sauce, all of it covered in some sort of cheese. The first taste was filled with nutmeg and cloves and onion, along with potato and cheese. The meat was not beef or pork, but it was delicious, I thought maybe lamb or goat. My stomach rumbled as I ate, as if just the taste was enough to remind it that it was empty.

Merry rambled on about what she was going to teach me, and something about another memory spell, but I was too busy eating to pay close attention. By the time I had cleaned my plate, I was all but asleep. Merry cleared the table, then urged me up, taking me down a long hall off the kitchen. The room was small, but there were two twin beds and my duffle bag sat at the end of one.

It didn't take much to convince me to shed my jeans and crawl in, though it felt odd with Merry there watching me. She adjusted my blankets to her liking, then sat beside me, her hand brushing my hair away from my face. It had gotten long and was starting to revert to its natural state of thick, black curls. I couldn't even remember when I had seen a salon last, and it required maintenance every four to six weeks.

"Close your eyes. Rest," Merry said softly, her hand covering my eyes. "*Epistrofí mnímis, Epistrofí mnímis, Férte píso tis iméres tis paidikís ilikías.*"

I was already drifting toward sleep when she stood, and I could hear her leave the room and shuffle down the hallway. Sleep pulled me under quickly. My dreams were almost like a tour of my childhood: sitting with my mother on the greenhouse porch, working with ward stones; on my father's lap in the living room, opening and closing the front door with words and gestures; teaching my little sister some small spell I'd learned. They turned darker and colder after that, after my father's death. There was a repeat of that memory, in all its gory detail, and the aftermath. There was my mother's voice, desperation making her words tremble as she taught me how to use *prostatévo* to keep an attacker at bay, even a memory of using it once against a bully in school, which earned me a very strict lesson in when and where magic was allowed.

Near to morning, I fell into a memory I had wanted desperately for my whole life, but would come to despise, the days that led up to the moment when my mother had hidden my identity behind a wall and left me on a bench outside a police station.

We lived in an almost picturesque cottage on the eastern coast of the United States, huddled and hiding. Mother had not enrolled us in school, and she kept our interaction with the world to a minimum. Daria spiked a high fever one day and fell ill. We had been running and hiding for almost three years, ever since the number of Brotherhood assailants had grown beyond my mother's ability to protect us. Mother left me to watch Daria while she went out to get supplies for a potion to cure her.

To my knowledge, I had not used my unique power since the day my father had died, but in the gloom of a house with the shutters drawn and only a small desk lamp to chase the shadows, I didn't know how to help Daria, other than to comfort her, so I had crawled into her bed, pulling her tiny body up against mine. The fever raged, her skin so hot to the touch. Her dark hair was plastered to her head with sweat, and she shivered, whispering nonsense in a voice gone rough whisper from her cough.

I tried to soothe her, caressing her skin, and whispering that I would keep her safe. When she went still, every fiber of my being called out for me to save her. She was dying there in my arms. I pressed my mouth to hers and called the illness out of her, feeling its dank, ugly heat fill my mouth. I swallowed and called again, and again…until her skin cooled and her body settled with the tiniest of sighs as she lapsed into a restful sleep.

When my mother came home, I was in the bathroom, letting the blood drain from me as it had when I had eased my father into the next life. Her face was drawn and pale and I could taste the fear. I didn't fully understand it, but I knew she was terrified by what I had done. I apologized over and over, tears burning my face. I could not have lived with myself if I had let Daria die. I was her big sister, and it was my job to protect her. My love for her was so big that it filled me, even when I knew that I wasn't supposed to use that gift. My mother was a fighter though, and she buried her fear to help me, teaching me how to use sanitary pads and making me a potion to help speed the flow.

We couldn't leave until it was done, you see. The men who wanted to kill me employed those with specific gifts to track the smell of my blood. If we left before I was done bleeding, the men would find us. Of course, what she didn't say was that if it took too long for it to be over, they would find us there, in that little cottage.

It took almost two days. My mother gathered up all of my pads and left me alone with a fully recovered Daria while she went to dispose of them. She said it would leave a false trail, give us time to leave. We spent days in the car after that, zigzagging up and down the coast, then inland, then back to the sea in hopes of throwing them from our trail. Then, the morning before my birthday, they found us.

CHAPTER 17
MEMORY TRAP

IT WAS REALLY EARLY, NOT EVEN DAYLIGHT. MOM HAD STOPPED US AT A REST stop sometime through the night to grab a few hours of sleep. We were just inside New York state, though Mom hadn't said where exactly we were heading. The memory was so vivid inside my dream I felt like I was once again a nine-year-old waking up in the backseat of the car needing to pee.

I could see the bathrooms through the front window. I probably should have woken Mom but decided I could go and be back before she woke up and I did my best to make no noise as I got out of the car and ran for the building with the bathroom. The air was nippy, the taste of autumn in the air. I did my business, trying not to sit on the metal commode knowing it would be ice cold. I washed my hands and went to the door of the bathroom, something making me slow and look around the area.

The boy looked out of place. He had to be about fourteen or fifteen, skinny and wearing clothes that didn't fit. He dashed for me, pushing me back inside. "Don't let them see you. I'll lead them away, then you run."

I was confused but nodded. He ran back out, calling out, "*Aderfia*, the girl went this way."

Several men in black, their bald heads reflecting the street lamps that lined the sidewalk, ran past me, following the boy. When I couldn't hear them anymore, I raced for the car, opening the door, and shaking my mother's shoulder as I got in.

We drove away, probably faster than it was safe to drive. I couldn't have known that my mother had already made the decision that would alter the trajectory of my life.

What follows that is less clear, blurred no doubt by the actions my mother was taking. I remember ditching the car and a bus ride, a lunch in a little diner along the way, and that night we got a motel room.

Mom consulted a big book I had seen out on the greenhouse porch back home, sorting through ingredients from the big bag she had brought with us as we left the car.

There was a small pot on the hotplate next to the sink and it bubbled as she murmured words and added ingredients from the bag. Once Daria was asleep, Mom called me to her. "We're going to do a spell, Thána. One that should help us to be safe for a long time."

I nodded solemnly. "What spell?"

Her smile was sad, and she kissed the crown of my head. "Just sit here and I will show you." My next true memory was of waking up on that bench, an officer talking to me.

I woke then, half surprised to still be in Merry's guest bedroom. Memories continued to flash through me as I got up and went in search of a bathroom. I relieved myself, then decided that if I couldn't remember when my last shower was, I should probably get cleaned up. I found towels and started some hot water flowing, then stripped out of my underwear, shirt, and bra before climbing in.

I tipped my head back under the spray, closing my eyes as memories darted through me of other showers in other places, at a dozen different ages. It was like a hyped-up, high-velocity deja vu that left me trembling when I finally rinsed myself clean and stepped out of the shower. The landslide didn't stop then, however. Everything I did came with echoes of every other time I had done the thing, from putting on my clothes to brushing my hair.

By the time I headed for the kitchen, my whole body was shaking with adrenaline amid the earthquakes and tremors of reliving thirty-two years in tiny snippets of time. I jumped when I heard Cambious speak, but only his voice penetrated my awareness, I couldn't understand his words. I stumbled back from the perceived threat, my eyes wide open even though I couldn't see my surroundings. I stumbled into a wall and laid both hands flat against it, looking for some stability. I blinked and leaned into the wall, willing the onslaught to stop.

There were warm hands on my back, and for a moment I couldn't differentiate them from every other pair of hands that had ever touched me that way. I groaned and tried to pull away, but there was nowhere to go. Voices echoed around me, and I couldn't tell which were real and which were memories.

"*Páfsi!*" The word screamed out of my lungs as I clung to the wall and my sanity. "Stop. Make it stop."

Hands grabbed my face and a deep voice spoke words that did not cause a series of overlapping memories, "*Zamyg khyalbarchlakh.*"

It took a moment, but the landslide slowed. It didn't stop, more like it lagged. Like a film all out of sync or something. I blinked against hot tears I hadn't been aware I was crying and Cambious appeared in front of me, his amber eyes filled with deep concern. "Really, Merry? Thána, can you hear me now?"

I nodded slowly, afraid each movement was going to start the assault again. "Okay, good. I'm going to take you downstairs. Can you move?"

I tried. I did, but two steps later I had to squeeze my eyes shut. Cambious muttered curses and scooped me up like a child. It had been a long time and a lot of pounds since anyone had been able to do that, let alone had tried.

I grabbed a hold of his shirt, my hands fisting tight as I put my forehead against his neck. Each jarring step down the stairs sent rivers of fear through my veins, but apparently, there had been very few times in my life I had been carried down a flight of stairs. My breathing slowly leveled out as we reached the bottom, and Cambious set my feet down on the floor. I didn't let go right away, leaning into his strength.

"Here, sit." Cambious guided me back until I could feel the stool behind me. "Are you okay?"

I nodded cautiously, daring to open my eyes. I could see the room and superimposed on it was a loop of the day before, but it was far less anxiety-invoking than the rest, probably due to the limited amount of time I'd spent there. "What is this?" I asked, my voice sounding strangely frail to my ears.

Cambious sighed as if the entire idea of it was exhausting. "Merry was a bit…overly enthusiastic with her spell work yesterday. All will to bring back your memory, no control over how fast. There was a reason your mother worked her spell the way she did, both the taking of your memory and the controlled way it would come back to you, so carefully. Memory spells can split a person into pieces. I warned her to be careful."

"But you did something that helped?" I rubbed my eyes and experimented with turning my head.

"I gave you some space, but at this point, all you can do is ride it out."

That did not sound like an answer I wanted to hear. "Ride it out?"

"We'll keep you down here, where it's relatively free of trigger memories and hopefully that should let it all unspool in a less traumatic way."

"How long is this unspooling going to take?" I asked.

"I don't know. It is not an exact science, this is magic of the mind and heart, not one of stones, herbs, and potions."

"And if I can't…ride it out?"

Cambious didn't answer that, just turned for the stairs. "I will bring you some breakfast, and something to help fortify you against this fight. Try to stay still, the more you try to do, the more the memory will fracture and slam you about."

"Right. Stay still." I watched him go. "Have you even met me?" I asked the empty air, cringing as I was offered evidence that the phrase was one I repeated often. I would have to find new expressions for my sarcasm.

In case that isn't clear enough, let me explain that I don't actually know **how** to stay still without something in my hands to play with or work on. I never have, as was evident by my cascading memories. I turned on the stool to the open book we had left on the table, but just that had me wanting to scream out again. The cacophony of similar turns and myriad books over the years was too much. I squeezed my eyes closed and held onto the table until the assault slowed, and I could try again.

Cambious hadn't been telling tales about staying still if something as simple as turning on the stool was enough to incapacitate me. I heard the door above, and Cambious's heavy tread as he came down the stairs. Almost as an afterthought, the smell of bacon and eggs wafted down the stairwell, but even that was too much and by the time Cambious reached me, I was on the floor under the table, knees to my chest and my eyes pressed down against my knees.

Not that it did anything to stem the tide, but somehow it made me feel a little better.

"Here." Cambious took my hand and put a cup in it. "Drink this."

I sniffled as I lifted my head, pulling the cup closer. "Do I want to know what is in it?"

He smiled gently. "It is a potion to shore up your defenses. The next few hours will be trying for you. Drink it all."

Dutifully, I drained the cup, making a face as the taste hit me. It was like that cough medicine my first foster mother would give me, some homemade glop that she insisted tasted like orange candy. I was fairly sure she had never actually tasted orange candy. Once I had handed the cup back, Cambious handed me a plate. "I know this might be hard, but you should eat."

I eyed the plate suspiciously. Already I could feel the memories queueing up to flood my head. I tried a bite and almost dropped the plate as every memory of eating scrambled eggs bubbled up. "I can't," I ground out through my teeth, giving him the plate back and dropping my head back to my knees.

"Let me help you." Cambious sat on the floor with the plate and lifted a forkful of eggs. "Thána, please try." I blinked at him and nodded. He put the fork in my mouth, smiling at me. The memories that came then went back to infancy, my mother or father feeding me in an endless barrage. I chewed and swallowed, keeping my eyes closed as Cambious put food into my mouth.

By the time I had nearly finished the food, the memories had resolved themselves into something resembling chronological order and I was able to cope with them a little better. "Thank you," I said to Cambious, returning my head to my knees.

"Do you need anything?"

I wanted to be snippy but didn't have the strength. "Coffee might be nice."

"Stay still, Thána. I will return."

I didn't watch him go. I kept my eyes closed, pressing them into my knees as if I could somehow stop the rapid-fire memory snippets with the pressure alone. He did bring me coffee, but I couldn't even hold the cup as every memory of every cup of coffee I had ever had in my life became bullets in the gun held to my sanity.

At some point, Cambious brought down the mattress from one of the twin beds and made me a bed of sorts, a nest of blankets and pillows I tried to use to insulate me from myself. I don't know if you've ever tried to hide from yourself, but here's a clue: you can't. A lot of the next two days is something of a blur, spent in a half-comatose state punctuated by moments of clarity when Cambious tried to feed me or give me water to drink.

I slept only when my body was so wrung out it just couldn't function anymore, though it was more a state of involuntary unconsciousness than it was actual sleep. I woke suddenly, soaked through with sweat and cold. I reached for the glass of water Cambious had left nearby and downed it before I realized that I wasn't spinning my way through every memory of drinking water in thirty-two years.

Cautiously, I sat fully up. I had a jackhammer-wielded-by-elephants headache and felt like I had gone ten rounds with Mike Tyson, my entire body feeling bruised and beaten, but I was functioning. I was disgustingly in need of a hot shower and a good meal, but I had survived more or less intact.

I pressed myself up off the mattress, which was going to need a good airing out after my sweat-fest, moving gingerly lest I set something off again. That was when I noticed Cambious. He was sitting with his back against the nearest wall to my nest, head slumped down to his chest, his legs splayed out in front of him. The glamor was gone, and he looked nearly peaceful, even with the horns and all.

Figuring I should let him sleep, I tiptoed to the stairs and made my way up, emerging into the room off the kitchen. A vague red light was starting to stain the deep blue-black of the skies as I went to the sink to splash cold water on my face. I itched with the sweat starting to dry on my skin, but my stomach was making enough noise to raise the dead, so I grabbed an apple in a fruit bowl on the counter, taking it with me as I headed for the bathroom.

My first bite stopped me in my tracks. The outside looked like an apple, but inside the flesh was a light purple in color and the taste was something like a blueberry. My stomach let me know it didn't care how it tasted, it wanted it and it wanted it now. It was gone by the time I got to the bathroom, and I left the core on the counter while I showered.

I was running out of clean clothes, and I would have to ask Merry if she had a washing machine…or whatever this world's equivalent would be. I pulled on my clean pair of jeans and the last T-shirt from my bag and headed back toward the kitchen to see if I could figure out coffee and maybe breakfast, but Merry was already there, looking haggard and sleep-deprived.

Her eyes brightened when she saw me. "Thána! Look at you. Has the spell finished its work then?"

I wanted to be angry with her but discovered that my feelings were more akin to annoyance than anger. "You could have warned me what was going to happen," I growled as she put a cup of coffee into my hands. "But yes, I seem to be past the machine gun memory stage, if nothing else."

"I am so relieved. Of course, I never meant for…well, that. It's been a long time since I have worked such a spell. I may have set too much intention and will with too little caution."

Something tickled in the back of my memory, something my mother had taught me. "Be careful what you wish for."

Merry chuckled and returned her attention to the eggs and potatoes in her pan. "Yes indeed. Your mother's spell was overly cautious. You would have regained all of these memories eventually, but if you are to come into yourself enough to go save her, her spell needed a push."

"Congratulations," I said wryly, lifting the coffee cup to taste. "You shoved it right off a cliff."

"Oh, yes, Cambious was quite cross with me. He's scarcely left your side since he returned from feeding."

"How long?" I asked. I took the coffee, which tasted an awful lot like salvation, to the table and sat on one of the benches.

"Around fifty hours, all told," she replied.

Fifty hours. I could tell that everything wasn't completely sorted inside my head, things were jumbled and out of order, but if I focused I could remember my mother teaching me the words and gestures, I could remember the feeling of pulling that power from inside of me. I could remember the taste of the illness I had taken from Daria and using the *prostatévo* spell to defend the two of us one day when the Brotherhood had found us.

It wasn't everything, but it was a hell of a lot more than when I had started.

CHAPTER 18
ON THE RUN AGAIN

Cambious stumbled up the stairs about an hour later, looking disheveled and like the sleep had done absolutely no good. He did smile, seeing me sitting at the table with Merry, our dirty dishes pushed to the side as we worked on refreshing my skills with my set of ward stones.

"There's still some breakfast on the stove," Merry told him as I murmured the incantation she'd been teaching me, bringing the stones to life. "Good, good, now move them slowly."

I kept my focus on my hands, slowly separating the six piles of stones until they formed a circle around my coffee cup. The air between the stones shimmered a faint green and within the stones, my coffee cup disappeared.

Cambious ambled over, rubbing at his eyes. "Did you just teach her *ekleípo*?"

Merry was just about bursting with pride. "She really is quite talented. Alana was right about that."

I canceled out the spell and bit back a yawn. "She is also exhausted. I could use a nap."

"You've been through a lot," Cambious agreed. "You should rest now. I heard from a friend last night that there has been an increase in Brotherhood activity in the area. They may know that we're here."

"Great." I pushed myself up from the table. "That should ensure a good sleep."

My thoughts rambled over the whirlwind of the last hour as Merry tested my memory of the things I should have learned up to my tenth birthday, and then beyond, as my mother had been trying to cram as much knowledge and skill into her hunted daughter as she could, probably hoping it would be enough to protect me in some way. I understood we had just been starting to go over the more advanced uses of the ward stones before she decided to try a different method of protection. I had remembered the word, *ekleípo*_and asked Merry to show me while she quizzed me on the other uses of the stones.

Merry had also filled my head with the things a blood witch was expected to be capable of, well beyond the healing of otherwise incurable diseases. The details had been lost over the years, but family memory told tales of blood being used in various protective spells, to seal things closed, like the door that held our portal safe, and for those suitably advanced, that blood could become a weapon, infecting others with the disease she had cured in another. I could see into the past and the future, down the bloodline, and connect with those still living who shared my blood, as we had already learned.

The blood trackers who the Brotherhood used to find me were said to be male blood witches. They couldn't "eat" disease the way we could, simply because they lacked the physical mechanisms to expel the disease, but they had many of the other traits and abilities, which allowed them to track us.

There was more, an entire field of study had been made of the unique gifts of a blood witch. Unlike all of the other kinds of witches, and there were many kinds, the blood witch stood alone in that she was born with gifts that couldn't be learned. Lucky me. Most of that knowledge had been lost over the centuries however, the gift becoming more and more rare as we were hunted and killed off. The last blood witch in my mother's family before me had been the first in almost a hundred years.

I crawled into the bed that hadn't been ravaged to provide me comfort in the basement, hoping I could get past the learning and the fear and sleep. For a long time, my brain just spun around and around, but eventually, exhaustion won, and I slept.

My dreams were much more focused than they had been, focused on my ancestors specifically. I saw Althea again, her sham trial and execution, her fear coursing through me as if I were the one being chased through the woods, stripped, and bled out. Whooshing through centuries, I saw a young girl of maybe thirteen, dripping blood from a cut on her hand into a wooden cup, mixing it with herbs before lifting it to the lips of a woman very definitely in hard labor. Then, an older woman shaking her head sadly as she held the hand of a woman on a pile of animal furs. "If I had been called sooner, perhaps…"

"*Adelfés tou aímatós mou, érchontai.*" The speaker was a woman of my age, maybe a little older, with patches of white decorating her otherwise black hair. She stood within a circle, a small fire burning at its center and ward stones around its perimeter, though I had never seen a ward so red as this. It was difficult to see outside the wards, though I couldn't be sure if it was because of the warding or because it was night.

Around the circle, the air shimmered and slowly figures began to form, none solid, but all clearly there. Eight women, in clothes of varied style, each holding up a hand with a cup or chalice in it. One by one they moved to the fire, tipping their cup, and letting something drip into the cauldron that hung over it. I knew somehow that this was blood collected from their menses, and the blood became real as it fell from their cups. When they had all done so, they returned to their places and again held up their hands.

"*Échoume synkentrósei gia na plirósoume tin timí tou aímatos. Hathus, sas parakaloúme, párte tin prosforá mas.*"

The nine women began to move in a circle, just inside the wards, faster and faster until the ground was shaking and then outside the wards, a dark shadow appeared. It was shaped like a man, but bigger than any man I had ever seen.

A voice deeper than Cambious's and louder than an air horn shook the circle. "*Déchomai tin prosforá sas, kóres tou aímatos. I gi eínai dikí sou edó kai chília chrónia.*"

One by one the specters of the women vanished until only the one present in the flesh remained. Taking the cauldron from the fire with her hands insulated by her skirt, she moved to the side of the circle where the shadow still hovered. With a nod, the wards fell, and she was face to face with…I had no context for what he was, but he towered over her and held out his hands. She tilted the cauldron and poured its contents into his hands.

From there, I fell into something that was not memory, mine, or an ancestor's. I was pulled to that tower cell, and my heart leaped as my mother looked back at me. I wanted to cry, to apologize for all the years I had been so angry with her. More than that, I wanted to feel her arms around me again.

I woke to Cambious's urgent whisper. "Thána, wake up."

He was crouched beside me, his glamor back in place. When I opened my eyes, he put his finger to his lips. I nodded my understanding. "We have to go. Now."

It had gotten dark, meaning I had slept much longer than I had intended to. Cambious had my duffle bag as he moved to the door of the bedroom, keeping himself low. I followed his example, stopping for my shoes where I had dropped them. Merry was waiting in the kitchen with a canvas bag which she handed to me. "Keep quiet and keep to the woods. Zo will find you."

I had to assume that this meant the Brotherhood had found us. Spontaneously, I hugged her, the closest thing to family I had had since my mother abandoned me. Cambious took my hand and guided me through the house and down a different set of stairs, which took us into a root cellar and then into a dark tunnel that moved away from the house at a slightly downward angle. After a while, Cambious let go of my hand and fumbled with something that became a handheld light, like the lanterns he'd lit our picnic with.

The tunnel seemed to go on forever, but after about a half-hour of walking, Cambious stopped us and pointed to a ladder. In silence we climbed, with him leading the way. At the top, he cautiously opened a hatch of some sort that I couldn't see around him, sticking his head up to scout the area. Then he was up and out, reaching back to take the bag, then my hand to aid me. I emerged into a dark forest, the air filled with the comforting smell of pine trees.

Cambious paused, looking around us before he pointed. "The road is this way."

I followed as he set out, having to hurry to keep up with his long steps. "Is the road going to be safe?" I asked.

"Safer than Merry's."

"Do we have a plan?" I asked as he changed directions.

"Right now, the plan is to not get caught by the Brotherhood," Cambious answered, his tone curt. "We'll figure out next steps once we're away from here."

"What about Merry? Will she be okay?"

He stopped and looked back over his shoulder, then at me. "She can handle herself, and she isn't who they're looking for."

"Yeah, but neither is my mother, and they've been keeping her for who knows how long."

"Yes, but your mother can lead them to you. Or could have, before you came here."

Something about that answer filled me with dread. Did it mean that now that I was here where they could track me, they had no need of her? Would they kill her before we could get to her? Which did nothing to help me figure out exactly how we were going to get to her. I mean, I am not exactly a fighter, and I certainly wasn't in supreme physical condition.

My chest tightened and I found breathing difficult. Cambious touched my hand. "We mustn't linger, Thána. It won't take them long to pick up your trail again if we do."

"That's reassuring," I muttered, letting him draw me onward. The night was dark around us, filled with the hulking shadows of trees, with softer gray spaces between them. After we'd walked about a mile, we came to what appeared to be a one-lane road where there was a vehicle waiting.

It was old and rundown, a dull blue marked in places with a darker color. Unlike the car we had taken to Merry's, its engine made some noise, vague knocking sounds in a rhythm that might have made my teeth hurt if we weren't in such dire straits. Zo was behind the wheel, and she gestured for us to hurry. Cambious held open the back door for me and advised me to lay across the seat. "Keep down, at least for now." He lifted a blanket off the floor and covered me before putting our two bags, and a backpack I hadn't noticed before, on the floor, then proceeding to the passenger side.

"I can get you into the city," Zo said, "but you'll have to make your own way from there."

"We should be fine. Get us to Stroya's."

"Are you sure?" Zo asked, her voice showing clear concern.

"We'll be fine," Cambious responded. "The bartender owes me a favor."

We drove in silence then, and slowly I began to hear the sounds of civilization. Traffic moved past us, and light punctuated even through the blanket. I could hear people talking, laughing. "It's probably safe for you to sit up," Cambious said, reaching back to tug on the blanket. I sat up, turning to look out the window. If I hadn't known we weren't back home, I'm not sure a first glance at the city outside my window would have told me differently.

There were storefronts and restaurants, what looked like office buildings, and here and there smaller standalone shops with signs with images of herbs and stones, cauldrons, and more. Zo pulled up in front of a bar with a neon sign in the window saying "Stroya's."

"You two be careful."

"Thank you, Zo," I said, touching her shoulder while Cambious opened my door and reached in for the bags. I climbed out with the canvas bag that Merry had given me and lifted a hand in farewell as Zo drove off. "What is this place?"

"This is just a bar," Cambious said, pointing to an alley between it and the next building. "We're going there. Which is also just a bar, but one for those of us who are not human."

He led me into the alley to a short staircase leading down to a door. "Stick close to me and don't talk to anyone you don't have to. Oh, and no glamors allowed in here, so...don't stare." He opened the door and escorted me in. There was a small room with a security guard on a stool. The guard appeared human, though a bit short. He nodded to Cambious and waved a hand at the door beside him. When it opened, I was nearly blown back by the sound of merriment and music and glass clinking.

"Are you going to stand there all night?" the guard asked me, startling me out of my hesitation.

Cambious led me in. It wasn't a huge place, but it wasn't the corner bar either. There were tables scattered around the room, most of them occupied, and stools along the bar, which seemed to be carved out of a dark wood, one long slab that had to be at least ten feet, and the edge was filled with carved figures, ornate and beautiful, at least where I could see it through the bodies.

Oh, and those bodies. I recognized some as incubi because they looked like Cambious, and I assumed that the women who looked similar were succubi, but the others…everywhere I looked I saw strange things I had once thought of as myth, if I'd thought of them at all. Cambious lifted a hand in greeting as a woman came toward him, all smiles and happiness.

She was pretty, in a sparkling silver blouse over a dark skirt…and the hairiest legs I'd ever seen. I brought my gaze back up quickly, taking in the wide face and soft brown hair, out of which grew an almost dainty set of horns.

"Ah, Celica, how have you been, my dear?"

"Cambious, you look well."

They hugged briefly and I felt her eyes sweep over me. "Oh, you know she won't make Stroya happy."

"Stroya can suck it," Cambious responded. "We won't be here long. I came to call in a favor."

"Then I shan't keep you." She kissed his cheek and moved away.

"Celica, she's the satyr I traded with," Cambious said with a grin as we moved to the bar. "Come on. I see Toman."

He slid onto a stool, putting my duffle bag in his lap. I took the stool beside him, trying to keep from drawing attention. To my left was a mountain of fur that was vaguely shaped like a man, but at least eight feet tall. I wasn't sure I even wanted to know what he was. Beyond him was another satyr and beyond him was a tall, impossibly slender, androgynous being who seemed more or less human, other than his curved and pointy ears and the pale blue of his skin.

Behind the bar, the person I assumed was Toman approached us. "Bringing a witch into my place, really Cam?"

"It couldn't be helped, Toman," Cambious said.

Toman put napkins in front of us, followed by glasses into which he poured a dark red wine. I caught myself staring at his hands, which weren't so much hands as they were talons. I glanced up at him, blinking a little. His face was decidedly birdlike, his nose and mouth protruding out in similarity to a beak. His red hair was filled with feathers of a deep wine red and black. And he had wings. Like, actual wings.

Cambious touched my thigh to draw my attention away. "I'm here to collect that favor you owe me," Cambious said to Toman. "We need a vehicle and a few minutes with Sibyl."

CHAPTER 19
SIBYL

"You don't want much then," Toman said darkly. "If Stroya finds out I let you in to see Sibyl, he'll have a fit." He blinked, drawing my attention back to his face, which was when I realized that he had two sets of eyes. Two were set very close to his nose/beak, and the other two were slightly higher and set wider.

"So, don't tell him," Cambious replied, lifting his glass of wine to sip. "Do I need to remind you what you owe me? This will not come close, and yet, if you arrange it, I will call us even."

Toman's face darkened and he clucked at Cambious. "Give me a few minutes. Gavin, cover the bar, I have something I need to do."

As he moved away, I could see that like his hands, his feet were talons that clicked against the floor when he walked. Cambious turned to me with his glass in hand. I frowned at him and took a sip of my own wine. It was rich and lush and fruity on my tongue. "What exactly does he owe you for?" I asked softly.

Cambious shook his head. "That is between him and I. Suffice it to say that this favor does little to restore the balance."

"And who is Sibyl?"

He smiled tightly. "You will see soon. I warn you, however, she is…not exactly sane."

Something tickled the back of my brain, something from high school English class and the section on Greek myth. "Is she…I mean, the Sibyl I know about was an oracle in ancient Greece."

He nodded and sipped his wine. "As are all Sibyls. Unfortunately, having access to all that knowledge tends to drive them mad."

I shook my head because that made about as much sense as the fact that I was sitting in a bar next to an incubus and a…Big Foot.

"Let me ask the questions though," Cambious said, putting his empty glass down on the bar. "She'll only answer three, and if you distract her, we might not find out what we need to know."

"And what is it you think she can tell us?"

"How to get your mother out of the Kourt, I hope. Ah, Toman." He gestured toward a door where Toman was waving to us.

I followed him through the door and down a long, ill-lit corridor where Toman paused to unlock another door and open it. "You have fifteen minutes. Any longer than that and Stroya will know. Your vehicle will be waiting out the back when you are done."

Cambious held out his hand. "Thank you, my friend. I shall not ask any more of you from this night on."

"Damn well better not," Toman muttered as he walked away.

"Remember, stay quiet." Cambious headed down the dark staircase and I followed, clutching the bag Merry had given me and realizing suddenly I hadn't even looked inside it to know what was there. There was a soft yellow glow as we neared the bottom of the stairs, and the air was increasingly warmer. At the bottom, we turned the corner into a small room dominated by a huge fireplace with a large fire burning, the air filled with the strong scent of the wood burning and something more fragrant, something that sent my mind whirring.

In front of the fireplace was a rocking chair and in that chair was a woman. Or what I assumed was a woman. She was tiny and frail-looking, all wrinkled skin stretched over bone. Her feet didn't reach the floor and her eyes were hazy and milk-white, likely blind. A plain white nightgown hung off her gaunt frame and gray and white hair hung in streaks from her balding head.

Unerringly, she turned her face toward us as we came to a stop. "Who comes?" she asked, her voice shaky and low.

"Pilgrims seeking guidance," Cambious responded. "May we approach?"

"What gift have you brought me, pilgrim?"

Cambious gestured at the bag in my hands. I opened it and reached inside, coming out with an old-looking bottle with no label. I handed it to Cambious who in turn held it out to the woman. "We bring a fine brandy aged a hundred years in the dark ranges of the Amerin mountains, in a cave where the ghosts of ages past fill the casks."

She gestured for him to come closer. He put the bottle in her hands. "It is a fine gift, pilgrim, but I have no need of such spirits. The ghosts of ages past fill me daily." Her face turned to me. "This woman is a blood witch."

Cambious stepped toward me protectively. "She is, but not mine to give."

The old woman smiled. "I would have a gift of her. I will answer your questions three, but once I have you will leave her with me. I would have her heal me."

I wasn't sure there was anything wrong with her other than advanced age and the blindness that came with it. Not to mention, I had no idea how my gift worked. Every time I had used it, it had been instinct. "It's okay, Cambious," I murmured. "I can try."

He looked into my eyes, judging my resolve before he nodded. "Very well then."

"Come, pilgrim, and give me your hand." As Cambious knelt in front of her, she lifted an odd-looking tube from the small table beside her and put it to her lips, inhaling deeply and holding her breath for an impossible length of time. When she exhaled, a purple mist escaped her mouth and she put the tube down, taking Cambious's offered hand.

"You have three questions. Ask them well."

"We seek the blood witch's mother who is held prisoner by the Brotherhood of God at the Mauno Kourt. What must be done to free her?"

The room was still, the only sound that of the crackling fire and when the woman lifted her head, her voice had taken on an odd inflection, stronger than it had been and deep. "Seek your way on rocky ground, find the one that must be found. He smells your blood and knows your way; his freedom is the price you'll pay."

Her head nodded back toward her chest and for a moment I thought she was asleep. "Your first question is answered. Ask your second."

Cambious licked his lips, considering his options before he asked, "The Brotherhood seeks the blood witch and will kill her if they find her. How can I keep her safe?"

Again, she lifted her head, her voice strong as she responded, "Safety is forgone and lost, and in the Kourt, you pay the cost. Look to the gods, look to the sky, her blood will spill while death is nigh."

Cambious looked over his shoulder at me, actual fear in his eyes. "One question remains, pilgrim. What will you know?"

He inhaled and let it out slowly. "Can we stop the Brotherhood?"

"Father of Brothers speaks hate, and others follow. He will burn in the fires of Apollo. Still, they will rise another day, hate born of hate finds a way."

She dropped her head to her chest again and Cambious stood, backing up. When she lifted her head, she was once again the frail old lady. "Your questions asked, your questions answered. Now leave me with the witch."

Cambious drew me back a few steps. "Be careful, Thána. I'm not sure what she will ask of you, but I promise it will not be pleasant."

I nodded, not trusting myself to speak. If I was honest, I was terrified of what she was going to ask me, not to mention terrified of what I thought her answers meant. If we couldn't destroy the Brotherhood, would I ever be safe? And what of my blood being spilled? I didn't like how any of that sounded. When Cambious could no longer be heard on the stairs, she beckoned me closer.

"I'm not sure what I can do to help you," I said cautiously, taking one knee in front of her. "My gifts are...unpredictable."

"Your gifts are strong, and I ask only that you give me a taste of them. On the mantle is a blade, bring it."

I was even less sure of what she was asking, but I got up and went to the fireplace. The blade looked to be made of black glass, shiny and sharp. I brought it back to her and went back to my knee. "Cut your arm and give it to me."

I stared at her until her eyes narrowed and her face grew hard. "You have a price to pay, *mágissa*, do not think to escape it." Her tone softened and her hand patted mine. "I won't take much, but my bones are cold."

Swallowing hard, I lifted the blade and after a couple of aborted attempts, managed to make a shallow cut about 4 inches above my left wrist. Blood beaded along the edge, but it wasn't enough. With a shaky hand, I drew the blade over it again and her hand pressed down on mine, making me slice deep enough that I gasped and had to fight the urge to drop the knife and cover the wound. Her hands pulled my wrist up toward her mouth and I had to stand to ease the odd turn on my shoulder. Leathery lips closed around the wound and a strange sucking sensation followed.

I was starting to feel faint when she finally released me and I stumbled back toward the fireplace, catching myself on the mantle. I did cover the wound now, though it was bleeding enough that I knew it would take more than my bare hand to staunch the flow. She started laughing, my blood painting her lips, and, in the firelight, shadows danced across her face, making her seem...younger somehow.

She was still laughing as I raced for the stairs, bursting through the door, and falling into Cambious.

"Are you okay?" Cambious asked, his hand going to where mine covered my bleeding arm.

"Let's just get out of here," I responded. He gestured down the hallway in the opposite direction of the bar. As we stepped out into the night, he tapped the talisman on his chest and his whole being shimmered as the glamor returned. As promised, there was a car waiting, a boxy-looking thing that didn't look big enough to even hold Cambious. It was dark grey, with a short front end and an even shorter back end with no back seat.

"He could have gotten us something made in this century," Cambious griped.

"Does it matter, as long as it runs?" I asked, moving to the passenger side, and using my wounded hand to open the door. I felt blood rushing as I flexed the muscles and must have paled because Cambious was suddenly at my side, supporting me as my knees gave out.

"Thána!"

He got the door fully open and sat me on the seat. "Let me see it." He pried my hand away and made a sound between a gasp and a growl. "Had I known that was what she wanted…" He pulled something out of my duffle bag and folded it, pressing it over the wound, then pressing my hand back over it. "Here, hold this. Press down tight."

Cambious helped me get my feet into the car and closed my door, then went around the back, dropping the bags and the bottle of brandy in the trunk before he squeezed himself into the driver's seat and started the engine. "There's a pharmacy up the street. We can get some bandages at least, if their healer is on duty, we might get lucky."

I was woozy when the car stopped, but Cambious helped me up and held me while the world spun around me. The shop in front of us looked similar to the Walgreens where I went to buy aspirin and Band-Aids, though its neon signs said "Healer on Staff" instead of something about a drive-through pharmacy window. Cambious got us in the door, with me still pressing down on what I could now see was one of my T-shirts. The place was well lit and nearly empty, but that would be expected at whatever hour of the night it was. Cambious helped me through several aisles until we came to what looked like any clinic in a pharmacy back home.

He got me sat down and went to the window beside a door. I couldn't hear him talking, but then I was busy trying very hard not to pass out. A few minutes, or possibly longer, later, the door opened and a guy who reminded me of that grandpa at my first foster family's Christmas dinner came out of the door, took one look at me, and told Cambious to bring me back right away.

Cambious helped me up, but my knees had become less solid than Jell-O which hadn't set completely and he ended up scooping me up and carrying me through the door. I realized as he set me down on an exam table that I had lost the T-shirt and I tried to get up to go find it.

I was pressed down, and Grandpa pulled my blood-soaked hand away from my arm, exposing the wound. "How did this happen?"

"I dropped the knife," I said, my words slurring.

"I'm sure," Grandpa responded. "For starters, let's get that blood flow under control. How much has she lost?"

Cambious shook his head. "I'm not sure."

Grandpa turned away and when he came back, he had a stick of some sort, the end of it glowing. "This is going to sting." He pried the wound open and put the glowy stick into it, tracing along the full length internally. Sting was not the word I would have used to describe that particular sensation. I screamed, my back arching up off the table. Cambious pressed me back down, but I still tried to squirm away. "Hold her still."

Once again, Grandpa turned away, and this time he came back with gauze that looked damp. He used it to clean the blood from my arm and wiped it over the wound. "There, now I can see what's going on."

I couldn't see what he was doing as he worked and twice, I swooned enough that I'm not certain I didn't actually lose consciousness. Then, Cambious was picking me up off the table and thanking the Grandpa witch doctor with a warning to him to be sure to clean up well if he didn't want unwelcome company. My arm was bandaged, and I was starting to feel a little more with it as we reached the car.

"I need your help here, Thána," Cambious said. "Can you stand?"

I nodded and he slowly lowered my feet to the ground and opened the car door for me. "We need to move, if the blood tracker is anywhere in Thelos he will have picked up our trail with the amount of blood you left in there."

Once I was in, Cambious closed my door and went back to the driver's side. "Where are we going?" I asked as we set out.

"Away from here."

CHAPTER 20
OUT OF THELOS

I woke to daylight painting the windshield a golden color. Beside me, Cambious was asleep behind the wheel. Outside the car, we seemed to be in a parking garage, and I could just make out the faint shimmer of wards outside the car. My left arm was an angry, screaming toddler who had been told he couldn't have the last cookie and I needed to pee badly enough that I wasn't sure I could get out of the seat to do it, even if there had been a bathroom nearby.

I tried to stretch, but the tiny cabin of the vehicle didn't give me much room. I could only imagine how much worse it was for Cambious. I shifted as much as I dared, seeing as I was now wearing the only jeans I had left, and to my dismay, they were stained with my blood. It wasn't a lot, but if Cambious was right and the Brotherhood was on our tail, this could lead them straight to us.

"How are you?" Cambious asked into the silence of the car, causing me to jump and nearly lose the hold I had on my bladder.

"Holy mother of—warn a person before you do that," I exclaimed, shaking my head. "I'm okay, but I need a bathroom."

"As do I. If you are capable of walking, we are someplace where we can do that as well as replace our clothing and get something to eat. Then we should once more be moving on."

"Right. And where is it we are going?" I asked, opening my door, and moving gingerly so I didn't wet myself.

"Toward Mauno Kourt, for lack of any other direction," Cambious responded, also climbing out of the car. He dismissed the wards and moved around picking up the stones. "We won't rescue your mother from here."

I had serious doubts about rescuing her at all, but I didn't say that. Instead, I concentrated on my steps and followed Cambious to a stairwell. He had parked us on the fourth floor of the parking structure, which I found was attached to what looked suspiciously like a mall. My disillusionment with my Fairy Kingdom was nearly complete.

Fortunately for me, there were bathrooms near the entrance, so I was able to relieve myself of that particular problem fairly quickly. Our next stop was a small boutique that sold clothes that, while they weren't exactly the height of fashion back home, wouldn't have been completely out of place either. We quickly picked out a few items—some pants and several shirts—paid, and then backtracked to the bathrooms so we could both shed our bloodstained clothes and get dressed. I took a few minutes to clean up as well, taking some wet paper towels into the stall with me.

I stuffed my bloodstained shirt and pants into the bag I took the new shirt and pants out of and dressed as quickly as I could. I was starting to get anxious, though I wasn't sure of the cause. We seemed relatively safe for the moment. I picked up the paper towels from the floor where I'd dropped them, then shoved those into the bag too. Cambious had said we could use them to lay a false trail, though I wasn't sure how that was supposed to work.

Besides, Cambious had promised me food.

My stomach growled then, as if it needed to be reminded that I hadn't had food since breakfast the morning before. We moved through the mall, which was starting to get busy, dodging weary mothers with toddlers pulling them or dragging behind them. I could smell something delicious as we neared what I was no longer surprised to find looked just like a food court in just about every mall I had ever been in.

We walked around each of the restaurants so I could see what there was to choose from, finally stopping beside a place serving sandwiches and what looked like burritos. I ordered a sandwich filled with eggs and some sort of sausage, with a side of coffee and left Cambious to order and pay while I found us a seat where we could see most of the food court.

Cambious brought our food and we sat, both of us keeping our eyes moving while we ate. The bag with my bloody clothes sat at my feet still, next to the bag with our other purchases and we were both aware that it could give us away. We ate quickly and as soon as we were done, we all but ran back toward the car.

"How far are we from the Kourt?" I asked when we were on the road, the bag of bloody clothes in my lap.

"It's about a two-day drive, but first we're going in the other direction to drop these clothes. So, a little longer than that."

"Do you think just dropping bloody clothes by the roadside and driving in the other direction is going to work?"

He grinned at me. "No, but I have other plans."

I understood a little while later, as we pulled into a mammoth train station. Cambious directed me to the ladies' room with instructions to put the bag in the trash, then rejoin him at the ticket counter. A half-hour later, we were back on the road, with two train tickets to a city called Aténa to the north and west of Thelos. I tucked the tickets under my seat with the hope that the combination was enough to make the Brotherhood think we were trying to get away and not suspect that we were headed for their base of operations.

"Okay, so…what Sibyl had to say about this insane scheme of ours, have you given it any thought?" I asked when we'd both been quiet for a long time.

Cambious nodded slowly. "Some. You?"

"Seek your way on rocky ground, find the one that must be found. He smells your blood and knows your way; his freedom is the price you'll pay…" That one seemed the easiest for me to focus on. "We're going to need someone's help, and I'm guessing it's a blood tracker?"

"That is what I deduced as well," Cambious said. "Legend tells us that the Brotherhood uses male blood witches, trained to use their powers to sense their own kind. They can smell your blood. The best can sense it just by being in proximity. They are rare, however. I have never met one."

"Fabulous." I shook my head, a vague detail from a dream coming to mind. "How does the Brotherhood get them to do it?"

"They are usually stolen in their early childhood when possible and indoctrinated in the Brotherhood's beliefs. The older ones are simply tortured until they submit. They are enslaved, treated hardly better than the women they hunt."

There was a boy in the background of my dream of Althea's death. Clad only in a diaper-like garment, covered in dirt and half-starved, he had been on the platform, a collar of some kind around his neck, held in place with needles that pierced his skin. I shuddered and pushed the image away. There had also been that boy with the Brotherhood who had spared my life when I was still a child. "So, we're supposed to find this person, without alerting his…handlers, and convince him to help us?"

"I've thought about that too," Cambious said. "As I said, Sybyl can be difficult to understand, but it should become clear as we draw closer."

"Okay, so what? We find some kid and promise him he'll go free if he just helps us find my mother?" I asked without even attempting to keep the doubt from my voice. "Sounds easy. Sure, let's do that."

"Perhaps he will find us," Cambious countered

We were leaving the city of Thelos, headed south and east on a freeway that was slowly getting less congested. "So, we get to the Kourt, we find this guy, he leads us to Mom…then what?"

Cambious shrugged as much as was possible in the tight little space of the car, which only made me realize that even if we rescued this blood tracker and my mother, we had no way to get them to safety. I skipped over the middle prophecy and moved on to the last. "Father of Brothers speaks hate and others follow. He will burn in the fires of Apollo. Still, they will rise another day, hate born of hate finds a way. Which means what? Apollo, the sun god? How do we convince the sun to burn a man?"

"Ah, a point of mythological differences. Apollo is a god of eternal flame, light, heat…" Cambious offered. "I warned you that she often makes little sense. The fires of Apollo may mean any number of things."

Great. Exactly what I wanted to hear when the middle prophecy had talked about my blood spilling and death being nigh. I was starting to wonder if it wouldn't just be easier to find some tall building to jump off of. I rubbed a hand over the bandages on my arm, wishing it would ease the pain there.

"Safety is forgone and lost, and in the Kourt, you pay the cost. Look to the gods, look to the sky, her blood will spill while death is nigh."

Sibyl's words echoed in my head and spun into a mini-tornado. I wasn't ready to acknowledge them, or the fear that bloomed under them. I wasn't ready to think about killing **or** dying. In fact, I was beginning to wonder what exactly I was doing. I wasn't a cop. I wasn't military. I had no idea how to break into a fortress, let alone evade bloodthirsty killers, rescue an old woman and escape in a car built for two.

But my father's ghost had told me to find her and all of my repressed anger at her abandonment was floundering under the desperate love of a ten-year-old's desire for her family.

"You should rest," Cambious said. "We have a long drive."

The world outside the windows of the car was getting increasingly gray, with thick clouds forming on the horizon. "Looks like rain," I said softly.

"Snow more like. Thelos is in a temperate zone, but it **is** winter here."

We were quiet then for a while and I dozed off. It wasn't really sleeping, but I wasn't awake either. It was that weird spot somewhere between the two, where I was vaguely aware of the world around me, but not engaged with it. Maybe I could just stay there and stop worrying about the strange turn my life had taken.

Eventually, the road beneath our tires changed and we slowed, pulling me out of my stupor. Cambious pulled off the road and into the parking lot of some hotel. The gray skies had grown black and just as Cambious had predicted, snow was falling. One more thing I hadn't come prepared for.

"I'll get us a room." Cambious was gone before I could say anything, not that I knew what to say. He came back to the car and opened the trunk, pulling out our bags and the bottle of brandy before leading the way to a door marked with a symbol I assumed was a number.

It looked like any hotel room I had ever stayed in, with a dark brown rug and walls painted beige. Two double beds were covered in ghastly bedspreads that looked like the product of a night of hallucinogenic drugs mixed with confetti shots and paint. There was a flash of memory, of a room just like this with my mother and sister, and a lot of fear. I shook my head to clear it and turned to find the bathroom, thinking I needed to wash my face and get it together.

We still had no plan for what we were doing. I had no idea what to expect, other than the flashes I had seen inside the fortress where my mother was being held. I had no delusions that I was equipped for this. I turned the water on and reached for the pristine white washcloth folded in a fan shape on the counter. My reflection stared back at me, with black smudges under dark green eyes and hair that was rapidly reverting to its natural state of fuzzy black curls.

I washed my face with cool water and thought about just running away, hiding somewhere that even the Brotherhood wouldn't find me, though I had no idea just where that might be. With a heavy sigh, I turned back into the room to find Cambious on the end of one bed, his glamor gone and his whole body looking heavy. His eyes were puffy and red. He was exhausted.

"You should rest," I said, pulling his attention to me.

"I need to feed," he replied. "The constant drain of the glamor is too much."

"Is it safe to…find someone here? I mean, I saw a bar at the corner, but…" Thus far we hadn't had to have this particular discussion, but I got the impression from his mother that an incubus wasn't exactly welcome in a lot of places.

"Likely not. I'll have to be discreet." He lurched back to his feet, his hand reaching for the amulet.

"Cam, you can barely stand." I pulled his hand away from the amulet. "How about you sleep for a while, and we can go to the bar together." He sat back down, and I went to one knee to help him with his boots. Which was when the solution came to me. "Or…we could…I mean, I could…"

He seemed to get the gist of what I was going for and shook his head minutely. "No, I couldn't ask that of you."

I grinned up at him. "You aren't asking. I'm offering. God knows I haven't had sex in a while, but I think I remember how it works."

CHAPTER 21
INTO THE WOODS

I SET THE HEAVY BOOTS ASIDE AND SLID MY HANDS UP CAM'S LEGS, NUDGING them apart so I could move between them. "You've done so much for me," I said softly. "Let me help **you** for a change."

He wanted to argue, I could see it in his eyes, but his exhaustion won the fight and he let me move closer, sliding a hand up under his shirt, urging it up and he responded with a shrug that brought it up to his neck before he pulled it off. I couldn't quite look him in the eye as my hands glided over his dark skin.

Cambious was a big man, built solid and strong. Randomly, I wondered if that was true before his transition, if he'd been big and solid muscle as a succubus. I shook off the distraction and turned my attention back to getting Cambious out of his clothes.

The jeans he wore did little to hide his arousal now that he had given in to the need. I leaned back to pull off my shirt, dropping it behind me as his big hands unzipped his jeans and he shimmied a little to get them down.

My surprise when he had bared himself almost threw me out of the moment. I had expected big, he'd implied that, but what I wasn't prepared for was the peachy-white skin. He followed my eyes and chuckled a little. "You saw she was white, obviously. There are ways to make it match, but I've never bothered."

"No need," I said, my voice huskier than normal. My body was certainly responding to having a naked man in front of me, even if he did have horns, and I stood to shed my own jeans. I shivered a little as I dropped my pants and panties on the bed, suddenly self-conscious of my soft, flabby body next to his, but if it was repellent, Cambious didn't show it, drawing me back to him with a gentle hand.

"You don't have to," Cambious said softly.

"I want to." If I let myself, I could reach back to the day we had met and the lust that had filled my head. It flushed through me. That rush, that need, and I was more than ready for what came next. I didn't know how the feeding thing worked, but my body certainly remembered how the sex thing did.

Cambious slid his large hands up my arms, then around my back to unhook my bra. His kiss was surprising somehow, soft lips on mine as he guided me to the bed. His skin was hot against mine as we lay down, his lips leaving a damp trail down between my breasts and over my belly. I wasn't thinking about my unfit body when his mouth moved further down, his hot breath sending a thrill of need straight into my sex. My orgasm took me by surprise and even more surprising was the accompanying sensation as Cambious sucked up the energy discharge that came with it.

I was still riding the tremors when he moved, spreading my legs apart to move between them, his own need obvious. I held my breath as he entered me, letting it out only after he started a slow pull back. "Thána, are you okay?" Cambious asked, his voice tender.

I nodded, opening eyes I hadn't realized I had closed. The air between us sizzled with energy that I vaguely recognized as coming from me, and as I ramped up to a second orgasm, Cambious breathed it in. It felt as if he were sucking my entire being out of my body and I fisted my hands in the bedspread beneath me, unable to do more than pant as I shook beneath him, my orgasm an extended experience that took my entire body to the brink of collapse.

I passed out, coming to only when Cambious started using a cool cloth to wipe the sweat from my skin. My limbs were heavy like I had run a marathon, or what I assumed it would feel like after running a marathon. I was still trembling as he lifted me like I was still a child and got me nestled into bed under the blankets. He kissed my forehead, and I wanted to say something, but my brain was already mid-shutdown procedure, so it came out as sort of a low moan.

"Sleep," Cambious said in my ear, and that was one command I had no trouble obeying.

The smell of coffee and bacon roused me sometime later and I sat up, forgetting I was naked, to see Cambious setting out breakfast on the room's small round table. "I figured you'd be hungry," Cambious said, keeping his back to me to give me time to find my clothes.

I dressed, or at least pulled on my panties and shirt, and moved to the table to join him, just as Cambious set a container filled with a mound of scrambled eggs and what looked and smelled like bacon in front of me. I reached for the cup of coffee first, peeling off the lid and sipping the hot liquid into me, feeling the warmth spread down my throat as I swallowed. My stomach rumbled and I picked up a small plastic fork to eat with.

Cambious sat opposite me, tucking into his own meal with less enthusiasm than I did. I watched him for a minute, then sat back with my coffee. "This isn't going to get awkward, is it?" I asked, pulling his eyes off his food to me. "I mean, I have no regrets, and you look restored, so…we're good, right?"

"If you mean that, yes," Cambious said, putting his empty plate on the table.

"Of course, I mean it. I wouldn't have offered if I thought I would regret it later. And I think it was pretty obvious how willing I was." I raised an eyebrow at him, nearly daring him to contradict me. "And I don't think I've ever slept harder, thank you very much. No dreams, just warm, fuzzy nothing until I smelled coffee."

"Well, I did drain you pretty good." Cambious seemed to be slowly letting go of whatever guilt he had been sitting with but wasn't all the way there.

"If I sleep that good after, you're welcome to drain me that good anytime you want," I said, blushing a little as I said it. "Seriously, Cam, I mean that. If you need it, tell me. You've done so much for me I can't begin to repay. This barely touches that debt."

He nodded, a half-smile turning up one corner of his mouth. "I will admit, I have never fed with a blood witch before. It was an amazing rush."

"There you go," I said, setting down my coffee to go back to my bacon. "So, what's up for us today? How far are we from the Kourt?"

"At least another day's drive. And we have to cross a border out of Spítia into Otadž."

I had a fleeting memory of those names. Spítia was my mother's homeland, with Thelos as its capital city. Otadž was a newer country, born out of a conflict that had torn the previous empire apart. When my mother was a girl, that country had split into Otadž and one named Orŏn to the north. That was about all I remembered. "Is it going to be a problem?"

He shrugged. "It is hard to say. The government of Otadž is in a terrible state, and most of its military has been recalled to the capital to protect what remains. Their Premier has been rocked by scandal and the parliament is so divided that nothing has been accomplished. The Brotherhood and a few other militant sects have stepped up in places to secure towns and demand adherence to their religion and rules. I do not know if they have made it so far as to the border crossings. I have not been this far from your portal in a very long time."

"So, we could be driving right into their hands."

He nodded slowly. "Perhaps, but there are places to cross where it is less likely we will be seen as a threat. There is a small town that straddles the border, we can cross there."

"And then we just have to find a fortress, rescue my mother, stop the Brotherhood from hunting me and get home before I lose my job." Because none of it mattered if we didn't find a way to get the Brotherhood off my trail. Chances were good my job was already gone. I'd lost track of how long it had been since we fled, a situation not helped by my days in a stupor after Merry's memory trick. Two days without word from me probably would have Bonnie ready to fire me. "You know this whole thing is insane, right?"

"So you have said." Cambious stood, crossing to the small window, and parting the heavy drapes just enough to peer out. A blade of light cut across the dingy room, making me wince and pull away from it.

"I'm going to shower." I stood and drank the last of my coffee before grabbing my duffel bag and heading into the bathroom. I looked like I was on the bad end of a hangover, my eyes dull and the smudges under them bordering on bruised. I stripped out of my dirty clothes and turned on the water, pausing to peel back the bandages on my arm. The cut was mostly closed, scabbed over in several places. Whatever was in the medicine they used here needed to find its way home with me, when and if I ever got to go home.

The thought gave me pause. I'm not sure when I had started to consider the house in California as home, but somewhere in the whirlwind, it had become an anchor, a safe place. I hadn't had that since the day we had left it when I was still a child.

I showered quickly and dressed in the other set of clothing Cambious had purchased for me. I had no way to straighten my curls, so instead, I finger combed them into something I could live with, promising myself an indulgent spa day when this was over that would include returning my hair to my preferred style.

By the time I emerged from the bathroom, Cambious looked like he was ready to get going, his glamor safely in place. Not for the first time, I wondered how many other races I had already seen but couldn't tell because of their glamors. And if this society was so far advanced, why did he have to hide who he was? I put the question aside for another day and followed Cambious out to the car.

I put my duffle in the trunk, pulling out the book on the Brotherhood and the blood witch primer to take into the car with me. As Cambious drove, I devoured the information the books could offer me, reading up on the various gifts peculiar to blood witches, before switching to the Brotherhood's history, up to about fifty years ago, when the book had been published. The Kourt was the ancestral home of a line of blood witches, built by a Duke as a place for protection and study. The Brotherhood had come in the night, like something out of a B-movie, with torches and spears, storming in to cleanse the Kourt, and slaughtering every living being in its halls.

The Kourt sat atop a small hill, with two roads that snaked around the hill to reach the stone walls. At the base of the hill, circling it, was a graveyard. Once a place of honor for those who had served the duke, or studied in his libraries, it had become the final resting place of generations of Brothers and was said to be protected by spells and enchantments, and creatures who guarded the Kourt.

"Great," I murmured, looking up from the book. We were driving through a wooded area, gently climbing. The snow blanketed the trees, but the road was clear, even as the snow continued to fall. "So, to get into the Kourt, we have to cross through a graveyard that the Brotherhood has warded with god only knows what."

"I expect it will include enslaved manticores at the least. I understand the Brotherhood considers them to be symbols of Jeus himself."

"Manticores?" My face scrunched up as I searched my memory. The word was familiar, but there was no easy recall.

"They are not unlike a lion, if a lion had wings, a tail like a scorpion, and the intelligence of a man," Cambious supplied. "They are extremely dangerous. One sting from a manticore's tail can kill a grown man in under ten minutes. Their claws are deadly. And they fly. There could be phoenixes as well. There was a news story a few years back about a phoenix who had escaped the Brotherhood. They also fly and can breathe fire. Toman is a phoenix. Their talons can be deadly as well. Oh, and a point of interest, they were said to guard the entrance of the cave of Apollo, where the sacred fire was kept."

"Okay, that's terrifying," I mumbled. "This rescue operation just gets better and better."

CHAPTER 22
THAT'S THE PLAN?

We reached a small town close to the middle of the day. There was a sign as we approached, welcoming us to Sigur, home of the award-winning poet, Timurline, whoever that was. The town itself looked like something from a postcard of some rural European town that had never fully stepped into the twentieth century, let alone whatever century it was here.

The buildings were all dark timber and whitewashed stone with slate roofs that sloped down from the center nearly to the street. The whole town was one street lined with shops, though I imagined that there were houses beyond that we couldn't see from the car.

In the center of the town, there was a monument that stood a good twenty-five feet tall, of a woman with a torch in her hand. "It is said that she was the first to settle here," Cambious said, steering us into the roundabout that circled the statue and its pedestal. A sign warned us that we were crossing into Otadž as we reached the center of the giant roundabout. We passed without fanfare, and I relaxed minutely as we carried on unimpeded.

"That wasn't so bad," Cambious murmured.

"Don't jinx us," I responded. Ahead of us, more buildings lined the road, but fewer of them seemed occupied. People were scarce and when we did see them, they were scurrying between doorways. It didn't feel particularly safe. There were no men on the streets with guns though, which was what I'd been expecting, if I'm being honest. I didn't even know if they had guns here.

We continued down the road and past the sign telling us we were leaving Sigur. Ahead of us was open road through a deep, dark forest that was blanketed with snow. It would have been beautiful if it didn't hide the men who wanted me dead. As we continued toward the fortress that held my mother, I continued my reading, wanting to fill my head with as much knowledge as I could in the hope that it would lead to a plan of some kind that didn't include my death.

A thought occurred to me, and I turned my head to look at Cambious. "So, I'm assuming that you aren't just a pretty face and pheromones, right?"

He frowned, glancing aside at me. "How do you mean?"

"Well, can you, you know, fight? Pick locks? Something like that?"

"I don't tend to go around getting into fights if I'm honest," Cambious replied. "Particularly here. I am a good deal stronger than most humans."

"Okay, that part is good." My brain was spinning out possible scenarios. I had access now to whatever knowledge my mother was able to impart to me before she left me, but it was admittedly not enough. I was ahead of my age group, to be certain, and she taught me protections most nine-year-olds would not learn for years to come, but protection spells and wards were not going to get us into a fortress. "Wait, I think I remember something about locks." I dug deep into the place where all of that knowledge seemed to reside, setting the Brotherhood book aside and going back to the blood witch primer. "My blood can fortify a lock but can unlock stuff too? Particularly if it was set by another blood witch."

"Are you certain?"

I shrugged. "No?" I thumbed through the primer, scanning for anything about locks. The problem was, this book was not written as a training tool. It didn't have instructions, just information. "It's theoretical anyway. I never tried it. It was in a book I read on the theory of blood magic. A lot of it went over my head, but I was only eight." Idly I wondered what had happened to that book. I remembered taking it with us when we fled, reading it in the car while Mom drove, but she must have taken it from me when she left me. "So, we can try that. If we get that far."

"Perhaps you will be able to sense your way, seeing as the Kourt was once home to the blood witches of the time?"

I shrugged again. "I guess we'll find out. And then we just have to get inside, find Mom, break her out, wipe out the Brotherhood…yeah, should be a walk in the park." I ran the words of the old woman through my head, trying to reason out how they could help us. "

Seek your way on rocky ground, find the one that must be found…He smells your blood and knows your way; his freedom is the price you'll pay. Safety is forgone and lost, and in the Kourt, you pay the cost. Look to the gods, look to the sky, her blood will spill while death is nigh. Father of Brothers speaks hate, and others follow. He will burn in the fires of Apollo. Still, they will rise another day, hate born of hate will find a way."

No matter how I turned it around in my head, it sounded like we would have to kill the leader of the Brotherhood to get them off my scent. Though, if it was as big an organization as it seemed, killing one man didn't feel like a solution of any kind. In fact, I had to wonder if it wouldn't just make it worse, turning the man into a martyr. I also wasn't sure I could do it. Kill a man I mean. Of course, I already had, when I was just a child, but I wasn't that person anymore.

I shook my head to clear it. "How far are we now?" I asked.

"Not far, another hour or so."

"We should eat. And make some kind of plan."

He nodded and pointed out the front windshield. "There is a cafe not far ahead of us. Or there used to be. We can stop."

True to his word, a few miles down the road, the trees gave way to a gravel parking lot and a little building with a faded sign in three languages, declaring the best pie in the precinct and we pulled in, parking beside a beat-up older car that vaguely resembled a Volkswagen Beetle. "I haven't been here in years, possibly since you still wore pigtails," Cambious said as he opened his door. "Used to be run by a little old man and his wife, they're probably gone now."

I kept forgetting Cambious was that much older than me, and I found myself wondering if that made the sex thing weird for him. I mean, it was weird enough for me with him being a creature stepped out of ancient superstition, but considering he'd known me since I was little, how strange had that have to have been. Unless incubi didn't have those sorts of taboos.

I put the question away for a time when we weren't an hour away from the stronghold of the men who wanted me dead, provided that time ever actually came.

The cafe had a long counter with stools and a handful of booths. A tired-looking woman with dark red-brown hair pulled back in a ponytail nodded to us. "*Sedi bilo gde.*"

Cambious nodded back. "*Hvala vam.*"

"How many languages do you speak?" I asked as Cambious led us to a booth near the back where we'd have the most privacy.

He seemed to think about it for a moment. "Fluently? Five, but I can manage in another six or so. Of course, those are languages here, I've found that on your side of the door, they've changed enough that I don't always understand them."

That made sense. Language evolves over time and could evolve in unexpected ways as cultures come together or splintered apart. We sat and the tired-looking woman approached with menus. I couldn't read it, or even figure out what language it was written in, but Cambious pointed out a few dishes he thought I might like and when the woman came back, he ordered for both of us.

He waited until she had walked away and pitched his voice low enough it wouldn't carry. "To find our way in, we will first have to get past the manticores."

"And any other creatures, plus wards or spells they've put up."

Cambious nodded. "Yes."

"Putting the mythological creatures to the side for the moment, what then?" I asked, glancing up to track the waitress.

"Well, that's going to depend on what we find once we get there."

"Right. Remind me how long the Brotherhood has been there?"

"A long time," Cambious replied. "I think we can assume any way in will be locked in some fashion. So, we deal with the lock. Then it gets tricky."

"I can tell you that my mother is in a cell up high, in a tower I think."

"Well, that narrows it down some. There are only four towers."

"So, we search them all?" I asked. "And how do we do that without being seen, caught, and killed?"

Cambious lifted a hand to the amulet that secured his glamor. "I was thinking we just walk in. We'll have to build you a glamor too. And steal some clothing."

"Okay, that sounds doable, provided we can do the glamor thing…I know Mom taught me some simple ones when I was little, but I can't promise I can make one work. From there we just have to avoid any confrontations and look like we belong."

"Simple," Cambious said, his tone indicating he thought the exact opposite.

We both sat back as our waitress brought our plates, simple enough sandwich-like meals with fried chips of some kind. They looked like potato chips, except for how they were kind of a pale blue in color. They tasted similar to potato chips, but for a bit of a sharp bite like old cheese.

"Okay, so let's get back to the mythological creatures that will want to kill us. Any ideas?" I asked as I swallowed my second bite.

"Perhaps. It will depend a great deal on the manticores themselves. I think we should probably take our time with them, watch their patrol patterns. Maybe we can avoid them altogether. We should make a circle around the Kourt itself before we settle down somewhere for sleep."

I nodded, not sure what he would have in mind, but figuring anything we planned now with our limited information would likely be useless later anyway. But at least we had the start of a plan. As we got close to finishing our food, the waitress brought the check, and with it a paper bag.

Cambious handed her a payment card and thanked her. "I ordered food to go. There's no guarantee we will find a safe place to eat later."

When she came back with his card, we got up to leave, but I detoured to the bathroom. Who knew when we'd have an actual bathroom again? I relieved myself and stopped to wash my hands, glancing in the mirror at my reflection. My hair was nearly full curl, and frizzy with the lack of product in it. I almost didn't look like myself anymore. In fact, I looked like the women in the pictures in my book. I looked like Merry when she was younger.

Cambious had the car started and turned toward the road when I came out. We drove in relative silence for a while, until the forest thinned out yet again, and we began to see gravestones in front of us and on the side of the road. Cambious turned us to the right as the road dead-ended just before the graves began. Several rows back, a four-foot stone wall erupted from the ground, blocking our view of the rest of the graveyard, as well as the base of the hill upon which the Kourt stood.

I leaned forward to look up, my eyes tracking rocky terrain until I could just make out the foundations of the fortress above us. With the wall between us and what we needed to see to plan our entry, not to mention our later escape, we were going to need to actually get out of the car at some point, but first Cambious was determined to drive completely around it, in order to get an idea of what our first obstacle would be.

CHAPTER 23
GLAMORS, NOT GLAMOROUS

The first gate we found in the wall was manned by two guards in black military uniforms, with weapons strapped to their waists, and in their hands. Unlike the Brothers I had encountered before, they both had full heads of hair, one blonde, one brunette, cut close on top and shaved on the sides.

We didn't slow down, but as we drove past, I got an impression of the graveyard beyond that wall, a road through it that bore to the right before I lost sight of it.

The second was guarded the same, but the stonework around the gate seemed to need some work, and through the gates I spotted, or thought I did, the creature Cambious called a manticore. I shivered involuntarily as we drove past but grabbed Cambious by the arm a few minutes later. "Stop."

Cambious pulled us off the road well out of sight of the guards, a question on his face. I wasn't sure I could put into words the feeling that swelled up within me. Near the wall was a neat row of graves, with stones so old the words etched into them couldn't be read, at least not from the car. Something there wanted my attention. I opened the door, my eyes scanning around us to make sure we weren't being watched.

"Thána, what are you doing?" Cambious hissed at me, but I shook my head, crossing the street and feeling my way toward whatever had called out to me. Nearest the wall was a stone that once had been white but was marred now by time and what looked like the damage of fire. I squatted beside it, brushing soot and dirt from the etched name, but it was still unreadable. It knew me, which I know makes no sense at all.

I could feel Cambious behind me, his concern palpable, even at that distance, but I ignored him, laying my hand flat against the stone, where the name had once been. As my palm connected I got a flash of the graveyard beyond the wall, not as it was right then, but as it had been when this witch had been laid there, and beyond that, the rocky face of the hill, a tumble of rocks, a hidden cave part way up, only visible when you were nearly upon it.

I heard Cambious open his door and stood, waving him back as I crossed the street back to him. "Go," I said once I had the car door closed. "There's a secret way in. Or there was. Whoever buried that witch left a… map, of sorts. I just felt it."

Cambious didn't respond, just continued us on down the road. Before we had made a complete circuit around the Kourt, we found a dirt road that took us back into the forest, and about fifteen minutes later, Cambious pulled us to a stop, nodding. "We can get some rest here. Work on your glamor."

I nodded. "Okay, but we can't sleep all night. We're going to need the darkness to protect us."

Cambious snorted. "For all the good it will do. Manticores have excellent night vision."

"Humor me? I got a look at that thing. I don't need to see it in the daylight again."

"I suggest you set up some wards, give us a good fifty feet inside, encompass the car. I'll get us set up for working."

I wasn't sure what he needed to set up, or where it was going to come from, but got out of the car all the same, pulling the bag of ward stones from the pocket of my jeans and eying the area around us, trying to figure out the boundaries of a fifty-foot circle. I decided to keep the car as the boundary to our east, setting the first set of stones about five feet from my door. I paced out the circle without activating the stones, making sure I had an even placement, so we were equally protected from all sides.

Once I had the spacing figured, I retraced my steps, marking the spot in the dirt, pine needles, or leaves so I would know where to return the stones, then brought them back to the car, arranging them on the hood in their respective pairs. I sorted through the various incantations I had learned to use with them and settled on the one that would make us disappear, as well as keep anyone from hurting us. I felt Cambious watching as I activated the pairs before holding my hand above the obsidian cubes, murmuring, "*Ekleípo.*"

Green light flared and formed a dome around the circle of stones. Cambious joined me, his pride palpable. "Very good, Thána. We now must move them in tandem." He reached for a pair, and I reached for its opposite. Very carefully we moved toward the edges of the circle I'd marked out, and I could feel the dome stretching with us. We returned to the hood for the next pairs and the next, until with the last the dome stretched over our heads and all around us in a circle.

While I'd been working, Cambious had started a small fire and spread a blanket down beside it. I noticed it was the same blanket as he'd used the night we had dinner together beside the portal. He must have put it in his bag before we left his cabin. My duffle bag was on the blanket, my books stacked beside it.

"I guess it's time to learn how to glamor?" I asked as I sat.

"Unless you would prefer to sleep first?"

I shook my head. "No, let's do this." I pulled the stack of books to me, setting my own spellbook aside. Glamors would have been beyond my skill level then, even if they would have come in handy. I chose the family book first, kind of remembering seeing something about glamors in its pages.

"The thing to remember about glamors is that they are an energy drain," Cambious said softly as I turned the pages. "They are easier to maintain if you have something to anchor them, such as my amulet." His hand lifted to caress the talisman gently. "And they are easier if you do not shift too much of yourself. I think for this it should suffice to change your appearance to be more masculine and shorten your hair. If you've noticed, the brotherhood either shaves their head or wears it cropped close. There was a monastic order as well that didn't ever cut their hair, but they are all but gone."

I nodded, tucking the information into a corner of my brain while I sought out the page I was looking for. "Okay, here it is." I set the book on the blanket in front of me, my eyes scanning over the page in an attempt to commit the information to memory. There were a number of incantations and their translations on the page. I chose the simplest to try first. *"Krýpse me apó tous echthroús mou."*

Nothing happened, at least nothing I could see.

"Breathe deep and center," Cambious said. "Cover your face with your hands."

I did as he suggested and tried again. This time I felt something akin to bubbles under my skin, like pouring peroxide on an open wound. Something in my face shifted, blurred even and when I lowered my hands, Cambious was smiling.

"Good."

I got up and crossed to the car to see my reflection. I was still me…sort of. My hair was lighter in color and my lips fuller, my nose longer. Anyone who knew me well would see past the disguise, but someone I'd never met wouldn't be able to pick me out of a lineup.

I crossed back to the blanket and sat again, pulling the book closer. I could feel the pull of the glamor on my energy, and instinctively murmured, "*Elefthérosi.*"

"You are getting better at this," Cambious said.

"Don't go praising me yet. That didn't do much to make me look like a man."

"It's a start. Here," he pointed to an incantation halfway down the page, "add that to the first."

I nodded and read over the words a few times before I lifted my hands up toward my face, hovering just centimeters away as I reached inside of me and murmured, "*Krýpse me apó tous echthroús mou. Anatrépste to fýlo.*"

Again, I felt my skin bubble and shift, even the bones in my face felt like they were shifting. This time when I got up to look, my face was wider, my forehead thicker and my black hair was neatly shaved on the sides of my head, the top just shy of an inch long. This was a bigger drain, and I wasn't sure I could hold it for as long as we would need. "This is work," I said as I returned to Cambious.

He nodded. "Let's tweak the look first, then we'll find you an anchor item."

My hand lifted to the place under my shirt where my mother's necklace lay warm against my skin. "I know what we can use. But how do we tweak it?"

"All you have changed is your face. You need to make the rest of you more masculine as well. Stand up and cross your arms, put your hands on your shoulders and repeat after me." I did as he said, breathing into my center as I awaited the words. "*Evreís ómous. Epípedos thórakas. Stenós gofoí.*"

As the words left my mouth, I felt the changes happening. It wasn't painful, exactly, but it wasn't very pleasant either. My shoulders seemed to shift outward and upward, my breasts reduced to what they had been before puberty and my hips pulled in, making my natural curves disappear. I was panting by the time it was done.

"Good. Very good. How does it feel?"

"Damn weird," I said. "I'm not sure I can hold it."

"You must, or we will need to start again." He stood and took a step toward me. "Take out your anchor item and hold it in your dominant hand."

I moved carefully, as if movement would destroy the illusion altogether, pulling the necklace free of my shirt. I held it in my right hand and looked for my next instruction. "Essentially what we are doing is saving this exact look into the anchor, much as you would a file on a computer," Cambious said. "Cover the pendant with your other hand. Feel its weight and shape. Ask it to keep the spell safe...in your mind, in your body. No need to speak it out loud.

"Feel the dimensions of your image, memorize how it feels, take the measure of it and when you are ready, the word is *Apothikéfsete*."

I felt silly asking an inanimate object for something, but I did it, closing my eyes and feeling like it shifted in my hand, a feeling as if it had opened to receive what I would give it. It took me a while to feel like I knew this new me well enough to commit it to the pendant, but finally, I said the word and felt a sort of pull, as if the pendant was dragging the information into itself.

"Very good. You are learning quickly," Cambious said. "You can release it now."

"*Elefthérosi.*" There was a flush of power draining from me and I swayed a little on my feet. Cambious caught my elbow to steady me.

"You should rest before we continue. I'll get our food."

I sat on the blanket, and he went back to the car, returning with the bag from the cafe. We ate in comfortable silence while I read through the rest of the page on glamors. As I finished my sandwich, I fingered the pendant. "*Anáklisi.*" The changes rippled through me. "*Elefthérosi.*" And I was back to myself again, this time without the feeling like I was going to pass out.

Here in the forest, we couldn't see the skies, but the woods around us were getting darker as night settled in. While I practiced with the glamor, Cambious cleaned up what was left of our food. I was glad our little protective dome helped to trap some of the heat from the small fire. The night was definitely colder than I was prepared for.

"You should get some sleep," Cambious said as he approached.

"What about you?" I asked, yawning as I dismissed my glamor and stretched. I suddenly realized that Cambious too had let his glamor dissipate.

"I'm fine. I need less sleep than you, remember?"

I shook my head. "Not what I meant. Do you need me to—?"

Cambious seemed to catch my meaning before I said it. "No, I am okay."

I frowned at him and stood. "Look, I know it's weird, okay? I get that. But we're going into the lion's den in a few hours, and I need you at your full capacity. What happens if your glamor slips because you're too drained to keep it? Or you don't have the strength to do whatever it is we need to do?"

"Thána, I—no, you're right. It would be a disaster."

"Assuming that it isn't already a completely bad idea," I murmured. "Here by the fire, or…"

"Well, it's been a long time since I've done it in a car," Cambious said, humor in his eyes. "I'm not sure that would work so well."

I chuckled and started to undress. "Here it is then. Just, don't let me sleep too long after. We need the dark."

CHAPTER 24
THAT WAS TOO EASY

I woke shivering a few hours later, my body pleasantly sore, the kind of sore that only comes after really vigorous sex. I was wrapped in the blanket and settled onto the passenger seat of the car. I sat up, my hand drifting to my mother's pendant as it shifted across my skin.

Cambious sat near the fire, though I couldn't make out what he was doing. I opened the car door, but as I moved my feet to get out, I found my clothes all folded neatly on the floor beneath me. I paused to pull my shirt on, shivering again as the cold cotton slid over my head. I didn't want to drop the blanket to pull my pants on but figured out quickly I didn't have a choice.

I shook my pants out before I moved enough to get them over my feet, losing the blanket almost at the same time. I stood quickly, yanking the pants up before sitting back down to get my feet off the cold ground.

"Your shoes are on the floor on the driver's side," Cambious said, standing now and starting to stamp out the fire.

I nodded, though I knew he couldn't see me, and reached around the steering wheel for my shoes, with my socks tucked inside. I got them on and stood, glancing around me. "We ready?" I asked as the domed space got even darker without the fire.

"As much as we can be," Cambious responded with less enthusiasm than I'd wanted to hear.

"Okay, then I guess we go."

I dismissed the wards and collected the stones and we both got into the car without speaking. We drove in silence to the spot I'd found the day before, slowing and pulling off the road. "This is a bad idea," I murmured as the car stopped.

"We don't have to go in."

I looked at Cambious, once again safely behind his glamor and I reached for my anchor, activating my own. "No, we do. I just haven't figured out how we…get back out again."

Cambious patted my knee. "If we can get in, we can get out again."

"I hope so."

I opened my door and got out, rubbing my hands over my arms to warm them. The night was clear, the heavens above us dotted with unfamiliar stars, not that I'd ever paid too much attention to the stars at home to know the difference. Off over the dark hulk of the Kourt, there was a silver sliver of a moon, and I realized with a start that there was more than one. I shook off my surprise and tried to focus my energy on the task at hand. Or at least the first one, get over the wall.

"What about the car?" I asked.

"Wait here, I'll ditch it somewhere, just don't be seen."

I crossed the road and made my way back to the grave I'd found before. Its pull wasn't as strong now that I'd gotten its message, but I found it easily enough, kneeling beside the stone and laying my hand on it again. My mind filled with the location of the entrance, the hidden climb up to it, then the cautions and warnings about the men who had taken the Kourt. Whoever had buried this message had done so after the Kourt's fall to the Brotherhood, but before the wall had been built. I'd been hoping for more though, like maybe a map of where this hidden entrance would take us, and where to go from there, or maybe an idea of the spells and wards the Brotherhood may have placed on the grounds. On those counts, however, the stone was silent.

Instead, I tried to use my time waiting for Cambious to try to determine what awaited us beyond the wall. I moved closer, and stilled, listening for any sounds that might give away the monsters that wandered the graveyard, or the humans who kept them there. I set my hand to the wall, hoping for another message, but the wall had been built by the Brotherhood and it only whispered of violence and death. The night was quiet, no sounds of footsteps or heavy breathing or flapping wings, at least not until Cambious reappeared.

He nodded and offered his hands to boost me up. I scanned the area as I moved, checking for any sign of the beast I'd glimpsed the day before. Nothing moved beyond the wall as I straddled it and reached down to offer Cambious a hand he didn't need. He merely put both hands on the top of the wall and pushed himself up and over before he helped me down.

First hurdle jumped. We squatted in the shadow of the wall, listening, and watching. My heart was slamming so hard against my ribs I was sure they could hear it all the way back in Thelos. "There," Cambious whispered after a long time, pointing off to our left.

I could just make out the sense of movement in the distance but couldn't see the beast. "We need to get to that rock," I whispered, my voice barely audible as my breath plumed the air. I pointed to the right.

"Okay, stay low and follow me." Cambious moved cautiously, keeping gravestones between us and the place we thought the manticore was. We stopped often, kneeling beside some monument or bush. We both knew that if we were even seen the whole thing would be over. Once the alarm was raised, we didn't stand a chance of infiltrating the Kourt and getting out alive.

Not that I liked our chances to begin with. It was highly likely this whole thing ended in death. *"Look to the gods, look to the sky, her blood will spill while death is nigh."* The words echoed through my head, and I had to shove them aside before the icy fear filled me and froze me in place.

Cambious moved again, taking us slowly closer to our target. I caught the movement to my right before my brain registered it, grabbing Cambious by the arm. I could smell it, the manticore, like an animal's cage at the zoo mixed with stale blood and vomit. It was moving closer, each step bringing it within reach of finding us.

We moved as slowly as we could, soft steps so that we made no sound, putting a tall stone monument between us and the beast. A memory hit me, and I lifted my hands to cover my face and murmured, *"Krýveo."* It was one of the earliest spells my mother had taught me, along with *prostatévo* and *ánoixe.* Cambious and I held our breath as the manticore passed. It stood nearly as tall as Cambious in his true form, its wings folded along its flanks. His head was crowned with a mane worthy of the king of beasts, but his face…his face was nearly human, but not quite. I shivered, though this time it had nothing to do with the cold.

After a small eternity, Cambious pointed and got us moving again. I was suddenly reminded of the time I had snuck into the campus of an all-boys school with Sandra Teller when I was a senior in high school, only this time the stakes were a whole lot higher.

We reached the last bit of cover we would have and stopped. I didn't know how long the spell would hide us, and there were maybe ten feet of open ground between us and the rock face. In the dark, I couldn't make out the path up that I knew was there, but I could sense something else. It had the feel of static electricity against my skin. Beside me, Cambious nodded. He felt it too. Wards. "Now what?" I asked as softly as I could.

Cambious seemed to weigh the question, lifting up to get a better look around us. "Where?" Cambious mouthed back to me.

I shook my head and moved a few steps to my right. I could just make out a ledge about six feet up. I pointed. I knew from the images I'd gotten from the stone that at one time there had been an easier way to get there, but it looked as though it was long gone. Our only choice would be for Cambious to boost me up, and then hope I had the strength to pull him up behind me.

"When I tell you, move quickly. I won't be able to hold the wards open for long without setting off alarms." Cautiously, he stood, his hands moving as he whispered the incantation *"Ftiáxe mia porta."* His glamor shimmered but held and I felt the hole he made in the wards. "Now."

I nodded and moved to the wall, keeping to a crouch until Cambious had joined me. We were horribly exposed as I put my foot to his hand, and he shoved me upward. I scrambled onto the ledge and lay flat as he scurried back to cover. I lay there panting, my eyes scanning the graveyard, clocking two, no, three of the death monsters patrolling. I held up a hand to let Cambious know to wait, then rolled onto my stomach, and held my hand down for him when the coast was as clear as it was likely to get.

Cambious repeated his incantation, then sprinted, his hand grabbing mine, and he jumped while I pulled, rolling away from the ledge as he pulled himself onto it. The ledge was barely wide enough for the two of us to lay side by side, but neither of us moved as we fought to catch our breath. I was the first one to recover, kneeling up to find our next step.

Cleverly concealed behind a wall of stone that blended in with its surroundings, I could just make out a trail of sorts, what had once been steps but was now just a steep trail that looked a bit treacherous. I moved for it, keeping low even after I was safely behind the wall of rock. It wasn't so tall that it would hide me from view completely. I didn't look to see if Cambious was behind me, just trusted that he would be.

I ended up staying on my hands and feet, crab crawling up a path strewn with smaller rocks and pebbles. I was sure the cacophony made by the stones as I sent them hurtling downward would rouse the guards, but there was no sound of alarm.

My calves were making me aware that they were not fans of this, and so was my lower back. I told them to suck it up, knowing I'd pay for it later...provided we survived. The trail leveled out a bit after around twenty feet, then curved in toward the hill, entering a cave that clearly wasn't a fully natural feature of the rock. I paused just inside the deeper dark for my eyes to adjust.

Cambious joined me, his sharper eyes scanning around us.

"That was too easy," I said barely aloud. "What next?"

He gestured deeper into the cave, and we moved slowly. I kept one hand on the wall as we moved, all but holding my breath and expecting something to jump out of the dark at us. Eventually, we found the tunnel blocked by a metal barrier of some kind. I felt my way around it until I found a lock. "Here," I whispered, putting my hand flat against it, and taking a deep breath to center myself and feel inside the lock. I still had no idea if I could make this work, but I turned to Cambious. "I need a knife or something to prick my finger."

He took something from a pocket, and I heard a folding knife snick open before he put the handle into my hand. I pricked the middle finger of my left hand with the tip of the knife, then handed it back before I pushed along the line of the finger, encouraging blood to flow. When I had a small bead of blood, I put the finger to the lock, spilling the blood inside. "*Ánoixe kleídoma aímatos.*" It was a simple enough incantation, and I could only hope I had remembered it correctly as I **pushed** the lock with my thoughts, with my will for it to open.

It seemed to take forever, and I was beginning to think I had been wrong when I could hear the faint metal-on-metal sound of the tumblers moving. The gate moved under my hand and just like that, we were in. I stepped through the gate, feeling my steps without light and with no idea what to expect.

Cambious was close behind me. I was wishing we'd thought to bring a flashlight or something when I noticed that the dark ahead was not as black as the dark behind us. It wasn't light but seemed to be drawing us toward something. My hand touched a surface that I expected to be stone but felt more like wood. I pressed a hand against it, hoping I could feel my way through it. As I did, I felt a rush of something race up my arm and a word filled my head, "*Diávasi.*"

I straightened up, pushing my hand against the wood, and spoke, "*Diávasi.*" The wall moved, swinging silently open and dropping us into a dark hallway where the floors were the same stone as the tunnel, but the walls were clearly man-made.

We were, thankfully, alone in the hall. When we had stepped through, the door closed just as silently, and when flush with the wall, it seemed to disappear. I felt along the wall but couldn't find the seams. "Okay, we're in," I whispered. "Remind me, what comes next?"

Cambious started down the hall and I followed. We moved slowly and tried to minimize the sound our feet made, easing up to a corner where faint light pooled. Cambious peeked around the corner. "I don't see anyone."

I moved around him and into the next corridor. Dingy yellow light dotted the length of the corridor, from ancient-looking light fixtures every ten feet or so. The walls reminded me of some medieval castle in some movie, all dark grey rocks of varying sizes. I half expected to find we were in a dungeon or something, but the irregular doors were wood, and there didn't seem to be anyone being tortured or imprisoned.

We came to another corner, where our corridor crossed with another. To our right, there was a flight of stairs. To our left, the corridor moved away into utter darkness. "Well, we have to go up eventually," I murmured, taking the lead.

The stairs ended with a doorway. I stood and listened, hoping it wouldn't open onto a room full of armed men or something. Cambious put a warm hand on my back, I suppose for reassurance, and I turned the nob, pushing the door open.

We both waited breathlessly, anticipating capture.

CHAPTER 25
PETER

When an ambush didn't happen, I took the last step into the room. Shelves lined the walls, and boxes and crates were stacked haphazardly, leaving little aisles between them.

"Storeroom?" I asked, turning to look around us.

"Looks like," Cambious agreed, moving toward a nearby shelf full of books. "Some of these are ancient." He turned toward me, then froze, his eyes on a dark corner. He pulled me closer. "There is someone here," Cambious whispered, his lips brushing my ear so he could keep his voice almost soundless.

I could hear something, frightened breathing, and the near-silent shuffle of skin against stone.

Cambious gestured for me to go left around the stack of boxes between us and the corner, as he moved to the right. It didn't make sense…this was no guard hiding in the shadows. I had a feeling I couldn't place.

"*Ko je tamo?*" a tremulous voice asked, and a sudden light flared ahead of us. I got the brief impression of a slight figure before the light blinded me. Cambious moved swiftly and the light fell, rattling against the rock as that tender voice yelled out.

I scrambled for the dropped light and Cambious shoved the small figure against the wall I could now see. "Cambious, stop," I said, moving closer with the light.

We could see now that the figure was just a boy, barely eleven or twelve, judging by his size. He wore little more than rags, his feet bare and covered with sores. "He's just a boy."

Dark eyes met mine, the pupils contracting in the bright beam of the flashlight. "You…you're *Thanátou*."

"I'm not here to hurt you," I said softly. Kids were not my forte, ask any one of my friends who had them, but I could see the terror in his eyes. "How do you know—" Oh, right. I slowly made the connection between his ragged clothing and my feeling. You can tell what I am?" He nodded. "Cambious, put him down."

"He can raise the alarm." Cambious cautioned, even as he set the boy on his feet.

"He can, but he won't. He knows what I am because he is a blood witch, like me," I said, smiling at the boy. "What's your name?"

"Peter." His voice shook, his eyes darting between me and Cambious.

"Peter what?"

He licked chapped lips and swallowed. "Peter Suelo."

"What are you doing hiding down here in the dark, Peter?" I asked.

"N-nothing. Why are you here?"

I glanced at Cambious, but his face was unreadable. I weighed my options. This might well be the person we were supposed to find, according to the madwoman. "Well, Peter, we're looking for someone."

Cambious grabbed my arm, but I shook my head. "I'm Thána. This is my friend Cam." I realized after I said it that I still looked like a man, but figured the kid already had me pegged as a blood witch, so it wouldn't matter. "Did the Brotherhood take you away from your family?"

He nodded, wiping his nose on his shirt sleeve. "Two men came when I was on my way home from school."

"Suelo isn't a local name," Cambious said. "Where are you from?"

"Juavez."

"That's three thousand miles from here," Cambious said aside to me. "How long have you been here?"

The kid shook his head. "I don't know. A while, maybe a year?"

His last name rattled around in my head until I remembered where I knew it from. "Suelo is Spanish for ground and Peter means rock. Rocky ground," I said softly to Cambious. "Are you trying to escape, Peter?"

His eyes dropped to my feet, but he nodded. "I want to go home. These men hurt me. They said they'd kill me."

"Not if we kill them first." Cambious's voice was darker than I could remember hearing it and here in the dark, it was kind of terrifying.

"We can help you, but first we have to find someone," I said softly. "A prisoner. She's in a tower cell."

Peter nodded. "They took us up there when they brought us here."

"Us?" Cambious asked.

Peter looked up at him, his eyes wide and filled with fear. "Me and Ashkān, and some bird-lady."

"Thána, we need to talk." Cambious drew me away from Peter. "We can't trust him."

"Do we have a choice?" I asked, glancing back. I could barely make out Peter's shape in the darkness. "The old lady said we to find rocky ground and that he would be able to smell my blood. He's a blood witch whose name means rocky ground. It doesn't get much more on the nose than this."

"That is what I'm afraid of. He could be a plant," Cambious said, his voice low and dark. "They know we're coming."

"Maybe," I conceded. "But he's had a lot of time while you and I are over here whispering about him to call for help. Besides, can't you see how scared he is?"

"If we take him with us into the Kourt, he may betray us as soon as we are inside and cut off from escape."

"I agree, but he knows where she is." I shook my head. "You heard what the old lady said, Cambious. You're the one who told me she's always right."

There was a low rumbling growl that took me a minute to identify as coming from Cambious. "We are going to regret this."

We went back to where Peter stood, shivering in the cold night air. "If we promise to help get you home, can you help us find the tower cells?" I asked softly. Peter inched back into the shadows.

"I know where they are," he answered tentatively. "But I don't want to go back up there. They're looking for me."

I nodded slowly. "Can you give us directions?"

He squirmed uncomfortably, his eyes darting from me to Cambious and back. "What if they find me?"

"Hide better," Cambious said, his hand drawing me away. "We're wasting time, Thána."

"Hold on, just give me a second." I squatted to put myself at Peter's height. "If you come with us, we can keep you safe."

"Promise?"

I nodded. "I promise."

He launched himself at me, wrapping his arms around my body and burying his face in my shirt. I let him cling for a moment, then gently loosened his grip. "Just stay close."

Cambious took the light and shined it around us, but it didn't penetrate the darkness for more than a few feet. I took a deep breath and held it, imagining all of the things that could go wrong. "This is insane," I muttered.

"How do you want to do this?" Cambious asked. Peter moved so that he was touching me, not quite clinging, but clearly wanting to stay away from Cambious.

I was not usually a person who did things without a plan, but I was so far out of my depth that I was pretty much making it all up as we went. I had a vague idea of the order of things that I'd like to see happen: uniforms or other clothing that would let us pass, find my mother, free her, and then get us all out without any of us dying. I didn't think about the whole notion of killing the head honcho. I still wasn't sure I had it in me to kill again.

My memories of that first kill were like most memories of a five-year-old, fuzzy in places and uncertain in others. I took his pain inside me though, I sucked it up, and with it, his life. I did it instinctively, and with a heavy dose of fear and rage. I wasn't sure I could do it a second time.

"Thána?"

I glanced up, realizing that I'd been off inside my head while they waited. "Right, let's go." I set out with a false bravado, hoping that doing would make it so, as one of my foster fathers used to say. "I guess first thing is to figure out where we are in relation to that tower? Any idea, Peter?"

Peter pointed one trembling hand in the direction opposite where we had come in. We picked our way through the maze of accumulated junk until we came to a large wooden door.

"We have to go through there, and then up to the main floor."

I nodded to Cambious, who opened the door. Peter's hand clutched my shirt, and I reached a hand down to try to comfort him, resting it on his back, just between his shoulder blades. He shuddered. Under my hand, I could feel his skin raised and welted. I glanced at Cambious and inclined my head toward Peter's back. Cambious lowered the light and flashed it at the torn blue of Peter's shirt, I could just make out what looked like scars from a whip of some kind, maybe a belt. I lifted my hand, and it came away bloody.

What kind of person tortured a child?

I didn't vocalize my question, but I know Cambious heard it anyway.

Maybe Cambious was right in that they knew we were coming, and they wanted to draw us in. Maybe this was how they captured me so that they could bleed me dry. The images of ancestors hung upside down while men in black cut into arteries filled my head and I shook it to clear it. Getting hung up on that would probably get me killed. We needed to be smarter than them. We needed to act in a way that they weren't prepared for.

There was no more light in the next room than there had been in the first and it seemed to go on forever, though it probably felt longer than it was due to the darkness and our own fear. And make no mistake, I was afraid. I was hoping it didn't show, that Peter couldn't feel it the same way I felt his, but my heart was pounding a rapid staccato against my ribs as we found a door. There was no telltale light seeping under or around it, so either it was also dark on the other side, or it was better sealed than most doors.

The hallway beyond was not quite as dark, a distant light coming from further down the hall. The walls were the same grey stone as the others we'd seen, but the floor had been covered with what looked like wood.

I stepped out, reaching back to draw Peter to me. He was trembling in fear, but he came easily enough. He pointed with one shaking hand toward the light. Cambious came behind us as we tried to walk as quietly as possible toward the light, which turned out to be just beyond a turn in the corridor. It was a vaguely yellow light shining out of a discolored sconce on the wall. In my mind's eye, I could imagine it had once held a torch…or maybe Hollywood had influenced my imagination too much.

Still, I cautiously turned the corner, glancing in both directions as the hallway formed an L shape. To my left, the hallway was dotted with heavy doors the same color as the stone walls. I couldn't see an end in that direction with the minimal light. Straight ahead was a shorter corridor, with a light at the end, illuminating the only door that way.

I turned left, easing down the hallway. The doors here were metal, with no indication of what might be behind them. Peter tugged on my shirt as we reached the fourth one, pointing to where the next light was. "Stairs."

I didn't respond, just started walking that way. We passed another four or five doors, more or less evenly spaced, all on the left side of the hall. At the light, we came to a crossroads of sorts. A corridor crossed the one we were in. Peeking around the corner, I spotted the stairs to the right. It was eerily quiet, particularly knowing that this fortress could easily hold a thousand people or more. I didn't want to jinx our luck by vocalizing my observation. "What's at the top of the stairs, Peter?" I asked in a whisper.

He shrugged a little. "Storerooms and stuff, I think."

"We're going to need to find clothing fast," Cambious observed. "I don't know what to do about the boy."

"Robes and stuff are easy enough," Peter offered. "If we go to the laundry. I worked there for a while when they first brought me here."

"Of course, you did." Cambious looked at me, his eyes betraying his doubt. "And I suppose you know how to get us there?"

Peter nodded. "Up three floors to the south hallway, it isn't far."

I let Peter take my hand and lead us up the stairs, turning us to the right. There were more stairs then, but Peter pulled us back and after a moment, I heard why. The sound of feet on stone, soft leather slapping the floor as two Brothers passed the top of the stairs. We waited a few more heartbeats after the sound of their feet passed before we headed up the steps. Peter stopped to poke his head out at the first landing before tugging on my hand and starting up the next flight.

When we had reached the top of the third flight, Peter pointed around the corner. I noticed his hand wasn't shaking nearly as much as earlier, but I had no way of knowing if it was because he had a role in our clandestine invasion or because he was closer to giving us away.

"You should let me go in. Just in case someone's there. Give me a few minutes." He darted away before I could stop him.

"I don't like this," Cambious said, leaning forward to watch Peter dash into a doorway. "We're exposed here."

"I know." I was itchy with nerves and sure we were about to be betrayed, especially the longer it took for Peter to return.

He did return though, in a brown jacket over a white shirt and dark pants, his arms filled with a bundle of black fabric. He grinned as he passed the bundle to Cambious. He adjusted the jacket. "The boys who serve upstairs dress like this."

Cambious took us down to a turn in the staircase where we had a line of sight in both directions and deposited the clothing on the floor, opening the bundle and sorting through it, tossing pieces to me before he stood and started to strip down. "Keep watch, boy."

"His name is Peter," I hissed at Cambious as I too started to strip so I could pull on the black pants and a navy-blue shirt. Peter had done pretty well at guessing our sizes, though the pants Cambious was now wearing were a little short and the suit jacket I pulled on was a little long in the sleeves. There were two deep crimson robes as well.

"Robes can get you past a lot of guards," Peter offered. "You should call me *slúga*. It's what they call the servant boys."

Cambious balled up the clothing we had come in, tucking it under his arm and hiding it with his robe. "Okay, now what?"

"Now we find our way to the holding cells," I said, looking to Peter.

The boy paled considerably. "I don't like it there."

I squatted to put myself closer to eye level with him. "I know you don't, but someone important to me is being held here, and we need to get her out. Can you help us do that?"

CHAPTER 26
STEP ONE, GET INSIDE

It took Peter a minute, and I could see him marshaling his fear before he nodded. "It won't be easy, but I'll try."

I smiled tightly. "Fast is good but unseen is better, you understand?"

He nodded again, glancing both ways down the hallway. "This way, we have a few hours before morning work begins, we can get through the kitchen to the back stairs." He set out and Cambious and I fell into step behind him, hoping we looked like we belonged there. I was starting to feel the strain of maintaining the glamor, but I pushed my fatigue away. There would be time enough to rest when we were safe.

The long hallway led us to another long hallway, then into a large room filled with tables. I could almost see them filled with witches of all ages, stacks of books punctuated with plates of half-eaten food from a time when it had served as both dining hall and study. Peter led us down one long side of the room, the wall lined with tapestries that depicted gruesome scenes of death and dying and war. A large archway waited ahead of us, with only the low flicker of a banked fire to see by.

The arch gave way to a neat and orderly kitchen, where a fire burned down to coals cast everything in a ruddy glow that was more color than light. A sturdy wooden table, looking as if it were old enough to have been built long before the Brotherhood, occupied the largest space, its surface worn smooth over years of food prep, its edges marked by knives and vague dark stains of heat. At one end of the table was a basket of not-quite-apples and another round fruit I couldn't quite make out in the dim light. Peter drew us past the table, one finger to his lips as he pointed to a door with his other hand. "The two cooks sleep in there," Peter explained in a whisper. "Very loyal."

Cambious grabbed fruit from the bowl, tucking it into the inside pocket of his robe, and I followed his lead. We would eventually need to eat.

We moved lightly, eyes stealing to that door over and over as we moved to a large pantry stocked with enough food to feed a small nation. There, Cambious grabbed what looked like sausages, strung along the front of shelves, and a box of something that I didn't see. The pantry led us out into a hallway that looked much the same as all of the other hallways we'd walked down, only somewhat better lit.

Peter led us off to the left, moving down the hall as if he were on a mission. We found the stairs he had promised and started up them. One floor up, he gestured at the hallway. "Armory is down there, and the library over there. On the opposite side of the floor is the door out to the parade grounds. That's where the road goes out and down the mountain and where they punish prisoners." He shuddered and shook his head.

"Where to next, Peter?" I prodded gently.

He looked up at me with wide brown eyes and swallowed hard. "We need to get past the guards on the stairs up to the tower." He pointed in the direction he'd said held the library, but Cambious put a hand on my arm before I could move in that direction.

"Maybe we should go by the armory first?" Cambious said softly. "The only weapon we have on hand is my knife."

"What kind of weapon are you thinking we need?" I asked, though I nodded to Peter to lead the way.

"Anything is better than nothing," Cambious replied. "I've used guns before, though it's been a while."

"Okay." I had never used a gun. I couldn't remember ever seeing a gun in person, other than the handful of times I'd dealt with the police. I'd always equated guns with bad guys, and it had never occurred to me that I might one day need to use one.

As we approached the door that Peter indicated was our destination, two Brothers were approaching from the opposite direction, deep in conversation. I froze, pulling Peter closer, but the men just nodded at us and kept walking.

"I can't go in," Peter said once they were gone. "I'll wait here."

Cambious and I exchanged a look filled with trepidation, but we had already gotten this far, and if Peter was going to betray us, there wasn't much we could do. Cambious handed him the bundle of our clothes, then opened the door, and strode in as if he had every right to be there. I followed a step behind. Inside was a spacious room lined with locked cages that held every type of weapon imaginable. There was a counter and a weary-looking Brother in rumpled clothing. He straightened up when he heard us come in. "Good morning, Brothers. What can I do for you?"

"I will tell you, Brother," Cambious said with a rather convincing smile. "This young Brother requires some work with his pistol before we are sent out in the field. I was hoping to get in some target practice before breakfast."

The man behind the counter smiled and nodded. "Very good. Do have a specific weapon in mind?"

Cambious leaned casually against the counter, and I got the impression he did *something* that made the brother go a little moon-eyed. "Why don't you surprise me."

The man blushed and turned away, disappearing into the rows of lockers behind him. I slapped Cambious on the shoulder. "What are you doing?" I hissed at him.

He glanced after the man, then back at me. "Hopefully confounding him enough to get what we need without too much trouble."

The Brother was back then, two guns and a box of ammo in his hand. He put them on the counter, then turned to his computer, punching in some information, then scanning the guns and ammo before looking up. "If you would just put your hand on the scanner..."

I was shaking, sure this was the end of our little rescue operation, but Cambious just leaned in closer, his hand skimming across the other man's arm and down to his hand, caressing it lightly as he clearly exuded pheromones directly at him. I watched in disbelief as Cambious got their hand positions reversed and the scanner beeped in recognition.

Cambious pulled back with a smile and grabbed both guns and ammo. "Thank you, Brother."

We turned for the door and Cambious handed me one of the guns and the box of ammo, which I promptly hid beneath my robe as he tucked his gun into a pocket. "We need to find a place to drop our clothes," Cambious breathed as we exited back to the hallway. Peter was leaning against the opposite wall but stood up quickly as we appeared.

I set off down the hall back toward where Peter said the library was. "We don't need anyone finding them."

"Yes, but I need my hands free," Cambious argued, taking the bundle back from Peter

"There is a closet near the tower stairs," Peter offered. "I hid in there the first night I ran."

"What kind of closet?" Cambious asked.

Peter shrugged. "It had cleaning supplies and stuff. Mostly used by the servants at night."

"We'll have to come back down from the tower," I offered.

Cambious nodded. The corridor widened slightly and there were several doors spaced about fifteen feet apart. "Library," Peter said.

Idly, I wondered how much time had passed since we'd found our way inside, how close we were to being surrounded by the waking life of the Kourt. Even if Peter didn't give us away, we could be discovered at any moment.

As if my thought had brought them to us, a group of Brothers in their black pants and light blue shirts rounded a corner and headed toward us. There were five of them, younger than I, possibly in their twenties, though the tallest one had a face covered in acne, so possibly younger.

They all snapped to attention at the sight of us, stopping and stepping back against the wall. "Good morning, Brothers." They said it in unison, their eyes skipping over us, then snapping to the floor in submission.

We acknowledged them with slight nods but continued moving. I could hear them murmuring behind us about Cambious's stature and I turned, my eyes sweeping over them. They blushed and hurried away.

"We're running out of time," I said to Cambious. "The whole place will be awake, and we'll have no way out."

"What do you suggest we do?"

I shook my head. "First we have to make sure she's there. Then we can figure out..." I shook my head. I had no plan for what came next, but I knew that the more of the Brotherhood we ran into, the less hope we had for actually escaping, especially once we were carrying my mother. "Peter, where do we go?"

He pointed further down the hallway where I could see a wooden door beside the first steps of a staircase. We hurried to the closet, where Cambious secreted our bundle of clothes and the food he had pilfered from the pantry, and we paused to load our guns. Then, we straightened ourselves up, adopted our best serious faces, and we strode to the staircase.

We did our best to look like we belonged, like it was normal for us to be climbing a staircase toward cells that held the prisoners of the Brotherhood. The staircase curved and climbed, taking us closer to our destination. We were stopped by two Brothers in military uniform who snapped to attention as we approached their desk on a wide landing. Behind them, bars blocked the way up the steps. Obviously, we needed to talk our way past them.

"We are here to question the mother of the blood witch," Cambious said, his voice deep and resonating.

"Yes, Brother." The man on the right turned to a board with pegs that held keys. "Here you are, third floor, last cell on the left." He handed

Cambious the key and his companion moved to open the gate in the bars to allow us to pass. "Are you taking the *slúga* with you?"

I looked the man in the eye. "He needs to learn a lesson about obedience. Perhaps you also need a lesson?"

He paled visibly and shook his head. "No, brother, I am sorry."

I pulled Peter to me and pushed him ahead of us so that he was the first up the stairs, with Cambious and I right behind him. As we neared the first floor of cells, the smell of caged animals filled the air, and I wrinkled my nose in an effort not to sneeze.

The stairs opened to a large room segregated into cages filled with…I wasn't fully sure what they all were. I could see a manticore, but he looked to be no older than Peter, if manticores aged the same way people did. His wings drooped downward, and his face was dirty, his eyes dull as they watched us. Further down was a man-sized bird of some kind, with bright orange and red feathers, but the face similar to a woman's, her nose and mouth extended in a sort of beak that went from the orange of her skin to dark black, as if it had been burned. She reminded me of Toman, the bartender.

"Phoenix," Cambious said aside to me. Past her was a lizard-like thing, as big as Peter, slender, but long with a tail adorned with a dangerous-looking club-like end.

"Is that what I think it is?" I asked as Cambious pulled me toward the next set of stairs.

"If you think that it's a dragon, yes. Juvenile. Haven't seen one outside of the mountains in Ver Char in a lifetime. Come on."

My disillusionment with my magic kingdom lifted a little. Maybe it wasn't filled with fairies and castles, and came with malls and credit cards, but at least it had magical creatures. I glanced back and the dragon was now a child of maybe ten, his skin tinged blue along his hairline, his tail wrapped around his legs.

"Do all dragons do that?" I asked, a hand on Cambious's arm to slow him. He turned to look and smiled.

"Of course."

I started to return to climbing the stairs but noticed that Peter was no longer in front of us. He was at one of the cages, speaking in an approximation of Spanish to the manticore inside. I went to get him, my eyes carefully on the creature in the cage as it came to the bars. His eyes widened as I approached, but Peter stuck a hand through the bars and slid his fingers into the barely-there mane, scrubbing against the manticore in what I took to be a soothing gesture. "*Estan conmiago.*"

"Peter, come." I touched his shoulder gently, my eyes on the young manticore.

"*Volveramos por ti.*" Peter smiled and pulled his hand back.

"Peter, be careful." The manticore's voice was pitched higher than I'd expected, and he shuffled closer to the bars.

"I'll take care of him," I responded, pulling Peter along to the stairs. "Who is that?" I asked when we were far enough away.

"My friend, Ashkān. We were brought here together. They're training him to work in the *Zidna*, the graveyard guards. They've been having trouble with the older manticores." Peter took my hand. "We can take him with us too, can't we?"

Because we'd be so much less conspicuous carrying my mother with a manticore in our company. I sighed and squeezed his hand. "We'll do our best."

CHAPTER 27
MOM

My mind was still on the manticore and the idea that Peter had made friends with the thing as we climbed to the second prison level. The smell was not as bad here, more the dank kind of smell of caged human bodies. It was dimly lit, but I could make out lumps of human shape in each of the cages.

I couldn't make out much more and Cambious kept us moving up the stairs to the third and final level. My breath caught in my throat from far more than the climb as we reached the top, and my heart began to thump loud enough for the others to hear. My mouth was dry as Cambious handed me the key. The cages here were empty, and the air was filled with expectation as I took each torturous step down the row of them, until at last, I could see her, much as she had looked in my vision.

Her long hair was streaked with gray, dirty and matted like it hadn't seen a brush in months or longer. Her skin was drab and gray, her dress a dirty white that was ripped and torn in multiple places. As she lifted her head, I could see the tracks tears had made in the dirt on her face, the dark circles that smudged her eyes so that they appeared sunken.

"Wasting your time," she said in a voice that trembled, though I couldn't tell whether it was in fear or anticipation or sheer exhaustion.

I fit the key into the lock and turned it, opening the door, then just standing there for a long time looking at her, trying to find the beautiful woman I remembered from my childhood. "M-om?" I asked, blinking unbidden tears.

She squinted at me and for a moment I had forgotten the glamor that hid me from prying eyes. I glanced back at Cambious to be sure we were alone, then touched the pendant, letting the glamor fade. I crossed to her and knelt beside her as she started to come up from her slouch.

"You shouldn't be here, Thána," she said, even as she pulled me into an embrace. "They will kill you."

I shook my head. "I couldn't just leave you here."

This close to her, I could smell something off about her, some disease… an infection. I could taste it on her skin as I kissed her cheeks. "We needed to make sure, but we can't leave just yet. It's too close to morning. But maybe I can…" I moved to place my mouth over hers, but her hand on my chest pushed me back.

"You mustn't. Their trackers will be able to find you, glamor or no if you start bleeding."

I nodded tightly, brushing away the tears I couldn't hold back. "No, you're right. Of course, you're right." I kissed her cheeks again. "We should go before we get caught, but we'll be back tonight, I promise."

She caught my hand as I started to stand, pressing her lips to my palm the way she had when I was small. I swallowed hard and turned to go before I could change my mind and try to force our way out.

I activated the glamor as I exited the cell, locking it behind me, but the tears were still falling when I rejoined Cambious and Peter. "How is she?" Cambious asked.

I shrugged. "Sick, starving, afraid. I told her we would come back tonight. We should find ourselves a place to hide, rest."

"The closet?" Cambious started us down the stairs, so he didn't see me shaking my head.

"Too close, don't you think?" I asked. "Won't they suspect I've come for my mother?"

"They're looking for me," Peter offered. "I could let them chase me."

"No, I don't think we're that desperate yet." We were approaching the guard station, so our conversation ended while I handed back the key.

"That was quick," one of the men commented.

"She requires more time to consider her fate," I replied. "We will return."

"His Excellency is returning from his latest mission to the capital today. Perhaps he will have better luck."

I struggled to keep my face neutral as I nodded. "Perhaps he will." I strode down the stairs quickly but stuttered back a bit when faced with a group of young men in their late teens moving swiftly through the corridor at the bottom. Cambious set a hand on my back to keep me from falling backward and turned us in the opposite direction.

We kept moving until we were back to the closet, stepping inside to catch our breath. Once we were a little more together and had collected our things, we stepped back out into the hall. We started walking swiftly out of the area, and I let the others take the lead until I had lost track of where we were in comparison to the tower, or anything else for that matter. "Peter, where are we?"

He shrugged. "I don't know. I've never been here before."

"Great." I looked up and down the hall, counting doors. "It looks like maybe a residential area. Dorms, maybe?"

"Well, all these men have to sleep somewhere."

I nodded and moved to one of the doors. I knocked lightly, then tried the knob. It turned easily and I opened the door just enough to peek inside. Two sets of bunk beds lined the room, with a wardrobe between them. Uniforms like the Brotherhood military wore hung on the end of one of the bunk beds. "Dorms. This one is clearly occupied, though no one is home."

"Probably at breakfast," Peter suggested.

"Try the rest," I said, moving to the next door.

"What are we looking for?" Cambious asked as he mirrored my movements on the opposite side of the hall.

"One that's empty," I responded. We made our way down the hall to the opposite end, but all of the rooms showed signs of having residents. "So much for that idea."

There was a window at the end of the hallway, showing that the sun was well on its way to risen. Below us, there was a small courtyard lined with trees that had lost most of their leaves. I could see the walls of the Kourt on either side, and I thought that it put us in the northwest corner of the fortress, at the L-junction that divided the original Kourt building, where we were, from the newer construction that was added when it became a school. If the information in my book was to be believed, we would find classrooms and more sleeping quarters there.

I knew we did not want to be anywhere near the classrooms come time for classes to begin, but perhaps we might find an empty room among the sleeping quarters. As we came to a junction in the corridors, I felt the same odd pull I had when I'd found the tombstone outside the wall. "This way."

I let it guide me, hoping it was a long-lost ancestor or other blood witch and not some Brotherhood trick. We turned right, then left until we found ourselves in front of a door. "Here." I whispered the word, feeling almost as if the place was sanctified or something. The knob turned easily under my hand, and I peered carefully into the room before I slipped inside.

At one time it had been a beautiful room, judging by what was left behind. The stone walls had been paneled with light-colored wood, and the floor bore the remnants of a thick carpet, though the color was lost to time and the low level of light. There were two beds with nothing left on them but old moldy mattresses and a vanity with an ornate mirror.

"We should be safe here," I said, though I couldn't say how I knew that to be true. "Peter, close the door."

Once the door was closed, Cambious and I both released our glamors and I sagged in relief. Peter started at the sight of Cambious in his natural state, his eyes wide, but to his credit, he didn't run or try to hide. Without a word, Cambious dropped his bundle of our clothing and the food on one of the beds, moving with me then to the vanity so we could push it to block the doorway. Peter scrambled out of the way, ending up in the far corner, under a tightly shuttered window.

"Why is this room left empty like this?" Cambious asked.

"They think it to be haunted," a soft, female voice said, making us jump.

Peter was pale and shaking as we turned to find a young woman or her ghost at least. Her skin was darker than mine, her black hair braided tightly along her scalp and left to cascade in tiny braids over her shoulders. She wore fitted pants, what looked to me like the pants you would wear horseback riding, with boots that came to her knees and over that a tunic with elaborate beading along the hem and cuffs.

She smiled broadly. "They are not wrong. I died here, in this room." Her hands spread out to the sides. "Ironically, it was not those bastards who did it. I died of a cancer no one could cure."

"I've never seen a spirit so…fully in this world," Cambious said.

"And I don't often show myself to…those of your kind." She made a face and looked at me. "What brings you to this awful place, Sister?"

I licked dry lips and tried to make words leave my mouth, but I was still processing the idea that I was talking to a ghost. "My mother," I finally managed to say. "She's a prisoner in the tower."

"They will kill you if they find you."

I nodded in agreement. "I know. But we've come this far."

"I have done what I can to help hide you, but aside from that, there is little I can do to aid your quest. You should rest while you can." She turned then to Peter, who looked frantically to me for help as her hand lifted to cup his cheek. "Brother of my line, you do us honor in your duty to our sister. Serve her well, and you will see your home again."

She offered one last smile, then vanished.

I fell back against the vanity and closed my eyes. I had to say the whole magic kingdom thing was beginning to live up to the stories in books, what with dragons and ghosts now.

"What…what did she mean?" Peter asked into the silence that had followed our ghost's departure.

"I assume she meant that you are, in some way related. She had the look of someone from your region," Cambious supplied. He nodded toward the beds. "You both should sleep. I will keep watch."

"You need rest too," I argued.

"There are only two beds," Cambious countered. "Two very small beds."

"I can sleep here," Peter interjected, already sliding down in the corner. "I don't mind. I usually sleep on the rock floor."

Honestly, I didn't like the idea of not giving Peter the comfort of an actual bed, but I could not think of a better solution. I moved the bundle of clothes and the sausage, with what I could see now was a box of some sort of cracker, to the vanity and took off my robe, depositing my fruit with the other food, then taking the gun from my pocket, grateful we hadn't needed to use it.

Peter's breathing had already evened out, meaning he was either already asleep, or really good at faking it. "Ah, kids. Can fall asleep anywhere," I said softly. I lay down on the mattress, covering myself with my robe and pillowing my head on my arms. I doubted I would have as easy a time falling asleep.

I watched Cambious fuss around the room, and realized belatedly that he was setting up wards, though I hadn't seen that particular configuration before. It was related to *ekleípo*, I could tell that, but it wasn't quite the same.

"It projects itself to be what the viewer expects to see, in this case, just a door no one opens. It should also muffle the sound," Cambious said as he came to sit on the opposite bed.

He looked tired and worried, even in his terrifying natural form. Except it wasn't actually terrifying to me anymore. I lifted my head and propped it on my hand. "Do you need me to…"

Cambious shook his head. "I am fine, Thána. Thank you."

"Because, if you do, I'm here," I said, pushing myself up to nearly sitting. "And I'll sleep after, we both know that."

He sighed and I felt a little guilty for it. We hadn't really discussed it, whatever **it** was. Slowly he nodded, dropping his robe onto the bed, and reaching for the zipper of his pants. "But only a little, and we must be quiet."

I sat up, easing my own zipper down and shimmying out of the pants. This time I went to him, reaching down to help him before I moved in, my eyes darting to Peter to make sure he was sleeping. For a moment I got distracted by the idea that our ghostly benefactor might also be watching, but I managed to pull myself back to the business at hand.

Cambious got me back onto my bed, and back into my pants when it was over, covering me with my robe and letting me sleep.

CHAPTER 28
STEP TWO, RESCUE MOM

I WOKE TO MY STOMACH GROWLING AND A DESPERATE NEED TO RELIEVE MYSELF. There was no way to tell what time it was with shutters closed and no lights to speak of in the room. I opened my eyes in the half-light, my glance skipping over Cambious, who was still asleep, to the corner where I had last seen Peter.

He wasn't there.

I sat up fast, my eyes skipping around the room until I found him. He was curled up under the vanity. Okay, so he hadn't run off. Yet.

I stretched and stood, surprised to find that Cambious had even gotten my shoes back onto my feet after I had passed out. I had again slept better than I ever had before sex with an incubus. Guess that made the whole relationship sort of mutually beneficial. I tiptoed to the first of the two doors in the room, hoping to find a bathroom, only to find a closet.

The next door, the one across from the beds, yielded better results. The bathroom was small, two stalls and two sinks, with a door to what I assumed was an adjoining room. I relieved myself, hoping that whoever was in the adjoining room was off to evening meal or something or too spooked by the supposed haunting to come investigate. A quick washing of my hands and I let myself back into the bedroom.

I went to the window and opened the levers on the shutters just enough to get a glimpse out. The sun was just starting to set if the lighting outside was to be believed.

When I turned, I found Cambious watching me. "Not dark yet, but getting there," I said softly.

"We probably shouldn't wait too long. It might be suspicious, us going up to the cells in the middle of the night."

I nodded and crossed to the vanity, coming back to the beds with our food. "Plus, Head Honcho guy was supposed to have come back from somewhere today. We don't know what he might have done to her."

"Okay, so do we have a plan?" Cambious asked.

"Sure, rescue Mom, escape and…try to take out the Brotherhood?" I said, my own doubt tilting the words into a higher register than my normal. I'd been taking this whole thing one step at a time, so no, I had no plan. Cambious took one of the sausages he'd stolen and cut it into pieces with his knife, passing me a few pieces.

"I have an idea."

We both turned to see Peter standing between the beds, rubbing his eyes. He climbed up on the end of my bed and took one of the apples. "Take me up there, say you're locking me up again. At least, that gives you a way up to the cells."

"But not the right keys," Cambious said.

"Can't you do that thing you did with the guy in the armory?" I asked, passing Peter some of the sausage.

"If either of them is into guys, maybe," Cambious answered. "There's no way to tell until we're too far in to get out easily."

I nodded. "Okay, it's a start. How are we getting back out again? Especially with Mom so sick?"

"We could steal a car," Peter offered with a little more confidence. "I mean, if you can drive."

A facility like this would certainly need to have a number of vehicles bigger than the one Cambious had hidden before our entrance. "Where?"

Peter shrugged and chewed for a moment. "I just know that *Patoras* has a car, and there are the trucks that bring people here." He nibbled on his sausage. "They brought someone today. I can smell her."

I was tempted to sniff the air, see if I could sense her the way Peter did.

"But that means the *Tragač Krevlju* has returned as well. You need to be careful."

I glanced at Cambious for a translation. "Essentially, their top blood tracker," Cambious supplied. "He'll be devoted to their cause and might even think he's doing it willingly." He looked at Peter. "How old is he?"

Peter shook his head. "A man. He sometimes was with them when I was punished, telling me I needed to know what I was." His hands shook and he put his apple down.

"Great." He wouldn't need me to bleed to find me. If I got close enough to him, he'd know, glamor or not.

"Okay, Cambious, what if we split up? You go find us some wheels, Peter and I go get Mom."

"No, I'm not leaving you alone." Cambious shook his head. "Besides, how are you going to get her down the stairs and past the guards?"

"And don't forget Ashkān," Peter said.

"And the dragon, the phoenix, and whoever they brought back with them. If she's a blood witch, they're going to bleed her to death," I added with a sigh. It was impossible. The whole thing just got more and more complicated with every step we took. "We're going to need a distraction to get back down the stairs." I looked at Peter. "Your friend, can he fight? If we get him out of his cell, can he go roaring down the stairs, maybe incapacitate the guards?"

Peter shrugged. "He was pretty beat up yesterday. They're trying to break him so they can train him like the others."

I shook my head. "I guess we play it by ear. Are we ready?"

No one moved, so I did, standing and wiping cracker crumbs from my stolen uniform and tugging at the shirt to try to pull the wrinkles out. I closed my hand around my mother's pendant and felt the glamor ripple over me. Cambious followed my lead and then we moved the vanity so that we could get out of the room.

There were more people about than there had been when we'd gone into the room, mostly what looked like upperclassmen in any private high school back home. They snapped to attention as we passed, some of them murmuring a greeting which we acknowledged with nods. We got out of that wing and maneuvered ourselves back toward the tower. Here too there were more people than before, men in uniforms and suits.

Few spared us even a glance as Cambious put one hand on the back of Peter's neck, using the contact to thrust him forward. As we neared the landing with the guard post, I began lecturing, as if I were angry at the poor kid. "You will learn, boy. I think a night or two in a cell will teach you to obey your betters."

Two different guards stood as we approached. "Problems with your *slúga*?"

"He is a willful, lazy *kravu*," Cambious said. "We are going to teach him a lesson. First, a good beating, then a few nights with no bed or food should do the trick."

One of the guards chuckled and reached for a set of keys. "Put him with the animals, the smell should help."

I could tell Cambious was flooding the area with pheromones and was starting to see a response in at least one of the men. He brushed his hand as he took the keys and handed them to me. "Go on, get started. I'll be along in a moment."

"Come on, *slúga*. Get moving."

I pushed Peter up the stairs and onto the floor where his friend the manticore and the juvenile dragon were being kept. On the wall near the cages were a paddle and a flogger. I pointed to them as I let go of Peter. "Make it sound like I'm beating you, I said softly as I looked at the keys in my hand. I went first to Ashkān's cage. He was hunched down in the back of his cell, his dark red eyes on me as I fit the first key in the lock. "Ashkān, I'm Thána. I'm going to help you out, but you have to promise not to hurt me."

Peter hit the wall with the paddle and let out a small yell. "It's okay, Ashkān. She's a friend." Peter hit the wall a little harder and yelled again. It took me three tries to get the right key and open the cell. I left the door slightly ajar and moved toward the one with the phoenix. She raised an eyebrow at me as I started trying keys and Peter continued to make it sound like I was beating the life out of him.

I could see she was injured and the wings on her back appeared to be clipped together in what must be a painful manner. She wore what looked like khakis and a torn shirt that might have been white once, her taloned feet bare. I got her door open, and she moved toward me slowly, every step of her taloned feet clicking on the stone floor. "I suppose you think that disguise is going to let you walk out with all of us?" she asked as she exited the cell. She towered over me by at least a foot.

"Well, I figured I could try," I responded. "Can I help you with that?" I gestured at her back, and she turned, bending her knees so I could see the metal bands that held her wings together. It took me a minute to figure out how to loosen them and by the time I was done, Cambious had appeared, holding the key to my mother's cell. "Go on, I'll finish here."

Cambious nodded and sprinted up the stairs while I turned to the last occupied cell. The dragon was at the door watching us, deep blue eyes tracing every move as I came to him. "Hello," I said softly. I tried keys until I found the right one and opened the door. In his human form, he was naked, and I could see rags that might once have been his clothes, likely shredded during a transformation...or maybe I'd seen one too many Hulk movies. "Would you like to come with us?"

He nodded shyly and reached for my hand, pulling it to his face and rubbing it across his cheek. I smiled for him and turned to find our fantastical menagerie had been joined by Cambious carrying my mother with a young woman of maybe seventeen trailing behind him. She was dressed much like any teenager I had ever known: jeans torn at the knees, sneakers, and a T-shirt with some logo I didn't recognize. She was pale, with fiery red hair in two messy braids and there was a bruise blossoming across one cheek. She held herself stiffly and moved like there were more injuries hidden by clothes.

"Those two guards won't stay dazed for long," Cambious said. "I suggest we get moving. Everyone, follow me, we are going down the stairs and into the closet at the bottom. Peter, you're my lookout."

No one spoke as Cambious and Peter took the lead. I took the rear with the young dragon's hand still in mine. We congregated for a moment at the guards' landing while Peter made sure the hallway below was clear enough for us to achieve the closest hiding place. It was going to be a tight fit, but it would be easier to move around the Kourt after the bulk of the building's inhabitants had gone to bed.

Both guards seemed to be dazed, heads lolling on their shoulders as we moved past. Cambious hissed at us to hurry, and we went down the stairs to where Peter held the closet door open. It was a bit of a squeeze, the eight of us in a supply closet, but we managed. Cambious set my mother on her feet and shifted her weight onto me while he pulled out his ward stones and began working on keeping us hidden. It was a fair bet that someone would eventually realize that the prisoners had all escaped, but hopefully, they would turn their search to other parts of the fortress, and we could find our way out.

It was a lot to hope for.

I turned away from what Cambious was doing to look at Mom. She didn't look much worse than she had the day before, so I hoped that meant she'd be able to hold her own. Her face was gaunt, but her eyes sparkled when she looked at me. I kissed her cheek and turned to the rest. Quietly I pretended I knew what I was doing and that I was in charge. "Everyone, my name is Thána and this is my mother, Alana. The big guy warding us in is Cambious. I know Peter and Ashkān's names, but the rest of you are a mystery." I looked to the phoenix, and she nodded tightly.

"Sabina Nephus."

I looked at the teenager next. "Ciara Connelly." I smiled at her and turned to the dragon, who was clinging to my hand still.

He blinked at me. "What's your name?" I asked.

"Reyansh," he answered quietly. "Kalya."

"Okay, good. I guess we should get as comfortable as we can. We're going to wait for night to fall fully before we move out."

Around me, the group shifted and got sat down. I encouraged Reyansh to go sit with Sabina so I could get Mom settled in. "Rest, Mom. It's going to be a long night." Once she was sitting and leaning against the shelves I moved to where Cambious stood guard at the door. "Okay, now what?" I whispered.

"I got those men to give me some information. The garage is just off the parade grounds. We just have to get there and steal a truck." Cambious closed his eyes and drew in a deep breath, letting it out slowly. "We probably need to split up. A group this big is going to get caught."

I nodded. "Okay. You take Mom and the girl, and Sabina. I'll take the kids. We meet in the garage. Do you know how to find it?"

Cambious nodded. "You should take Sabina though. You need some protection, and she looks like she can fight."

I grinned. "I've got a manticore and a dragon, I'll be fine. Besides, you'll have your hands full with Mom. I'm counting on you to get her out."

CHAPTER 29
STEP THREE, HIDE

About an hour later, we heard a lot of muffled commotion through the door, booted feet pounding up and down the stairs, and yelling. I had settled in next to my mother, letting her lean on me. It didn't seem real, that this was the woman who had raised me and hidden me away, the woman who had been gone from my life for more than twenty years, and here I was holding her in a closet with a bunch of strangers.

We didn't talk, all of us afraid that even a whisper would give us away.

It seemed to take forever for the noise to die down and we waited a whole hour more before we began shifting around, stretching stiff muscles, and standing. "Cambious and his group will go first. Keep quiet and follow his lead," I said before hugging my mother to me. "I'll see you soon, okay?"

"Be careful, Thána. *Patoras* Javonic will do anything to get your blood."

"Is that his name?" I asked. "Well, I'm still using my blood, so he's going to have to wait. Go with Cambious, he'll keep you safe." I turned to Ciara. "Can you glamor? Even a little bit?" She nodded, glancing at Cambious, then back to me. "Okay, you should try to look like a man, you'll draw less attention."

Ciara closed her eyes and put a hand to her chest as if she was trying to reach inside herself. Slowly her shape shimmered and in her place was a thin young man with bright red hair. "Good. Remember, it's only as good as your concentration, and it won't save you if a blood tracker gets too close." Cambious had disabled the wards while I was getting Ciara ready.

I looked up at Cambious and nodded. "Get going. We'll meet you in the garage. Be careful."

Cambious took off his robe and draped it around my mother, pulling the hood up to hide her better. That left only Sabina with no disguise.

"I'll be fine," she said, as if she sensed my thought.

Cambious cracked open the door and peered out, nodding once before drawing my mother out into the hall. Ciara and Sabina followed, and the door closed, leaving me with the three children. Peter had shed his brown jacket and given it to Reyansh to cover his naked form. Ashkān sat in the back of the closet, looking tired and wary. Of the three, he was in the worst shape, and I was tempted to try to help him, but Mom was right about that blood tracker finding me if I did.

I glanced at Peter who was moving to sit with his friend and an idea started to form. "Peter, have you ever tried blood magic?" I asked, my voice just above a whisper. He shook his head, his eyes wide. I wasn't even sure my crazy idea would work, but he was a blood witch, and the old woman had wanted my blood to heal her, so it stood to reason that his blood held the same healing properties that mine did, and if the crazy old oracle could get healing from my blood, maybe Ashkān could get it from Peter's.

"I have an idea of a way to help Ashkān feel better without giving away our hiding place with the smell of my blood," I said, squatting down in front of the boys. "Can the tracker smell your blood?"

Peter shook his head. "Sort of, but not really. We smell different, the boys."

I pulled Cambious's knife from the pocket of my stolen pants and looked Peter in the eye. "Our blood can heal, I've seen it. If Ashkān drinks some of your blood, it may make him stronger, and give us a better chance of escaping."

Peter's eyes were wide and scared, and he actually shuffled away from me. "It is forbidden." He shook his head and closed his eyes. "Forbidden."

Leave it to me to find a taboo. "Maybe it is, and maybe there's a reason for that, but right now, we need to get Ashkān healed up so we can escape." It took a few long moments, but Peter finally gave in, nodding.

I looked at Ashkān. "Can you do that?"

He shuddered. "It will make me strong?"

"I hope so." I handed the knife to Peter. "Not too deep, and not someplace where the wound will hinder you." I gestured at my arm, where the old woman had cut me, and backed off to let them work out the details. Reyansh came to me and clung to my side. I suppose he needed comfort, which I'll admit is not my strength, but I put a hand on his shoulder and hoped it helped.

I heard Peter hiss and looked back to find him holding his bleeding arm up to Ashkān's mouth. For a long moment Ashkān just looked at the blood welling along the line of the cut, then he tentatively opened his mouth and leaned forward. He sucked at the blood and Peter held himself still with his arm up and his eyes wide. There was fear there, but bravery won out and when Ashkān released him, Peter clamped his other hand over the wound as his eyes found mine.

I looked around me and found a bag of cleaning cloths. I rummaged through it until I found one that would make a makeshift bandage. The blood had already stopped flowing by the time I got the bandage wound around Peter's arm and tied it off. "I heal fast," Peter offered.

Tucking that information away, I turned my attention to the manticore. We would know soon enough if my theory was correct. A male blood witch couldn't eat disease because he would have no way to expel it, but if that was the only difference, Ashkān should be up to moving before too long. We were going to need to move fast, and hope Peter could lead us safely to the garage.

It wasn't the best plan, but there was no way I could glamor them, I was running low on energy due to the extended use of my own glamor and I wasn't sure it was something I could do anyway. I paced the small space afforded me between the door and where Ashkān sat. There was no noise outside the door, as if everyone had abandoned the tower once the prisoners were all gone.

Time was against us, and my anxiety was only ratcheted up by the need to wait for Ashkān to be ready. After what seemed an eternity, Ashkān rose and shook himself before nodding to me. "I'm ready."

I exhaled slowly. "Okay, Peter you go out first. We need to keep to the most unused corridors, but we need to get there fast, okay?"

Peter opened the door, sticking his head out to make sure the area was clear. He stepped out and I gestured for Ashkān to follow before I tucked Reyansh to my side and followed. The hallway was eerily empty, and a part of my brain was whispering to me about a trap, that they knew where we were going, and they would ambush us there.

I shook it off and we headed out, not the way we had come, but down a hall we had never used. It took us to a staircase that we slipped down. Peter stopped us as we reached the bottom, leaning out past the wall to look before he moved on. He led us down a hall that seemed to be lined with storage rooms, with automatic lights that came on as we moved.

The lights made me nervous, but Peter kept moving until we found another staircase. "There's probably Brothers down there," Peter said, turning to look at me. "I can check."

"Stay here," I responded, peeling Reyansh from my side, and moving down the stairs. Peter was right. I could see a small cluster of men, armed with some kind of guns. They appeared to be guarding a door. I climbed back up to where the kids were waiting. "There are four of them, guarding a door. Peter, which way do we need to go?"

He pointed straight down the stairs. "Okay, I'll distract them, Peter, you lead the boys away and I'll join you.

"We need to go that way, then down another floor. That will be the library floor."

"Good. Get yourselves to the library. I'll find you there," I said.

Peter stopped me with a hand on mine, lifting his wounded arm and pulling the bandage off. "Smell."

I leaned down and sniffed at the cut, but I couldn't say I smelled anything other than the slight tang of blood. "Deeper," he said. "Clear your mind and breathe it in. If my blood can heal, then you should be able to track the scent of others like us."

I raised an eyebrow as I looked up at him, suddenly more confident than he had been before now. "Okay, I'll try." I closed my eyes to block out the shifting shadows as the boys moved around us restlessly. I breathed in, letting the feeling of air moving into my lungs pull my attention inward, to the core of me, as Merry had taught me. I let it out slowly and set my nose all but on Peter's arm before I breathed in as much as my lungs would allow.

There, just there. I don't think I can explain it well, but there was an earthy sort of smell, like rich soil and rain, with a vaguely metallic taste at the end. When I pulled back, Peter rewrapped the bandage around the wound. "Now, you should be able to find me, no matter where I go."

I was still marveling at the things I continued to learn about myself and what I could do as I got back to the bottom of the stairs. I wasn't sure exactly what I was going to do to distract those men, but I'd been improvising this entire operation, so I figured something would come to me. I took off my robe and gave it to Peter. "Take this."

At the bottom of the stairs, I squared my shoulders and lifted my head, putting on an authoritative air like it was a coat before I stepped off the stairs and turned straight toward them. I could tell that they were chatting about something not related to their duty, but I couldn't make out what it was. When they saw me, they fell silent and snapped to attention. "Lazy *kravus*! Our prisoners have escaped and here you stand chatting like children!" I reached inside of me and murmured a word I hoped I was remembering correctly, "*Sýnchysi*." I felt a wave leave me, spreading confusion toward the men.

I moved past them, eying them up and down, pulling their eyes toward me, and away from the place where Peter and the others waited. "I should have you disciplined."

"Sir, we only—"

I held up a hand to cut him off. "You are to be attentive and aware at all times, are you not?"

"Yes, Brother."

"Good. I do not want to see any more of that behavior. Understood?" Between two of the men, I could see Reyansh and Peter moving swiftly into the corridor beyond where the men would be able to see. "And stand up straight, straighten up those shirts. You look like you just rolled out of bed."

All four of them fussed with their clothes and I moved back toward the stairs. "Keep vigilant, Brothers. There is a blood witch loose on the grounds."

I heard them muttering as I started to walk away. "Brother, may we ask your name?"

I turned back. "You may. However, I do not have to tell you. I outrank you, that is all you need know."

"Perhaps you are one of the fugitives using a glamor. If there is a blood witch, she would be capable of that."

I could see that the confusion I had caused was wearing off and suspicion was taking its place. "Very well. I am Brother Caspin. I came in with *Patoras* yesterday. Would you like me to ask him to join us to vouch for me?"

The one who had spoken blanched a little white. I crossed my arms and met his gaze with my own, hard and a little angry. "I applaud your suspicion, Brother. Continue your vigilance. I must return to the search."

"How hard can a group like that be to find?" I heard one of them ask as I headed for the corridor. "You'd think at least the freaks would stand out."

He wasn't wrong, thus the sneaking around. I didn't run, but I moved quickly until I came to the stairs, and I took them as fast as I dared. The corridor at the bottom was familiar. We had been here before. Now all I needed to do was find the library.

CHAPTER 30
STEP FOUR, ESCAPE?

THE CORRIDOR WHERE I FOUND MYSELF WAS BETTER LIT THAN I WOULD HAVE liked, and I saw at least two pairs of Brothers patrolling as I moved in the direction that I believed would take me to the library. I nodded in greeting as I passed two of them. They stopped walking and I could feel their eyes, or maybe I just imagined it, but I was sweating until I heard their footsteps resume.

The second pair found me just as I was opening the door to the library.

"Little late for study, Brother," the first one said.

"I thought everyone was hunting for our escaped prisoners." The second of them was taller and older than most of the guards I'd seen so far.

I turned and offered them a smile. "Indeed. I just left my robe here earlier. It's getting chilly out there." I was shaking and hoped it didn't show. That was when I smelled it. Another blood witch and it wasn't Peter. If I could smell him, he could smell me. I swallowed, not daring to look to see how close he was. "Carry on, Brothers. I'm back to the hunt."

I pulled the door closed behind me and moved away from it as fast as I could in the dark room. Tables and chairs and bookshelves were dark shadows against the faint light coming in the nearby windows. My heart was trying to beat my ribs out of its way as I kept moving, trying to escape the scent.

Peter emerged from the shadows between two sets of shelves, looking pale and gaunt in the odd lighting. He held a finger to his lips and beckoned me into the shadows where the others were hiding beneath my robe. "We can't stay here," I whispered. "And we can't go out there. That blood tracker is here."

"Where else can we go?" Reyansh asked, his fear evident in the way his voice shook.

I leaned out and looked out the nearest window. "Out there," I responded. I went to the window, moving books aside from the shelf in front of the window to make room for us to climb out. The latch was an old-fashioned sort of thing that wouldn't budge. I inhaled and reached inside me again, putting my hands together and opening them while I whispered "*Ánoixe*." For a moment I was worried that it wouldn't open, but slowly the latch moved, and I put my hands to the bottom of the window, pushing it up. I leaned out to check for patrols or other Brothers, but there was nothing out there but a small yard that I hoped would give us a way out to the garage.

"Come on, boys."

Ashkān came first, pouncing up to the window ledge and then outside, then Peter. I had to help Reyansh up and out. I stepped through the window, reaching back through to put the books back, then pull the window down. "*Kontá.*" The latch closed easier than it had opened.

Inside the library, the door opened, and lights came on. I threw myself down so I wouldn't be seen. Peter grabbed my shoulder, pointing at a dark arch. I nodded and crawled with them toward it. I don't think I'd ever been as scared as I was right at that moment. I was certain it was the blood tracker who had entered the library, and I knew that he knew what I smelled like now because I knew what he smelled like.

We made the archway and in the deep dark on the other side, I stood. "Everyone okay?" No one answered, but I figured that was at least an affirmation that they all were good. I needed to get my bearings, figure out where we were and where the garage was, and how to get us there from the wrong side of the Kourt.

"Any idea where we are, Peter?" I asked, feeling along the wall in the dark. It wasn't going to take them long to figure out where we had gone.

"Never been here before."

"Great." My hand traced the stones in the wall and suddenly I felt the same thing I had when I had been drawn to that tombstone. I pressed my hand to the rock and got the immediate impression of another tunnel, one that ran through the walls and could get us to the parade grounds.

"They're out there." I heard the words clearly and pulled the boys closer as I reached in front of me to find the entrance.

Here, Adelfí. I laid a hand on the stone wall and whispered "*Diávasi,*" as I had when Cambious and I had made entry into the Kourt._I was genuinely surprised when the wall gave way, swinging inward to let us in. I hurried them inside and closed the door, feeling the rock welcome it back in place. It was even darker in the tunnel, and I had no light. Not that I would use one at that moment, not if it might give us away.

"They must have gone over the wall. Her scent ends here." The words were muffled, but I felt a rush of relief still the wild staccato of my heart.

We waited for a long moment before moving or speaking. "Everyone hold hands." I said it with almost no sound and felt Reyansh put his hand in mine. The tunnel went to our left and our right, and I had no idea which way to go. I tried to still and center and *feel* it, but all I felt was the anxiety to catch up to Cambious and my mother, running alongside the fear of being caught.

I let my indecision keep me immobile far longer than I should have, then chose to go to the right. I switched Reyansh to my left side and used my right hand to guide us by keeping it on the wall. Here the wall seemed to be brick, rather than stone. The tunnel wasn't very wide, just slightly larger than an average person, with low ceilings that would have made Cambious have to stoop over.

We inched our way in the dark, Reyansh squeezing my hand as if he was afraid I would let go of him and lose him in the dark. The tunnel turned and the wall under my hand was once again stone, not brick. It was impossible to tell how much time passed as we made our way in the absolute darkness, and I had lost all sense of direction when I felt wood under my fingers. "Stop, I think this is our exit," I said softly, reclaiming my hand from Reyansh and feeling over the wood until I found a latch. I pressed my ear to the door, trying to hear whether anyone was on the other side before I tried the latch and opened the door just a crack, pressing my face into the space and looking around.

I couldn't tell where we were, but the door seemed to let us out into a colonnade of sorts, with columns and arches that opened into an empty expanse, hidden by the lights on every third column. I eased through the door, holding the boys back until I could get around the door to get a better look. The colonnade stretched a long way down, took a left turn, then continued along the building, ultimately forming a giant U around what I took to be the parade grounds.

I beckoned the boys out and closed the door. Like the one we had entered the tunnel from, once closed no one would know the door was there. On this side, it looked just like the stones around it, and there were no seams to give it away. It was as if the door itself was warded with an invisible warding. Which I suppose, now that I think about it, wasn't outside the realm of possibility.

Across the parade grounds, I could see the lights of the opposing colonnade, and I could feel that my mother was nearby. "Where is the garage from here?" I asked Peter.

It was Ashkān who answered though. "Over there, behind." He lifted a paw and pointed with one deadly sharp claw to the opposite side of the grounds.

"Okay, I think we'll be safest if we cut across the square, where it's darkest."

Just as I was about to lead them out of the lighted colonnade, a nearby door opened and four men in the Brotherhood's military uniforms stepped out. "They think some of them got out over the wall into the Ring, but those mangy manticores should deal with them," one of the men said.

"Hey!" a second of them had spotted us and was pointing his gun in our direction.

"Go, boys!" I pushed Reyansh and Peter toward the nearest archway, preparing to try the *Yperaspízo* spell, but before I could even bring my hands up, there was a deep, guttural growl and Ashkān launched himself at the nearest man, claws raking over his face before Ashkān pounced at the second.

He moved so fast I could barely keep track of him and in a matter of seconds all four were down and the area was splattered with blood. Not a single shot was fired. I didn't even get my own gun out of my pocket. I looked frantically around us, hoping no one had heard the commotion. "Come on, Ashkān, we need to move."

I didn't want to think about the fact that I had just watched him kill four men, I just wanted to catch up to Cambious and get everyone out in one piece. Ashkān and I raced across the square, finding Peter and Reyansh hiding in the shadows of a pillar. Ashkān was shaking, the rage still clear on his face. I squatted down in front of him and wiped some of the blood from his face with my fingers. "Are you okay?"

He nodded slowly. "They would have killed us."

"Yes, they probably would have," I agreed.

"I've never...well, I did fight back when they came for me, but I don't think anyone died."

"You were amazing," Peter offered, throwing his arms around his friend to hug him. "You saved all of us."

"Okay, let's get ourselves hidden a little better." I stood and looked to Peter for direction. He nodded toward the end of the building. As we neared it, I could see that a paved street ran out to the gates that I assumed would open up to the road that would take us to freedom. The paving led us back toward a hulking shape that I hoped was the garage.

I was pretty sure the Brotherhood would have put guards on the garage, and in fact, I was starting to wonder just how stupid this head guy was that he didn't have the entire grounds crawling with men. We should have run into a lot more than we had. Maybe they weren't as big an operation as I had believed. Maybe we stood a chance.

I pulled my gun out and kept us in the shadows, moving slowly along the building toward the light being spilled from a large open door. Shadows were moving through that light with tight, military precision.

I could see at least six of them. There were probably more. Suddenly, they snapped to attention. "Vigilance men, they were seen coming this way. <u>Patoras</u> thinks they will try to steal a vehicle." I could just make out the shape of the man who seemed to be in command.

He was tall, thin, and not very imposing physically. That made me think he'd risen to command levels by other means. The scary for us kind of means. Cunning, savagery, and intelligence.

There was no way we were getting through or around them. We inched back into the shadows, and I squatted down, gathering the boys in close. "We need to find another way."

"Can't you distract them like before?" Reyansh asked.

"There are too many of them, and I don't think these men would fall for it." I was wishing I knew where Cambious and my mother were when I smelled **him** again. "Shit."

"Thána, is that you?" The question came from behind us, whispered and yet carrying to my ears all the same.

I moved the boys further back along the wall to find the other half of our misfit gang. Cambious looked exhausted. Mother looked even worse. Sabina was sporting a few new bruises. Only the girl looked relatively unscathed by their adventure. The blood tracker was getting closer. I had to do something, or we would all be caught. The trouble was, there was only one thing I could think of, and it was nuts.

CHAPTER 31
CAPTURE

"Cambious, if I can clear the garage door of men, can you get everyone into a truck and out of here?" I asked in a whisper, my eyes on my mother's face. All of this had been to get her out, and if we failed to do that, we lost everything.

"I think so," Cambious responded. "What are you thinking?"

I shook my head. "Just keep them safe." I hugged my mother tight and whispered in her ear, "I'll see you soon," before I pressed my lips to hers and let my sense memory guide me, sucking the sickness and the pain out of her body and into mine.

I knew it wouldn't take long for the bleeding to start, not with that much illness burning inside of me. My body would need to get rid of it before it could start to take hold inside me. I turned and ran for the light, slowing only a little as the men realized I was there.

I smirked at the commander as I lifted my hand to my mother's pendant and released the glamor. I brought my hands up, shouting "*Yper-aspízo,*" sending those closest to me stumbling backward, then ran like hell for the dark on the other side of the garage. They clamored after me, shouting as I was swallowed up by the dark. I didn't look back to see if they were all coming for me, just trusted that if anyone was left over, Cambious and the others could deal with them.

The start of the bleeding nearly knocked me off my feet, soaking into my stolen pants and running down my leg. If that tracker hadn't already traced my scent, he would now. I rounded a corner blindly, knocking into a patrol that was responding to the alarm behind me. I dropped the first man simply with the force of our collision and got a couple of shots off before the gun was knocked from my hand.

I kept fighting my way forward, fighting like my life depended on it, which it did. I dug nails into places I knew would cause the most pain, stomped on feet, even bit one man as he tried to pull me backward, his arm around my neck. Remarkably, I found myself free of them and took off running again. I wasn't sure where I was going or what I was going to do when I got there, I just knew that the longer they were chasing me, the more time Cambious had to get the others out.

There was a blur of color above me as I found myself back at the parade grounds, and I recognized Sabina as she touched down. I changed my course and ran toward her, just as a big truck lumbered up to the gates. The truck rammed the gates and pushed through them, while Sabina and I ran toward them. I was running out of steam.

"I can't carry you; you have to keep going," Sabina said. "I'll slow them down a bit."

She took flight again and suddenly behind me I felt a heat that hadn't been there. Orange-red light lit up the night and a glance behind me showed flames eating across the carefully groomed grass. I pumped my arms and legs and ran with everything left in me, but the glamor had taken so much energy to maintain for as long as I did that there wasn't much left in the reserve tank.

Men were screaming, shouting commands, but I was almost to the gates.

And that was when it hit me.

I wasn't sure at the time what exactly it was, but I went down. I went down hard, crashing into the pavement and rolling until I hit the tumbled wreckage of the gate. Pain lanced through my shoulder, my face, my side. I hadn't even begun to feel it all when a man squatted down in front of me, his hand squeezing my chin. "Where are you going, *thanátou*?"

I recognized him, the smell of him, but also his face. I had seen him before…before all of this craziness started. In El Paso, even before Finneas had made his appearance. He was the one who had set the assassins on me.

His fingers pressed into my side, pulling my attention to the metal that pierced me and held me in place. The gate that had been my road to freedom now impaled me with the twisted metal left behind after the truck crashed through. I screamed as his fingers traced the metal into me, then again as his hands yanked me free of the gate.

"I let you escape once. It won't happen again."

He grabbed my shirt and hauled me to my feet, though he had to support me as I wobbled on knees that weren't entirely sure they remembered how to be knees. By the time he had shoved me into the gloved hands of two large men, I was fairly soaked in my own blood, and they had to all but carry me. We went into the Kourt, into a large hall with portraits of men in the black uniforms of the Brotherhood.

My thoughts were sluggishly trying to catch up as the memory of that rest stop, and the boy who had drawn the hunters away from me, bubbled up.

My captors dropped me onto a beautiful marble floor, white with threads of gold and black and the tracker came to stand beside me. He gave a salute as booted feet approached us. "*Patoras*, Thána Alizon."

"What a bloody mess you are." He squatted in front of me, a middle-aged man with a streak of gray in his black hair. He wore the military uniform, his boots highly polished. His face showed disgust as he turned my head to look at the scrape across my face where skin had met pavement at high velocity. "Get her cleaned up for the trial. And plug her up, I don't want that tainted blood spoiling the rest."

The way he said the word **trial** made me think it wasn't going to be so much a trial as a declaration of my guilt. The two big men pulled me back up and when my knees gave out, one of them scooped me up and threw me over his shoulder like I was already dead. I passed out somewhere along the way and only woke when I was dropped, none too gently, onto a cold exam table.

The room around me was some sort of medical clinic, the walls and floor a pristine white, and vaguely familiar machines filled the space near the head of the table. Two men, completely covered in white with only their eyes visible, approached. One had a tablet of some kind which he was tapping as the other reached for me. He poked at my shoulder and fire bit me there, spreading out into the surrounding skin.

"Gunshot, left shoulder, looks clean." He reached for my side, which was screaming at me in a language I had never heard from my own body. "Oh, this is a mess."

I screamed as his fingers pressed into the wound. "Likely from the gate, Patoras said she hit it at high speed. Probably has some internal bleeding as well. We may have to stitch it up so there's enough blood left for her bleeding." His hands moved to my thighs, pushing them apart. "She's killed someone already tonight, look at this."

I wanted to argue that I hadn't killed anyone, but I wasn't sure that was true. I know at least one of the shots from my gun hit flesh. I lost my train of thought then as they stripped me and washed me, awakening every single injury from head to toe. There was no care given to my pain as they scrubbed my skin and stitched up cuts and otherwise made me presentable, including shoving something akin to a tampon into my vagina to stop the blood.

When they were done, I was dressed in a simple white shift that came to my knees, my hands bound behind me in a position I was sure was designed to make my shoulder shout obscenities at me. I was forced to walk on bare feet, and one very swollen ankle, out of the medical room and down a hall. My mind filled with the memory of Althea Anagnos and how they had killed her centuries before.

My blood still stained the marble in the hall as they pushed me out the same doors we had come into, only in front of the colonnade, where there had been only grass, there was now a platform, as if it had sprung out of the ground. Of course, it could have. I'd just helped a dragon, a manticore, and a phoenix escape a fortress. I was willing to believe almost anything at that point.

They pushed me up some stairs and onto the platform. The parade grounds were lit up like it was already day, and it was filled with what looked like every person that lived in the Kourt. I was surprised to see that most were little more than boys standing in the front row. This was to be part of their indoctrination.

Patoras Javonic stepped up to me, his smile of victory sickening. I wanted to spit in his face, but my mouth was dry as I contemplated the death I was about to endure.

"I held her here for two years. I beat her, burned her, starved her. She never once told me anything, but she still gave you to me." He spoke directly into my ear, his hand holding the back of my neck. "And now I will bleed you just as we have done for millennia. Your blood will keep me in power for decades." He pressed a gloved finger against my scraped-up cheek, just enough to get it to bleed a little for him, then he licked the blood clean. "Did you know that less than half an ounce of your blood once a week will keep me strong and healthy? The last one of you that we bled gave me almost fifty years. Yours will do the same."

My brain stuck on what he was saying. It wasn't just that his order wanted blood witches dead. Our blood could keep him alive well past a normal lifespan. Most of the rank and file couldn't know that. It went against everything I knew about the Brotherhood. How did they not see it? Had no one even noticed he'd been alive that long? And why didn't he bleed the men too? Peter had implied that he and that lead tracker weren't the only ones, and we'd proven that his blood was just as potent.

He shoved me forward. I pushed the thoughts aside and tried to focus on what was about to happen.

"Thána Alizon, you have been convicted of being *thánatou*. Your punishment is death by *Aimorragía*."

Two men came forward and pulled me toward the scaffold from which they would hang me to bleed out, and from that position, I could see something I hadn't in Althea's memory. There were holes in the platform through which tubing protruded, tubing that ended in large bore needles. I imagined that underneath the scaffolding, there were bottles or vats or something to collect it.

In the distance, beyond the destroyed gates, the sun was just starting to rise, staining the horizon in shades of orange, red, and pink. My hands were untied and one of the men raised a knife to cut the shift from me, but he stopped as a cry rang out from the back of the ranks of men, and the ordered lines split apart.

A giant manticore tore at the grass as he ran, roaring at anyone who came too close. Then came the fire, raining down out of the sky as Sabina dove at the men, setting several alight before she took back to the skies. She wasn't alone, at least five other manticores were diving into the chaos they had created. The screaming was deafening, punctuated by the sound of the flames and the stench of burning flesh.

I pulled away from my captors, but there wasn't much of a way to go to get free of them. I shoved at the closest one and ducked under Javonic's hand to grab at the gun of one of his guards. I brought it up, only to drop it as I got punched in the face. I staggered backward, and almost off the platform.

My body was yelling at me to stop, but at the same time there was an adrenaline rush fueling my fear and rage and I somehow managed to slip free again, aiming for the stairs. The parade grounds were a swirling cacophony of fire and blood and the screams of dying men. The big manticore charged toward me and at the last second said, "Duck."

I dropped and his huge, clawed foot raked the throat of the man who had been about to grab me. His blood covered me, and the manticore's face. "I will get you out. Climb on."

"What?" I wasn't sure I'd heard him right, but he squatted down and nodded his head toward his back. He was bigger than that horse I'd ridden as a teenager, but I climbed on.

"Get a good hold. I can't fly anymore, but I will get you to your mother."

I dug my hands into his thick mane and tried to squeeze my knees against his powerful muscles and he started to run, knocking anyone who got in our way to one side. I saw Sabina make another pass, saw her focus on the platform, felt the heat of it as it took to flame.

But then it was all I could do to just hold on as my great steed rammed through a clump of men, slashing at them as we passed. The jostling broke open stitches and blood oozed through the side of the shift. That was the last thing I remember of that moment because the adrenaline was fading and the blood loss was too much, and I passed out again.

I woke with a start as I started slipping from the manticore's back, grabbing onto his mane and pulling myself upright again. We were in the cemetery. The smell of smoke was strong and the skies behind us were orange against the deep blue of the last vestiges of night. Ahead of us, the sky was starting to lighten with the rising of the sun.

"Are you alright?" He was slowing now, and I was able to sit up a little bit.

"I think so. I mean, I've been shot, stabbed by twisted metal and I have road rash on my face, but I'm alive, so yeah. I'm good."

Of course, I wasn't sure how long that would stay true. Blood was still oozing from my side, and I was fairly sure that something inside of me was bleeding as well, but for the moment I wasn't actively dying. We stopped and for a moment I just wanted to lay back down and sleep.

"Thána!" My mother rushed toward me, looking much better than she had when I last saw her and her hands on my waist helped me slide down off my rescuer's back. She turned my face to look at my cheek, but I just tugged her into a hug.

"I'm okay. Thanks to the big guy here." I turned to him. "I don't even know your name."

He inclined his head. "I am Bijan. Ashkān is the son of my brother. You freed him. I have repaid the debt."

I shivered in the cold not-quite-morning air and looked around me for Cambious. He was sitting with his back to the wall, the glamor off and his black skin was strangely ashen. "Is he okay?" I asked, pressing a hand to my still bleeding side.

"He will be. He needs rest and to feed," my mother responded. "I'm more worried about you."

I was only upright at that moment because I had a hold of Bijan's mane. I figured I was due to collapse soon, probably needed a hospital...or at least that grandpa witch doctor at that clinic.

"We should move, survivors are coming down the hill." Ciara was suddenly beside my mother, green eyes sparkling. "You don't look so good."

I nodded my agreement, but it set the world spinning. "Not much you can do for me unless you're secretly a surgeon. I'm pretty torn up in here. Where are the boys?"

"Waiting by the truck."

"Let's load up then. What about you?" I asked Bijan as I shifted my weight and reached for Ciara's shoulder.

"I will see to my people. If you could send Ashkān to me, please."

On top of the pain, the cold was creeping up from my bare feet, and the thin cotton of the shift did little to help. I leaned heavily on Ciara and together we moved slowly for the truck. Around us, manticores were landing, and I could see at least six of them now, plus Bijan. They were all bloody. Behind them, Sabina came, circling low before setting down beside us.

She helped Ciara get me into the truck's cab, then went to help Cambious up into the back where I could hear Peter and Ashkān saying their goodbyes. I drifted in and out as everyone else got settled in and when I looked up, my mother was in the driver's seat. "Where?" I asked

"To get you taken care of, then home."

I nodded my agreement. I'd like that. Home. It seemed a lifetime since we'd left.

CHAPTER 32
FREEDOM

I could hear my mother and Sabina talking about the wisdom of trusting anyone this close to the Kourt. I blinked and lifted my head. We were parked outside what seemed to be a hospital, Mom and Sabina standing on my side of the truck with the door partially open. It dawned on me slowly that my mother was wearing clothes that were not what she had been wearing.

I felt sluggish, probably the blood loss. The side of the shift was soaked through and there was blood on the seat.

"May not have a choice," I slurred. "Bleeding out over here."

"I'll take her and Peter in," my mother said. "You stay out here, keep an eye on Cambious and the other boy."

"Reyansh," I offered.

"Yes, Reyansh." My mother pulled the door open and slipped her hand behind my back. Gently she guided me to my feet and supported me as she called out for Peter to join her. We were halfway to the doors under the giant sign that I assumed meant "Emergency" in whatever the local language was when someone saw us and came running with a gurney.

The man lifted me easily and then we were running, and I felt dizzy before we stopped. My mother vanished and in her place were several men and women in green scrubs and hands all over my torn-up body. I remember screaming at one point, my back arching up off the bed and being held down. I managed to answer some of their questions before I passed out again.

I don't know how long I was out, but I could tell, as I started to wake up that they had drugged me to keep me under. I also felt nicely insulated from the pain. When I opened my eyes, I found my mother in the chair beside my bed, her hand on mine. Her eyes were closed, her face peaceful.

"Welcome back to the land of the living," Cambious said from my other side.

I turned to look at him, and even with the glamor in place, I could see that he had fed, and hopefully, slept. "You look better. How long was I out?"

He shook his head lightly. "Not long, they had to operate to get the bleeding under control."

I had figured that much out, though it didn't feel like I'd been operated on. "You should be up and around soon." He pointed up to an IV bag of blood that was nearly empty. "Our teenage friend was a match; she was happy to donate."

"I thought I heard voices." I looked up to find a woman in a lab coat at the door. "I'm Dr. Straub, I was the one who patched up your insides."

"Thanks for that, Doc," I said. "I feel almost as good as new."

My mother squeezed my hand, and I glanced her way.

"You should take it easy the next few days. I'll set you up with a course of antibiotics, to stave off any chance of infection, but I think as soon as that IV is done, we can cut you loose."

I waited until she left the room to shake my head. "We need your medical knowledge back home. I'd probably still be halfway to dead back there."

Mom moved to sit on the bed, brushing a hand over my forehead. "Without the magic, we aren't that much more advanced."

I gestured at Cambious. "Tell him that. We're nowhere near being able to do that kind of thing."

Mom chuckled. "Well, true. But it was more than Dr. Straub's magical training that saved you."

We were all quiet for a long moment, ignoring the fact that we had somehow managed the impossible. "What about the Brotherhood?" I asked softly.

Cambious inhaled deeply and let it out slowly. "Reports are still coming in, but between the phoenix and the manticores, I'd say we hurt them badly. There are some survivors here, or there were, I'm not sure anymore."

"The military has moved in to clean up the mess. I guess they finally decided to enforce the law." My mother's voice was bitter. I guess she had a right to be.

"The manticores?"

"As far as I know, all gone back to their homelands," Cambious said.

"Apparently, we interrupted their plans for a rebellion." He chuckled, leaning back in the chair. "To hear Bijan tell the story, anyway."

"And the kids?"

"With Ciara and Sabina. We thought it best to not flaunt the idea that we have a dragon kid and a phoenix. Some of our people aren't fond of... well, folks who are different."

"Okay, so what's next?" I asked.

"Merry is on her way to take you, your mother, Ciara, and Peter back to her place. She has connections that can help us find their families and get them home. Sabina and I will see Reyansh home," Cambious said.

"So, it's just...over?"

Cambious shook his head and stood. "Remember Sybyl's words, it may be over for now, but as she said, hate will grow back. I'll give you two some time alone."

My mother held my hand as he left, smiling softly down on me. "I thought I would never see you again. And when I saw you there, I thought it was another one of his tricks."

"I'm sorry," I whispered.

"Sorry?"

"I didn't come sooner, that you were there so long."

She shook her head. "I'm the one who is sorry, Thána. I never wanted to leave you like that, but I was convinced it was the only way to get them off your scent."

"I did okay." I wasn't going to tell her how angry I'd been at her when I'd discovered that she had blocked my memory, hidden my gifts. I could see the pain in her eyes. "And I've kind of had a crash course in magic since Finneas Connor showed up in my life. Though I have to tell you, it was a bit of a disappointment to discover that the magical land on the other side of that closet door looked a lot like home."

"You were expecting what? Something like the Lord of the Rings?"

"Something like that." I shook my head. So much had changed. "So, we go home? Back to the house in California?"

"We could. But we should go get your sister first."

"Did you wipe her memory too?" I asked, feeling a little jealous that she had likely had more time with our mother than I did.

"No, though she might have been better off. And she was more than a little angry with me when I left her."

"Where is she?"

My mother sighed and stood up to pace the room. "Through another portal, in a land they call Vaneesh. We stumbled on the portal when we were up in the Amerin mountains and thinking that it would get us back to you, and get the Brotherhood off our trail, we went through. Only the world on the other side of that portal was not the one where we had left you. I was so tired of the running. You would have been about thirteen, I guess. We'd been running for almost seven years."

"So, you stayed?"

She nodded. "Yeah, for a long while." She came back to the chair and sank into it. "The Brotherhood didn't make an appearance for almost ten years. By then we were settled into this apartment I loved, and we had friends, some of them in rather high levels of the government. Those first few men just kind of disappeared. Then they stopped coming."

"But eventually you left her?"

"Eventually. She was married, with a son. I wanted to check in on you, and see if the Brotherhood's power here had waned. I told her I'd be back. She knew better though. She has your father's gift of seeing into the future. We fought and I left."

"How long ago?"

"At least two years, on that side of the portal. I think. Time is different there, and it's easy to lose track of time when you're being tortured."

I could believe that to be true. I'd only had a taste of what she'd endured. "So, we go get her. Then we go home." I yawned, but I didn't want to sleep. I wanted to spend time with this woman I had fought so hard to get to.

"Sleep, Thána. We have all the time in the world now that we're together again." Her hand brushed lightly across my face and as if her words were a spell, my eyes closed even though I wanted to keep them open.

When I woke, Cambious was back with clothing for me, and a bag filled with takeout sandwiches. "They aren't great, but you'll want them on the road. Merry and your mother are downstairs."

I was happy to see that I was no longer bound to an IV, and while I was still sporting a few bandages, I felt great. Maybe great is an overstatement, but I certainly didn't feel as though it had been less than twenty-four hours since I had been shot and stabbed in the gut with wrought iron. I put my feet to the floor and stood, a little wobbly but otherwise just fine. There wasn't even a twinge in the ankle I had sprained. "Yeah, I think I like the doctors of your world a whole lot more than the ones back home."

Cambious chuckled. "You say that now but wait until you have to find one to reattach your...never mind. Get dressed. I'll wait outside."

I pulled on the jeans he'd brought and realized that they must have been the clothes I'd left at Merry's when we ran, because they were my own, as was the shirt. The shoes were new though, because those were somewhere in the Kourt, probably on the floor of that medical ward, where they had cut my clothes off of me. They looked sturdy enough and though a little stiff, they fit well. Once I was dressed, I grabbed the bag of sandwiches and met Cambious in the hallway.

"Merry took care of the bill," Cambious said as he led me to a bank of elevators. "She still feels really guilty about dumping your brain box the way she did."

"She should." I wasn't angry anymore. In fact, I was kind of grateful. Who knew if we would have succeeded without it? "You're looking well fed." If I didn't know better, I would have said he blushed, but it's hard to tell on skin as dark as his.

"Yes, I am."

I raised an eyebrow but didn't press further. I didn't need to know who he was getting his meals with, though I was beginning to think it was Sabina, just from the way he wouldn't meet my eyes. My mother gathered me to her side almost as soon as the elevator doors opened, escorting me to the front door where Merry waited beside a beat-up old car with one red door and one blue fender while everything else was a dark green.

We didn't talk much as Merry took us from the hospital to the hotel where the others were waiting for us. Reyansh ran for me before I'd even cleared the door of the room, wrapping his arms around me, and burying his face in my shirt.

"Hey, Reyansh, I'm fine," I comforted as best I could, eventually peeling him off of me so I could sit on one of the beds. I felt great, but I seemed to be tiring easily. Reyansh climbed up to sit beside me, taking my hand in his. It was nice to see him dressed in something more than that brown jacket Peter had given him.

"You're really okay?" Peter asked, his face showing his worry. He too was wearing new clothes and he had a little more color in his face than the last time I'd seen him.

I nodded. "Good as new. Better even because we got out."

If I was honest with myself, I had never really expected we would. But here we were. Now we just had to worry about the ones that survived and seeing everyone home to their families. "What do we know about the Brotherhood?" I asked, putting an arm around Reyansh.

Sabina stood away from the corner where she'd been leaning, clad in dark red jeans and a deep orange shirt. The combination played up her natural coloring. "I did a recon flight earlier. The Kourt is basically deserted, the only activity was some military firefighters putting out the last of the fire. I guess most of the residential area was destroyed, some of the walls collapsed on that side."

"Survivors?" I asked.

She nodded. "I'd estimate a couple dozen escaped the Kourt, and there are probably a number of them who were off on missions."

"What about *Patoras* Javonic?"

"We aren't sure," Cambious said. "Sabina said he was caught in the fire, but identifying the dead is going to take a while."

Mom came to sit on the opposite bed. "We're safe enough, for now. Even if he lives through this, it is going to take them time to recover, and at least now we have the government of Otadž involved. Their new Premier has vowed to extinguish the Brotherhood."

"Well, I guess all that's left is to get these kids home."

"If we have a home left," Ciara said. I hadn't even seen her over by the bathroom door. "The Brotherhood killed my mother when they came for me. I haven't seen my dad in years. He left when we learned what I was."

Merry cupped a hand to her face. "If there is no home left, you are welcome in mine, *paidí*."

I stifled a yawn.

"Do I have to?" Reyansh asked into the silence left hanging around us.

"Have to what?" I asked.

"Go, with them. I want to stay with you."

My mother came to kneel in front of him. "A dragon belongs with his own people, there is no place for you where we're going."

I kissed the top of his head. "Mom and I have something we need to do, but when we come back, I'll have Cambious bring me to visit you, how about that?"

"Really?" He brightened considerably.

"Yes, really."

Cambious nodded to Sabina. "I think that's our cue. Come on Reyansh, I'll race you to the car."

CHAPTER 33
RECOVERY

Before we left for Merry's house, Mom and I went back to the Kourt. I needed to see for myself. The place was deserted in the late afternoon, charred remains still smoldering in places. Smoke lurked along the stone floors and clung to doorways.

Whatever was left of the Brotherhood had gone into hiding, so there was no one to lay claim to the property. We picked our way past the ruins of the platform where they were going to kill me and into the marble-floored hall.

The place where I had first met Patorus was marked with black where the fire had burned the blood I'd left behind. I turned away from it and turned down the hallway that I thought would lead me to the library.

The walls of the hallway were blackened, and the fire had burned away all of the wood doorways and tapestries. I had a vague notion that the Brotherhood had filled their library with all of the books they had forbidden others.

The library doors had burned away, and the damage inside was extensive. What hadn't been destroyed by fire was waterlogged and smoke damaged. I stopped beside the window that I had led the children out through. "He saved my life once," I said into the silence.

"Who did?" my mother asked.

I turned to face her. "The tracker. Do you remember? When the Brotherhood caught up to us at a rest stop, but we got away?"

She nodded.

"They were using a young boy then as their blood tracker, but they hadn't broken him yet. He drew them away so I could get back to the car."

I sighed. "I can't imagine what they did to him after, but the blood tracker who caught me was the same boy."

I wandered over to the least damaged section of the library, trailing a finger along the spines of books, eyes scanning titles. My finger tingled as I touched on a particular book, and I pulled it down. If nothing else, I'd had a crash course in trusting my instincts in recent weeks.

The book was old and permeated with smoke, its black cover faded and the pages inside it were like creamy old parchment, thick and elegant. With a provocative title like "Blood Magic," I had to believe that it was something that could help me find my way.

I tucked the book up under my arm and continued perusing titles. I ended up with a book on portal construction and a grimoire of defensive and offensive magics titled "The Dark Art of War" that promised to teach me to be a better protector.

I came out from between the shelves to find my mother holding a burn-damaged book with a forlorn look on her face. "You okay?"

She held the book up, letting the burned pages flutter. "It was one of the foremost books on blood witches and their peculiar type of magic. Probably the only copy still in existence. The rest of the shelf this was on is ashes."

I shrugged and showed her my haul. "I found some interesting books, so not a total loss." I suddenly remembered the collection of books in the storeroom Cambious and I had made our way through, where we had found Peter. "They may have more."

I let instinct guide me through the smokey ruins, down into the underground levels, and back to that storeroom.

My mother gasped as her eyes swept the shelves. She grabbed at the books, stacking them until she could hardly hold them. I took several as well, so she wouldn't try to carry even more. I gestured toward the stairs with my chin. "We should probably get moving. Sun will be down in a while, and we don't want to get caught here after dark."

Merry's car waited for us just inside the destroyed gate. I tossed my books in the back seat and climbed in beside my mother. "I am very proud of you, Thána," Mom said as she started the engine. "So very proud."

I was uncomfortable with the sentiment and muttered a thank you in barely audible tones. We headed for the graveyard, leaving the smoldering ruins of the Kourt behind us. As we neared the gate in the outer wall, Mom slowed us down.

All around us, the air shimmered with ghosts hovering over their graves, arms raised as if to thank us for returning their home to them. Tears burned at the corner of my eyes when the ghost who had kept us safe on our overnight in the Kourt stepped closer. She was more solid than most of the others, and her gratitude was obvious on her face.

I raised a hand to acknowledge them before Mom took us out onto the road and toward the hotel where we would spend one more night before heading back to Merry's.

The morning saw us all up early, dressed, and ready to hit the road. Peter was taking it in stride, though he seemed sad to be without his friend Ashkān. Ciara was quiet and sulking, though I suppose I would sulk in her position too.

I sat behind my mother, with Peter between me and Ciara, one of my stolen books in hand. It wasn't written specifically for blood witches, but it did go in depth on the theory of blood magic that could be done by other witches and had notes in a tiny, neat hand about alterations for blood witches.

Like so much else I had learned over the last few months, the more I read the more I realized I had to learn. It was a good thing I now had time to learn it, and eager teachers in my mother and Merry.

I spent most of that drive buried in the book, devouring it, and making plans to start testing some of the spells in it once we got back to Merry's. I dozed off at some point and woke to the smell of rain. The world outside our window was gray and wet, but I could tell we were almost to Merry's house.

It startled me, as our drive to the Kourt took much longer. "How long was I asleep?" I asked groggily.

Mom turned to look at me. "Quite a while, I'm afraid. You didn't even wake up when we stopped to switch drivers."

"Must have needed it. Maybe it's the near-death experience." I stretched, yawning and shifting, which woke Peter who had been lying against me. "Sorry."

He blinked at me blearily but smiled.

We made the turn onto Merry's street and into her driveway. Zo was waiting on the porch, rushing out to greet her mother and then mine. "I thought we'd never see you again."

My mother's smile was sad as she accepted the hug. "I am here now, thanks to Thána."

Zo pulled me into the hug too. "Thank you for bringing my favorite cousin home to me."

"No sweat," I replied, gently pulling free. I wasn't comfortable with displays of affection. "Um, this is Ciara and Peter. They helped too." Peter hid behind me, but Ciara nodded in greeting.

"Let's get everyone settled in," Merry said, making motions toward the house. "Zo, put on the kettle, we'll be wanting some tea."

Mom slid her arm around me as if I needed her support to go into the house. I didn't pull away, though I kind of wanted to. For all of the work to get her there, I still only barely knew her. The next hour or so saw us making sleeping arrangements. Merry's house was bigger than I had imagined it, with enough bedrooms for everyone to have their own.

Once that was decided, I settled at the kitchen table with my book on blood magic in an effort to stay out of the way while Merry and Zo made dinner. The front door opened a few minutes later, and two women who looked a lot like Zo came in all aflutter.

"Is it true?" one of them asked as Zo went to greet them. "Is she here?"

The older of the two dropped several shopping bags as my mother joined them, grabbing my mother into a big hug. "If by she, you mean me, yes," Mom said, pulling the other woman into the hug too. "It is so good to see you! Thána, come here. I want to introduce you."

I inhaled and let it out slowly before I stood and went to meet them. "Thána, these are two of Merry's daughters. This is Zeph and this is Zelda. Merry really likes the letter Z. And this is my eldest daughter, Thána."

I smiled and nodded my head. "Pleasure to meet you both."

"Zo called and let us know you needed clothes, so of course, we just cleaned out our closets for you," Zelda said. She had Merry's eyes and a sprinkle of gray highlighting her black hair.

"And I pulled some things out of storage for the girl and the boy," Zeph added. "What were their names again?"

Right about then, Peter appeared on the stairs. "This is Peter," I said, nodding for him that it was okay. "These are cousins of mine, Peter. They brought you some clothes."

Zeph picked up one of the bags and passed it to Peter. "These might be a bit big on you, but they'll do."

"Thank you," Peter said, his voice small.

Mom drew her cousins into the living room, and I returned to my book, but as word spread, more and more relatives appeared, and I realized that I wasn't going to get any reading accomplished. I took the book back to my room, stopping outside Peter's door. He was sitting on the floor with Ciara, working with some ward stones.

Ciara looked up at me and rolled her eyes. "I couldn't deal with all of those people, so I figured I could teach Peter some magic."

"I hear you. I spent most of my adult life thinking I had no family. To suddenly be awash in them is overwhelming."

"Most of my family is gone, one way or another," Ciara said, her face sad.

"I have a lot of family," Peter said once he'd gotten the stones activated. "I miss them."

I rubbed a hand in his hair and gave him a smile. "Tomorrow we start finding them so we can get you home. We just have to survive this family reunion."

Family. It was such a foreign concept. But Merry's living room and dining room were full of it. There were cousins, aunts, and uncles. And they were all keen to know me.

With a sigh, I headed back down the stairs, slipping into the living room where Mom was telling a story about the world where she and Daria had been living.

She looked up at me, her eyes shining with love, and held out her hand. I went to her and took her hand, sinking to the couch beside her. "Thána, this handsome fella is your uncle Christophe and his lovely daughter Emily."

"Hello." My uncle Christophe was a mountain of a man, easily six foot five, with broad shoulders and a full beard that came to his chest. Emily was a slight young woman by comparison, thin and short, with red-brown hair and glasses. It felt like the whole room was staring at me, expecting me to speak. "Um, I guess you want to know about me?"

"Well, you are a bit of a mystery to us," Zeph said.

"Not so much a mystery. I'm just a mid-level corporate manager who discovered I was a witch and followed an incubus into a land where magic is real."

"Oh, there's a story or five in that." I looked at the speaker, an older woman with gray hair cut in a short bob whose name I couldn't remember.

I shook my head. "Some Brotherhood thugs attacked me, I came through the portal, and here I am."

"I hear you all but demolished the Brotherhood," Emily said. "Is it true?"

I shrugged. "Well, their leader is not likely to live for long. He was pretty badly burned. There were a fair number of them killed or injured, but they'll regroup. Or that's what Sybyl said."

I was uncomfortable being the center of attention and I shifted my weight a little as if it would help. "You should write a book about it," Christophe said. "We have several authors in the family."

I put a hand on my side where my injury was and yawned. "I'm pretty wiped out. Still healing, you know. I'm going to go lay down."

Mom stood with me, walking me toward the stairs. "Are you okay?"

I nodded. "Just tired. And overwhelmed."

She kissed my cheek. "I understand. Let me know if you need anything."

I wanted to say that I was a big girl now and had been taking care of myself for a long time, but I didn't, just left her standing at the bottom of the stairs.

I don't know how long the house was filled with people, but it went well into the night. The air was filled with voices and laughter and punctuated with singing from time to time.

Idly, as I lay there, I wondered about the house in California, and my father's ghost who had told me to find my mother. I still wasn't sure how the ghost thing worked, but I couldn't help but wonder if he knew somehow that I had found her.

California felt like a lifetime ago as I lay there, staring at the wall. I had no idea when or if we would go back. Mom wanted to go to Daria, but she had mentioned that the portal was quite a hike from where she could park a car, so she wanted me to recover more before we made the trek.

Who knew what would follow that? Would we end up staying there? Would we come back here? There were no solid answers. Just the looming questions and familial obligations.

A NOTE FROM THE AUTHOR:

This book has been a labor of love, which I know is cliché as all get out, but this character has become a friend, and she has a lot of me in her DNA.

I love that this genre, and the world of publishing as it is today, allow me to play with characters like these and create worlds like this for us to frolic through. These characters are diverse by design, without apology. All genders, all orientations, and all races are represented (or even made up) and magic brings them together.

I hope you enjoyed this journey and will come along for the sequels.
Thank you!
Natalie J. Case

GLOSSARY OF TERMS

A

Adelfí: Sister
Aderfia: Brothers
Ánoixe: Open
Ánoixe kleídoma aímatos: Open this lock by my blood
Apokalýpto: Reveal

C

Kravu: Cow

D

Dimiourgió: Break

E

Ekleípo: Disappear (used with ward stones)
Éla: Come
Eleuthérosi: Release
Evlogim Patoras: Second Father

F

Ftiáxe mia porta: Open a door

I

Irémise: Quiet

K

Kapnastís: Disease eater
Kleidóste sto aíma mou: Lock to my blood
Kontá: Close
Krývo: Hide

M

Mágissa: witch
Makrá vlépinta: Ability of a blood witch to see past/future
Mikros: Little one

P

Páfsi: Pause
Paidí: Child
Pigaíno: Go
Prostatévo: Protect

S

Slúga: Servant
Sýnchysi: Confusion

T

Teíchos: Wall
Thanátou: Death bringer, angel of death
Thráfsi: Break

X

Xekleídoma: Unlock

Y

Yperaspízo: Defend
Ýpnos: Sleep

MÖRDERIN

NATALIE CASE

You know who you are. You know what you did.
Thank you, from the bottom of my heart.

CHAPTER 1
FAMILY

I looked up from the book I was studying when I heard footsteps on the stairs. Mom smiled over a tray with a teapot and a couple of cups. We'd been back at Merry's for nearly two weeks while I finished recovering physically. I still tired easily, but Merry had made me a little concoction I could add to my coffee or tea to give me some pep.

I had taken to spending the afternoons in the basement, trying to learn everything I could. While the purges of blood witches in the past centuries had pretty much decimated any books that would teach me how to use those gifts, I wanted to at least get some basic magic under my belt. I hadn't yet graduated to the tomes I had taken from the Kourt, all of which went well beyond my meager knowledge.

"I thought you two could use some afternoon sustenance," Mom said as I cleared a space at the table for the tray. She set it down revealing more than tea, but a plate with sandwiches as well.

She poured the tea and handed a cup to Ciara who sat across from me cutting up herbs she'd gotten from Merry's gardens to brew *something*. She had probably told me what, but I'd been more focused on the spells I was learning for defense and combat. I'd bet things would have gone much better for us if I'd known some of these, and since we didn't know what was coming next, it would be good to learn.

"Thanks." She took half a sandwich and settled back on her stool. She'd been quiet since we came back, but I'd learned that she had only discovered her specific gift at fourteen and that it made her a pariah to her family.

"What book do you have your nose in today?" Mom asked before tipping it aside so she could see. "Oh, yeah, that one is... very dry. There's another one that is probably better for you to start with. That one's all theory, which is nice if you're an academic, but not so much for practical use. I'll see if Merry has a copy."

I put the book down and rubbed my eyes in agreement with her assessment of the book's dry theoretical approach. I'd been reading it for hours and couldn't tell you much about it. "I heard from Cambious this morning," I offered as I took my cup of tea from her. "They found Reyansh's clan, and are staying a few days to help him settle in. Then he said he'd head back to the gate."

"It will do Reyansh good to be back with his people, even if he would have rather stayed with you." She took the only empty stool and poured her own cup of tea. "And Merry thinks she may have found your aunt, Ciara. It looks like you might be related to Thána, on her father's side."

Ciara made a face. "Aunt Greta? She won't want me. Dad's side of the family is very anti-blood witch. They might even be the reason the Brotherhood found us."

My mother frowned deeply. "You can't believe your own family would... do that?"

Ciara shrugged. "Mom thought so. That's why we moved around so much, hoping Dad's side of the family would lose track of us." She chewed for a minute, then swallowed. "Honestly, I'd rather stay where I'm wanted. And Merry has a great book collection. I could learn a lot here."

Mom smiled. "Yes, you could. Since you're nearly eighteen, we probably won't even need to do any legal paperwork to keep you, but I'll have Merry's daughter do some checking."

Peter's family had been easier to find, and his parents had traveled to come take him home. He'd been so happy to see them, and they were beyond grateful that we brought him back to them. They believed he had been killed.

I sipped at my tea, then reached across the table for the tablet Zo had loaned me, swiping the screen to the last thing I'd been looking at. I turned it to Mom. "So, it looks like *Patoras* died of his injures yesterday." When he had been found in the ruins we left behind, his body was covered in third-degree burns, bringing the last of the prophecy to fruition. We found Peter and he helped us find my mother. My blood had spilled when I'd slammed into the torn-up cemetery and now, Patoras had died by phoenix fire, said to be sacred to Apollo.

Mom took the tablet, her eyes scanning the news story. "Good riddance."

There was a lot about the destruction that sat sick in my stomach, the number of men and boys who had died was high among them. Not a single one of the youngest men had survived. We had no idea how many did make it out, but we were fairly certain no one was coming after me, at least for a while. Still, the loss of life was too much to think about.

"Meanwhile," Mom turned to look at me, "I hope you're ready for the madness that will descend on us tomorrow."

I nodded, even though I wasn't sure that what I was could be called ready. Anxious. Nauseous. Sort of terrified? "As much as I can be, I suppose," I said, trying to keep my tone neutral.

"It will be nice to see my brothers and sister," Mom said, "but I worry about the rest of them. I'm hoping they won't be too much for you."

Her hand caressed mine until I pulled it away. "Yeah, me too." I was uncomfortable whenever the word family was used. I'd gone a long time believing I had no family, and now I was being asked to participate in some sort of family reunion. I had no context for how to feel or what to expect. "And they all… know?" I asked, glancing at Ciara before looking Mom in the eyes.

There was a sort of apology there, in her eyes. "At this point, I think the whole family knows that we have a blood witch in the family again."

I licked my lips and swallowed. "How do I… navigate this?" I had spent some time with Zo who had warned me not to let myself be sucked into playing savior, that there were bound to be family members who would want to see me demonstrate my powers, including a few who might be expecting miracles.

"Merry's told everyone to not expect you to be some sort of super-witch," Mom said. "But I'm told that there is at least one who could use your help. He doesn't have long, and the cancer is too far spread for any magic but yours."

I flushed and my stomach sank. I still had no idea how to control those gifts, or if I could rely on them. "I don't want them all staring at me."

Mom smiled sadly. "I know. We'll get through it."

The earthy scent of what Ciara was cutting up smelled strong and reminded me of the inxbane that Cambious had brought me. I found the absence of the big man strange. So much of my life since arriving in California had involved him. I had given up trying to figure out exactly how much time had passed since that first meeting.

The spot in my side where the fence had ripped me up was still tender and the stretch for a book near Ciara's elbow made it twinge. The ache in my shoulder from the gunshot wound made itself known at least once per day as well, but back home, I'd likely still be in the hospital, if I had even survived.

I snorted. Back home, none of this would have happened.

"Stop fussing, you're beautiful."

I snorted and turned to look at her. "You're biased, Mom." My hair was shiny and clean, the curls more defined than I had ever allowed, thanks to some product Mom had given me. Part of me was starting to like the look.

I finger-combed a little more, turning my head to see the side in the mirror. "People have started to arrive," Mom said, touching my arm.

"Lovely," I muttered, my tone only mildly sarcastic.

"Best to get it over with." Mom's hand slid down my arm and into my hand, tugging lightly to get me moving. Voices drifted down the hall as we moved toward the kitchen Merry was positively beaming as she was swarmed by small humans. Mom led me through the kitchen and into a room I had never seen before. It was spacious enough to hold fifty people comfortably. At the moment, there were maybe ten.

"Anna!" Mom let go of my hand and pulled a woman into a hug. She was my height, her hair dark and pulled up to show a graceful neck. She pulled off a soft yellow coat, and handed it off to a man beside her as she smiled at my mother.

"Alana!"

They hugged like long-lost sisters before my mother pulled me in. "This is Thána, my oldest."

Anna's dark eyes met mine and I held my breath for a moment, unsure how my newfound family would feel about me. Anna smiled and hugged me tightly. "We've been worrying over you for years, Thána. Welcome home."

"Thank you," I managed to say, looking to the man she was with as she touched his arm.

"My husband, Guntar."

He nodded to me, and I returned the gesture. He was the opposite of his wife, his hair so blond it was almost white, his eyes a pale ice blue. "We heard you were injured, Thána. I trust you are recovering?" Guntar said, his accent thick and somewhere between German and Russian, at least to my ears.

I nodded a little uncomfortably. "Better every day." My hand went to my side involuntarily, as if I could feel the scar through my sweater. A door opened on the other side of the room and cold air blew through along with the sound of rain. A crowd of people entered, and my mother left to go greet them.

Over the next half hour, I met an impossible number of relatives that included my mother's siblings and their offspring, various and sundry great aunts and uncles along with third and fourth cousins. I was dizzy with introductions. As Mom settled in with her brothers and sister, I withdrew to the kitchen where Ciara was helping Zo and Merry move the trays and trays of food into the large formal dining room.

Helping them gave me a reprieve from the large group of people who were all far too keen on knowing me. It reminded me of Christmases in foster care, where I was the odd one out and everyone felt the need to make awkward small talk. The table was overfull by the time we were done and Merry went to call everyone in to eat. I grabbed a plate and filled it before the crowd could block me into a corner and took it to the other room.

Ciara joined me, her eyes skipping over the others. "I don't think I've ever seen this many people in one place."

"Unsettling, isn't it?" I asked. "How are you doing?"

She shrugged and picked at her food. "You know… I'm dealing."

I wasn't sure how to talk to her or give her what she needed. An awkward silence fell, until it was broken by a tall, lanky cousin who came and plopped herself on the floor in front of us. I knew I'd been introduced, but her name escaped me. She grinned, clearly reading the loss on my face. "Helen. And you must be Ciara." She balanced her plate on her lap and reached out a hand. Ciara took it with a tight nod.

Helen was the daughter of one of my uncles, I couldn't remember which, somewhere in her early twenties. She wore her hair shaved close on the left side, the rest of it flopped over to the right in a thick blanket of black. "My mom always said that there were no blood witches left, and here I sit with two of them. That is awesome."

"Sure," I replied dryly. "Awesome. As long as you don't count the people who want you dead because of it."

"There is that, for sure," Helen agreed. "But the things you can do! I've been fascinated by blood witches my whole life. Did you know that at one time they were practically revered as gods? And some of them became so powerful that they could raise the dead."

I chuckled a little. "Merry says that's hogswallop, that the patient was declared dead prematurely."

Helen shrugged. "There are stories, not just family stories either. There was a blood witch from Frenko who specialized in curing the blind, back around a thousand years ago."

"Yeah, and she was probably bled to death by the brotherhood as a reward," Ciara said bitterly.

Helen frowned. "I don't know, I'd have to look it up."

"While I appreciate your enthusiasm," I said, "you have to understand that both of us have suffered very recently for being what we are. Not quite ready to embrace the history just yet."

Helen accepted that with a nod. "I can understand that. My family is sick of me talking about it. Even as a kid I'd wished I'd been born one."

Ciara stood abruptly and left the room, leaving Helen gaping after her. "The brotherhood killed the only family that accepted her for who she was," I said softly. "She's alone in this world." Not unlike I had been all those years.

"I didn't mean to upset her."

"I know, just give her some space," I replied. I nibbled on the hot potato dish that Merry had made. Not for the first time, I wished I had her skill in the kitchen.

"So, what about you, then?" Helen asked.

"Me?"

"I hear that you've used your gifts. What is it like?"

I inhaled deeply, not sure how to answer. "Scary. Weird. And not knowing what I am capable of makes it worse." My mind flashed back to the day my father died, how the pain called out to me, begging me to ease the agony, then to the day I had taken the illness from my sister. I had been led by instinct. The one book I had on blood witch magic said I shouldn't have been able to do it at that age. But those limitations didn't seem to apply to me. "Mostly just instinct."

"Helen, I told you not to bother Thána," a voice said from the doorway. I looked up to find Uncle Christophe which meant Helen was Emily's sister. "She's been dying to talk to you since we found out you were here. Please forgive her impertinence."

I smiled a little. "It's okay. I like her curiosity. It's a refreshing change from people wanting to kill me." I stood to take my plate to the kitchen, hoping to find a quieter spot to hide out without actually going into hiding. Two boys went running and slid past me on the tile floor, laughing. I moved back out of the way, which was when I nearly stepped on a third boy I hadn't seen behind me.

He was maybe thirteen, but small for his age and painfully thin. His face was pale and his eyes dark. I apologized and his gaze met mine. I could instantly tell he wasn't well. Something inside pushed me toward him. "Are you okay?"

"Devin, there you are." A woman only slightly younger than me bustled up to the boy. "I told you not to wander off."

"He's okay," I said, touching his shoulder. The sense of disease intensified. I wanted to help him. More than that, I knew that I could help him. "Do you..." I pressed my lips together as she looked up at me. "You're Adria, right?" My mind was climbing back through introductions and trying to place her in the family tree, but this was definitely the boy Mom had told me needed my gifts.

She flushed a little, pushing red-brown bangs out of her eyes. "Yes, and this is my son, Devin."

"Is he... he is sick?"

Her eyes were wide, and she nodded. "Yes, you can tell?"

"I can smell it." I bent so that I could look into his eyes. "I think I could help, if you'd let me?"

Adria was holding her breath, a spark of hope in her eyes. I was suddenly aware of other eyes as well. "But how about we go someplace quieter?" Adria nodded and followed me as I led the way upstairs to the bedroom I had claimed as my own.

I closed the door on the others that had followed us. I did not want an audience. "I'm not promising anything," I said cautiously. "I've only done this a few times."

"Anything. The doctors cannot cure it."

I nodded and gestured toward my bed. "Why don't you sit down here, Devin, and I'll try to explain what I'm going to do." Adria pulled him into her lap, and I sat next to them. "Okay, Devin. I'm going to put my lips on your lips, kind of like a kiss, but I need you to keep your mouth open a little bit, okay?" His eyes grew wide, but he nodded. "Then I'm going to take a deep breath, and your body should let me pull the sickness out of you."

"Will it hurt?" he asked, his voice barely above a squeak.

"I don't know, I've never asked anyone what it felt like."

"What happens to it?"

"What, the sickness?" I asked. He nodded. "Well, I take it from you and then I get rid of it."

"You won't get sick?"

I shook my head. "Do you want to give it a try?"

He looked up at his mother, then back to me. He nodded and I offered him a smile. "Okay open your mouth just a little. Good." I set one hand on his cheek and guided his head back, then leaned in, barely touching my lips to his. I took a second to center and reached inside myself for that spark of magic. The cancer was riddled throughout his small frame, I could almost see it attached to his organs and even along his ribcage. I thought for a moment it might fight me, but as I breathed in, it leaped out of him, as though it had been waiting there for someone to come for it.

I swallowed and took a second breath, then a third, gulping it down as fast as it would rise up out of him. It was more than I had ever attempted, and by the time I could no longer sense the disease, I was starting to gag. I dashed out the door and across the hall into the bathroom, dropping to my knees as the cancer came roaring back out of me.

My head was filled with white noise as I vomited up black masses of gunk, retching until my stomach hurt. When I could finally raise my head, I felt drained and as I stood up, my body began the other process for ridding itself of the illness I had taken from Devin. I took my time getting cleaned up and brushing my teeth to get rid of the terrible taste. I was only shaking a little as I opened the door, just as my mother had been about to knock. I smiled weakly and gestured toward the bedroom. Her arm slipped around me, and she helped me to the bed.

"Are you okay?" she asked as I sat gingerly.

"I will be. How is Devin?"

"A little shaky, but already so much better. Adria's got him out there eating."

"Good, he needs it. He's also probably going to need a good night's sleep."

"So do you." She patted the bed to encourage me to lay down. "I'll let everyone know that you're okay, but that you need some rest."

CHAPTER 2
BACK TO BASICS

"Okay, so what you're saying is that there are portals, like ours, that are created and some that are naturally occurring?" I said, squinting at the words in the book on the table in front of me.

"Yes, exactly," my mother agreed.

"And they go to different places?"

She nodded. "This is the list of the known portals here that terminate in your world."

There were twenty or so places listed, with the locations on this world to the left and their corresponding locations on my world to the right. "But Daria is on a completely different world?"

Mom smiled and reached across to turn the page. "Yes, there are only two known portals between here and there, however. The one was only documented when I came back through it."

"Cambious told me that they are often in out-of-the-way places, sort of making you work to get to them?"

She nodded again. "Most of them are, yes. Then there's the world where Daria is right now. They have a central location where eight portals all converge from eight different worlds."

"Okay. I can accept that. I think." I rubbed my eyes and sorted through the information I had already absorbed. Mom was ready to leave to go to Daria, but she wanted me to have a little more than theoretical knowledge. "So, the magic that creates these portals is what, exactly?"

She paced around me before coming back to the book on the table. "Well, it depends on the witches that cast it, largely. For example, our portal was created with a combination of opening, traveling, and destination magic several centuries ago. It took a coven of thirteen here, plus three on the other side."

"That must have been fun to coordinate," I muttered, already rejecting the idea of the math that would have been involved. "What makes the natural ones?" I could feel myself frowning and rubbed a hand over my forehead.

"No one knows, exactly. They do seem to happen near other mystical places, liminal spaces."

"Like a cave or something?"

Mom smiled. "Yes. Caves, tree corridors, even volcanoes, or stone arches."

To complicate matters, there was also the fact that some portals were permanent structures, and some were temporary, and if I was understanding correctly, the magic involved was both intense and draining. Thus, the reason it took so many to complete it.

"So how many worlds are there out there? And are they…different planets? Or… what?"

Mom chuckled. "So many questions. You've always been inquisitive. I'm not sure anyone really knows, but it seems logical to think of them as different planets."

The more I learned the more I was sure that I would never fully understand anything here. "So, this world of Daria's? Are they magic too?"

Mom sorted through the piles of books, taking some of them back to the shelves. "Some. As I understand it though, magic isn't inherent. Some of the natives have the ability to learn to use it, and with that many portals, they've become something of a varied population of different species. Each bringing with them their own values, gifts, and magics."

"Like here? With the dragons and phoenixes and incubi?"

"Not exactly the same. I've met Pixins who look a lot like Native Americans but have no gender. And there are Dealthians, like Habros who are big, but mostly human-looking. Aside from their coloring, of course."

"Oh?" I asked, watching her move around the room tidying things up.

"Most of the native races on that world are shades of aqua and blue."

I felt a bit like I was spinning out of my head. "Did you ever visit any place else? Like, go through other portals?"

She shook her head. "I was pretty content to just stay in Vaneesh, but Daria did a few field trips with her school to a place called Callipha. She and Habros also honeymooned there."

"I promised Merry I would practice those spells she gave me. Got any pointers?" I held up my spell book. I had taken to jotting down new spells with notes about what they did and what I needed to know about them. Merry had been giving me new spells each day to practice.

Mom came back to the table, smiling. "Maybe take those attack spells outside? Unless you want to spend the afternoon cleaning up down here."

"Fair point. What are you up to today?"

She sighed and hitched a thumb toward the stairs. "I am off to pick up the car that will get us to the portal, and then I'll be packing us up."

"We head out tomorrow?" I asked, gathering up some of the supplies I'd been sorting through for my casting practice.

"If you're still up for it."

She'd been keeping a close eye on my healing and stamina because it was a long hike up a mountain to get to the portal that would take us to Daria. If I were honest, I wanted another week to work on my stamina, but she was anxious to get back. "I'm up for it."

We climbed the stairs then, emerging into a kitchen flooded with morning light. "You'll need a jacket."

I rolled my eyes. "Yes, Mom." I kissed her cheek and headed for the backyard where I could throw spells at targets Merry had set up for me. It was weird, this relationship I was building with her. The memories of my early childhood with her set certain emotional attachments that were hard to escape now that I remembered them, and yet here I was just getting to know her as an adult.

I set my book and supplies on the table beside the fire pit and stretched my arms up over my head, twisting at the waist to loosen up. I ran through the basics rapidly as a warm-up to the more complex spells. I tried to practice the entire list of spells I'd learned each day, kind of like spelling practice when I was a kid. The more I used them, the less likely I'd be to forget. I started with those Merry taught me that first day: open, close, come, go, and the others, about twenty in all. Most were simple things, good for day-to-day stuff, but of little use in the fight for your life when facing other magic users.

I went to the defensive spells then, starting with *prostatévo* and *yperaspízo*, both of which were quick means to block or push away an attack, but only in the direction they are cast. Next, I tried *teíchos*, which took me a few tries to get right. Both arms pushed out to the sides, hands upright. A wall of power slammed up when I finally got it correct, in a square around me. It would hold as long as I kept it powered, protecting me from just about any magic attack. Similar to basic wards, but only for as long as the witch could hold the spell.

I turned to my book then, flipping pages until I found the list of more offensive spells. "*Spróxte.*" I made the corresponding pushing motion with one hand, aiming it at the nearest wooden targets at the other end of the yard. The target moved back a few inches. The second time, I used both hands and it toppled over backward. Merry had taught me that it was more about my will than the words or gestures. The words help focus the will, and the gesture gave it direction. I could only imagine how much stronger my will would be if I needed to use it to save myself.

That led me to the next couple of spells which were more than one word and gesture. The first two I had successfully cast several times. One was akin to actually punching someone while the second combined projected confusion with a cloaking spell. That one would have been handy to have in my arsenal at the Kourt.

The new spells were meant to be physical, and dangerous. The first would cast fire out of my hands, supposedly. I took a solid stance and raised my right hand, pointing it toward the target. With a deep breath, I reached for the magic inside me and murmured the words, barely audible. At first, nothing happened. There was a growing warmth in the palm of my hand and when I looked, I had a small ball of fire. I willed it toward the target, and it would have been amazing if I could actually aim.

Instead, it sort of flopped onto the ground at my feet, catching the grass until I stomped it out. There was a spell for that too, I just didn't remember it. On the third try, I hit the target, then had to run to douse the fire. I set the target back onto its feet and shifted it back to its original position.

After checking my list, I set myself up for the next spell. It was meant to break whatever you were casting at, like a locked door or what-have-you. Conceivably, it could break bones, or so Merry had said. It had limited applications if stealth was important because Merry said that it made a lot of noise, but it was a good one to learn. I picked up the stick Merry had told me I would need and held it up, looking past it to the target. Trying to focus on both points was harder than I had imagined, and I wasn't entirely sure I understood how to throw the energy from the stick to the target.

My first attempt sent the unbroken stick flying. The second resulted in a broken stick. I was forced to stop trying when I ran out of sticks to break. At least I was starting to feel the energy created when the stick snapped. I was also feeling the strain of the work. I had learned that magic was about energy and in order to use magic we needed to transfer that energy, whether we took it from an action, like breaking the stick, or from our own bodies.

Which was why it was so draining.

I suppressed a yawn and gathered my things to go back into the house. Mom was anxious to get moving, which meant that if I was going to get anything more out of Merry before we left, I needed to pin her down.

My first thought, as we parked the car in a remote and difficult-to-find spot on the side of a mountain, was that I wasn't sure I had a ten-mile hike in me. I'd been imagining a nice, gentle walk in the woods, but gazing up at our destination, my thighs were already complaining in advance.

Mom smiled at me over the roof of the car. "It's not that bad."

I shrugged. "I didn't say anything."

"I can see it on your face. Daria wasn't a fan either."

I circled to the trunk to pull out my pack. It was a proper backpacking-style pack, complete with a rolled-up, magic bedroll that Mom hadn't shown me how to use yet. I shrugged it on and took a look around. "Is the car going to be safe here?" I asked.

"It will be fine." She locked the car as I closed the trunk and we turned to survey the mountain.

We were already deep into the Amerin mountain range that ran along the southern end of Spítia, my mother's homeland. It had been almost three weeks since our spectacular escape from the Mauno Kourt and the magic-augmented surgery that had saved my life.

Merry had been thrilled to have students in the house that she could teach, and she had enthusiastically answered my million and one questions, shown me how to use spells, and gave me a crash course in potion making, which was one of her specialties. I'd hardly slept, using Merry's potion to keep myself awake and alert. It was better than coffee, and I don't say that lightly. I'd had an illicit affair with coffee since my teens.

"Okay, so where is this trail?" I asked as we started toward the trees.

"It isn't a trail so much as it is a… let's call it a path." She smiled. "Don't worry, Thána. I know where we're going."

I was skeptical, but I followed her. The ground was fairly level and the trees around us were a mix of what I took to be maple, or maple adjacent, and some sort of evergreen. It was hard to be certain here. So many things were just like home, but most of the time they were just off from what I saw as normal. Like the apples that Merry grew on a tree in her yard. They look just like nice Fuji apples until you bite into one. Then it's all purple flesh and tasting of blueberries. Delicious, but off-putting the first few times I tried one.

After a half mile or so, our path turned west and started to climb. Here and there the ground showed signs of an actual path; leaves and grass worn down to dirt from feet that had trampled this way over time, but much of it was only a hint of that, the grass sparse and thin. As we continued climbing, the high canopy of leaves became a ceiling and despite the early afternoon sunshine, the path we walked grew dim.

"So why were you all the way up here?" I asked a little breathlessly as we paused by a fallen tree to rest. I took the canteen from my hip and took a big swig of water.

"There's a cabin further west where I was hoping Daria and I could spend the summer. It belonged to a friend's family when I was a girl. I thought it might keep the Brotherhood off our trail."

"And this portal just... happened to be what you found first?"

She shrugged. "It seems to be one of the naturally occurring ones, though the only naturally occurring portals I'd ever known about before this one went to your world. Of course, I knew about man-made portals opening into other places, but never even considered that a natural one might."

"So how far do we have to go?" I asked, looking up the slope.

She turned and let her gaze sweep the trees. "A couple of hours to the place we'll camp tonight. Tomorrow around noon should put us at the portal."

I nodded, still skeptical about the magic sleeping bag and lack of tent, since it was still technically winter, and even here in the middle of the afternoon, it was cool. It would turn positively cold as the sun went down.

In the weeks since we had somehow pulled off the most impossible rescue, I had gotten the chance to get to know the mother who had loved me enough to hide me away. She took any memory of my life before that day and abandoned me to a life without her in a last-ditch attempt to keep me safe.

With my memory of her finally restored, I was glad to discover that despite being a prisoner of a religious cult for two years, Alana Alizon was much the same woman as she was in my memory of her. Her smile was warm and comforting and her voice stilled some need in me that I couldn't even name.

Her laugh was richer than I remembered, and her hair had lost the glossy black of her youth, faded now into a mix of gray and silver and white that I thought made her even more beautiful. There were lines around her eyes and deeper lines between them. Her deep blue eyes sparkled whenever she spoke of my sister Daria, Daria's son Kota, or my father.

She was a very tactile person though, something I was struggling to get used to. Having spent eight years of my life in foster care, I had developed an aversion to being held or even touched in some cases. Not due to anything bad happening, but none of the foster families I stayed with were physically affectionate. It rubbed off and kind of became my default over the years.

Still, she was fond of casual touch, of a hand on my arm and spontaneous hugging, and I was trying to cope with it. To be fair, she caught on pretty quickly and had curbed her need to constantly touch me. Maybe she was just reassuring herself that I was actually there.

"Hey, you ready to keep moving?" Mom asked, pulling me from my thoughts.

"Sure, lead on." I leveraged myself up off the log after reattaching my canteen to my belt. Several hours later, we emerged from the trees to find a lake, with flat grassy land for camping on and there was even a fire ring already built.

We shrugged off our packs and Mom sent me back into the woods to forage for firewood. By the time I came back with an armful of dry wood, she had cleared a good 20-foot circle around the fire ring and was setting up her new set of ward stones. "We'll need some bigger logs to get us through the night," she said without looking up.

"Okay. I saw some dead stuff, but it's all too big to carry."

She looked up then. "The word is *tomí*. Center, touch the wood where you want to cut it, and say tomí."

I headed back into the tree line and angled toward where I had seen the downed branches. The whole tree was dead, but most of it was still standing. I circled the pile of branches, looking for ones that were substantial, but that I could still carry, and finally pulled one branch thicker than my calf from the pile. I took a moment to breathe in slowly and let it out just as slowly, reaching inside me for the spot at my center that Merry had taught me was the place my magic lived. I set my hand on the wood and murmured the word.

Under my hand, the wood cracked and split cleanly. I grinned to myself and moved my hand further up the branch and repeated the spell twice more until I had six decent-sized pieces of wood.

I had a harder time stacking it all so I could carry it than I did cutting it, but eventually, I got it all up and headed back to my mother. She had a tidy fire going with the wood I had already brought back, and her ward stones looked ready to deploy. The field generated around the small circle of stones had a vague red tint to it, so it had to be some variation I had yet to learn. Most of the ones I knew tilted toward blues or greens.

She had food prepped to cook, the cast iron frying pan sat on the stones around the fire ring, filled with a fish. "I was gone ten minutes," I said as I stacked the wood a few feet from the fire. "How have you already caught and cleaned a fish? You didn't even pack a fishing pole."

She chuckled. "I'll teach you how to call them to you. First, let's get our warding up."

I moved toward her, bending down to take the first pair as she took the opposite pair. We moved away from each other toward the places she had already marked. We repeated the steps for the rest of the pairs, stretching out the field until it formed a dome barely over our heads. "There, that should help us stay warm," Mom said, moving back to the fire.

CHAPTER 3
CAMP

The fire ring was dead center of the circle covered by the wards, and I could already feel the heat generated by the fire bouncing off the wards and filling the air inside with warmth. Mom squatted next to her pack and pulled out a metal grill, unfolded its legs and put it over the fire.

The frying pan went on the grill and she sat back, her face the picture of satisfaction. Even with everything I had learned since Finneas Connor had appeared in my life and changed everything, I could still be surprised. My mother had insisted on doing the packing, and while I knew she had used some form of magic, I was still amazed at how much she had fit into the two packs.

I pulled the magic sleeping bag off my pack and unrolled it. It didn't look a whole lot different than any other sleeping bag I had ever seen. I shook it out and picked a spot far enough from the fire that if it sparked, it shouldn't set me ablaze and spread it out.

Mom looked up from where she was seated beside the fire, cutting up onions and carrots, or what looked like onions and carrots. "Okay, put your hand on the middle of the bedroll, center, and set the intention in your mind for it to inflate. The word is *fouskóno*."

I did as instructed, closing my eyes and trying to picture what the sleeping bag was supposed to look like when it was inflated, and I said the word almost inaudibly. Merry had been teaching me that a practiced witch didn't even need to speak the words, but I wasn't all the way there yet. Under my hand, there was movement and I stepped back as I opened my eyes. Below the sleeping bag there was… well, it was almost a mattress. I put my hand on it, testing the firmness. It was firm enough to hold me and

I turned to sit, marveling again at the combination of magic and technology my mother's world had to offer.

As I sat, my body began to make me aware that it was not a fan of the day's walking. My legs were aching and my feet pounding inside my hiking boots. My hips were even complaining, particularly on the side that recently had wrought iron shoved into it. The injury could have taken my life, if not for a doctor who was also a witch. Still, it would ache when I overdid it with physical labor, or when I got cold. It would start there, where the metal had pierced my side, then spread up toward my shoulder and down toward my hip.

"Are you warm enough?" Mom asked as if she could hear my internal dialog. So far, I was pretty sure she couldn't actually do that, but she sometimes made me wonder.

"Yeah, I'm good." It was weird, getting to know my mother as an adult. All my memories of her were either from before my tenth birthday or from the last few weeks. That twenty-two-year gap sometimes sat between us like a stone. There was still some lingering anger in the deep, dark places where I shoved emotion that I didn't want to acknowledge or deal with. It fit in right beside my simmering self-doubt and the strange feeling when I discovered Cambious had found other sources for feeding.

I untied my boots and loosened them up to give my feet some room to swell. The smell of the onions cooking filled the air around me as Mom spooned the melted butter and vegetables over the fish, making room in the pan for the delicious, potato-like things that Merry called *patátí*. The taste was something similar to a cross between a regular gold potato and a yam, with a touch of peppery flavor. They cooked faster than either a potato or a yam, their orange-red flesh absorbing heat in a way I had never seen.

But then, I was no kitchen witch. My meals were often something I could throw into the microwave. Mom seemed to be nearly at home in the kitchen as Merry was. Or, in this case, she was at home over an open fire. I yawned, suddenly exhausted. Not surprising really. The day was more exercise than I'd had in years, and I was only three weeks out from nearly dying.

Above us, the skies were getting dark. If the food wasn't done soon, I was going to be asleep before it was ready. Again, as if reading my thoughts, Mom handed me a plate. It was a light wood, she had told me what kind, but I'd forgotten. As I started eating, she inflated her bedroll and situated it so that our heads would be close together. We were quiet as we ate, and I could feel the exhaustion pulling on me. Of course, that exhaustion was not just from the outdoor exercise. All the spell work and lack of sleep were catching up to me now that I was away from Merry's kitchen and her supply of herbs to brew my little stay-awake potion.

I finished the food on my plate, and murmured, "*Kathárise*" over it, watching the remaining food bits vanish. That was one spell I had found to be super handy. I set the plate aside because I didn't have the energy to return it to the pack.

Unzipping my sleeping bag, I slipped my feet out of my shoes and climbed in, leaving it open because I needed to be able to get out fast. I hated the feeling of being zipped in. It was too constricting. I was vaguely aware of my mother moving around, cleaning up, before she set two of the bigger logs onto the fire. She stirred the coals to be sure they caught, then she too was slipping into her sleeping bag and silence fell within the wards.

I woke early, with sunlight just starting to trade out the deep black of the skies for a dark crimson that would fade to orange. The dome of our wards had kept most of the cold out, but a chill hung in the air as I stuck my feet into my boots. The fire had burned down to a half-scorched log and an ash-covered bed of hot coals. I took one of the sticks from the pile and rolled the log to the side, then stirred up the coals before feeding some kindling into them. It took a bit of coaxing to get the fire burning again, but I had a tidy little flame I could build on.

By the time I could roll the half-burned log back into the fire, my stomach was rumbling, and I really wanted some coffee. Fortunately, Mom had foreseen my needs and packed a small percolator and some grounds. I moved around our warded space as quietly as I could, letting her sleep as I dug into my pack, coming out with the silicone pouch filled with a smaller pouch holding my coffee and a package of filters.

To get water, I had to dismiss the wards and untie the percolator from the outside of my pack. By the time I'd made it down to the lake and back with water, Mom was stretching and sitting up. I smiled my good morning to her and set the cooking rack over the fire before taking the percolator and coffee supplies to my bed.

"You know how that works?" Mom asked, her tone a little sassy.

I shot her a look. "I think I can manage to make coffee, thanks. Breakfast is on you though."

She stood up, turning her torso to work out the kinks before she sighed. "I'm going to go relieve my bladder. I'll start breakfast after."

It wasn't all that different from our mornings while we were staying with Merry. I was usually up first, made coffee, and settled down with whatever book I had decided to explore that morning. Mom would join me soon after and either she or Merry would make breakfast for the four of us, because inevitably, Ciara would stumble down the stairs, drawn by the smell of coffee.

When Mom got back from her duck into the woods, I made my own trip out to relieve myself. When I returned, Mom handed me my wooden plate with thick porridge on it, smelling of cinnamon and raisins. I was jealous, if I'm being honest, of the ability she had to just make food happen. Thus far my attempts to use magic in my cooking had resulted in some pretty spectacular messes and ruined food. I figured I was better off sticking to things I could put in the microwave.

The percolator was just finishing, so I untied my cup from my pack, grabbed hers, then went to pour the coffee. She murmured her thanks and set aside her plate of porridge to bring the coffee cup to her face. Closing her eyes, she breathed in to savor the smell. She could rib me all she wanted about my love affair with coffee. I could give it right back to her. Still, I had to admit it smelled wonderful. Merry only kept the good stuff on hand. It was grown on some island in the Adria sea, and it was some of the best-tasting coffee I'd ever had.

I settled in with the coffee and porridge, my thoughts on the day ahead. We had another day of hiking to get to the portal, which would deposit us in a place with a name that translated to something like Portal Park. From there, we had to make our way to my sister's house, some four miles away.

The porridge was made from some local grain, similar to oatmeal, but with a taste that leaned toward quinoa. Mom had sweetened it a little and added cinnamon, just like she used to do with my oatmeal. It was the kind of meal you needed if you were planning to climb a mountain, hearty and stick-to-your-ribs food, as one of my foster mothers used to say.

We finished eating as the skies grew lighter, the blacks much bluer than they had been. I took to cleaning and repacking everything while Mom brushed out and braided her hair. She had contemplated getting it cut, but in the end had decided that the growth from two years in captivity was a reminder of her strength, so she let it go. Most of the time, she kept it braided and pinned up.

My hair had grown too, though it was hard to tell as it had completely reverted to its natural state. I had decided to embrace the curls, even if they took work to maintain. From my pack, I dug out my comb and a tube of product Merry had made up for me. I squeezed out a nickel-sized dollop of the stuff and rubbed my hands together before applying it to my hair, combing it through with my fingers, and then the comb. The product helped to keep the humidity from turning my hair into the equivalent of black dandelion fluff and gave my curls a glorious shine that no salon had ever managed.

When we were both done with our respective grooming routines, we went about striking the camp. I dumped the coffee grounds onto the remains of the fire, then took the filter and percolator down to the lake. The filter was good for three or four pots, or so Merry had told me, just rinse it, dry it, and use it again. I rinsed both the filter and the pot, then filled the pot with water and brought it back to dump on the fire. With the filter laying on my hand, I murmured, "Stegnós," and watched it dry on my skin.

Mom showed me the valve on the side of my bed, and I opened it. Air whooshed out and the whole thing began deflating, but slowly. I couldn't see how I was going to get it rolled up tight enough to tie back onto my backpack. Mom laid her hand flat on top of hers and said, "*Kylíste sfichtá."* With a snap, all the air seemed to deflate as if someone had vacuumed it out, and the whole thing rolled up tight as could be.

I followed her lead and tied the roll to my pack before hefting the whole thing up and onto my back. "Lead on, Mother Dearest," I said with a smirk.

She rolled her eyes and pointed into the trees opposite the ones we had come through to get to our camping spot. The sun had started to warm the air, even if it did seem to be stuck on the horizon, hovering, and watching us leave the lake.

Under the cover of the trees, it was chilly, even with the exertion of the fairly steep climb. We paused for water a few hours later. My thighs were complaining enough that I knew better than to sit down. I might never get back up again. I leaned against a tree and sipped from my canteen. "So, Mom," I said, "what kind of reunion are we expecting?"

She cracked her neck and shook her head. "Honestly, I don't know. Daria was pretty angry with me when I left, and it's been a long time."

"You said two and a half years, right?"

She nodded. "More or less, I think. The time differences confuse me."

I could understand that, even with the conversion model that Merry gave me, I wasn't sure how long ago California was. "So, Daria was angry at you for leaving because she saw what would happen?"

"Not in specifics," Mom replied. "That's the problem with that particular gift. It's all abstracts and emotions. She knew that my leaving would be a tipping point of some kind, and that bad things would happen, but even she didn't know exactly what."

"But we assume she meant that whole business with the Brotherhood?"

"I'm not sure what else it could have meant."

Neither did I, honestly, but the closer we got to the portal, the more anxious I was getting. She gestured onward and I nodded. I wasn't sure what I had to be nervous about, aside from the fact that I would soon be meeting the sister I hadn't seen in twenty-two years, plus her husband and kid. "Daria's husband... what's he like?" I asked as we resumed our hiking.

She considered the question for a moment. "He's a Dealthian, from one of the Dealth underground cities."

"Which tells me exactly nothing," I said straight-faced.

"Right. Um... the closest approximation I can think of would be dwarves? Though Dealthan's are not short. In fact, Habros is over six feet tall. They are miners though, and most of them who move aboveground work in the financial systems, at least in Vaneesh. To be honest, I don't know much about the other countries. There were some tensions with a country south of Vaneesh before I left, and there were some internal groups that wanted the government to curb some of the immigration from other worlds, but for the most part, Vaneesh embraces the differences in the people who settle there."

"So Habros is a banker?" I asked.

"High-level broker," Mom corrected. "Daria met him through a mutual friend, a Pixin named Xen."

I tucked that information away, including a note-to-self to ask what a Pixin was. This was at least the second time my mother had mentioned them. "What does Daria do?"

"She runs a small shop selling magical plants, potions... that sort of thing. She gets that from your father as well. She can get anything to grow anywhere. Though for a while she considered joining the Vaneesh military. Right out of high school they were recruiting her heavily. Like your father's mother, Daria's got some heavy-duty defensive skills. She even saved your life once."

So many questions circled my head, and I wasn't sure which one to chase after. "When?" I asked finally.

"Oh, you were nine, I think, and we were in Atlanta when a Brotherhood spy narrowed in on us. Daria saw him before I did and instinctively threw *prostatévo* at him. I'd never seen her use it before then, but it was one of the strongest I had ever seen. Beat yours hands down. As she got older and began actual study, she became capable of so much more."

"So why didn't she go into the military?" I asked.

"By then she had met Habros and they were contemplating marriage. Habros wasn't too hot on the idea of her being deployed for months on end. So, she turned them down and raised the capital to buy some property and opened her shop."

Daria sounded like someone I'd really like to know, but I was still nervous about meeting her again after all this time. That thought sat in my head as we hiked. I wanted to know so much more about this place we were heading, but Mom had said she didn't know much about any of the countries outside of Vaneesh, where she had settled with Daria some twenty years before.

I did know that they had made friends in the government, friends powerful enough to protect them when the odd Brotherhood thug showed up looking for them. "What about you?" I asked as we paused by a creek to refill canteens.

"What about me?" Mom asked, looking up from where she squatted by the water.

"What did you do there?"

"Well, in the early days I worked in the Office of Magic Permits and Regulations."

"They have regulations and permits for magic?"

"Depends on what kind and what it's being used for." She stood, capping her canteen and attaching it to her belt. "In Vaneesh, we human witches are a minority. Most of our workings are not under the jurisdiction of the Office. But other races and their magic is. And if we wanted to do something big, like say build a house or clear a lot of trees and rocks, we need a permit. And medicine. If you're practicing magical medicine, you need a permit." She turned to me. "I'm going to have to check on their laws for you. Not sure where blood witches fall on that spectrum."

Somehow, I found it unsettling that I might have to tell the government about my ability, especially when I didn't really have control of it or understand completely how it worked.

We resumed walking. It was starting to warm up as we got closer to noon. "Not far now," Mom said, pointing up to a spot where the trees gave way to rocks.

"I still can't believe you found this by accident." It was getting harder to talk and walk at the same time as the air around us thinned.

"We got turned around back there where that fallen tree was. We were supposed to go left and instead we went right. The cabin we were aiming for is about a mile that way." She pointed off to the south. "I'd realized we were going the wrong way just before I saw the portal."

We hiked in silence until we were free of the tree line, stopping for a moment to sip water and catch our breath. "That boulder there." Mom pointed to a large boulder about fifty feet away. I couldn't see the portal from my position, but I believed her.

"Well then, shall we?" I said, putting my canteen back on my belt.

She smiled and we set off, circling the boulder until I could see the portal. Unlike the one at home, there was no door, just a jagged rectangle in the rock. Through the hole appeared a fairly desolate place, a sort of ring of rocks with portals, and beyond them a gray sort of nothing.

Beside me, Mom was frowning. "What's wrong?" I asked.

She leaned closer to the portal. "I'm not sure. That should be a park filled with flowers and grass."

"Do portals ever... change destinations?"

She shook her head. "Maybe there was a firestorm, they don't usually strike inland though." She put a hand on the rock and was about to step through when I touched her arm.

"Reality check. Are you sure you want to go through without knowing what happened?"

She shrugged. "I want to get back to Daria. And the only way to do that is to go through this doorway."

I nodded. She was not wrong. Unless we could gather up a coven of sufficiently powerful witches to force a new portal open come Beltane. And how that was an actual sentence I strung together in my brain was just a little mystifying. Less than a year before, my reality was completely different from this. "Okay. Then we go."

CHAPTER 4
PORTALS

Mom ducked and stepped through, snagging my nearest hand, though whether it was to encourage me, or for her own fortitude, I couldn't be sure. I shivered a little as I passed through the portal and set my foot onto the soil of yet another world I had never known existed. Idly I wondered how many of these there were… how many portals, how many worlds.

Beneath our feet, the ground crunched, and I bent down to examine the blackened remains of plants. It had the crunch of being frozen but the grass was black and scarred as if from fire. I had no idea what would cause the effect. I stood to get a better look around me. The skies were a dull gray with heavy black clouds that threatened us with rain. Around us, the boulders and rocks formed a circle of sorts, the gray of granite with splashes of black, punctuated with eight portals, all doorways to other places. Beyond the rocks there were trees, though they, like the grass, looked burned, the limbs twisted together and devoid of leaves.

In several places, the circle of boulders was dissected by dirt paths leading toward the trees. Mom dropped my hand and turned, her eyes scanning around us, her mouth open as she took in the destruction. She pointed toward one of the paths and hurried toward it. I followed, still trying to discern if anything I was seeing was normal. The thought of normal *fled* as we entered the trees and got a look at what lay beyond them.

The skyline that greeted us was broken and desolate. Buildings hulked in the half-light, ragged against the gray sky, as if their tops had been ripped off by some rampaging monster.

"Mom? Is that normal?" I pointed to one of the nearer buildings which seemed to be crumbling before our eyes.

"No. I… it wasn't like this…"

Okay, I had figured that much already. We kept walking toward what I thought must have been a street at some point but was now a stretch of broken concrete blocks and shattered glass dotted with burned-out vehicles. We left the crunchy grass for the crunchy glass and I snagged Mom's hand. She looked like she needed the support. "Daria…"

"We'll find her," I said, not sure it was a promise I could keep. We both stopped dead between two blackened vehicles. The smell of sulfur wafted past us. "What happened here?"

Mom shook her head, turning to look around. There wasn't another person to be seen, human or otherwise. "Okay, let's start with what we know. How do we get from here to Daria's?" I asked, tugging on her hand to get her to look at me. "Mom, focus. I need you here with me."

She nodded, though her eyes still looked haunted. "I'm here. It's going to be a hike."

"Good thing we came prepared for that." I smiled, though it wasn't my most reassuring.

Mom pointed up the street from where we stood. The road had been wide, but all that remained traversable was the center, the sides crowded with debris. We had to pick our way over and around the detritus of a city that lay in ruins; a city that only two and a half years before had been a vibrant, thriving home to hundreds of thousands of beings.

The buildings that lined the street had been stores or businesses, judging by what remained. Broken mannequins, most of which looked more or less human, lay amid dirty clothing and glass. Metal bars were twisted and charred.

It reminded me of a post-apocalyptic movie. We walked in silence, and silence was all that greeted us in return. I could feel my mother's growing fear. It wasn't helped by the darkness sinking in around us as the clouds drew closer. We were going to get wet.

We climbed up a hill and paused at the top to catch our breath. "We won't get there before this rain hits," Mom said. "We should find a place we can make secure and stop until morning."

I was not feeling very secure at all at that moment, but I kept the feeling to myself. "We should be able to find something in one of these buildings," I offered, eyeing the advance of black clouds. Light split the sky and beneath us the ground rumbled, nearly knocking me off my feet. The first drops of rain hit near me, smelling of ozone and sulfur.

"That's not rain!" Mom shouted, already starting to run for cover. Great, now I had to worry about acid rain, or worse, too. We moved quickly, but the clouds seemed to be keeping pace with us.

Mom jumped into a broken display window, with me just steps behind her. Rain found my skin before I reached shelter, an icy burn, as if I'd been hit with freon or something. I yelped and leaped for cover. As the wind picked up, we pulled deeper into the store, ending up behind what I assumed had been the sales counter.

Once we were relatively safe, I turned my hand up so I could see the skin where the rain had hit. There was a blister forming and the skin around it was angry and red. Mom shrugged out of her pack and opened a front pocket to pull out her first aid kit, but she could only stare at it for a long moment. "I'm not sure how to treat it," she admitted, looking up at me.

I likewise shimmied out of my pack before looking into her kit. "It's sharp and so cold that it's burned me, so water to flush it, then bandage it to keep it clean, I guess."

She nodded and pulled the canteen from her belt. I held my hand out away from our packs so she could pour the water over the burn. I hissed as the liquid rushed over my skin, but instead of helping, it only caused more blisters to form. I yanked my hand away. "Okay, not that." I instinctively blew on the skin to ease the sensation of burning as it spread.

The only other idea I had was one I wasn't sure would work. The theory on self-healing was filled with contradictions, but I pulled my knife from my back pocket and cut a slice across the palm of my other hand before clamping it over the blisters.

"Thána!" My mother reached for me, but I covered the blisters, working at not screaming in pain as hot blood went to work thawing the icy burn. When the burning sensation eased, I lifted my hand. The blisters had stopped spreading. The skin was still red, and under the blisters, it looked black. I couldn't tell if it was just the heat of my blood or if being the blood of a blood witch had done the trick.

Mom immediately took my cut hand and started to treat it, wiping it clean before smearing some of that magic ointment over the cut and winding gauze around my hand. "Did you know that would work?" she asked as she took my blistered hand to carefully wipe the blood away.

"Nope, but I was out of other ideas," I said.

Lightning strikes split the skies and thunderclaps loud enough to wake the dead shook our shelter. "Well, whatever caused all of this damage clearly wiped the place out. Was it this rain, do you think?"

She shrugged. "Not by itself. I mean, that rain isn't hurting the buildings."

True enough, though the rain was slamming into the ground in a pretty good attempt to drill down to hell, the ground didn't yield. "Well, it might explain the lack of people," I offered, pulling out my flashlight to get a better look at the damage on my hand.

"I can't tell if this is magic… or something else." She looked distressed and I could only imagine she was worrying about Daria and her family.

It was hard to tell, huddling there in the destroyed store, just how far the damage went, or whether we'd find the rest of the world out there unchanged outside of the city center. My gut told me that what we would find though was even more devastation. Something bad had happened here.

The rain continued until it was pitch black and we were left alone in a silence so profound it seemed to demand we speak in whispers. In that strange silence, we set about making sure we'd be safe, deploying ward stones set in a configuration that would hide us from prying eyes. We had no idea what dangers awaited us beyond the rain. Our dinner was protein bars washed down with water, and we set up our bedrolls after we'd cleared the space of debris.

I'm not sure I actually slept. I dozed in and out, suddenly aware of my mother's breathing or the wind, and at times certain I heard it raining again. As the skies started to lighten, I extricated myself from my bedroll and dismissed the wards, stumbling away from our little camp to find a place to relieve my very full bladder. I found a spot that looked like it had once been this world's equivalent of a bathroom and the mostly unbroken commode it held.

As I unzipped my jeans, I was reminded that both my hands were injured. In the left, where I had sliced myself open for the blood, there was a dull ache, probably mostly healed from the magic ointment. My right hand though… the blisters had all hardened over and the skin around and under them was black, like the grass. They didn't hurt as much as they had the night before, but I was having trouble using my hand.

It was stiff and felt swollen, even if I didn't see any swelling. My fingers were numb and even the simple task of pulling my pants down was something they didn't seem capable of. I struggled through before making my way back to our cold camp. Mom was still fitfully sleeping, so I turned to the task of packing up my things so I'd be ready to move out once she awoke.

I made my way to the front of the store, stepping out onto the street to look around. There was a weak yellow light in the distance that I took to be the sun. The light wavered and danced along the horizon before being absorbed into the cold gray sky. As before, the street was eerily silent. I came back just as Mom was sitting up and stretching slowly.

We shared a quiet meal of dry granola with raisins, washed down with the lukewarm water from my canteen. "We should get to Daria's inside an hour," Mom said as we got set to go.

"And then what?" I asked as she helped me heft my pack and get it settled on my shoulders. She caught the hand that had been burned by the rain.

"This isn't looking good."

"It doesn't really hurt, just a deep ache." The sky went from the dark gray I was beginning to think was natural for this world to a sort of gray-white, with two bright watery spots, one to the left and one straight ahead of us. "Is that a second sun?" I asked, pointing.

Mom squinted up at the sky. "Actually, that's the sun." She pointed at the other bright object. "That is the closest of the moons. They have three moons. This one is almost always visible."

I'd never really been what you might call a fan of science fiction, or even really studied science beyond what I needed to get through school, but I had a vague knowledge of planets with more than one sun or moon. There was a lot about it that made little sense to me, but I didn't need to understand it to accept it as real. After all, that had pretty much become my life. When this whole crazy mess had started, I hadn't believed in witches either, but there I was.

I was grateful yet again for the medical magic that had spurred the healing of the cut when I flexed my hand. It had become one of my favorite things about this place—that place, seeing as the place we were in was completely different. Who knew what new wonders this world had for me to find?

We were quiet as Mom directed us through a city that had been devastated. The further we moved from the city center, the worse the damage seemed to be. As the commercial streets gave way to residential, there were fewer and fewer buildings left standing.

Mom stopped me with a hand on my arm, her free hand fluttering up to cover an open mouth. There, nestled between two buildings burned to studs stood a small, quaint building, all but untouched by the destruction around it. Over the door was a sign I couldn't read.

"Daria..." Mom left me standing in the street and raced up the steps to pull on the door. It didn't budge. I joined her as she began pounding on it. Through the window, I could see a tidy shop with displays of jars and bottles. A hulking shadow moved through the dim light. The shadow slowly became a man... of sorts.

He bent down to squint out the dusty window, then his eyes widened in surprise and the door opened. Mom rushed in, and he pulled her into a hug that felt a little bit desperate... or maybe it was just the look on his face that made me think that. Eventually, Mom disentangled herself from his huge arms, wiping tears from her face. "Habros, I..." She shook her head and took a deep breath, collecting herself. "Habros, my eldest daughter, Thána."

He nodded his head tightly and moved back to make room for me to enter, then closed the door and threw the lock. He was at least six foot five and built like a boulder. His forearms alone were as big as my thighs and twice as muscled. His skin was vaguely blue, his long hair a pale blond and also vaguely blue as we moved from the shadows of the store and into the light of the hallway. He had a warm, kind face with large eyes that told stories of a weary man. A full beard and mustache hid the lower half of his face and as he tucked a stray strand of hair behind a rather large ear, I noticed his fingers were long and thick.

No one spoke as he led us into a more residential space. We entered a kitchen. Sitting at the table was a young man, tall, but thin, and topped with a shock of red hair. "Grandma?!" The chair knocked over as he raced to reach her, letting her arms fold around him. "I've been so worried!"

Mom put him at arm's length and swept her eyes over him. "Kota look at you. You've grown nearly a *kepke*!"

"You've been gone a long time," Kota said, rolling his eyes.

"So I noticed." My mother turned to me, drawing me closer. "Kota, this is your Aunt Thána."

He nodded his head politely, then returned to his seat, putting the chair back on its feet before sitting. I could all but feel my mother's need to ask about Daria, but something was holding her back. Maybe the look in Habros's eyes.

"What happened here?" I asked when the silence had become more awkward than I was comfortable with.

"War," Habros answered. "War happened." He sighed heavily, then gestured at the table. "Sit, I'll make lunch."

CHAPTER 5
WAR

"We don't have much." His accent was thick and reminded me of Russian. His English was very good, however. Habros set a plate in front of me with some fruit that resembled blackberries and a piece of what I thought was a pita pocket filled with some sort of fish. "Our rations for this month are pretty much gone, so we're down to what we can grow or hunt."

We ate in silence for a few minutes before I found the nerve to open my mouth again. "How long has it been like this?"

"A long time," Habros seemed to sink into himself across from me. "First it was more Kabeshi rhetoric and threats, then Loland joined them. No one knew they had magic workers, not until the first of the bombs hit. They wiped out border towns in days. They had more ground troops than anyone could believe. Everywhere the bombs landed, the fallout lasted weeks. The storms came next. Rain that burns, thunder that can collapse buildings. They have poured so much magic into the city the storms come every night." He gestured toward the outside. "Daria managed to protect us, protect this place, but we couldn't hide forever."

The room was silent as Habros sobbed into his chest. "They took Mom," Kota said softly.

"Who they?" I asked, reaching a hand to touch his.

He pulled back and licked his lips. "Kabeshi shock troops. They took her to one of the camps."

I looked at Mom, but she was as bereft as Habros. "Why? What do they want?"

"To purify Vaneesh of everyone who is not native to our lands, to end the invasion of outworlders and their toxic influence." Habros shook his head. "You're both lucky you weren't spotted getting here, and so far they haven't found any magic user with the power to close the portals. Not that they haven't tried."

I could feel the despair rolling off my mother. I didn't know what to say to make it better, so I lifted my pita sandwich. Habros hissed and reached across the table to take my rain-burned hand. "You need to treat that, before it spreads."

"I used… my magic to stop the burn when it happened."

"Kota, get your mother's kit." He turned my hand to get a better look. "The blisters are filled with an acidic compound. If we don't drain them, they will eat into your body. Left untreated, they could kill you."

"Oh."

His fingers moved over the hardened skin around the blisters. "It isn't bad and doesn't appear to have spread much. We should be able to save the hand."

"Save the hand?" I asked, pulling it away.

"If we can't stop the infection topically, we'll have to amputate to keep it from going systemic."

Kota returned and put a box on the table. Habros opened it and rummaged around, coming out with a knife that looked very sharp and a cloth that he spread out on the table. He tapped it and I assumed he meant that he wanted me to put my hand over it.

"This is going to hurt." He took my hand in his as if we were going to arm wrestle, his grip hard.

I thought I understood the word hurt, but as he set the blade to my skin, I had to redefine the word. I bit down on the scream that tried to escape me, my free hand gripping the table tightly enough to leave marks. Habros peeled off the first layer of hardened skin with the edge of the knife. Underneath was just as black. He looked apologetic as he set the blade against my wound for the second time. As he pulled the third layer off, I couldn't hold back the scream and unconsciously tried to pull free.

Habros kept a firm grip and as he set to it again, the sudden pressure released as the first of the blisters broke and a red-black liquid leaked onto the cloth. Habros scraped until my hand was a raw, red monster and all the black skin was in a pile between us. He pulled a bottle out of the box and thumbed it open, sprinkling a white powder over the wound.

It bubbled and foamed like peroxide would. Habros released his grip and recapped the bottle. "Very lucky it hadn't gone deeper."

Under all the foam, I now had a two-inch-long gash on the outside of my left hand. It no longer felt swollen though, so that was something.

"Let it finish its work, then we can dress it." Habros gathered up the cloth, which I could see was starting to look like Swiss cheese as the acid ate away at it. He stepped out a side door and when he came back, he no longer had the cloth. "I'm not sure how it works, exactly, but it doesn't become toxic until it interacts with flesh. Specifically, human flesh."

"Great." I glanced at my mother. "Why do I keep going places that I'm not wanted?" She didn't appear to hear me. "Mom, are you okay?"

"She knew." Mom shook her head. "Daria knew something bad was going to happen. I didn't listen."

"You can't blame yourself. You didn't start a war," I said, then realized I didn't know that for certain. I hadn't been here. Who knew what chain reaction of events set this thing in motion?

"No, she didn't," Habros said. His big hands pulled gauze out of the box then drew my hand toward him. He wrapped the gauze around it and taped it down. "We'll need to check it every few hours, make sure we neutralized all the acid, but it should heal now."

We were all quiet then. Kota and Habros seemed to pull into themselves and I couldn't read my mother's face. To get this far only to have Daria gone must have been painful for her. After a while, Habros shuddered and wiped his eyes. "Kota, best get to your lessons."

Kota nodded and kissed my mother's cheek before disappearing down a hallway. "Mother, your room is as you left it. Thána, let me show you where you can set up."

He led us down the hallway and opened a door that hid a flight of stairs. At the bottom was a cozy family room. There were several doors along the far wall. He opened one and smiled at me. "Consider this room yours for however long you are here."

I lugged my pack into the room. It wasn't big, but it would do. The walls were a dusty blue color, and the bedspread was a deeper blue. There was a small table near the head of the bed and a dresser near the door.

I dropped my pack on the bed and huffed out a breath of frustration. Okay, maybe fear too. My life had always been mundane. Traditional school, a career that paid the bills, and no real excitement before the day that I had met Finneas Connor. Since then? Well, there hadn't been a mundane day in a whole lot of days, however long ago it had been when my world turned inside out. And now I found myself in the middle of yet another conflict that shouldn't have anything to do with me, but which I knew was going to get very personal before we found our way home.

If we ever found our way home.

To calm myself, I spent the next few minutes unpacking. I wasn't carrying a lot in the way of clothes, but I put what I had in the dresser, then arranged my toiletries and such on the top. I propped the pack with its assorted hanging pieces in the corner between the dresser and the wall.

"You okay?"

I turned to look up at my mother, who was leaning on the door frame. "Honestly?" I sighed and sat on the bed. "I'm not sure. What about you?"

Her eyes were red and I wondered if she'd been crying in the few minutes she was in her room. She hugged herself. "I'm scared."

I understood that. "What do we do now?"

She shook her head. "I don't know."

It was a war in a world I knew nothing about. It was safe to say that there wasn't anything we could do. Other than leave. We could conceivably attempt that. Maybe even take my nephew and brother-in-law with us. One look at my mother and I knew that wasn't happening. She still wanted to find Daria.

"Whatever you're thinking, stick a pin in it," I said, standing again. "We have no idea what we walked into, and there is clearly magic happening here that we have no understanding of. It would be suicide to try anything."

She closed her eyes and nodded. "I know. I know. But Daria…"

"Is out of our reach," I responded, taking her hand. "At least for now. Besides, if Habros couldn't save her, what are you and I going to do?"

"Habros isn't a witch," Habros said. Mom turned revealing the large man behind her.

"I'm barely a witch," I countered. "Haven't even been that for very long."

He glanced toward the stairs. "I'm trying to keep Kota strong, but I don't know how much longer it will be before he figures it out."

I frowned, crossing my arms. "Figures what out?"

"What they're doing to outworlders who have magic, gifts. Especially ones we can't replicate."

"Like Daria." My mother licked her lips and drew me close. "Some magic can be learned, some is there inside you when you are born, like your blood magic. This world had no magic of its own before the first outworlders arrived."

This was sounding suspiciously like a battle I'd already fought once. I swallowed around the lump that was suddenly filling the back of my throat. "So, what is it they're doing?"

He seemed to crumple, leaning against the wall behind him. "I've heard rumors about the experiments, torture." He closed his eyes. "Mind control."

"Is there no one left of the Vaneeshi army? Government?" my mother asked, the fear echoing in her voice.

"They're north of Meerat. In the fortress at Hazuul, last I heard. Trying to regroup."

"Well, we're not going to solve it standing here in Habros's hallway," I offered. My head was buzzing with doubt that there was even a solution to be found between just the three of us. And I couldn't begin to know what should come next.

The dreary half-light that was the daytime of this ravaged country faded toward true darkness and I did my best to mostly stay out of the way while Habros and my mother prepared dinner. That left me sitting with my nephew in a small parlor. I had a book I'd taken from my sister's bookshelf downstairs, hoping to get a handle on some of the history of the place. I'd been surprised to find anything written in an approximation of English, but Mom had told me there were many here in Vaneesh who spoke some dialect of it.

Kota was reading as well, stealing glances at me as if he had questions that he wanted to ask. He was tall like his father, though of slighter build. His eyes were the darkest green I'd ever seen, set in a slender face that had a spattering of freckles. His hair was the color of my father's, and like Habros, his skin had a cool tint to it, rather than the warm pink I was accustomed to seeing. It occurred to me that I didn't even know how old he was.

I closed my book and looked at him. "So, Kota, how old are you?"

"Nine years, four months, and two days old," Kota replied. "How old are you?"

I smiled. "Honestly, with the time differences in all of these worlds, I have no idea. I was thirty-two years old when I left home, and that was months ago."

"Why did you leave?"

"Well, there were some men who were chasing me, and I needed to find my mother."

"Grandma told me when she left that she would come back, but she was gone a long time."

I nodded. "The same men who were chasing me had taken her. I only just found her. The first thing she wanted to do was come back here to see you."

"If she came back before, she'd be where my mother is now, so maybe it's good that she didn't."

"Tell me about your mother," I said.

"She makes this soap that makes me giggle." He chuckled a little. "And she makes these cookies I really like. She helps me with my homework." He was quiet for a long moment then he sighed. "I really miss her."

"How long has she been gone?" I asked.

"A month and a week." I got the impression that my nephew was decidedly precise when it came to numbers of any kind. "My friend Mali was taken too. And their father."

We were quiet for a long time before he shifted in his chair. "I was afraid that they would take me too, but I pretend I don't have magic. No one knows."

I didn't know what to say to that, but my mother saved me from needing to say anything as she announced that dinner was ready. It was weird, having a sit-down meal with family. Even with having spent almost a month at Merry's, we seldom all sat down to eat at the same time.

I volunteered to help clean up and was making an effort to wash dishes when I heard voices. I glanced over my shoulder as Habros came into the kitchen with someone beside him.

Clad in black from head to toe, including most of their face, the newcomer looked small next to Habros but was a bit taller than me with broad shoulders. I pulled my hand out of the soapy water and dried it on a towel before turning around expectantly.

The stranger pulled back their hood and tugged down the mask covering their lower face. Underneath was deeply tanned skin that had a ruddy hue, not at all unlike a Native American. Black hair cropped short on the sides made the face seem particularly angular, while the long locks on top, tipped in blue, fell down the right side. Their eyes were solid black and wide set, almost enough to be off-putting. Cheekbones that looked sharp enough to cut bone gave the face a gauntness that belied the strong body below. I couldn't distinguish gender from my first look, and I didn't want to stare, so I switched my gaze to Habros.

"Thána, this is Xen, one of our good friends. Xen, this is my wife's sister."

Xen nodded at me, and I returned the gesture. They took off their jacket and draped it over the back of the chair. "Are we safe to talk?"

Habros nodded and took his seat. "She wants to find Daria too."

Xen paced between the table and the doorway that led to the shop. There was agitation in their movements. "The intel isn't great," Xen finally said. "Getting out of the city is going to be next to impossible."

"Getting out?" I asked. I rinsed off a plate and set it down before drying my hands on the towel again.

"Daria is being held in one of their camps, south of the city, so getting out of the city is our first step." Xen shook their head and took a seat. "The only way out is through checkpoints. Getting caught means getting dead or ending up in the camp ourselves."

I joined them at the table, glancing up as my mother came into the kitchen. "And then we have to get to the camp. Right now, I don't see a way for us to do that in a vehicle," Xen said.

I nodded, seeing the problem. We would need a vehicle to get to the camp, wherever that was.

"Unless..." We all looked at Habros.

"Unless what?" Xen asked.

"What about in one of the Kabeshi vehicles?"

"None of us are Kabeshi. The first soldier who saw any of us driving it would stop us," Xen replied.

"That's easy enough to fix," I said, looking up at Mom to confirm it was okay to talk about that particular magic.

"Thána is right. We can definitely handle that portion." Mom moved closer.

"More magic?" Xen asked, glancing between me and Mom.

Mom took the remaining chair. "Nothing big, just a glamor for the driver."

Habros nodded. "Yes, that's what I was thinking. If we can get our hands on one of their prisoner haulers, it could get us through the checkpoint."

Xen processed that information and drew in a deep breath. "That gets us out of the city, and maybe even into the camp. Then things get dicey."

"Dicey?"

Xen looked at me, their dark eyes holding mine. "Yes. Very. My information tells me that the camp guards have orders to kill anyone attempting to get out on sight. Add to that most of the prisoners have been starved, beaten to submission, tortured. Maybe even programmed to aid the Kabeshi. They are going to be difficult to get out."

"And then there's the question of where we go once we do," Habros added. "Anywhere south of here is nearly one hundred miles from any place we could consider safe."

The whole thing sounded even more hopeless than the idea of Cambious and I rescuing Mom. I pulled my fingers through my curls, trying to fathom what all would be involved in mounting this kind of rescue.

"Daria and I were originally planning to evacuate to Dealth before the Kabeshi army moved north. It's closer to Kabesh but safer than here."

Xen shook their head. "Intel says that they've taken Dealth too. Our choices are north or west. North gets us to Hazuul, west takes us over the Le'ano mountains to the Wilds."

"Wilds?" I asked.

"The Wilds are populated by kooks and criminals, with only a few natives," Mom responded. "Harsh terrain, harsh weather, animals that want to eat you. No central government, no rules."

Yeah, that sounded fun in the way that Australia had always sounded fun, which is to say, not. "I vote for not there, then," I said.

"There is a third option." We all looked at my mother and waited. "We could escape through a portal."

We were silent, the words sitting on the tabletop between us as if they were physical things. Xen shifted. "That sounds like running away."

"And actual running away to the Wilds doesn't?" I asked, earning a harsh look from Xen.

"Look, Outworlder, I was born here. These are my people. I'm not leaving this world to be overrun by these *muokas*."

I held up my hands in surrender. I wasn't sure what a muoka was, other than an insult of some variety, but the tone of voice was absolutely clear.

"How many are with us?" Habros asked, and that seemed to soothe the ruffled feathers.

"We must stay small. A large force will give us away," Xen said. "Dyn and myself for combat, you for the physical needs, Katyk to manage communications."

"And me as the driver," I added, noticing Mom's look of alarm. "Who are Dyn and Katyk?"

"Dyn is one of my birthmates. Katyk is a witch with a knack for tech. She was living in Benkar when the Kabeshi attacked. She speaks Kabeshi and has experience with their magically enhanced weapons."

"And we trust her?" I asked, glancing at Habros who had stiffened at the mention of her name.

"She has no love for Kabesh," Habros answered, making a face. "But much is unknown about her."

"Native?"

Xen shook her head. "I do not know her world of origin, but she is not from any of this world's lands."

"Not much of an army," Habros said softly.

"That is because the army went north." Xen stood. "I should be getting back before the patrols come back this way. I'll send word when I know how and where we are getting the vehicle."

I stayed sitting while Habros walked Xen through the store. Across from me, my mother looked deep in thought. "So, are we really talking about doing this?" I asked.

She pulled in a long, slow breath and exhaled just as slowly. "What other choice do we have?"

I shrugged. I am not a coward, but the thought of what was being considered had me thinking that it would be totally acceptable to sneak back down to the portal park and go back to Spítia. I knew my mother wouldn't leave though, and after all the work to get to her, I wasn't about to just walk away. I sighed. "This won't be like what Cambious and I did in Otadž, which technically should not have worked. We need a real plan."

Mom nodded. "I know."

"Even then, we're more likely to die than to succeed."

She nodded again. "I know. But it's Daria. I can't... just do nothing."

I got up to finish washing the last of the dishes. "So, Xen said that she was born here. I thought that natives were blue, like Habros?"

Mom came to dry the dishes. "No, Xen is Pixin. And not female, by the way. Pixin are agender. The city has a good-sized population of Pixin. They came through a portal around a hundred years ago, fleeing from some natural disaster."

She moved around me to put the dry dishes in the cupboard. "Native Vaneeshi are generally light-skinned, in a blue-green sort of color. Kabeshi are much darker in color with thick hair that covers their skin just about everywhere. Some evolutionary thing that stems from the Kabeshi environment."

I tried to file that information in some sort of order in my brain so I would remember it. "They speak English though? I mean, I understand Habros would have learned it from you and Daria, but Xen's English was good too."

Mom grinned. "The Pixin are good with language, can pick up a new one in days. Most of them speak ten or more languages. Xen and your sister have been friends for years."

"I can barely manage one language," I muttered.

The day was wearing on me and my bandages had gotten wet while I washed, so I was going to need to change them. I stifled a yawn but didn't argue when Mom told me to go get some sleep and she'd finish up in the kitchen.

Downstairs, I went to my room and dug the first aid kit out of my pack before sitting on the bed to peel off the wet gauze. My hand still looked like it was angry with me, the skin around the wound red, but at least it seemed to be starting to heal. I wrapped fresh gauze around it, then stripped down to my underwear and t-shirt and climbed into bed.

I tried to count backward how many days I had been gone from California. I kept losing count and eventually abandoned the attempt. It seemed like a lifetime in a lot of ways. The time differences didn't help, and math was never my best subject.

I drifted off, wondering if the Brotherhood thugs had destroyed the house, and how we would go home if they had.

CHAPTER 6
MAGIC

I discovered that my sister kept a workroom, much like Merry's back in Spítia, complete with a large fireplace, several cauldrons, and all manner of herbs and flowers hanging from the rafters to dry. Unlike Merry's, it was also equipped with what looked like the supplies you might find in a science lab.

Sipping at my coffee, I circled the room, eyes dancing over books in languages I couldn't hope to decipher, and then to the desk stuck in the back corner. The surface was scattered with papers and as I shifted them around, I found a tablet computer.

I sat, setting my coffee aside in favor of the tablet. It turned on with a touch, and the screen filled with a recipe of some kind. I scanned through it, deciding the end result would be an ointment to promote hair growth, or possibly inhibit hair growth, depending on the way it was mixed, and any will imparted while mixing it.

I found the tablet incredibly intuitive, much more so than any I'd used back home. Some books had been translated into English: an entire folder full of Daria's recipes for potions and spells, a detailed plan of the garden I hadn't even known they had behind the building that was both shop and home, as well as programs for translation, accounting and more.

Then one particular icon caught my eye. I pressed it and found myself looking at Daria's diary, for lack of a better word. The entry left off mid-sentence, and I found myself wondering if that had been the day they came for her.

Meerat is completely lost. We should have run when the evac orders came. Habros is worried. I am very publicly a magic user and the Kabeshi will stop at nothing to clear the land of us. There is still small hope we can escape if I can get the spell working. I came close last night, but the portal closed before I could...

And that was where it ended. "Portal?" I murmured, picking my coffee back up. "What were you up to, Daria?"

"Thána?"

"In here," I called in response to my mother's voice. She appeared in the doorway.

"I was wondering where you'd gone."

"Just trying to get to know my sister a little bit." I held the tablet up. "She was working on some spell before they took her."

"She was always working on something," Mom said with a smile.

"She says something about a portal. I thought you needed a bunch of witches to create a portal."

Mom nodded. "You do. Ripping open the veil that separates the worlds isn't easy. It takes a lot of power."

"I wonder what she was trying to do," I muttered, reaching for my coffee. "Any word yet from our agender friend?"

My mother shook her head. "Not yet. Might take some time to find what we need."

"I'm going to need some pictures of Kabeshi soldiers if I'm going to get a glamor ready."

"Oh, I thought..."

I frowned at her. "You thought you were going to be the driver?"

"Well, I am more experienced."

"You are also not going with us." I stood.

"What?" Her face clouded over, though I couldn't tell if it was anger or confusion.

"I busted you out of a prison once, I don't want to risk losing you to a different prison."

"Thána, I'm a grown woman."

"Yes, you are. But you are also my mother, Kota's grandmother. Someone is going to need to stay with him because we can't bring him along on this crazy joy ride."

She looked like she wanted to keep arguing, but I had learned that when it came to family, she'd sacrifice almost anything. I had serious doubts about this whole venture, but this I was sure about. The only reason I hadn't just said no to the whole thing was because of her. She wouldn't leave without Daria and I wouldn't leave her here, especially not after discovering the place ravaged by war and knowing that she would be in danger if I left her there.

My coffee had gone cold, so I headed toward the kitchen with Mom following. I dumped the cold coffee and poured more. "Hey," I said as a thought occurred to me. "If they're rounding up magic users and putting them all in one place, why aren't they combining their power to escape?"

Mom frowned. "That is a good question."

"They hobble them." Habros had come in the back door, his arms full of vegetables of some kind.

I moved so he could get to the sink with his bounty. "Hobble them how?" I asked.

"With a marriage of magic and science." It was my mother who answered. "It was developed years ago, as a means of controlling witches that went bad. There was a spree of crimes where magic was being used to steal. When the culprits were caught, the choices were to find a way to hobble their power, keep them under armed guard, or execution."

"So, they found a way to hobble them." It made sense but wasn't anything I'd really considered before. I'd spent most of my life with my powers hidden away inside me, not even knowing they existed, and while I'd only had access to them for less than a year, I already couldn't imagine having them taken away. "So, we can't rely on them to help in any way. Good to know."

My brain spun through many scenarios then came back to Mom and Kota. Leaving them here wasn't the wisest choice. They would still be in danger. I had no idea how to get them out of the city so we could meet up with them, provided we survived.

"Mother, I think you should take Kota back to Spítia and wait for us there," Habros said as if he had heard my thoughts.

"What?" The scowl on her face was deep.

Habros held up both hands as if to placate her. "I need to know that you are both safe. It is easier to get you to the portal than it is to get you out of the city."

"I've been thinking the same thing," I added.

The look of betrayal on her face stung. Tears welled in her eyes. "I can help."

"The fewer people we have to keep track of the better," I countered. "If the two of you are safe, that's one less thing that can go wrong."

I hadn't figured out yet how we would get back to Spítia ourselves, but I had learned in the last rescue operation that I could go with the flow and take each problem as it presented itself. The master plan was just a high view of what had to happen. How we made that happen was open to interpretation and improvisation.

"Fine." She stormed off, but I knew she would come to understand, so I turned my attention to Habros.

Before I could say anything, he gestured to my hand. "How does that feel?"

I nodded distractedly. "It's okay. Still a little stiff. I'm going to need you to fill me in on as much as possible… about the Kabeshi, about Vaneesh history, about my sister. Every detail could be important."

He nodded. "Of course."

By the time the evening storm passed through that night, I felt as though my brain were bleeding out my ears, but I knew a lot more than I did before about the precarious politics that underpinned the current crisis, as well as just how ambitious my sister was with her work. Habros had shown me how to see hidden entries in Daria's journal, plus where to find her handwritten notes on the spells she'd been practicing. Daria was a big note-taker, a habit I had never really gotten good at.

While Habros started to make dinner, I went back to Daria's lab to find the notebook Habros had told me to look at. It was a beat-up-looking thing, a leather cover over something not unlike a composition book. I flipped through it, finding myself stopping every few pages to read. There was a spell to create light, though her notes said that the energy cost was prohibitive to wide usage. And I found several that dealt with gardening needs, from perpetual watering to weed inhibition. Near the end of the book, there were a bunch of references to various books, then a list of words and those words in various combinations.

Reading through her notes had me highly intrigued by an idea. I could see where the work was going. I took the book and headed back to the kitchen. My mother had rejoined Habros and was setting the table. "Mom, does Daria create new spells?"

"She likes to tinker with new ideas."

"Have you ever heard of a portal that doesn't go to a different world, but to a different location in the same one?"

She frowned. "No. How would that even work?"

I showed her the notebook with the list of words. "I think that's what she is trying to do here. See she's got *tomí* for cut, *síranga*, which I think means tunnel. *Ánoixe* to open." There were other words I wasn't sure of, but it seemed to be a spell to create a wormhole or something, bridging the gap between two spots within the same world.

Mom took the book, her eyes skimming over the page. "It doesn't look like she got it to work."

I nodded, helping Habros bring food to the table. "She said she was getting close. She was hoping to use it to get everyone out of the city."

The spell kept me distracted while we ate. I took the tablet and notebook with me to my room, lying across my bed to investigate further. Her journal entries detailed which combinations she had tried, and their results. She'd been working on it for well over two years. The catalyst seemed to have been the onset of hostilities with Kabesh. She was looking for a way to get her family to safety, knowing that to take Vaneesh, Kabesh had to take Meerat.

Chewing on my lip, I sat up and took a deep breath. Her closest attempt had been the words for open and tunnel and then what I assumed was a place name. "Okay, what the hell." I put the notebook on the bed and lifted my hands in an approximation of Daria's sketch, wrists together, hands open, arms stretched out in front of me. I centered myself, closing my eyes, and summoning the magic that lived within me. I chose the only place name I knew. "*Ánoixe ti síranga pros tin Hazuul*."

My palms burned and a sort of orangey light started to glow in the space where my wrists were touching. It felt like all the magic inside me was surging up, from my center, to my arms then out through my hands. At the same time, the rest of me felt like I was breaking apart.

The air in front of my hands shimmered and seemed to tear. The slit widened a bit, and I could see houses and some tall building through the hole. Every centimeter it opened made my body quake harder until I wasn't able to hold it any longer. I pulled my hands apart and sank down onto the bed. I shook from head to toe, rocking the bed. My stomach squeezed and my head pounded to the entirely too fast rhythm of my heart. I wasn't sure if I was going to hold down my dinner.

The room spun when I tried to open my eyes, which pushed me over the edge. I raced for the bathroom, bouncing off the hallway walls like I was the ball in a pinball machine. I managed to reach the toilet, depositing everything I had ever eaten. I was still there when my mother came in. "Thána, are you okay?"

The shaking had diminished, and the nausea seemed to have abated. "I think so." My voice sounded strange to my ears, like it was coming from somewhere else.

"What happened?"

I pushed myself up off the floor and flushed the commode, then washed my face with cool water and rinsed my mouth. "I tried Daria's spell. I opened a rift of some kind, but… it was…" I wasn't sure how to describe it, and the jackhammer that had taken up residence in my head wasn't helping. My hands trembled as I released the counter, my legs weak and my knees threatening to give out.

Mom's arm snaked around my back, pulling me up against her body. "I've got you."

She supported me back to my bedroom. There was nothing there to give away that magic had just taken place. "It can be done."

"Not tonight." She helped me take off my shoes and tucked me into bed almost as if I were a child again. She kissed my forehead. "Sleep."

I did not need to be told twice. In fact, I doubt I could have stayed awake if I wanted to.

———

I've had a few hangovers in my life, but none of them came close to what I woke up to the next morning. I was cold and everything ached. I was half-convinced that there was a herd of elephants stampeding through my brain.

I pulled myself out of bed, bringing the blanket with me. I wrapped it around me as I stumbled toward the stairs. "Coffee," was the first thing I said, and my voice still sounded strange.

"This is the last of it." Mom poured a cup and handed it to me, one hand rising to press against my forehead. "I imagine you're hurting."

I sort of nodded, pulling the blanket closer and sitting. "What in the actual hell happened to me?"

She smirked at me. "You tried a spell that is lightyears beyond your training, that's what. I'm surprised you managed to even summon that much energy."

I closed my eyes and sipped my coffee. For a minute I thought it might come back up. When the wave of nausea passed, I turned my attention to the spell. "Okay, it takes a lot of energy, I get that, but I got it to open, Mom. I saw houses and some tower before I had to let it go."

We were quiet for a moment. I worked over the words, over what it was I wanted it to do. "It needs something to stabilize it, and maybe a stronger command."

"You're not going to let this go," Mom said, sipping at her own coffee. It wasn't a question.

"And at least one more person with magic or the ability to at least add energy to the casting." I inhaled and tried to let go of it, at least until the elephants stopped dancing. "My head is killing me."

"Daria should have some pain potions in the shop. I'll go look."

I put my coffee and my head down on the table. The surface was nice and cool. I almost fell back to sleep, but felt eyes on me. I turned my head and found Kota standing there in his pajamas, those intense eyes watching me.

"Are you sick?"

"Yes, Kota, I am."

He looked at me, tilting his head to the side. "Is it in your head? I can hear it go *boom, boom, boom.*"

"You can hear it?"

He stepped closer, lifting his hands. He paused then and met my eyes with his. "May I touch you?"

Curious, I agreed. His hands were warm as he touched my face. His eyes closed and I could sense him centering himself, gathering that core of who he is, and then, relief flooded through me. It started in my face, where his hands were, but like a wave of warm water, it flushed away the pounding in my head, the heavy ache of my limbs.

I blinked as he stepped back, sitting up straighter. "How did you do that?"

He shrugged. "I just do. Mom calls it my gift."

My mother returned from the hall to the shop, two different potions in her hands. "I'm good," I said as she started to hand me the bottles. "Kota made it better."

Mom frowned and looked at Kota. "He did?"

"He put his hands on my face and it just washed away."

"Huh. That's *diádikasía*. Extremely rare. Related to your magic, but different." She turned to Kota. "How long have you been able to do that?"

He shrugged again. "A while. It only works on some stuff though. Not on blood stuff."

"Like cuts?" Mom asked.

Kota nodded. "But Mom told me not to let anyone know. Just family."

"Probably safer that way," I said. "Thank you, Kota."

"Well, for future reference, this one works on most headaches, while this one settles the stomach." She handed me the bottles. The headache one was a soft green and the stomach one was white, with a hint of pink.

"Good to know." I went back to my coffee. "Have you two talked about the trip?"

Mom stiffened but started pulling out food. "Not yet."

"What trip?" Kota sat at his usual spot at the table. "Are we getting away from the soldiers?"

I smiled. "Yes. You and your grandma are going to go somewhere safe."

"What about Mom?"

"Your dad and I are working on that."

"When are we going?"

I looked up at Mom. "We haven't quite decided yet, but soon."

"How long will we be gone?" Kota asked.

"I don't know that either." I sighed. We only had the vaguest outline of a plan. I wasn't convinced it would work, and even if it did, that only liberated a small number of prisoners. It did nothing to push the Kabeshi army out of the city or eliminate the hateful rhetoric.

"I heard from Xen," Habros said as he entered the kitchen. "We have a window of opportunity to get our hands on one of the haulers in five days. It will be due for maintenance, so we can steal it from the garage."

Five days didn't give us a lot of time to plan. "I better get working on that glamor." I needed a crash course in driving their vehicles as well as time for crafting a convincing glamor. I was also determined to get Daria's spell working. It might be the solution for how we escaped. If I could open a rift between the prison camp and the portal park, we could walk out of one portal and into another.

After breakfast, I took some pictures Habros had given me of Kabeshi soldiers into Daria's lab, along with her tablet and notebook plus my own spell book retrieved from my pack. My first attempts were dismal. I'd never tried to glamor myself into another species before. I knew it could be done, of course, that was, after all, how Cambious got by in my world, and in the parts of Spítia where incubi weren't welcome. I'd done a fair bit of studying on the mechanics of glamors and learned various ways to change the projected image, but it had all been theory before now.

I found skin tone to be the hardest thing to replicate, at least until I attempted the body hair. I looked something like a hairy Smurf. I released the glamor and breathed in deep.

"How's it coming?"

I looked up as my mother came into the room. "Slow," I responded.

"Here." She handed me a blue crystal cut into an oval shape. It was clear and faceted so that it sparkled as she set it into my hand.

"What is this for?" I asked.

"Two-fold. One, you're going to need an anchor for your glamor, or you'll wear yourself out. And two, you said something about a stabilizing force for the portal spell. This is kelcimite. It stabilizes volatile potions and spells as well as exudes a calming influence."

I could feel the calming influence as I held it on my open palm. "How would that work?"

"Show me the spell, without casting it."

I stood, handing the crystal back to her, and put my hands in the correct position. Without centering, I said the words. She nodded, then put the crystal between my hands, cupping them slightly closer together to hold it. "Cast through the stone."

I frowned. "Do what now?"

"This position means you are casting your inner magic core through your hands. To stabilize the responding magic, it needs to be passed through the crystal as it leaves your body."

"Okay, let me try."

"If I might suggest," Mom said, setting a hand on my arm. "Perhaps try it with a less powerful spell, at least until you get the hang of it."

"Probably a good plan." I cast about in the chasm of my memory for something less taxing and settled for simple. Closing my hand around the stone I cast *ánoixe* so that the crystal ended up on my open palms. The cool surface of the stone was slightly warmer as all around me books ruffled open. The feeling of the energy leaving my body was slightly different, more of a controlled stream rather than a burst. Like everything else since learning magic was real, it was going to take some time.

"Xen is here," Habros said from the hallway. "They'd like to talk about the plan."

"I'll be right there." I pocketed the stone and snatched up the notebook and tablet. Mom followed me out to the kitchen, which had become a tight space because Xen was not alone. I recognized the person beside them as Pixin, they had the same build and coloring as Xen, but their hair was a curly mop of bright reds and shades of brown.

"This is Dyn, who has been doing recon for us," Xen said, gesturing to the Pixin. "Hedron is our inside man."

Hedron was a big guy wearing a military uniform of khaki brown with ribbons on his shoulders that I assumed conferred rank. Thick blonde hair covered his blue skin, what I could see of it anyway. Even the backs of his hands were covered in it. The only skin not full of hair was on his face, but I couldn't tell if that was natural, or if he shaved. He nodded tightly. I was about to turn my attention to the last of the newcomers when I noticed something no one had told me about.

Hedron had a tail. Like an actual tail. As far as I could tell without turning him around and subjecting him to an exam, it protruded from around six inches above his waist and was a good three feet long. It too was covered in hair, all the way down to the tip, which twitched as I continued to stare.

"And I'm Katyk." The last of the group reached out her hand, pulling me away from my startled examination, and I shook it somewhat distractedly. "Human, mostly." She smirked and pulled her hand back.

Hedron spoke in a deep, guttural language and Xen murmured their agreement. "We can't stay long. Hedron has to get back to work." They pointed at a hand-drawn map on the table. "We're here." Xen's finger touched a spot on the map, then dragged it closer to the middle. "Hauler will be here. Hedron will get it there and adjust the computers to give us access out of the city. Then it's down to us."

Dyn spoke aside to Xen in a language filled with clicks, then put their finger down on the camp location. "This is our target. Once we are out of the city, we then must access the camp."

Hedron spoke again and Xen tilted toward me, one hand settling on my arm. It was warm and oddly comforting. "You sure you can do this? Driving and looking like him?" They gestured at Hedron.

I took a deep breath, then nodded. I wasn't, actually, but I was going to try. "I'm sure. What's the plan for getting through the gates?"

"Hedron will put a prisoner transfer on our mission," Dyn said. "They move prisoners regularly. It keeps them confused and away from any who might attempt to rescue them."

"And then what?" I asked.

"Then we haul ass out of there and aim for a border," Katyk said, slapping her hand down on the table for emphasis.

CHAPTER 7
FLIRTING

The plan sounded vague, but it was more than I had planned when Cambious and I decided to infiltrate a fortress to rescue my mother, and we had time to work on it. Katyk stood and I found myself looking her over. She had a familiar air about her, something I couldn't quite name. Deep mahogany skin coupled with bright blue eyes, and the kind of body that woke up my lady parts. "My grandmother was a succubus," she offered as she caught me looking. "I got the pigment, but not the horns." She patted her dark auburn curls where Cambious's horns emerged from his head.

Hedron spoke again and clicked his heels together before he left, exiting out the back door. "He bids you farewell. He must return to his duty."

"Hedron is Kabeshi?" I asked. "Why is he helping us? And why isn't he driving?"

"He's part Kabeshi, his mother is an outworlder," Katyk responded. "They've put her in one of their camps."

"If he is absent his post for too long, they will kill her," Xen added. "The Kabeshi often use family to turn those who might benefit their cause."

"When are we doing this?" I asked.

"Four days from now. You will need to be here by the third hour, any later and we will run into trouble. I will bring you a uniform. You should wear it from the time you leave here. They will not question a Kabeshi of rank walking through the streets."

"I'll get us there," Habros said.

The two Pixin spoke to one another in that clicky language, then gestured toward the door into the garden. "We will leave you now. You should study this map, but hide it. If you are found with it, our plan fails." I watched Xen as they left, more than a little intrigued by them. I turned expectantly to Katyk. "Oh, I have nowhere to be. I thought we should talk."

I frowned at her. "Talk about what?"

Her smile was devious. "For starters, about the way you were just looking at my ass."

My mother cleared her throat beside me. "On that note, I'll go back to getting Kota and I packed up."

"And I have gardening to attend to," Habros added quickly.

Katyk waited until they were both gone to plop herself back into the chair and kick her feet onto the table. I rescued the map, rolling it up and setting it on the counter.

"They going somewhere?" Katyk asked.

"Who?"

"Your mother and the kid."

"Hopefully someplace a little safer than here," I replied. I felt a little off-kilter, not unlike when I'd had that crush on Muriel Hart in college. I had to admit, I liked the way she looked. "Habros might not like your boots on his kitchen table."

I started some water for tea because I felt like I should be doing something. "So, tell me about you," Katyk said as I started the water heating.

"Me? I figured Xen would have filled you in."

"Xen told me you were an outworlder with magic. That's it."

I shrugged and turned, leaning back against the counter. "That's me. Nothing too exciting."

"Oh, I don't buy that." Katyk took her feet down off the table, turning her chair to look me up and down. "You strike me as someone who knows her way around exciting."

I shook my head. "Not really. I'm not even all that much of a witch, honestly. I've only known I was one for a few months."

She frowned. "That sounds like a story."

"Not so much. My gifts were hidden from me to protect me from the Brotherhood." I kicked myself because that just basically outed me as a blood witch to someone I'd just met.

I needn't have worried though. Katyk shuddered and rubbed her hands over her arms as if she were cold. "Crazy fuckers."

"You know who they are?"

The water kettle screamed at me and I pulled two mugs from the cupboard. "I'm having some of this tea my sister made, if you want some."

I didn't wait for her to answer, filling the teapot with first the tea ball, then the water, and putting it on the table along with the mugs.

"I know enough. Religious zealots of the seriously crazed kind. Get worked up about blood witches, has nearly wiped them out at this point."

"That's about right." I poured the tea and sat across from her.

"So you're a blood witch then?"

I nodded. "Guilty as charged. What about you?"

She played with her cup and her eyes dropped to the table. "Nothing as big as all that. My particular gifts are all related to my succubus grandmother. Sex magic, that kind of thing."

I hadn't even known there was sex magic, aside from an incubus or succubus feeding, but I was intrigued. "Like what?"

"There's a whole bunch of stuff you can do with the energy created by sex," Katyk responded.

"Do you… I mean, I've been with an incubus before…do you have to feed?" I blushed even as I said it, memories of sex with Cambious filling my head.

Katyk chuckled. "No, I'm only a quarter succubus. But I can collect the energy and use it in a number of ways. And that explains it."

"Explains what?" I asked.

Her hand snaked across the table to caress mine. "I don't usually have to work this hard. But I'm guessing you're inoculated against the pheromones and that's why you haven't figured out that I'm flirting with you."

The blush on my face was intense if I could judge by the heat that filled my cheeks. I cleared my throat and pulled my hand back to sip at my tea. "Oh, that. I have never been good with that. But yes, I drank that god-awful potion."

She smiled, those startlingly blue eyes sparkling. "Well, I guess I'll have to do it the old-fashioned way."

I wasn't sure how to respond, so I drank my tea and tried to think of a new subject that wouldn't be as uncomfortable. "You haven't said where you're from, but Xen said you aren't a local," I finally said.

Katyk brought one foot up to the chair, her knee almost at eye level, and cradled her cup. "This is home, but no, I wasn't born here. I come from this tiny, tiny town in Spítia, but my sister and I left there when I was seventeen and we've been portal hopping ever since. We always seem to come back here though."

It sounded like there was probably a lot of backstory I wasn't ready to delve into. I had to keep my focus on getting to Daria, not developing a new love interest.

"I tend to stay out of politics wherever I land, but Kabesh hasn't made that easy," Katyk said. "I'm tempted to just head through a portal, but like I said, I've come to think of this place as home."

"How many portals have you traveled through?"

She seemed to be counting in her head. "Five, no, wait, six. If we're counting new worlds and not actual passages through the door. Spítia, here, a place called Trough where there are tribes of nomads and only one permanent village that we found. There's a place similar to here development-wise but where there is a very strict matriarchy in power, and right after that, I found myself nearly getting burned at the stake for being a witch. I didn't like that place much. And then there was Gazaby. I could have laid on the beach for months, crystal clear water, white sand for miles. The problem there was the fish-people. Very aggressive."

"Fish-people?" I asked, intrigued if she meant mermaids.

"Ugly things. Feet like flippers, hands like claws, covered in scales." She shuddered. "And teeth... they were the worst."

We talked a while longer, Katyk regaling me with tales of her exploits, though I got the impression some of the details were exaggerated a bit to impress me. We lapsed into a comfortable quiet for a few minutes before I put my cup down. "I should probably get back to work on that glamor. There's a lot of detail to get right." Especially now that I knew it included a tail.

"I never was any good with those. Probably a good thing. I would get into so much trouble if I could make it work." She grinned. "It was very nice to meet you Thána. See you in a couple of days."

I watched her go before I put our mugs and the teapot into the sink and headed back down to the lab with Daria's notebook and tablet. I flipped through the notebook to the pages where Daria's notes were on the portal spell as I sat at her desk. I rummaged until I found a pen and scribbled a note in the margin of the page about casting through the Kelcimite.

Pulling the crystal from my pocket, I turned it over and over in my hand, contemplating the other side of the equation. I couldn't do anything about having a second person with magic to amplify my strength without calling Mom, but I was thinking about the power of the words themselves. Essentially, the spell was a command to open a tunnel from here to there, wherever there ended up being. What I needed was a little more oomph. I looked back through the list of variations Daria had experimented with and tried to come up with additional words of power, ones that were stronger versions of those she had already tried.

I scribbled down *káno*, which meant make or create. Merry had used it in an effort to teach me some magic in the kitchen. I also put down a few ideas to ask Mom about, mainly things like words for push, rip, and tear; slightly more violent actions to open and make. Then another thought occurred to me and I wrote down *burn*. I would need to get the correct spell words for those and try them.

But first thing was to keep working on the glamor. I cleared my mind of the portal idea and turned my attention back to the glamor. Now that I had seen a Kabeshi in person maybe it would be easier, but then I still had to figure out how to work the tail into the mix.

Several hours later, exhausted and dripping with sweat, I showered and crawled into bed. It was exhausting work, and I was no closer to a workable glamor. I'd gotten a fairly good approximation of skin tone until I added the hair, then my blue turned kind of green. I'd managed a stumpy sort of tail once or twice, but lost it when I tried to add the proper skin coloring.

It was a good thing I had a few days to perfect it. I fell asleep and immediately into a dream where I was running blindly, terrified and certain there were monsters in the dark intent on hurting me. I was pulled to a stop by Xen, pressed into a dark recess. Their hand was in mine and we huddled together as the danger passed. When we moved again, we were not alone. The woman who joined us I knew to be Daria. What followed was more running, screaming, and blood.

I woke with a start, half expecting to be scratched up and bleeding. I had no context for the dream, but it had the same urgency as the ones in the past, connected to being a blood witch. I somehow found my mother because of it. I gathered the blankets around me and sat cross-legged on the bed. It had been something I wasn't in control of before. I had zoned out in the car and something inside me found my mother in her prison cell.

The dreams had mostly been about the past though, and this was definitely not the past. I drew in a deep breath and reached inside, soaking my thoughts in the fiery center of me that was my magic. Then I drew up the image of Daria's face from the dream. She was fair skinned like our father and her hair was a few shades darker red than his, a sprinkling of freckles across her nose. She had Mom's eyes but narrow set and deep blue. I held the image in my head for a long moment before I cast it away from me, following as it led me zooming across the city and away until I came crashing to a halt in a room with medical equipment.

Daria lay on an exam table, strapped down, her breathing labored. Her eyes were closed, her hands fisted as a Kabeshi man moved around her. I couldn't see what was being done to her, but Habros had talked about torture. She screamed and I had to let the vision go, collapsing backward, once again lying on the bed. I was panting, but it solidified for me that someone needed to help her, and if not her family, who else would it be?

I was wishing I'd brought more of that mix Merry had made to keep me going on marathon nights of studying and practicing. I needed to up my game. I got up and wandered back to Daria's lab, wondering if she had the same plants and whether or not I could remember how the recipe went.

I found Mom there, sorting through some of the beakers looking for something. "Hey, do you remember that potion Merry made for me to help me stay awake and get work done?"

"Hmm?" She glanced up before resuming her rummaging. "Yes, why?"

"Can we make it here? Or something close? I have a lot of work to do."

Mom put her hands down on the table, her mouth pursed in a scowl, like she was going to scold me. "Thána, you know you shouldn't rely on those things. Eventually, you're going to burn out."

"I know," I responded, adopting my best chastised expression. "But I can't keep sleeping when I should be working. I promise that I'll stop as soon as I get the glamor down, and I'll sleep properly before we leave."

She sighed but looked resigned. "Fine. We can't do that exact potion, since we don't have all of the ingredients, but I can whip you up something similar."

She moved around the lab, collecting herbs and a smaller cauldron. "Will I distract you if I ask some questions while you work?" I asked, moving so that I could watch what she was doing.

"No. Ask away."

I licked my lips and tried to figure out where to begin. "Can you use English words as spells?" I asked first, surprising myself a little. I hadn't even been aware of thinking that at all.

She shrugged her shoulders. "I suppose. It is more about the intent than the words. The words help frame your intent. Our ancestors all wrote down words in their own language. We just kept using them."

"How do you know which are more powerful. Like the difference between *prostatévo* and *yperaspízo*?"

"In that case, one is passive and the other is active. With *prostatévo*, you are casting to merely not allow an attack to harm you. In the other, you are turning the attack away. Done well, back at your attacker."

An earthy smell was rising from the cutting board she was working on, and it reminded me of Merry's kitchen. "Okay, that makes sense. So, with this portal spell, I can get it to open using *open* and *tunnel*, but it won't stay open without a lot of effort and is not big enough to pass through. Would something like *rip* or *tear* work better?"

She nodded, adding the dark green herbs she'd been chopping into the cauldron. "Yes, but you have to be careful with words like that, Thána. They intimate violence, and with magic, violence is hard to control."

I nodded in understanding. "I probably shouldn't try *burn* or *stab* then," I said chuckling.

She raised a brow at me but kept her attention on the knife in her hands as she cut something that looked a lot like a vanilla bean. I let her work in silence for a while before I cleared my throat and spoke softly. "I saw Daria."

She froze for a second before continuing what she was doing. "How?"

"The same way I saw you in that cell. I don't remember what Merry called that."

"*Makrá vlépinta*," Mom said, the area around her eyes tightening. "Which you still shouldn't be able to do. It takes a lifetime to control your power well enough."

"And yet..."

The silence settled over us again until she scraped the mush that had once been a dried bean into the cauldron. "Bring me that bottle with the blue flowers on it." She pointed and I went to grab it. Inside was a foul-smelling liquid that was thick, like cough syrup. "How is she?"

"She seemed okay," I lied. I tinkered with a coin I found on the work surface so I had something to look at other than my mother's face. "Tired, worn. You know."

I couldn't read her face as she finished mixing the ingredients. Part of me was sure that she knew I was lying. How could Daria be fine in a prison camp, her powers hobbled while she's being tortured?

Mom stuck her fingers into the mixture in the cauldron and murmured words I didn't quite make out, infusing the mix with energy. Then she covered the cauldron and washed her hands. "That needs to sit overnight, then it should be good to go, which means you can get some sleep."

"I napped earlier. I can work for a few hours."

"You never did like to be told to go to bed."

"I have a lifetime of learning to make up for." I patted her hand reassuringly. "But I promise not to overdo it and get a good night's sleep."

"Good, because after tomorrow you won't have me to nag you about it. Or Kota to help you deal with the hangover."

It was my turn to raise an eyebrow. "Oh?"

She breathed in deep and let it out slowly. "I would still rather be here to help, but you and Habros are right. Kota needs me, so tomorrow night, he and I will sneak down to the park and head home."

"Good." I smiled for her, knowing she wasn't happy.

"Which reminds me," she pulled something out of her back pocket. "I'm not even sure why I brought it, since it won't work here."

Mom handed me one of the small phones they used in Spítia. "Merry's combo is in there. Call me when you and your sister come through the portal, so I can come to pick you up."

I took the phone and tucked it into the pocket of my jeans. "By the way, did you think that the tail thing was something you might have mentioned when I volunteered my services as the driver?"

"Oh. Didn't I?" She looked genuinely surprised, frowning a little as she went back to looking for whatever she'd been searching for when I came in. "I could have sworn I did. I sometimes can't remember if I thought a thing or said it out loud."

It was part and parcel of her long captivity, I knew, so I couldn't be upset. "Well, how about you help me figure out how to get the glamor right and I'll forgive the oversight," I said.

"Deal. Tomorrow morning. Right now, I need to find, ah, there it is." She lifted a dial that had been hidden under a bunch of papers. "Daria really needs to keep this lab in better shape."

"What is that?" I asked. She held it out to me, setting it on my upturned palm.

"It's a lock your sister and I developed. It wasn't going to do much good with so many magical folks around, but if you set it with blood magic, it should hold against anyone who isn't a blood witch."

"What are we locking up?" I asked, letting her take it back.

"Whatever you need. I figured it might come in handy. I'll show you how to use it tomorrow." She dusted her hands together. "I'll have a nice kit built up for you before I leave."

"Kit?"

"Tools, medicine, first aid. You never know what you're going to need."

"You do think of everything."

"That's what mothers are for. Don't work too late." She kissed my cheek and I turned to my books.

I glanced through a number of pages in my spell book, turning the kelcimite over and over in my free hand. "Okay, let's try something easy first." I bit my lip and closed the book before taking a half step back from the worktable. I centered, breathed in, and thought *ánoixe* without making the gesture. It took a few tries, but eventually, the book fluttered open. I just needed to remember how the connection worked inside me.

That part was still clumsy for me, not just because I was a novice, but because some small part of me still had trouble believing. I pushed the doubt away and focused again, this time, instead of *kontá* to close the book, I just thought *close* at it. After several tries, with nothing happening, I made the corresponding gesture at the same time.

The book snapped shut with a jarring finality, as if I'd slammed the cover closed. At least it worked. I picked up the kelcimite and thought about the wisdom of attempting the portal spell on my own.

CHAPTER 8
CASTING

Glancing over my shoulder as if expecting to get caught, I licked my lips, then squared my stance and brought my hands up, cupping them to hold the stone while also pushing them forward, toward the wall.

Deep breaths filled my lungs before I closed my eyes and sunk my consciousness into the core of me, into the fire of my blood and magic. I didn't speak the words, not aloud. I repeated the same incantation as I had tried before, opening my eyes as the magic traveled down my arms and shot through the stone.

The rift formed a little faster and this time I could see through it more clearly, but it did not grow, and I'd learned not to keep holding it if I wanted to keep working.

I released the spell, sagging into the desk chair and panting. Sweat slicked over my skin from the exertion, but the spell had definitely been more stable. Once I caught my breath, I stood to try again. I simplified the spell even more, issuing just the simple command to tunnel.

The result was a hole about the size of my head at chest height. It didn't seem to take as much energy, but I couldn't tell you what was on the other side of that hole. I hadn't given it a destination and there was no light or movement I could see. I released the spell and once again sat to rest.

"It needs to be bigger..." I said aloud to the empty room. It had to be more than just the intent of the spell, or it would have been big enough for a train. I pulled Daria's notebook closer and read over the page again and again, as if somehow re-reading the words would make something jump out at me.

After a long time, I stood once more. I set my stance, cupped my hands, and reached inside. I set a solid intention, a tunnel to the kitchen then spoke the words.

It felt as if my insides were being pulled out through my hands, which were burning as blue light poured out of the crystal and my body shook. The wall seemed to open and the hole grew until it was roughly as tall as I was. I stumbled forward, almost pulled through the hole.

I got the briefest glimpse of the kitchen table and the sensation of falling and then… nothing. I'm not sure how much time passed as I lay on the cold tile floor of the kitchen, but when I came to, there was dried blood on my face and my whole body hurt.

Pushing myself up, I could tell it was still nighttime, the skies outside the kitchen window dark. My right hand was still painfully clutched around the stone. I climbed to my feet and shoved the stone in my pocket before stumbling to the sink to wash the blood off my face.

It didn't feel like I was injured, but my nostrils were raw, telling me that I'd likely had a nosebleed. Beyond all reason, I'd made it work. Okay, it was only on a small scale, but I'd opened the tunnel and used it.

My equilibrium was next to zero as I made my way down the stairs to my bedroom. I wanted to make notes on what I'd done but figured it could wait until morning. I shimmied out of my jeans and crawled into bed. Sleep came quickly.

Dreams of running and being chased filled my head, and as I drew closer to waking up, it was Daria's face I kept seeing, over and over, hearing her scream, her eyes dark and filled with tears.

"Thána?"

I cut off the scream that tried to follow me out of my nightmare as I jumped. My mother was worried, I could see it on her face. "Are you okay?"

I nodded, pushing my sweaty hair aside. "Yeah, sorry. Dreams."

"It's nearly midday."

I didn't feel like I had slept that long, though some of that could be the hangover from the spell. "I guess I needed some sleep." I reached for my jeans and tugged them on.

"How late were you up?" Mom asked as I joined her to head to the lab.

"I don't know." It wasn't a lie, exactly. I had no idea what time I had crawled into bed. Or how long I was unconscious on the kitchen floor for that matter. For some reason I couldn't name, I didn't want to tell her that I'd gotten some version of the portal spell to work.

Of course, that thought was predicated on there being no lingering signs that magic of that variety had happened, though I figured she would have said something if she'd found any. The lab was much as I'd left it, my books still on the worktable. If I squinted, I imagined faint traces of something on the wall the hole had burrowed through, but I was probably projecting.

"Show me what you have so far," Mom said, pulling a stool up to the table.

I followed suit, perching on my stool, and reached for my notes. "My problem seems to be combining elements."

"Hmmm. Show me."

I exhaled and dug deep, then lifted my hands and murmured the incantation that had come the closest to being what I wanted to end up with, the skin and tail close, but the body hair and eyes still lacking.

"Ah, yes. I wondered if that was where you were getting stuck. Basically, you're trying too hard. Too many instructions."

"What do you mean?" I asked. "That's how I worked the glamor I used at the Kourt." I let the changes fade.

"It's fine for small changes. But for something this big you can't string together all of the different individual components. There's too much that can go wrong, too many ways for them to interact with each other."

"Okay, so then what do I do instead?"

"Let's start with Hedron. Can you picture him in your mind?"

I closed my eyes and imagined him as he'd been in the kitchen the day before. "Yes."

"Good, now imagine him with darker hair. Most of the Kabeshi have blue-black hair."

I altered the image in my mind, giving my Kabeshi soldier a shaved crew cut of dark hair, making the hair on his hands darker too.

"Remember his tail," my mother murmured. "Now, *álleji*."

I whispered the word to myself and felt the familiar bubbling and shifting.

"Better. Much better."

I opened my eyes. I didn't feel like an alien, but a glance down told me I looked like one. The skin on my arms was a deep blue with thick dark hair and out of the corner of my eye, I saw movement. Turning, I found it to be my tail, though when I reached for it, my hand passed through, and in my surprise, I let the glamor release.

"It isn't real, remember?" Mom said with a chuckle.

"Oh. Right." I'm not sure why I thought I could touch what was, essentially, a figment of my imagination, but it looked real enough. "I guess that means it will work?"

"You still need to tweak it. Spend some time with those images Habros gave you and see if you can make it your own. You can't just mirror someone; you need to create your own person."

"Okay. Thank you for the help."

"You were always good with glamors. Do you remember your first?"

I dug through my memory to find it. "When I tried to hide the bruise on my cheek? I... fell down the stairs?"

"You tried to ride the banister after your father told you no. You thought you'd get in trouble, so you tried to glamor the evidence away."

I chuckled as I remembered how my father struggled between wanting to chastise me for the stunt, and pride at what I'd accomplished. "Dad saw through it though."

"That he did. He was so proud of you though."

"If I remember correctly, I'd watched *you* do it."

She nodded. "Yes, even then I knew we were going to need more than just the wards to hide you."

I sighed, lost for a long moment in the piles of returned memories of the time before I found myself alone with no memory. We had been a happy family. The love that filled those memories was so profound that it could knock me to my knees if I let it. It was the thing I'd craved most in the years between that bench outside the police station and the moment when the memory spell spun out.

"I'm sorry," I said into the silence, tears stinging the corners of my eyes.

Her hand covered mine, warm and offering comfort I wasn't sure I had the strength to accept. If I did, if I let myself feel all of that again, I wasn't sure I'd be able to let her go.

"You have nothing to apologize for," she said softly.

I lifted our hands and turned hers so I could press a kiss to her palm, the way she had always done to me as a child. "You could have had that happy life if I wasn't what I am."

She cupped my face in both hands and drew me close enough that she could kiss my forehead. "If you were not what you are, how do you know my life would have been happy? We cannot change what we are, Thána. We must embrace it for all of the joys and all of the pains."

There had been a lot of pain, that was a sure thing. For both of us. We sat in silence for a few moments, and I was starting to feel awkward when she inhaled and stepped away, reaching for the cauldron on the end of the worktable. She set it in front of me and pulled away the cloth that had been covering it. The smell was pungent, almost astringent. "Promise me you won't misuse this?" she asked.

"Promise."

"This is a bit more potent than what Merry made for you." She tilted the cauldron so I could see the result of her work. It was a dark powder. She opened a drawer and dug around in it, coming out with a small black leather pouch, which she handed to me. "Hold this open."

I pulled the pouch open and she grabbed a funnel from beside the assorted beakers, set it into the pouch, then poured the powder into the funnel. The mixture Merry had made for me I had used like a tea, but this didn't seem to be a tea.

"You can put it in anything really or even take it dry," Mom said. "But only a pinch at a time, and at least four hours between doses, and absolutely no more than two doses in a day. Understand?"

"Yes. I understand."

"Good. I'm serious, this can be addictive, Thána." Spontaneously, she pulled me into a hug. "You keep working on that glamor. I'm going to go check on Kota. He has been carefully considering which books to bring with him. Left to decide on his own, we'd still be here three weeks from now."

I searched through my things for the images Habros had given me. Of the four or five different Kabeshi, I couldn't see a single tail, but they were all facing the camera. I couldn't read their rank from the insignia on their shoulders and chest. Hell, I probably couldn't have read them had they been American soldiers. They all had darker hair than Hedron did, though the hair on the one in the white uniform was more brown than black.

Most of them wore the hair on their head either closely cut or completely shaved, and most of them were clean-shaven of facial hair as well. I set the pictures down and centered myself, building a Kabeshi image in my mind based on pieces of this face and that build, that chin, and that nose. I held it there in my mind, memorizing its every nuance before I whispered the word, "*Álleji.*"

The change was more profound, and it felt like the air itself was trembling, but when it stopped, and I looked down, I was impressed with the changes. The illusion was striking, even before I went to find a mirror.

I was in the bathroom, admiring my work when I heard Kota yell. He came flying at me full of nine-year-old fury, screaming incomprehensibly. I instinctively put out my hands to keep him from actually hurting me, dropping the glamor at the same time. "Kota, Kota stop. It's me."

He shook from head to toe as he realized what I was saying. His eyes were still filled with anger and his face was a mask of contempt. "Kota, calm down." I touched his cheek with one hand to bring his attention to my face. "It's okay. It was just a glamor."

Tears welled in his eyes and he covered his face with his hands. I had no idea how to handle that. I never have been great with kids. Fortunately, Habros appeared in the doorway. "I'm sorry. I was working on the glamor and came in here to look in the mirror. He must have thought—"

Habros held a hand up. "It's okay." His big hands came down on Kota's shoulders and the boy turned, burying his face in his father's shirt. "They were pretty violent when they came for her." He pulled Kota away and knelt in front of him. "See, it was just a magic trick. Aunt Thána is not really a Kabeshi soldier."

Kota looked at me shyly and I offered a weak smile. "You looked like them," he said.

I nodded. "But I don't now, right?"

"I didn't want them to come take me."

"No one is going to take you anywhere that I don't say is okay," Habros said. "And tonight, you are going with your grandmother to a safe place where you don't have to worry about Kabeshi soldiers at all."

Habros stood and got them turned to leave the bathroom. "Let's go make sure you're all packed up."

While they did that, I headed upstairs. I wanted to study the map Xen had left with us again. As a kid living in Upstate New York, I'd always had a good sense of direction, and that had followed me to El Paso. Since stepping through the portal though, I couldn't tell you which way was north if my life depended on it.

I stopped in my tracks when I heard something from the kitchen, inching closer until I could peek out of the hallway. I sagged in relief when I spotted Xen by the table. They looked up at me and lifted a hand in greeting. "Wasn't expecting to see you," I said amiably as I entered the kitchen.

"I bring word from Hedron," Xen responded.

"Okay, what word?"

Xen hesitated. "Are you well?"

I frowned. "What?"

"You look… tired."

"Exhausted, but I'll be fine. What's the news?"

"Daria has been moved." Xen continued looking at me with concern.

"Is it a problem?" I asked.

"No, it is better for us. This new camp is to our east. Closer to the front lines."

"Which means closer to escape." I exhaled, though the relief was minimal. "Good, but that changes some of the details." I pulled the map down from the cupboard where we'd hidden it. "Show me?"

Xen took the map and spread it out, one finger tracing along the streets we'd already identified. "This remains the same. Once you have the hauler, our route moves here." Their finger followed a different route, taking us east and out a different checkpoint.

"My information says the camp is here, near the foothills. The difficulty in our escape will be that the Kabeshi army is arrayed here." Their finger swept across an area just north of the camp. "However, it will make us less obvious also. The army has many outworlders enslaved, to power their weapons."

"So a Kabeshi soldier with a Pixin aid will be seen as normal. That's good." I'd only just started worrying about the language problem, but if I could have Xen in the cab of the hauler, they could translate for me.

"Perhaps having Katyk as your aid would be a better use of our skills."

"You're the translator, right?"

Xen smiled. "Yes, but on this particular mission, I serve another purpose. Katyk is also a witch, and she has access to some communications tech that I do not."

I wasn't sure why that made me uncomfortable, but it did. "Okay, I'll trust you on that." And I did trust Xen. Maybe it was the way Habros trusted them, or that they had known my sister, but Xen just fit into my understanding of this world. They rolled up the map and handed it back to me.

"I should head back. Dyn is due home from his recon of the new gate."

I found myself not wanting Xen to leave. "I could make us some tea… if you can stay a little while."

"Thank you, Thána. If times were different, I would love to sit with you and drink tea. Alas, there is still much for me to do before the night's storm comes through."

I watched them leave out the back door, smiling to myself. I had work to do too, not the least of which was getting my mother and Kota safely to the portal park.

CHAPTER 9
SNEAKING OUT

WE WAITED FOR THE EVENING STORM TO PASS, LEAVING THE STREETS EMPTY AND smelling vaguely of something akin to sulfur. With Kota watching me, I triggered my glamor, offering us some small safety from casual observers.

Habros carried Kota's bag as we ducked out the back door of the shop, through the largely depleted garden, and into an alley that ran between what was left of two large buildings. Near the end of that alley, we paused, listening to the stillness of the occupied city, making sure there were no passing patrols before moving out onto the street.

Like it was the night my mother and I arrived, the skies were strange, the moons hidden behind dark smudges of clouds that seemed to sit on top of the city. We kept to the shadows, inching our way between abandoned vehicles and partially destroyed buildings until we could see the trees of the park ahead.

Boots against pavement brought us up short just before we were about to dash across the main street through the heart of the city. We pulled back, pressing into the alcove of a doorway. I peeked out as the sounds grew closer, trying to get a look at the enemy in action.

There were four of them in brown khaki uniforms that vaguely reminded me of Germany in WWII. They moved down the cleared center of that main street, occasionally poking long sticks into vehicles or stopping to examine the buildings around them. One of them turned our way and I pulled back, barely breathing.

It seemed an eternity before they moved on and the sound of their footsteps diminished enough to feel safe moving out of the alcove. We moved slowly, quietly to the corner, and paused again, listening and looking, half certain we were about to be discovered.

Mom and Kota went first, dashing out of the shadow of the building and into the shadows of the trees. Habros and I followed, breathing a little easier when we were swallowed up by the ring of trees that guarded the stone circle full of portals. The circle was much as it was when we had first arrived, with no signs of any activity.

My mother gestured and we followed her to the portal, though I had no idea how she knew which one went to Spítia. I had a plan that would fix that, just in case we managed to get back here once we had Daria. Habros went to one knee beside his son, speaking quietly to him before pulling him into a hug.

My mother offered a weak smile. "You be careful."

I nodded. "I will. And we'll be fine."

She hugged me tight, whispering soft words of a protection spell before she let go. Habros hugged her then and when he released her, Mom adjusted her pack and took Kota's hand.

"Are you ready?"

"Does it hurt?" Kota asked, eyeing the portal suspiciously, then looking at me.

"Not at all. It's just like walking through a door," I assured him.

Mom tugged on his hand and they took the few steps to the doorway, then they were through and on the other side. I held up a hand in farewell, then took the lock my mother had given to me and a knife from my pocket.

"What are you doing?" Habros asked.

"Making it so she can't come back here to help, and so that no one else can go through this portal to Spítia."

I pricked my finger and smeared the blood around the locking mechanism before lifting it and planting it in the center of the portal and holding it there. "Kleidóste sto aíma mou." Similar to using wards, the field grew from the lock and covered the opening, the lock suspended in the middle. "There."

"I've seen Daria tinkering with that lock, I never understood how it worked."

"As of right now, no one passes through that portal until my blood unlocks it." I hadn't told my mother I'd planned to do it, knowing she would argue. I'd also figured she was likely to get Kota to safety and come back in a misguided effort to help. An effort that was likely to get someone dead.

"We should go. The longer we're out here, the more likely we are to get caught."

We made our way back to my sister's home the same way we came, encountering two more patrols that we had to hide from. Once we reached the safety of the garden, I relaxed a little. The danger drove home the notion that this was essentially a suicide mission.

On Daria's tablet, I'd found my way to an archive of news that followed the breakdown of treaty talks, to the first forays of conventional weapons that Vaneeshi magic users defended away, to the less conventional weapons fire. This was followed by invasion, followed by more magic weapons, which was what had caused the daily acidic rain that had nearly taken my hand, engineered to specifically take out offworlders. Then came the occupation and several attempts to close the portals in the park, which caused further damage to the buildings and people surrounding the park. Many of the citizens of Meerat had escaped north, and those that remained were culled of magic users and put under curfew.

Daria hadn't believed the Kabeshi would take down the city's defenses. Her diary spoke with admiration of the defense squad made up of friends she went to school with and other people of great power. That was why the family hadn't left when the city was evacuating. That, and wanting to be there when Mom returned.

The house was quiet as we entered, and I let the glamor go. It wasn't perfect yet, but it was close enough for our little outing to the portals. Of course, I was very aware that if I were approached, I wouldn't even be able to speak in their language and the whole charade would come to an end.

That wasn't the only peril either. This whole thing depended on me being able to drive this vehicle. From what I had seen, their transportation wasn't hugely different from what I was accustomed to. Unlike the cars in Spítia, they had actual steering wheels instead of levers and buttons.

Habros was going to teach me, but we only had access to a smaller vehicle, and I wouldn't be able to drive it anywhere, due to that being forbidden by the occupying Kabeshi military. So, it would all be theory until I got behind the wheel of the hauler in a few days.

As if he had followed my thoughts, Habros set a hand on my shoulder. "Tomorrow we will teach you to drive."

"Okay, good. I think I'm going to work a little more on this glamor before I sleep." In truth, I had no intention of sleeping, not when there was so much to do. I watched Habros disappear behind the door to his bedroom and went to the lab. I put my hands into the pockets of my jeans, coming out with the crystal and the pouch. Filling a glass at the sink, I took a pinch of the powder and sprinkled it in, stirring with a finger before drinking the whole thing down in one go. It was not as disgusting as Merry's mix, which I had to hold my nose to drink, but it left a sour taste in my mouth.

It didn't take long to work, either. Like fingers crawling out from my stomach, the magic of it crept through me, infusing me with energy that flushed the fatigue away. Cracking my neck, I tried to decide where to begin. I figured I should get the glamor perfected, so I opened my spell book to the pages with my notes, marked with the images Habros had given me.

My eyes were not as big as the ones in these pictures, and I needed a stronger chin. I also wanted broader shoulders. I needed to be imposing. For several long hours, I sat in that lab, setting and resetting the glamor until I decided that I could do little better. I saved the image into the crystal, glad that was something I'd learned to do. The glamor unanchored could drain me in under an hour and I was going to need it to hold for many hours.

I turned my attention then to Daria's notebook, thumbing through it. My sister was a talented potion maker and made quite a good living selling her wares to the Vaneeshi, both those without magic and her fellow witches. She had a section about ward stones where she ruminated on whether or not she could learn to make them, and I found a handful of wooden cubes about the same size as ward stones scattered under some receipts on her desk.

They didn't feel like ward stones exactly, but I could sense something of magic in them. I cleared a space on the worktable, moving a rack of test tubes and beakers off to the side, and sorted the cubes into pairs like I would ward stones. The wood was dark, almost black, with a fine grain and polish on them like varnish. Curious, I set four pairs and held my hand over them, whispering, *"Prostatéfste kai apothéste aftó to choro."*

The field flared, a soft green dome building above the stacked pairs. I took the pen I'd been taking notes with and tried to pierce the dome. I could push against it, pressing the field inward, but couldn't penetrate it. I ran through the other variations I knew and found them all to work to some degree, albeit none of them as strong as the wards generated by the stones.

I'm the first to admit that I had no idea how they worked. But clearly, Daria had figured it out. I was starting to worry that my sister was so far beyond me that we would have nothing in common. I was also worried that if the Kabeshi knew how powerful she was, they would stop at nothing to bend her to their will.

The Kabeshi had found ways to mix magic with weaponry only because they had corrupted Vaneeshi magic workers through blackmail, bribery, and for the strongest— torture. That was what I'd seen in my vision. Torture.

I sat in the chair and closed my eyes. The energy still running through me from Mom's powder made it hard to focus enough to activate *makrá vlépinta*. I breathed in, centering, and calming myself. It was night, and I could hope Daria was asleep, that maybe I could somehow let her know that help was coming.

For a long time I sat, just holding the image of Daria in my mind, trying to sense her somewhere in the world around me. I was about to give up when I felt something. It was faint, but I turned the chair to face in that direction, following the trail the way I had before.

"Daria." I breathed the name as I saw her, hoping she might hear me. She shifted on the floor of her cell, her eyes barely opening. She was thin, almost painfully so, and her skin was ashen. "I'm coming, little sister."

I dropped the effort and sagged into the chair. I wasn't supposed to be able to do it at all, so it was little wonder why it wore me out. The first time I had basically passed out, like I had when I got the portal to the kitchen open. It was beyond my skill level. But then, I had lost more than twenty years in which I could have been learning how to be a blood witch. It was Merry's daughter Zo's theory that my abilities had grown as they normally would even while blocked from my conscious use, and that I would find myself able to do a good number of things that others had to grow into, once I learned what they were.

There was more to her theories about my abilities. Things to do with genetics that I didn't remotely follow. Blood witches were a part of both of my family lines, that much I knew. I'd been told that my father's family opposed the marriage for just that reason. They came decidedly down on the anti-blood witch side of the argument.

I exhaled and weighed my options for what to work on next. I didn't want to practice any of the fighting spells I had been learning in the lab. I might break something important. I could work in the garden though. There was nearly nothing left there to ruin.

I paused to make myself a second dose of anti-fatigue powder, which needed a better name, and downed it before heading for the kitchen and letting myself outside.

There were no stars above, though I could see the vague, watery light of two of the three moons through the cloud layer. Rubbing my hands together to warm them, I set myself up in the open space between rows of planters and inhaled deeply. I started with the easy ones like *prostatévo*, crossing my arms at my wrists. I could feel the wall of energy that would separate me from whatever attack was coming. Then I cast *yperaspízo*, pushing that wall toward whatever was coming. I ran through my list of *defense first* spells.

I rolled my neck and thought of something else. Mom had said that the magic wasn't in the words, but in the will and power of the witch casting the magic. Okay, maybe I could try English. I started again with the easy stuff: protect, defend, move, throw. A memory came to me of that day at Mano Kourt, of Sabina breathing fire at the Brotherhood, and my first attempts at casting fire back at Merry's. I didn't want a ball of fire, I wanted a stream.

I refocused, stuck my hands out in front of me, and imagined flames coming from my fingers as I said, "Fire."

Nothing happened.

I shook off my disappointment and tried again. I grew frustrated around my tenth attempt and shook the tired weight off my arms, pacing around in a circle.

"Your focus is too broad," a voice came from the shadows, causing me to jump. "Try pointing just one finger. Focus on the tip." Slowly, Katyk emerged from the shadows, a crooked smile on her face.

"Oh. Hello." I found myself frowning and tried to stop. "What are you doing here?"

"I figured you'd still be up, practicing."

Something about her appearance in the garden seemed strange, putting me instantly on the defensive. "Just getting myself ready."

"If all goes well, you shouldn't need any of that," Katyk said, coming closer. Her walk was sultry, her hips moving with each exaggerated step, her eyes on mine as she licked her lips.

"When does that happen?" I asked, subconsciously mimicking her lick on my own lips.

"Fair point." She was beside me now, her hand on my arm, sliding it down to my hand and lifting it. She folded my fingers in, all but my pointer finger. "Here, try it again."

"I thought you only do sex magic."

She had moved behind me, I could feel her breasts against my back, her breath on my neck. "Sex is fire," she whispered. "Do it."

I was too distracted by her nearness, but I tried. Again, nothing happened. Her hands slithered around my body and slid into my jeans. They pressed in just above my groin and heat pooled there beneath her fingers. "Feel it here," she whispered, switching to my left ear. "This is the seat of your fire. Let it burn."

Despite myself, I let her voice seduce me, falling deeper into the arousal she was stoking before I exhaled and cast. Red-orange flames shot from my fingertip across the garden. Her hands delved deeper, pulling a groan from me. Fingers danced through my sudden wetness, pressed against my clitoris before I managed to find my head and step away.

"What?" she asked, pouting at me.

"Nothing. Just… I'm not…" I wasn't even sure what it was I was trying to say.

"Certainly seems like you are," she replied, holding up her fingers. Then, she dropped her hand. "Sorry, I thought— well, it doesn't matter what I thought, I suppose. Here." She pulled a bag I hadn't noticed off her shoulder and handed it to me. "The promised uniform."

"I thought Xen was bringing it?" I found myself disappointed that the Pixin wasn't the one bringing me the uniform.

"They got tied up. Expanded patrols in their section of the city. It was safer for me."

I took the bag with a nod of thanks. "Good. Thanks." She stood there, smirking at me and I found myself wanting to put my hands through her hair. "I just need to focus," I said, licking my lips again.

"Focus is good." She stepped closer, her hands moving to my hips.

"What are you doing?" I asked.

"Focusing," she replied, her lips only a breath away from mine. Her kiss was fire that filled my mouth and burned down to meet that hot, molten spot inside me she had stoked.

Some part of me wanted to step back, to stop whatever this was from going any further, but the not-thinking-things-through side of me slammed that door and drew us toward the house. We fumbled and stumbled our way into the kitchen. She shoved me against the wall, her hands finding their way in through my zipper and under my jeans while her lips burned their way down my neck.

I involuntarily rocked against her hand and she chuckled darkly against my throat. She nipped at my collarbone and licked up to my ear. "How's that focus?"

My answer came in the form of my hands on her face and my tongue invading her mouth. I spun us around and shoved her against the wall. I bit her lower lip lightly before sucking at the skin of her neck. I shouldn't have been that out of control, but the lust in my loins was overriding logic, which is, I suppose, the whole point of lust to begin with.

"Downstairs," I growled, pulling away, then pulling her with me. Maybe that whole lust inoculation was wearing off and this was the succubus thing? I didn't care in that moment. My skin radiated heat as I pulled her into my bedroom. I shut the door before pushing her against it, fumbling with the buttons of her black leather pants. She shoved them down once I cleared the last button.

I stepped back, toeing off my shoes, and shed my jeans. I pulled my t-shirt off, dropping it on the pile of denim as Katyk stalked across the room toward me. She pushed me to the bed and straddled me so that our groins rubbed together.

It had been a while since I'd been with a woman, but that didn't seem to matter as muscle memory and arousal took the lead. Katyk caressed over my skin, from my hips up to my breasts, then slid down and reached under me. I arched up enough to give her room to work the clasp of my bra, nipping at her lips.

We were breathing heavily as she tossed my bra aside. I pulled on the hem of her shirt. She shifted against me, grinding down as I won the fight to her skin. She wore no bra, leaving her breasts bare to my hands.

Her lips were dry, chapped even as they pressed to mine. One hand snaked between us and I lifted my hips to press up against her. Her fingers found their way inside me and I groaned into her mouth as her hot tongue met mine. I lost myself in the heat of my orgasm, surrendering to her insistent fingers.

She rode the tremors, then kissed her way down between my breasts, stopping just below my navel. Her grin was wicked, maybe more so than her fingers, and I took the moment to flip us so that she was on her back beneath me.

"My turn."

We exhausted ourselves in turns, finally collapsing to sleep in the wee hours of the morning.

My dreams were replays of being chased, and Daria screaming. I woke to Katyk getting dressed. I stretched, letting the sheets slip down to my stomach. Katyk turned and smiled. "Morning."

"You leaving?"

She nodded. "I need to get back."

"Back where?" I asked, sitting up.

"Back to my side of the prep," she responded, turning to steal a kiss. Katyk sat on the bed to pull on her shoes and pulled a hand through her hair.

"Your side?"

"We all have jobs to do." She stood and I pouted at her. "Including you. I interrupted last night."

I had to concede that point. "But you helped too."

"Good." She stood. "You got the glamor locked in?"

I yawned and stretched, reaching for my pile of clothes on the floor. "I think so. Today is about learning to drive."

"Good luck with that."

I fished around for my bra, eventually finding it half under the bed. By the time I had it on, Katyk was at the door. I pulled on my shirt and jeans and followed her to the stairs. The floor was cold beneath my bare feet and I wished for a moment that I'd thought to put socks on.

CHAPTER 10
PREP

Habros raised an eyebrow at us as we emerged into the kitchen, but he said nothing as I walked Katyk to the back door. "See you soon," she whispered, kissing me deeply before she disappeared.

"I hope you got *some* sleep," Habros said, pouring me a cup of the dark tea he preferred.

"More than I had planned," I replied.

"Good." We were quiet for a few minutes, each in our thoughts. Mine were an unsurprising mix of spells, sex, and worry. I pulled the pouch of powder from my pocket and sprinkled a pinch of it into my tea. "Is that wise?" Habros asked quietly.

"If you want me to function it is," I replied. "Especially since this world doesn't seem to have coffee." I sipped at the tea and contemplated the day ahead. Habros was going to teach me the basics of how their vehicles work, and I wanted him to review my efforts at the glamor, making sure it was as accurate as possible. Beyond that, I wanted to work on the portal spell and continue my efforts in learning how to defend myself.

I stood after draining my cup and took it to the sink. "I'm ready for this lesson if you are. I just need shoes."

Habros stood as I came back with socks and my hiking boots on, the chair scraping across the floor. He placed his cup beside mine in the sink. "Come on then." He led me out to the garden, and through a door to the building behind his. "They just left the vehicles," Habros said as we descended a cement and steel staircase. "The apartments in this building were abandoned in the first days of the bombing."

We went down a few floors, then through a door marked with a character I vaguely recognized as the local language's version of numbers. It was dark in the garage, the lights long gone when the building above was damaged.

Habros pointed to the first vehicle I could see. It was a dark blue and squat, nearly square. There was no trunk and what I took to be the engine compartment looked almost like an afterthought. In some ways, it reminded me of that ugly Cube car Nissan put out back home.

"Your sister has terrible taste in vehicles," Habros said, his voice warm with affection. "Get in."

He handed me a black fob as I opened the driver's side door. "The hauler is obviously going to be bigger, and likely will have the driver's side on the opposite side."

"That's okay, that's what I'm used to."

He pointed to a slot on the dashboard. "The key goes here."

I slid the fob into the slot. "And then press this." He pointed to a button above the slot. Under me, the car rumbled to life. It wasn't loud, but I could feel the engine thrumming.

Habros pushed the door shut before coming to the other side of the car. He sat in the passenger seat, looking a lot like Cambious had in the ridiculously small car he'd gotten us in Thelos. "Clearly, the wheel is for steering. This lever here," he pointed to a silver lever on the right side of the steering column, "is how you control speed. It is currently in brake. Pull down one stop to go very slowly, each step down makes the vehicle move faster. These buttons here control whether your movement is forward or backward."

I looked the console over, my hands moving to the lever and buttons before returning to the steering wheel. "We should be safe enough to drive around the garage," Habros said.

"Okay." I was nervous but told myself that it was just like driving back home, only the controls had moved. I pushed the button for forward, then eased the lever down. We edged forward out of the parking spot. The steering wheel was super responsive, and I almost clipped the bumper of the nearest car because of it. I kept us at the slowest gear for our first circle of the parking garage, then eased into the next faster and the next.

As we completed our fourth circle, I slowed back down, then came to a stop before putting it in reverse and backing into the parking spot. "That wasn't bad," I said.

"Remember, the hauler will be distinctly larger."

"I've driven big vehicles before. I should be fine."

"Good." He opened his door and got out. "I'm going to go pack up a few of Daria's things, so she'll have them when we free her."

"I should go through the kit Mom packed me too." I was itching for us to get started now that it had come to this point, but we still had a few days to wait. I was determined to use my time wisely.

My bedroom still had the vague scent of Katyk hanging in the corners and on the bedsheets. I grabbed the small backpack my mother had packed before she left and sat on the bed. My first aid kit was on top, followed by several pouches like the one in my pocket, labeled with information about what was inside. I'd worked with a few of them before. There was a mix that, when properly used, could hide all signs you were ever in a place, even to the point of removing footprints.

Mom had told me that my father used to use it when he would make Bigfoot tracks for me to find in the backyard during a phase when I was obsessed with Bigfoot. He'd strap on these oversized feet after a good rain and tromp through the muddy yard, then he'd sprinkle the powder over the last few feet of tracks to make it look like he'd vanished or jumped the fence or something.

There was a pouch of sleep powder and another of mixed herbs, that combined with ward stones would offer protection against all but the strongest of magics. Under that were the rest of the protein bars we'd packed back at Merry's house and a small batch of potions in plastic jars labeled for various ailments, including the ones for pain and stomachaches.

I repacked the bag and added my full canteen to it. I had no idea how this insanity would turn bad, but I wanted to go in believing I had prepared as much as possible for the inevitability that it would.

That done, I turned my attention to the uniform Katyk had brought me. It was going to need a good pressing to be ready to wear, especially after spending the night in a bag. I shook it out and put it on. The pants were a little long and the shirt fit tight across my chest. I rolled the cuffs of the pants under, so they fell right across the top of my shoes, then moved to the mirror to see if I needed to make adjustment to my chest or if the glamor would be enough to cover me.

I had to go back to my jeans to fetch the stone, and slid it into the pocket of my uniform pants before I triggered the glamor, feeling the familiar bubbling as the spell rearranged my features.

I still wasn't completely happy with the eyes, but when I'd tried to make them bigger, they had just looked like a child's drawing of an alien, and nothing at all like the Kabeshi I had for reference. I wandered out of my room, heading toward the room Habros shared with my sister.

"Habros?"

He startled when I appeared in the doorway. I smirked. "Does that mean I pass muster?"

"You what?" Habros asked once he'd recovered.

"Um, the glamor is good?"

"Turn around, let me see."

I stepped into the room and made a slow turn so he could get a look at the tail. "Yes, it is convincing." He lifted the bag he was packing, testing its weight. "Daria says I pack like I'm never going to see home again." He grimaced and put the bag back onto the bed. "I... miss her."

Letting the glamor drop, I nodded. "I know you do. But we'll see her soon."

"I hope so." It was the first time I'd heard doubt in his voice. "We are taking a lot of risks."

"Yes, we are. But they've worked for me before." I brushed my hand down his arm. "To rescue Mom, Cambious and I had to glamor ourselves and steal uniforms too. We got out alive."

Of course, I didn't tell him how much more complicated this glamor was, or that for Mom's rescue, I'd had the advantage of working with other witches, a phoenix, and some mutinous manticores. I didn't expect to have that advantage this time around.

I spent the remaining hours before departure, from that moment until around eight hours before we were to leave, working over the portal spell and practicing with offensive types of spells. I used a combination of spell words in both the Greek-like language of my mother's homeland and in English, sometimes in combination with various gestures and motions, sometimes not.

I'd created a portal from the kitchen to my bedroom twice, and managed to not pass out the second time, though my nose bled quite a lot. It wasn't going to teleport us out of the camp but could be useful in getting away if we were being chased. I even got the casting down to the set intention and a clear vision of where I wanted to go.

Habros came and got me from Daria's lab for dinner on our last night. I was trembling and soaked with sweat. I hadn't taken a dose of my anti-fatigue powder in hours because I had promised my mother I would sleep before we left. I nearly fell asleep in the soup Habros had made with the last of the vegetables from the garden, and I stumbled downstairs afterward, zombie-like.

The exhaustion of nearly forty-eight hours of spell work hung heavily on my body as I crawled out of my pants and into bed. I vaguely remember hearing Habros come down the stairs, and then nothing until the dreams hit. Xen and Daria, escape, running, wounded and bleeding. Shortly before Habros woke me, the running became hiding in caves of some kind and forcing Daria to drink my blood to keep her from dying.

"Thána, it's time."

I sat up with a start, gasping as I pulled a hand through my sweat-soaked hair. I set about getting ready, brushing my hair, and pulling it back into a short ponytail before donning the freshly pressed uniform. Habros had even pressed in the turned-up cuffs of the pants.

I triggered the glamor as I got to the top of the stairs with the backpack over one shoulder. I had my ward stones and anti-fatigue powder in one pocket and the kelcimite in the other, and had tucked my mother's pendant into a pocket in the backpack for safekeeping.

Habros had a cup of tea on the table for me and a bowl of what passed for oatmeal. There were no raisins or sugar to be had with Kabeshi soldiers shutting down most of the markets and keeping food that was available down to basics. We made quick work of breakfast, and set out, going through the garden to the street beyond it, the way we'd taken Mom and Kota to the portals.

Beside me, Habros wore black and carried the bag he'd packed Daria's things into. He was quiet, but I could feel his nerves. It wasn't quite dawn and the streets were quiet. We passed the one market in the section of the city that was allowed to open just as the lights came on inside.

We crossed a few streets and made a left onto the first I'd seen that wasn't lined with derelict vehicles and debris. The buildings were all standing and near the end of the street, there was our first real test of the glamor, the Kabeshi checkpoint.

There were a few non-Kabeshi around at that point, I'd spotted a Pixin and one I thought was Dealthian, like Habros. I had no idea what rank my uniform said I was, but as some junior officers passed, they saluted me, fist to chest and I responded in kind.

Habros dropped back a step so that he was behind me as we approached the pedestrian gate of the checkpoint. The Kabeshi at the gate gave me a once over and nodded to his counterpart who buzzed me through. Behind me, Habros stopped, produced his paperwork, and spoke to the soldier briefly. We'd agreed I would keep walking. We did not want them to think we were together.

We would meet up again once we were out of sight of the checkpoint. I made it to the corner and turned, slowing my steps so that Habros could make up the difference. Here, in the center of the Kabeshi-controlled city, there were a lot more people moving around. I felt Habros behind me and resumed my previous pace, though he stayed a few steps behind.

"Left," Habros said, just loud enough for me to hear. I crossed the street and could see the garage just a few blocks up. It was a big one, with a wide gaping mouth and the smell of grease mixed with kerosene.

There were two large vehicles inside the maw of the open bays and a third waiting outside. I could see people working as we approached, wearing grease-stained coveralls and strange collars around their necks.

There was an office where I spotted Hedron with paperwork in his hand. Xen appeared to my right, slipping a tablet into my hand. It would contain our mission and my authorization to take the hauler. For this part, I was on my own with only Hedron for assistance. I would pick up the others a few blocks away.

I took a deep breath and entered the office, clicking my heels and saluting Hedron. His face looked tense, but then, that might just be his normal face. He nodded to me and held out his hand for the tablet. I handed it over, flicking my eyes over the very interested man behind the desk. He seemed human and was also collared. He shrank away behind his terminal when Hedron looked at him.

Hedron spoke in Kabeshi, then handed the tablet back to me and gestured toward a door. It led us into a hallway where we passed a few men in the same brown uniform who snapped to attention as we approached. Hedron barely acknowledged them. We emerged into the weak morning sun and Hedron pointed to a vehicle parked directly in front of the bay doors.

My hands were shaking and my nerves rattled from feeling of being very exposed. Hedron walked me to the driver's side and handed me the key. I saluted him again before I set my foot to the runner and leveraged myself into the cab. I breathed a little easier when I pulled the door shut. I glanced over the controls, put the key in its slot, and brought the engine to life.

It rumbled louder than the small car did, a rumble I could feel in my ass. My feet shifted under the console, subconsciously looking for the brake and gas peddles that weren't there. I eased the lever down one gear and the truck lurched forward. I kept it slow as I pulled out onto the street and turned toward our planned rendezvous. I didn't take it much faster once I was on the street, keeping it at two or three, and easing back to one to make my turn.

I didn't see my passengers at first, but as I came to a stop, Xen stepped out of the shadow of the building wearing a collar like those I'd seen at the garage. I braked the vehicle as Xen climbed up on the passenger side. "I take it you had no trouble."

"Smooth as pudding."

"Let us hope that it is a good sign of what is to come." Xen glanced back at the building. "We should get started." They pressed a button on the console. "Opens the back. This one," they pointed, "unlocks the cages." Xen pushed that button too. Their eyes met mine and their hand patted my leg, as if for luck.

With a nod, Xen got out and headed to the back. Dyn and Habros followed Xen, but Katyk climbed up into the cab, also wearing one of the collars. She leaned across the seat and kissed me, one hand rubbing over my thigh. "Don't start something we don't have time to finish," I said.

Her eyes sparkled and her grin was wicked. "Gotta keep the motor running." She rolled her eyes and pulled away. She held out her other hand and I opened mine where she deposited a small device. "It goes behind your ear, so we can communicate."

I nestled the device into the space between my ear and my neck, surprised as it felt like it was melting into my skin. "Good, now press it to connect us."

I did as she said, tapping the spot. An odd sensation rippled out from the dot, making my head feel strangely muffled and like I was being held in place.

She smiled. "Okay, the next bit isn't quite as easy, but it should let me talk for you, from inside your head."

CHAPTER 11
CHECKPOINTS

"That doesn't sound pleasant," I said.

"It isn't very, but it might be the only way we survive to get out of the city, so just relax. Close your eyes and center yourself. Try not to tense up."

That was easier said than done. I closed my eyes and took a few slow breaths, sinking my conscious thought into my center. I was about to open my eyes and look to see if she was still there when I felt… well, I'm not sure what I felt. It was like a tickle, only not in a physical way. Katyk cupped the back of my head with one hand and the tickle wiggled into me, almost like a finger pushing into Jell-O. Or something. I don't know, I suck at metaphors.

The wiggle grew in pressure, then thickness until I thought she was drilling into my skull with a tree branch. My body clenched tight, fighting the intrusion even as I tried to stay relaxed. "Thána, take a deep breath."

I did as I was told and there was a *pop* inside my head as the pressure released. A weird sensation took its place, like I was no longer alone in my head. "Okay, I'm in. Can you feel me?"

"I feel something." I slowly opened my eyes.

"Turn your head and look out the side window so I can… yeah, that's good." When I moved my head, the sensation of Katyk followed, almost like a ghost. I turned to look at her and she pulled back a little. "Okay, that part is weird, seeing myself like this."

With what felt like fingers outstretched, she sought out the parts of me she needed to control. "There it is." The words were hers, but it was my mouth saying them.

Next, she spoke Kabeshi and my mouth moved, the words spilling from my lips.

My head was full. It wasn't painful, exactly, but I was going to have a headache when it was over. "I'll try to be as still as I can and not do anything unless you need me to," Katyk said. She kissed me and settled into the passenger seat.

I heard the back door close and the clang of the cage doors. They needed to be locked inside in case we were inspected. "Let's go," Katyk said, her voice in my ear though her mouth didn't move.

"Okay, hold on to something," I responded.

"You remember where you are going?" Xen asked, their voice coming from the communications dot.

"Yeah, I think so." I put the hauler in first gear and got us started, moving into second after I made the next turn. Two more turns got us moving east. In the distance, I could see the blockade of the road. Nervously, I pulled the tablet with my mission orders closer on the seat. I could feel the intrusion of Katyk in my head as if there were a physical tether binding us together. My heart was racing and some part of me was sure this was going to end right there at the checkpoint.

"Focus," Katyk said softly.

"You reading my mind, Katyk?" I asked.

"No, but I can feel your tension. Take a deep breath. You can do this."

I still had my doubts, but I downshifted as we neared the checkpoint. I licked my lips and hoped we weren't about to die. A soldier held up one hand and I put the brake on, grabbed the tablet and lowered the window.

He took the tablet, nodded, then asked me a question in Kabeshi. Katyk's words came out of my mouth in response, then she translated that he wanted to inspect the cargo. I pressed the button and the back door opened. The hauler lurched as someone climbed in.

It seemed to take forever and I was already thinking about just ramming the gate when I heard the door close. The soldier handed back the tablet, spoke something in Kabeshi, and waved for the gate to be opened. I held my breath as I took the brake off and eased us through.

I didn't exhale until we were through and out onto the open road. That was the first hurdle. "Well done," Xen said in my ear. The rest of the plan was not as clearly laid out as this last part had been. Our next step was just to get to the camp.

The terrain around Meerat was largely flat, with what looked like orchards on the right and stretches of tract-like housing on the left for the first few miles.

It was a straight shot from Meerat to the camp. The highway seemed well maintained, and we were nearly an hour out before I saw signs that we were approaching the foothills. To our north, I saw evidence of the army, with vehicles and tents that became denser the further east we went. There was a barricade across the road, and as we got closer, I could see that there were tall wire fences around a camp, with evidence that they had someone who knew how to work wards.

"Okay, what are we doing?" I asked, slowing down.

"We talk our way in," Xen replied.

"And then what?" I asked.

"We hope the fake orders Hedron created for us work and we can take as many prisoners as we can fit in this thing."

"And if they don't?"

"Then we improvise," Xen said.

"Great." The gate loomed ahead of us and again I gave thought to just ramming through it, but that would give us away before we even had a chance to try this charade. We were stopped by a bored-looking soldier in the black uniform of the Kabeshi Special Forces.

Again, I handed off the tablet, watching as he read it over. He waved to the men inside the gates, and a team of them appeared. The officer handed the tablet back, then said something in Kabeshi. "The team is going to scan the truck. Open the back door," Katyk said quietly.

Five men surrounded the vehicle with machines of some kind in their hands. One approached me, the scanner aimed at the console. I had no idea what they were looking for as they moved around and then one of them got into the back. After a few tense minutes, they withdrew and the gate opened. The gate officer gave me instructions and Katyk replied to him through my mouth.

I drove us into the camp, trying to ignore the feeling that I was driving us to our deaths. Inside the fence, there was a wooden building to our left and a series of tents on the right. My directions were to park in front of the building and present my prisoners to the commandant. My hands trembled as I opened first the back door of the vehicle, then the cages.

As I got out of the hauler, another black-uniformed officer approached. The hair covering his skin was darker than any I had seen and thick. Even his face was mostly covered with hair, with only the area around his eyes and forehead free of it. "Salute," Habros said in my ear.

I clicked my heels together and brought my fist to my chest with a nod of my head. Soldiers lined up Habros and the others behind me while I handed my orders to the officer. He scanned the tablet and handed it back, then asked me a question in Kabeshi. Katyk's answer was short, and I had no idea how she was hiding the fact that she was the one speaking. I didn't dare look.

Fortunately, I didn't need to worry too much about understanding because the officer waved me toward the building. Another uniformed Kabeshi waved me over to a desk under an awning. He held out his hand for the tablet and I gave it to him. The others had been told to follow. "They are reviewing the orders," Katyk said into my head. "They will gather the prisoners Hedron indicated in our orders."

I waited, watching the man at the desk review the orders and compare it to his own screen. He nodded tightly. "*Ja. Wer haver mehreren gafangene beroit. Wer werver Irre gafangener vorüberehend unterbringer, währen wer volkehrunger treffer.*"

He put my tablet down on the desk and looked up, glancing over my team. "They're putting us in temporary holding," Katyk said. "*Meyn bevel ist, sie nacht aul meyner augen zue lasser.*" Katyk's words felt weird in my mouth. My anxiety ratcheed up, my hands sweating and my mouth dry. Any moment now we would be discovered.

"*Kommer zie.*" The man stood and handed the tablet back. I fell into step beside him and we moved away from the building and toward the tents. Several men saluted us and the man beside me acknowledged them absently.

Inside the tent, there was a cage large enough to hold as many as ten prisoners. He pressed a badge of some kind to the lock and the door opened. I had no idea how far Katyk's tether would stretch and there was no way I could fake being Kabeshi without her.

"*Zie zind hiar sichen urd wer werder die anderer bringer. Bas dahen könnin zie unsere anrichtunger nutser.*"

"He says that he will bring the prisoners they are sending with us, and you are free to use the facilities," Katyk said in my head.

"I need to find Daria," I thought as loudly as I could in her direction, hoping that connection went both ways.

"*Ich würne gerner dae deildunskammer seher,*" Katyk said through my mouth.

"*Ja. Jut, ich werder nes tir seigen.*"

"*Dring dae hiexĕ de Daria Komen. Zie körnte atwas dilbung gebraucher.*" The man gestured at Katyk.

I felt terrible leaving Xen, Dyn, and Habros behind, but it was Katyk I really needed at that moment. "We're going to their torture facility," Katyk told me.

For a second I froze, the dream of Daria screaming filled my head. The torture facility didn't sound like any place I wanted to go.

"That's where your sister is," Katyk responded.

We entered the building and saluted guards who opened the door. Inside the room, there was a medical table like the one I had seen Daria strapped to. There were trays of instruments that looked like something out of a horror movie, and the wall was lined with implements of pain. I did my best to look like I was dispassionately examining the facilities, but as I turned to finish surveying the room, I came upon small cages. There were five, two of them filled with people.

They were folded up to fit in the tiny space. It had to be painful. There was no room to shift or move much more than turning their head, and even that was limited. I took a step closer. The woman in the nearest cage opened her eyes and I almost gasped.

"Daria." Behind me, Katyk coughed to cover my blunder and I snapped my attention back. I had to keep it together. I walked to the wall and chose a black leather paddle, testing its weight against my hand. The officer looked at me with suspicion. Now, so was Daria. This could fall apart with one wrong word. I moved back to the cage holding my sister and set a hand on it. "*Ver ist des?*" I had no idea what Katyk was saying but was trusting her to steer us around this carefully.

"*Thartnäckile hiexĕ. Nenkt, zie karn urs vidersteher. Aven vir verder zie brecher.*"

My head started to pound like it was pushing against Katyk's invasion. The strain of the glamor wasn't helping. My hand rubbed against the pocket holding my pouch of anti-fatigue powder. I couldn't very well take it while this officer was watching.

He moved to the cages, lifting the keycard to the locks. They popped open and he reached into the man's cage first where he gripped his hair and dragged him from the cage. I stepped in before he could do the same with Daria, my hand cupping the back of her neck rather than her hair.

Daria looked ready to fight, aside from her nakedness and unsteady feet. "Clothes?" I said in my head to Katyk.

"*Kleidang für des gefengenen?*"

The officer grunted and gestured at a metal cabinet. I crossed to it and found thin white pajama-type clothes. I pulled out two sets, but when I turned back, the officer was eyeing me suspiciously. I glanced at Katyk for help, but she just took the clothes from me, a ghost of some emotion I couldn't name on her face.

The officer reached toward my arm, his face clouded. I had hoped to get through this without tipping my hand, but it looked like I was going to need to get my hands dirty… or my pants bloody.

"*Sýnchysi,*" I murmured as he touched me, urging the confusion that would let me close enough to ensure he took a very long nap. I gripped his lapel and dragged him toward me, pushing my mouth over his. I didn't want to kill him, but if I took enough of his life force, he'd be unconscious for hours. Maybe days. He struggled against me and for a long moment I wasn't sure I could do it, then I felt it… like something inside him had torn free and surged out into me. I staggered back, falling against the cabinet as he crashed into the exam table.

Now I would have to contend with bleeding on top of everything else as my body expelled what I'd taken from him, but it was that or violence and I'd already proven I wasn't overly good with violence.

"Who are you?" Daria's voice wavered.

I stopped halfway across the room and turned back, touching the kelcimite in my pocket to release the glamor. "I'm Thána, your sister."

She frowned at me, staring with dull eyes. "Mom found you?"

"I don't have time to explain just now. Get dressed and I'll tell you the whole story once we're out of here."

I didn't look at her. I couldn't look and still function. She was wounded and scarred and who knows what all they did to her during her time there.

I gathered myself and pulled the pouch of powder from my pocket. I pinched out a dose and dropped it straight on my tongue.

The taste of it concentrated like that was intense and the effect kicked in fast. Energy surged through me and I was able to think clearly again. "Okay, we need to get back to the others," I said, looking around us. "He'll be out for a while, that should buy us some time. We walk out of here calmly, get them, get in the truck and haul ass."

Daria got into the clothing I had given her, then reached for the keycard on the officer's belt. I stopped her with a hand on hers.

"Collars," Daria said in her scratchy voice.

I nodded and took the card myself. "We'll deactivate them once they're in the truck."

I reactivated the glamor. "Okay, nice and smooth. We can do this." All we needed to do was get back to the others, get everyone into the truck, and drive away. It was that simple.

Of course, nothing is ever that simple.

We moved as though we belonged there and had a purpose. Daria and the man whose name I hadn't gotten were behind me, with Katyk bringing up the rear. We made it across to the tent where we'd left the others. There were another five people crammed in with them. I walked up to the cage, and pressed the key card to the lock, stepping quickly out of the way as Habros pulled Daria to him, weeping openly into her hair. Daria was slow to respond, but when she did, she clung to her husband desperately.

The display was starting to draw attention.

I slipped the hauler key into Habros's hand. "I'm going to lay down some defenses, you get the hauler started."

"Thána, you're the one with the glamor," he protested.

"Just trust me. I'll get them in the back, you drive like hell."

I lined my prisoners up, sandwiching Daria in the middle. "We should hurry," I said quietly, leading the way to the hauler.

I directed them toward the open door. Dyn went in first and I passed him the key card so he could deactivate the collars. I glanced at Xen, who had an arm around Daria's back, then to Katyk who was hanging back, watching around us. The five prisoners we were supposed to be taking to another camp were in. That left Xen, Daria, Katyk, and me.

I nodded to Xen and moved to a more defensive position. If I could just get everyone on board before—

"Halte es. Tiese deiben geher nacht."

So much for that. I looked up at the approaching commandant. He was gesturing at us and speaking emphatically. I guessed the officer I had put down had been discovered. I stepped between him and the prisoners, hands already lifting as I reached inside for a spell, pulling out a defensive shield that pushed him back two steps. "Get Daria in," I said over my shoulder to Xen. I heard the hauler's engine come to life. I only had to hold him for a few more moments. My body chose that moment to begin bleeding. I decided it was time for more than defense and lifted my right hand. "Fire."

Flames shot from my hand, but I was burning through my dose of the anti-fatigue powder fast, so I wasn't going to be able to hold it for long. Xen and Daria were on the truck, but men were surrounding us.

"Habros, go!" I screamed, even as hands closed around me from behind, pulling me off my feet and spinning me away from the commandant. The hauler was moving, the back door waving as it sped away. Xen and Daria were on the ground with weapons leveled at them.

"I really wanted *you* anyway," Katyk's voice was dark in my ear. "The others don't matter. I've kept the prize. Don't let her touch you, she's powerful."

Her presence in my mind became louder and overpowering and the last thing I saw before I passed out was the hauler smashing through the gates.

CHAPTER 12
CAUGHT

I woke up confused. Everything felt off, my skin was too tight, my head too big. There was something over my head, some type of hood, and around my neck… I swallowed hard against the panic rising to choke me. It was metal, the collar, and it fit tight against my throat. I could move my head to some extent, but the collar was wide enough that my chin would touch it if I tilted forward.

The surface under me was cold and hard and my right hand was restrained in something that felt like metal. My left ankle was as well which meant I couldn't do much beyond shifting around.

Daria. I could almost see the look on her face when she realized we had been betrayed as the truck drove away. *Katyk.*

Katyk had seduced me and got me to trust her, and she betrayed us. I shifted as much as I could, trying to feel out where I was.

We had failed.

Tears stung my eyes thinking about Daria stuffed into that tiny cage. I had no idea how long I had been out, but I was still bleeding so it couldn't have been that long. With any luck, Habros and the others had made a clean escape and were hauling ass to the nearest border and safety.

"Okay, Thána, think," I muttered.

I heard movement and froze. "Is she awake?" The voice was heavily accented and nearer than I'd like.

"Yes, I think so." That was Katyk, and right by my head. "Aren't you?" She poked my shoulder. "Have a nice nap?"

I turned my head toward her. "Bitch."

"Ow, you hurt my feelings."

"Katyk, stop playing, and bring her."

Hands moved over my ankle and wrist, freeing me from the restraints, then forced me off whatever surface I had been chained to. I was between two big soldiers, stumbling blindly as they compelled me along. I realized belatedly that my feet were bare, and the clothes I was wearing were light, loose against my skin.

The floor beneath me was wood, so I assumed we were in the building. Then wood gave way to tile and the horror of my new situation started to sink in. A door closed somewhere behind me, and then the hood was ripped off, leaving me blinking at the sudden rush of white light.

I looked around, hoping I was wrong, but no… there I was in the room where they tortured prisoners until they broke. I held no delusions about my ability to withstand pain. My throat closed as I spotted the cages. Daria had been returned to the one we had taken her from and Xen was in the one beside her. Both looked dazed.

"I wouldn't worry about them." A voice pulled my attention to the medical bed. Beside it stood a Kabeshi dressed all in white. He was arranging implements on a tray. Katyk stood beside him. She was dressed in clothes like the ones I'd found there for Daria, though hers bore a blue symbol on each sleeve.

"Bring her."

The two soldiers holding me dragged me to the table. I didn't resist, it seemed like resistance at that precise moment would be futile and just a waste of precious energy. I was lifted and forced to lay on my stomach before my arms were pulled down to restraints on the side of the table. My feet were likewise spread apart and restrained.

"Very good. Now we can begin."

"I think you should know that I have nothing to give you," I said. "I'm barely trained. I have no special gifts."

His hand touched the inside of my thigh where my menses had turned the rough white cloth red. "Oh, I think you do. Our friend here tells me that you are something they call a blood witch."

"Yeah, okay, I am. I am a blood witch. But it's not something you can weaponize."

"We shall see."

Cold hands pulled my shirt up, exposing my back and one hand laid possessively on my skin. "When you arrived, you looked like one of us. How did you achieve that?"

I shook my head. He had to know the answer to that. From what Mom had said about the number of magic users in Vaneesh, it didn't make sense that they wouldn't know about glamors.

Fingers pinched the skin under my left shoulder blade, pulling it taut, then something clamped down, like a clothespin only bigger and stronger. "I asked you a question, *bluathexe*." He repeated the pinching on the right side, pulling the skin of my back tight.

I turned my head away from him. I didn't want to look at his face. Something struck the stretched-out skin, laying a strip of hot, angry welt along my spine. I bit my lip and closed my eyes against the tears burning in the corners. After a second blow, my tormentor moved his hands down a few inches, once again pulling my skin and pinching it with a clamp.

By the time he had three clamps on each side, I was breathing hard through my teeth in my attempt to remain silent. He struck me repeatedly, sometimes with hard, stinging blows and others with teasing hits, leaving me panting.

"Now will you answer?"

I'll be honest. I had forgotten what the question even was. His hand stroked down my hot skin. "How did you disguise yourself?"

Oh, that. Right. "It was a glamor," I said through clenched teeth.

"Is that your magic? The magic of a blood witch?"

"What? No." I shook my head. "Just… magic. Any witch…" I bit down on my lip to stop myself from talking.

"I see. Is this true *hiexĕ*?"

"Yes, Commandant. Most witches can learn it."

"Honesty. I like this. So tell me then, what is your special magic? Why are you called a blood witch?"

"I can… heal people." I could only hope that telling him what my magic actually was would turn him from the idea that I might be of use to him. "I can… eat disease, for lack of a better description."

"And this?" His hand moved over my wet thighs again.

"How my body gets rid of it, the disease, the bad energy."

"Who did you heal?"

"What?"

His hand toyed with one of the clamps, dragging a curse from me. "Who did you heal?" With each word, he flicked one of the clamps.

"No one." I gasped. "I just…"

"You attacked one of my men."

I swallowed hard. "Yes. I knocked him out."

"That does not sound like a method of healing."

I knew that, of course. It was how I had killed the man who killed my father. Instead of pulling out a disease, I pulled out the energy that kept them alive. The body shed it like a disease because it was foreign. He hit me again and this time I did yell. "You will show me how this was done."

I shook my head. "No. I won't."

A man appeared at the door, clicking his heels. *"Obersut Artoz, su wirst gesacht."*

"Maybe not today, but you will."

That sounded ominous. I fought the desire to pull at the restraints holding me. My entire being wanted to break free, but wasting energy wasn't the way.

"Perhaps you need some time to think about it." He snapped his fingers and the soldiers returned. The clamps were pulled painfully from my skin and my hands and legs were freed. They yanked me off the table and threw me toward the cages. I balked when I realized what they were about to do, fighting as they dragged me closer.

"No." I shook my head vehemently and fought with every bit of my resolve, but then the collar around my neck buzzed to life and a shock reverberated through my body, dropping me to the floor like a fish flopping around on the ground. I was still pulsating as they folded me up and shoved me into the tiny cage.

I passed out and my next true awareness was of someone was talking to me, and it wasn't the Kabeshi doctor.

"Thána, are you okay?"

Xen. That was Xen's flat-toned voice. I blinked and opened my eyes. The room was dark, and we were alone. "Thána?"

I was supremely uncomfortable in the small space, my back pressed against the bars, my knees bent up against my chest. My right hand was trapped between my body and the bars and my head was pressed forward against my knees. "I… I think I'm okay," I responded finally. I wasn't. My back was angry, hot, and itchy, almost like a sunburn. And my claustrophobia was rearing its head.

It wasn't the small space so much as it was a small space that I was locked into. I've never been good with being locked in anywhere. The small space just made it worse.

"Xen, are you okay?" I asked, trying to divert my mind from the rising panic.

"I am unharmed," Xen said.

"Daria?" I tried to turn my head enough to see her, but the cage restricted my movement, and they had me facing away from Daria and Xen. "Daria?"

"Quiet. They'll hear."

Her voice was tiny and tremulous, barely audible even in the stillness of the otherwise empty room. "It's okay, Daria," I said softly. "We'll get out of this. Habros—"

She gasped and made a weird sort of half-choking sound.

"He's fine." I had no way of knowing that, of course, but I needed her to believe it. "And Kota is safe. Mom took him back to Spítia."

"Kota..."

"He's safe, I promise." I turned my attention to the locking mechanism on the cage. I couldn't see anything from that side of it though. "Xen, any ideas on how we get out of this?"

"Not at the moment."

Great. So far the great escape was neither great nor an escape. Maybe Habros and Dyn would be able to mount a rescue. I doubted Habros would keep going in the other direction once he knew Daria wasn't in the hauler. Of course, attacking the prison camp wasn't the brightest of ideas either, and a repeat of the plan that got us here in the first place wasn't going to work.

That left it firmly on us to figure something out and there were no rebellious manticores to come to my rescue this time. At least I didn't have a gaping wound and internal injuries. Yet.

In small favors, it felt as if my bleeding had stopped. The blood soaking the pants they'd put me in was drying and was going to chafe if I wasn't allowed to change, but that was the least of my worries. No, I needed to focus my attention on the rest of my worries: surviving, escaping, not dying.

As goals went, not dying was pretty high on the list. Not getting seriously injured was right up there too. I reached up to feel my way around the locking mechanism. I wondered if I could convince it to open the way I had other locks. A little blood, a little push. I wasn't finding any opening I could bleed into though.

"If you are thinking of using your magic, I would advise against it," Xen said. "The collar will make it most painful if you try."

"Just exploring the options," I said. "Do you have anything to add to this mess besides an ability with languages?"

"It is most difficult to fight while locked in this cage. I can tell you what was said in Kabeshi, if you like."

"Who is this guy? Daria?"

"The man who called him away called him a colonel by way of rank. I assume he is one of their scientists," Xen responded.

"He is the devil," Daria whispered. "Opens up your brain and plays."

"Yeah, he's a barrel of laughs." Okay, so I couldn't magic us out of the cages, and they'd taken everything I came with. That line of thinking was not helping my claustrophobia. I pushed the panic down inside me, but it kept climbing its way back into my throat. I wanted to scream and thrash, but I'd only succeed in hurting myself, and that would not help us at all.

I told myself to focus, but that just reminded me of Katyk. I couldn't feel her inside my head, but that didn't mean I was free of her. I imagined a wall made of brick in the back of my mind where she had tunneled into me. If magic was mostly intent, maybe it would be enough to keep her out.

CHAPTER 13
PAIN AND BLOOD

My voice was hoarse and grating, my screams disintegrating into ragged sobs. Artoz wiped his hands on a towel as he moved away from me. My blood seemed dark against the white of his uniform. Thus far he seemed far more interested in hurting me than actually asking me questions.

He picked up the glass flask that held about a pint of my blood and held it up to the light. "Tell me, *hiexĕ*, is it true what our mutual friend has said? Is this blood a miracle cure?"

The table was tilted at a forty-five-degree angle, with my head on the bottom, which did nothing to help the booming headache I'd been left with after Katyk's recent attempt at breaking my mind open. My ragged back was pressed against it, laying down a bass beat of pain to underscore the day's melody being played on my hands. They were splayed flat against wood slats with clamps that used screws to pierce the skin between my knuckles. The counterpoint was played by the two missing fingernails on each hand.

It wasn't a symphony. It was more of a clash metal song played by teenagers who had never picked up an instrument before. Or ever heard music. I let my mind continue to chase that ridiculous analogy, rather than answering the man's question.

Something pressed down against the bloody nail bed of my right index finger, pulling my attention back to Artoz. "If I pour some of this blood onto your wounds, would it heal you?"

"I don't know." I panted the words around gulps of air to keep myself from screaming again. "I don't know," I repeated when it looked like he was going to repeat the pressure on my finger. "Haven't learned."

He smiled at me, the blue tint of his skin darkening around his lips. "Shall we find out?"

I figured that was a rhetorical question, because even if I said no, he was going to do what he wanted. He turned around to the tray of tools on the counter behind him, coming back with an eyedropper. He withdrew some blood from the flask, then dribbled it onto the two fingers of my right hand where he had pulled out the nails earlier in this session of torture.

I hissed as the cooled blood fell against hot and angry flesh. Nothing happened. At least, not immediately.

Artoz shrugged and returned the flask and eyedropper to the counter. "How about the wound of another? Will it heal that?"

He gestured and Xen was shoved closer, their arm pulled across my stomach. Artoz lifted a surgical blade and dispassionately drew it down Xen's arm. Xen hissed, their eyes on mine as Artoz brought the flask over the bleeding skin and poured my blood over it.

His fingers smeared my blood into the wound, earning another hiss from Xen. Xen's wound didn't immediately close, but it looked like the bleeding was slowing, the skin tightening. "Very interesting," Artoz said.

Xen's eyes held mine, and I wanted to apologize, but before I could say anything, Artoz slammed his knife into Xen's stomach. I yelled and pulled on my pinned hands as Xen doubled over. Artoz pulled Xen back, leaning them up against the table. He held the wound open with one hand and used the other hand to pour what was left of my blood into it. Xen gasped while his fingers played in the wound. I couldn't see what the reaction was from my angled position.

Artoz seemed satisfied, however, releasing his hold on Xen and nodding to the soldiers. Xen was dragged out of the room. "Perhaps you are ready to show me this skill of yours? This disease eating?" He snapped his fingers and the guard at the door opened it. Two soldiers dragged in a man in ragged prisoner clothes. He was emaciated and looked feverish. As they dragged him closer I could feel the disease burning through him. I had no name for it, but he was dying of it.

Artoz removed my restraints. As soon as my hands were free of the clamps, I cradled them to my chest. I was forced to stand up and the man was dragged closer. Previously, they had brought me others, trying to induce me to repeat the energy-sucking I had done on the guard to incapacitate him and I had refused. I guess they thought I'd see curing this man as a blessing. Of course, I'd just be curing him so they could torture him more.

The prisoner wouldn't look me in the eyes. That was okay because I couldn't look in his either. "He's too sick," I said hesitantly. "All I can do is make his death painless."

I wasn't sure that was true, not without touching him, but in his position, I think I'd opt for death over healing. I didn't think about the fact that I actually was in his position, he was just further along in the progression of our predicament.

"Show me," Artoz said, nodding to the guards who brought the man closer. Artoz touched the collar around my neck with his keycard and I felt a blush of returning control.

I balked at the idea, but I couldn't see any other choices. Licking my lips, I nodded to the man. I had no idea if he understood what was happening... what I was about to do. As tenderly as I could I used a thumb on his chin to open his mouth and reached inside me. I closed my eyes and pressed our lips together. The infection in him was a raging fire that tasted of ash and sulfur. I pulled at it and it came sluggishly, bringing his life with it. When I had swallowed, the man slumped, dead before the men holding him could put him down.

I stumbled back against the tilted table, sliding to the floor myself.

"Most impressive, *Mörderin*," Artoz praised, his hand petting my hair. "You will make a grand assassin."

I shook my head in denial. I was already sinking into a pit of guilt for what I'd just done, even though the man would likely have been dead in days if I hadn't. "You have earned a reward." Again, he snapped his fingers and one of the men came forward with a small plastic cup. I lifted both hands to take it, unable to grip it without pain and holding it between the palms of both hands. The water inside was brown and had the faint smell of something that wasn't water, but I didn't care. I couldn't remember the last time I'd had anything in my mouth that wasn't screams or blood from biting my tongue.

I swallowed fast before he could change his mind and take it away from me. I dropped the cup before it was gone, splashing the last of the water to the floor. All told, it was no more than a few tablespoons and it sank into my stomach like a stone. While Artoz retrieved the cup, his men took my arms and dragged me to the cage beside Daria's, re-enabling the collar before opening the door. At least when they shoved me in, they had me facing her and they let me arrange myself to take the strain off the worst of my injuries.

We were left alone then, just Daria and me. "Daria?" I could just see her eyes which were watching me. She hadn't said much in the days we'd been locked up together and most of it had been to tell me to stay quiet.

"Are you okay?" Daria whispered, her fingers reaching through the bars to touch my knee.

"I will be," I assured, though I wasn't sure how. Thus far I had yet to be able to do much to find a way out. "How are you?"

She pulled her hand back. "Better."

That wasn't surprising. They had left her largely alone since I had come into the picture. "The drugs are mostly out of my system."

The particular drugs that Artoz had used in an effort to break my sister down far enough to brainwash her into working for them were long-lasting hallucinogens that amplified every terrifying thing Artoz did to her. I'd learned that in the quiet times between torture sessions. Sometimes, when the drugs had Daria in their grip, she would cower and shake. Other times she screamed or talked herself hoarse to someone who wasn't there.

Fortunately, my sister was stronger than I would be in the same situation. Artoz hadn't graduated to the drugs on me. Yet. The pain was already bad enough that I had considered giving in multiple times. I wasn't going to try to pretend I had what it would take to continue to withstand Artoz's torture. I was weakening each time they took me out of the cage, whether it was due to lack of food or loss of blood, or my aversion to the pain.

"Do you think Habros is okay?"

It wasn't the first time she had asked me that question. "I hope so, Daria." It was the same answer I gave every time. I did hope so, but I had serious doubts. The plan was nebulous beyond getting to the camp, and we had no way of knowing if Artoz had sent troops after them, or even if the prisoners he had taken through the gate could be trusted.

I had come to understand that Katyk was one of Artoz's broken dolls, a magic user who he brainwashed, and her job had been to deliver him more witches, particularly those he could break and use. She'd played along with our plan until I had shown her my power, and that was when she'd betrayed us.

I closed my eyes, wishing for the thumping in my head to subside or the screaming pain in my hands to go quiet or even just to pass out enough to sleep for more than a few minutes. As part of the added fun of being the current favorite projects of the head torturer, we got the awesome benefit of sensory and sleep deprivation on top of everything else.

As if sensing my thoughts, the light in the room turned up to eleven, flooding our special hell with the whitest, brightest light I had ever experienced. It was bright enough that I couldn't even see the torture table. Seconds later the noise pollution started, an endless loop of the most horrific sounds that ranged from the screams of people and animals, someone vomiting, horns, and sirens of all kinds.

And again, I was bleeding out the life I'd taken from that poor man, adding a lovely bouquet of blood to the overall stench of the room. If I'd had any water to spare in my body, I'd have cried, but all I could do was whisper my new mantra in my head, "Just stay alive."

I tried to shift around, but there was no room. I needed to take my mind off of the cage and the terror nibbling at the corners of my conscious thought. "He called me *Mörderin*. Do you know what that means?" I asked Daria.

Her eyes were bloodshot and rimmed in red as she turned to look at me. "Killer."

The difference between Artoz calling me a killer and Patoras calling me a *thanátou* was that Artoz wanted me to kill and Patoras had wanted me dead.

The air around me took on a watery wave like nothing was solid. It had all become Jell-o. My skin was alive with fire, the sounds of torment piped in to drive us crazy amplified in my ears and became real in my body, ripping at my skin and jabbing at my stomach.

"Thána?" Daria seemed to be far away.

Sweat dripped into my eyes and I tried to wipe them only for my hands to become raging monsters of pain slapping at my face. "Hallucinations," Daria said.

Right. Drug. None of it was real. The water had been drugged.

"Just ride it out. The worst will be over soon."

Sure, ride it out, as if it were a motorcycle taking me to anywhere but here.

I was still in the grip of the drug when they came back. Artoz loomed over me, pulling my hand to him to examine the two fingers he had doused in my blood. To my addled brain, he seemed as tall as a house, his hands huge, his fingers thick. I tried to pull away but my arm turned into rubber and stretched out between us. The floor wobbled under me as I was dragged to the table and strapped down again. I couldn't understand the words that were flowing around me, but I understood the bite of pain as my hands were once again clamped down, the screws eating into the soft tissue. I think I was screaming.

Katyk came then, all sultry fire slinking over my bare skin, blocking out Artoz and his aides, filling up my senses with sex until I was writhing on the table, not from the pain, but with arousal. As I approached orgasm, a knife sliced into my thigh and I arched off the table to the sound of Katyk chuckling in my ear.

I was returned to the cage after a long time, more of the drug fingering my nervous system, ratcheting up the terror that was already a living part of me. The lights and sound returned and it was all I could do not to scream myself mute.

By the time I realized the noise and light had been stopped, I had completely lost track of time. It could have been hours or even days lost in the jumble of thought, memory, and terror, riding the hallucinogen through an ocean of pain. I was surprised when the door of my cage opened and I was dragged out by my hair. "I grow tired of this game, *Mörderin*," Artoz said, pulling on his gloves. "I have decided to take matters further."

The guard who had pulled me out, put his arm around my neck, putting pressure on the collar and pulling me off balance as another one did the same to Daria. She was pushed to her knees on the floor and her eyes were wide when they looked at me. Artoz grabbed my chin and forced me to look at him. "You will kill this man, and you will do so now, or I will kill *her*." He turned my face and my heart sank into my stomach.

"Thána, no!" Daria screamed.

His eyes flicked toward her, flinching as if seeing her like that was more than he could bear. A shiver ran through him and when his eyes met mine he was resigned. He made the most minute nod to me, acceptance. Permission.

"Habros! Kill *me*, leave him alone!" Daria tried to pull away from the guard holding her but stilled when her collar started to buzz.

What I wanted to do was grab Artoz and suck his life into me, but he wisely stayed well out of my reach. Not that I could have held him with my busted-up hands. "Please, don't…" My throat closed around the words and for a moment I couldn't convince my lungs to continue working.

I was pushed closer to Habros.

"Thána, please don't."

I couldn't look at her. I think we all knew that forced to choose between my sister and her husband, I would invariably choose my sister. Even if she would never forgive me. I licked my lips and nodded slightly. The guard eased up his hold on me, letting me move under my own power. He turned the collar off as Habros was pushed to his knees. I stroked his cheek lightly with the backs of my fingers before leaning in to kiss his forehead.

"Forgive me?" I whispered.

"Forgiven," he said, his voice deep and warm.

I could hear Daria sobbing and it wrenched my heart into a pretzel. I pressed my mouth to his and for a moment we both just froze, stuck in a twisted tableau of surreal intimacy so much deeper than any kiss. As I opened my mouth, he opened his and surrendered. It took me three tries to get myself to breathe in, and more than twice that to really mean it and feel the force of him, the energy that kept him alive move at all. It was too much to take in one go and I had to pull back, choking against it in my throat.

My ears burned with Daria's sobs. Habros was sagging, his strength sapped. He tasted like no one I had ever done this to, so alive, so strong.

"Finish him," Artoz said beside me. His hand pushed my head back and held me in place.

"Too much," I gasped.

"Do it, or they both die."

I closed my eyes and went back to Habros's mouth. When I was done, Habros lay dead at my feet. My sister screamed and I fell to my knees choking up a strange combination of bile and something white and stringy. I hadn't had food in long enough that it could only be a byproduct of what I had just done. I collapsed, blacking out as my hands hit the floor and the pain overwhelmed me.

CHAPTER 14
ESCAPE

I sort of surrendered after that, giving Artoz what he wanted, but hiding inside myself. I crawled deep and refused to be teased out. Even when he started cutting. I couldn't tell you how long we were there in that room, how many days went with little to mark their passing but endless pain and amplified horror.

The hallucinogenic became a part of every game and at first, as it slipped through me, I welcomed the rush of pain relief and euphoria that came with it, but that didn't last. All too soon, that euphoria became paranoia and the relief circled back to pain.

The horror of nearly dying at the hands of the Brotherhood danced with the horror at hand, especially when Artoz made shallow but painful cuts around the scar in my side. His face was distorted and elongated, eyes bulging, his mouth filled with fangs. In the bright white light, I thought I saw demons coming to play with my brain. Sometimes when the pain was more than I could stand, I left my body, floating in a cloud of euphoria akin to physical arousal.

In the absolute dark that followed, I heard horrible things whispered through the bars of the cage. They condemned me, those voices that called me *thánatou*.

Daria's tears ripped at me and I know that I apologized repeatedly in my drugged state, until my voice grew ever more raw. I tried to catalog the various injuries, but couldn't be sure which were real and which were imagined. I thought he had cut me and burned me, but I couldn't localize the pain, outside the fire of the pain in my hands.

They brought me others, threatening Daria each time to make me kill. Each time I did, Artoz's smug satisfaction only made the guilt pooling inside of me worse. I did the only thing I could, I stopped. I couldn't scream anymore. I couldn't fight. I was merely existing and waiting for the end.

It wasn't until an explosion sounded nearby, rocking the building that I remembered myself, found a way to climb back out. Daria reached through the bars to touch my knee and I shifted so I could see her clearly. "What was that?" I asked, my voice sounding like my throat had been scraped across gravel.

"I don't know."

We hadn't spoken much since Habros. She had to hate me and I couldn't stomach that.

The door to our torture chamber burst open and Xen appeared, their arms full. Xen dropped the contents of their arms on the table, coming to the cages and squatting to look at us. They held up a key card and opened the cages. "We must hurry. I brought clothes. Get dressed."

Daria was the first to understand what was happening. She and Xen had to help me out of the cage and over to the table. Among the piles of uniform clothes was my backpack, along with what had been in my pockets when I was caught. My eyes fell on the pouch of powder and I fumbled with it, my swollen hands making it difficult. Daria took it from me, opening it and sniffing the contents. She took a pinch out and held her fingers up to my mouth. "Open."

I did as I was told, savoring the feeling of heat that fingered its way through my battered body as I swallowed. Xen had to help me get into the clean clothes as my left hand was only marginally functional and my right was worse. The bruises extended down most of my fingers and up past my wrist as reminders of the hospitality of our host who had repeatedly used those hand clamps and screws to torment me. Xen released us both from our collars, their hand lingering on the side of my neck for a moment in a gesture I found strangely intimate. Daria grabbed the backpack as I picked up the kelcimite with my left hand, sticking it into the pocket of my stolen uniform pants.

"We do not have a lot of time," Xen said. They led us to the door, listening for a long moment before opening it and leading us out. Another explosion rocked the ground. "The distraction won't keep them busy for long."

The air was cool against my hot skin and I wondered if I was feverish. I could hear yelling and gunfire. We emerged into the weak sunlight of a late afternoon that reeked of waste and charred flesh. The tents that housed the prisoners were aflame and prisoners were darting about. The fence line nearest to us was down and prisoners raced through it, chased down by soldiers.

Daria and Xen supported me between them as we moved toward a vehicle. We were cut off by two men in the khaki brown uniforms of the infantry as we approached. Xen moved quickly, kicking and punching while they barely had time to react.

Guns sounded nearby and we pulled back against the building. "This rescue needs a rescue," I grumbled. Xen took up a defensive position. A thought occurred to me. I fumbled in my pocket for the stone. It hurt like nothing I'd ever felt, and that's including wrought iron in my gut, but I got the stone up and forced my hands to take position with it.

I don't know if Daria knew what I was about to try, but she moved so that she was behind me, her arms around my waist to support me. Gunfire sprayed the wall and men circled us. The anti-fatigue powder combined with the adrenaline of refusing to return to the torment and the absolute terror of the faces around us, all morphed by the hallucinogenic running through me allowed me to drag strength up from somewhere I didn't know existed.

I was screaming, the spell tearing through me and out through my hands. The hole opened in the air in front of us. I had no idea where the portal went as my only intent was "away from here" when I cast. Daria started to propel me toward the portal, then Xen crashed into us from behind, throwing us through and we crashed to the ground on the other side, tumbling and ending in a tangled heap.

I lost the grip on the stone when we landed and the portal snapped shut with an audible click. For a long moment, none of us moved, then Xen rolled off and offered a hand to Daria, leaving me gasping for air. My nose was bleeding and everything hurt, like every organ inside me had been pummeled.

"How did you do that?" Daria asked.

"Where are we?" Xen walked in a tight circle around us.

I rolled onto my back, looking up at a rapidly darkening sky. The ground beneath me was hard and dry and it made my back scream. I sat up slowly, rubbing my aching head with the palm of my left hand.

"I don't know," I responded. It was the answer to both questions. "Your notes," I said, looking up at Daria and sort of waving one hand. "I had been practicing. Never got more than from one room to another though." Daria's face seemed almost demonic and my stomach tilted to one side.

"Well, we are far enough away from where we were that it is almost nightfall." Xen looked around us. "And judging from that, and the terrain, I'm guessing the eastern edge of The Wilds."

"Well, that's not good," Daria said. She slipped the backpack off and squatted down to sort through what was in it. She pulled the canteen out and took a long drink before she brought it up to my lips. The water was warm but tasted like heaven. She pulled it away before I was done. "We need to ration it. No telling how far freshwater is."

"I will gather firewood," Xen said. "Stay alert."

"What's not good?" I asked, my sluggish thoughts finally catching up.

"The Wilds," Daria responded. She was still sorting through the contents of the backpack, laying the supplies out around her on the ground. "Good. This is a good kit. Let me see your hands while there's still light."

She sat and I gave her my right hand. The two missing fingernails had started to grow back a lot faster than the two on my left hand, proving that yes, my blood could heal even myself when used to treat wounds. Those two fingers were bruised and swollen and probably broken. In my drugged state they seemed to be huge and with the dark coloring, they resembled tree branches.

Daria opened the first aid kit and set about carefully cleaning the wounds that punctured the skin between my knuckles. They weren't deep. They hadn't needed to be. The pain was searing and terrible with every flex of every finger.

I hissed as the antiseptic touched the open wounds, but Daria kept to her task, her focus firmly on what she was doing. "Daria." Her eyes flicked up toward mine, but then back to her work. "I'm sorry."

She flinched and shook her head. "Don't. I can't..."

Xen came back with an armload of wood and they set about making a small fire. I didn't see how Xen lit it, but it didn't matter as long as there was heat. "I found a small river. There are fish." Xen grabbed the canteen and held it to my mouth. "Drink, I will refill it."

I gulped down the water as fast as I could but pulled back before it was gone, nodding to Daria. She took the canteen and drained it before handing it back to Xen. She smeared the healing ointment onto my hand and carefully wrapped bandages over the wounds. She wound gauze around the two broken fingers, binding them together and turning my hand into something resembling a lobster claw. If lobsters were white. Of course, then that was all I could see, so I closed my eyes.

My mind drifted a little as she did my left hand. I was suddenly stuck on the look on Habros's face just before I killed him.

"Thána?"

I blinked back to my sister's face in the gathering dark. "What?"

"I asked if there was anything else I should look at? Your back?"

I nodded sloppily, turning so she could lift my shirt. My back was a mess of welts and bruises, half-healed cuts, and scrapes. I'd truthfully lost track. I remembered the clamps and switch, a heavy paddle, something like sandpaper, but there had been more. Maybe my mind was protecting me from remembering more. Or maybe it was the drug.

She examined me. I could feel her fingers glaze over my skin and I hissed when she touched an angry burn near the place where the wrought iron had pierced my side at the Kourt. "I don't like how this looks, but there isn't enough light to see it properly." She continued to walk her fingers over my skin, making tsking sounds and from time to time, leaned in close. She eased the shirt back down. Rummaging through the pack, she lifted something toward my mouth. "This will help the pain."

I let her pour the potion in and swallowed it. It was a deep fruity flavor and felt slick on my tongue. She then opened a protein bar and broke it in half, giving me a piece. "Go slow or you'll get sick," Daria cautioned.

My stomach howled out its hunger at just the scent of food and while protein bars were not my favorite things to eat, I didn't care. I couldn't remember the last time I had eaten anything solid. For Daria, it had probably been even longer.

We sat in uncomfortable silence until Xen came back carrying a fish that was still wriggling and the canteen. By the time Xen had the fish cleaned and had skewered pieces of it on sticks to roast, the sunlight was gone completely, leaving us with only the light of the fire. As hungry as I was though, my body was less interested in food than it was in sleep.

I groaned as I lay down, relishing in the ability to stretch out after so long crammed in that cage. The only way to lay that didn't cause more pain was on my stomach, a prospect generally prohibited by the size of my breasts. Right then, though, it didn't seem to matter.

I was vaguely aware of Xen and Daria talking softly, of the crackling of the fire and Daria setting up wards, then nothing. That nothing didn't last though. The fire of the drug inside me seemed to wake up as I slept, and Artoz chased me through ruined cities and into a desert, growing to stand over eight feet tall, his steps shaking the ground. I couldn't run far enough or fast enough and each time he caught me, he would laugh maniacally and mark numbers in my skin with his blade.

I jumped awake at some sound. The fire was little more than embers. Xen and Daria were asleep, the three of us laid out in a triangle around the fire. The night air was cold, even with the wards.

Shifting enough to reach the small pile of wood near the fire, I tried to coax the coals to catch. Out of the corner of my eye, I thought I spotted movement in the dark. I froze, scanning around me. I convinced myself it was the fear induced by the drug and went back to tending the fire.

The night sky was clearer than I'd ever seen it in the time I'd been this side of the portal. One of the three moons was hanging low on the horizon, its yellow-white light giving the landscape an even eerier cast than if it had been pitch black.

The sound of something moving nearby made me freeze again. A low growl stalked across the ground from beyond Daria. My breath came in short bursts as I strained to see what was out there. Yellow eyes emerged from the brush. As it came closer, I could make out some sort of cat.

It moved closer, belly slunk low to the ground, sniffing the air. It was nearly at the wards, behind Daria, looking like a cross between a lynx and a bobcat, though its fur looked darker than either.

I don't know if it could feel me watching it, but it was unprepared for Xen, who suddenly woke and lunged toward it. They hit the wards at almost the same moment and the cat yelped, running into the shadows again.

Daria awoke then too, and none of us would be going back to sleep. Daylight crept along the horizon, painting dark reds and oranges over the black of night.

We split two protein bars between the three of us and once the sun was fully up, we put out the fire and wordlessly set out. Our first stop was the river, which was fast-moving, but not very wide.

"Let's get you cleaned up," Daria said to me, putting the backpack down. "I want a better look at your back."

I didn't argue and let Xen help me get the shirt off. "This is a mess. Sit down."

I sat on a rock beside the water while Xen refilled our only canteen and handed it to Daria who was murmuring some incantation over it before decidedly cold water poured down my back. It fizzled against my wounds, especially the burns. I pulled away involuntarily, but she held me in place by holding my shoulder.

"We don't have bandages that will cover this mess," Daria said after smearing ointment on most of the places that were screaming in pain. "We'll need to keep a good eye on it."

She helped me get my shirt back on, then dumped out the rest of the canteen and went to refill it. Now that it was properly light, I could see the terrain around us. Ahead and to the right there were mountains, the most distant of them capped in snow. To the left was a great expanse of high desert with mesas and scrub brush. The river flowed down from the mountains and cut across the plateau we had landed on, before dropping somewhere behind us, down to an oasis. Or that was my assumption.

"So, now what?" I asked. My throat was raw and my voice sounded thick.

Xen looked around. "I think I know where we are. Dyn and I came camping in the Wilds as children. There is a clan of natives we befriended."

"What are our options?" Daria asked, helping me drink from the canteen.

"Well, my first choice would be for Thána here to do that thing that got us here again, only dumping us somewhere safer." Xen looked hopeful, but Daria quashed that immediately.

"She's in no shape to try. It's a miracle she did it the first time."

"Our other options are less pleasant." Xen made a face and pointed toward the mountains. "Over the mountains. We might get lucky and find someone along the way willing to provide us with transportation, but we might just find bandits or worse. Or, down there." Xen pointed in the opposite direction. "There is a small town where we might be able to make contact with someone who can help us. If we are very lucky, a member of the clan will find us first."

Daria shielded her eyes and looked down into the valley. Neither prospect sounded like something I wanted to do. I wasn't at all convinced I physically could, though sitting where I was was not appealing either. "Which is closer?" Daria asked.

"The town, by some margin," Xen responded.

Daria pulled the pouch of anti-fatigue powder from her pocket, taking a pinch for herself before offering a pinch to me and Xen. "All right, then. Let's get moving."

CHAPTER 15
THE WILDS

For most of the first hour, I plodded along, occasionally with my sister's support when my knees got rubbery. I was still getting the odd flash of terror, but the powder was burning off the drug at an accelerated rate, which should mean I'd be more functional soon.

The air was fairly warm and getting warmer as we went. We sipped at the water sparingly as we had no idea when we would find more. I was sweating and starting to worry about sunburn when Xen stopped us to rest in the shade of a stand of trees that smelled like cedar but had leaves of golden-brown that shimmered when the wind blew through them.

My hands were starting to feel better, less swollen at least. I was able to move the fingers of my left hand a little without pain. My right hand throbbed in time with my heart, which was complaining about the exertion. The salt in my sweat made the wounds in my back unhappy too.

Complaining about it wouldn't do any good. Xen and Daria knew I was miserable, though Xen couldn't know all of the reasons why. As I sat there on the hard ground with my eyes closed, all I could see was Habros's face, his surrender. Like me, he'd save Daria first. My throat constricted and my stomach churned. Daria's screams as Habros died only twisted the knife in my belly and I lurched up enough that my vomit wouldn't land on my legs.

It was hot and filled with bits of protein bar along with bitter bile. I pulled away from hands that tried to help me, not wanting the comfort they offered. "I'm fine." I reached for the canteen, using a small amount of water to rinse my mouth of the taste of bile.

Neither of them told me I wasn't fine. In fact, no one spoke, and I was grateful for the silence.

We sat for a while longer, then one by one got to our feet, and headed out again. I realized as we walked that I never figured out how long the days were here, so I had no idea if we were close to midday or not. The heat continued to rise and I was seriously doubting we were going to make it to anything that resembled civilization.

Xen put a hand on my arm to stop my forward momentum and I looked up to see why. In the wavy distance, the dust was rising and the cloud was coming our way. There was nowhere for us to hide out there on the open plain, so we took a defensive stance with Xen in the lead.

As the cloud of dust came closer I could see that there were animals of some sort, with man-shaped riders. The animals were bigger than horses and shaggy, with hair that formed dreadlocks and bare faces shaped more like a hippo than a horse.

The person on the animal in the lead nodded his head in greeting. At least I think it was a *he*. It was hard to tell behind the scarf, hat and goggles. There wasn't an inch of skin showing anywhere. He said something in a language I had no hope of understanding, but it was clear that Xen did.

Xen responded in neutral tones. It sounded as if they were negotiating. The other two riders sat and waited. Xen nodded. "These hunters are part of the clan Dyn and I befriended. They are willing to give us a ride and shelter."

"Do we trust them?" Daria asked quietly.

"Do we have a choice?" I asked in response, gazing up at the monstrous beasts.

"It will give us a chance to rest, and tomorrow he will show us the way to the town or take us to the road over the mountain," Xen said before they returned to speaking with the rider.

Each rider gave a command to their mount and the animals knelt down like I had seen camels do on television. Xen motioned for me to go to the right. The rider reached a hand down and clasping it around my forearm, he pulled as I climbed. The girth of the thing was almost too much to straddle and I nearly fell off as it lurched to its feet again.

Their hooves made almost no sound, even with the hard ground beneath them and despite their size, they had a smooth gait. Still, I clung to the rider in front of me, keeping my eyes closed and pressed to his back to protect them from the dust.

When we stopped again we were beside what looked to be a rather small house, low to the ground, with a roof of clay tiles covered in sand. Our mount lowered itself to the ground before the rider in front of me threw his leg over the beast's neck and jumped off. He turned to offer me a helping hand. Once on the ground, I could see that what I mistook for a house was merely the entrance, with stairs leading down and a door five feet below the surface.

I drifted toward my sister and we followed the leader and Xen into the home, which was much more spacious than the visible building would lead you to believe. The door opened into a large room. Fabric streamed from the center of the ceiling out to the walls, then draped down, giving it the feel of a tent. The lead rider called out while he was removing his scarf and goggles.

A woman in a long red robe and a bright yellow scarf that covered her head and cascaded over her shoulders appeared from behind one of the curtains. Instantly, the three riders put their hands together and bowed from the waist. Xen was introduced to the woman and the men all disappeared behind the same curtain from which she had appeared.

She and Xen spoke quietly before she came to Daria and me, extending one hand to each of us. She looked to be, at least partially, a native to this world, in that she had similar coloring as Habros, though she was slight of build and her hair was a dusty brown. A light spattering of blue freckles adorned her nose, cheeks, and forehead. Her smile was warm. Her eyes were narrow, her pupils oblong, not unlike a cat, or maybe more like a lizard.

Her language was musical and mesmerizing. I had to blink to clear the spell of it. She drew my bandaged hands closer and asked Xen a question. When Xen responded, she nodded knowingly. "This is Alaya," Xen said by way of introductions. "This is her hakhem, the clan home."

Alaya gestured toward a comfortable-looking side of the room where a carpet woven of reds and golds and several low couches covered in pillows looked made for entertaining.

"Sit. Sit." Alaya said, gesturing.

"You speak English?" I asked.

"Some little. Sit." We chose spots while Alaya returned to the place where a doorway was hidden behind the fabric. I could hear her speaking, hands clapping and when she returned there was an older woman with her, carrying an ornate wooden trunk. The woman came to me and set the trunk on the floor before sinking to her knees.

I looked to Xen for an explanation but they just shrugged at me. "This Ganzh," Alaya said. "She…" Alaya held out her hands, then turned to Xen to explain.

"She is their healer," Xen told me after a few moments.

Up close, I realized her skin was made up of tiny scales, also not unlike a lizard or snake, and so smooth that it looked like human skin from a distance.

Ganzh took my right hand between hers, closing her eyes and murmuring to herself before she set to unwrapping the bandages. She made sounds like the sight was horrifying and turned to spit on the floor behind her. Under the bandages the whole back of my hand was black with bruising, the edges purple, yellow and green. The three spots where the screws had penetrated my skin were inflamed and swollen. The pointer and middle fingers were mottled red and blue and the knuckles huge.

She once again sandwiched my hand between hers, and heat moved between our skins. She opened her trunk and said something to a little girl I who had snuck into the room without me noticing. She scampered away and came back with a jug of water. The girl was maybe nine or ten with dark hair pulled back under a royal blue scarf that slipped to her shoulders when she knelt beside the healer. She poured water into a wooden bowl that Ganzh was holding.

The girl looked at my hand, then rummaged in the trunk, holding up a bundle of herbs. Ganzh nodded and the girl pulled several leaves off the bundle and dropped them in the water. Ganzh covered the bowl with one hand and chanted as the girl brought a huge crimson feather out of the trunk. Tied around the quill end of the feather were several beaded strings that clinked together almost musically. Once Ganzh had taken the feather, the girl was up again and moving toward one of the lights with a candle in her hand. I hadn't realized that the lights were flames, so steady inside glass domes.

She lit the candle and returned, kneeling again and lifting a different bundle of herbs. This she lit from the candle, whispering prayers over it before walking behind Ganzh and waving the smoking bundle over her head. The smoke was fragrant, soothing, and it settled around Ganzh's shoulders. Ganzh used the feather to guide the smoke down over the water, both of them still chanting low and soft.

I let the sound pull me away from the pain in my body, my eyes closing as she ministered to my abused hands. The feather danced over my skin, spreading the water and calming the pain. I barely noticed as she moved from my right hand to my left.

Xen's voice startled me, and I blinked up at Ganzh who gestured something at me. "She says to remove your shirt and lay down so she can tend your back."

I felt a little self-conscious stripping myself in a strange place with people I didn't know, but the combination of the scented smoke and the gentle ministrations had me easily compliant. The girl helped me and set my shirt aside before coming to help me arrange myself on the couch. The healer's hands were soft and steady as she repeated her ritual. I'd have to get Xen to explain what the woman was doing to me. Just not right then. I was too tired and heavy.

My next real awareness came hours later. The lights were dimmed and the room quiet except for the soft breathing of Daria on the next couch. I let my eyes wander the room, eventually finding Xen curled up on pillows across from me. Xen wasn't sleeping though. They were watching me.

I wanted to stretch the muscles in my back, but I was afraid I'd rip open the scabs forming. I settled for shifting onto my side, suddenly remembering that I was naked from the waist up. I guess it was too late for modesty at that point.

The fingers on my right hand were splinted and bandaged, soft linen wound around my hand all the way down to my wrist. I had a little more movement in it than before. I used the heel of my left hand to shift upward, wincing as the pressure reminded me that it was also still injured.

I'd been one-handed a time or two in my life. I'd had surgery for carpal tunnel at one point, leaving me without the use of my dominant hand for a few months. I'd managed, but this having two hands out of commission was turning out to be very limiting.

I rolled my head to get my neck to crack and stood, reaching for the shirt I'd taken off. The back of it was crusted with blood. Xen was beside me then, holding out a saffron yellow robe. "Ganzh left this for you," Xen said softly.

They bunched up the robe and lifted it. I was self-conscious as they settled it over me, fussing with the sleeves and sliding the soft fabric over my naked skin. There were ties in the back to close it, then a scarf of the deepest purple. Xen smiled as they helped me adjust the scarf to some approximation of the way Ganzh had worn hers.

"Are you hungry? Alaya left food."

"Starving."

Xen gestured toward the pillows where they'd been reclining. There was a short stool holding up a tray with an array of foods that seemed familiar and yet not. I settled onto one of the pillows and looked the plate over, opting for a cracker and what I thought was cheese. I wasn't wrong. The soft cheese had a mild flavor similar to mozzarella. The cracker was savory with the taste of fennel and rye.

My stomach chose that moment to growl as if to remind me that I'd thrown up what little food it had gotten in the last… however long it had been since that tea with Habros.

Habros.

I closed my eyes and pushed the thought of him away. If I let myself wallow in that guilt I might not be able to keep going. I focused on the food in front of me. There were olive-shaped fruits that tasted of sweet onion and a pot of what looked like honey with small cake-like cookies and rolls of some kind of meat.

I ate in silence, forcing myself to go slow even though what I wanted to do was shove it all into my face at once.

"How do you feel?" Xen asked, pouring water into a ceramic cup for me from a silver pitcher.

"Better, I think." We kept our voices pitched low to let Daria sleep. Her trauma was not as recent as mine, but she'd still been through hell.

"Ganzh treated her remaining injuries as well," Xen said as if reading my thoughts. Xen's eyes traced over my sister, then came back to me. "That magic you did, is it a thing you could do again?"

I swallowed the piece of fruit in my mouth and shrugged lightly. "I don't know? Maybe?"

Xen didn't look at me. "Meerat is a long way from here. And we have no transportation."

Which was the reason for the question about the portal spell. "What about our hosts?" I asked hopefully.

"We have nothing of value to trade."

That was a fair point. They were under no obligation to help us, and they had already done much more than simply let us shelter under their roof. "To be honest, that was the first time that spell worked for me, other than very short range. I don't know how or why it worked this time."

"I've been thinking about that," Daria said as she sat beside me, cross-legged on the floor. I hadn't noticed that she'd awoken. "I think some of it was fear and some of it was me, and the boost from the xýpna powder."

"Is that what it's called?" I asked.

"That's what Mom always called it." She reached for some of the cheese and meat. "If we work together, we may be able to make short jumps, but we'll need to rest each time."

"Many places between us and Meerat are not safe," Xen offered into the silence between us while Daria ate. "There are dangerous animals who hunt the Wilds, and most of the people here are not as generous as our hosts."

"The Wilds were used as a prison back in the day," Daria said. "It was difficult to get to and from, so criminals were sent here."

"But not anymore, right?" I asked.

"It created a culture of outlaws," Xen replied. "Or several micro-cultures of them, with little to no moral compass. Ayala and her clan are among the few native to the Wilds, and their numbers are dwindling."

"Great." I sighed and rubbed the spot between my eyes with my left hand.

"Headache?" Daria asked and I sighed again.

"It's fine." It was just a dull ache, nothing compared to the pain in my hands and back.

"What was your intent when you cast that spell back at the prison camp?" Daria asked, pouring herself some water.

"I'm not sure I had a clear intention, just 'get us out of here'."

"But you said you'd made it work before?"

I nodded. "Your lab to the kitchen was the first time it worked, knocked my ass out though. I woke up on the kitchen floor with a bloody nose."

Daria fished in her pocket and came out with the kelcimite. "And this?"

"Mom gave it to me to help stabilize the spell."

"That makes sense. She was gone by the time I started working on it. Probably would have told me I was nuts to try."

"She didn't seem to think it was nuts, but she also wasn't convinced it would work." I fumbled with my water, eventually managing to pick it up with my left hand.

Daria reached for my right hand, cupping it between the two of hers. "How is the pain?"

I tugged it back. "I'll live." Somehow it bothered me that she was being kind. It was one thing for us to work together to get to safety. It was completely another for her to take care of me after what I had done.

"So, if we can make it work?" I hid my discomfort behind the redirect of the conversation and ate a piece of fruit.

Xen sighed. "We will need a way to defend ourselves."

"And to know where we want to end up. Randomly jumping from place to place isn't going to help," Daria added.

I frowned. "I assumed we'd want to get back to the portal to Spítia?"

"We do not know what awaits us in Meerat," Xen said.

"Is there somewhere else we should go?"

Daria's face hardened. "We should do what I should have done to begin with, join the Vaneeshi army, and drive those Kabeshi bastards back over the southern mountains."

I looked at my bandaged hands, wondering if I'd even be able to cast with them this broken. "Daria…" I didn't know what to say though. I understood her desire.

"I didn't go when the Minister asked me to, because Habros didn't want me to fight. Now Habros is…" She bit off whatever she'd been about to say. "This is my home, Thána. I've lived here for more than fifteen years. I can't just abandon it."

"What about Kota?" I asked.

She flinched. "You said you locked the portal. He's safe enough with Mom while we fix this."

I looked at Xen who had stayed quiet. "Like Daria, this is my home too. I was born here."

I was outnumbered. I held no delusions that I had anything to offer in the war, but the least I could do to fill the hole left when I took Habros's life would be to get the two of them to a place where they could contribute to the effort.

"Okay, so what does that mean?" I asked. "Where do we need to go?"

Xen rearranged the food items left on the tray. They put one of the cookies on my side, then arrayed some of the fruit across the middle, with another cookie on their side of the tray and a meat roll on either side of it. They pointed to the cookie on my side. "This is us. This is the mountain range dividing the Wilds from Vaneesh." They pointed at the other cookie. "This is Meerat, with the Vaneesh army to the north and the Kabeshi army to the south."

"Any idea how many miles that is?" I asked.

"A lot," Daria responded.

CHAPTER 16
ATTACK

Xen and Daria continued talking, planning our best course of action to get out of the Wilds and back to Vaneesh. I withdrew, in part because I had no input there but also because the pain in my head was increasing. It wasn't like any headache I'd ever had.

The pressure was growing, like my brain was pushing against my skull in an attempt to escape. I sat back against the wall, pressing my bandaged hands against my temples in an effort to hold it in. My head was filled with white noise, and I was pretty sure that some alien was going to burst out of my head.

"Thána."

Hands touched my knees, but when I opened my eyes, everything was gray, clouded over. "Help me move her." That was Daria's voice. They dragged me away from the wall and I curled in on myself, hands now around the back of my neck to keep my head attached to my body.

I vaguely heard Daria setting up wards around me, but I *felt* it when they were complete, like something had snapped clean and an attack had been blocked. It took me a few minutes to realize the pain was gone and I could breathe again. Slowly, I sat up inside a circle of wards, with Xen and Daria staring at me from outside. "What was that?" I asked breathlessly.

"Someone trying to get into your brain," Daria responded.

"Who would— Katyk." I covered my mouth with my left had and shook my head.

"Katyk?" Daria asked.

"The woman who betrayed us," Xen supplied. "She escaped me before I came to get you."

"I take it she's a witch too then?" Daria asked.

"Part succubus too. We needed her to get to you." Of course, Katyk had just been bringing us to our eventual deaths.

"Well, it looked like she was pretty close to getting in." Daria squatted outside the wards. "I wasn't sure the wards would work though. How's your head?"

"Better. It hurt more this time."

"This time?" Daria asked, glancing at Xen.

"The witch convinced us that she could speak Kabeshi through your sister's mouth," Xen answered.

Daria nodded. "She hijacked you. I've read about it but never seen it done. Makes you more susceptible to her."

"Great." We weren't going to get far if the only way to escape Katyk's psychic attacks was to hide inside wards. "How do I keep her out?"

Daria sighed. "I don't know. If Mom were here…" She shook her head. "Tell me what you know about her?"

Xen paced around the wards. "She came to us about two weeks after they took you, said she had escaped from a prison camp in the south, near the border with Loland."

"I'm thinking she didn't so much escape as she was sent to infiltrate you and deliver more of us to the Kabeshi," Daria said. "That's how they got the weapons they've been using. They break us and brainwash us and get us to help them." Her hands trembled and her face paled. Flashes of my own torment at the hands of the Kabeshi colonel filled my head and I looked away. I couldn't deny that I would have eventually broken.

"Do you think she's trying to find us?" I asked.

Daria shrugged. "Possibly."

"They would not come to the Wilds while they are fighting a war with Vaneesh, would they?" Xen asked.

"Maybe not them, but I could see Katyk coming after us." I envisioned Katyk angry and shivered. All of that passion was hot as anything when it was focused on pleasure but turned into anger, it would be downright scary.

My cheeks burned with the memories of that passion that filled my head. Xen groaned, making me look up. "Tell me you did not have sex with her."

I frowned up at them. "What?"

Daria rubbed her hands over her face. "Succubus. Sex magic."

"I—" Honestly, I had no idea what sex magic could do, or even really what it was. "I mean, it's embarrassing, considering her betrayal, but…"

"But nothing," Daria shook her head. "There isn't anything we can do here. I need supplies." She paced, muttering, and counting things off on her fingers.

"Supplies for what?" I asked, standing now myself.

"To get her hooks out of you," Daria responded. "Which means we need to get out of here and get somewhere where I can get what we need."

Behind Daria, the curtains moved and Alaya appeared, putting her hands together and bowing slightly. Xen and Daria mimicked the gesture, and I followed clumsily. Xen went to talk with her and Daria turned to me. "There's a town on the Vaneesh border. I know someone there who might have what we need."

"Okay, how do we keep her from crippling me between here and there?" I asked.

"There isn't much we can do, at least while we're moving, but if we get wards set up anytime we stop, we might keep her off you while you're resting at least."

That didn't sound like a plan I was going to enjoy, especially if I also had to manage to continue using the portal spell.

Xen came back to us as Alaya went back behind the curtain. "Alaya has offered us the use of three of the glouses, and an escort as far as the base of the mountain."

"Glouses?" I asked, looking to Daria for an explanation.

"The animals we rode here on."

Alaya returned moments later with a young woman carrying a pile of cloth. She spoke to Xen, then nodded to the woman who approached Daria. "Clothes for us," Xen said. "Better for traveling in."

Daria took the clothes with a nod of appreciation and set them on the couch where I had slept. "I'm going to release the wards," Daria said. "Be ready. I'll bring them right back up after I hand you the clothes."

She sorted the clothes then lifted a hand and dropped the wards. I didn't immediately feel the pressure of Katyk trying to get in my head but was still relieved when I felt them close back up around me.

Getting undressed and then dressed again was not easy with my hands in that condition, but I managed to get the boots off, then the uniform pants. I struggled a little getting the sand-colored pants on. The fabric was heavy-duty, like denim or canvas which would provide protection from flying sand. Likewise, the shirt was much heavier than the uniform shirt that was crusted with my blood. I pulled it on over my head and thrust my arms through the sleeves, a task that my hands were not happy with. I shoved my feet back into the boots, though I wasn't going to be able to tie the laces by myself.

That left a pile of sand-colored cloth that I wasn't sure about until I saw Daria sit on the couch and wind hers around each leg where the pants met boot. Xen looked like they wanted to help me get finished, but the wards were preventing them from getting close.

I took a deep breath and stuck my left hand out, dismissing the wards. We all froze for a moment, waiting to see if the attack would resume. When it didn't, Xen came to me, helping me get my shirt tucked in and the pants done up, then they knelt to tie my boots and wind the lengths of cloth around my legs. As they stood, they picked up the scarf I had let fall to the ground and smiled slightly as they draped it over my shoulders and tucked a strand of hair behind my ear. It was a familiar gesture and I lifted a hand to theirs, smiling a little awkwardly.

Xen returned the smile, their face softening as their cheeks blushed a little. The whole thing felt oddly intimate and comfortable. In my vulnerable state, I had to rely on them, which isn't easy to do when you're accustomed to taking care of yourself. It was made somewhat easier by their willingness to help and the friendship that was developing.

Daria packed up the ward stones and whatever else had come out of the backpack. I was itching to get moving now that we had at least a marginal idea of where we were going. There was also the hope that Katyk had only found me because we had been still for too long.

Xen was talking to Alaya again, nodding and glancing back at us. A man emerged from behind the curtain, dressed the same as the men who had helped us the day before. He handed a bag to Xen before heading out the door.

Xen slung the bag over her shoulder crossbody.

"Safe journey you," Alaya said in her broken English.

"Thank you for your help," I replied with a slight bow.

We headed up the stairs to find our guide waiting with our mounts all kneeling. He helped me climb awkwardly onto mine, handing me the reins that ran up to a harness just in front of the animal's ears.

Once we were mounted, the guide clapped his hands and the animals all lurched to their feet, settling in behind the leader as we headed into the not-quite-dawn morning. The sun was somewhere behind us, creeping slowly up to stretch red-gold fingers of light out across the scrubland toward the mountains. As we moved, I huddled into myself, cradling my right hand to my chest and imagining every few seconds that I could feel Katyk pushing her way into me.

The sun was high in the sky when our guide called us to a halt. The scrubland had given way to forest and the path seemed well traveled.

"This is as far as he goes," Xen said, dismounting their glouse. "We walk from here."

He came to help me down before turning our glouses around to return home.

"What's in the bag?" Daria asked, nodding toward the one Xen had clutched at their side.

"Some food, water, bandages for Thána's hands."

"So, does this path lead all the way through these mountains?" I asked, squinting into the distance.

"There's a road further north," Xen said. "This path will take us to it."

We stood there looking into the trees for a long moment, then Daria held out the kelcimite. "Might as well try it now. If you show me what you did, I should be able to duplicate it, so we can take turns."

I nodded, taking the stone in my left hand. "Okay, you were behind me, arms around me." We assumed that position, with Xen beside us.

"Start small," Daria instructed. "Aim us for the furthest spot you can see ahead of us."

I squinted up the path for a likely destination and lifted my hands, doing my best to get the stone in position. I closed my eyes and reached inside, but for the briefest moment, I was paralyzed with fear. Daria's arms tightened around my waist just enough to knock me loose. With a deep breath, I directed my intention to the spot ahead of us where the path disappeared from view and cast the spell out through the kelcimite.

The hole that opened was jagged and a little shaky, but it held. Xen went through first, then Daria and I walked through together, her arms still around me.

I sagged against her as we emerged, more or less in the spot I'd aimed for. "That makes no sense," Daria said. "You didn't…" She was frowning as she turned me to face her. "That wasn't my spell."

"Yes, it was." I was confused. "What do you mean?"

"I've never seen that."

I shook my head. "I just followed the lead you left in your notes."

"What combination of words ended up working?"

That was about when I realized what she was getting at. Just like when I'd gotten us out of that camp, I didn't use any words. Just pulled magic from my center and shot it out of the stone toward my intended target. "The first time I got it to work I used tunnel as the catalyst, but since then I think it's just been the intent, no catalyst."

"That isn't supposed to be possible," Daria said. "All the theory is based on words and gestures."

"Welcome to my life," I muttered. She frowned even harder at me. "Sorry, just… apparently, I do that. Things that shouldn't be possible. Maybe because I don't know that they shouldn't be possible? Like *makrá vlépinta*. It's how I saw you." I wasn't sure if I had even told her about that.

Daria shook her head. "Well, Mom always did say you were gifted."

"I'm still learning. I didn't even know I was a witch for twenty-two years," I said defensively. "I just know it worked when I tried it."

"Can you do it again, maybe a little further this time?" Xen asked.

I wasn't positive, but I didn't want to tell them that. "Just give me some of that powder. What did you call it?" I asked Daria.

She pulled the backpack off and reached into it, coming out with the pouch. "Xýpna, and you need to be careful using it."

"Mom warned me too." She opened the pouch and pulled out a pinch. I let her drop it on my tongue, feeling a little ridicuous. It was better mixed in with a drink, easier to swallow, but this worked faster. I curled my tongue back and swallowed, closing my eyes as the warm rush of energy filled me. "Okay, where are we going next?"

Daria looked like she was trying to calculate distances or something. "What about the road east? Is that concrete enough?"

I shrugged, wincing as it pulled on the scabs across my back. "Won't know until we try."

Daria stood behind me, her arms circling my waist. This time I could feel her there, the strength of her latching on to me. I lifted my hands and the kelcimite even though my right hand hurt immensely. The position to hold the stone put a strain on my broken fingers and made the puncture wounds on the back of my hand scream. I put the pain out of my mind and focused on sending us to the road. I had no idea what it looked like or where it was, but I set the intention to take us there anyway.

When I was sure it was set, I cast the spell out through the stone. The hole opened, a little unsteady at first, but holding. Through it, I could see trees and what might possibly be a road. Xen stepped through and Daria and I moved toward it, but the portal was starting to wobble and my body was on fire. Daria pushed us through and I stumbled into Xen, who kept me from falling down.

Sweat dripped down my face, and I used my scarf to wipe it. "I think I'm going to pass out now," I said, sinking to my knees. Xen eased me down, sitting on the leaf-covered ground to cradle my head on their thigh.

We were still in that position when I came around, and it was evident that some time had passed. Daria had put up the wards and a small fire warmed the space. My back was cussing at me in languages I understood all too well. It did not like me laying on it. I shifted, looking up at Xen who seemed to be asleep sitting up. I scooted away from them, which wasn't easy without using my hands.

"Feeling better?" Daria asked.

"A little," I responded. I was still shaky and had dried blood on my face from a nosebleed that started when I went down. I used the corner of the scarf to clean it off before moving a little closer to the fire. Daria handed me a canteen of water and a piece of a piquant jerky.

I sipped the water first, then tried the jerky. It was spicy and meaty. "This is good."

Daria nodded, but her gaze stayed cast on the fire. I felt the need to apologize again, but I knew she didn't want to hear it. My apology wouldn't make me feel better and it would just remind her that I had killed her husband.

"Mom and I fought..." Daria said quietly. "Before she left. My last words to her were in anger."

"I know, she told me."

"I saw you. I mean, the vision I had..." She gestured around her. "This whole mess. I knew if she left, if she brought you back here, this would happen. Well, not specifically. I see flashes, bits and pieces, and I have to figure out how they fit together." She poked at the fire with a stick. "I shouldn't have yelled at her. None of this is her fault."

CHAPTER 17
AND WE'RE WALKING

"You were one of the first concrete memories I got back when Mom's spell started to unwind," I said when the silence was getting awkward. "I think you were six and you got very sick. Mom had to go out to get medicine for you."

Daria looked up from the fire. "I vaguely remember that. You climbed into bed with me."

I nodded and smiled. "I was so worried about you, and I knew I could make you better, even if Mom told me not to."

"Because of the Brotherhood," Daria said. She crinkled her nose and mouth in an expression of disgust. "I remember them too." She breathed in deeply and let it out slowly. "I was so angry with her over leaving you like that. But she was scared and she was running out of options."

"Well, it worked. I have no idea how much spellwork she had to have done to erase our trail and block my scent, but I had twenty-two years of safety." Until Finneas came into my life and turned it upside down. He had come through a portal armed with something that the Brotherhood didn't have: the name I was living under. That was the only reason that he got to me before the brotherhood did. What I had never figured out was why the Brotherhood chose then to come after me and not before.

"How are your hands?" Daria asked.

I looked down at them, trying to find the best way to answer that. "They hurt, not gonna lie. The position I have to hold my hands in to cast that spell is painful."

"I could feel you struggling."

"What about you?" I asked, realizing that while I wallowed in my own pain, I hadn't even asked about hers.

"The worst for me was the hallucinations," she said quietly.

"I know he hurt you. I saw it." I chanced a look at her.

"I heal fast," Daria said. "My back will never be the same, and I'll have some scars on my legs, but I'm alive because you came for me."

She was also a widow because I killed her husband. She must have seen the apology in my eyes, but before I could speak it, Daria held up a hand. "Don't apologize again. I'm not angry with you. I mean, I am, but I know it's irrational. You did what you had to. If you hadn't, we'd probably both be dead."

Behind me, Xen woke. They stood and stretched before joining us by the fire. Daria tossed some of the jerky to Xen who thanked her. I yawned, the heat from the fire was relaxing, and it reminded my body of how little I'd been sleeping even before the torture.

"You should sleep more," Xen said, a gentle hand on my arm. "We should be safe enough here until morning."

"Not sure I could," I responded.

"I can fix that," Daria said, pulling the backpack to her and rummaging inside. She tossed me the black pouch with sleep powder in it. "Put a pinch in the cap of the canteen, then add water. It's hard to swallow without water."

I took the cap off the canteen and followed her instructions. It had a taste that reminded me of charcoal and I fought to swallow it at first. When it finally slid down the back of my throat, I recapped the canteen and set it between me and Xen.

Laying down on the leaf-covered ground, I pillowed my head on my left forearm, staying mostly on my stomach to give my back a break. I wasn't sure the powder was working and stared into the fire waiting for it to kick in. Soon, my eyelids were filled with lead and I slept.

Almost immediately, dreams chased me, one blurring into another, all of them filled with blood and screaming. None of it made sense, all disjointed and scrambling through memories of pain and fear mixed with horrific imaginings of what was to come.

I woke with a start, pushing myself up before remembering the state of my hands. I tried to calm my breathing as I looked around, half-convinced there would be pursuers of one kind or another coming for me. There was nothing outside the wards but the slice of light illuminating the road as the sun rose.

I took stock of my condition and decided that I needed to relieve myself, but I didn't want to leave Xen and Daria unprotected, so I got to my feet and moved to where I could touch the wards. I tried to remember what Mom had taught me about opening doorways in the wards.

It took me two tries, but I got it and stepped through. Outside our little circle, the world was chilly. I was glad for the bandages covering my hands.

I found a spot and struggled to get my pants open and down before I squatted near a tree for support and did my business. When I was done I managed to get as far as buttoning the first button on my pants, but I couldn't get the other two by myself.

Xen was up and moving around as I got back and let myself back into the wards. "I feel like a child over here. One who can't button their own pants.

Xen chuckled and crossed to me. "It is a good thing you are with adults who can help you then." Xen buttoned my pants and gestured back the way I had come. "Let me out?"

I reopened the doorway for Xen and considered just taking the wards down, but then I remembered Katyk and decided to stay safe inside until we were ready to go. Daria groaned as she sat up and stopped mid-stretch with a strained look.

"Are you okay?" I asked.

"Stiff, sore but not stuffed into a tiny cage or dead, so yeah, I'm okay," Daria responded. "I have a couple of bad spots on my back from that damn *peitche*." She must have sensed my confusion and gestured with one hand in a solid downward motion. "The hard one, like a riding crop."

I nodded at that. I had a few of those too. Artoz had an affinity for it. He also liked to use the point of a blade on the resulting injury to deepen it. "Should I take a look?"

She shook her head and got to her feet. "Xen put some ointment on them last night. They'll heal."

I looked down at my bandaged hands. We'd put the ointment on those wounds and on my back. Any other time I'd used it, the wounds healed miraculously. It didn't seem to be working this time. Maybe the trauma to my hands was a kind that the ointment couldn't treat. My back at least felt better.

Xen came back and Daria let them into the wards, letting herself out at the same time. "So, what's the plan for today?" I asked as Xen brought out a loaf of bread from the bag we'd been given.

"Daria and I talked about that last night. I think we should walk for a while before you try the spell. There's no point in us exhausting you, then having to spend most of the day resting."

Xen broke off a piece of the bread and passed it to me before tearing off another piece to eat. I wasn't going to argue with not wearing myself out.

If I had to pass out every time I cast that spell for any amount of distance, we'd get where we were going faster if we just walked.

I nibbled on the bread while we waited for Daria to return from her ablutions. It had a nutty flavor that surprised me, but I also found it very filling.

Once Daria returned, we made sure that the fire was out and collected our things before dropping the wards and collecting the stones. We didn't speak, just stepped out of the shade of the trees and into the sunlight that illuminated the blacktop. The road headed straight up the mountain, disappearing into the trees.

We walked in silence for hours, our pace held by the steep climb. The air warmed around us and as we topped a rise, the breathtaking view brought us up short. In the distance, the rugged line of mountains served as a hazy backdrop to a valley painted in shades of green and blue, dotted with splashes of red and yellow. A river danced happily through the scene and far off to the north I could see a bridge spanning the river. The road ran along the edge of that valley, plunging from where we were standing, then following a lower ridge to the bridge.

"How far do you think that bridge is?" I asked.

Daria shaded her eyes and sized up the distance. "A few miles at least."

I fingered the kelcimite in my pocket. "Do we want to try the portal now, when I can clearly see a destination, or wait until later when I might not be able to?"

"Are you up to it?" Xen asked, their eyes pointedly looking at my hands.

"Yeah, I think so." I took the kelcimite out and got ready. Daria stepped in behind me, her hands on my hips. I took a deep breath, set my intention, and cast. The hole opened a lot smoother and stabilized quickly. Xen was looking at the bridge in the distance.

"I can see the other end," Xen said before they peered through the hole.

"Can't hold it forever, Xen," I said, gritting my teeth at the strain. Xen stepped through, then Daria and I followed.

I sagged against my sister for a moment, but my rubbery knees held and I was only a little worse for the wear. I pocketed the stone. The river was loud as water tumbled over rocks and around boulders.

"If there's a way down, I can refill our canteens," Xen offered. We crossed the bridge and not far from the end of it there was a trampled trail leading down through the trees. "Wait here, I'll be right back."

Xen took the canteen that had come with me and the one Alaya had given us and scrambled down the slope, leaving me and Daria by the road.

"We haven't seen a single car all day," I said.

"This road doesn't get much traffic in the best of times. With Vaneesh at war, I imagine very few people are traveling."

That made sense, even if some part of me clung to the hope that we might be able to flag down a ride. Our current mode of transportation was going to get us to the Vaneesh border in about a year.

Xen came trudging back up the slope, the canteens in hand. We all took a sip of water and set out walking again. My head was lightly buzzing and while I wasn't zapped completely like I'd been the night before, I was starting to feel the drain. "If I'm going to do that again, I'm going to need some of the xýpna powder."

"How many doses have you had?" Daria asked, her face full of concern.

I shrugged. "Since Mom made it for me? I have no idea."

"This stuff can get addictive, Thána."

"Do you see other choices here that I don't?"

She sighed and pulled the backpack off her shoulder to pull out the pouch. "No. I wish I did though." Daria gave me a pinch and I swallowed it down with another sip from the canteen.

I eyed up the road ahead of us. "Let's walk to where the road curves up there, see if we can spot a likely destination for our next jump."

That curve only showed us the next curve, then the next, so we ended up walking for over an hour before I found a spot where I could clearly see a likely spot for the portal. The road descended from where we stood and ran through another valley before climbing a steep hill. "I'm going to aim for the top of that hill," I said, readying myself.

Before Daria could get into position behind me, the sound of an engine brought me up short. We all stepped back out of the road and a vehicle lumbered past us, heading into the Wilds. The driver looked at us in surprise. I put them out of my mind and turned my attention back to the spell.

Daria's hands were strong and sure on my hips, and we breathed in as one, our magic coming together. I opened my eyes when I was ready, focused on the spot I wanted to land, then cast my spell through the stone. The portal stabilized quickly and Xen stepped through with us right behind.

"You know, I think we're getting better with that," I said. Of course, that was when I realized I had another bloody nose. I wiped the blood away and pinched my nose when the bleeding didn't stop immediately. I could still feel the buzz of the xýpna powder working in me.

From the top of the hill, we could see for miles. On either side of the road, there were sheer rock faces in the dusty blue-gray that seemed to be the norm here. Further up, small caves dotted the cliff faces. In the distance, there was another ridge running parallel to the one we stood on, though it was significantly taller.

I could hear water running nearby, likely the same river we'd already crossed. I figured I had one more jump in me before I exhausted myself and was considering the next likely spot when the vehicle that had passed us by earlier came up from behind.

Xen pulled me out of the road, but the truck didn't pass this time, it slowed down. There were two men in the cab and three in the back. Xen's hand tightened on my arm.

The man on the passenger's side was eyeing Daria up and down, then turned his gaze on me, then Xen. He spoke, his tone dripping with superiority and menace. I was pretty sure he was speaking Vaneeshi, at least it sounded like it. He was clearly of mixed parentage, judging by the Vaneeshi coloring and the fact that his hands were four claw-like fingers that resembled talons.

Daria responded to him, her voice likewise hard and challenging. One of the men jumped down from the back and came toward us. Xen pushed me aside and took a defensive posture between us. They didn't wait for the man to take the first swing. Xen's fist connected with his nose and a swipe of their right leg took the man down.

Of course, that just made the whole lot of them mad. The other two jumped out of the back and the passenger opened his door, catching Daria on the chin. She stumbled back into me, shoving me up against the rock.

Talon-hand clawed at her and I could smell blood almost instantly. Daria screamed and shoved her knee into the man's groin. He went down, but not before he drew a bloody line down her arm.

Xen was holding their own against the three others, but one of them was attempting to get a loop of rope at the end of a pole around their neck. I wasn't entirely sure what was happening, but I was not in the mood for this bullshit. I sidestepped closer to Xen, thrust my arms around Daria's waist with the kelcimite in my left hand, and cast.

"Where—" Daria stiffened in front of me.

"Trust me," was all I said. "Xen, now!"

Like before when we escaped the camp, Xen threw themselves at us and we tumbled through the portal, landing on hard rock and rolling away into a dark place. For a long moment we lay there stunned before I remembered that Daria was bleeding, and I extricated myself from the pile of limbs, squinting in the dark.

"Where are we?" Xen asked while I tried to figure out where Daria was hurt.

Behind us, the mouth of the cave let in some light, but it didn't penetrate very far. "Somewhere those assholes can't get to us," I replied. "Help me get Daria closer to the light."

Xen and I got Daria near the mouth of the cave. I risked a glance down, then wished I hadn't. I could see our would-be captors trying to figure out where we had disappeared to down below. It was a long way down.

Daria groaned and I turned to look her over. Her face was whiter than normal, and blood soaked her shirt on the left side, from up under her arm and the wound curved down along onto her stomach. The cut on her arm wasn't as deep or as long. "Okay, we need the first aid kit."

Xen helped me maneuver Daria enough to get the backpack off of her, then pulled out the kit. "We need to stop this bleeding."

My hands were next to useless all wrapped up in bandages so I started pulling at them.

"What are you doing?" Xen asked.

"Just help me get them off."

Xen blinked at me for a long moment, then did as I asked. When my left hand was free, I pressed it to Daria's side to try to staunch the flow. Xen got my right hand free of the bandages, giving me slightly more movement. "Daria? Hey, Daria." I cupped my black and blue hand to her face and she opened her eyes. "That's it, stay with me. How bad is it?"

"I'm fine," Daria slurred, her eyes sliding shut again.

"No, I need you to stay awake."

"That looks like a lot of blood," Xen said.

"Yeah, that's what worries me." I moved the torn bits of shirt out of the way so I could get a better look. Near the top of the gash I could see bone, but as it progressed down to softer places with organs that could get damaged, the laceration became more shallow. That was a good sign. "I don't think there's any internal damage though."

I thought through our options and started to formulate a plan. "Okay, I need a knife, that ointment, the pain potion, and some bandages. In that order."

Xen looked skeptical but pulled a knife from the bag Alaya had given us and handed it to me. While they rummaged in the backpack for the ointment I turned so that Xen couldn't see my next move, which was to pull the blade across my right palm and press the bleeding wound to Daria's side.

"Here." Xen held out the ointment already opened so that I could dip the ring finger of my left hand in for a healthy dollop which I smeared over the place where my blood mingled with Daria's. "Do her arm." I nodded to myself as Xen applied the ointment on the less serious gash on Daria's arm, then exchanged the ointment for the potion bottle. I could already see the worst of the gash starting to close. I brought my cut hand up and moved it over the mouth of the bottle.

Xen pulled it back. "What are you doing?"

"My blood has healing power, we just need to get it into her."

Xen brought the bottle back and I squeezed my hand to coax more blood from it. When I'd filled the bottle back up I told Xen to shake it to mix it thoroughly, then they put the bottle to Daria's mouth. Her eyes opened briefly but fluttered closed again when Xen tipped the bottle.

"Let's get these bandaged up, then I'll have a look at you."

CHAPTER 18
A LONG ROAD

"I am uninjured," Xen said as they handed me bandages and tape.

"That guy clocked you pretty good," I responded. "You could have a concussion."

"I have a hard head. I am more worried about you." They looked pointedly at my hands.

I finished bandaging my sister and sat back, my hands in my lap. "Not going to lie, they hurt."

With the bandages off I could get a better look at the damage. The bruising on my right hand was starting to add yellow and green into the color scheme, but the puncture wounds were closed and scabbed. The two broken fingers were purple and black in their splints and the fingernails were halfway grown back in.

"Maybe I should smear my blood all over everything," I said.

"You could take some of the potion?" Xen asked.

"I'm still not clear on how a lot of my magic works. I don't know if it would help or not."

"Will it cause more trouble for you?"

I shook my head lightly. "I don't think so."

Xen held out the bottle. "Then take some. I will keep watch."

I took a swig from the bottle and passed it back. "I don't think we need to worry, there's no way anyone can get up here." My eyes burned with fatigue and as the potion worked its way into me, I drifted closer to sleep.

A hand touched my shoulder, pulling my attention back. "We should stay close together. It will be cold tonight and we have no fire to warm us."

I stirred and gestured at Daria. "Get the ward stones. I think I can set up something to keep the worst of the wind out."

I rubbed my burning eyes and dug through my memory for the right configuration. I'd only done it once, and it took a fair amount of energy because it made a solid barrier that would keep out just about anything. I spilled the stones into my hands and sorted them out into pairs, kneeling just a few feet from the entrance. "You might want to move her now if you're going to. Once this is up we won't have a lot of light."

Behind me, Xen coaxed Daria up from the rock floor and helped her further into the cave. They helped her lay back down while I set the stones up in their positions, two on the bottom and one on top at each corner of the opening. "*Frágmi anémo,*" I said softly, calling up the magic. A dark green wall sprang up from the stones, filling the natural opening.

Inside the cave, the amount of light was cut in half. I pushed at the wards to ensure they were strong and nodded to myself. "There, all tucked in for some sleep." I sat down near Daria scanning her once more to assure myself she'd be okay for the night. Xen moved between us, laying so that Daria was spooned up against their back. I laid down, letting Xen pull me in close so that we were nearly nose to nose.

Xen's body radiated heat that made me want to snuggle in. "Are you always this warm?" I asked.

Xen responded by putting an arm over my hip and tugging me a little closer. "I am approaching my time to join. I will continue to warm until the chosen day."

"I thought you were all non-binary, um, agender?" I asked.

"We are. However, when we achieve a certain age, we join together with our birthmates and we are made one."

"I don't understand."

"I have many birthmates, those born from the same joining. We will join in a ceremony that combines our genetic material. And from this comes the next birthing."

"Oh." Yeah, witty response.

"I am told it is a beautiful ceremony." I could feel their breath on my lips. "It is a time of great change for us. Some will devote themselves to the raising of our offspring. Others choose to withdraw to study and become our future leaders. Some go adventuring."

"And you? What do you plan?"

Xen was quiet for long enough that I thought they had fallen asleep. "I have not yet decided." Their dark eyes stared into mine and I was suddenly very aware of the tight body pressed into me. "Much will depend on what happens between here and there."

"You mean the war?"

Xen moved so that our noses touched and I smiled, though in the dark they wouldn't see it. "I mean many things, Thána."

Something about the way they said my name made my stomach flutter. "How long?" I asked.

"It will be soon, but there is some time. You should rest now. Come morning you will need your strength to get us down from here."

It was comforting, laying there beside Xen, like I had known them forever and we had always been this close. My eyes drifted closed and sleep came hard, no doubt riding a chariot pulled by the double team of the day's exertion and the pain potion. Dreams came twice as hard, slamming me from one painful experience to another and back again, landing me in the grip of the drug-enhanced terror of Artoz's torture chamber. I thrashed about, trying to grab onto something to pull me from the nightmare.

I could feel Katyk digging away at me, like a nail digging through the back of my head. I felt Artoz pull out each fingernail, over and over. And in the midst of the pain and terror, I felt something else. My whole body flushed with it. The soft heat of arousal pooled in my stomach. I knew in some way it was Katyk fucking with my head and not me, but my body didn't seem to care.

While Artoz hurt me over and over, his hallucinogenic drug making every pain, every sound, every touch a monster towering over me, she was inside my head, taking turns with arousal and fear until I couldn't tell where one ended and the other began.

I woke with a start, sitting up and pulling away from both Daria and Xen. I was trembling and breathing hard as if I'd just run a mile, or had sex. I drew shaky hands through my hair and tried to slow my breathing. I hadn't remembered those things, and to be honest I couldn't tell if they were real or not.

The wards were still solid, so I didn't think Katyk had actually gotten into my head again, but I couldn't be sure. I was beginning to wish that Artoz had me demonstrate my abilities on Katyk.

I crawled to the pile of our things, sipping at one of the canteens and chewing on a piece of the bread. My left hand seemed to be a lot better, though my nailbeds were raw and they had bled while I slept. The bruising was not as spectacular as it had been and my grip was improving. I couldn't say the same for my right hand.

Spots on my back were starting to itch, which I took as a good sign for the healing going on back there. The burn on my side was worse though, I could feel it. It was crusty with broken scabbing and it radiated heat into the tissue around it. I could not reach it to do anything about it, so I'd have to wait until Xen or Daria were awake.

I stood, moving to the wards. The sun was up, hanging low just barely over the distant ridge of mountains. With the wards still up, I couldn't see clearly enough to make decisions about where our next portal jump should take us. At the same time, I wasn't ready to release them, not with the nightmares still hanging in the corners of my awareness.

"You okay?" Daria asked sleepily behind me.

I turned to find her sitting up, one hand pressed to her side. "Me? You're the one who tried bleeding to death yesterday," I responded. "How's that?"

She wobbled her head a little. "I'll live. I expected it to hurt more."

"Well, I helped." I held up the almost closed cut on the meaty part of my left palm.

I couldn't read the look on her face in the dim light. "Hungry?"

Daria shook her head. "Need to pee though."

"Yes, me too," Xen said, shifting so that they could sit up.

I nodded in agreement and set about dismissing the wards. I was rewarded with a blast of cold air. "Well, that's bracing."

Daria came to me and took my hands in hers. "We should get these bandaged back up."

"The bandages make it hard to use my hands." Of course, so did the actual injuries.

"Okay, let's at least protect the open wounds and tape those fingers."

"That burn on my back is unpleasant too." She cleaned and bandaged the fingernail beds of the four fingers missing nails, as well as taped the two broken fingers that were less swollen and a little less black than they had been the day before. Then I turned and pulled my shirt up so she could get a look at the burn.

She hissed between her teeth. "This needs debriding, but we can't do that here." Her fingertips touched the skin around it gently. Daria grabbed the first aid kit. "We're almost out of the healing ointment Mom sent with you, but I can try something else that might take some of the heat out of it." She opened one of the jars and whispered while she covered the burn with her hand. Whatever she smeared on it made a brief sizzling sound, then spread a cooling sensation over my skin. "How's that?"

"Better. Thanks."

While Daria and Xen gathered our things, I stood at the mouth of our cave and eyed the expanse of early morning mountain beauty.

Daria joined me when they were ready. "What are you thinking?" she asked.

"That spot there." I pointed to what looked like a vista point where there was space for parking. It was further away than anything I had consciously tried.

"That's a bit of a reach. Can you do it?"

I shrugged. "Only one way to find out. Xen, you might want to stay close. We might have to move fast if I can't hold the portal."

Without the bulky bandages, it was much easier to form my hands around the kelcimite properly. I inhaled deeply and found my center, then focused my intent on the overlook, closer to the road than the edge so a rough landing wouldn't send us crashing to our deaths.

The portal opened and wavered, then stabilized. I could already feel blood dripping from my nose. Together, the three of us crowded into the opening, emerging on the other side with a minimum of stumbling and no falling. I caught myself on Xen's shoulder as my knees tried to buckle under me.

Xen supported me until I uttered my thanks and was able to take a step on my own. Daria came to check on my nosebleed, but I waved her off. "It will pass, it always does."

"You get these often?" she asked, her tone slightly chiding.

"Only when I try magic that I shouldn't," I said, grinning as I wiped my nose on the back of my hand. The bright red stood out in stark contrast to the bruising there.

I walked to the edge and looked down at the drop into a deeply forested canyon. "It's beautiful here."

"Beauty can be deceitful," Xen said as they joined me. "In those trees are venomous snakes that can kill you in under a minute, several breeds of large, carnivorous cats and very large bo'ra." Xen looked to Daria, a question on their face.

"A kind of wolf," Daria supplied. "They are the size of horses and have a long, narrow face with teeth that are sharp like needles."

I raised an eyebrow and stepped back from the edge. "I suggest we avoid all of those things."

Daria chuckled. "You okay to start walking? We should be able to find a place to relieve ourselves just up the road."

I nodded and fell into step beside my sister. Xen took up the other side. We were quiet until we found a spot that looked safe enough to duck into the trees and take care of business. Xen stood watch for predators, while Daria and I relieved ourselves, then we did the same for them.

"Hopefully, those assholes gave up looking for us after we disappeared on them," Daria said as we got back to the road.

"Any clue how far we still have to go?" I asked. The road ahead of us dipped down, disappearing into a bunch of trees. I couldn't see where it came back out again.

"I would estimate that we are halfway through the pass," Xen said.

That was discouraging. The silence that settled between us wasn't as awkward as it had been the day before. I don't know if that was just us actively choosing to not remember what we'd been through or what we'd done, or because we were finding the company less of a chore. I was still sure Daria hated me. Or would hate me once she'd had time to process her husband's death.

That, of course, dropped me back into that memory. I had not known Habros long, but in that time I had found him to be a gentle and loving man who very clearly adored my sister and my mother. And yet, I had taken his life. I had pressed my mouth to his and called his life's energy out of him while my sister screamed.

I dragged myself out of that dark spot and told myself I'd have time to wallow there once we were someplace safer. Not that I knew when or where that would be. As we reached the bottom of the slope where the road leveled off and ran through dense forest, I spotted movement off to the side and froze in place. I tried to track what I had seen. Squinting into the trees, I wanted to believe it was just my imagination.

"What?" Daria asked, turning.

I shook my head, still not sure. "I thought I saw—" I didn't scream, exactly. It was more of a strangled exhalation as a snake slithered out from behind the rocks. It was easily as big around as a basketball, with a diamond-shaped head that turned our way, dark eyes set in brown and green skin that would make it impossible to see if not set against the blue-grey of the rocks.

Xen's hand was on my arm, but I didn't need to be told not to move. The snake lifted its head, eyeing us as if trying to decide if we were a threat. After a long staring contest, it lowered itself to the ground and continued on its way, winding its impossible length around the rocks and back into the trees.

I didn't breathe again until the final inches of its tail had disappeared. All told, it had to have been nearly fifteen feet long. None of us moved until it had been gone for quite a few minutes. When we did start walking again our pace was just a bit swifter than it had been and the trees looming ahead gave us all just a bit of pause.

The world around us got darker as we got to the point where the trees crowded the road on either side, their canopies growing together over our heads. My left hand was in my pocket on the kelcimite, fingering it nervously. I really wanted to get us out of there, but I couldn't see far enough ahead to feel safe. I didn't want to open a portal that dropped us off a cliff or something.

CHAPTER 19
THERAVEE

The road curved before it emerged from the trees, and then started climbing again. I was sweating before we'd gotten very far up the hill where Xen deemed we were probably safe enough to sit for a few minutes and have some food.

We picked a spot with a few boulders that looked good for sitting and Xen checked the area for any snake-shaped interlopers before we broke out the bread and some of the dried meat Alaya had given us. If nothing else, by the time I'd gotten home I was going to be in much better shape than I had been when I left.

I took a deep drink from one of the canteens and passed it to Daria. The scabs over the puncture wounds in my hands were itchy and I rubbed them a little, fighting the urge to pick the scabs. It was a terrible habit I had all my life and was the reason for the chickenpox scar at the base of my throat.

"With any luck, once we get to the top here, I'll be able to see someplace for us to jump," I said after swallowing the last of my jerky. Following the jump we'd made that morning, I was thinking that creating a portal from a height actually increased the distance that I could make in a single cast. I was hoping to test that theory.

"We should look for a place where we can camp for the night when we jump," Xen said, brushing crumbs from their lap before standing.

"It's early yet," Daria said.

Xen nodded. "It is at least an hour to the top. Then the jump, which will mean Thána can't do much for a while, and I'd like to get us safe inside wards before nightfall. Besides, that should get us close enough to Theravee that we get there by noon tomorrow."

I took a last sip from the canteen and gave it back to Daria to put back in the backpack, then stretched cautiously so I didn't break open any scabs on my back. I rolled my head, pressing it to each side, hoping that whatever pressure was building there at the base of my skull would dissipate. It didn't, but then why would my body decide to make things easy at that point? At least I wasn't actively bleeding.

My thighs and ass told me in no uncertain terms that they were not fans of this uphill malarky long before we reached the summit of the hill. The pressure in my head climbed as we did, and belatedly I realized that it was probably Katyk. I shook my head and grabbed my sister's arm. "Daria."

My knees buckled and I hit the pavement, bloodying my knees. Both hands went to the back of my head, trying to keep her out.

Daria knelt in front of me and took my head in her hands, forcing me to look at her. "Thána, listen to me. You have to fight her."

"Don't know how." I ground the words out through gritted teeth. The pressure was bending into pain. Suddenly a sharper pain cut through and brought me up short. Daria's hand was pressing hard against the burn on my back, the scabs breaking. Blood rose to the surface.

"Focus on this," Daria said, keeping the pressure on until I was able to meet her eyes. "Now, push it back at her. Take this pain and build a wall with it."

I had no idea how to do what she was telling me to do, but I nodded and imagined a wall, sharp with spikes of pain, then pushed the whole thing toward where Katyk was breaching my brain. I thought I heard a scream, then the pressure released so suddenly that I fell forward into Daria, resting my head on her shoulder.

She held me while I caught my breath, then helped me stand again. "We should get you behind wards sooner rather than later."

I concurred. "She's closer than she was before." I didn't know how I knew that, but I did.

"Okay, what do you think?" Daria and I surveyed the landscape before us.

There wasn't a lot to choose from. The countryside was gorgeous, but we were in rocky terrain with little hope of shelter. "Do you think we can make that ridge?" I asked, pointing in the distance. It was even further than the distance we'd jumped that morning, but it looked like the best place to make camp for the night.

"You're the one who has to do the work," Daria said, putting the choice back on me.

"Okay, give me some xýpna and we'll give it a go."

Daria fished the pouch out without giving me her standard warnings about overusing it. She held it out to me, letting me take my own pinch, which was only marginally awkward with my forefinger in bandages. I took slightly more than I meant to, and I meant to take more than she had been giving me. I needed the kick it would give me.

Daria handed me the canteen once I'd swallowed so I could wash it down. We were getting dangerously low on water. I let the powder work its magic, nodding when I was ready. Daria held my hips and Xen placed their hand on my arm as I pulled the stone from my pocket, keeping my eyes on the spot I had chosen. I was surprised by a flow of energy that came from Xen. It wasn't… magic, exactly, but it was easy to weave into the sharing of energy I had established with Daria.

I tightened my focus until I was sure I could hit the spot, then reached deep and cast. The space between me and our destination appeared to fold in on itself as the hole opened. Blood dripped from my nose and my head was imploding as we stepped through together. I went down as soon as we cleared the portal, graying out.

Daria helped me fall gracefully and pried the stone from my hand. I squeezed my eyes shut and pinched my nose to try to stop the bleeding. A few minutes later, Xen touched my shoulder. "Can you move? We found a good spot for camp."

I offered them my hand to help me up, my eyelids squeezed shut. Xen gripped my elbow and did most of the work getting me on my feet. Xen supported most of my weight as we moved. I dared open my eyes as we stopped, regretting it almost instantly. The sky was red, but the sun was still bright and glaring and my head rejected the light almost violently.

Xen eased me back down to the ground and I think I passed out for a while because my next real awareness was Daria cleaning up my bloody face. We were safely behind wards with a small fire warming the space and I could smell meat cooking.

Outside the wards, the skies were much darker and I could see two of the moons, one nearly full and the other just a crescent.

"We found a spring for water and Xen caught a greckle."

"What's a greckle?" I asked, attempting to sit up. I hissed as the burn wound reminded me of its presence.

"Small animal. Tastes like pork." Daria helped me sit and finished wiping my face. I could see why they had chosen the spot. Behind me, a cliff rose, giving us protection from the wind and predators. The wards were set up so that they abutted the stone.

"You remember what pork tastes like?" I asked, remembering that Daria had left the world we had been born to when she was pretty small.

"Not really, it's what Mom said."

"Oh." I guess that made sense. It struck me how vastly different our childhoods had been. "What do you remember?"

"About your world?" Daria asked, sitting beside me. "I remember the smell of the ocean and crying when we left you. I also remember chicken nuggets and French fries. I remember even less of Spítia."

Because of Merry's memory spell, I had a near-perfect recall of my childhood, of my entire life really, but there was a time when I had no memories before ten. Daria was eight when Mom took her to Spítia, and not even ten when they had come to Vaneesh.

My whole body felt bruised, like each time I cast that spell I was compressing and throwing myself into a rock wall. At least a few places on my back were bleeding, not the least of which was the burn. "I think I want some of that pain potion," I said into the quiet.

"Eat first, then I'll give you that and some of the sleep powder."

I didn't argue. Xen passed me a stick that held roasted meat and I agreed, it did taste like pork. My stomach growled even as I ate, and it was gone quickly. I took my medicine and tried to find a comfortable position to sleep in before Xen beckoned me closer, guiding my head down to their thigh. It was just enough to calm me.

I listened to the crackle of the fire and Xen's soft voice as they told a story about the last time they had been home to their birthplace. Xen's hand stroked through my hair and glazed over my temples and cheeks, lulling me into sleep. The dreams came then. Katyk's lips on mine, our bodies sliding skin to skin, the sensual heat of her against me. Arousal rushed like lava through my body and I hungered for each touch. My body began to orgasm and the stimulus went from sensual to painful, my body arching to both as we burned against each other and the metal of Artoz's heated blade pressed against my back.

I woke screaming, my skin hot and fevered, my body letting me know that the arousal, at least, wasn't completely in my head. I could feel the xýpna still working inside me, contributing to the heat. Daria and Xen were looking at me, the question on their faces without saying a word.

"I'm okay," I demurred, gesturing for them to lay back down. "Nightmare."

Daria's pained expression told me that she knew the same fears and had similar nightmares. She closed her eyes again, but I'm not sure either of us slept any more that night. By the time the sun was rising in the distance, I was restlessly pacing the space inside the wards. I was afraid that Katyk was going to catch up to us, that somehow her intrusions into my head had allowed her to find us. Daria had said she could help sever the connection once we got to civilization and Xen thought we could reach that town by noon.

I didn't know what I expected Katyk to do to us if she found us, but suspected her handlers wouldn't let her chase us on her own. We had to hope we could reach this town, get me free of her claws, and then find our way to the Vaneeshi command. No problem. Piece of cake. We'd be done by sundown.

Sarcasm had always been my first coping mechanism.

By the time Daria and Xen were ready to head out I was fairly jittery. I steeled myself mentally when Daria released the wards, but nothing happened. Xen pointed me in the direction of the road and we hiked down from our camp, which turned out to be further off the road than I had anticipated. It showed how out of it I had been. We didn't talk much and I set a pace I knew I wouldn't be able to maintain. I just wanted distance between me and wherever Katyk was. The road led us along the ridge for nearly a mile before it dipped below the rim and wound its way down toward a river that flowed lazily in the direction of a village I could just barely see.

I played with the stone in my pocket for a long minute, trying to judge distances. I didn't want to incapacitate myself again, but I also wanted this trek to be over. "I'm going to aim for the bridge," I said, pointing.

Daria didn't argue, surprisingly. It would put us just across the river from the town. It was likely close to the same distance as our last jump. Daria held up the xýpna pouch, but I shook my head. "Save it for after."

She nodded and we took position, Daria behind me and Xen beside us. Daria's hands held my hips, but this time, she pressed herself into my back and I felt the connection of her magic with mine in a nearly audible snap. Her energy mixed with mine, and once again, Xen's. I set my intention, raised the stone, and cast.

The hole was almost instantly stable, and I could see the bridge through it. Together we stepped through. I released the spell, sagging a little against Daria, but this time, her energy held, flowing into me to help offset the effects of the spell. I found my feet and nodded my thanks. We were starting to get good at this thing.

As one, we turned to the bridge and I scanned the village ahead. It reminded me of Vail, Colorado in a way. I had no idea what to expect. We still had nothing of value to trade to get us what we needed, but Daria had said that she knew someone there.

Xen was the first to start walking and we followed, crossing over a lazy river flowing down past the town before moving underground. The main street was lined with shops and the smell of baking bread made my mouth water. The buildings were nothing like what I'd seen in Meerat. They seemed cozier somehow, made of wood and plaster rather than concrete and glass.

Daria led us to a sidewalk, made from what looked like paving stones, and past the bakery, a meat seller of some kind, and a shop that seemed to carry a variety of goods and smelled of incense.

It was early yet since we'd made the jump so far, but the door to the shop was open and Daria led us in. At the far end, there was a person who appeared to be marking prices on small jars. They looked up as the door chimed, and a smile spread across their face. "Daria, *bawo ni iyanu!*"

Daria let her friend sweep her into a hug. As I got closer, I determined the person was most likely a woman, but I had never seen anyone of her race. She was tall and willowy, with grace in her movements that made her look like she was moving through water. She was bald, though I couldn't tell if that was genetic or a choice, and the vague blue of her skin suggested she was a native to the world. Her nose was a sharp slope that softened to a rounded end above full lips that were painted with a dark burgundy lipstick. She had flat cheekbones that made her face look angled and large ears that were decked in silver earrings, from the lobe all the way up and around the curve at the top.

Daria stepped back and gestured to me. "*Eyi ni arabinrin mi,* Thána *ati ore mi,* Xen. *A nilo iranlọwọ rẹ.*" Daria looked at me and Xen. "Thána, Xen, this is my friend, Eniyii."

Eniyii took Daria's hands and kissed them both. They withdrew to talk, and Xen and I busied ourselves looking around her shop. It reminded me of one of those boutique gift shops back home, with the candles and jewelry, bath products, and the like. I was drawn to a display of jewelry near the window. The stones were deep blues, darker than most sapphires, set in silver. There were earcuffs, like the ones Eniyii was wearing, bracelets, and a pendant that more than the rest seemed to call to me. I could almost see myself in the stone.

It was heavy, both the stone and its setting. As I lifted it, a sense of calm flowed through me. Then I felt Katyk again, violently shoving herself at me, into me. I dropped the pendant and it clattered to the ground. I grabbed my head and tried to shove back against the invasion. I reached around my side, shoving my thumb into the burn, and tried to do as I had the last time she'd attacked.

I could hear the others talking, but I couldn't understand anything. Panting and stumbling toward Daria, I felt Katyk breaking through my defense, seething anger flooding into me. She screamed from my mouth, trying to get my arms to grab my sister. I threw myself backward, flailing as I hit a display and slid to the floor with the products.

Katyk wanted to kill them and make me do it. "Fight, Thána."

I was pulled out of the cascade of candles I'd toppled, then there was a weight straddling over me, a heavy blanket of calm and restraint. Katyk was still in my head, but we couldn't move.

CHAPTER 20
RELEASE

I was aware of two things at the same time. Inside my head, Katyk was furious and shoving against whatever magic had been used to restrain me. Outside of me, Daria and Eniyii were creating a circle in chalk on the floor around me while Xen stood watch at the door.

Eniyii drew symbols inside and outside the circle, chanting musically as she went. Then came candles and more chanting. Eniyii's soft robes moved with her as she danced around the circle with an instrument that made a rattling noise.

Katyk laughed and told me that nothing could get her out of my head now and soon the village would be overrun with Kabeshi troops. I tried to open my mouth to warn Daria, but nothing came out.

The panic started to build as I struggled against Katyk, who stoked the fear while also stoking my arousal until the two were so intertwined I couldn't tell them apart. I was writhing under the restraint, my hips moving against the floor, then arching up. Daria knelt beside me and I felt wards rise, felt Katyk's hold starting to slip, then a different kind of wards. Katyk flailed and fought, and Daria grabbed my chin and forced my mouth open. I tasted blood and swallowed.

Daria's mind pushed into me, shoving at Katyk. "My blood is stronger than your sex. Get out of my sister."

They grappled for a long minute, but ultimately, Daria won and Katyk slipped away.

"They're coming," I gasped, grabbing at Daria's hands. "She said they're coming."

"I know. Let's get you squared away first. I need you to stay in this circle while Eniyii and I gather what we need to permanently break her hold on you."

Eniyii handed something to my sister and she placed it over my head. "The pendant has protective power," Eniyii said in a very heavy accent. "I saw you were drawn to it. It will help you."

I let Daria settle it around my neck, welcoming the weight of it. "Rest. Xen will be here to watch you while we work."

I couldn't rest, not when Katyk knew where we were and she was coming. We were putting the entire town in danger. The heaviness of the magic holding me in place was comforting in an odd way, or maybe it was whatever magic was in the pendant. I closed my eyes. Part of me wanted to turn onto my side as my back protested the pressure of the floor, but it seemed like too much effort.

Xen moved from the door to sit just outside the wards protecting me. "I will not let Katyk near you," Xen said softly.

"I'm not sure I could fight her off again." Even through the wards, I could sense their concern. In that moment, I felt certain that was notworthy of concern, at least not in this. I had let Katyk in. I had let her seduce me. "It's too quiet. Talk to me."

"What is it you would like me to say?"

"Anything. Tell me a story."

"As you wish." Xen shifted a little, their eyes skipping to the door and back again. "Shall I speak of the day I met Daria? I had been assigned to the school's defense preparedness team, teaching hand-to-hand combat skills. Daria was feisty and ambitious. I knew that day we would become very good friends."

Xen's voice was soothing, and I let it lull me out of my fear. While I don't think I slept, I did doze, drifting in a quasi-sleep space that wound around me in a mix of nightmares and memories. The sound of my mother's voice sang a lullaby to Daria when she was small, the feeling of never belonging, the desire for family, the smell of my father's hands after working in the garden. They swirled around me, taking me from comfort to terror and back again.

I'm not sure how long I lay there on the shop floor before Daria was back, stepping carefully over the lines of the circle and sitting beside me. The heaviness lifted and Daria sat me up with a soft smile. The room was darkened and when I looked up I found that Eniyii had closed shades over the windows.

Xen once again stood by the door, their eyes on me, though I could not read their expression. "Let's start with getting you out of your clothes," Daria said softly.

"Really?" I asked, my voice surprisingly ragged.

"We are going to bathe you. I'm going to need to douse your head and be able to reach your *ọpọlọ yio*." Her hand cupped the back of my neck. "The place where she enters. And your *gbongbo*, where she found you." With that, Daria's eyes fell to my groin and I blushed.

Daria's hands were gentle as she helped me out of the shirt. I could tell it was crusty with blood and dirt, and I felt strangely vulnerable without it. I was never an overly modest person, but somehow this felt naked in ways I'd never been. The pants came next, leaving me on the floor of the shop stark naked.

Once again Eniyii began circling me, her rattle moving in rhythm to her chants. Daria put a stone bowl in my lap and had me put my hands to either side to hold it. She poured ice-cold water into the bowl and the cold seeped into the stone and my thighs. Next, Daria sprinkled in an herb mixture that smelled sour and sharp, like lemons that had begun to ferment. Her finger stirred the water while she murmured her spell. I couldn't make out the words, but they seemed to be in Spítia's not-quite Greek native tongue.

The water continued to swirl long after her finger was removed and she reached for a thick orange sponge. She continued murmuring as she dunked the sponge in the bowl and squeezed it, then stood and moved behind me. Eniyii's voice raised in volume as Daria squeezed the sponge, sending the ice-cold water cascading into my hair. I shivered before it even touched my scalp.

The water filtered through my hair, dripping onto my forehead and down my neck. Daria dipped the sponge again and again, squeezing the water out onto my head and skin, then scrubbing the sponge over me. She focused on the base of my skull, then continued down my back before coming to face me. She washed my face and neck, over my shoulders, and down each arm.

She helped me stand then, the bowl still in my hands, though my broken fingers were not amused with that. She was gentle as she washed my breasts and down my stomach, and looked apologetic as she guided me to spread my legs a little wider so she could clean between them, then down both the front and back of my legs. When she was done, she took the bowl from me and had me sit back down.

Daria then walked in a counter-clockwise circle around me, the opposite of Eniyii's path, her voice a sing-songy rhythm as she completed her spell. I didn't feel any different when it was over, just cold and vaguely embarrassed. Daria squatted beside me. "Sit while we take down the circle. Eniyii has said that we can stay here while we sort out our next step. I'll get you some clothes and you can take a nap."

"Katyk—"

Daria offered a tight smile. "Don't worry. This town is not without its defenses. And now it has *me*."

I wasn't sure what that meant, but I let it go and waited until I felt the wards close. Daria came back with a soft robe of light green. She helped me up and into the robe, then Xen came to walk with me toward the back. Like Daria's home in Meerat, Eniyii's shop had a hall that led to a tidy little kitchen, a cozy living room with a fireplace, and probably more, but we only got as far as the living room. I was offered the couch and dropped onto it gratefully, sighing as I sank into the softness of its cushions. After sleeping on the ground the last few nights, that couch felt like heaven.

Xen stood for a long moment in the doorway before moving to sit in a chair. "You don't have to stay with me," I offered, shifting to see them better.

"I told your sister I would," Xen replied.

"In case this didn't work." That was fair enough, I supposed. Without knowing specifically what Katyk did to break into my brain, Daria was mostly guessing at what would work.

"Also, I cannot help with the magic, so it is best to stay out of the way."

"Okay."

"You should try to sleep."

I certainly was tired enough to. The combination of the long-distance jump, the attack by Katyk, and the heavy weight of the magical restraint that kept Katyk from using my body to try to kill people had worn down my already run-down body. Not to mention the whole escape from torture and all the insanity that entailed. I yawned as if tallying the reasons I should be tired made me more tired.

I drifted, but some part of me was aware of Xen watching me and of Daria and Eniyii doing something nearby. There was energy stirring. An explosion rocked me from my doze and I sat up quickly. Xen only looked at me strangely.

"What was that?" I asked.

Xen frowned. "What was what? I heard nothing."

It took me a second to realize what it was. Wards, but on a scale I had never seen. Like a shield around the entire town. "Oh, it's… never mind."

Xen raised an eyebrow at me. "I take it that it is something to do with your sister's magic?"

"Yeah, I guess." I cocked my head to one side. "You have no awareness of it? Magic, I mean?"

They smiled. "Only when I can see it, like when you open those portals. We Pixin are not inclined magically. Our gifts lie elsewhere, in languages and communication, and for those of us trained, defending our people, even against larger opponents."

"Oh, I guess I kinda figured that Daria's friends were all magic folks. I don't know why." Maybe it was because everyone in Spítia had skill with some kind of magic and I figured that friends of Daria's who were not native to this world would also.

"I am a master of Pixila. Our style of defensive fighting."

"That's what you taught Daria?"

Xen nodded. "She is quite good, though her side kick still needs work."

"Huh."

"She is strong, but like you, her nightmares are severe. She would not want me to tell you this, but she is not well."

I sat up a little straighter. "She hasn't said anything."

"And she will not. It is not her way. She is a caregiver and protector. As long as she has someone who needs her, she will ignore what she needs."

"How... how bad is it?" I asked, though if I had given more than a few minutes thought to anything outside myself, I'd have realized that of course she wasn't well. She'd been in that place a whole lot longer than I was, undergoing Artoz's torture for at least a month.

"Physically she is mostly recovered. She has waited until you were asleep to have me treat her remaining wounds. Your blood in the pain potion helped considerably."

But mentally, she had to be dealing with a lot of the same terror I was. That drug had been in her system for weeks before we got there. I'd been under its influence for much less time.

As if sensing the direction of my thoughts, Xen said, "Daria tells me that Artoz was harder on you, tried to break you more quickly because he saw you as a weapon. Daria's gifts are defensive more than offensive."

"How do I help her?" I asked, shifting uncomfortably.

"I do not know if either of us can help her. But be careful how much you rely on her helping you. She must process what was done to her, not hide inside caring for you."

"How—" I stopped myself from blurting out that I didn't think she could care for me. I looked down at my hands, which were starting to look better. "Did she... tell you? What I did?"

"She told me that you had to choose, between her and Habros. And you chose your flesh and blood."

I bit my lip and couldn't look at Xen. "I didn't want to."

Xen sat beside me, one hand on my thigh. "She knows that. She told me that afterward you sobbed and begged for forgiveness."

I shook my head. "I don't expect her to forgive me. In fact, once we get through this, I'll leave so she doesn't have to look at me and see that in her head."

"I do not believe she desires that. She has grown to care for you a great deal. As have I."

"I— what?"

Eniyii appeared in the doorway. "If you are hungry, I have acquired food."

My stomach rumbled in response and I stood, wavering a little as a wave of dizziness swept over me. Xen slid an arm around my waist and together we followed our host back to the small kitchen where the table was set with a loaf of brown bread and a pot of something that smelled like stew.

Eniyii served up bowls of the stuff and tore off pieces of the bread to pass around. I wolfed down half of mine without even looking up. I felt as though I was still an empty hole after going so long without food.

Daria joined us and took a seat beside me. "Well, that should give anyone trying to cross that bridge some trouble." She took her bowl and glanced at me. "How are you feeling?"

"No signs that Katyk is trying to make a comeback, so that's something," I replied. "How about you?"

She nodded tightly. "I'm good, though we need to talk about what comes next."

I put down my spoon. "Okay."

She swallowed hard. "I'm thinking that maybe you should stay here."

"What?" This was where she finally told me she hated me and never wanted to see me again, no matter what Xen believed.

"This isn't your fight, Thána. Xen and I live here. Xen and I were the targets of the Kabeshi offensive. Stay here, where you'll be safe."

"I'm not going to be safe if Katyk figures out a way to break through your wards. Even if the Kabeshi didn't know I exist, they do now and that makes me just as much of a target as you are." I pushed my bowl away. "Besides, Katyk isn't just going to let me go. She's furious that I got away from her. She was punished for it." At least, that's what I'd felt behind her most recent attack.

"We're going into an active war zone," Xen said. "Daria and I are prepared for that."

"So, get me prepared," I responded. I looked at Daria. "I promised Mom I would get you to her safely. I'm not letting you leave me behind."

CHAPTER 21
DEFENSE

We spent the next two days with Eniyii, Daria attempting to teach me more and more complex defensive spells, and Xen trying to teach me Pixila. Daria was infinitely more successful. Even with enforced weight loss due to being starved for however long, and the increased stamina due to the inordinate amount of physical activity I had endured since embarking on the adventure to find my mother, I was nothing near physically fit.

I spent more of my training time with Xen on my ass on the ground than I did blocking their attacks. "You are thinking too hard," Xen said when they had knocked me down for the hundredth time.

"And moving too slow, I know." I climbed to my feet and dusted off my ass. My hands were wrapped up in tape to keep them from further injury, though they were mostly healed but for the broken fingers. Nothing I was doing was helping those heal faster. I had nearly full fingernails on my right hand and the bruising was now little more than brown and yellow dusting over the skin.

Daria had even gotten the burn to start healing, but not until I had endured her excruciating debridement that I thought was never going to end. The infection was disgusting, the tissue she pulled out of it a frightening shade of black before she was able to apply some healing ointment and bandage it up.

Daria appeared at the door to Eniyii's meditation room where Xen and I were working. "They're here."

I inhaled and let it out with a nod. "Where?"

"The bridge. Katyk is picking at the wards, but she's not getting in."

I had walked the wards with Xen earlier in the day and I knew they were strong, possibly stronger than any I could ever cast. Daria had used the natural landscape, essentially turning the rock faces to our north and south into ward stones, then using the boundary of the river, and the energy inherent in the water, to build on. She'd explained the magic theory behind it, but at the time, my thoughts had been more on making sure they were as strong as Daria had claimed them to be.

I had met a few more of the townsfolk, most of whom seemed to be the same race as Eniyii and none of whom seemed to have hair, so I guess that meant it was likely to be genetic. They all had that same graceful build as well, tall and lank, with long arms and legs. I felt positively short beside them.

"So, what's the plan?" I asked, picking at the tape on my hands to start unwinding it.

"Let them stew. Besides, I want to introduce you to someone." She led me out to the living room and gestured at the screen on the wall that resembled a television. Instead, it was more like a video phone. On the screen, there was a Vaneeshi woman in a military uniform. Her brown hair was clipped short and her features were narrow, with harsh lines and slim lips.

"Minister, this is my sister, Thána Alizon."

I nodded in greeting and the minister returned the gesture. "Daria tells me that you are responsible for her escape from the Kabeshi."

"I played a part in it, yes," I responded.

"You should know that at least twenty other prisoners escaped that camp at the same time."

"I'm glad, but to be fair, that was Xen's doing, not mine. I was pretty out of it at that point."

"And yet you performed magic unlike any your sister has ever seen."

I chuckled a little. "Born of desperation, I assure you. And I was following groundwork that Daria created."

"Even so, I look forward to a demonstration when you arrive."

"I take it that means we have a plan?" I asked, looking to Daria.

"The Minister is sending a troop to help us deal with Katyk and friends, then we'll be going to the front with them."

"When are we expecting arrival?"

"They should be at the town's borders in a few hours," the Minister said. "Colonel Devets has two of our magic corps with him."

"Thank you, Minister," Daria said. "We'll handle this small incursion and be with you soon."

The minister inclined her head and the screen went black. "So we're doing this thing?" I asked, glancing aside at my sister.

"Looks like. I'm headed out to get a look at how many men Katyk's got with her, want to join me?"

We turned in unison. Eniyii raised a hand in greeting as we passed through the shop, though she was helping a customer. There were more people on the streets than I had seen before, gathered in clumps around store windows or strolling down to gawk at the enemy. Daria and I fell into step behind two people holding hands. I was finding it harder to determine gender among people of this race, then realized that it shouldn't matter anyway.

I could see the faint shimmer of the wards before we had cleared the last of the buildings and caught glimpses of the men between the bodies of the people ahead of us. Nearly twenty townsfolk were gawking at the people beyond the wards. I stepped around the couple that had stopped in front of us, getting my first look at Katyk.

She wore one of the khaki brown uniforms of the Kabeshi infantry, her hair pulled back severely from her face. It made her cheeks seem sharp and her forehead larger than it was. She was raging, stalking across the end of the bridge. I knew it the moment her eyes caught sight of me. She stopped and turned to face us.

I raised an eyebrow, stepping out onto the bridge despite Daria's warning hand on my arm. I touched her hand in what I hoped was a reassuring way. "You finally caught up," I said when I was close enough to the wards that I knew Katyk could hear me.

"I am going to rip your mind to shreds, *Mörderin*," Katyk growled at me.

"You can try," I responded. "But I don't think the odds are on your side."

"I have back up. What do you have? A bunch of hicks?"

"Oh, I think you'll find these hicks a match for you, Katyk," Daria said, stepping in beside me.

"Still hanging out with the sister that killed your husband I see," Katyk taunted. "How long will that last, I wonder. How long before she turns on you?"

"You're starting to sound desperate, Katyk," I said. "I'm betting Artoz blamed you for our escape."

Katyk made a face that was either disgust or fear, I couldn't be sure. She slammed her hands against the wards. "I will get in there, and when I do, you will find out what I am capable of."

"Good luck with that," I said over my shoulder as I turned around and headed back toward Eniyii's shop. "I counted twenty men or so."

Daria nodded. "Same. I didn't see any heavy artillery either. I didn't expect they'd be able to haul big guns, not over the pass, and not with enough time to catch us. But we shouldn't assume that means that they can't do some damage."

"Can standard artillery take out the wards?" I asked, stopping to look back.

"Eventually, yes. And their magically enhanced weapons even faster. They shredded Meerat's wards in less than two days."

"Great."

We walked past Eniyii's shop and down to the bakery to pick up some of the savory bread that tasted of rye and onion and from there, down to a small park where we sat on a bench to eat. Children played nearby, bundled up against the chilly air. It had gotten increasingly colder while we'd been in the village.

For a long time, we sat silent, not entirely uncomfortable with each other for a change. "I remember that day when you saved my life. The first time, I mean," Daria said softly after a while. "I remember how scared you were. You cried."

"I did. I thought you were going to die," I replied.

"And when Mom came home, she was terrified of what you did. For a long time, I believed it was because she wanted me to die."

"What? Mom would never—"

"I know. Now. Back then I didn't understand why she was afraid." She nibbled on her bread. "When we had come to Spítia, after we hid you, we were staying with Uncle Adrian. Well, it was his house. He was somewhere else. The Brotherhood found us. One of them had grabbed me and when his hand touched my skin, I saw..."

I waited for her to go on, but when she didn't, I glanced up from the bread in my hand. She seemed lost in her thoughts with a faraway look haunting her eyes.

"Daria? What did you see?"

She inhaled sharply and shook her head. "I saw what they would do to you. That was when I understood Mom's fear."

"Oh." The memory was visceral, bringing a tremble to my hands. They didn't get the chance to do it, but it had been a close call. They had planned to string me up and bleed me, slowly and painfully. Fortunately for me, the manticores had been itching for a chance to rebel. Which still seemed like a ridiculous thing to say. "I survived," I said finally. "And more importantly, I got Mom out."

Daria nodded but was silent for a long time. "I don't hate you, you know? I miss him. I love him. But I knew he would die. I knew that two years ago. I was just holding my breath, waiting."

"You knew?" I asked, resting my hand on her shoulder.

"Not how or when, but yeah, I knew. Like I know Kota is going to live to old age, and you are going to teach him how to use his magic."

"What about you?"

She shrugged and brushed tears from her eyes. "I never see myself. Just everyone around me. It's a pain in the ass."

"I can't even imagine." It was weird enough being able to see bits of my bloodline's past and sometimes being able to see them in the here and now, I couldn't imagine glimpses into the future. "Do you remember Dad at all?"

"I think I remember what he looks like," Daria answered. "But mostly he's just soft feelings, like home and family."

"I saw him. Well, his ghost. At least I think it was his ghost. At the house in California, before I went to Spítia."

"Wow, that's rare."

It was my turn to shrug. "He told me to find Mom."

Daria smiled. "And you did. Maybe that will let him rest."

"I haven't been back, so I don't know. I'll be surprised if the house is still standing. Cambious and I went through the gate while Brotherhood thugs were dismantling our wards."

"Cambious, the big guy with the horns?" Daria asked. "I thought I made him up. He terrified me when I was little."

I chuckled. "Hell, he terrified me as a grown adult. Granted, at the time I knew nothing, well, very little, about any of this, so he seemed quite impossible. I thought maybe I was delusional." And now the notion that my childhood home held a portal to another world, guarded by an incubus with whom I had sex more than one time seemed nearly sedate. "And here I sit, not even a full year later, in yet another world, getting ready to go to war with another group of assholes who want to use me or kill me."

"I thought the Brotherhood just wanted you dead?" Daria asked.

"Most of them yes. Their leader, on the other hand, had discovered that he could stay alive by drinking the blood of a blood witch, so their method of killing us is generally to drain our blood, which then goes into storage for *Patoras* to drink at his leisure."

"What happened to him?"

"The fires of Apollo," I said dryly. "A phoenix named Sabina and a tribe of manticores burned the whole thing down. He eventually died from his injuries."

Daria actually laughed. "You have had a strange life."

"To be fair, it's only been the last… however many months that have been that strange. Up until then, I was just a mid-level manager at a manufacturing facility."

"Thána, I want you to be careful with Minister Brek," Daria said suddenly, licking her lips.

"Don't you trust her?" I asked, frowning.

"I do, at least in some ways, but she's ambitious and has a tendency to use people up to get what she wants. She's been in power a long time because of that."

"Because she uses people?" I certainly knew other politicians like that.

"Particularly people with unique abilities, like you. She's going to try to recruit you, even offer you citizenship. She has no real understanding of magic and how it works and just demands people figure out a way to do what she wants done."

I nodded. "Okay, watch my back. Got it." Daria was anxious, I could feel it. "Is there more?"

Daria shrugged and looked at a young boy who went running past. "I have a strange question first."

"Okay… " I waited, but it took her a moment to collect her thoughts and turn to me again.

"Did Artoz do something with Xen and your blood?"

That moment filled my head, the look in Xen's eyes when it happened. It was a strange look, not about the pain or fear, but something was significant about it. "Yeah, he wanted to see how my healing thing worked. He cut Xen, then poured my blood over the wound."

Daria nodded and nibbled at her bread. "That explains it."

"Explains what?" I asked because from where I was sitting it explained nothing.

"Pixin are different from us, Thána, and Xen's behavior since our escape… specifically their behavior toward you, had me a little worried. But, if there is a blood bond…" She shook her head. "You need to stay close to Xen. Let Xen protect you."

"Protect me from what?" I asked, becoming more concerned.

"I'm not sure. I just know that you're going to need Xen to get through what comes next. And, I know that Xen is going to need you. I didn't see more than that." She sighed and rubbed a hand over her face. "We should get ready. Colonel Devets will be here soon."

"And then?" I asked as we stood.

"And then we fight."

CHAPTER 22
OFFENSE

I was just finishing up getting dressed in the black uniform that Xen had brought me and tying my boots when Xen came to tell me it was time. I felt kind of badass if I'm honest. The pants were a bit tight, but not in a way that restricted my movement, and in fact, they felt almost like they enhanced my movements. The boots were honest-to-god combat boots, all black and perfect. I wore a black tank top under the uniform shirt and over that a vest full of pockets which I had already filled with my kelcimite, ward stones, and the pouch of xýpna powder.

I emerged from the shop to find the street filled with olive-green uniforms. Daria's red hair caught my eye and I went to her. "Here she is now. Colonel, my sister Thána. Thána, this is Colonel Devets."

I nodded a greeting. "Glad you're here, Colonel."

"I'm not. Let's get this over with so I can get back to the real war."

"Nice," I murmured aside to Daria. "This shouldn't take long. They only have about twenty men."

"And Katyk," Daria amended. "Don't discount her."

"She the witch?" Devets asked.

"Yes sir," Daria responded. "But don't worry, Thána and I can handle her."

"We can?" I asked Daria so that he wouldn't hear.

She put a reassuring hand on my shoulder, then gestured toward where Katyk and her men waited. "The Minister wants her taken alive," Devets said.

"Not a problem," Daria responded. "I assume you have working restraints?"

Devets waved to one of his men who came trotting over. He had a pair of metal cuffs in his hand. "Should lockdown any magical ability."

Daria nodded. "That will do."

Devets's men were ranged along the wards, weapons at the ready. Beyond the wards, I could see the enemy similarly ranged. An idea was starting to form. I put my hand on Daria's to get her attention. "What if I could jump behind them, take men with me? Just as you drop the shields, we'll be on both sides of them. They won't stand a chance."

"You can do that?" Devets asked.

I nodded. "I can, but if Katyk sees me doing it, she might anticipate the attack." I stood on tiptoes to see over the assembled men. "There's enough room back there for at least ten men."

Devets waved again and an aide trotted up. "Bring me Róisín and nine of the men with the new shields." He nodded and ran off behind us. "Róisín is one of our magic workers. She goes with you."

I stood on tiptoes again to get a good look at our destination. When Róisín and the men arrived, I took the kelcimite from my pocket. "Can you manage this and the wards at the same time?" I asked Daria.

"I have another idea. Xen, come here."

I wasn't sure what Daria meant for Xen to do, but she just guided Xen into the position she normally took. Xen's hands found my hips and their body lined up against my back, warm and comforting. "Xen may not have magic ability, Thána, but they have a strong core of energy you should be able to tap into."

I looked at the men. "I'm about to open a portal that will put us directly behind the enemy. You're going to need to move quickly because I can't hold it open for long."

"How is this possible?" Róisín asked, her brow lifting. She was fair of skin and her hair the palest blond I had ever seen. It was nearly white.

"It just is," I said.

"Are we ready, Colonel?" Daria asked, a hand lifted to drop the wards. I could vaguely feel her hold on them. They mostly stood on their own once up, but in order to collapse them, she'd needed to keep a tether.

"Ready when you are."

Xen's hands tightened on my hips. We were turned away from the wards, hidden from Katyk's eyes by the line of men and their weapons. "Now or never I guess," I muttered, lifting the kelcimite and setting our destination in my head. The casting was nearly effortless with our destination so close. The portal opened in front of me and I dared to open my eyes. "Now."

Daria released the wards and I held the hole open as the men dashed through, following as the last of them cleared the hole.

I stumbled a little, but Róisín caught my elbow. "You're going to have to teach me that trick."

She waved a hand in an intricate pattern and the shields held by our men came to life with crackling blue energy. The enemy was already in chaos, with guns coming from the other side of the bridge, while we pushed them closer and closer.

There was a sudden explosion in the middle of our line and two men went down. I backpedaled as Katyk burst through the opening in the line. Energy crackled around her, surging red between her fingers. Fire exploded with her fury, eating the distance between us.

I deflected it with a version of *prostatévo* Daria had taught me, turning it from fire to water. The water splashed my legs as it hit the ground in front of me. We had anticipated that she would come with fire.

Katyk growled and charged at me, but Róisín blocked her with a spell I didn't see, knocking Katyk to the ground. I pounced forward, pushing her from her knees until she was prone on the ground. "*Város.*" The spell would feel like my entire body weight pinned Katyk to the ground where she lay. It was the same spell Daria had used to keep me down when Katyk had invaded my mind. "Struggling will only make it heavier," I said as I accepted Róisín's aid to get to my feet.

"This isn't over," Katyk growled.

"I'm sure it isn't," I agreed, looking around. The fight, such as it was, had already ended. There were two men down that I could see. The others were kneeling on this side of the bridge, weapons down, and were being taken into custody.

Despite the ease of the victory, my heart was thumping. Daria approached with the man carrying the magic cuffs. Together with Róisín, he roughly moved Katyk so he could get her into them. Once she was secure, I released the spell so that they could get her up and move her toward the vehicles.

Xen slipped an arm around my waist. "That went well."

"It did," I agreed, smiling. "I'm glad."

"As am I." Warmth graced their cheeks and they let go of me as we started back over the bridge. "I should go get our things together."

I nodded and Xen headed briskly for the storefront. "Well, that was easy enough," I said as Daria approached.

"Don't get used to it. That was a small group of light infantry that had been marching for days on end. Our next battle won't be so easy."

Xen headed into Eniyii's shop to get our backpack and the bag Alaya had given us. Eniyii leaned on the doorway, watching as the soldiers secured the prisoners. Daria drew her friend into a hug, thanking her for the hospitality before Xen gestured at a hauler, not unlike the one we had stolen. "This is our ride."

I let the uniformed Vaneeshi man by the back of the hauler help me take the large step up behind Xen. In the place of the cages that had filled our last hauler, this one had benches. I sat next to Xen and Daria slid in next to me. "Well, this sure is comfy," I said sarcastically.

"It is not too late to stay behind," Xen offered.

"I'll take my chances." The vehicle roared to life, vibrating around us.

"The Colonel is leaving a few men behind to guard the pass," Xen said after a few minutes. "I doubt we need to worry about anyone coming from that direction. Most of the people in the Wilds are insular. Kabesh should have no interest in them."

"How long a ride is this going to be?"

"A couple of hours." I looked up as Róisín and a man in a similar black uniform joined us. "This is my partner Ragna."

I lifted a hand in greeting. "I'm Thána, my sister Daria and our friend, Xen."

"Pixin, right?" Ragna asked, taking a seat beside Daria. "My best friend as a kid was Pixin, but we lost touch when they went off to the joining."

"It changes many of us," Xen acknowledged. Ragna was heavier set, and I guessed more or less human, with curly brown hair and sparkling brown eyes, maybe twenty or so. Róisín sat across from Xen and sighed.

The vehicle started moving, making a wide U-turn, and rumbled toward the road out of town. "So that trick you did," Ragna said after a while, leaning forward to see me around Daria. "What was that?"

"Just something I do, I guess." I was uncomfortable under his intense gaze. "Daria here doesn't get how I do it either, and she's helped me cast it several times."

"Is that so?" Ragna asked.

Daria shrugged. "I've done some research into the idea before, but Thána has taken it to a whole new level. It's not like any magic I've seen before."

"You'll have to show us. See if we can learn it. Would certainly come in handy." Róisín said.

"Would have ended the battle for Meerat right quick," Ragna said, sitting back.

"Well, it takes two to cast it, so maybe you'll get the chance." I don't know why it bugged me that they were interested. It just did. I could see it as a valuable tool though, so I tried to push away my annoyance.

"My sister's magical education wasn't the most traditional," Daria said. "And her innate gifts are pretty rare."

"Is that so?" Ragna leaned forward again. "What are they?"

"Ragna!" Róisín slapped his knee. "You know better."

"No, it's okay," I said. "It's not a big deal. I'm a blood witch."

"Oh, I've read about those," Róisín said. "I thought they were all gone."

"Not many around, that's for sure," I answered.

"I've never even heard of one," Ragna said. "So you… use blood magic?"

I shrugged. "I can, though mostly I'm a healer I guess. I can take disease out of the body, cure a lot of things that medicine can't."

"Things like?" There was his hyper-keen interest again.

"Cancer, infections. The downside is then my body has to eliminate the disease before I get sick, so I menstruate. The bigger the disease, the bigger the mess."

That got me the disgusted look I'd expected. "What about you?"

"Me?" Ragna asked. "I'm air. Need some wind? I'm your guy. Good for knocking people around, pushing weapons out of alignment, that kind of thing. I also helped design those shields you saw in action."

"Those were nifty," I said. "Looked like some variation on wards?"

He grinned and nodded. "Nice eye. Instead of creating eight points around a specific piece of land, they create a field between eight points within the metal frame, with the stone, albeit much smaller ones than normal, embedded directly into the frame. Then it just takes one of us to bring as many as fifteen online."

"Kelsha got twenty up but can't maintain them. Which means we can't deploy them on a large scale, because we don't have that many magic workers," Róisín added. "At least not ones that can work wards."

By the time we'd been on the road for an hour or so, my butt was numb and I shifted my weight, trying to get feeling back. I was startled when I felt Daria take my hand.

"These are looking better," she said, her voice low as her fingers glazed over my broken fingers.

"Yeah, they're okay," I responded.

"When we get to the base, we should have a proper doctor have a look at them. And," she looked up at me, then glanced at Xen and back. She reached across me to Xen, bringing their hand to mine. Xen's skin was warm, nearly hot to the touch. Daria glanced at Róisín who appeared to be asleep and back again. "Xen is your partner."

There was something in her tone, a warning of some kind. The way she said the word partner… I wasn't entirely sure what she was implying, but I nodded. Daria wanted Xen to protect me, that much was obvious, she'd already said as much, but when she put Xen's hand into mine, I also got the sense that I needed to protect Xen just as much.

The skies got hazier and colder as we progressed toward the base and I was shivering as the hauler came to a stop. I followed the others out, emerging into a late afternoon where the damage to the environment kept the light in a strange orange state that darkened into red on the horizon.

Xen stepped close to me, their hand slipping into mine. I didn't mind, I just wasn't sure what was going on. Xen had become a comfortable companion, someone I trusted implicitly, which was rare. I looked at them in a vaguely amused way. "Not that I'm complaining," I said so only Xen could hear me, "but why are we holding hands?"

"I will explain when we are alone," Xen said softly.

"Folks, the Minister is waiting for you." Colonel Devets gestured toward a dark green tent, then led the way. Two Vaneeshi in green uniforms held aside the tent flaps and we were ushered inside.

A woman turned, her face familiar. "Daria, it is good to see you again."

Daria nodded and extended her hand. The minister met it with hers, but rather than shaking, they merely hovered without touching and both pulled back. "My sister."

I followed her lead, though the gesture was odd to me. "Thána, I am very happy to make your acquaintance."

"And I thank you for the ride. All that walking was exhausting," I said.

She smiled and gestured us over to a table with a bunch of chairs. "I tried to recruit your sister directly out of school, but she wanted to be a wife and mother. Please sit. I have food on the way."

"Well, I'm here now," Daria said, her tone a bit dark. "So, how can we help?"

"We've taken back the northern half of Meerat, but holding it is a problem. We need to reinforce our warding before Kabeshi forces regroup and get their big guns up and running again. We managed to hit them during our last raid, but they already have replacements coming. You saw what they did the first time."

Daria nodded. "I can probably help there. Knowing how they shredded the first time, I can shore up against those specific weapons."

"That's only good if they haven't come up with new tech," Xen offered from behind me.

"Ah, Minister, this is Xen. They and my sister are partners."

"Not often a Pixin bonds with anyone other than another Pixin," the minister said with a touch of surprise.

Xen's hand touched my shoulder a bit possessively. "Our bond is not breakable." Again, I got the impression that this meant more than I was understanding. There was some cultural weight attached to the interaction. I lifted a hand to caress over theirs where it rested on my shoulder.

The minister held up both hands. "I'm not one to argue. If your skills are anything like my other Pixin, you are a welcome member of the team."

I let the conversation flow around me, focused more on figuring out what it was Daria was up to than on what was being said. I looked up when Xen squeezed my shoulder. There was a plate of food in front of me. It didn't look particularly appetizing, but I figured that at that point any food was worth eating since I had no idea when I'd get to eat again.

"If you'll excuse me, I have some plans I need to review. When you are done eating, my aide can show you to your quarters."

The minister left the table and Xen took the chair next to mine. The three of us ate in relative silence and when we were done, Daria gestured to the man in military garb that was standing nearby. He snapped his heels together and approached. "If you will follow me."

Neither Daria nor Xen said a word as we were led through a confusing array of tents and buildings before the aide stopped beside a tent that looked pretty much like all the rest. He saluted us, his hand snapping to his shoulder and then down. Xen ducked inside first, scanning the interior before calling us inside.

It looked like any military quarters I'd ever seen on TV or in movies. There were three cots, a small table, and a metal wardrobe. Daria closed the flap of the tent while Xen explored the four walls. "Ward stones." Daria held out her hand and I passed them over.

In moments she had secured the inside of the tent with a set of pretty impenetrable wards, the kind designed to muffle sound as well as protect. "What the hell, Daria?" I asked when they both relaxed. "I thought these were your people?"

Daria sat on one of the cots, dragging her hands through her hair. "I'm probably being paranoid, but Róisín has scars on her hand." Xen lifted my left hand, petting over the scars and the last of the bruising on the knuckles. "You may have noticed that Katyk has them too?"

I hadn't actually. Daria lifted her left hand. "It's one of Artoz's favorite games, especially when he thinks you have something of worth to offer."

I had never noticed the tiny scars between her knuckles. I swallowed down the rising bile. "Do you think she's been turned?" I asked.

"I don't want to take any risks, but I also don't want to say anything to Minister Brek without knowing for certain."

"What about Ragna?"

Daria sighed. "I didn't see any signs, but I think at this point, after Katyk, we operate on the assumption that any magic-user may have been compromised."

CHAPTER 23
BONDING

I did not like how that sounded. "So now we need to protect ourselves from our allies too. Great." Xen's hand was still holding mine and it was warm, comforting. Until I realized that it was warmer than it had been before. "Are you okay?" I asked, lifting my free hand to touch their face.

"I am close to the time of joining," Xen replied. "In normal times, I would journey to the birthplace east of here now. It progressed faster than I anticipated."

I saw concern on Daria's face, but also that she had known this, and it was a part of the reason she wanted Xen and I together. "What happens if you don't go to the joining?" I asked softly.

"Xen's body temperature will continue to rise, and eventually they will lose their ability for rational thought," Daria said.

"What does this have to do with Xen pretending that we're partnered?" I asked.

"We're past pretending," Daria said. She rubbed her hands over her face. "When Artoz used your blood to heal Xen, it started a process called bonding."

"Pixin who do not go to the joining have two choices. They burn out or they choose to bond. Any Pixin will be able to tell that I have not completed the process."

"How?" I asked. "How would they know?"

"Pixin are telepathic," Daria answered.

I turned to look at Xen, surprised. "They are?"

Xen inclined their head. "Yes, it is how we learn languages so easily. Do not worry, your thoughts are safe. We have a strict code. However, when a

Pixin takes a bond, it changes the fundamental vibration of our being. Another Pixin will know in only seconds if we are not bonded."

"Why do I feel like I just got invited to a shotgun wedding?" I asked.

"It's not like that. Well, not exactly." Daria said. She stopped her pacing in front of Xen. "You don't have to."

"If we are not bonded, others will know and that will give them reason to doubt us," Xen said. "Doubt can only cause us harm." Xen met my eyes briefly, then looked away. "There is not much time before I start to feel the effects, perhaps a week."

"Wait," I said. "Stop and explain to me what you are talking about."

"I explained about the Pixin joining," Xen said. I nodded. "When the time comes, we must join, or risk our sanity. It is rare, but on occasion, two Pixin form an emotional bond that transcends the joining. Even more rarely, we can make a bond with a being of another race."

"Okay, but what exactly does it mean?"

"During the joining, our genetic material is combined and from this, the next generation is born. When we bond, our blood is brought together. This was already begun when I was cut and your blood was used to heal me. Since that day I have felt you inside of me, but because the bonding was not completed, you cannot yet feel me."

"So, you need to bleed into me?" I asked, not sure I was liking the sound of that.

"It is not that simple." Xen moved to sit on a cot. "And it is at the same time. We both cut our arms and our wounds are bound together. As the blood moves between us, we become one. I will take on traits of yours. You will take on traits of mine." Xen's eyes locked into mine. "We will become one, and no other will have access to what is ours."

"I… what?" I shook my head. "I don't even know what that means."

"The magic corps works with partners, based on their skill sets," Daria said. "One offensive and one defensive. You don't get a choice who you're partnered with and you have to let them into your head. If you are bonded to Xen, only Xen has access to that head. They can't force you to work with someone we can't trust."

I narrowed my eyes at Daria. "What about you?"

She paced away. "I have a partner. Sort of. We were paired when I took basic training that last year of school, before Habros proposed. I happen to know that he's never been compromised, and he lost his partner recently. I trust him."

"Okay, this doesn't seem like something we need to rush into," I said. "I mean, is this something we can undo later?"

Xen shook their head. "A bonding is for life. Once we are bonded, we are one."

"Doesn't this seem a bit... I don't know, extreme?"

Xen took my hand and drew me away from my sister. "Is there someone else you are bonded to?"

I shook my head. "No. I've never considered myself the marriage kind of person."

Their hand cupped my face and they smiled. "I always assumed I would go to join with my birthmates. I have never considered bonding before, however, I have grown quite fond of you and would give my life to keep you safe."

I opened my mouth but didn't really have words, so I closed it again. "What about the joining? I thought you wanted that."

Xen looked down where they still held one of my hands. "The closer I have come to time for the joining, since I have been with you and Daria, I find myself reluctant if I am honest with myself. A bonding will negate the physical need to join. Our bond will afford me protection from the Sickness, and you protection from Katyk, or any others who may wish to get inside you."

"Partnerships are bonds of a sort too. You have to be able to link up telepathically. You don't have the skills you need to keep someone from taking whatever they want once they have access to you. That's how Katyk was able to manipulate you," Daria said.

"You can also use my strength and stamina to aid you, as you have been with your sister."

I was starting to get a headache. "Do we have to decide right now?"

"The process will take most of the night." Xen let go of my hand. "But I will not force this on you, Thána. It must be a choice you make freely. And you must understand what this will mean for you."

"I'm still not sure I understand," I said, sitting on the nearest cot.

"Pixin are not... sexual beings, Thána," Xen said. "I will never give you children, or physical satisfaction."

I shook my head. "I'm thirty-two, if I had wanted kids, I would have had them already. And sex is... not a big part of my life as it is." I rubbed my hands down my thighs, trying to ground myself. "What about you? Is this something you want?"

Xen smiled and shook their head. "I would be most happy to bond with you."

"Forever?" I asked, the pitch of my voice climbing.

"If you will have me as your bondmate, yes."

I still wasn't sure. I mean, I liked Xen. Considered them a friend. Maybe more than a friend. And I certainly didn't want them to go mad. I'd be willing to fight for them, and this seemed easier than fighting.

I had always been a solitary person, but Xen fit beside me in ways I had never felt before. I had no idea what the actual parameters of this bonding would be, or how it would work, but I slowly nodded. "What do we need to do?"

Xen took my hand and guided me to the middle of the space and had me kneel, taking their knees across from me. "When we mix our genetic material, it will bond our minds. We will be one. It will take nine hours for our joining, time in which our physical bodies will be looked after by our guardian and our minds will merge so that we will know each other more intimately than is otherwise possible. I will hold nothing back. Likewise, you must hold nothing back or the bonding will not be secure. You will have my confidence and I will have yours. Nothing will come between us."

That was a lot of commitment. I swallowed or tried to, but my mouth was suddenly very dry. "Breathe, Thána. The pain is brief, the joy is forever."

Xen held out their hand and Daria placed a rather large knife in it. She laid out the strips of cloth that had once kept sand out of our boots, one on each side of where we knelt. Xen kissed the blade, then held it to my lips. I followed suit, feeling a little bit goofy.

That feeling fled as Xen brought the blade down, lifting my right arm to meet it. They drew the blade across the outside of my arm, from elbow to wrist. I hissed as the blood welled up in its wake. They followed the same motion on my other arm. Neither cut was super deep, but they weren't completely superficial either. Xen handed me the knife and nodded for me to do the same to them, offering me the insides of their arms.

I exhaled and made the cuts, wincing a little. Daria took the knife from me and set it aside, then took my right arm and pressed the bleeding wound to Xen's matching wound. She lifted the cloth and wound it around us, holding our wounds together. Daria then took my left arm, to do the same.

I was feeling woozy, but at the same time on fire. Almost like the brush of fingers on my forehead, I could hear Xen's thoughts, then they rushed into me and mine into them. The dizzy dance had me breathless. I could see their life in a tapestry of moments, of people and places, feelings and desires. At the same time, I was aware of Xen inside me, of my own life spread out for them to understand and partake of. We were drawn together, then washed apart over and over again, like we were riding the waves of two separate oceans that could not resist one another.

Xen had never felt to me like a person ruled by emotion, but I had never been so wrong. There was an exuberance within I had never noticed, joy and pain. The loss of Habros and the presumed loss of Dyn cut deep rivers of grief inside them. The anxiety that had been building over the joining was palpable, underscoring what I now recognized as their affection for me.

Every conversation between us changed in meaning now, seen through Xen's eyes instead of my own. Every touch, from the moment they helped me out of that cage, was filled with affection that I'd been too blind to see.

Slowly, I became aware of the world outside of the bonding. My body ached from a night spent kneeling on the floor, my shoulders unhappy about the position my arms had been held in for hours on end. Daria had removed the bindings and Xen was stirring. I opened my eyes and blinked.

Xen's eyes met mine and I could see the question in their black depths. I smiled to let them know I was fine, then groaned as I moved. The cuts Xen had made to my arm were all but healed, leaving a fine red line on both arms. Xen's arms bore matching scars.

"Well, that was intense," I muttered as I let Daria help me up off the floor.

"Yes, it was," Xen agreed.

"You should both get some sleep," Daria said as she dismantled the wards. "I can buy you a few hours at least. I need to find Amblin and get a better understanding of the tactical situation."

I yawned as if I needed to be told I was tired. Xen tugged me closer, arms around my waist, and led me to one of the cots. I went down easily, sleep claiming me quickly.

I woke later, startled out of my sleep, but uncertain what had startled me. I sat up, spotting Xen on another cot. Otherwise, the tent was empty. Either Daria or Xen had removed my boots after I fell asleep, and I found them at the foot of the cot. By the time I had them on, Xen was also awake and sitting up. They blushed when my eyes caught on theirs.

It was kind of adorable.

I rubbed my face and tried to clear my head, which was suddenly all Xen, all the time. "That will pass," Xen said, coming to sit beside me. "The first few days can be a bit overwhelming."

"I'm not usually so sappy," I said as Xen rubbed a hand warmly over my back. "Sorry."

"Do not apologize." Xen stroked my hair, tucking a stray curl behind my ear. "If you are ready, we should find Daria."

"I need to pee first."

We exited the tent, made a pit stop at the latrine, then made our way back to the command tent. It felt natural to hold hands, even though touch seemed to intensify the connection between us. I was aware of Xen in a way I'd never imagined. I couldn't read their thoughts exactly, but I could sense their general path and the emotions attached to them.

Daria stood with a group of people in the black uniforms of the magic corps and we crossed to join them.

"Amblin Jeflow, this is Thána Alizon and her partner Xen. Thána, Xen, this is Amblin, my new partner."

"There have been rumors all over camp this morning about you, Thána," Amblin said, his voice a rich baritone with a lilting, almost Irish brogue. He was not a tall man but looked to be solidly built, all muscle. His hair and beard were the color of flames, his eyes a deep blue. His smile was infectious.

"Is that so?" I asked, looking to Daria.

"Apparently, our friend Róisín has been telling the entire corps about your magic," Daria explained. "Everyone is eager for a demonstration."

"I see. Well, I'm happy to oblige once I've had something to eat."

"We were just talking about heading to the mess tent for food ourselves," Amblin said amiably. "Please join us."

Xen's hand snaked into mine again as we headed back out of the tent, following Daria and Amblin. The mess tent was situated near the middle of the base, and it looked like we had missed the lunch rush. Only a few soldiers were still sitting at the scattered tables as we passed along the buffet set up with an odd variety of foods. I took a sandwich with some kind of meat and a fat sort of banana and followed Daria to a table. The others all took seats at nearby tables, leaving just me, Daria, Xen, and Amblin at ours.

"Did you sleep well?" Daria asked as we tucked in.

"Like a baby," I responded.

"Those cots are not very comfortable," Amblin observed.

"When you've been sleeping on cold rocks, it feels like heaven," I countered.

He chuckled warmly. "That is a fair point."

I watched him for a moment. Something in his mannerisms made me think he wasn't native and he wasn't from Spítia. "May I ask where you're from?"

"Me? No place you would likely know," he said. "My mother and father were raised in a city called Gavlescore but were run out because they were believed to be witches."

"Which they were," Daria said.

"Oh, aye, they were." Amblin chuckled. "The good townsfolk didn't take kindly to witches. Eventually, we came here. It was a big culture shock, let me tell you. In Gavlescore they barely have indoor toilets, and here this place is with all this tech?"

We ate in silence for a few minutes before Xen left the table and returned with glasses of water for the two of us. "So, what about you two?" Amblin asked.

"Us?" I glanced at Xen and back. "What about us?"

"How long have you two been, you know, you two?"

"Not long," Xen answered, "though it feels like a lifetime." They smiled, slipping a hand into mine.

I found myself returning the smile and leaning into their warmth. All too soon the food was gone, and I was starting to feel eyes on me. "I guess we should do this thing."

Outside the mess tent, we found an open space that would work for demonstration purposes, and the magic corps team created a circle around the space, gently urging others out so that there was enough room. I felt very self-conscious with all eyes on me. I looked to Daria and squeezed Xen's hand before letting go. I knew I'd need to work with Xen again eventually, but for the first go in front of strangers, I wanted to have the variables under control.

I picked a spot about fifteen feet away, still within the circle, and got the kelcimite out of my vest pocket. "Okay," I said to no one in particular as I lifted my hands.

Daria's hands landed on my hips and our energy connected instantly. I cast, watching the hole form. Without a word, Xen stepped through, emerging on the other side of the circle. A ripple of murmuring voices came at me like a wave, even as Daria stepped back.

"Now that is impressive," Amblin said. "May I?"

He gestured at the hole that I had been about to close, and I nodded. He ducked his head and stepped through, laughing raucously from across the circle as he emerged. I dropped my arms and closed the portal. Amblin came bounding back to us, a grin on his face. "You must show me how it works."

I looked at Daria who nodded, guiding Amblin to stand beside me. "She needs to draw on your energy to create it, so open up." She put Amblin's hands on my hips, and I paused to center before I tried to find his energy behind me. He was like a solid column of flame, hot energy contained in his body yet easily tapped into. I lifted my hands again and cast.

Once again, the hole opened and this time several of the magic users rushed through to the other side. Amblin stepped back when I closed it, scratching his head. "I told you," Daria said.

"I know you told me but seeing it for myself..." Amblin turned me with a hand on one shoulder. "How exactly did you do that?"

I shrugged. "I don't know exactly. I just do."

"Remarkable."

The rest of the corps was coming at me with questions and requests until Xen stepped in beside me and I felt their calm slide between me and the collective energy of the group. "Everyone, please. If you overwhelm her, she will not be able to answer your questions."

"I don't know that I can answer them anyway," I said. "The first time I made it work at any distance, I was drugged and desperate and I just wanted an escape."

"And the distance nearly killed her," Daria added. "Short distances like this aren't useful practically, but longer distances are dangerous, and not just because of the energy drain."

"Right, if I am not familiar with the landing zone, and I can't see it clearly, I could end up sending us off a cliff or into a rock, that kind of thing," I added.

"What about size? How big a hole can you make?" The speaker was a short woman with dark skin and a hooked nose.

"I've only ever tried about this size. Enough for the three of us."

"Except in Theravee," Róisín said as she joined us. "Ten of us went through then."

I nodded. "True, I had forgotten that. We went in five across then. But it was also a pretty short distance, maybe fifty yards?"

"Around twenty locks," Daria said to nods all around us.

"Locks?" I asked.

"Unit of measure. About a yard and two-thirds."

I tucked that knowledge away, hoping for the ability to recall it if the need should arise. "I wish I could explain it to you folks."

"Perhaps if you were to allow us all to try it with you, as you just did with Amblin, one of us would be able to figure it out," Róisín said, a half-smile on her face.

Xen took my hand, something I was starting to understand to be a protective gesture. "Thána has not yet fully recovered from her ordeal. It would be best not to tax her."

"How taxing can it be?" one of the others asked.

"She's punching a hole in time and space, so pretty damn taxing," Amblin answered before I could. "Give her some space."

"Can you show us a longer distance?" someone asked.

"Where do you suggest?" I asked.

Xen slipped their arm around me. "How about the command tent. You know where that is and how it is laid out," Xen said.

"Yeah, I can do that." I turned toward where the command tent was. It wasn't the longest jump I'd tried, but there were people on the other side, and I didn't know what would happen to them if my portal opened exactly where they were standing. I decided to focus on the sidewall of the tent, essentially opening a new door, just one that came from across the base.

Xen moved so they were behind me, wrapping their arms around my waist and putting their body flush against my back. Warmth flowed between us and in that heat, I felt a strong source of energy I could use. I lifted the stone and closed my eyes, picturing the tent. I cast a hole wide enough for at least three across. It wavered slightly but stabilized quickly. "Can't hold it forever, people. If you're going, do it."

Xen held me as they trickled through the open portal, then we followed. I dropped the portal and sagged a bit against Xen. The magic corps folks were all talking amongst themselves, and several of the people in the green uniforms of the non-magic soldiers were joining in.

CHAPTER 24
IMPOSSIBLE

"That was an impressive display."

I turned to the speaker, finding the minister and her aide. "Thank you." I didn't know what else to say. My knees were a little rubbery and I gestured toward a chair near the big table. Xen came with me and I sat to rest. It wasn't as bad as some of our jumps, but it was draining.

"We should talk," the minister said. Amblin and Daria joined us at the table. The others all wandered back to the corner of the tent where I had found them earlier.

Minister Brek took the head of the table, holding out her hand for something. Her aide set a tablet in her hand. "It is fortunate that you have arrived now. We are preparing our next assault on Meerat. The Kabeshi army has taken back the downtown district and the city south. We want to push the Kabeshi army out once more."

"Amblin and I can provide support—" Daria said, stopping when the minister held up her hand.

"Of course, you can, but it's Thána's ability to create portals that I want to utilize."

"I'm not sure that I can really be that much help, ma'am," I said. "I need to be able to see the target or know it well enough that I'm not opening a portal someplace deadly."

She smiled, making her face seem even more hawk-like. "Amblin is a far-seer. I'm sure the two of you can work something out."

I frowned at Daria who returned the look. "I'm not sure it works like that, Minister. Thána is not a fully trained witch. She's never worked with anyone other than myself and Xen."

"Didn't she let Amblin help her cast just now?"

"That is a bit different, Minister," I said. "I only needed his energy to open the portal. I can't see what he sees in his mind."

Xen cleared their throat. "I remind you, Minister, we are bonded. No one can enter Thána's mind but me."

Minister Brek tapped her fingers on the tablet and the sidewall of the tent became a screen with a map of Meerat. "The enemy holds this section of downtown." She stood so she could point. "Which means they hold the portal park, the financial district, and all of the south end. We want to insert a strike force here." She pointed to the portal park. "This will be a team of shock troops mixed with magic corps bombers. Their job will be to use our targeted bombs to take out the troops along this area." Her finger moved to the west and north of the park. "That will open up this main route for the bulk of our troops. At the same time, we want to have our troops ready with magic shields to push southward along these streets." She pointed to the part of the city that had been our escape.

"And you want me to open portals for these troops?" I asked.

"The element of surprise. They won't be expecting it."

I shook my head. "I can't do two at once. And at that distance, I'm not even sure I can do one without it knocking me out."

"I want my city back," the minister said, sitting back down.

"With all due respect, Minister," Daria said, "What you're asking is not possible."

"We need for it to be possible. You have three days to figure it out." She stood and stalked off with her aide trailing behind.

"I don't have that kind of power, Daria," I said.

"I know." She got up and went to the map. "The park should be easier. You've been there, you know the layout."

"That's at least fifty catres," Xen said. "The most we've done so far is maybe ten."

I could see Daria's mind racing ahead of the problem and starting to work backward. "The problem is the amount of energy required." She turned to Amblin. "Did you ever get that energy bridge working?"

"Energy bridge?" I asked.

Amblin nodded. "Yes, it is meant to allow several magic users to combine their energy. We have used it to create wards strong enough to repel the Kabeshi *megischor* bombs. There are two problems with that idea though." He stroked his beard, his eyes crinkling as he thought about the problem. "The first is that it renders the bridge team unable to defend themselves as long as the spell is active. The second is that it renders everyone locked into the bridge useless, which decimates the magic corp."

I stood, shaking my head. "You're ignoring the fact that I can't do what she wants."

Daria turned to me. "We won't know that until we try."

"I'm pretty sure I know that right now." I stalked away, out of the command tent.

"Thána! Stop, let's work the problem."

I stopped and turned to face my sister. "Daria, she wants something I can't give her."

"I think you can, at least the first part. Come back inside, let's get our heads together." What she didn't say was that I owed her this much, after everything I had taken from her. I still heard it though, deep in my gut.

I sighed, suddenly very tired. "I need a nap or some xýpna. I'm exhausted."

"How long since your last dose?" Daria asked.

"Honestly, I have no idea. It's been at least a day."

"How's your head? Your stomach?"

I closed my eyes and breathed in, letting it out slowly. "Vague headache, but it isn't bad. Why?"

"If you're showing signs of withdrawal you shouldn't have more but if you're okay, I can give you some."

"Daria, I'm a grown woman. I think I'm capable of deciding that for myself. Besides, I'm the older sister, remember?"

"Well, I am a licensed practitioner of the medical arts. I have an oath to uphold. It would be irresponsible of me to let you become reliant on a stimulant."

I made a gimme motion with my hand and she pulled the pouch out of a pocket, tossing it to me. I took a pinch of the powder and dropped it on my tongue. Rather than give her back the pouch, I tucked it into one of my own pockets. I had the feeling I was going to need it.

Back in the command tent, Amblin had traded the projected map for a paper one that covered most of the conference table. He was bent over it, his fingers tracing along a street that ran parallel to the park a few blocks over. His finger stopped on a blue circle. "Here."

A man I didn't know, wearing a uniform with a lot of silver pins that showed rank squinted and traced the street back to the outskirts of the city where there was another blue dot. "That's a lot of underground to cover without letting them know we're coming."

"Indir and Chal can take care of that," Amblin said, checking in with Daria as we rejoined the table. "They can muffle the sound." He pointed to three more blue dots on the map. "If we can get them into the underground, they can split up and come out at these three stations when they get the signal."

"That's a big if." The man straightened up, his eyes falling on me. "Can you do this?"

I shook my head. "I don't even know what *this* you're talking about."

"Amblin here says you can get a strike team into Portal Park."

"Maybe," I responded. "But I can't help with the rest of these troops."

"You let us worry about them." He snapped his fingers and started hurling out orders to the men and women in uniform who appeared in response. "The Minister says we do it— we do it."

"I'm beginning to see why they lost the city," I muttered to Xen.

"They did not react quickly enough, that is how they lost Meerat," Xen said. "Now they are trying to compensate for that error."

"Yeah, by jumping the gun. I don't think I can do this."

"You can," Xen said. "I have faith."

"That makes one of us." I shook my head and moved to where I could see the map. "I'll never reach it from here. You're going to need to get me closer." I pointed to a spot north and west of the city. "At least here. Closer is better."

The military man nodded his agreement. "We can arrange that. Lieutenant, I leave you to the magic details." He turned on his heel and headed off, barking orders as he went.

"He means well," Amblin said in the silence he left behind. He turned to a woman beside him that I hadn't even noticed. "Get the corps together. I need a complete skills inventory of our available people. Send Indir and Chal to my quarters in a half hour. Oh, and round up any low-level magic folks and match them up to any of our people who can siphon energy from them. We're going to need a lot of power."

She saluted him and left. Amblin turned his attention to me. He pointed to a spot on the map marked by black boxes, then to a spot north and east of us. "This is our practice area. I'll have markers put out at increasing intervals and build you up to this big jump."

"This is going to take a lot more than xýpna powder," I said aside to Xen. A lot more.

"Give me an hour to get everything set up," Amblin said.

I let Xen take my hand as we left the tent, aiming for our assigned quarters. "This is a mistake," I said once we were inside the relative safety of the tent. "I can't do this."

"You can," Xen raised my hand and pressed their lips to the dusty bruises still hanging on my knuckles. "I will be right beside you."

"I know. I've never been good at this kind of thing." I hated being the center of attention unless I was good and angry. "Do you remember where the showers were? I could use some hot soapy water about now."

"Yeah, come on." Xen led me back toward the latrines, then took a left and stopped in front of a small wooden structure. "Showers."

I opened the door, then looked at Xen. "Are you coming?"

"I did not wish to presume."

I rolled my eyes and gestured for them to join me. Xen had seen everything I had to display both physically and mentally. I realized as I stepped into a basic shower set up with several wooden stalls and hooks for clothes along one wall that the reverse wasn't true. I had never seen Xen unclothed. There were cubicles full of towels and I crossed to grab two as Xen began removing their clothing. By the time I had returned, Xen was naked from the waist up.

Their arms were strong, well defined, as was the rest of what I could see. Xen blushed a little. I stopped looking to afford them some modesty, turning my attention to getting naked myself. Behind me, the water turned on in one of the cubicles. I hung my vest, shirt, and pants and put my boots under the bench before turning to find Xen tipping back their head under the water stream.

My curiosity was strong, but I also didn't want to make Xen uncomfortable. "It is okay," Xen said, holding out a hand. I took it and joined them in the cubicle. "We are one."

They drew my hand to their chest, which was flat, with no nipples, just muscle. I slid my hand down, rounding their hip and over the hard round of their ass. "Is all of you this hard?" I murmured.

"No, not all," Xen replied, guiding my other hand down between their legs.

I'm not sure what I was expecting, but where I had the opening to my sex organ, Xen had only a soft mound of flesh with a small opening for waste. Xen's hand echoed mine, gentle and exploring. We turned so that I was under the water. Memories from the bonding flooded between us such as the various times either of us had showered in the presence of others, not like what had happened to me after Merry's spell, but more controlled, more emotion-driven.

Xen chuckled as I tossed my wet hair, which was long enough now that when wet it covered my face. "Turn around, let me help." I wasn't sure what help they were offering, but then their hands were scrubbing through my hair and the smell of soap filled the air. It was unbelievable how good it felt to get clean. I couldn't remember the last time I had managed to shower. Xen scrubbed down my back, gentle over still healing spots, then we turned again so I could return the favor.

"I promised Daria I'd get you to the infirmary so the doctor can examine your remaining wounds," Xen said as we rinsed off and reached for our towels.

"I'm fine," I insisted. Everything was healing nicely, even the broken fingers were starting to look better.

"At least let us go get your fingertips rebandaged?" Xen cajoled.

I had to agree the bandages protecting my ruined nail beds had gotten dirty and the wounds themselves were still tender. "Yeah, okay. By then, Amblin should be ready." We dressed quickly and I finger-combed my curls into something that wouldn't dry into a hideous mass.

It was comfortable walking together, even holding hands. That was not a thing I had ever done, yet there I was. The infirmary tent was quiet. There was one soldier asleep on a bed, and two people in scrubs. One of them was clearly a Pixin, and the other Vaneeshi.

The Pixin spoke in the guttural language that Xen and Dyn had used between them and Xen responded. The Vaneeshi came toward me, his eyes on my hands. He said something and I shook my head. "Sorry, I don't speak Vaneeshi."

"I said, those Kabeshi are cruel."

"It's mostly healed." I let him lift my right hand to examine. "I just need new bandages for my nail beds."

He raised an eyebrow. "Are you a doctor?"

I blushed and shook my head. "No, sorry."

"Come, let's have a look."

I was led to the back of the tent where there was an array of equipment, and up to what looked like a copier. The doctor raised the top and put my right hand down on a metal plate, moving my fingers so that they were spread before he lowered the top. I was surprised when it conformed around my hand, all soft and squishy. A few seconds later, he did the same with my left, nodding to himself as he looked at a screen.

"Soft tissue damage is healing nicely, though there is some scarring that could cause you trouble in the future. Those fingers though, I'm going to need to set them properly if you ever want to be able to use them again. Jya, can you warm up the *scholacht*?"

The Pixin doctor nodded and moved to one of the other machines. "We're going to improve the circulation to take care of the last of the swelling and bruising and see if we can encourage those nails to grow. But first, let's deal with your fingers."

He gently removed the tape that was holding the two fingers together, right up until he pulled on the first finger. I bit my tongue to prevent the scream from coming out as he pulled and the bones shifted. Instantly I could feel the difference where the broken bones had been misaligned. Jya beckoned me over to sit on the nearest cot, bringing a set of sleeves that were connected to the machine by thick cables. Jya helped me guide my hands and lower arms into the machine, then flipped a switch.

Instantly, my hands felt as though they were suspended in water, warm water that was getting warmer. The sensation of waves rippling over my skin was massage-like, bringing a tingling feeling as the blood rose to the surface. Xen sat beside me while the machine did its job.

Jya came back about five minutes later to unhook me. I was amazed at how much better everything looked and felt. The last of the swelling was gone and the movement much improved. The Vaneeshi doctor nodded as he examined my hands. "Better. Let's get you bandaged up."

In just a few minutes I had a splint for the two broken fingers with artificial skin coating the nail beds that still needed protection. Xen and I left the infirmary and headed for the command center. I flexed my wrists, made fists, and nodded to myself. "We really need this kind of medicine back home."

Daria was standing outside the command tent as we approached. "Amblin's ready."

"Okay. I'm as ready as I'm going to get."

Daria led us out to an open range where target practice had taken place at some point. There were distance markers I could see leading off into the horizon. The weird lighting didn't help visibility at all.

A thought occurred to me as we walked toward where Amblin was waiting. "This air, from the bombs and stuff... is it safe to breathe?"

Daria shrugged a little. "It's not great, but there's enough oxygen in the air and the pollutants are being dispersed by the winds, so it should be fine."

Should be. I sighed and tucked the knowledge into the "other things to worry about" compartment of my brain so I could focus on the task at hand.

CHAPTER 25
PRACTICE MAKES PERFECT

AT FIRST, IT WAS JUST THE FOUR OF US: ME AND XEN, AMBLIN, AND DARIA. The warm-up distance was little more than what I had done with everyone watching earlier in the day. Xen and I worked well together, despite the fact that they were not magically inclined, their energy was solid and strong.

As expected, as the distance grew so did the work required to reach it. By the third marker, I was sweating, my head hurt, and I was tiring out. Daria stepped in to add her energy to mine and Xen's. That got us to the fourth marker, which was just on the edge of visible from where I stood.

I held up my hands. "I need a break." I slid to the ground with a groan, my hands trembling as I put the kelcimite in my pocket. Daria handed me a canteen which I accepted gratefully, swallowing down large gulps of water before fishing the xýpna from a pocket. I took a generous pinch and washed it down with even more water.

We had been joined by five people in black uniforms and a few more in the green uniforms of the army. "Thána, this is the start of our bridge," Amblin said, drawing my attention. "This is R'essa, she's going to be our point person."

"And that means what?" I asked, greeting the Vaneeshi woman with a nod.

"I will be the one who gathers the energy and forms the bridge so that I can pass it to you," R'essa said. "And these are our volunteers. For the actual event, we'll have more people, but this should be sufficient for us to teach you how it works."

I held my hand up to Xen who leveraged me to my feet. "Okay, show me."

R'essa communicated to the volunteers in Vaneeshi and I watched them lay on the ground, side by side, hands joined. After a few moments of R'essa speaking some spell, I could feel the build-up of energy.

"We're ready," R'essa said, turning back to me. She was vaguely glowing, her eyes unfocused.

"Xen, I need you here," Amblin said, directing Xen to stand in front of R'essa and lifting R'essa's hands to Xen's shoulders. Xen shivered but nodded when I met their eyes to make sure they were okay. "And Thána, right here please."

Amblin guided me into position, Xen's arms around my hips, my body pulled tight against theirs. "Good. Now Thána, you should already be feeling the energy building up."

I nodded, eyes closed as I let the energy move into me. "Okay, nice and easy, do you know where the fifth marker is?"

"Only vaguely," I replied, scanning the horizon. I tried to envision the marker, setting my intention to open the portal right beside that marker. It wasn't as precise as being able to see the destination, but intent had been enough for the first jump, and even the second.

I lifted the stone and drew on the combined energy behind me and cast. I knew instantly I had overshot the goal by a fair amount, but the portal was stable, and Amblin sent one of the soldiers through and back. The pounding in my head was getting louder and I cracked my neck to try to find some relief, but that only made it worse. I touched Xen's hand that lay against my stomach and stepped away, wiping at a suddenly bloody nose.

"I think maybe that is enough for now," Amblin said. "Let's take a break until after the evening meal."

Daria handed me something to wipe my nose. "That was good."

I shook my head. "I overshot. If I do that when we're aiming for the park, I could put us right through one of those portals. That wouldn't do any of us any good."

"You just need practice," Amblin countered. "Take a break."

"I don't think I have it in me to walk back to the mess tent," I said. "I'm just going to rest here."

"It is getting cold," Xen said. "And you need food."

"I'll see about getting some jackets." Daria slung an arm around me and got me turned toward the tents. "We're expecting snow tonight."

"Great, just when I thought I'd escaped the cold wet stuff." My childhood had been filled with snowy winters, blizzards and ice storms had been normal from mid-October through to March.

Daria wasn't wrong about the snow, it was falling steadily by the time we'd finished eating and moved back to the range. The coat she'd brought helped cut some of the cold, but after just a few attempts I was shivering and my hands cramping around the kelcimite. I had also burned through the xýpna at a faster rate. I couldn't tell if it was due to the cold, my fatigue, or if my body was building up an immunity.

I let Xen help me back to our tent as I was physically wiped out, even if my mind was racing around the situation I had gotten myself into. Not even a full year ago, I had been mostly happy, living in a warm desert city with a solid idea of what my future would bring.

I sat on the cot I had claimed and pulled off my boots, a chore made all the harder by arms that weighed a ton. A few minutes later, Daria slipped into the tent, holding up a bottle and three cups. "I don't know about you, but I could use a drink," she said, handing a glass to Xen and pouring in a smokey, dark liquid. She handed me a glass and poured some into it before pouring her own.

Sniffing the glass told me it was some kind of whiskey. I sipped at it and nodded appreciatively. "I stole it from Amblin. He always has the good stuff," Daria said.

"Are we celebrating something?" I asked.

Daria shook her head. "I need something to shut my head off. Figured you might too."

I downed a good swallow of the whiskey, letting its smokey flavor wash over my tongue and burn its way down my throat. It was like a smooth Canadian whiskey had been stuck into a smokehouse for a week.

"Mmm, this is good." I finished it off and set the cup on the floor by the head of my bed. Taking my vest off and hanging it at the end of the cot, I slipped under the blankets while Daria set up the wards to keep us warm. "What's going on in your head that you need booze?" I asked sleepily as she and Xen prepared for bed.

"This…" She gestured around her. She sighed and sat to pull off her boots. "Minister Brek wants me to go with the main army, to help man the shield line."

"Is that an issue?" I asked.

"It means I can't be with you," Daria said after a few moments.

"I will be," Xen offered. "I will keep Thána safe."

"I know," Daria said. "And you'll both need to keep aware. There's something else I need to tell you. It's about Katyk."

I was instantly alarmed, sitting back up. "What about Katyk?"

"Brek seems to think they are deprogramming her. They're talking about putting her in the bombing unit."

"What? Are they crazy?" I asked.

"She's responded well to the treatment, apparently. Renounced the Kabeshi, says she just wants to go home."

"No, she's playing them. You don't deprogram someone in two days," I said. All of the rage Katyk poured into me when she was inside my head came roaring back. It went beyond whatever Artoz had done to her. She had funneled all that fury into getting to me, and she wasn't going to just let go of it because she was now a prisoner on the other side.

"Which is why I think I need to stay with you," Daria said with a sigh.

"Katyk will not harm Thána," Xen said. "I will see to it."

Daria scrubbed hands over her face. "I know, Xen, I do." She tossed back the last of the whiskey in her glass. "I cannot make Brek see reason. The magic corp is stretched tight, and Katyk apparently knows how the Kabeshi weapons work. Brek thinks she can use Katyk to sabotage the big guns."

"Won't matter if I can't make the distance anyway." I laid back down, hoping my exhaustion would drop me into a sleep without dreams. I pushed Katyk out of my conscious thought. "Let me worry about that first."

I woke to distressed sounds coming from Daria, going from asleep to standing upright as she screamed. She flailed at her blanket, hands and feet thrashing as I crossed to her. "Daria?" I kept my voice soft and my touch gentle, soothing a hand down her arm. "Daria, I'm here."

Her eyes popped open and the terror in them was palpable. I swallowed and touched her cheek to get her to focus on me. "It's okay. I'm here."

She blinked at me for a long minute, her face pale and sweaty. She sat up, rubbing her eyes. "Want to talk about it?" I asked.

Daria shook her head. "No point. Just… nightmare."

"Okay." I went back to my cot. Now that I was awake, I needed to pee, and my stomach was growling. I pulled on my boots and reached for my jacket. "I'm going to hit the latrine and grab some food."

Daria shoved her feet into her boots and stood. "I'll come with you."

We dismissed the wards so that Xen wouldn't be trapped if they woke while we were gone and were greeted by a blast of frigid air. The world outside our tent was white and gray, and it was early enough there wasn't more than a single set of tracks in the snow leading from the tents toward the latrine. We trudged through ankle-deep snow, leaving two trails of shuffling footsteps. We took care of our business and washed our hands before we trudged down to the mess tent.

Space heaters were keeping the tent toasty warm, and a handful of officers were finishing up breakfast before their shifts as we entered. "Tea?"

Daria asked as I headed for the food. I nodded and she went to where the tea was set up. If nothing else, I wanted the heat from a cup of tea.

I loaded up a plate with some of that fennel and onion bread toasted and spread with something akin to cream cheese, a handful of some sort of nut, and added a small bowl of the local porridge, which had a flavor like rice pudding. Daria had put two mugs of tea on a table and went to fill her own plate.

We sat quietly eating for a few minutes before Daria cleared her throat. "It was Artoz." I looked up but didn't say anything. "I guess the thing with Katyk stirred it up. I know what she went through, before…"

"Yeah, but she broke. You didn't," I countered, pulling my mug of tea closer and wrapping my hands around it for the warmth.

"You don't know how close I came." There were tears in the corners of her eyes and she wiped at them. "If you hadn't come…" She shook her head. "He had left me alone for weeks, just drugging me, letting me heal so that he could begin again. The mind games were almost worse than the torture."

I sipped at my tea and waited to see if she was done. She ate a piece of the green fruit I hadn't yet tried and when she swallowed, she glanced toward the officers who were clearing their table. "If I had taken my commission when the minister had offered it, I never would have been taken. The city might not have fallen."

"You don't know that," I said, touching her hand.

She pulled it away and the look in her eyes told me that she did, in fact, know that. "I wanted to stay with my family. I could have helped defend Meerat during the first volley, rather than after the fact when it was too little, too late. And now Habros is gone and Kota might as well be, and I don't know…"

"Daria." I didn't have any words of wisdom, but I wanted to take away the pain in her voice. "We can't change what we did," I swallowed and pushed away the image of Habros, "or didn't do. We can only do our best going forward."

I felt Xen and looked up, smiling as they entered the mess tent. "There you are," they said, rubbing warm hands over my shoulders.

"Here we are. I woke up with a desperate need for food."

"I am also hungry." Xen turned to the buffet.

Daria seemed to be pulling back into herself. "I promised Amblin I would go over the shield formations with his second in charge this morning," she said, standing and lifting her plate. "I'll meet you out on the range after I'm done."

"Okay." She deposited her plate in the bin set up for soiled dishes and left the tent, pulling her jacket closed.

Xen joined me a moment later as I pulled the pouch of xýpna from my pocket. I dropped a healthy dose of it into my tea and stirred. "Did you sleep well?" I asked as Xen tucked into their food.

They nodded. "Is Daria well?"

I shrugged. "I don't know. She had a nightmare. This thing with Katyk has her spooked and she's second-guessing her decision not to join the magic corps before the attack on Meerat."

"That is probably Brek's fault," Xen said quietly, glancing around to make sure they weren't overheard. "Brek tried to recruit Daria right out of school, which was where she had worked with Amblin. They made a great team. Then came to her again when Kota was small. Both times Daria turned her down. Then came the war. Brek tried a third time when it became clear that Kabesh had magical weapons. She does not like being told no."

"I know the type." Unfortunately, I didn't know how to help my sister other than taking back the city she loves so I could reunite her with her son. If anyone had told me a year ago that I would be going to war in a place I had never heard of, I'd have thought they were crazy. I drank my xýpna-infused tea while Xen ate and when we were done, I cleared our plates.

"Do you want to go to the command center?" Xen asked as we exited the mess tent.

I shook my head. "Let's just head out to the range. I'd like to get warmed up before everyone else gets there."

We walked hand in hand until the cold was too much and we both shoved our hands into our pockets. The range was cold and empty, but the dark targets stood out against the snow, making them easier to see.

The xýpna powder was working its magic, and the energy swelled inside me, almost enough to make me believe that I could accomplish the task I'd been handed.

CHAPTER 26
BUILDING BRIDGES

I started my warm-up solo, seeing if I could cast a portal around ten yards away without even Xen to back me. It felt like I was pushing wet cement through the kelcimite, but it opened and stabilized before I let it go. "Not doing that again," I said to no one in particular.

"That is what you have me for," Xen chided, stepping into place behind me.

I felt our connection come to life and instantly all of their energy was at my disposal. I cast a portal out to the last distance I had done the day before without Daria's help. It came a little easier than it had then, but I also hadn't been casting for hours yet. "One more?" I asked Xen over my shoulder. I felt their nod and set up to cast out to the fourth marker. The portal wobbled precariously before it stabilized and was large enough to get a person through. I dropped it quickly so I wouldn't drain myself.

The crunch of footsteps on snow made me turn to find R'essa approaching with steaming mugs in her hands. "I brought you some tea," she said, passing us each a mug. "Thought you might need it to warm up."

"Thank you," I wrapped cold hands around the mug and brought it up where the steam could warm my face.

"How are you feeling today?" R'essa asked. "You had quite a workout yesterday."

"I'll be fine. I slept well." I sipped the tea, relishing the warmth.

"I asked my team to bring out some benches this morning, so we have a place to rest during breaks."

"That's great," I said, though my attention was drifting back out to the range.

"I was wondering if I could offer you some of my observations from yesterday? Just don't take any of it as criticism, more suggestions that might be helpful."

"Okay."

R'essa's eyes dropped to my hands where I was playing with the kelcimite. "When you cast, I notice that you expend a lot of energy, like you're forcing the magic out of you."

"That is what it feels like."

"You might be able to go further and hold it longer if you control it better, make it a stream rather than a burst, that way you have energy in reserve."

I frowned a little as I tried to sort out what she meant. I lifted the kelcimite and chose a spot just about five yards from where I stood and tried to control the flow of magic. It stuttered out of me, the portal flickering even as it was forming, but it did form.

"Good, how did that feel?" R'essa asked.

"Like I was trying to pull out my own teeth," I responded. "But yes, I can see how that is a better use of energy."

"You'll find it gets easier with practice." R'essa turned as the sound of people reached us. "And here's my team."

The group seemed almost jovial as they carried two benches out, and behind the benches came a table and a space heater. While it wouldn't warm the whole range, it would give us a space to warm up, and the passive participants a hope to not freeze to the ground.

Bringing up the rear, Amblin and Daria came, their faces grim.

"What's wrong?" I asked as Daria joined me.

"We just got word that Kabeshi troops bombed our positions in the north part of the capital early this morning. We took heavy casualties," Amblin responded. "Including two of our most advanced magic users."

"Brek wants to step up our schedule. We go in at first light tomorrow. She's already moving the ground troops into position outside the city," Daria added.

"I don't know if I can be ready by tomorrow," I said aside to Xen.

"We will make it work," they responded, squeezing my hand.

I was still unconvinced. I sipped my tea, then set it down on the table. R'essa started to stage her team. They sat three to each bench with two standing behind the benches and R'essa between them so they were all in contact. I exhaled as Xen took position in front of R'essa and I stepped back into Xen's arms.

I chose to go straight for the fifth marker, trying to do as R'essa had suggested. Time seemed to get sluggish and stretched out as the energy gathered within me, and I wasn't sure anything was going to happen for a long time. The magic was building, and eventually, the portal formed. Xen's arms tightened a bit and I dropped the portal. "That was a little closer to the mark, I think," I said looking at Amblin for confirmation. He nodded.

"Try again, hold it a little longer," Amblin directed.

I lifted my hands and this time the stream of energy was more consistent. Around me it seemed everyone was moving quickly. Daria and Amblin raced to the portal as I held it open. They were back through almost immediately "Right next to the marker," Amblin said as I dropped the portal. "Ready to try the last marker?"

I pocketed the kelcimite and retrieved my tea, using it to warm my hands even as I lifted it to sip. "Yeah, okay."

Amblin pulled a map out of his pocket, pointing to a spot for me. "This is where we are. This is the fifth marker." He pointed to the spot I'd just hit, then dragged his finger up a few inches. "This is the sixth."

I finished off the tea and set the cup aside. I was starting to feel the fatigue building, so paused to have another dose of xýpna. I could feel Daria's concern but chose to ignore it, moving back to my spot. Xen's hands found my waist and the bridge snapped back into place. I tried to envision the marker while at the same time setting the intent to go past the fifth marker, hoping it would be enough.

The magic came up a little faster, building up and streaming out of the stone. When the portal opened, Daria stepped through partway, shaking her head. "Nope, less than halfway between the markers."

I dropped the portal and took a few deep breaths before trying again. The strain was making my arms and shoulders ache. I cast again but staggered back against Xen before the portal fully formed. My nose was bleeding as Xen guided me to a spot vacated by one of the bridge team. Daria squatted in front of me, offering me a cloth to wipe the blood from my face.

"Sorry."

"Don't apologize. We're asking a lot of you, especially since this is so new to you."

"I can get there, I think. I just need a break."

My stomach rumbled as I sat there reveling in the warmth from the space heater. My eyes kept lifting as if I could see the marker if I just stared at the horizon long enough. At least I knew what I was aiming for when we did this for real.

Xen touched my hand and gave me another cup of tea. I looked around us to find soldiers filling up the table with food and a big pot of tea. It didn't feel like we'd been out there long enough for it to be lunchtime, but more time seemed to have elapsed than I was aware of.

Daria brought me a plate with some bread and a thick slab of what looked and smelled like beef, along with some vegetables that reminded me of the meals Habros had made for Mom and me. I pushed the thought of Habros aside and thanked her, digging in as my stomach growled for food.

All around me people gathered in pairs or trios, chatting comfortably. R'essa came to sit beside me. "You doing okay?"

I swallowed my mouthful before I responded. "I think so. But, something was different. I felt... strange."

"How so?" R'essa asked.

"Like time wasn't moving for me." I wasn't sure that explained it. "Daria seemed to be moving at least twice as fast as normal."

"And that didn't happen before?"

I shook my head. "Like I said, weird."

"Hmmm. It did seem to take you a long time to cast." She nibbled on her food, her face a mask of concentration. "If I knew how you were doing this, I might be able to figure it out, but Amblin tells me that it isn't like anything he's seen, and he's our most experienced witch."

"Yeah, Daria can't figure it out either. I wish I knew how to show it to you." I focused on eating and mulled over the way it felt the last two times I had cast the portal spell. It was almost as if time had slowed as I pulled the energy from the bridge through Xen and had only resumed once the portal was stable. "I guess we add it to the list of things I do without knowing how or why."

"You are a most peculiar witch, Thána," R'essa said, admiration in her voice. "It is a pleasure to work with you."

I blushed a little and turned my discomfort into looking for Xen. They were standing with Daria near the tea, so I got up and joined them. Daria instantly turned my head to check my nose bleed, then checked my hands after Xen took my mostly empty plate from me. "These look a lot better today."

"Feel better too. Still don't have much movement in the broken fingers though. I suppose that's a good thing. Don't want to hurt them even more."

"How does the casting feel?"

"Weird, but it's not hurting my hands at all anymore."

"That's good."

Xen slipped a warm hand into mine, and it was comforting. "So, tomorrow?" I asked Daria.

She grimaced and closed her eyes. "We'll talk when we're done here. Once you hit the distance, we're going to bring in the squad that will be going through the portal. We want them to have a few practice runs."

That seemed fair. "I'm ready when everyone else is, other than needing a trip to the latrine. I'll be back in a minute."

Xen came with me. We didn't speak, it didn't feel necessary. We both relieved ourselves and washed our hands, then headed back. It had started snowing again, but at least the air had warmed up a bit. Everyone moved into position again as we approached, and this time Daria joined Xen and I as we lined up.

"Take a minute and breathe, center," Daria said softly to me. I followed her instructions, digging deep to find my center and breathing into it. "Good, now connect to Xen. I want you to see the energy they are holding for you and I want you to feed that into your core. Picture your target. The number six in red on a black background."

It dawned on me that I had no idea what their six looked like. I shifted the kelcimite to my right hand and held out my left hand, palm up. "Show me?"

Daria's finger drew a symbol on my hand, leaving a tingling residue. I thanked her and lifted my hands back into the correct formation. I re-centered and fixed the symbol in my head. I started the pull of energy from Xen, gathering a ball of it before pushing the spell outward and into the kelcimite. I kept my eyes closed as the stream of magic continued, the hole forming slowly, but sure and steady. I was sweating and my breathing was getting ragged, but the portal was open and holding. Amblin stepped through and let out a whoop.

He came back grinning. "Right on target!"

I dropped the portal and sank to the ground. The heater had melted the snow but left the grass muddy and wet. Xen and Daria got me up to the bench, Daria once again moving in with the cloth to clean up the blood, but I waved her off as nausea hit me and I doubled over, my head swimming as I vomited up the lunch I'd just eaten.

Xen's hand was on my back, rubbing in small circles while Daria held my hair out of the way. I was shaky as I sat back, taking the cloth to both clean up the blood and wipe my mouth. Amblin offered me a mug of tea which I took gratefully.

"I told you, the distance isn't doable," Daria said, her tone dark. "We can't ask this of her."

"It's fine, Daria," I said. "I can do it."

"At what cost? This could kill you."

"I only have to get it open and hold it long enough for everyone to get through."

"No. We have to find someplace closer for her to work from." Daria stomped a foot down as if to make sure we all knew she was upset.

"We can't spare the men to secure any place closer," Amblin said. "You heard the minister."

"I heard fine. I just don't agree."

"Daria, I can do this." My nose had stopped bleeding and I stood, letting Xen keep me steady. They guided me away from the little pile of vomit. "I need more energy. It isn't enough."

R'essa said something in Vaneeshi to one of her people who jogged off into camp. "Drink some more tea, and if you can, eat something."

My stomach lurched at the thought of food, but the tea was warming and soothing. I moved to the other bench and sat while someone cleaned up my mess. Daria came to sit beside me.

"You don't have to do this," she said softly.

"No? Your minister seems to think I do."

"Forget Brek. Tell me now and I'll make her do it another way."

I rested my head on her shoulder. "I can do it. I just need more oomph."

"Don't let them push you so far that it kills you," Daria said.

"I promised Mom I would reunite you. I can't do that if we don't take back the portal park."

"You're stubborn like her." Daria pressed a kiss into my hair. "But if you need to tap out, tell me."

"I will, I promise."

Daria and I stayed huddled together on the bench even as a group of people began to congregate. It was a lot more people than I had been expecting. Then I saw her.

I stood abruptly, drawing Daria's attention. Katyk looked at me, a brief, flickering smile on her lips before she schooled her face and she glanced down at the ground as if she were ashamed. I didn't buy it.

"I don't want her here," I said to Amblin, pointing to Katyk.

He held up both hands to placate me. "Minister Brek is insisting we need her."

"No." I trembled and it had nothing to do with energy drain.

"Thána, please—"

"She betrayed us. We cannot trust her."

"Hello, Thána."

I didn't look at her at first, but out of the corner of my eye, I saw something I didn't expect. Around her neck was a small metal collar with a blinking green light. Beside her was a Vaneeshi woman in the black uniform of the magic corps. She held up something in her hand. "If she steps out of line, she gets zapped. She's here strictly to help us fire up some of our trickiest bombs."

Katyk put a finger under the collar and looked at me. "Anyone pushes that button, I go down like a sack of *polora*."

I had no clue as to what polora was, but I liked the sound of dropping her on her ass. Behind me R'essa was setting up the team, which was twice the size it had been earlier, making sure they were staged in a way that they could all touch at least one other person in the chain.

"I'll be back in a few minutes," I said to Amblin, stalking away toward the latrines again. My stomach roiled with fury at having to see her and to work with her was beyond belief. What I wanted to do was pummel her into the ground. I made it to the building and went inside, surprised to find Xen right behind me. I had been so caught up in my rage that I hadn't heard or felt them behind me.

I went to the sink to splash water over my face. It was bracingly cold and it served to snap my attention back to the task at hand. "Sorry, I couldn't..." I said to Xen in the mirror over the sink.

"Do not apologize. You are correct in your anger. They cannot control her, even with that technology. Her presence puts all of us in danger."

I sighed. "I want that zapper so that when she comes at me I can drop her, and I don't want her to know that I have it."

Xen smirked at me in the mirror. "I think that can be arranged. I will speak to Daria."

I splashed a little more water on my skin, then dried my hands and nodded. "I'm ready. The sooner we make this work the sooner I can get some sleep. I have the feeling that tomorrow is going to suck."

We walked back hand in hand. I didn't say anything to anyone and I didn't look at Katyk or any of the strike team. I didn't need to know who they were or what their job was. I only had to get them there. We took our spots and I tried to soothe my still angry insides, though it took a few times through the centering ritual Merry had taught me to get me there.

"Be ready to move," I said as I took my stance and lifted the crystal. "I can't hold it forever."

The power that surged through my connection to Xen was incredible and it made for a strong and steady casting that opened the portal wide enough for five or six across. "Go," Daria called, and the group surged toward the opening. By the time the last of them was across to the other side, my temples felt like they were imploding and my nose was bleeding again.

"Get them back," I said through gritted teeth. "I can't..."

Daria yelled for them to return but it was too late as I started to feel the bridge falter. The portal flickered and then crashed, taking me down with it. I heard Daria and Xen, but they were miles away.

I woke with a start, confused. I was no longer on the cold, wet ground, but on a cot in the infirmary tent. Amblin and Daria stood at the end of the bed, Xen sat beside it on a stool. I could taste blood in my mouth and my head was pounding. "What happened?" I asked, my words slurring.

"You pushed too hard," Daria chastised.

"But you made it work," Amblin added.

"Give my patient some room to breathe." I recognized the voice as the Vaneeshi doctor I had seen the day before. He came around Daria with shooing gestures.

"I'll be back, Thána. We need to go have a word with Minister Brek."

My sister and Amblin left us then, which let me see that R'essa was there too. She lifted a hand and then followed the others.

"I'm going to get spoiled if you keep coming in here," the doctor said jovially.

"I just couldn't wait to see you again," I offered, my words a little less slurred.

"Looks like you bit off a little more than you could chew."

"Story of my life, Doc." I tried to sit up, but my head and stomach both protested and Xen's hand on my shoulder kept me from trying any harder.

"Your sister tells me that you've been relying on a stimulant to help you function," the doctor said while he leaned closer and flashed a light in my eyes.

"I wouldn't say relying," I protested.

He sat back with his arms crossed. "No? Are you using it every day?"

I conceded that point with a nod.

"More than once per day?"

Again, I had to nod.

"Sounds like reliance to me."

"I just need it to get through this fight. I need the energy boost to get the portal open."

"You sound an awful lot like an addict, my friend."

I opened my mouth to protest, then realized that protesting would be exactly what an addict would do. "I promise to back off it just as soon as tomorrow is over."

"I'm going to hold you to that," the doctor said. "Now, some of your test results are back. You are very dehydrated, your... I don't know the English word." He looked at Xen. "*Antasrávī?*"

Xen blinked a few times before nodding. "Endocrine, I believe."

"Yes, your endocrine system is not functioning properly and you bumped your head when you went down."

"I just need a good meal and some sleep, Doc," I said, once again making the effort to get up.

"Do not make me restrain you," Xen said. There was humor in their tone, but I also didn't doubt they would do just that.

"We are going to get some fluid into you, along with a special vitamin mix we give the soldiers. Your friend can bring you food from the mess tent if they like, but I'm keeping you here where we can keep an eye on you and make sure you rest."

I could tell that fighting would get me nowhere, so I acquiesced, laying back in defeat. "Good." He patted my knee and got up, calling a nurse over to give him directions.

Xen leaned in and kissed my forehead gently. "I will bring you dinner."

"I'll be here… I guess." They smiled and headed for the front of the tent, leaving me alone. It was the only time I'd been alone on this world other than the few minutes between picking up the hauler and picking up the team.

CHAPTER 27
INTO THE STORM

The quiet didn't last long. A few minutes later I had nurses getting me hooked up to an IV system, and drawing blood for more tests. I managed to doze for a bit once they were done, waking when Xen returned with a tray filled with a rich-looking stew, bread rolls, and some mixed fruit.

Xen sat with me while I ate, though we didn't speak much. My mind replayed the last spell casting over and over. "Tomorrow shouldn't be so traumatic," I said as I finished eating. "I'll be starting fresh, and so will the bridge team."

"Your sister is worried for you," Xen said. "She and Minister Brek have been arguing about the prudence of this plan."

"I get that. And believe me, I would rather she was with us when this happens. We'll be fine though." I smiled with more confidence than I truly felt. "You just keep Katyk away from me."

"That reminds me." Xen slipped a hand into their pocket and came out with a small remote just like the one Katyk's handler had. "This is for you."

"What's the range on this thing?"

Xen grinned. "I doubt you could incapacitate her from here if that is what you are asking."

"I would never!" I declared, taking the remote. "But I feel better having it."

We sat in comfortable silence as the infirmary emptied of people. The night nurse came to introduce herself and check my IV. My mind wandered over the expectations for the morning, and there was a part of me that was terrified something would go very wrong.

All I had to do was open the door. That was literally my only job. Once that was done, I could rest.

Xen left to return to our quarters and I settled in to try to sleep. About an hour later, Daria reappeared with Xen in tow. She looked angry. The infirmary tent was quiet, as I was the only overnight guest and there was only one person there to keep an eye on me.

I frowned up at my sister. "What's wrong?"

She pulled the stool closer and sat. "Xen and I have had a long talk." She seemed to be trying to decide something. "So, change of plans."

"Okay," I tried to read her face, but I didn't know her well enough.

"I'll be leaving in a few hours with Amblin and the shield team. Well before dawn, you and Xen will head to your jumping point with the strike team. All of that stays the same. However, I want you and Xen to follow the strike team through and find a safe place to hunker down. As soon as I can break away, I'll come to find you."

My frown deepened. "Why? What's changed?"

She pressed her lips together and glanced at the nurse who was sitting at a desk not far away. Her voice was only just above a whisper. "This is a war Vaneesh cannot win, not with Brek burning through our magic corp like she is. I'm done. We're going back to Spítia."

"Who we?" I asked. I looked up at Xen who caressed my knee.

"I will go where you go."

I wanted to ask what Brek had done, beyond expecting me to risk my life to open this portal, but I could tell that was a conversation for another time. "Okay. We go to Spítia then." I rubbed a hand on her hand. "Mom and Kota will be so happy to see you."

She looked down at our hands. "I miss him. Them."

I took my hand away. I couldn't share her grief when I was the cause of it. "We'll see them soon. By tomorrow night we'll be back on the other side of that portal. Of course, we will have a long walk ahead of us with no food or shelter, but we'll be closer to our family."

She offered me a small smile. "Sometimes you sound so much like Mom. It's easy to forget you didn't spend your whole life with her like I did. Leave the prep to me. I should be able to put together something to see us through."

"I may have only had the last few months with Mom, but it's been good getting the chance to know her."

"I never did ask you how that happened."

I thought about it for a moment. "Long story short? Cambious and I decided we could storm a castle and rescue Mom, so we did. With the help of a phoenix, a dragon, and a couple of manticores."

"Wait. You're telling me that those... they're real?" Daria asked, her voice incredulous. "Like, actual manticores? And a phoenix?"

I chuckled. "Oh, yeah, they're real alright. It does sound like the setup for a bad joke though: An incubus and a witch invade a castle with a phoenix, a dragon, and a manticore..."

Daria shivered. "And it sounds like a myth."

"Yeah, that's what I thought too. I'm surprised with all the cross-population here that you don't see more like Katyk."

"Katyk?"

"Part succubus, according to her. But those types of species in general. Unless they're using glamors." I thought about that for a moment before discarding the idea. It would take too much energy to maintain a glamor long term.

"We've had people who claim to be part this or that, even had a supposed werewolf run for a government position a few years back, but mostly they're mocked, not believed. Humans, and several human-like species, but none of the mythical ones."

"I would never have believed it if I hadn't seen it," I responded.

"Daria."

We looked up to find Amblin at the door to the infirmary. Daria nodded, and reached for my hand, lifting it to kiss gently. "Be safe and I'll find you tomorrow."

I nodded. "You be safe too."

I watched her leave with Xen behind her and tried to settle my brain enough to sleep. When I finally did, my dreams were of Habros and my sister, fantasy scenes of the two of them together, rapturous and in love mixing with flashes of blood and death and memories of home.

It was still dark with no sign of sunrise as Xen and I met the strike and bridge teams. We were all clad in the same black uniforms, with impact-resistant vests packed with a combination of survival supplies and personal effects.

We loaded into two haulers, making sure Xen and I were in one and Katyk was in the other.

"Settle in," R'essa said as she took a seat across from me. "It's a long ride."

I leaned into Xen's warmth as we started moving, trying to keep my head on what was to come and not letting myself wallow in the past or worry for Daria, wherever she was. Xen's hand rubbed over my back and if I closed my eyes I could imagine we were somewhere else, preferably someplace warm, with a fire and some wine.

"Here," R'essa said, pulling my attention as she took something out of the pack on her hip. "These communicators will keep us in contact with everyone. Turn your head?"

I did as she asked as she opened a package and withdrew a small dot. She brushed my hair back and touched the object to a spot just behind and slightly below my ear. There was a prick that made me hiss, then a whirring sound. By the time R'essa had done the same to Xen, I was starting to hear voices calmly relaying orders.

"Say something," R'essa instructed.

"Like what?" I asked.

She smiled. "Just like that. To mute yourself, just tap the dot. Tap again to unmute."

I tapped the spot and left it muted for the time being. I didn't need our whole team to hear anything I had to say for now. They seemed to be a step up from the communications tools Katyk had given us for our rescue operation. "So what are we expecting when we get to our spot?" I asked.

"We secured the site late yesterday, and we have a troop to guard our perimeter while we work. They have set up a space for us. Once we're there and ready, we wait for the order to come through."

I slid a hand into Xen's. "And once we're through?"

"Once we get the strike team through, our job is done."

R'essa couldn't know that we had other plans, and once Xen and I stepped through the portal and I closed it, it wouldn't matter anyway.

Of course, a lot depended on luck. We had to get through, and we had to survive a battle that I had no way of understanding. Daria had to survive her end of the battle plan and find us. I had to get the portal unlocked and get us all through before anyone figured out what we were up to.

I tried to picture the portal park in my mind, the way it had been the day Mom and I came through. In the circle of portals, there wasn't much for cover, but the stones themselves and the grove of trees surrounding it offered a few places we might be able to hide.

The hauler slowed and I heard voices, then we turned and came to a stop. I let the bridge team get up before I did, stretching and yawning. I jumped down from the hauler, reaching into a pocket for the xýpna powder and dropping a healthy pinch onto my tongue before swallowing. Even if the whole mad situation wasn't over that day, Daria wouldn't need to worry about the health risks of the powder for much longer. I was nearly out. There was maybe enough for five or six more doses, a few more if I was stingy with them.

The distant horizon was streaked with deep crimson and orange as the sun began its ascent into the morning sky. R'essa drew us away from the trucks and up a small rise. The ground was slick mud that sucked at our boots until we got to the top where space heaters were drying things up. The space was set with an array of benches where the bridge team would form up.

On the southern horizon sat the hulking shadow of Meerat, the light of the dawn only starting to help it stand out from the night sky. "Where am I aiming?" I asked aside to Xen, who pointed. My gaze followed the line of their finger. "Good."

I heard Minister Brek's voice and turned to find her speaking with a man in the green uniform of the military. I was wary of her presence there but tried to put the random thoughts about her ambitions aside.

She came toward us, and everyone in the area snapped to attention, which she dismissed with the wave of one hand. "I hope you're prepared for this, Thána," the minister said.

"As much as I can be, Minister," I responded. "Like I said, I'm not positive I can actually do this."

She raised one eyebrow at me. "I'm sure you can. When this day is over, you and I will talk about how you can best serve Vaneesh."

I rubbed my bare hands along the arms of the coat Daria had found for me, shivering a little, though I wasn't sure whether it was cold or anticipation. Xen drew me away from the Minister and closer to one of the space heaters, stepping in close. "When the team is through?" Xen asked, glancing around to make sure we weren't overheard.

"We follow," I responded, not entirely sure why we were keeping it a secret but knowing instinctively that it was our only choice. I had no doubts that Brek would seek to stop us if she knew.

R'essa joined us with cups of tea. "It shouldn't be long. Amblin reported in an hour ago to say they were in position."

I took my tea with a nod. "Sooner the better."

"Katyk, with me."

I turned at the mention of her name. She was only steps away from me, but the man in charge of her was right there, gripping her shoulder.

"I just wanted to wish you luck," Katyk said to me with a shy expression. Her eyes though, her eyes told me that what she wanted was to beat me into the ground.

"Stay away from me, Katyk," I said with a snarl.

"I'm only here to do my part, Thána," Katyk replied, taking another step. She suddenly froze, her eyes wide with pupils full-blown while arcs of blue electricity danced between her collar and her skin. Her handler gave a small smirk, then dragged Katyk away, shoving her toward the rest of the strike team.

There was a burst of static in my ear and I jumped, making Xen chuckle. "It takes getting used to."

Voices replaced the static as the comms came online and various commanders were reporting the readiness of their squads. After a few minutes, I heard Amblin's voice. "Bridge team, this is shields. We are in position and ready to go on your mark."

R'essa nodded and the teams started taking up positions. "Roger that shield team. We're setting up now."

"Thána?" That was Daria's voice. I touched the dot to unmute myself.

"I'm good," I responded.

"Good. I'll see you soon."

I swallowed down some tea as a means of trying to keep myself steady, then handed off the cup and looked to R'essa for direction. She lined me up, then turned to make sure her team was all in place. I muted the comms again and leaned back into Xen's heat. "No matter what happens to me, get us through the hole. Even if it means dragging me through unconscious."

"If you are unconscious, won't the portal close?" Xen asked in my ear.

"Move fast," I said, turning and kissing them without thinking about it. We both froze minutely before I shook it off and turned back to face the city.

"Shield team, we are establishing the bridge now," R'essa said behind us.

Xen's hands circled my waist and pulled me tight. To my left, I could see the strike team pulled together in a tight five-by-five formation. Each person was armed with assorted weapons that I had never bothered to figure out. I'd see soon enough what they did.

I felt the energy as the bridge team, five extra people strong, connected to R'essa who in turn connected with Xen. The power flowed through them like a river and into me. I exhaled while I began to pull, lifting the kelcimite from my pocket and getting my hands into position.

The casting burst through me, though I tried to keep it as close to us as possible while still giving the strike team room to get through.

"Shield team, portal is open, you can commence the attack now."

The strike team took off at a run. Blood poured from my nose, but Xen got me moving. We were less than a few seconds behind the last member of the team, stumbling and rolling to the ground on the other side.

Before I could do more than roll onto my back, a blue burst of energy slammed through the ring at waist level. The casting team member stood at the center, her hands outstretched while the strike team all took a knee around her. The hair on my arms lifted in the aftershocks. I was reeling, holding on to consciousness by the thinnest thread as Xen pulled me back between two of the boulders that held the portals.

They helped me sit up, leaning me against the nearest rock and wiped at the blood on my face with a damp cloth they pulled from a pocket. Just beyond the ring of portals, I could see at least five brown-uniformed Kabeshi on the ground.

I took the cloth from Xen and held my nose until the bleeding stopped. In the clearing, the strike team broke into smaller teams, several of whom spread out to begin their bombing sweeps intended to drive the enemy into the Vaneeshi main force. My vision swam and I threw myself to the side, vomiting into the ground. Xen pulled me back up, their face showing concern. My fingers fumbled at the pocket for the xýpna powder, taking a small amount to try to fend off the impending unconsciousness.

All around us, gunfire penetrated the air and the skies lit up in a dangerous-looking red as the battle began in earnest. The circle of portals was empty now except for us, the strike team all deployed with their magically enhanced weapons. Smoke filled the air and explosions rocked the ground beneath us. Out of the corner of my eye, I saw a Kabeshi soldier and I turned, throwing up a *prostatévo* that was almost too late.

The bullet bounced to the side mere inches from my face. Xen jumped to their feet and launched themself at the soldier almost instantly. I clawed my way to my feet while Xen engaged the Kabeshi man up close, fists and feet flying. They snatched the gun from the man as he went down, then shoved me into a rock behind me as they fired into the ring of portals, taking down another soldier.

"We are too exposed," Xen said.

I nodded in agreement. "What do you suggest?"

They stood on their toes and craned their neck to look around us. "The bathrooms, perhaps?"

It was more shelter than we currently had if nothing else. Xen took my wrist and we inched out from between the boulders. Xen pointed with the gun to a small building that seemed a long way off. We had only made a few steps in that direction when a whistling sound caught my attention. I threw out the best defensive spell in my arsenal, pulling Xen down as the bomb came almost directly at us.

It overshot us and hit the ground just behind the boulder where we had been sitting. I grabbed Xen and pulled them behind the nearest boulder as the bomb exploded. It sent red dust through the air and rocked the ground. We gasped for breath as we moved away from the choking dust, ending up back inside the ring of portals.

Xen shoved me and jumped backward as a bolt of fire was hurled our way. It passed between us and slammed into the ground a few yards away.

"Katyk." I knew before I even turned around. Either she had slipped her handler or he was dead. Either way, she was going to try to kill me.

Another bolt of fire came at us and I stepped in front of Xen, casting *prostatévo* once more to deflect it. Katyk ran toward us laughing and I realized she had somehow gotten out of her collar. "Shit." I backpedaled, but Katyk kept coming, murder in her eyes.

Xen ran at Katyk, landing a solid kick to her stomach and sent her falling backward. Katyk rolled to her feet and came up ready for a fight, her fists clenched.

I tried to get around them so I could get her between us, but Katyk kept moving, her feet dancing as she threw a flurry of punches, most of which Xen dodged. One landed on Xen's jaw and they staggered backward. Katyk turned on me and pounced. We went down together, sprawling on the frosty ground and rolling until she was on top and had her knee pinning my right hand to the ground.

Magic danced along her fingers as she brought them to my face. "I'd like to make this hurt, but we don't have time for fun."

"Just do it and stop yammering," I said with far more confidence than I was feeling.

"Oh, I will. But first, I need to handle your friend here." She slapped her palm down on my forehead and my body froze. "Stay."

Xen circled warily. They had no defense against magic and Katyk had no compunctions about using that against them. I strained against the spell, but it held me tightly to the ground. "This is going well," I muttered.

The sounds of battle were intense and all around us. The chatter of the soldiers in my ear was distracting. I tried to tune it out and focus on the problem. Xen landed a few good punches before Katyk threw more fire. Xen dodged and ducked clear, then ran at Katyk, driving their shoulder into Katyk's waist.

It was just enough to disrupt the continuity of her magic, giving me the chance to wiggle free. I got to my feet and landed a kick to Katyk's head with enough force to knock her out. I helped Xen up and together we ran for the small building again. "Where the hell is Daria?"

The bathroom was small, with only two stalls and no insulation to protect from the winter cold. We were breathing heavily as we shut the door, hoping it would at least keep us from breathing whatever foul dust that bomb had released. My head was reeling with a combination of fatigue, xýpna powder, and the dust from the magic-enhanced bomb. I leaned over the metal sink and tried to slow the rapid beating of my heart.

Xen tapped their comm unit. "Shield team, be advised, the portal park is under siege."

"Roger that. Do you require assistance?" That was Daria's voice.

I nodded to Xen. "Affirmative Shield."

"I'm closest," Daria said, though it didn't seem meant for us. "Hold tight, I'm on my way."

"We need to get the portal unlocked," I said to Xen, once my breathing was under control.

"We need someone to clear out that smoke first," Xen responded, moving to the door to peek out. "It will not kill you right away, but the more of it you breathe in, the faster you die."

"I could try something." After all, I was already doing things that everyone said shouldn't be possible. I weighed the options, trying to decide on an option that wouldn't kill everyone. If I just tried to blow it away, it could relocate someplace that would lead to people dying. "What do you know about it?"

Xen sighed, then coughed. "I know that it is some magic linked to a conventional bomb. The red smoke is emitted when the bomb explodes."

I'd already known that much. "But what is it made up of? Magic doesn't create something out of nothing."

Xen shook their head. "Daria might know."

"Okay, let me try something." I moved to the door, the idea still forming in my head. I pulled it open and stepped outside. I held my breath as I cast a bolt of fire at the nearest eddy of red smoke. The dust particles in the smoke flashed and popped, leaving the air clear when it had burned out. "Okay, not spectacular, but it's something." I tried again, but static and shouting over the comms pulled my attention and my attempt fizzled out. "How do I turn this off?" I asked Xen, my hand covering the unit.

Xen pulled the piece out of my head, leaving behind a sore spot that I rubbed at. They tucked the unit into one of the pockets of their vest and I refocused my attention on trying to burn away some of the smoke. It was slow going, in large part due to my exhaustion.

I was sweating when I'd cleared a path from the door of the bathroom to the nearest boulder. I reached behind me for Xen's hand and together we inched out. I tried to see everything at once as we moved, hoping to see Daria, and hoping not to see more Kabeshi soldiers.

Red smoke lingered in the ring, making visibility low. I burned off the smoke as we moved, though it closed in behind us again. It was work just to keep a buffer of breathable air around us as I tried to figure out which portal led to Spítia, and my mother.

Out of the smoke, I felt, rather than saw, Katyk coming at us again. She charged, growling as she launched herself at me. I dodged, but she still managed to ram her shoulder into my hip, sending us crashing to the ground. Xen pulled her off of me before she could pin me to the ground, but the smoke was starting to affect them as it closed in around us again and they lost their grip on Katyk's shoulder.

I rolled away and got back to my feet, readying another blast of fire to clear the air. Katyk was coughing, but her eyes never left me. I burned away the particles in the air around Xen, moving closer to them as Katyk watched us closely.

"You're awfully hard to kill for someone so… soft," Katyk said, wiping her mouth with the back of her hand.

"Maybe you just aren't trying hard enough," I quipped. I took the kelcimite from my pocket as Xen and I inched backward. Through the smoke, I spotted the lock that was suspended in the portal to Spítia. "Stay close," I said as Xen started to move around me to go after Katyk. I cast the portal before Katyk could react, pulling Xen with me as I jumped through.

It wasn't a large jump, and Katyk would find us again quickly, but it put us at our destination. It also set off my nose to bleeding again, but that meant I wouldn't have to cut myself to open the lock.

I smeared the blood on my hand and pressed it to the lock, murmuring the spell my mother had taught me to open it. I felt the lock give and fall into my hand. "Door's open. Where is Daria?" I asked Xen.

"Nearly here," Xen replied. They pushed me behind them as Katyk came again, her hands glowing with fire energy. The smoke was starting to dissipate as they traded blows, but Katyk's face was streaked with red soot and her wild eyes were bloodshot. Xen had landed some good blows to her nose and cheeks, dusting her face with bruises.

"Thána!" Daria's voice called over the sound of the fight and the general din of the battle being fought around us.

"Here!" I held a hand up over the smoke so my sister could find us.

My distraction cost me. A bolt of energy slammed the side of my head and sent me reeling. I nearly lost my grip on the kelcimite before I could pocket it to protect it. I saw the next one coming and dodged it before taking a play out of Katyk's repertoire and charging at her. I grabbed her around the waist and slammed her to the ground.

All the lessons Xen had tried to drill into me went through my head, but the memory of a schoolyard bully preceded them, and the satisfaction of getting the better of them was behind the fist I hit into her face.

Our momentum took us back to the center of the ring of portals and for a moment I was disoriented. I looked around for Xen or Daria. Katyk shoved me to the side, landing a punch of her own to my jawline. I got to my feet, circling warily, but Xen grabbed Katyk from behind, lifting her off her feet and tossing her to one side.

Daria grabbed my hand, her face hidden behind a gas mask. My eyes burned and my chest hurt, but we dashed toward the portal. We had no supplies, and the walk down the mountain in Spítia was going to suck, but anything was better than staying there.

We'd only taken a few steps when an explosion rocked the ground and we stumbled backward.

"That was close," Daria said.

"Too close," Xen agreed.

"Um, guys..." I pointed to where I could see Kabeshi soldiers with weapons entering the circle.

"Get behind me," Daria said, her left arm lifting a shield I hadn't realized she was carrying. It came to life just as someone started firing.

"Got any more of those shields?" I asked, my eyes picking the soldiers out of the smoke. We weren't surrounded, but it was getting close.

Katyk was somewhere nearby laughing at us. I could hear her, even if I couldn't see her. We were swiftly becoming trapped. "We need to get to the portal!" I said with urgency. The problem was, I had lost track of which one was the right portal. I thought that maybe I had one more small jump in me if I could figure out where we were going.

"Stick close to me," Daria said behind me. We moved in tandem, trusting Daria knew which portal we wanted.

"Down!" Xen shouted, yanking on my arm.

Something went whizzing over my head and impacted the ground ten feet away. The concussion pushed us closer to the boulders. Another blast sent us careening toward one of the portals, but at least the bombing was keeping the troops off of us.

"Thána, two portals down," Daria said, pointing. "Can you get us there?"

I shrugged, once again taking the kelcimite from my pocket. "I can try."

Xen grabbed my waist with one hand as they held Daria's shoulder with the other. I got set, my eyes focused on our destination, and prepared to cast. As the portal formed, Katyk was suddenly on me, reaching to knock the kelcimite from my hand. At almost the same moment another blast hit, close enough that I lost my footing and fell into Daria and Xen, sending the four of us tumbling through the portal behind.

The portal I was casting opened just as I cleared the one we'd stumbled through, landing us in a tumble of limbs and bodies in cold mud.

My head was exploding and I was pretty sure I was going to need a blood transfusion by the time the day was over as blood once again oozed out of my nose.

Xen was the first to recover, getting to their feet to help extricate us into separate people.

"Katyk?" My voice sounded like I was drunk and I was close to passing out. I couldn't see Katyk, but I knew she'd come through the first portal with us. Maybe she didn't manage to jump into the second one.

Daria looked me over for injuries while I tried to figure out where we were. The ground beneath me was wet and cold, more mud than anything. The air was wet too. It wasn't exactly raining, it was more like a fine mist.

We found ourselves in a field of sorts. The land around us was flat, and we were in the open. With no idea where we were, or for that matter where the portal back to Vaneesh was, I couldn't guess what came next.

The sky above us was cloudy, but there were spots of blue, and in the distance, the sun was shining down.

"Can you move?" Xen asked me.

I held my hand up for an assist in getting to my feet. Xen and Daria both helped me up, but I was unsteady and wobbly. They supported me between them. "Where are we going?" I asked, my words slurring together.

"There is a building in the distance," Xen said. "We need shelter and I do not want us in the open."

That made as much sense as anything else, at least in my exhaustion. My head was buzzing louder and louder and I wasn't sure I could stay conscious. I shook my head in an attempt to clear it, but all that did was make it worse. "Gonna pass out now," I mumbled just before I did exactly that.

I was vaguely aware of Xen and Daria shifting my weight so that Xen could pick me up, and the smell of animals before I fell deeper into a state of exhaustion-driven sleep. I have no idea how long I was out, but when I came to, I was nestled into a bed of hay. The smell of animals was stronger here, despite the wards I could just make out.

"We're still alive?" I asked, rubbing my eyes. My head hurt worse than any hangover I'd ever had in my life and my body felt like I'd been in a car accident, then wrung through one of those old-fashioned washing machines.

"So it would appear," Xen said, humor in their voice. "Are you well?"

"Nothing a stiff drink and three thousand Tylenol wouldn't fix," I muttered as I sat up. Despite the pain, I didn't seem to be injured anywhere. "Figure out where we are?"

It was pretty obvious that the *immediate* where was a barn of some kind.

"I did some recon," Xen said. "There's a city not far from here. The farm we are on consists of this structure and what appears to be a home."

Farm. That explained the smell.

"Any sign of Katyk? Or the portal?" I asked, moving closer. Daria handed me a packet of something that smelled like jerky.

"Neither, I am afraid," Xen said.

"Now that you're awake, we should head for the city," Daria said. "Maybe we can find someone who knows about the portal and can direct us." As Daria moved, I realized she was shrugging into a larger backpack and was startled to recognize it as the one I'd brought with me from Spítia.

"You went back to your house?" I asked. It took me two tries to get to my feet, and my knees were a bit on the rubbery side, but I was up. Daria released the wards and we headed through the barn door.

"It's why I was late," Daria answered. "There were some things I needed."

Several large animals stuck their heads over stall doors as we moved. They were not completely unlike cows, but they were taller and their fur ranged from a milky sort of lilac to a deep blue and their horns were white like ivory. Some of them were shaggy and some had large ears that moved like an elephant's ears.

"I don't think we're in Kansas anymore, Toto," I said, earning only blank stares. "Never mind." I shook my head. Of course, they didn't get the reference. At least I thought it was funny.

Xen checked outside the doors, then waved us on. We moved as fast as I could go under the circumstances, hoping to reach a road or something without incident.

Just as the road became visible, we heard someone call out. I contemplated telling them to run for it but knew I wouldn't get far.

We turned to find someone standing on the stairs of the house with a bat of some kind in their hand. The house was two stories, though more log-cabin than modern house, with clean white paint and a roof tiled in dark shingles.

Xen took the lead and approached the house. I could tell as we got closer that it was a woman, dressed as you might expect a farmer from the nineteenth century, her dirty pants worn and patched at the knees. They spoke and I thought I understood some of the words, but how would I? Unless Xen's knack with languages was contagious, or part of our bonding thing.

Xen responded hesitantly and again, some of the words made sense. It dawned on me that this was some derivation of English. Or possibly an offshoot of Old English. Once upon a time, I'd had a pretty good grasp of Old English.

The woman grunted and gestured toward the road. Someone else appeared behind her, a man with a full beard and hair that cascaded down his back in a brown curtain. He appeared to have just gotten out of bed, wearing a long chemise-like garment with a robe. He spoke to the woman, then turned to us. "*Commen.*"

We were escorted into the home, the woman bringing up the rear. She did not look amused that we were being invited in. They looked human, or human-adjacent anyway. Nothing immediately stuck out as being different.

The man smiled and spoke to Xen, gesturing to the chairs around the kitchen table. "This is Edda and Aldrich Comly," Xen said as we sat. "This is their farm."

Aldrich bustled about the kitchen, bringing plates and cups. He poured something into the cups that looked and smelled an awful lot like coffee. Onto the plates, he heaped meat and eggs and bread. "*Ete. Ablissé.*"

The woman stood at the end of the table watching us until he drew her away. "What's happening?" I whispered to Xen as I pulled the cup to me and breathed in the aroma.

"Hospitality is an important aspect of this society," Xen said. "To refuse their generosity would not have been good."

"Which means you know where we are," Daria replied.

I sipped the liquid in the cup and tasted something so like coffee it barely warranted listing the differences.

"Yes, the woman's language gave it away. It is not a good thing." Daria sighed. "We are in Amblin's homeworld."

"Gavlescore?" I asked. I could feel the color drain from my face. "The place that doesn't like… witches?" I whispered the last word.

"Gavlescore is the name of the nearest city. We will need to be very careful."

"And get the hell out of here as soon as we can," Daria added.

Out of the frying pan, and once again into the fire. Somehow, I seemed to have become very skilled in being where I was not wanted. Spítia, and my mother seemed further away than ever.

GLOSSARY OF TERMS

A

Ablissé: Drink
Adelfí: Sister
Aderfia: Brothers
Ánoixe: Open
Ánoixe kleídoma aímatos: Open this lock by my blood
Apokalýpto: Reveal

B

Bluathexe: Blood Witch

C

Commen: Come

D

Dimiourgió: Break

E

Ekleípo: Disappear (used with ward stones)

Éla: Come
Elefthérosi: Release
Ete: Eat
Evlogim Patoras: Second Father

F

Ftiáxe mia porta: Open a door

H

Hiexĕ: Witch

I

Irémise: Quiet

K

Kapnastís: Disease eater
Kleidóste sto aíma mou: Lock to my blood
Kommer: Come
Kontá: Close
Kravu: Cow
Krývo: Hide

M

Mágissa: witch
Makrá vlépinta: Ability of a blood witch to see past/future
Mikros: Little one
Mörderin: Killer

O

Obersut: Colonel

P

Páfsi: Pause
Paidí: Child

Patoras: Father
Pigaíno: Go
Prostatévo: Protect

S

Slúga: Servant
Sýnchysi: Confusion

T

Teíchos: Wall
Thanátou: Death bringer, angel of death
Thráfsi: Break

X

Xekleídoma: Unlock

Y

Yperaspízo: Defend
Ýpnos: Sleep

FROM THE AUTHOR

Thank you for joining me on this journey! These characters are very dear to me and telling their story has been a wonderful experience. Making conscious choices to include diverse characters with rich backgrounds is a passion I bring to each book, to every story I aim to tell.

Representing the LGBTQA+ community is important to me and I want to tell stories that are true to my family and friends who are a part of that community.

I hope you enjoyed the ride, and will follow Thána and friends into the next journey.

HÊALIC

NATALIE J. CASE

For my father

CHAPTER 1
GAVELSCORE

My first taste of coffee in more than a month was a heaven that belied the supposed hell we had managed to find ourselves in. At least my mouth believed it was coffee. It looked, smelled, and tasted like coffee, with a dark roast that was slightly sweet.

"Gavelscore is the name of the nearest city," Xen informed us once we had been left alone in the small kitchen. Edda had gone back out the door we had come through and Aldrich had disappeared up some stairs.

"This is going to complicate our finding the way back to Vaneesh," Daria added, her eyes skipping around the room and coming back to us. "We can't just go around asking people how to find the portal."

"Our best bet is still to head to town," Xen said. "I could not turn down the hospitality once it was offered. Not without offending them, and Edda looked fairly offended to start with."

"What did you tell them?" Daria asked quietly.

"That we were travelers who had been robbed on our way to the city," Xen replied. "Once I heard them speak, I knew where we were. Their speech is distinctive. One of their minor deities is the Faceless Stranger, who commands that those who honor him extend hospitality to all."

"Amblin isn't the only one you've met from here, is he?" Daria asked, turning to her food.

"No," Xen replied. "When my birthmates and I were young, one of the caretakers was a woman from a town on this world. She told us many stories."

"I really need to stop going places where people want me dead." My magic hangover was starting to ease up with the liberal application of food and coffee. I wasn't going to be up to casting any time soon, but at least I didn't feel like my head was going to implode.

Aldrich reappeared then, clad in a dark blue dress, with a wide skirt covered in an apron, his long brown hair plaited and styled in circles around his head. He smiled broadly at us as he refilled our coffee. He asked a question, which I caught about one-third of, and Xen wiped their face on a napkin before responding.

He was moving around the kitchen as they spoke. Daria and I ate quietly, not entirely sure what we were meant to be doing. "Yes, *andyttan*," Xen said, rising from the table. They started helping Aldrich clear our plates, giving me a look when I began to do the same. I sank back into my chair and finished the coffee in my cup instead.

Once the kitchen was tidied, Aldrich handed Xen a basket filled with leftover sausages and bread, then walked us to the door. Edda reigned in the two beasts pulling a wagon, like something out of *Little House on the Prairie*, if Pa Ingalls had horses that looked like overly large greyhounds. She grunted and jerked her head toward the bed of the wagon behind her.

"Our host will take us into town," Xen explained. They climbed up first, then offered a hand to each of us. We were barely seated before the wagon lurched forward. Aldrich waved as we pulled out onto the road.

"Quick things to know," Xen said in a hushed tone. "Gender roles are very strict here, and the reverse of what you may be used to. The society is matriarchal; the women control everything from religion to government. I have told them we are from a town many days' journey from here. You must let me speak for us in most situations. There are many ways we may endanger ourselves here."

"No argument from me," I said, rubbing my face.

The road was fairly smooth, though in places the wagon bounced over rocks and potholes filled with water. Now that the sun was fully up, the day was warm and the air thick with humidity. The road was dirt and gravel, passing first through open fields, then as we neared the outskirts of the city, a sluggish river sidled up to the left side of the road, and trees filled the right.

The city was surrounded by a rock wall topped with parapets and punctuated by huge wooden doors that stood open but guarded. The wagon rumbled through the doors and made its way through streets lined with carts, shops, and taverns.

When it stopped, our benefactor said something to Xen and gestured with her chin toward what looked like an inn or tavern with a sign painted in faded yellow featuring a dragon and what looked like Wyld Wyvern for a name. Xen thanked her and drew us toward the doors. Inside, the tavern part of the building was largely empty. There was one woman at a table, laying out tiles with symbols on them, and one woman behind the bar. It was like walking onto the set of an old Western movie.

The bartender nodded at us. "*Canne help êow?*"

Xen glanced at me, then stepped closer. "*Min frig and hir sweostor were uppan by bandits. We seke scead and werk. Mastery Comly lean êow rím agan arstafa.*"

I was definitely thinking that Xen's talents with languages were actually affecting me through our connection because I understood most of that. Either that or my Old English wasn't as rusty as I had thought it was.

The woman behind the bar gave a stiff nod. "*Cannae êow cran mete?*"

Xen nodded. "*Ay bâm til rostian.*"

"*Ay pro fremung weargbr on cycene, ford forth hêdan rýmet yonder. Day wyrht for in wýscan rýmet.*"

"*Aye, dances êow.*"

The woman came out from behind the bar and gestured toward the stairs. We followed her up and down a mezzanine that overlooked the bar, then into a corridor marked by doors. She took a ring of keys from her belt and unlocked a door at the far end, then handed the key to Xen.

The room was small, with a bed that might fit two of us if we didn't mind spooning. Beside the bed was a small table with an oil lamp and a basin with a pitcher. There were a few hooks on the walls for clothes and not much else. Xen thanked our host and waited until she was gone to sigh and close the door.

"This is the only room available," Xen said. "I will work in the kitchen in return for the room."

"We need more than just a roof over our heads." Daria tested the bed and sat with a sigh.

"Do we have anything we can sell?" I asked, joining Daria. "A city this size must have a way we can make money while we figure out where the portal is."

"Do you think you could jump us straight to the portal?" Daria asked.

I shook my head. "I doubt I could jump at all right now, and I saw absolutely nothing as we came through, so I don't think I want to risk it."

Daria nodded. She pulled off my hiking backpack and set it on the bed. I shrugged out of the smaller backpack and did the same. We didn't have a lot, and what we did have would not go over well in a world as backward as this. Daria dumped out her backpack on the bed and I followed suit. Together we sifted through the contents, none of which looked promising.

Daria had filled the large backpack with some food rations, a large first-aid kit, some pictures of Habros and Kota, and various trinkets, none of which promised any great return monetarily.

In the smaller backpack, I also had a few rations, a small amount of first-aid stuff, and our communication devices, which probably wouldn't work there. From the pockets of my vest, I pulled the bag of ward stones, with my mother's necklace inside, xýpna pouch, and the buzzer for Katyk's collar.

Xen pulled something from a pocket. I couldn't see it, but I got a wave of anxiety from them as they examined it, then held out their hand so we could see. It was a dark red stone, faceted so that it caught the light, set in what looked to me like silver.

"That's beautiful, Xen," Daria's voice was soft, reverent.

"It was a gift from Elder Pya, one of my forebears. It comes from our homeworld. It is said the stone was made in the fires of Havek Dor, the volcano that made our world and then destroyed it."

I shook my head. "You can't sell that." My hand moved to the pouch holding the ward stones. I had less attachment to my pendant than Xen's to theirs, and I realized slowly I was still wearing the pendant Daria's friend had given me. Between the two, we should be able to at least pick up some more appropriate clothing for the three of us, if we could find someone interested in buying.

Xen had tears in their eyes but held their head up. "We can not eat this, nor wear it. I will ask the good Mastrey where I might find someone interested."

"Mastrey?" I asked.

Xen nodded. "Yes, I believe that to be the safest title." They repocketed the gem and its chain. "I should get down to the kitchen. You two should probably just stay here, for now."

I raised an eyebrow. "What? Just sit here?"

"You don't speak the language or know the customs."

"We can still walk around," Daria said.

Xen sighed. "Do not be gone long. We know very little about this place."

"All the more reason we should look around," Daria countered, standing.

I shoved the pouch into the pocket of my pants, then our things back into our packs before tucking them under the bed. I shed my vest and untucked my shirt to make my clothing a little less conspicuously foreign.

Daria followed my lead, then we headed out. Xen paused to lock the door, then handed me the key. I pocketed it, and Daria and I headed for the front door while Xen headed toward where I supposed the kitchen was hiding.

We paused outside the door, glancing around to get our bearings. The streets were muddy, though it seemed that under the mud was a packed layer of clay that didn't give way under the hooves of the various pack animals. Across the street from us was a storefront with large glass windows with hats on display and beside that was a store window filled with dresses. Most of them were fairly plain like the one Aldrich had put on before we left, but there were a few fancier ones as well.

Daria pointed up the street and we started in that direction. The mud streets gave way to cobblestone and the buildings seemed newer, cleaner, and a little higher class. Here there were restaurants with painted windows and homes with gables and dormers, painted in colors I thought might have been bright at one time, but the heavy mist that seemed to be the constant state of the weather made them seem dull.

"It feels like London, circa 1880," I muttered, tucking damp hair behind an ear.

"Where?" Daria asked.

I shook my head. "Never mind."

"There's a jewelry store," Daria said, taking my hand and drawing me with her across the street.

The pieces on display in the window showed skill in metalwork, with silver and bronze trinkets with and without gemstones. Daria craned her neck to look further into the store.

"We could just go in," I said, nudging her.

"Do we dare?"

I rolled my eyes at her. "Come on."

I stepped up into the store, which was narrow with a glass-top counter that held the seller's wares. A well-rounded woman with rosy cheeks and a quick smile emerged from behind a curtain, bobbing her head in our direction. "*Goode marn, cannae serve?*"

I smiled and ignored Daria grabbing at my shirt. "*Goode marn*, um …" I exhaled and ran through a hundred responses. "*Doon ye* … um … *buy?*"

"*Nun local?*" The woman chuckled. "*Gese, Ay buy. Cannae see?*"

Daria was tense beside me, but I ignored her and pulled out the bag that held my ward stones, opening it carefully, even as her hand tightened on my elbow. I extracted the pendant, which was precious to me but had less overall sentimentality than Xen's did. Mine was a family heirloom. Theirs was an heirloom to an entire race of people.

If Daria recognized it, she said nothing. It was a heavy pewter and ruby necklace that had belonged to my mother, and her mother before that, back down the Alizon line. The ancient pewter had been cleaned and polished and the ruby in its center was smooth and unfaceted. I set it in the woman's hand, and she nodded appreciatively before reaching under the counter for a soft velvet cloth that she laid on the counter.

She set the pendant on the cloth, then turned behind her, coming back with a pair of glasses with a jeweler's loupe over one eye. She examined the pendant, turning it over and examining the chain, nodding to herself. "*Es go'd. Ay cannae go ye fiftig duckels.*"

I had no idea if that was a good price, but I nodded in agreement, then reached under my shirt and pulled off the other necklace. The shopkeeper took it from me, examining it the same way. "*Ay cannae go ye thiftig duckels.*"

We needed money if we were going to get by. I nodded again. A few moments later, I had a purse full of coins and we left the shop.

"We should make an effort to blend in," I said as we headed back toward our accommodations. Everything about us made us stand out, from the length of our hair to the cut of our clothes.

"We passed a barbershop," Daria said.

"And that clothing store," I added, tucking my newfound wealth into a pocket.

———

Several hours later, both of us sporting new haircuts in styles that would help us blend in and new clothes for ourselves and Xen, we returned to the tavern and our room above it. I had opted for a cut that would minimize the frizz that my hair liked to default to in the humidity we were dealing with.

The barber had cut it back, shorter than I'd worn it since my teens, parted on the right, and slicked down with a pomade that made it both shiny and mostly straight. She had thrown in the pomade as well. Daria had opted for something a little longer, a straight cut at about the level of the bottom of her ear.

I stripped out of the black uniform I'd been wearing since we had left the Vaneeshi army camp and pulled on the trousers I had purchased. They were black also, but lighter weight. Over that, I had a blousy white shirt with tapered sleeves that buttoned at the wrist and a vest that matched the pants in color and fabric. I had a jacket as well: a smart double-breasted number that came to my knees. I kept the boots I'd been wearing and topped the whole thing off with a hat that hit somewhere between a bowler hat and a top hat.

Daria was similarly dressed, though she had opted for a deep brown fabric for the vest and pants, with a jacket that came to the top of her boots.

We had learned a good amount and had figured out communication with most of the people we encountered, though some were admittedly harder than others. The small city we were in, Gavelscore, was ruled over by a governor named Belle MacInster who ruled in the name of the Duchess of Ellover.

Between us, Daria and I had worked out a story that covered for our odd clothing and dialect, though we said as little as possible in that regard. We purported to have journeyed from far away, lands outside of the duchy, and may have implied outside of the country.

Once we were dressed, Daria and I headed downstairs to the tavern, choosing a table near the giant fireplace that was warming the room. A different bartender was on duty, a woman in a striking red suit with a high collar and tie. Like perhaps half of the townsfolk we had encountered, she was dark-skinned, her hair cropped close.

Her smile was bright as she came to us. "*Ye moost eren ûser ednîwe. Bae wel.*"

Daria nodded to me, so I looked up at our hostess. "*Bae wel. Ay de ic Thána. Daet ic Daria. We wolde liketh onlic supper,*" I said, introducing us and asking for dinner. The dialect seemed to be a weird combination of Old and Middle English, with obvious differences due to developing in a completely different culture. My high school and early college fascination were going to serve me well.

"*Goode. Doon ye foreberan stewe or venison?*"

"Stewe," Daria replied.

I nodded. "Stewe."

The bartender nodded to us and disappeared behind a door I assumed led to the kitchen. She reappeared moments later, going to the bar before bringing two glasses containing what looked like beer, somewhere between a lager and a brown ale in color. She put the glasses on our table and went to other customers.

"You seem comfortable here," Daria observed.

"I considered getting my college degree in English Language History." I sipped the beer in my glass and nodded appreciatively. It was nutty and thick, with a subtle caramel flavor on the finish. "I love how languages evolve. I couldn't figure out how that sort of degree would earn me enough to live on though, so I switched over to a management track. The owner of the bookstore I worked in kept me well-stocked in books though."

She raised an eyebrow at me but didn't respond as Xen appeared, an apron over their uniform and two steaming bowls in their hands. They smiled warmly as they set the bowls down. "I see you've been busy. How did you manage?"

"Took your idea," I said, lifting the spoon they set down beside the bowl. "Sold some jewelry. Now you don't have to sell yours."

"What jewelry did you have to sell?" Xen asked.

"Just something that used to be my mother's. I haven't worn it since … well, since Mom and I got to Vaneesh. It was buried down in my backpack.

Nearly forgot I had it. Transferred it into the bag with my stones before we headed for Meerat."

"We got you some clothes too," Daria said.

"I should get back to the kitchen. I should be done soon."

We had a lot left to figure out before we could begin looking for the portal back to Vaneesh. It would be dangerous to go around asking people about a magic portal. I also had not forgotten that somewhere in the world, Katyk was possibly free and probably looking for us.

Daria and I ate, sipped our beer, and watched as people came and went. As I was finishing my beer, a lively card game of some kind was happening at a table near the front, five women in moderate garb drinking and laughing as coins clinked in a pile between them. "I guess some things are the same everywhere," I said.

A young man with dark hair pulled up in a low bun approached us, his dull blue skirt covered with a dirty apron that had once been white. He gestured to our plates, and I nodded, passing them to him. A few moments later, Xen joined us, their eyes skipping around the room before gesturing toward the stairs. Together, the three of us went to our small room, shutting the door as Xen collapsed onto the bed.

"Are you okay?" I asked, sitting next to them, and lifting a hand to rub over their back.

"I will be. Just tired. It has been a long while since I have worked on my feet all day."

Somewhere in my memory, there was knowledge of what Xen had done before the war, something I'd seen during that long night of our bonding. They had been teaching at the University, languages, and Pixila, but prior to that, they had worked as a line cook while attending classes.

"You two seem to have adapted well today," Xen observed, gesturing at Daria's clothing.

"It was her," Daria countered. "You would have been impressed."

Xen grinned at me. "Oh, I am."

"We got you some stuff to help you fit in better." Daria handed over the bag that contained undergarments, two pairs of pants and two shirts, and an apron.

"Great. Thank you." Xen set the bag aside and bent down to untie their boots.

"With any luck, we can find our way home soon," Daria said.

"It may be a while," Xen countered. "From what I have picked up on today, this place is pretty backward."

"We noticed," I said. "So far, we know the local governor's name, the Duchess's name, and that there is a Queen."

Xen nodded. "There is also a city Healdor, or Mayor, and a Steallere, or constable. Big news stories of the day included a dead body they found down by the riverfront—a man who had his stomach sliced open and his genitals removed. And the preparations for the centennial celebrations in a month. Apparently, we'll be expecting a royal visitor."

"I overheard a little something about the dead body," I said. "Speculation is that he was a low-rent body-boy, which I took to be the polite way to say he was a prostitute."

"That was the speculation I heard as well." Xen yawned.

I echoed the yawn, suddenly lulled by the beer and heavy food. It was still early, the world outside our one small window just starting to get dark. "I'll go see if I can get us some extra bedding," I said, standing.

CHAPTER 2
SETTLING IN

I LEFT THEM SORTING OUT ARRANGEMENTS AND HEADED BACK DOWN TO THE tavern, where I ran into the same young man who had cleared our dishes. "*Canne Ay geten ... um ... blankets and a pillow?*"

He looked at me confused, so I put my hands together and set my head on them like they were a pillow.

"*Oh, ya, canne geten. Commen.*"

He led me to a curtained-off doorway, disappearing within, and returning with a stack of blankets and a pillow. "*Dances ěow.*" Before I could return to the room, there was a commotion that came spilling through the tavern doors.

"*Tey âmyltan anooder oon!*"

The speaker was a man who looked to be in his forties, with stringy black hair that hung about an ashen face marked with sores. Almost as one, the women gathered in the tavern got to their feet and bustled outside.

I followed, blankets and pillow held to my chest as I tried my best to see over the crowd that had gathered at the mouth of an alley between two buildings. Women in what I took to be police uniforms were holding the crowd back. "*Deos ys it, Mary?*" someone called out.

"Jackie Barren," one of the policewomen said. "*Te manslaga ynterrupted.*"

The crowd seemed disappointed and began to disperse, allowing me to see into the alley. The man was splayed out in the mud, his skirt hiked up, exposing his partially removed genitals. The chest of his bodice was bright red with blood. I turned away, swallowing against a sudden urge to vomit as I hurried back to Xen and Daria.

"What took so long?" Daria asked as I pushed the door shut behind me. "Are you okay?" she asked when she saw my face.

I was shaking as I handed her the pillow and blankets, shaking my head. "There was another murder, right across the street."

Xen sat up from where they had been nearly asleep in the bed. "Another one?"

I nodded, pulling a hand through my shorter-than-normal hair. "Looked like the killer tried to take off his balls but got interrupted."

"You saw it?" Daria asked incredulously.

"Only a little. He was in the alley." I shivered and put the image out of my head before I sat to take off my boots. Xen was on the side of the bed closest to the wall and Daria was making up a bed on the floor. I stripped out of my new clothes, hanging them on the hook before sliding into the bed in just my underwear and the tank top I'd kept from my uniform.

Despite the early hour, I fell easily into sleep. The day had been long and trying, and I was still recovering from the overuse of my magical abilities. I had also not allowed myself to have any of the remaining xýpna powder. We were dangerously low, and I might need it to get us home.

Thunder woke me in the early hours of the morning. I eased myself up slowly, not wanting to wake Xen or Daria, and pulled on my pants before tiptoeing to the door to find the bathroom. It was little more than a closet with a seat over a hole that looked like it fed into a pipe that flushed the waste out to someplace I didn't care to think about, using a water sluice activated by a rope pull.

I did my business and flushed in the dark, then made my way back to our room. Xen was sitting up when I came in, their outline visible in the light from the moon outside our window. I picked my way around Daria and back to the bed.

"What time is it?" Xen asked, their voice barely a whisper.

"Early," I responded. I knew I was done sleeping and contemplated going downstairs so I didn't wake Daria.

"Let me up?"

I moved so Xen could get up, watching as they dressed as quietly as possible. Like me, Xen chose to keep their boots. Once they were dressed and I had put on my boots, we left Daria asleep on the floor and made our way downstairs.

Xen led me into the kitchen, a square room dominated by a large fireplace, with a prep table made of a good six-inch thick slab of wood, and a white enamel sink set into a wooden counter, the pump set to the right side. It reminded me of a fourth-grade field trip to one of those living history museums.

The air was chilled and I set myself to starting a fire, a task made easier by a hot bed of coals left from the night before. I used the iron poker to stir up the coals, then fed it some kindling from the woodpile, followed by a couple of logs. In a few minutes, I had heat flowing into the room.

Xen lifted a metal rack from beside the fireplace, fitting it into grooves in the walls, creating a cooktop over the fire. I hadn't seen that in any museums I'd been to. "If you want coffee, you will need to work for it," Xen said, a twinkle in their black eyes.

"Oh?" I watched them pull a canister from under a counter and place it on the prep table next to a piece of stone with a groove in the middle. Beside the stone was what looked like a stone rolling pin. I opened the canister to the welcome aroma of coffee. The beans inside were an odd reddish color, but the smell was perfect. "I guess I need to grind them?"

Xen smiled and took a pot to the sink, pumping water into it before taking it to the fire. I took a handful of beans and put them on the stone, lifting the rolling pin. It seemed to be made to specifically fit in the groove. The mechanics of it seemed easy enough. It would be so much easier to use magic, but if I got caught, I didn't know what would happen, so I resorted to manually pushing the rolling pin down onto the beans.

While I crushed beans, Xen moved around the kitchen, pulling together ingredients and tools, and bringing them to the prep table. I paused my grinding to watch as they began piling a dark brown flour on the surface, making a well in it. The eggs they took from a bowl on a counter were larger than chicken eggs, with a vaguely green color, speckled with purple dots. They cracked the eggs into the well.

Xen looked up at me, a question on their face.

I smiled. "Where'd you learn to cook?" I asked, though I knew the answer. I just liked hearing them tell stories of their life. I went back to my work, glancing up as they continued working.

"When I was a child, I was apprenticed to a chef for five years. He was very patient with me and taught me many things."

"As a child?" I asked. For as close as we had become and all of the sharing we'd done during the bonding ritual, there were a lot of things I didn't quite understand about their race and culture.

"You would likely not consider me a child at the time, but Pixin do not age as humans do." Xen had turned the pile of flour into a mound of dough that they were kneading. "We spend five years in each of several disciplines. We all begin with languages with a mentor who translates, either for government or for bookhouses. Then, we choose those things which interest us to learn. I chose cooking, painting, sculpture, and martial arts."

"That's an interesting combination." I lifted the rolling pin to examine my progress. "I think I'm done."

Xen looked over at the grounds and nodded. "Good. Near the sink, you will find a carafe. There is some cheesecloth in the middle drawer." They nodded toward the stack of drawers under the counter behind me. "Put the grounds in the cheesecloth and fold it up like an envelope."

I followed Xen's instructions, thinking I could see where this was going. "And put the grounds in the bottom of the carafe?" I asked. The carafe was ceramic, painted white with purple and blue flowers.

"Yes. Check the water; it should be hot enough."

I went to the fireplace to get the pot of water, carefully pouring it into the carafe.

"Let it steep," Xen said, covering their ball of dough with a towel. They crossed to a door I hadn't seen and opened it, stepping into a spacious pantry, and emerging with two mugs. "Are you hungry?" Xen asked.

I shook my head. "Not really. My stomach's a little unhappy." It wasn't upset exactly, but the thought of food unsettled it. "Maybe after coffee."

"Our benefactor wants me to prepare breakfast for the guests. I am told that other than the three of us, there are five women staying here."

"I would offer to help, but me and the kitchen don't get along."

"I do not mind. I prefer having something to do."

"Yeah, me too." I wasn't good at sitting still. Never had been. "Maybe I should get a job too. If we had some money coming in, we could get a second room."

"Perhaps. You might speak with Mastery Claudette. The coffee is ready to be pressed. The plunger is there." Xen pointed to a stick with a rounded end. "Press the packet of grounds to release the strongest flavors. It is then ready to pour."

I followed their instructions, my mouth watering at the smell of coffee … or whatever this was, then poured some into each mug. I lifted the cup, savoring the smell before taking my first sip. "What do they call this?" I asked.

"Affe," Xen responded.

The door behind me opened and a pale light preceded the entrance of the young man I had met the day before. He was dressed plainly, his dress a dark brown. In one hand he carried a bucket with what looked like milk, and in the other a basket of eggs.

"*Sal morgen*," the boy said.

I moved to help him, taking the eggs, and setting them on the counter by the remaining ones from the day before.

"*Dank êow*, Calder." Xen took the bucket of milk and set it on the counter by the eggs. "*Canne êow getten som hekka?*"

Calder nodded and headed back outside.

"They have a cold room downstairs. It is where they store perishables."

I poured more of the affe into my cup. "I should get out of your way. I'll be out front."

Taking my cup, I headed for the front doors. The city was slowly waking up as I sat on the bench in front of the tavern. Wagons pulled by the horse-like animals were led or driven by women. A woman pulling a cart filled with produce stopped in front of me and hollered something I didn't understand.

Calder did though, appearing with a nervous laugh. The woman pointed to a basket filled with purple and orange carrot-looking things and some white fruits that resembled lemons. Calder took the basket with a sort of bow and scurried back inside.

"*Lasen cú.*" The woman spit the words before putting her hands back on the handles of the cart and moving on.

I sipped my affe and scanned the street. It felt like we had stepped into a movie when we'd fallen through the portal. Across the street, the alley was still blocked off, some barrels and wooden beams blocking the view. There was one uniformed woman standing guard. I wondered if the man who had died there was a body-boy like the one they had found down by the water.

"Hey."

I looked up to find my sister standing beside me. She motioned with her chin toward the cop. "That where it happened?"

I nodded, finishing my cup. My stomach still wasn't happy, and my head had decided it needed to get in on the noise. "Looks like they're keeping everyone out."

"Sounds like they have a problem," Daria said, stretching. "Have you eaten?"

I shook my head. "My stomach is queasy."

She frowned at me. "How's your head?"

I rubbed the back of my head where the pounding felt like it was just getting started. "Loud," I responded. "I just need more caffeine." I stood, then lurched as if the wooden porch beneath my feet had shuddered.

Daria caught me, lifting a hand to my forehead. "You're not feverish."

"If I didn't know better, I'd say I was hungover," I said.

She kept her arm around my shoulder as we went back inside. Someone had gotten a fire started in the main room. I shivered, as if the heat reminded my body that it was cold. Daria took my cup as I sat in a chair near the fire and disappeared into the kitchen. She returned a few moments later with the cup filled.

"How much of the xýpna powder did you use to get us here?" Daria asked, her voice filled with concern.

"Too much," I responded. The affe was warming, and the caffeine was helping, or I wanted to believe it was. "I'll be fine."

"Is there any left?"

"Some." I pulled the pouch out of my pocket and handed it to her.

"There aren't even five doses in here."

"Like I said, too much." I didn't want a lecture. "I'll take it easy today. Tomorrow I'll be fine."

Calder came from the kitchen with two plates that he set in front of us. A slab of that brown bread with a smear of butter was nestled beside a mound of scrambled eggs and a fat sausage that glistened with grease. I was okay until the smell hit me, and that was when my stomach decided to turn over and throw its contents up through my esophagus.

I bolted for the door, doubling over to drop the former contents of my stomach onto their new home: the muddy street. There wasn't all that much there, mostly affe and bile, but my stomach was at least enthusiastic about it. By the time I was done dry heaving, the pain in my head had tripled, my temples pulsing to the tempo of my heart.

Daria's hand rubbed my back as I tried to decide if I wanted to stand up or just sit down right there. I lifted a hand for Daria to help me stand up, wobbling a little as my head spun. "I think it's fair to say this is withdrawal."

"Yes, it is. The next few days are not going to be pleasant for you, I'm afraid." Daria helped me to a chair at an empty table. "I can try to see if I can find ingredients to make you something to take the edge off."

"Too risky," I said. "I'll make do with what we have." I had no experience with withdrawal, aside from whatever some television show or movie might have told me. "I'm going to go upstairs and lay down."

"Do you want me to come with you?" Daria asked.

"Eat your breakfast." I pushed myself to my feet and walked slowly to the stairs.

I could feel Daria watching me and I did my best to not fall on my face before I got to our room. I stripped down to my underwear and tank top and crawled into the bed, dragging the backpack to me so I could rummage through it for the potions that might make a small difference in how I felt. I took a dose of both the pain and nausea potions before laying down to listen to the pounding inside my head.

CHAPTER 3
FAKING IT

I wouldn't say that I slept, but I wasn't doing much more than existing when Daria came into the room. "How are you feeling?"

I pulled a hand across my eyes and groaned a little as I shifted to sit up. "About the same."

"I found an apothecary." She held up a small vial. "This should help a little. Put a drop of that under your tongue."

Daria handed me the vial and I opened it carefully, recoiling at the smell. "Seriously?"

"Sorry, best I could do given the circumstances. However, I did convince the apothecary to give me a job. We need to function until we can find our way back to the portal."

I used the dropper in the vial to place a drop under my tongue. It tasted as bad as it smelled. "How did you manage the language?"

She chuckled. "I faked it as best I could. There's enough English in the mix I can get the gist. Besides, science is its own language. She understood that easily enough."

"I was thinking I should find something too. Get us out of this one-room situation. I'm just not sure what that would be. My skillset doesn't exactly work well here."

"Let's get you back on your feet before you worry about it. How are you feeling now?"

I thought about it. The headache had been dialed back but wasn't gone, and my stomach was making noises that sounded vaguely like hunger. "Better, I think."

She nodded. "Good. One drop every two hours or so, and we'll see if that doesn't get you over the worst of it. I should go. I told my new boss I'd be back once I'd delivered this to you. If you feel up to it, Xen's got some broth and tea ready for you."

I watched her leave and debated whether I was up to attempting to go downstairs and decided that I needed to get something in my stomach. I dressed and headed down. Half the tables in the tavern held several women enjoying lunch and talking. I headed for an empty table and took a seat, my eyes scanning the room to get an idea of who these women were.

Calder appeared with dishes that he served to one of the tables. He smiled when he saw me and came to my table. "*Ora êow myne su booter?*"

I nodded. "*Canne êow telle Xen, Ay want sôm rop?*" I struggled with the exact words but figured it was close enough for him to figure out.

He scampered away and I let myself contemplate the people in the room. It was early afternoon, so I assumed these women had come for lunch. The table nearest me held a tall dark-skinned woman with striking blue eyes. She wore nice clothes, though they weren't new. There was some raggedness at the hems of her pants, and I saw signs of a patch on one knee. Her hair was cut close and slicked down, much like many of the others within the range of my eyes.

Beside her was a younger version of her, though I couldn't be sure if that meant daughter or sister. Rounding out their table was a larger woman in newer clothes with gray hair and a laugh like a raven's caw.

Nearer to the bar was a table of two who sat close together and kept their heads down and their voices low. They felt my eyes and looked up, scowling at me. I looked elsewhere.

Xen appeared then, setting a bowl of a rich broth on the table for me, followed by a cup of tea. "You okay?" Xen asked, concern in their voice.

I nodded. "Yeah, I'm fine. Thanks."

"I was worried."

I brushed their hand, then pulled back. I had no idea how public displays of affection would play here. "Just a little xýpna withdrawal. I'll get over it."

Xen went back to the kitchen, and I turned my attention to my broth. It was deep brown and smelled vaguely like beef. I took a sip and decided it also tasted like beef. I waited to see what my stomach would do and when it didn't flip over, I settled in to drink my tea and broth.

"*Not verray gêbed.*"

I looked up to find a woman in the uniform of the city's police force. I couldn't remember the words I needed so I resorted to pantomime and English. "Queasy stomach."

"*Steallere Brooklane. Ay wolde liket to ask êow a fewe acsungs.*"

I gestured for her to join me. She sat across from me and folded her hands on the table, looking me up and down. "*Êow nun local?*"

I shook my head. "*Non, mîn sweostor and mîn ...*" I didn't know how to describe Xen. "*Mîn frêond are,* um, traveling."

"*Thither did êower come?*"

"Um, south? That way." I pointed and she turned to look. I don't think she understood me. I tried to think of a town name that would fit this culture but was failing. "Inkshire," I finally said, gesturing vaguely again in the direction we had come from.

"*For hwon êow come?*" She was eyeing me suspiciously.

I thought she was asking me why we were there. I wasn't sure how to answer her. "*We seke werk.*"

"*Êow saw mord anihst niht?*"

I shook my head. "*Non. Ay âwihte heard te noise.*" I touched my ear to make up for my inability to work out words. It had been a long time since I had broken off my love affair with Old English and most of what I had retained were common words.

The constable nodded and stood. "*Bêo foreglêaw.*" She looked me over before leaving.

"*Wot was de uppan?*" The woman speaking had dark red hair and she was dressed in dusty brown clothes that reminded me of an old west gunslinger. She sat without being invited and I raised an eyebrow.

"*Non, jus âscung.*"

She kicked one dirty boot-covered foot up onto the chair next to me. "*Pucian dôcincel de oon. Ay* Anne Gothfried." She leaned forward and held out her hand.

I met her hand with mine and was rewarded with a firm shake. "Thána Alizon."

"I thought I heard you speaking my language."

I nearly dropped my spoon and had to swallow quickly to not choke on the broth in my mouth. "I beg your pardon?"

She grinned wickedly. "That's what I thought." She had a vaguely Australian-sounding accent, and her English was good. "Crazy, this place, right?"

I blinked at her, trying to decide how open to be with her. "I—how long have you been here?"

She shrugged. "A good few years. Got lost in a cave, fell through a hole, and landed here. Broke my leg. By the time I'd found help, I'd completely lost track of where I'd started."

The small hope that had flared with the knowledge that she had come from elsewhere and might know the way out died. I finished my broth and pulled my tea close. "I know how that is," I said neutrally. "Our story is similar."

"Figured as much. How long have you been here?"

"Just a few days. We're trying to figure out what to do next."

She nodded. "Sure. A few things you should know." She leaned toward me conspiratorially. "Keep a low profile. Stay this side of the river; there's a plague sweeping the slums. Stay off the streets once the sun goes down, especially in this part of town. There's a killer or two hunting the nights."

I nodded at that. "The body in the river and the one in the alley."

She sat back again. "Oh, aye, but there's those no one talks about too. High society girl cut up something awful a month ago, up northside of town. And a cousin of Steallere Brooklane's a few weeks ago. In their own bedrooms."

"Do they have any suspects?" I asked.

Anne raised an eyebrow at me. "Well, she did just ask you some questions."

"Is that why? She thinks we had something to do with this?" I shook my head. "We haven't been here long enough."

"You think that will matter if she decides you did it? Justice here doesn't have a very true aim. So, watch your step."

"Thanks, I will."

I was even more unsettled than I had been before she sat down. Calder came to take my empty bowl, nodding in respect to both Anne and myself before he headed back to the kitchen.

"At least they got that part right," Anne said, putting her feet back on the floor and standing. "Men in their rightful place, I mean." She chuckled. "If you're around later, I aim to have a card game going. I'll teach you how to play."

She sauntered away, nodding greetings as she passed people, and disappeared out the door.

I sat back with my tea, and let my thoughts wander through our conversation. I felt better, enough that I thought a walk might feel good. I wasn't sure when I'd become the person who went for a walk on purpose, but in the time since I had left California, I had been forced into doing a lot of walking. In fact, I had discovered that too much sitting still made me nervous.

I finished my tea and stood, determined to walk down to the river and try to get a better idea of the city's layout. It was bigger than I had at first understood. We were in one of the less advantaged parts of town but by no means the poorest. That honor went to the shantytown across the river, which flowed through the city's western side, cutting off the slum from the rest. There was one bridge that was barely large enough for a wagon or cart.

I made my way through the streets, trying to commit the layout of buildings to memory as I went. The inn and tavern we were currently calling home sat on one of three main arteries leading into the city. It ran right to the river before turning north. Daria and I had done some exploring but had stayed within a few blocks of the Wyvern.

I followed the muddy street, past a number of saloons and taverns, plus a few stores of various kinds. They gave way to boarding houses, which then gave way to what looked to be row houses, narrowly stacked side by side, punctuated with small alleys every five or so houses. The street here was not as muddy, due to a good layer of gravel. The houses to my left stopped as I reached the river. The water was murky and green, the current sluggish.

The river here was narrow and throttled with reeds of some kind. Further south I could see the city walls, with a large metal gate across the river, its bars sinking beneath the surface. The bridge was a few yards north from where I stopped to look across at the ramshackle buildings that reminded me of some of the slums I'd seen in third-world countries in movies and television shows. Built haphazardly from a mix of building materials, the whole place looked like it would go down in a strong wind, and a smelly smoke seemed to permeate the place, slinking low along the ground and slipping down to congregate in the reeds.

My curiosity was at war with my common sense. Anne had told me that the place was infected with some kind of plague, and that was not something I needed to mess with. As I got closer to the bridge, I saw that crossing it was probably not going to be possible anyway. There was a wooden wall smack in the middle of the span, with a door and a guard in elegant livery bearing a purple heart behind a black stag.

Seeing that I couldn't go that way, I turned instead to the north, wandering up the road a ways. It followed the river, and the homes became nicer, the paint fresher and cleaner. Trees crowded the bank on the other side for a while, thick with undergrowth and full of leaves. Further up I could see another bridge and beyond that a manor house of the grandest kind. Like the city, it was walled in, with gates standing open just beyond the bridge. I assumed that was where the town's Healdor lived. She was apparently related to the Duchess and appointed by her to oversee the city. I guessed democracy hadn't been invented there yet.

My head was starting to remind me that I was still going through withdrawal. I pulled the vial of medicine Daria had made for me from a pocket and dropped some under my tongue. Crossing the street where the bridge met the second major road through town, I found the streets were paved in cobblestones of a faintly pinkish hue.

The people here were more finely dressed, and the houses were opulent and large. Animals pulled fancy carriages more than wagons here, with women dressed like Victorian dandies with men on their arms, decked out in beautiful gowns. The men all seemed to have longer hair, pinned up in various artful styles.

It was like I had stumbled into a gender-bent Charles Dickens novel or something. I ambled down the street, finding a grand hotel with a large veranda and a restaurant from which I could smell fresh bread and meat cooking. There were bakeries and stores selling clothing, jewelry, fabulous hats, and more. The scent of something sweet filled the air and as I turned the corner, I found a candy shop with children gathered around the front window, watching a man inside pulling taffy.

I paused there for a moment, mesmerized the same as the children by the soothing and rhythmic movement of the candy looping and stretching. I knew it wasn't so soothing to the guy tasked with the job. I'd tried it once with a friend. I never took taffy for granted ever again. My arms ached for days.

At the next major street crossing, I turned back toward the side of town I'd come from. That was when I found the theater with signs declaring two sold-out shows of some sort of musical or opera. I didn't understand all of the words, so I couldn't be sure. There were several pubs or taverns in the area and some quick food carts with pastries and fruits on display.

My stomach rumbled, as if to remind me that all I had given it so far was broth, so I ambled over to the cart nearest me, nodding my greeting to the woman running it. I picked out what looked like a pear and handed her a coin from my pocket. It was probably worth more than the fruit was. I hadn't figured out their monetary system just yet.

I polished the pear on my pants as I continued my slow walk, then bit into it. The yellow-green skin gave way to a soft yellow flesh that tasted like a pear and an orange had a baby, a little sweet for my tastes, but good. I ate while I walked. The cobblestone gave way to gravel and that to mud, bringing me back to the street I had started on.

The apothecary sat on one side and across from it was a dry goods store with barrels of spices and displays of canned beans and the like. The afternoon was starting to chill and dark clouds were moving closer. I decided it would be good to head back to our room before I got drenched.

I made the turn and froze, certain I had just seen Katyk. My eyes scanned the faces in the area where I thought I had seen her, but I found no trace of her red hair or mahogany skin, just the regular city folk going on about their business.

CHAPTER 4
WITHDRAWAL

As I started back toward the inn, I heard a commotion behind me, from near the bridge over to the shantytown. A crowd was gathering, and voices were raised. Instinctively, I turned and moved closer. People had formed a circle around a young man. He couldn't have been even seventeen, rail-thin, and dressed in rags. He cowered from them, hands raised to protect his head as they screamed at him, calling him *haêg* and *wytch*. They were throwing things at him: small stones and produce.

The Steallere and several of her officers broke through the circle and shouted the crowd down. "*Wot hath sê doon?*" Steallere Brooklane asked the crowd as two of her officers grabbed the boy's arms.

"*Sê corse mîn dohter, Steallere,*" a woman said, pulling a young girl forward. The girl had a rash of some kind on her face. "*Lôc whot sê doon.*"

The crowd roared. The woman held out a cloth doll with straw for hair. "*Sê wîcan hera dês.*" She threw the doll at the boy's feet and spit on it.

"*Doth êow denie?*" the Steallere asked.

"*Ay am no haêg.*" The boy was shaking, his fingers fisting in the dirty cloth of his skirt. Under the skirt I could see he was barefoot, his toes squishing in the mud.

"*Hâftan hêo,*" the Steallere said to her officers, telling them to take the boy.

The crowd parted to let them through, dragging the still protesting boy away. One of the officers dropped a cloth over the doll and picked it up, taking it with her. The mother was still there, holding her daughter's hand as the crowd dispersed.

I stepped closer, holding up both hands. "*Forgefan, Mastery.*"

She looked at me with suspicion in her eyes. I smiled, angling to get a closer look at the rash. It reminded me of poison oak. "*Menen Ay sêo?*"

"*Are êow a l'âce?*"

I squatted down by the girl, using a hand on her chin to turn her face. I wasn't sure what the word meant but nodded a little. "*Doth it itch ... um, ôman?*"

The little girl nodded.

I stood and gestured to the apothecary. I took the girl's hand and led them into the storefront, which was pristine white inside, with shelves lined with bottles and jars. A woman in her fifties or so looked up as we came in. She came out from behind the counter, and I caught a glimpse of Daria in the back.

She stood and followed her boss out. The mother and the apothecary spoke while I turned to Daria. "It looks like a reaction to a poisonous plant. If she leaves it alone, it should go away, but it itches, so she'll keep scratching and spread it."

Daria nodded, looking the rash over.

"I don't sense anything wrong with her, so it's nothing internal," I said as softly as I could.

"Mastery, Ay 'ave ..." Daria shook her head and instead went to a shelf, retrieving a jar of ointment. She knelt beside the girl and opened the jar, sticking her finger in, then rubbing the ointment onto the rash.

The girl's eyes widened as the itching lessened. "Mama!"

Daria stood, handing the ointment to the mother before drawing me away. "That was a bit reckless."

"They're going to kill that kid and he did nothing but make the girl a doll," I said.

"And there is nothing you can do about it." Daria countered, her eyes flashing at me.

"I know. I know." I did know, but that didn't mean I wasn't going to worry about it.

The mother and daughter left after paying the apothecary.

"*L'âcedôm Gilder, mín sweostor, Thána,*" Daria said, introducing me to her boss.

The apothecary smiled and nodded. "*Êower môdwelig. Êow efne l'âce?*"

I was pretty sure she was asking me if I was a healer of some kind. Daria had used a related word as the woman's title, so I shook my head. "*Ay wiste âdlung, Ay knowe ...*" I fumbled over the words, scrambling through my decidedly limited recall of vocabulary I had known well in another life. "*Ay knowe lîchama?*" I gestured at my body, swiping my hand down my torso.

The apothecary nodded. "*Goode. Êow shold hycgan. Limpan l'âce.*"

I had no idea what most of those words were, but I figured I could ask Xen that evening. "I should go." I turned to leave, but as I got to the door, Daria called my name.

She took off the apron she'd been wearing and said goodbye to her boss, joining me at the door.

"Feeling better?" she asked as we headed back to the tavern.

"I was, but I'm getting queasy again."

The skies had gotten very dark and heavy with clouds. "Looks like we're in for a storm," Daria said as lightning cracked the sky and thunder shook the ground.

"I'll say." We hastened our pace, reaching the tavern door just as the rain began coming down. We dashed through the door to find the tavern full, a fire roaring in the fireplace, and music playing from an instrument I hadn't noticed before in the corner. It was not unlike a piano, smaller with a tinny quality to the sound. I pointed to the only empty table, the one near the door to the kitchen. We sat, looking up as Calder set two glasses of brown beer on the table.

"*Goode evnyng. Canne getten mete?*"

"*Yea, Calder, dance êow*," I thanked him.

"Little rowdy in here," Daria said, her eyes sweeping the room.

I turned my chair so that I could do the same, spotting Anne at one of the tables, one hand wrapped around a mug, the other holding cards. In front of her was a pile of coins. She must have felt my eyes and turned to wink in my direction.

"Who is that?" Daria asked.

I shook my head a little. "Her name is Anne ... something. I met her earlier. She isn't local either, if you take my meaning." I looked up as Calder set plates down. There was a pile of some mashed vegetables with a yellow-orange color to it, drizzled with a rich-looking gravy. Beside that was a hunk of dark meat and a piece of heavily buttered bread.

I paused to drop some of the medicine into my mouth, hoping that it would be enough to prevent a repeat of the morning. Once it absorbed into me, I turned to my plate. The meat reminded me of lamb. Daria and I ate quietly until Anne came across the room to our table.

"Heard you played doctor today," she said as a way of greeting. She sat in the empty chair between me and Daria.

"The girl had poison oak or something," I replied.

Daria cleared her throat.

"Anne, my sister Daria."

"Ah yes, the apothecary's new assistant." Anne nodded at Daria but kept her focus on me. "Maybe the two of you need to open up your own shop; lots of folks need doctoring around here."

Daria snorted and picked up her beer. "Yeah, that would go over well."

Anne turned to look her over. "Bet you could do some good."

"And what good do you do?" Daria asked, pinning Anne with dark eyes.

"Me?" Anne grinned and sat back. "I gamble some, drink a lot, and dabble in trade, mostly in the ingredients trade ... spices, herbs, exotic medicinals."

Something about the way she said medicinals gave me the impression that she meant more than aspirin. She leaned in toward me, glancing around to make sure no one was close by. "Watch your back." She nodded toward the door, where the Steallere and two of her officers stood. Anne slapped the table and stood, moving back to her game.

"That was cryptic," Daria said.

"Not so much," I countered, putting on a smile as the cops came to us. "*Evnyng, Steallere,*" I said with a smile. "*Canne joyn ûs?*"

"*No, dance êow. Wot doth êow witen aboot sê haeg?*"

I frowned up at her. "Nothing. Um, *nâht.*"

"*Êow stîd sê childe.*" Her face was stern as she looked down at me.

"*Aye, Steallere,*" I agreed. I had helped the kid. "*Hîe was âwihte a ... um rash?*" I looked to Daria who shrugged. "From a plant. Probably the stuff he used to make the hair." Of course, she wasn't going to understand any of that. "*Hîe doll haer.*" I touched my own hair. "*Loc at the cniht's hands. Sê willa same.*"

"Plague?"

I shook my head. "No, Steallere. *Hîe reaction.*"

Her eyes narrowed at me and for the longest moment she just stared, then she turned on her heel and stalked off.

"Remind me again how it is you know what they're saying?" Daria said, pushing her nearly empty plate away.

"It's very similar to Old English, which I studied in college. Clearly, I'm not fluent. Most of the materials I had to study were written records. It was a dead language at the time. My former professor would go nuts here, getting to hear it spoken."

"You need to be careful though. I didn't understand most of those words, but I know she was accusing you of something."

I shook my head. "Not really. She asked about the girl with the rash. I told her it was a reaction, and to check the boy's hands. He probably has the same rash."

"They'll still call him a witch though," Daria said with a sigh. "And they'll probably execute him."

She was probably right. I echoed her sigh. There was nothing we could do about it, no matter how much I hated it. My dinner, what little I'd eaten, was roiling around in my stomach like it wanted to escape, and my head was starting to pound again. I took another dose of Daria's medicine and sagged in my chair.

"You're not looking so great," Daria said, reaching across to lay the back of her hand against my cheek. "Maybe you should go lay down."

I nodded, but fatigue flushed through me, and getting up seemed like too much work. Daria stood and helped me up, her arm slung around my waist to support me as we made our way to the stairs. Getting up the stairs was slow and difficult, my limbs too heavy and my breath short. By the time we got to the room, I was sweating, and my head was pounding.

Daria helped me out of my clothes, which was to say that she undressed me because my arms were a hundred pounds each, and I couldn't lift them. I was shivering as Daria tucked me into bed. "Thána, I need you to open your eyes."

I hadn't realized I had closed them, but I blinked a few times and managed to look at her. She was holding a flask from the first-aid kit. "That's it. Just a little bit of this." She tilted the flask to my lips and spilled a lukewarm liquid into my mouth. I swallowed both the liquid and the sudden surge of wanting to throw up. "I was afraid of this."

Daria petted over my head and I wanted to ask what she was afraid of but couldn't make the words come out of my mouth.

The next twenty-four hours were brutal. My fever soared, then dropped drastically. I tossed fitfully on the bed, in turns drenched in sweat and shivering. Daria and Xen took shifts sitting with me, wiping me down with cool water, and administering various potions and mixtures in an effort to abate the symptoms of my withdrawal. I became aware of babbling at one point, then that the voice was my own. I had no idea what I was saying.

When I did sleep, I was beset with dreams of Katyk stalking me through the muddy streets and Artoz with his weapons of cruelty. There were moments when I felt like I once again was flooded with that hallucinogen, and the shadows became monsters bent on mutilating me.

My first clear thought was thirst. My tongue stuck to my teeth and swallowing was difficult, I was so dry. I opened my eyes to the dim light of almost morning. Xen and Daria were both asleep on the floor. I imagine I had thrashed around enough that sharing a bed with me was unpleasant. There was a cup on the table by the bed and I lifted it, hoping for water.

I wasn't disappointed. I drained the cup before I sat up fully, then scrubbed my hands over my face. I was wrung out, and I could smell myself. Right at that moment, I would have killed for a hot shower, but I was going to have to make do with a washcloth and the lukewarm water in the pitcher. My legs felt like rubber as I attempted to stand, so I kept one hand on the table to stabilize myself. Someone had filled the pitcher, so I didn't have to go looking for water.

I was nearly done washing my body of sweat when I felt Xen stirring. Warm hands slid over my skin as Xen hugged me back against their body. "Better today?"

I nodded, letting the comfort of familiar hands ground me. "Much."

"Good, you had us worried."

"Still have a bit of a headache, but I think I'm past the worst of it." My stomach chose that moment to growl loudly, making me smile. "Hungry, I guess."

Xen pressed a kiss to my neck. "I can fix that." They turned to get dressed and I followed suit.

Daria sat up just as I finished tying my boots. "You look better."

"Thanks to the two of you." I reached for Xen as I stood, my knees still wobbly. "I need some caffeine and some food."

"Go on. I'll be down in a bit."

Xen let me lean on them as we made our way slowly down to the kitchen. They pulled a stool in from the bar to let me sit by the prep table before they got started putting water on to boil for the affe and making the morning's bread.

"There was another murder yesterday," Xen said after a bit. "They're trying to keep it hushed up, but I heard that it was the daughter of a judge."

"Not likely the same person murdering body-boys then." I set myself the task of pounding the affe beans while they kneaded the bread. "Anne mentioned something about two other young women having been killed."

"Gossip says they are looking for a man of some means who perhaps was rejected by the girl."

"Wouldn't be the first time," I muttered. "What else did I miss?"

"It was pretty quiet otherwise." Xen worked quietly, setting the bread aside to rise, and pressing the affe before starting on the thick local porridge. "Though it is said that the plague has crossed the river. "

"That isn't good."

"Aye, I am still not certain what kind of illness it is, but it would appear to be plenty contagious."

Daria joined us as Xen poured affe, yawning and stretching. She came to me, turning my face and examining my eyes, then checking my temperature with her hands. "From now on, when I tell you to be careful, I expect you to listen."

"Yes, *Mom*."

She rolled her eyes and picked up her mug of affe. "Today is the holy day here. If you're feeling up to it, I was thinking it would a good day to explore a little, since neither Xen nor I are working."

"I think I can manage," I replied. "Once I've had some food and affe."

"We will go slowly," Xen said, one hand caressing mine.

CHAPTER 5
PLAGUE

THE STREETS WERE LARGELY EMPTY AS WE MADE OUR WAY FROM THE TAVERN. Here and there we saw people tending to mundane things, but the doors to the shops were all closed, and their windows shuttered. Our primary goal was finding the portal, but none of us had a clue how to go about it. It certainly wasn't safe to ask around.

None of us had any real desire to participate in a religion we probably wouldn't understand either. That left us to get to know the city we found ourselves stranded in. I led Xen and Daria down to the bridge to the shantytown, which I was surprised to see was open, though still guarded.

On our side of the bridge, there was a small group of men gathered, wearing black dresses covered with red aprons, their faces covered with red cloth, and heads covered in something akin to a nun's wimple. They were gathering supplies out of a cart: baskets filled with bread and other foods, plus what I took to be medical supplies.

They formed up into two lines of two in front of the gate on the bridge. A tired-looking woman joined them, her clothes the same somber black with a crimson collar. Her hair was buzzed close to the scalp and her hands were covered in black gloves. She lifted a mask in the same crimson, tying it over her nose and mouth before moving to the head of the column. At some signal I didn't see, they began walking, each nodding in greeting to the guard who stood holding the gate open.

"That's the poor side of town," I said softly. "Whatever this plague is, they've got it the worst."

"That's how it always is," Daria said. "Any idea what the symptoms are?"

I shook my head. "Not yet."

"Calder spoke of it," Xen offered as we stood watching. "Upper respiratory, with added boils that weep blood."

"How contagious is it?" Daria asked.

"It is uncertain. Thus, they keep the ill sequestered."

"The sanitary conditions around here can't be helping." I stepped off the wooden sidewalk, and Daria's hand stopped me.

"No."

I frowned at her, unsure what she meant. "No?"

"You are not going over there."

"I wasn't planning on it."

She raised an eyebrow at me. "You're not thinking about finding out if it is something you can heal?"

I rolled my eyes. "Well, the thought had occurred to me, yes, but I'm in no hurry to get locked up as a witch."

"Good. Keep it that way."

We resumed our walk, up toward the second bridge. "The home of the local nobility, I take it?" Daria asked.

"Seems a logical assumption, yes," Xen replied.

"This was as far as I went the other day," I said. "Then I went that way, and back to the inn."

"Did you find the church?" Daria asked as we continued past the bridge, following the street where it skirted along the river.

"No, but I wasn't really looking either," I replied. The homes along the street were more stately here than I had seen elsewhere.

"I am told that the square in front of the church is where they will hang that unfortunate boy," Xen said as we turned onto a street lined with gorgeous homes and stately gardens.

"Hang?" I shuddered. There were certainly worse ways to die, but the idea of public executions made me uncomfortable. "During the witch hunts where I come from, there were some hangings, but they also burned convicted witches." That was one way I did not want to go. The thought was rather terrifying.

"Barbaric," Daria said, shaking her head.

We came to a place where the street widened, then opened up into a public plaza of sorts. A large cathedral-style building dominated the northern side, while a hulking sort of pre-industrial monolith of a structure sat in the east. It was built of gray stone, with mammoth pillars holding up a portico and wide stairs that led down to the square. In the corner of the square between the two was a thick pole with crossbeams ten feet up, large enough to hang two people side by side on each end of the beams.

As we moved closer, however, I could see that hanging wasn't the only thing it was used for. It also seemed to serve a similar purpose to what a stockade would have been back home. Two young men were chained to it, sitting with their backs to the pole, arms chained above their heads, their feet locked down in shackles to the paving stones beneath them. Beside them, guards in a deep purple livery stood watch, with spears in hand and swords on their belts.

"What do you suppose their crime was?" Daria asked.

"I don't know about the guy on the left, but the kid on the right is the one they arrested the other day," I replied, my eyes skipping back to the church. It was an impressive building, with a gorgeous stained-glass window above the main doors, an octagon of colored glass that rivaled any of those I'd seen in the European cathedrals. "I wonder what their religion is like," I mused aloud as we paused to take in the enormity of the building.

"We could go in and find out," Xen teased, knowing I would definitely not want to do that.

"I think not." My eyes were drawn to the gray building where a door had opened and the Steallere was now standing, her eyes on us. "Perhaps we should continue walking," I said, smiling at the cop as I turned us toward one of the roads out of the square.

"Problem?" Xen asked once we were a few blocks down.

"She doesn't appear to like me," I responded. And considering that she could throw any of us in jail for any slight, it was best to keep on the right side of the Steallere and her officers. We meandered for a while through residential streets and shops. "Is that actually an alchemist's shop?" I asked as we stopped on the gravel street across from a blacksmith.

"Alchemy?" Daria asked.

I nodded, scanning the sign to be sure of what I was reading. "They condemn magic but believe in alchemy. That's rich."

"Are you going to explain what alchemy is?" Daria asked.

I sighed a little. "Depends on who you ask, I guess. It was a sort of pseudo-science back in a similar time period back home. Part medicinal science, part mad science. Some said they were the precursor to actual science. They got some stuff right, but a lot very wrong. One of their goals was to turn lead into gold."

I'd only done a cursory study on alchemy, as a bit of source material in my study of the language included alchemy texts. I was in it more for the language than the alchemy.

A few doors down there was a sign that I thought meant doctor. "L'âce means doctor, right?" I asked Xen.

"Roughly, though it can be used for anyone in the healing arts."

We took another turn and found ourselves back to the main street that would take us back to the inn, up near the tightly packed houses of the poorer families, just not poor enough to be pushed over the river.

Daria touched my arm and we stopped. A woman was weeping loudly outside a door where another woman in black was painting a red X on the door. "What do you think that means?"

"Nothing good," I responded.

"Plague," Xen breathed, drawing us away.

"Is she a doctor, do you think?" Daria asked.

The weeping woman seemed to be begging the doctor for something, but we weren't close enough to hear.

"Nân menen timbrân. Hêr bae wîte." The doctor shook her head and began walking away. This only increased the other woman's wailing.

"Poor thing."

I jumped at the words, surprised to find Anne beside me. "You startled me," I said almost defensively.

Anne smirked, but her attention was still on the woman. "Her daughter took ill yesterday. Looks like the plague has jumped the river. Things are going to get dicey around here. You three might want to think about moving on to another town."

"Where would you suggest?" I asked, watching the woman break down.

"Anywhere but here," Anne said. "If you don't get sick, you might end up a victim of one of these killers. And if you escape those, you might end up branded a witch. Any of those three gets you dead. Me, I'm heading north, I think. There's a sweet little fella in a place called Eveshire I took a shine to. Maybe I'll settle down for a while."

I chuckled. "You don't seem like the settling kind, Anne."

She shrugged. "First time for everything." She sauntered off with the tip of her top hat. The woman's wails were tearing at me, and I wanted nothing more than to go comfort her.

I hadn't even realized I had started moving until I felt Daria's hand on my arm. "Don't."

"Listen to her," I countered. "Maybe I can help."

"Do you think you could?" Xen asked. "Without showing yourself to have magic?"

"I don't know," I said. "It depends on what the plague is. And how far along it is. And whether or not my body can handle it."

"What are you going to do?" Daria demanded. "Go over there and ask her to let you in? What are you going to say is your reason?"

I did have an idea, but it was still risky. "I'll tell her that I am a doctor and that where we are from, I have successfully treated this disease."

Daria didn't look convinced, but I took Xen by the arm, and we crossed to the woman. I let Xen do the talking, watching the woman's face move from despair to hope. When she nodded, I reached for the door handle, then turned to Xen. "You should probably stay out here."

Xen looked like they wanted to argue, but nodded, moving instead to comfort the mother. I exhaled slowly and entered the home. It was dark and narrow and filled with the scent of death—not that anyone who wasn't a blood witch would smell it yet. Soon though, there would be no nose that wouldn't know that death had visited this home.

I followed the scent back past the common area, with its crowded kitchen, into an even darker room. On the bed, a small child lay. She couldn't have been but five or six. Her tiny face glistened with sweat from the fever that filled her. Two small boils sat on one cheek, and I could see a larger one on her arm. I moved closer and knelt beside the bed, lifting one hand to lay on her stomach. Her breathing was shallow, and I could feel the asthmatic wheeze in her chest.

She tossed a little in the grip of her nightmares. This was not unlike the illness I had saved Daria from all of those years ago. I was pretty sure I could heal her. I lifted myself up so that I could lean over her, put two fingers on her chin to open her mouth, and pressed my lips to hers.

The disease came easily, almost willingly, and I swallowed it down but stopped before it was completely gone. I couldn't perform miracles without giving myself away. I would go and have Daria compound a potion and mix a healthy dose of my blood into it. That would bring the girl the rest of the way.

I brushed a hand across her brow and she opened her eyes. They were a sharp green. "*Êow getten betera. Slêpte.*" I stood with a slight smile and found my way back out of the house. "Tell her to keep the girl in bed, and I will return tomorrow with medicine."

Xen nodded and translated. The woman started thanking me, but I sidestepped the embrace she tried to give. "No one should touch me until I've shed this," I said softly to Xen. "And we need her to quiet down before she draws a crowd."

Xen did what they could to calm the woman and get her to remain still while I joined Daria. "Well?"

"The girl will live," I answered. We started walking and Xen joined us. "It is a nasty little bug though. And I didn't heal her completely, just took the worst of it. I'll need you to make a cough syrup and we'll add some of my blood to it. That should finish the healing."

"That was a little reckless," Daria said, shaking her head.

I didn't disagree. "It was a lot reckless," I admitted. "I couldn't stand that woman's pain." I rubbed my forehead. "Damn, this is hitting hard." I could feel myself sweating and I was already starting to bleed as my body fought to rid itself of the disease.

We quickened our pace and as soon as we made it back to the inn, I ran up the stairs and into the closet with the not-quite-a-toilet. As I sat, my body heaved, and I was glad I'd made it before I'd started this on the street.

I wasn't sure how long I sat there, but Xen knocked on the door to ask if I was okay and to bring me a clean pair of pants, along with a folded rectangle of absorbent cloth and a damp cloth. I got cleaned up and changed my pants before emerging. "That was fun." I would continue to bleed for at least a few hours, but the worst of it had passed, and the makeshift pad would absorb the rest.

Xen smiled at me, taking the pants and bloody cloth from me. "I will do some laundry and make us some food. Daria is downstairs, so if you would like to rest, the room will be quiet."

"Thanks." I did want to rest. The disease was more virulent than I had anticipated. Nothing a good antibiotic wouldn't cure, but I was assuming these people had not yet invented penicillin.

I let myself into our room and lay down, wishing I had somehow managed to keep any of my books or even my notes. Most were back at Merry's place, and the rest were in Meerat at Daria's. It probably wouldn't have been wise to have them there anyway, on the off chance that someone could read them. Still, I needed to keep track of how I used my gifts and what the results were. With very little surviving literature on the subject of blood witches, it seemed prudent to document my journey of learning how to use that magic.

I knew Daria didn't want me doing anything that would put us in danger, and I agreed with that in principle, but knowing I had the capacity to heal someone and not doing anything felt like a betrayal of who I was. I was just going to have to carefully wing it and hope for the best.

There was a time when I planned everything, but that seemed as far away as that house in California.

CHAPTER 6
WINGING IT

I followed Daria to work the next day, greeting her boss with a smile and a nod before following Daria to the back of the shop. The lab was clean and filled with familiar equipment. Daria set about collecting the needed ingredients and mixing them together before setting the beaker over a small flame to heat it and melt the sugar that would make the syrup palatable.

Once it cooled, Daria went out into the front to make sure her boss was distracted and wouldn't see what I did next. We had debated over how much blood to use and came to a compromise that I hoped would work. I pricked a finger with the tip of the knife she'd used to cut herbs and held the wound over the beaker, dropping ten good drops in before sucking on the finger and swirling the syrup. It took on a pinkish-red hue as I mixed it.

When Daria returned, L'âcedôm Gilder came with her. Daria decanted the mixture into a bottle, put a stopper in it, and handed it to me. In return, I put a copper coin on the work table. *"Dances êow."* I nodded to the apothecary and touched Daria's hand. "I'll see you tonight."

I hurried up the street then, glancing around furtively because I was aware I wasn't supposed to enter the home. I needed to see for myself how the girl was doing though. I knocked at the door and waited. The woman opened it, looking like she hadn't slept all night. I held up the bottle. *"Tê wyrtdren Ay behât,"* I said, hoping I'd said it correctly. "How is she?"

"Better, L'âce. Please come in."

I followed her through the house to the small bedroom. The girl did look better, her skin not so pale or sweaty. She was sitting up in the bed, the remains of her breakfast on a plate beside her.

I sat on the bed and reached a hand to her face to be sure the fever had broken. The disease was still there, harboring deep in her lungs, but I had no doubt now that our concoction would bring her the rest of the way. I nodded and stood. "*Oon spōn, twâ ach day. Morgentide and eventide.*"

I turned to go, but the woman stopped me, trying to press coins into my hand. I shook my head. "No, I can't."

She was insistent though, talking so fast I couldn't pick out all of the words and folding my fingers around the coins. Finally, I acquiesced and took the money before excusing myself and letting myself back to the street. I turned to go investigate the alchemy shop but found myself face to face with the woman we had assumed was a doctor.

"*Nân menen timbrân. Hêr bae wîte.*" She pointed emphatically to the X on the door.

"*Nân wîte,*" I responded. "*Jus a cūg. Ay gotten sê wyrtdren.*"

She scowled at me and dragged me back to the door, knocking once before opening it and pulling me back inside and to the girl's bedside. The doctor stared for a moment, then sat to examine the child, sputtering about the plague and other words I wasn't getting.

"*Hû hast êow doon it?*"

I shrugged my shoulders. "*Ay hast síen it afore.*" I was starting to feel uncomfortable under this woman's examination.

"*Hû?*" she demanded, standing.

"*Êow wene l'aess. Ay shoon go.*" I stepped around her and continued toward the corner that would take me to the alchemy shop.

The door was propped open to let in the cool morning air. I stepped inside and let my eyes adjust to the gloom. It was a cramped and crowded workshop, reminding me of those shops in Harry Potter movies. I half expected to see a broom sweeping the floor on its own in the back.

Shelves were filled with paper packets and boxes tied in twine, jars of colored liquids, and various other things. An old man emerged from behind a curtain, his white coat stained and thick, dirty glasses perched precariously on his nose. He looked startled to see me and disappeared back behind the curtain. A few moments later, a woman appeared.

She was marginally more presentable, her suit clean and pressed. Her white hair was trimmed close along the sides, with a longer bit on top, not dissimilar to mine. Her face was thin, almost gaunt. Dark eyes peered at me from beneath bushy gray eyebrows and she looked at me like I was interrupting her favorite television show or something.

Which was ridiculous, I know. It was just the image that stuck in my brain.

"*Whut?*" she asked me, her voice a harsh scratch.

I raised an eyebrow and turned pointedly to peruse her shelves. "*Ay gâd innian …*" I hadn't thought far enough ahead here, and my mind raced over what little I knew of alchemy for something it was reputed to cure. "… Melancholia."

The woman nodded sharply and grunted before turning and pulling a number of packets from various places and taking them to the lab set-up, lighting a candle, and moving a beaker over it before performing what looked to me to be a fairly intricate spell that resulted in a dark green liquid, which she dispensed into a vial. "*Twê shingles.*"

I pulled coins from my pocket, fishing out the smallest of the copper ones and putting them in her hand in turn for the vial, which I pocketed, and headed back out.

It was nearing midday and I had no plans for the rest of the day with both Daria and Xen working. I found myself wandering down to the river, staring across at the shantytown. There was little movement there but for a few emaciated men in rags hanging sheets to dry on a line that stretched between two trees.

I watched them for a time before my stomach rumbled and I decided food wasn't a bad idea. As I headed back toward the inn, I noticed there was a small group of people outside of the home I had visited and a man was working at washing the "X" off of the door. I felt eyes on me as I hurried by. I didn't want or need that kind of attention.

By the time I got back to the Wyvern, I was aware of being followed. I ducked inside and took a seat at one of the tables. My followers congregated outside the open doors, watching me. It was uncomfortable.

When Calder appeared, I asked for whatever food Xen was cooking and tried to pretend I didn't notice them watching me. The other women in the tavern kept looking at them, then me, trying to figure out what was going on.

Finally, a young woman, maybe eighteen, but certainly not much older, gathered her courage and came into the tavern and directly up to me. "*L'âce, mîn faeder is ill. Canne êow commen?*"

Calder appeared then with my plate and the young lady blushed, stepping back out of the way. "*Hinder, plaes.*"

I tried to focus on the food in front of me, a nice thick slab of meat and the now familiar pile of mash, all smothered in Xen's thick gravy. I was very aware of the girl's eyes. Halfway through, I pushed the plate aside and beckoned her closer.

"*Whut is leger? Hû is sê ill?*"

"*Sê âspîwan and sê fêfres.*"

My best translation was that he had a fever and, judging by the hand to her stomach, I assumed he was sick to his stomach. I sighed and stood, gesturing toward the door. I knew I shouldn't do this, that I was risking everything, but if I could help, I knew that I would.

I was only just starting to come into my heritage as a blood witch, still learning what I could and couldn't do. My ancestors had combined the ability to eat disease with a thorough knowledge of the body and the medicines of the day. Fortunately, I had Daria for the medicine part.

The young lady led me down muddy streets and into a dark alley that stunk of human waste before opening the door to what was little more than a hovel. It was small, with a single bed shoved into the corner on which a dreadfully thin man lay, a nearly full bucket beside him, the smell of which turned my stomach.

He moaned when I laid a hand on his head to check his temperature, his eyes opening briefly, barely registering my presence. I could feel the fever, but it was the stomach where the problem lay. As near as I could tell, it was a form of food poisoning, though I couldn't say what had caused it.

I told the young lady to empty the bucket and bring it back, pointedly not looking at where she went to dump it. When she returned, I had her help me position him so that his mouth was over the bucket, then I stuck two fingers down his throat to force him to vomit. He gagged, shaking as he started to throw up. I kept him at it until all that came out was bile, then laid him back on his pillow.

That was as close I could come to pumping his stomach, and I hoped it was enough. I instructed her to give him clean water only for the next day, and then broth for two more days, and told her to come and find me if his fever didn't go away or got worse.

With a sigh, I left them, stepping into the stinky alley, unsurprised to find a young boy waiting for me. He didn't say anything, just took my hand to pull me toward a door a little further down. The smell of the disease hit me before we even stepped inside. Like the first place, this was small and dingy, with very little natural light. Two girls who couldn't have been more than nine lay in the bed. Both were near death and covered with boils.

On the floor, on the other side of the room, an older girl lay, likely teenage, but tiny and just as sick as the younger two. "*Thither êow môdor and faeder?*"

The boy shook his head. I wasn't sure if that meant that they were gone or that he didn't know. I wasn't sure I had it in me to even partially eat this much disease at once—not even if I only went as far as I did with the first girl. "Okay, Thána, let's not be stupid about this."

I needed to start by getting the boy out of the room so I could do my thing. "*Goone to te apothecary and bidden Daria for cūg wyrtdren for drîe.*" I took a coin from my pocket.

His eyes were huge, but he nodded and scampered away.

As soon as the door was closed, I knelt on the floor beside the bed. I started with the girl closest to me. I tried not to take too much, but enough that the medicine could take her the rest of the way, then moved to her sister and did the same.

By the time I had moved to the older girl, I was starting to feel the disease inside of me. I took a little more from her, expecting she would have to care for the others. I wasn't surprised when the boy returned with Daria in tow. She scowled at me but set the bottles on the table.

I was really starting to struggle, hoping the flow would hold off just a little longer. "You're insane."

"Just give me room to set these up. Distract the boy." I found a knife among their dishes and wiped it as clean as it would get on my pants before unstoppering each bottle and pricking my finger. I counted out the drops of blood, then pressed the wound with my thumb to get it to stop bleeding before stoppering the bottles and shaking them to mix the contents.

I found a spoon and moved to where the boy was hugging the oldest girl, who looked a bit bewildered. I held up one of the bottles and the spoon. "*Oon spōn, twâ ach day. Morgentide and eventide.*" I poured the liquid onto the spoon and fed it to her. "*Wiste?*"

She nodded her understanding and I moved back to the other two girls. I needed Daria's help to rouse them enough to take the medicine and, by then, I wasn't sure I was even going to get back to the inn before my body forcefully ejected the plague I had drawn into myself.

I fled down the alley, not even waiting to see if Daria followed, throwing myself up the stairs and into the small toilet closet. I was there so long, I nearly fell asleep. When the flow had slowed enough that I could manage with the sanitary products of the time, I emerged feeling like I wanted a shower. Or better yet, a hot bath.

I shuffled back to the bedroom we shared and almost cried with relief when I saw that Daria had anticipated my need to get clean. She'd brought up a bucket of heated water and a cloth to clean myself with before she'd left the room to allow me privacy. I found that part kind of funny; she'd seen just about all that I had to offer in the way of physical bits.

I stripped down and grabbed the small bit of soap that sat beside our washbasin, lathered up, and scrubbed myself down. It felt good to get clean. I even scoured a good amount of soap through my hair and rinsed it before I got dressed again.

My stomach was rumbling, but I paused to scrub my underwear in the dirty water and hung them on one of the hooks to dry before I took the bucket back to the toilet to dump. I headed downstairs then, spotting Daria sitting near the piano with a bowl of something in front of her. I nodded in her direction but headed first toward the kitchen with the empty bucket.

Xen smiled at me as I came into the room, but they were up to their elbows in flour and bread dough, so I just put the bucket on the floor near the back door. "Thank you for that," I said, peeking into the large cauldron bubbling over the fire. "This smells good."

"Mastery and her sister went out hunting yesterday and brought back a beast big enough to feed an army. Got some ground up for sausage and this should be enough stew for this place for a few days. And thank your sister."

I grimaced and turned to look at them. "How angry was she?"

Xen raised an eyebrow at me. "Pretty angry, but more worried. If word gets out, Thána …"

I shook my head. "Those were desperate people. They had nowhere to turn."

"Still, until we can figure out a way off this world, you need to be more careful."

I bristled, knowing they were right, but also knowing that I'd do it again. "I can't stand to see people suffer."

"Even if it means your own life?" Xen asked, eyes on their task. "Or your sister's?"

"Xen, I…"

"Or mine?" Their voice was so soft I almost wasn't sure I'd heard them.

I came around the work table and slid my arms around their waist, drawing them close. "I would never knowingly put you in harm's way. I promise to be more careful."

"That is all we ask."

"I'm going to grab some of this stew and go see if I can convince Daria to forgive me."

I grabbed one of the wooden bowls and served myself from the cauldron, thanking Xen with a nod as they cut me off a chunk of bread from the still-steaming loaf.

CHAPTER 7
FAITH

The evening's rowdiness hadn't even begun, though I could see a card game getting started at one table. Anne was noticeably absent, so I assumed she had taken her own advice and gotten the hell out of Dodge. I nodded to Calder near the bar and headed to sit with Daria.

I sat, letting my eyes sweep the room. "Everything good?" I asked quietly.

"Aside from you trying to scare me to death?"

"Daria—"

"No, I get it, I do. I wouldn't have been able to say no either." Her eyes swept the room and came back to me. "We *need* to remember where we are though, Thána."

I nodded and started eating. I was ravished. "So, in other news, I stopped by that alchemist's shop earlier. I'm thinking she's someone we should get to know."

Daria's face tightened. "L'âcedôm Gilder says she's a *hrýman*, which I take to mean crazy person."

I dug the vial I had her make me from the pocket of my pants and handed it to her. "Tell me what you think that is."

Daria took it and opened it, sniffing at the opening. "Mm-mm ... do I smell valer?"

"If that's related to valerian, yes."

"A depression remedy?" Daria raised an eyebrow as she closed the vial. "How did she make it?"

"Well, I didn't actually see her speaking words over it, but it looked a lot like work I've seen Mom do, like when she made the xýpna for me." I kept my voice low so no one would overhear me.

"Just be careful. I don't think the alchemist would appreciate you calling her a witch."

"I wasn't planning on it." I finished my stew and sat back in the chair. "Interestingly, alchemy is similar in a lot of ways to what your apothecary does. Much of it is based in herbalism, though steeped with a lot of superstition."

I noticed the inn's owner coming out of the back hall that led to her quarters. She looked like she hadn't slept in a week, her hair disheveled and her eyes sunken and dark. "What's up with her?"

Daria looked her way. "Calder said her daughter is ill."

"This plague?" I asked.

Daria shook her head. "I don't think so. He said something about a growth on her neck."

"That doesn't sound good."

"Not in the least. ... I do have some good news, however," Daria offered. "One of the rooms emptied out today." She held up a key. "No more nights on the floor."

Calder came to clear my dishes, bringing with him two fresh glasses of the dark beer that seemed to be the drink of choice, at least among those that spent time in the Wyvern.

———

It was odd how we settled into place there. Several days passed uneventfully. Xen and I would get up together in the mornings and I would help them in the kitchen, then walk with Daria to the apothecary. Most days I walked around the town, acquainting myself with the layout and the people.

One day I found myself outside the church. My curiosity pulled me up the steps and in through the open doors. The cavernous nave was filled with marble and glass; tall windows with colored glass marked either side. I had to assume that the colors had meanings beyond just being pretty, as they matched in pairs, from a pale blue nearest the doors and continuing through several colors until the final set nearest the altar were deep red.

It reminded me of the men I had seen preparing to minister to the poor, with their black and red garments. Looking toward the altar, it was easy to see that red was an important color to their religion, as the altar was draped in a cloth of deep crimson, and a carpet of the same hue marked the path from what would have been the choir in a European cathedral, off to two side chapels.

I stood just off the carpet, somehow loath to step onto it. As I stood there, attempting to figure out their faith simply from the layout and décor of the church, a door opened somewhere behind and to the right of the altar.

Three men appeared in black robes and wimples, carrying candles, a silver tray covered with a red cloth, and a pitcher of some sort. They stopped when they saw me, looking a little startled, then continued to stand in front of the altar. They bowed in unison three times, then ascended the stairs and set about putting the tray and pitcher somewhere under the altar before one joined their brother in replacing the altar candles.

The other man came toward me, bowing from the waist with his hands behind his back. *"Wilcumian, Mastery. Hwôn mêo Ay ambihtan?"*

I nodded my head in greeting, which seemed to be the accepted practice of a woman greeting a man. *"Aye wot ... um, frymdig?"* I gestured around us. I think I told him I was curious. I could have been wrong. It wasn't a commonly used word in any of the texts I had studied. *"Mîn trêowd is ... um ... miselic."*

"Êow ârian cyrten, Mastery. Aye hêre widwier wâgn Sâcerd."

He bowed again and left me standing there. For a moment, I watched the two who were still replacing the candles for a moment, then turned to survey the nave again. In any cathedral I'd ever been in, I knew instantly which faith was being practiced, but I had yet to figure out anything regarding this religion, other than assuming they worshipped a goddess rather than a god.

"Mastery, Sâcerd Mader Raffa."

I turned to find a stern-looking woman in a black suit and red collar that was not totally unlike the collar of the Catholic priests back home, just that it circled the neck entirely, stiff and precise. On her chest was a gold chain that ended in a deeply red stone nearly the size of a child's fist. I smiled and inclined my head to show my respect.

"Sâcerd Mader."

"Brôder Michel sod eôw rihtung?"

I wasn't sure what rihtung meant but barged on ahead anyway. *"Aye nun local. Mîn trêowd is som miselic. Ûser non ..."* Again, I gestured at the building around us because once again my limited vocabulary was hampering me.

The priestess nodded though, smiling. *"Êow commen leng? Doest êow worship Mader Killi?"*

I nodded too. *"Gese, Mader. Nun in a ... cathedral."* That was not their word, but I couldn't find the right translation in my head. "Um, *ûser worship in de gâstlic hearg."* Those were words I remembered from a book that passingly spoke of druids and their sacred groves.

With my broken language skills, I spoke with the priestess for nearly an hour, working out a bit of the way their faith lived out. There were many things that I thought translated fairly well to the medieval churches of Europe. And quite a few that I think would have gotten you burned at the stake. At one point, she set a hand on mine and I got the briefest flash of a shrine set among trees and what I assumed was Mader Raffa as a young girl. It startled me and I subconsciously pulled my arm back.

That was more Daria's gift than mine.

As the afternoon light shifted and the nave grew darker, I took my leave with heartfelt thanks and headed back toward the Wyvern. It was good to have at least some working knowledge of the religion, considering that it held the power of life and death in its hands.

On my way back toward the inn, I found a small bookseller and decided to see if there were any books to be found that might help me understand the religion better. I found a book of prayers and what I assumed was their sacred text, or one of them anyway. The other two were reserved for clergy. I made my purchase and returned in time to meet Daria for supper.

"You look pleased with yourself," Daria observed as we took our seats in what had become our usual places.

"It was a good day," I replied, setting the books on the chair between us. "You, on the other hand, look exhausted."

"My day was very long, but I think I finally got the formula down for a sort of antibiotic."

That got my attention. "Really?"

"I'm not positive it will work on this plague, but yeah. I should know tomorrow. Then I just need to find a willing test subject. They have some pretty remarkable plants here that I'd love to take samples of when we leave."

"That's incredible, Daria. It could change the course of this society."

"I'm just hoping to save lives."

I wanted to tell her what had happened with Mader Raffa, but Calder appeared with our beer and asked us whether we wanted roasted boar or what passed for chicken here, small birds that were everywhere. Once we ordered, I turned my attention to the books, lifting first the prayer book. I'd always been better with the written word than spoken language. Some of that was due to having the time to process the words and phrases, and not needing to hurry through them to respond. In the case of Old English, it also had to do with it being a dead language; thus, only those of us who studied it ever tried to speak it out loud.

"What's that?" Daria asked after sipping her beer.

"Book of prayers," I responded. "I thought it wouldn't hurt to learn something of their faith."

She nodded, then touched my hand and gestured toward the door. Her boss was entering with a black bag and the matron of the inn met her, both somber. They moved together toward the private rooms. "She's not doing well, poor thing," Daria said. "L'âcedôm Gilder said she can no longer eat solid food. The growth is impacting her trachea as well."

"Can they operate?" I asked.

"I don't know."

We looked up as Calder set our plates down. We settled in to eat and got about halfway before L'âcedôm Gilder appeared beside us, asking Daria to join her. Daria snagged my hand to bring me with them. Down the dark hallway, we entered a small bedroom. It was thick with the scent of the cancer that was going to kill the girl who lay on the bed.

She was small, rail-thin, and pale. The growth in her neck was visible, sticking out of the left side and across the front. I recoiled from the smell and Daria tightened her hand in mine.

"Cancer," I breathed the word and it seemed to sit in the air between us and the child.

"*Doest êow nâwan es?*" L'âcedôm Gilder asked.

I nodded tightly. "*Ay hast sienna som afor.*"

"*Hwon doest êow traht—ian sê?*"

I inhaled slowly and Daria's hand grew tight in mine. I squeezed it and let go, moving to kneel beside the bed. The girl's eyes were dark and sunken, but they followed me, and I smiled for her as I lifted a hand to touch the growth. "*Doest es heart?*"

The tumor was hard under my fingers, the skin tightly stretched and warm to the touch. She shook her head minutely.

"Daria, I'm going to need you to mix up something for me." I looked at my sister, hoping she knew I was asking her to clear the room. "Something with anti-inflammatory properties. Nothing too alkaline, and I'm going to need to augment it."

"Thána, are you sure?"

I nodded. "Mastery Claudette, *canst êow heald Xen to macian a … um … poultice. Sê nâwan es.*"

Daria drew the apothecary away and Mastery Claudette followed them out, leaving me alone with the child. I had never attempted anything of the kind while knowing what I was, and my plan was still forming. It couldn't be done all at once; for one, it was too much disease for me to handle and for another, it would do nothing but brand me a witch.

I glanced behind me to ensure we were alone, then covered her eyes with one hand and used that to tilt her head back. I put my other hand on her chin, opening her mouth. I leaned in close, but not quite touching her lips with my own. Closing my eyes, I breathed in deeply, calling to the cancer. She coughed and it propelled far more than I had meant to take into my mouth.

I pulled back, swallowing hard. I ended up on my ass on the floor, shaking my head. At least I knew this wasn't going to be a reticent form. I'd read tales of other blood witches fighting against cancers that latched onto their host and would not easily be tempted out.

The girl's mother returned with a wooden bowl. As I had anticipated, Xen had known exactly what I needed. The bowl was filled with a mix of milk and bread with some herbs. I nodded and set the bowl on the floor by the bed. There was no medicinal value in the poultice, but it would cover the magic part of what I was doing. A few minutes later, Daria returned with a jar in her hands.

Inside it, I could see a milky pink potion that would help disguise the fact that I was about to bleed into it. She also had a small knife that she handed me, with her body blocking me from view. I asked Claudette for a cup and while she was gone, I sliced into the meaty part of my palm, letting the blood collect in the jar, then used the knife to stir the blood into the potion.

When Claudette returned with the cup, I got up off the floor, showing her the jar.

I poured about a quarter cup of the potion into the wooden cup and showed it to her. "*Micle twâ ach day. Morgentide and eventide.*"

Daria helped me get the girl upright enough to drink the liquid, though her ability to swallow was hampered. I thought the growth was smaller already but was probably projecting. As an afterthought, I spilled some of the potion into the poultice, mixing it with my fingers and murmuring a healing spell under my breath. I squeezed the liquid out of the bread and laid it over the growth, packing it down, and telling Claudette to let it dry and stay there until it was time for the next dose, then replace it.

We withdrew from the room and I could feel my body preparing to shed the disease, so I left Daria to say my farewells and dashed up the stairs.

CHAPTER 8
DOMESTICATION

XEN AND I BARELY SPOKE IN THE EVENINGS; IT WAS ALMOST LIKE THERE WASN'T any need. I've never been more comfortable sharing space with a person before. I'd always felt so out of place, like I was just visiting in the lives of those around me but somehow there, in that backward place where our very existence was problematic, there in that small room with Xen, I was at home.

They came in from the kitchen, already pulling at the sleeves of their shirt before the door was closed. I was on the bed, reading by the light of the oil lamp. Xen pulled off their boots and dropped the clothes by my pile of clothes to be washed, then crawled up the bed to lay against the wall.

There was this connection between us, due to the bonding, and enhanced by our genuine affection. It wasn't exactly like we could speak into each other's minds. It was more ethereal than that. Like a caress. Xen was tired, and a bit melancholy.

I put down the book and moved to lie beside them. "Are you homesick?" I asked.

Xen sighed and shook their head. "Not exactly."

"What is wrong then?"

"Not wrong exactly." Their finger caressed my arm. "I have been thinking about you."

"Me?"

"Since our bonding, your memories sometimes fill my head."

I shifted so I could see their face. "My memories are making you sad?"

"Not sad, maybe worried." Their eyes met mine. "I am afraid that I will not be enough for you."

I could feel myself frowning. "Not enough?"

They sighed again. "I cannot give you …"

Suddenly, I knew what Xen was talking about. "Sex. You're worried that I need sex."

Their face blushed a bit, but they nodded. "I cannot give you the satisfaction that Katyk or Cambius or the others have in the past."

I moved close enough to press my lips to theirs. "I don't need sex, Xen. I told you that before we bonded."

"Yes, I know that. Yet those memories are intense."

I nodded. "Yes, they are. But look how much time stretches between them. I have gone years without sex partners. Besides, you give me so much more than sex."

"I do?"

"You give me this. This is something I have never had with anyone, sex partner or friend. I never knew I could have this kind of closeness." I kissed them again, just the light brushing of our lips together. "I love you more than I have ever loved anyone."

"And I love you more than I thought was possible with someone who is not Pixin."

We were quiet for a minute, just laying side by side. "What were you reading when I came in?"

"I picked up the local scripture. Thought it might be good to learn what not to do, and it lets me improve my vocabulary of the local dialect."

"You have done very well in regard to the language."

"Yes, I have to admit it's been kind of fun, but my vocabulary is limited, and the dialect here is a bit different than any I've studied."

"It is a bit trickier than some, yes." Xen yawned and I reached to turn off the lamp. "You can continue reading."

"You need to sleep, and truthfully so do I."

Xen's eyes closed and I reached to pull the blankets up over us. "I am going to be making jerky tomorrow before the meat goes bad," Xen mumbled softly. "If you want to help."

"Count on it." I settled on my side and Xen spooned up behind me. In only moments, I fell asleep.

I woke as Xen was getting dressed, stretching and blinking up at them. "Is it morning already?"

"Almost. Dawn is about an hour off. I want to get an early start."

"Okay. Let me get dressed and go pee, and I'll be down to help."

Xen sat to pull on their military boots. "I'll start the affe."

They left as I got out of bed and stretched, reaching for the last of my clean clothes and pulling on just the pants and shirt. There was no need to be formal if I was going to be helping Xen in the kitchen. I pulled on my boots and went to relieve my bladder before heading downstairs.

The tavern area was quiet. Calder was sweeping the floors and he lifted a hand in greeting as I passed. Xen wasn't in the kitchen when I got there, but I washed my hands and found the day-old bread scraps, tearing them up and putting them in a bowl to start the poultice for the girl, whose name I hadn't even learned.

I sniffed at the jug filled with the morning's milk, then poured a generous amount into the bowl before plucking some herbs from the small window herbery that I knew helped with inflammation and purification, and tossing them into the mix.

Letting that steep, I set about grinding affe beans.

"You almost look at home," Xen said, coming in the side door with a slab of meat.

"Just don't ask me to cook anything," I replied. Once the beans were ground, I picked up the bowl. "I'm going to go check on my patient."

"Be careful."

I grinned. "Always."

The door to the girl's room was open just a crack and I let myself in. She was asleep. I set the bowl down before mixing some of the potion into it and stirring it with my fingers while barely verbalizing a healing incantation. I set to removing the dried poultice so that I could apply the new dressing.

She woke before I was done, her eyes sparkling even in the low light of the room.

"*Goode morn,*" I said softly. "*Betera?*"

She licked her lips. "*Betera.*" Her voice was barely there, and her hand moved to the growth, feeling around it. The tumor was smaller and would continue to shrink, especially if I managed to "eat" more of it later in the day. It was a risk, but I didn't think I could have lived with myself if I let her die.

"*L'âce, goode morn.*"

I nodded in greeting to Claudette. "*Sê es betera. Âwunian sê L'âcedôm.*" I pointed to the jar and stood, letting the mother tend to her daughter.

"*Dances êow, L'âce.*"

I left the room and returned to the kitchen.

"Nice timing." Xen poured a cup of affe for me and handed it to me.

"So, what is it we're doing today?" I asked, sipping at the cup.

"I am going to get a start on breakfast. That needs to be cut into thin strips no more than this big." They held up two fingers that were just about two inches apart. "I'd put on an apron if I were you." Xen nodded toward the pegs on the wall near the door to the tavern where several aprons hung.

"I can do that." I selected an apron and put it on, tying it around my waist, then picked up a knife and set myself to the task while Xen started making bread.

Once they had it set aside to rise, they turned to the task of dicing up the starchy tubers that passed for potatoes there. They were kind of a cross between a potato and a turnip, with dark skin and orange flesh. Xen diced them and put them in a cast-iron frying pan, dropping in a big chunk of butter and some seasoning before moving the pan to the fire. It didn't take long for the sizzle of melting butter to fill the space.

We worked quietly on our separate tasks until the smells of the breakfast Xen was making made my stomach rumble. They chuckled lightly before dumping some eggs into the pan with the potatoes, a few other vegetables, and sausage they had chopped up and added in.

I was nearly finished with cutting the meat into strips, my hands bloody.

"Good," Xen said. "I prepared the spices. Look in the bowl on the counter."

A large ceramic bowl sat opposite me, near the sink. I took a moment to wash my hands again, drying them on the apron. "Okay, so I'm guessing we need to coat the strips with the spices?"

"Yes."

I looked from the bowl to the pile of meat strips and back, trying to decide the best way to do that. I ended up spreading out the strips and dumping the spice mixture over them, then massaging the spices into each piece, making sure they were thoroughly covered.

"I may just make a chef out of you yet," Xen teased as they came back to watch me.

"Funny," I responded wryly.

The side door opened, and Calder appeared, looking at me in surprise. Beside him was a younger boy, maybe thirteen. He was sandy-haired with freckles that covered his face and judging by the way his skirt barely reached his ankles, he'd recently had a growth spurt.

"*Pardon, Mastery. Mîn brôdor, Phillan. Sê commen ta fylst.*"

"*Goode, Calder. Wilcumian Phillan. Steort de swol en de smîchause. Lesan grênes, bout non swol. Phillan cannae getten eggs.*"

Calder nodded tightly and turned his brother around to head back outside.

"Did I do something wrong?" I asked.

Xen shook their head. "He is not accustomed to seeing two women in the kitchen. One is odd enough. It is men's work, after all."

I rolled my eyes. "I guess it would blow his mind to tell him you are neither, and if it means I get to spend more time with you, I'm all for it."

Xen stirred the skillet with the breakfast in it, then moved it to a higher rack so it would keep warm but not burn, and went back to their bread making.

"These are ready."

"Not quite. We need to put hooks in them so we can hang them in the smokehouse."

"We have a *smokehouse*?" I asked, surprised.

Xen pointed me to a deep drawer in which I found small hooks made of cast iron. "We do now," they replied with a grin. "I had Calder help me set it up yesterday so I could do this. It is only some canvas tented over poles, but it should be sufficient."

We dropped back to our comfortable silence, each of us intent on our tasks. When I had completed mine, I piled the meat into the spice bowl to make it easier to carry. Xen stuck two loaves of bread into the brick oven and dusted their hands before wiping them on their apron. They hefted the bowl up off the counter and led the way out the back door.

With a basket full of eggs in his hands, Phillan was coming back from the coop where the birds that gave us eggs were kept. Calder was piling green branches beside the dark canvas tent they had constructed. Inside the tent, six poles were topped with crossbeams that held the canvas flat above an entire line of fire that started and ended about six inches away from the poles. Xen and I made quick work of hanging the strips of meat from those crossbeams before Xen had me help lay more wood onto the already burning fire.

"We need to give it plenty of fuel before we add the green wood," Xen explained as they poked the fire and made sure it was burning well.

Calder came when Xen called him, his arms full of green branches and leaves. Together, we worked to cover the fire, and everything was already smoking well before we were done. *"Phillan, getten yon binn, plaes."*

Xen pointed at a basket by the kitchen door. It was filled with peels and rinds from all kinds of fruits and vegetables. Xen scattered them into the smoldering mass of greenery.

"Calder, hindrian onne welhwâ pro maesse, plaes." Xen took my hand, and we headed back into the kitchen.

"I smell like smoke now," I said. Not that it was a complaint. I'd always loved the smell of a fire.

"Hungry?" Xen asked, grabbing a plate and moving to the fire.

"Yes. And I need more affe." The little bit left in my cup was cold, so I dumped it into the sink and took the cup with me to the fire.

Xen handed me a plate filled with eggs and potatoes and sausage, all cooked together, then filled my cup.

"Go sit down. The boys and I have this covered."

I felt a little guilty, leaving them to clean up the mess made with the meat and spices, but Xen pointed me toward the door, and I took the hint. Instead of sitting at one of the tables, I went out the front door with my breakfast and affe. The sun was up above the horizon, if only barely, painting the street in a rosy sort of glow that would wear away as the people started coming out of homes and boarding houses to begin their day.

There was not a lot of pretty on that side of town, but at this hour I could pretend. The street was drier than normal, but the hulking clouds hanging in the west hinted that they wouldn't stay that way for long. I enjoyed the quiet, sitting in the wooden chair and eating my breakfast.

It was almost like being—if not home—someplace safe.

CHAPTER 9
MURDER

OF COURSE, JUST THINKING THAT WAS ENOUGH TO TEMPT THE UNIVERSE INTO reminding me I wasn't safe. Screams filled the air from across the street and a young man in a dress that had seen better days emerged from the alley, his arms flailing and his hair askew. "*Steallere! Steallere! Mord! Mord!*"

I stood, putting aside my empty plate and setting my affe on the porch rail before crossing the street. People were starting to respond, but I was the first to reach the nearly hysterical man. He pointed down the alley to the door into what I had been told was a cheap boarding house. I only made out about every other word the man was saying, but once I got a good look down the alley, I didn't need words.

The rising sun stabbed down on maybe the most horrific thing I'd ever seen. I swallowed hard against the urge to vomit. The metallic smell of blood filled the air and red painted the walls and ground dark. There was something off about the smell, but I was more grossed out by the sight of it. That, and him.

He was small, but not young. The skirt of his dress was torn open clear to his chest and his undergarments were yanked down. The killer had taken his time with this one. Even at a distance of at least five yards, I could see his innards. His genitalia had been removed and his intestines lay on the ground beside him. There were also cuts along his arms, the skin bathed in red around it. I was feeling lightheaded even as the Steallere and two of her officers arrived on the scene.

A crowd was starting to gather and I backpedaled out of the way, still fighting the urge to lose my breakfast.

"Thána!"

I felt Daria's hand on my shoulder and turned to bury my face into her shirt. I'd never really considered myself squeamish, but that was unlike anything I had ever seen. Daria drew me back across the street and got me to sit down at one of the tables. "Are you okay?"

I nodded, despite my shaking. The sight and smell of blood were bad enough on their own, but it had busted open the door in my head that kept memories I didn't want to think about locked away. Now they flooded me, from the day our father died to the violence at the hands of the brotherhood, to the torture by the Kabeshi. For a moment, I couldn't breathe or open my eyes. I felt every injury as if they had just happened and my body quaked with remembered pain.

Hands touched mine, stilling them, and pulling me out of my head. "Thána?"

I hesitantly opened my eyes to find Xen kneeling in front of me, holding my hands. Their presence settled on me like a blanket, pushing everything back into its hiding place and giving me room to breathe. "I'm okay. Thanks." I squeezed their hands as if that would prove my affirmation and offered a tight smile that probably looked more like a grimace. "The sight of all that blood just … shook loose some memories."

"I was worried that maybe it was Katyk again," Daria said. "We don't know where she is."

"For all we know, she went back through the portal to Meerat," I responded. "We know she didn't follow us through the second portal, so it is reasonable to assume she landed close to where we came through."

"Or she's out there somewhere, hunting for us," Daria said dryly.

"Or that," I agreed. It wasn't a pleasant thought. Katyk's eyes as we fought had been wild and filled with rage. She had been dead set on killing me. Suddenly, it dawned on me why. It filled my head like a movie only I could see. "They killed her sister," I said aloud as Xen was getting up.

"What?" Daria asked. "Who killed whose sister?"

"The Kabeshi," I said. "Katyk told me they had her sister. They must have killed her when we escaped. To punish Katyk."

"It's not like Katyk let us go," Daria said, still looking confused.

"No, but she brought us to them, and they were not the sanest people I've ever met. Why else would she be so furious?" In my head, the girl looked like a miniature of Katyk, with her mahogany skin and dark hair.

"Perhaps Katyk is merely an angry person," Xen said. "Let us hope she has returned through the portal."

"Are you going to be okay? I should be getting to work."

I looked up at my sister and nodded. "I'm fine. I think I'll spend today reading about the Upright Goddess and what is expected of those who serve her."

"I must return to the kitchen." Xen touched my shoulder in passing as they headed for the kitchen.

I stretched and stood, aiming for our room, but I was only a few steps up the stairs when I heard my name. I turned to find the Steallere at the door. I inclined my head in greeting. "*Steallere, goode morn.*"

"*Non fer sôm,*" Steallere Brooklane responded wryly.

"*Hû mêo Ay gieldan?*" I asked, unsure if her comment was meant jokingly or if she was as serious as her face suggested. I opted to assume she was serious.

"*Tê mord. Êower ware ot tê mord?*"

I shook my head. "*Ay wot hêr hwae yon man ... um ... galan,* I think is the word." Scream was not a word I often found in old English texts. I hoped it was at least close.

"*Tês twa êow ware ot a mord.*"

"*Non, būt a foregenga. Ay sele nâinc.*" I did not like the way she was looking at me. Foregenga was a new word I'd picked up reading. My understanding based on context was that it meant a bystander or one who did not participate.

She did not look pleased with my response. Fortunately for me, one of her officers called her back toward the scene. I took the opportunity to continue up the stairs and into our room. I was starting to think that this Steallere was going to be a problem.

I settled in to read, trading the prayer book for the bigger book of scripture that told the stories of the local faith. The first part had a fairly unique take on a creation myth, stating that the Upright Goddess birthed the world from her womb and that the first people were her children, conceived from her fertilizing the land.

I hadn't figured out why her title was the Upright Goddess, but this wasn't her only title. She was also called *Sâcerd Ide*, which I translated as Holy Queen and *Mader de Aemlic* or Mother of All. I had to admit, my geeky little heart was happier than it had been since my days studying the language at college. I wished I had been able to continue and find a use for the resulting degree that wouldn't leave me penniless and struggling.

If I'd only known I would end up there.

I was a little surprised to learn that the religion wasn't monotheistic. There was the Unclean One, a god who received the dead, and two lesser goddesses who ruled over the sun and the moon. The side chapels I had seen in the church were devoted to the two of them: Sunna and Mônna. And of course, the Faceless Stranger, who urged hospitality.

I immersed myself in my reading until there was a frantic knock at the door. Setting aside the book, I stood and crossed to the door. On the other side was a young boy of maybe twelve.

"*L'âce, commen.*"

Judging by the pallor of his skin and the smell of him, he was infected with this plague. "*Mîn mader. Commen.*"

I let him pull me out of the room and into the hall, then followed him down the stairs. On the street, he turned to the right and into a row of tenement-like buildings that lined the muddy street. The stench of excrement was nearly overpowering and as he led me to a door, I could see mice crawling openly over piles of garbage.

The boy led me up three flights of stairs and into a small apartment. The smell of the disease was strong and I almost recoiled from it. On a rickety bed in the main room lay a woman who looked like she'd lived hard and was probably younger than she looked, if the boy was hers. I would guess her to be close in age to my own mother if I didn't know better. Several children were huddled near a stove and a harried-looking man in a tattered dress came out of the kitchen area.

The woman wasn't moving and as my eyes adjusted to the gloom of the room, I found myself watching to see if she was breathing. No one spoke as I crossed to her and knelt beside the bed, one hand sliding to her wrist to feel for her pulse. It was weak, but there. I leaned in to get a better feel for how bad it was and turned my head away so the family wouldn't see my expression. She was close to death, maybe closer than even I could help with. I took a deep breath and stood, crossing to the father.

"*Ay hnot hycgan Ay cannae helpan hêo,*" I said softly. "*Daone medtrumnes es daette micel.* The disease is strong."

His eyes brimmed with tears and the boy started to wail behind me.

"*Cwêman, L'âce,*" the man pleaded. His hand delved into the pocket of his dirty apron and then he held that hand out to me.

I opened my hand, surprised when he filled it with coins. "*Et es all we âgan.*"

I licked my lips, looking down at the money and trying to figure out what to do. It was nearly suicide to try, especially with so many eyes on me. "Okay." I made a decision and told the man that they all needed to leave the apartment. I told him he needed to go to the apothecary, ask for Daria, and tell her that I needed the medicine she made, enough for all of them. I gave him back the coins to use to pay for the medicine.

He gathered his kids, a look resembling relief on his hard features. Once they were gone, I turned to the woman. Every time I helped someone, I was putting my life in danger. Mine and Daria's and Xen's. But this woman was probably the only one in the family who worked to support them. Without her, they would most likely starve or be sent to workhouses, or worse.

I went back to the bed, easing myself down to sit beside her. As I had done before, I moved over her, opening her mouth with a hand on her chin. I wasn't sure I could take enough of the disease for her to live, but if Daria's antibiotic was ready for a real-world test, there was a chance. I leaned in and called to the disease that was sitting heavy and hard in her chest. It was slow to respond but it did eventually come sluggishly up and into me.

The taste was vile, like rotten meat and sour milk combined, and I found myself gagging. I stumbled back from the bed, gasping big gulps of the fetid air in the hope that it would keep me from vomiting. When the urge passed, I turned back to my patient. There was very little sign of any change that may have happened as a result of my treatment.

Her skin still wore the sheen of her fever, and her face was so pale that it made the white pillow seem dirty. At least her breathing seemed to have eased some. I paced the room, watching her as I passed. I wasn't convinced I'd taken enough of the disease to ensure she would live. I didn't dare try again.

Eventually, the husband returned, telling me that his brother would watch his children until his wife was better. I made sure they would also take the medicine, because the boy at least was sick, then left him to tend to his wife.

The street was uncharacteristically quiet as the dinner hour approached. I passed several doors marked with the red "X" that marked them as plague houses. Someone inside was likely close to death or had already died. I shivered, suddenly chilled and feeling a bit like I was feverish. I shook it off and kept walking.

As I got back to the Wyvern, my back got stiff and cramps nearly doubled me over as my body attempted to shed the disease I had taken from the woman. I stumbled up the stairs and to the toilet closet, vomiting before I could try to contain it. Most of it went into the toilet, thankfully. By the time I felt as though the worst of the bleeding was done and I had managed to clean up my mess, I was weak and shaky.

I inched my way back to our room and sat gingerly on the bed. I didn't even bother to undress or take off my boots, I just laid down, pulling a blanket up to ward off the chill.

The door opened almost immediately and Xen was beside me in a heartbeat. "Thána?"

I smiled weakly. "I'm okay, Xen. Just need some sleep."

"Are you sure? You do not look good." Their hand brushed my face. "You feel hot."

I nodded, taking their hand and pressing a kiss into the palm. "It will pass. I've already expelled the worst of it."

"You did it again, didn't you?" Xen sat on the edge of the bed. "You're going to get yourself killed."

"I can't just do nothing, Xen. Not when I know I can help."

The scowl on their face was disapproving, but I could barely keep my eyes open. The exhaustion pulled me toward sleep and I couldn't begin to fight it.

I'm not sure how long I slept, but the room was dark when I opened my eyes again and Xen was asleep beside me. I'd never even heard them come into the room. I eased myself out of bed, nursing oddly sore muscles in my legs and stomach as well as the heaviness that filled my arms. It was like trying to move through oatmeal.

I relieved my very insistent bladder and attended to the other needs stemming from my latest healing efforts before I headed downstairs to let Xen sleep. The tavern was empty, the doors closed, and the fire burned down to mere coals. There was a chill in the air, like that first kiss of winter intruding on a pleasant autumn day.

The street outside was quiet. I guessed it was still an hour or two until dawn. I let myself into the kitchen and stoked the coals of the fire before feeding it some kindling, then a couple of logs. I put the rack in and went to the sink to wash my hands before filling a pot with water to make some affe.

I ground the beans and waited for the water, idly wondering what was happening in Meerat, or Spítia, or even back home. I'd been so busy surviving it had been a while since I'd thought about them. Once the affe was ready, I poured myself a cup and went to sit out by the windows so I could watch the street.

It had rained through the night and there were puddles of standing water in the ruts left by carts and wagons in the mud. For a moment, I was at peace.

Then I remembered where I was and that we needed to find our way home.

In the quiet, I tried to remember our trip through the portal from Meerat. I had been trying to cast the portal a short distance to get us to the doorway to Spítia. Between Katyk and the explosion, by the time I got the portal cast, we had been thrown through a totally different portal, and the casting dropped us haphazardly into a field.

I vaguely remembered a rocky terrain, mountains maybe, before we tumbled through the new portal. I pulled the kelcimite from my pocket and played with it. Not for the first time, I wondered if the intention to go to the portal would be enough. But I didn't know how many portals existed on this world. It was possible there was one back to Spítia, or maybe my own world, if I was to believe Anne's story.

I was on my second cup of affe when I heard someone coming down the stairs.

Daria stopped at the bottom, looking surprised to see me there. "You okay?"

I nodded and swallowed the last of the affe. "You're up early."

"I am going to get some anthorium and sedar bark. There's a place outside of town. Anthorium is best harvested while there is still dew."

"Want company?"

"Sure."

I stood, leaving my empty cup on the table. Together, Daria and I headed out, sticking close to the buildings to avoid the worst of the mud. "So, what are these things for?"

"The anthorium root is good for soothing sore throats and coughs. The flowers can be brewed in a tea and the leaves, when stewed and compounded with a few other ingredients, make a nice astringent. The sedar bark can be pounded down to a pulp to make a poultice of sorts that helps protect open wounds."

We walked in silence for a while, stepping around the worst of the puddles and trying to stay on the driest part of the road. There were more red "Xs" on doors and an eerie sort of silence that followed us as we walked.

The gates into the city stood open, and several women in their uniforms stood watch or milled about. They barely took notice of us as we passed. Outside the gates, we didn't have to go far. Along the road and on the banks of the river was a pale blue flower that Daria pointed to. We squatted down and Daria set a small basket between us.

"Grasp it here, near the ground, and pull up. Try not to damage the stalk." She demonstrated, pulling up a clump of dirt that clung to the roots of the plant. She shook off the worst of the dirt and put the rest in the basket.

"This reminds me of Mom, up in the mountains. Before she left me. We did a lot of gathering."

Daria smiled and nodded. "I learned a lot of what I know about plants from her. Though, some of it is inherited from our father. To hear Mom tell it, he was brilliant with plants."

"The greenhouse porch ... he would spend hours out there."

"I don't remember that," Daria said softly.

"You were very small when he died."

We continued working, filling up Daria's basket. When we'd gathered enough, Daria gestured toward the river. "We'll find the seder down near the water."

We moved down the bank where I could see a hardy little bush that reminded me of mesquite. Daria produced a small knife from a pocket and used it to trim small branches from several of the bushes. She laid them across the flowers.

"Daria …" I paused, not sure how to ask what I wanted to know. We didn't talk about things, not in any meaningful ways. "I—how are you doing? I mean, with all of this?" I gestured around me as if that would convey my meaning.

"I'm dealing," Daria responded, though her expression was more irritated than anything.

"I mean, you've been through a lot, and I know—"

"You don't," Daria countered. She closed her eyes and licked her lips before dragging in a deep breath. "You don't know how I feel, Thána."

"Okay, so tell me then. I can't help you if I don't know what you're going through."

She sighed and started climbing back up toward the road. "What is it you want me to say? There are moments in every single day when I miss him so much I can't breathe? Or that I cry myself to sleep thinking of Kota? That the nightmares don't stop when I wake up?" She shook her head. "As long as I focus on what I am doing and don't let myself remember, I do okay."

I didn't know how to respond to that. I couldn't apologize anymore for killing Habros, or for sending Mom and Kota through the portal. I couldn't apologize for bringing us here because it wasn't my fault. Of all of it, I understood the nightmares best. I'd never loved anyone enough for their loss to cut into my heart the way my sister was dealing with.

"I will find us a way home," I said softly as we neared the city gates again.

Daria didn't say anything, she just led the way back to the Wyvern. We stopped in front of the tavern. "Have you checked in on the girl?" Daria asked.

I shook my head. "I probably should."

"Let me know if you need more medicine for her."

"I will."

We stood there awkwardly for a few minutes before Daria turned and headed up the street toward the apothecary shop. I sighed. The rising sun painted the street in a soft golden glow and people were starting to appear in the doorways, opening shops and sweeping stoops. I watched Daria go before turning inside.

CHAPTER 10
IS THERE A DOCTOR IN THE HOUSE?

I could smell fresh affe and food cooking, which meant Xen was up and in the kitchen. I hesitated between the door and the hall, then headed for the small sick room, letting myself in quietly. The smell of the cancer had diminished significantly since my last visit and the tumor no longer protruded out of her throat. The girl opened her eyes as I moved closer and I offered her a small smile.

Her hand fluttered to her neck as I sat beside her and mine followed, feeling along the edges of the tumor. "*Micle betera*," I murmured. I picked up the bottle of medicine, which was starting to run low. "*Ay will getten mōr. Mene Ay?*" I gestured to her mouth and she nodded.

As I had done previously, I put one hand over her eyes to tilt her head back, and the other on her chin to open her mouth. With a scarce glance over my shoulder, I leaned in, hoping that from the door it would merely look like I was looking at her mouth.

I called to the cancer, urging it up out of her. It was a little more reluctant this time, but it came and I swallowed it quickly before releasing her. The chances were good that I couldn't completely heal her, even if I wasn't worried about being branded a witch, but I would at least give her several more years of life.

"*Dance êow, L'âce.*" The girl's voice was a little raspy but better than it had been.

"Thána," I responded. "*Callen* me Thána."

"And Ay am Calina."

"*Ay will âcirran.*" I excused myself and headed for the kitchen.

Xen looked up with a smile. "I was wondering where you'd gone."

"I went out early with Daria to harvest some plants she needed."

"There's fresh affe." Xen pointed to the carafe with the knife they were using to score the fat, round loaves of bread being readied for the oven.

"Thanks, but I need to go clean up after visiting Calina. I just wanted to say good morning."

"And how is she?"

"Better. I expect she will be sickly for a good long while, but better."

"I should have breakfast ready soon."

I kissed Xen's cheek and excused myself, heading for the toilet as my body processed the disease I had taken. An hour later, I was having breakfast and drinking a fresh cup of affe, sitting with my back to the fireplace and watching the people beyond the open door of the tavern.

It was starting to rain again, and people scurried inside in an attempt to stay dry. I was alone for the moment. I'd forgotten how much I loved to linger with a good cup of caffeine and people-watch. I was starting to get to know the people moving through this neighborhood. Not that I interacted with many, but I'd begun to learn names and routines.

A shadow darkened the doorway, pulling my attention from the man bent under the weight of wood he was carrying on his back. "You look comfortable."

I smiled a little, recognizing the voice. "I thought you were leaving the plague and murderers behind."

Anne pulled off her hat and shook her jacket free from the worst of the rain. "I did. Got bored."

I chuckled. "I imagine 'bored' isn't something you are often."

"Where is everyone?" She sat casually across from me, kicking muddy boots up onto the chair beside mine.

I shrugged. "Plague has hit pretty close to here. I'm guessing people are staying home. The rooms upstairs are nearly empty."

"And yet, here you stay."

I nodded and set my empty affe cup on the table. "Got nowhere else to be just now. I actually need to find a job to contribute to our funds so we can leave eventually."

"What kind of work are you looking for?"

I shrugged. "I don't know. I was a manager back home ... not a lot of need for that here."

"L'âce?"

I looked up at the tremulous voice and spotted the young boy whose family I had helped. I couldn't sense the disease in him at a distance, and the color had returned to his skin. In his arms, he held a bundle of something. He looked nervously at Anne, then back to me before thrusting the bundle at me. "*Min faeder makken fir êow, to dances êow.*"

I opened the clumsily wrapped bundle, revealing a lively blanket made from scraps of yarn in an intricate and beautiful pattern. Tears burned the corner of my eyes. "*Dances êow and êower faeder. Hu es êower mader?*"

"*Het hê betera, fey bût betera.*"

"*Ay will commen to sey afterword.*"

"*Dances êow.*" He dipped in a sort of curtsey and ran out the door again.

"What was that about?"

"His mother is sick. I did what I could to help."

Her hand snaked over the table to caress the blanket. "That is beautiful work. Probably worth a lot." She pulled her hand back. "You said you were a manager. Now you're a doctor?"

I shook my head. "No, just someone who likes to help people, I guess."

Her eyes narrowed and it felt like she was trying to read my soul. It was uncomfortable. "Well, I should put this away and run a few errands. Perhaps I'll see you tonight?"

"Perhaps."

I felt her watching me all the way up the stairs. Part of me liked her and the way her gaze lingered in certain places, but I had to admit, I was suspicious of her too. I spread the blanket on the bed, admiring the intricacies of the pattern. It looked similar to the crocheted stuff my foster grandmother used to always have in her hands, but different as well.

I checked my pockets for whatever money I had left. I wasn't lying about needing to find work. We were starting to run low of funds, and I didn't want Xen to think they had to sell their necklace. I pocketed the change and decided my first stop would be the apothecary, to get Daria to whip up some more of the medicine we had given Calina.

The streets were emptier than usual as the cold drizzle became a cold downpour. I ducked under the awning outside the apothecary's shop, shaking loose some of the water. The bell above the door rang as I entered. The apothecary looked up from her work and smiled. "Ah, *L'áce, goode morn.*"

"*Good morn, L'ácedôm. Mîn sweoster?*"

She gestured over her shoulder toward the back room.

Daria looked annoyed when I entered. "I'm working."

"I know," I responded. "Calina needs more of that medicine you made for her." I put a coin on the table. "No rush; this evening is fine."

Daria rolled her eyes and huffed at me. "Yeah, okay. I can do that."

"Good. Thank you." I watched her work for a moment before I leaned in a little closer. "I saw the young man whose family needed your antibiotic this morning."

She looked up at me, surprise and anticipation in her eyes. "And?"

I nodded. "He was much better. I plan to go visit his mother when I'm done here. You might want to make more. I have a feeling it's going to be needed."

"My boss was asking about you this morning. I don't think I understood all of what she was asking, but it seemed like she wanted you to come work for her."

"Me?" I frowned at my sister, then looked back to where L'âcedôm Gilder was working with some powdered substance. "What could I do for her?"

"She's not stupid, Thána. She knows it's you who has been diagnosing people and sending them here for medicine."

I started to say that I wasn't doing that, but it was true. I had been figuring out what the people needed and sending them to Daria. I left her to her work and went back to the front of the shop. "*L'âcedôm Gilder, Daria sâ êow reordian et me?*"

She raised an eyebrow and dusted her hands free of the powder she was working with. "*Êow wan werk? Ic non wîte nôgh? Ay mê scieppan bâm milde tîeme.*"

I inclined my head, accepting that there certainly was enough disease around to keep an actual doctor busy, but I wasn't a doctor. I wasn't sure how to respond. "Ay non ..." I gestured around us. "*Libban de nâteshwôn âsmêagan hîe es a rûmmôd.*" I hoped that I'd said that correctly. It was not a good idea to put myself out there as a healer. I'd gotten better at being able to read the body and identify diseases, but I couldn't just cure people. Not if I wanted to keep living.

"Commen." She gestured for me to follow her through a door beside her work counter. The room beyond it was small but already set up as a sort of clinic with a bed, a sink, and a counter stocked with various potions and salves. "*Êow scêawian te, pron ðe ic wenian te.*"

It was insane, of course. Absolutely insane. Not to mention dangerous. I shook my head, though my eyes kept sweeping the room. It would need cleaning and a divider of some kind for the privacy of patients. Patients. "*Dances êow, L'âcedôm Gilder,*" I said, glancing back through the open door to see if Daria knew what her boss was asking of me. "*Menen yfelhogian hîe?*"

She nodded and went back to her work. I was still a little thrown by the suggestion and worried that taking up the good apothecary's offer would put us all in danger. I left the shop, still thinking about the kind of good I might be able to accomplish. She wasn't asking me to perform miracles, just to figure out what was wrong with people so that she and Daria could give them the right medicine.

I let that swirl through the back of my brain while I headed for the home of the family we had given the first of Daria's antibiotics. I knocked briefly at the door and after a few seconds, it opened. The father's face opened into a smile as he saw me, and he stood aside to invite me in. On the bed, the woman I had treated was reclining, still pale, and her eyes and cheeks sunken, but much better than she had been.

I introduced myself and checked her over, though that was more show to cover for my real examination, which was magical. Her lungs were still congested and she had a long road to recovery, but it seemed she would live to tell the tale. I asked after the children and thanked the man for the beautiful blanket he had given me before I left and headed back to the Wyvern.

The muddy streets were slick and deep ruts made crossing them difficult. I was glad I'd kept the boots from my Vaneeshi uniform so I wasn't sliding around in the mud. Picking my way around the worst of the ruts, I found myself needing to pull back suddenly as a column of women in uniforms came marching from the city gates.

The deep crimson of their uniform jackets set them apart from any of the other authorities I'd seen in Gavelscore, some of them decorated with gold braids and black or white medals on the right-hand breast. In the lead was a tall broad-shouldered woman on a black horse-adjacent beast. She wore a helmet and a white cape that draped over the horse's backside. All around me people were stopping to stare.

"*Dêos weorð–mynd wyman?*" I asked the man who had stopped beside me.

"*Dêos se Mader's Wæpen, Stâlian Batorry,*" he responded, a note of awe in his voice.

The Mother's Weapon. I assumed that meant they were the militant arm of the church. Behind the troop of marching women came a carriage draped in black curtains with an emblem I didn't recognize emblazoned on them. It resembled a tree in some ways, a tree that burned at the roots. All around me people were bowing or dipping in a deep curtsey and I belatedly followed suit.

None of that boded well for the three of us.

Once the parade had passed, I continued on my way, arriving at the front doors of the Wyvern where I did my best to knock the mud off my boots before heading inside. It was a little early for the supper rush, and the only people in the tavern were our good hostess, Mastery Claudette behind the bar, and Calder, who was sweeping the floors.

Claudette smiled brightly at me. "Goode day, L'âce."

"Masterly Claudette, hoer es êower dohtor?"

"Betera tôdæge."

I passed into the kitchen to find Xen cleaning the prep table. "Hey, how's your day been?" I asked when they looked up.

"Busy. You?"

I shifted a little uncomfortably. "Weird. L'âcedôm Gilder offered me a job."

Xen frowned at me. "What kind of job?"

"She wants me to … diagnose patients, tell her and Daria what kind of medicine they need."

Xen held their breath and blinked. "What did you tell her?"

"I told her I'd think about it," I responded. "But it's impossible."

Xen didn't respond right away, which drew my attention away from the fire where I was warming my hands. "Right?" I asked. "It would be asking for trouble."

"Maybe. Or perhaps it would be the kind of cover you need to help people without giving away how."

"What?"

"Well, you aren't going to stop helping those who ask for your help, and doing it the way you have been is dangerous. If you are seen as a professional, then you are not putting yourself at as much risk."

"It's not like I'd have free rein to just … eat all the disease. I don't even know what that would do to me."

Xen came around the table and took my hands, their thumbs rubbing over the scars left from the torture in the Kabeshi prison camp. "I am not expecting you to perform miracles, Thána, but think of the good you could do when you can sense what is wrong so that others can treat it."

"I don't even understand how it works, Xen." I lifted their hands and kissed them before pacing to the door and back. "How do I trust that I'm saying the right thing?"

"You are from a long line of healers, Thána. I have seen it in your memory, in the visions that fill your sleep. Trust that. Trust your ancestors to guide you."

"We might have another problem. I just saw a military unit coming into town. They are with the church."

"So you will be careful."

"What about Daria?" I asked.

"What about Daria?" Xen echoed. "Daria will understand."

"I'm not so sure." I kept pacing, remembering the tension that had built between us since the morning. "She wants me to focus on getting us out of here."

"Right now, we have no way to do that. It would be best for all of us if we continue our current course until something more promising presents itself."

I wasn't convinced, of course. It still seemed to me to be a one-way trip to the gallows for me.

"All I am saying is that you should consider it." Xen went back to their cleaning.

I hesitated, unsure what to do with myself and feeling stuck between Xen and my sister. "Can I help you with dinner?" I asked after a long moment.

Xen looked up and gave me a nod. "I would be happy for the company. The bread for tonight should be close to done. Would you check for me while I finish this?"

I grabbed an apron and put it on, using the ends to open the oven door. The smell of fresh bread filled the room. I pulled out the loaves, transferring them to the counter to cool. After that, Xen instructed me on how to start the hearty meal they had planned. Together, we made a dish that was similar to the chili my assistant in El Paso used to make for potluck lunches, though Xen's version was not as spicy and contained tiny seed-shaped pasta.

While that bubbled away in the cauldron over the fire, Xen prepped some vegetables and directed me toward a large hunk of meat that they planned to roast with the vegetables. It didn't take long for the domestic peace to burn away the earlier discomfort I'd felt. No matter what else was wrong in my life, this was right.

CHAPTER 11
WITCH DOCTOR

The tavern was no longer empty as I brought my plate out of the kitchen and took a seat at one of the tables. The women that had begun to congregate were more sedate than usual, their eyes skipping around between the windows and door as they settled in for their usual card game. I recognized some of their faces, but not all.

Daria appeared shortly after I sat down, just as Calder set my glass of beer in front of me. She pointed to my plate and nodded to Calder, then sat with a huff.

"You okay?" I asked.

She rolled her eyes and nodded. "Yeah, it's been a day." She took a vial out of her jacket pocket and put it on the table. "That's for you."

I frowned at it before reaching across to pick it up. "What is it?"

"Antibiotic. I want you to take it as a precaution."

"I'm not going to get sick." I put the vial down and focused my attention on my dinner.

"You don't know that," Daria countered. "*L'âcedôm Gilder* told me what she asked you. And if you're going to be seeing patients, I want you protected."

"I hadn't made up my mind," I responded, though I thought we both already knew that I was likely to try. "But we also need the money and it's a way for me to get to know more people ... maybe find a way home?"

Daria only nodded as Calder returned with her plate. "What does Xen think?"

I sighed. "They said I should do it, thinks it might provide me some cover."

"I hadn't even thought about that part. It might."

We both ate in silence for a while. My thoughts wandered to how best to present myself, how to explain what I did. Random snippets of the scriptures I had read bubbled up, giving me an idea. I would need to research a little, but there was a chance I could cloak myself with their religion on top of having L'âcedôm Gilder as a sort of sponsor.

Before I was done eating, I had made up my mind to take the job. Daria excused herself when she was done, withdrawing to her room. I took our plates to Xen, scraping the remnants into the slop bucket that would be fed to the animals before taking them to the sink. "I'm going up to our room. I've got some reading to do."

"I will be up when the last of the dinner is done."

I headed up the stairs, lighting the small oil lamp and setting it beside the bed before I got the scripture book out of my backpack. I rifled through the pages, searching for a story I remembered. The Unclean One, who was named Ôs, was more than the god of the dead, he was responsible for disease as well. Ôs created a plague and Killi gave the people blessed healers, known as *Hêalics*, with the ability to cure it.

All I needed to do was to find a way to dress up my practice in a way that cast me as one such healer. Piece of cake. Sure.

I walked with Daria to the shop the next morning to tell L'âcedôm Gilder that I would accept her offer, and see about the supplies and such I was going to need. I made a list for her servant to get me: cleaning supplies, a room divider, some chairs for those waiting, as well as medical sorts of things, including bandages and the like. Once he had scampered off, I took off my jacket and rolled up my sleeves to clean the room. I wanted to be sure that there were no germs on any of the surfaces, and no trace of dirt to be seen. I even washed the front window, inside and out. Patients would come through the apothecary shop, but the window overlooked the street.

Once I was done with that, I took my leave and went to the dry goods store, looking for a journal. If I was going to practice, I was going to write stuff down. It would help me improve. I'd just need to ensure the language I used couldn't be read by the locals. I found a small leatherbound book and an inkwell and quill.

When I returned to the shop, L'âcedôm Gilder was watching as a young man was painting the word "L'âce" on the window in bright yellow paint. Beyond the window, I could see two young men arranging the divider so that the bed was hidden from both the window and the door to the shop.

I stood watching for a moment before I excused myself to head inside. The bed was filled with the supplies I had asked for, and I took some time arranging the office in what I hoped would be an efficient use of space. I'd never pretended to be a doctor before, though, so I was mostly guessing. When I was almost done, I heard a soft voice and turned. A young woman in a rumpled suit that looked too big for her held up a hand that I could tell was covered in little blisters, the skin red. "Bærnett?" I asked, gesturing for her to come in.

She sat on the bed and held up her hand between us. I could smell infection, but it was subtle and probably just getting started. I held her hand, turning it slightly so I could get a better look. The burn went part way up her arm, almost to her elbow, and it was at the wrist where I could see the infection. The skin there had broken open. As I laid a hand over the area, I got the sense of some caustic chemical, a powder she'd spilled while working in a factory. I could almost *see* it happen.

I took the time to clean the entire affected area, then asked her to wait while I went into the apothecary shop. "I need something to treat a chemical burn and infection." Daria nodded and came out from behind the counter, crossing to a shelf.

"Do you know what kind of chemical?" she asked.

I shook my head. "Small blisters, very red skin."

Daria handed me a small jar with an ointment inside. "Have her cover the affected area in bandages to help keep it clean. And it should be washed twice a day."

I relayed the information to the woman as I was dressing and bandaging her arm. I put the jar of ointment in her hand and told her to pay Daria. For a first patient, that wasn't bad.

Of course, it wouldn't stay that easy. L'âcedôm Gilder had a flier made announcing that she had a doctor on staff and had her serving boy Stephan plaster them around town. Within days, I was inundated with all manner of folks looking for a little healing. I wrote down each patient in my journal, took pulses, and listened to lungs and hearts, but it was really all for show. I was relying on my sense of smell and the sense that was my magic.

I was cautious, relying on magic to diagnose them, but not to heal them. I adopted some key phrases from scripture to paint myself as devout, even to the point of offering up prayer before examining them.

Outside on the street, the red uniforms of the Scealc, the Mother's military arm, were becoming a regular sight. They patrolled in pairs as the city geared up for several trials of those accused of witchcraft.

It was nearly a week before the first plague victim showed up at my door. I could smell it before she even made the doorway. She was sweaty and pale, her eyes sunken and dark and she was racked with coughs that shook her whole body, but made no noise. I met her partway and aided her to the bed, convincing her to lie down.

I scribbled down a note to Daria and sent it with Stephan, who had become my gopher, asking for antibiotics and cough medicine, all before I had even begun my exam. I turned back to my patient, taking her hand to try to calm her as well as to connect so I could determine how far the disease had gone. She was the first patient I considered healing. I even had a plan for how I would do it without getting caught. I reached for a bottle on my counter, bringing it close to her face.

"*Êðian slêac ðigen inweard,*" I murmured, telling her to breathe in deeply and slowly as I took the stopper off the bottle. "*Mader de Aemlic, wîsian mîn hands hælan ðêos cwene.*" I spoke the prayer softly, reverently and with just a slight magic touch to urge the woman toward sleep. Between that and the bottle of sleep gas, it would give me a few minutes of solitude to do my thing.

I glanced back over my shoulder to make sure that Stephan wasn't returning yet, then pulled open her mouth and sucked in as much of the disease as I thought wise. From the doorway, it should just look like I was examining her mouth. The foul taste confirmed that this was the plague that was sweeping through the poorer sides of the city. I swallowed, then turned to the sink in case it made me throw up.

"*L'âce?*"

I turned to the sound, smiling at Stephan who had two bottles in his hands. "*Argôd, Stephan. Dances êow.*" I took the bottles and turned to my patient, who was just rousing from her stupor. "*Oon spōn, twâ ach day. Morgentide and eventide. Bêga. Ge swefan. Slêpte es hæling.*"

She thanked me and tucked the medicine into a pocket. I had Stephan help her to the door, telling him to come back after to wash his hands. I went to the sink to do the same, then wiped down anything I had touched. I had no idea if the plague was airborne or left behind on surfaces, but I figured cleanliness would be key regardless.

As the holy day rolled around, Xen and I walked together down to the church square. The red uniforms of the Scealc stood at attention behind the stockade. Three men were chained there, all of them clad in little more than filthy rags.

"The witches, I presume?" I said softly to Xen.

"So it would seem."

The doors to the church opened and a tall imposing woman in crimson robes and a crown of sorts appeared, a staff as tall as she was in one hand. The entire square stilled and one by one, everyone went to their knees.

"*Mader's Wæpen,* I'm guessing this is *Stâlian Batorry,*" I said as Xen and I followed the crowd's lead and knelt.

"Calder tells me that she is a renowned witch hunter." Xen scanned the crowd.

Stâlian Batorry said a blessing over the crowd, then turned her attention to the prisoners. A phalanx of her soldiers opened a path from the church steps to the stockade and she descended the stairs. One of the three prisoners was crying openly and trying to pull his hands free of the rough rope that bound them. Stâlian Batorry approached the first prisoner, making a show of examining him, pulling at the rags to expose his chest, which bore the bruises of a rather violent beating.

From our spot across the square, I couldn't hear what was said between them, but when she moved on, it was clear she had condemned him. She repeated her show with the second man, who was more defiant, holding his head high and refusing to look at her. One of the soldiers needed to move in to control the last of them for her exam—the young man whose only crime was making a doll for a little girl. When it was over, Stâlian Batorry announced the verdict to the entire crowd. The three men were guilty and would be executed. The Stâlian promised that any other witches would be found and dealt with.

I wasn't prepared to watch three men hang that day, but I was transfixed by the tableau as nooses were lowered and placed around the necks of each man. With a clap of her hands, Stâlian Batorry signaled their deaths, and they were each pulled off their feet. I looked away even as the crowd roared.

"I am willing to bet that not one of those men were witches," I said, drawing Xen away from the milling crowd. They were restless now that the execution was over.

We walked back toward the river, and I shivered as the cold wind pushed at our faces. It smelled like snow, which would only make this place even more of a hell.

The snow started as we approached the tavern, a light dusting at first, but as the day wore on, it got heavier, and a strong wind moved in to drive it into drifts.

Daria joined us for supper, though the three of us were alone in the tavern. We took the table closest to the fireplace and sat in companionable silence as we ate. "Did they really execute three men?" Daria asked as Xen rose to clear our plates.

"It was awful." I shook my head at the memory of it.

"It does rather emphasize our need to get out of here," Daria stated.

"Yeah, I know."

"All these soldiers make me nervous." Daria moved a little closer to the fire. "Amblin was just a kid when they got out of here, and I always thought his stories were exaggerated, but …" Her voice trailed off and she seemed to retreat into her thoughts.

I felt the urge to apologize again, my guilt welling up inside me. I bit my tongue and waited for her to speak. "The nightmares were bad last night," she said softly, not looking at me. "*Very* bad."

I reached a hand across the table to touch her arm. "Do you want to talk about it?"

She inhaled deeply and shifted in her chair. "I know you get them too; I don't want to trigger anything."

I shook my head. "When they're bad, I have Xen to talk to. I can be that for you."

She nodded once. "It started with a … I *saw* something … Katyk, and murder, and then I got trapped in a loop of Artoz and his torture."

"You *saw* Katyk?" I asked breathlessly. "Like a premonition?"

She nodded and looked away. "I think it's safe to say that she didn't go back to Vaneesh."

I put Katyk out of my head for the moment and focused on my sister. "What was the worst? For you?"

Daria licked her lips and glanced up at me, then back to the fire. "The burns. I've always been terrified of burning, ever since I was a kid. He seemed to know that."

Artoz had several methods for burning his victims, from acid burns to metal rods heated red hot to open flames that he held to the skin. "There's a spot on my back …" Daria's hand moved to touch it. "He kept burning it. Over and over. Just to hear me scream."

"He did seem to like the sound of screaming." Of course, that just brought up the time I had been the cause of Daria's screams. I closed my eyes against the memory, Habros' face in my broken hands, the taste of his life passing into me. I cleared my throat and shoved it away. "He can't hurt us here." I said it half for myself.

Xen returned then with tea for all of us and our conversation turned to better things. We told one another stories of our childhoods and the laughter was a little like medicine. Mastery Claudette appeared to lock up and we took that as our cue to bank the fire and head up to our rooms.

CHAPTER 12
CALLED OUT

It didn't take long for me to settle into a rhythm. My journal slowly filled with observations and recipes for various potions, powders, and other treatments, including instructions for when and why to use them.

Daria and I worked well together, my diagnosis and her treatment; as long as I could identify the ailment, she would know how to treat it, even if I didn't. L'âcedôm Gilder was very pleased, both in how many people we helped and how much money she was making.

When things were quiet, I would help Daria make batches of remedies. We started putting together packages for the plague victims specifically, storing them in a cabinet in my office so that I didn't have to expose Stephan or Daria to any more of the disease than necessary. We kept our spellwork quiet and minimal, but a little magic went into every bottle. My mind was still on getting home, though I wasn't sure if I meant Spítia or California.

I also built up the tools at my disposal, and I invested in a spacious bag of canvas and leather, along with a version of a stethoscope, and other tools of the medical trade in a society like this one. I kept the bag stocked with the kits we were making with the antibiotic, cough medicine, and an ointment that was in many ways similar to that healing ointment that we got in Spítia. Two days a week, I went out to those doors with the red "Xs" and treated whomever I could. The rest of the week, I let them come to me.

At first, only about every fourth or fifth patient was sick with the plague. But, as word started to spread, I saw that increase to include almost all those I was treating. It meant that I needed to find a better solution to the method my body used to shed the illness. I was very cautious and took only what was necessary, but it still meant I was bleeding far more time than I wasn't.

By my third week playing doctor, L'âcedôm Gilder was paying me enough that we could consider moving out of the tavern and into a small place near the apothecary. The small apartment straddled the border between the poor side and a slightly more affluent neighborhood, furnished with three beds and a kitchen table with chairs. It was on the second floor with a window overlooking the street. The kitchen was barely that, with a wood stove to cook on, a small sink with a hand pump, and little else.

It was almost domestic. Almost.

One night, as we were preparing for bed, I sat holding the kelcimite in my hands, playing with it while I thought about the portal.

"What are you doing?" Daria asked as she pulled off her pants.

"Just thinking. Trying to remember enough about our trip through to cast us back there."

"Is that not a risk?" Xen asked.

"Yes, in more ways than one," I agreed. There was the risk of being seen, the risk of portaling into or through something solid, and the risk of getting stranded in an even worse predicament than we were already in. "I'm wondering if I could do it with a map. I mean, it's all about the intent, isn't it?"

Daria seemed to think about it. "Not all about intent, but largely so. How would you start?"

"I hadn't gotten that far," I admitted. I set aside the kelcimite and finished getting ready for bed.

"We do not even know which direction to begin looking," Xen pointed out.

"True." Because of the nature of the portal spell, it could be anywhere, in any direction.

For a long time, I lay in the darkness, staring at the ceiling, revisiting every second of the fight with Katyk that led us to our current predicament. The problem was that by the time we had stumbled through the portal, I was so exhausted that I think I actually blacked out.

No matter how many times I replayed the loop of memory, I just couldn't see any details of the terrain around the portal. Eventually, I drifted off to sleep and into dreams that repeated the battle in surround sound. I could feel Katyk's hands on me, pushing me down. That raced into feeling Katyk's hands on me, caressing my skin, and from there, into the invasion of her mind into mine.

I woke thrashing against her, breathless and sweating, half expecting to find her there in the room with us. It was still dark, and Xen was snoring lightly. Daria's eyes were open though.

"I'm okay," I said. "Just need to pee."

I pulled my clothes on and padded on bare feet out to the hall that led to our building's shared toilet. My feet were cold by the time I got back to the kitchen. I stoked the bed of coals in our wood-burning stove and added wood to both warm the place up and make some affe. There was no point trying to go back to sleep.

I lit the oil lamp on the table and settled in with my journal. We had been making small tweaks to our formulas, and I had taken to making sure I noted which patient got which version so that we could judge effectiveness, but we were relying on them coming back to see us when they got better.

There were a lot of people suffering that couldn't pay. L'âcedôm Gilder was keeping prices low, but she was a businessperson and anything we couldn't forage for cost money to produce. I was still sitting at the table when Xen came out of the bedroom, rubbing their eyes.

"You okay?" Xen asked softly.

I nodded. "Couldn't sleep."

They crossed to me, pressing a kiss to the top of my head before moving to sit so they could pull on their boots.

"Time for you to leave already?" I frowned and turned toward our dingy little window. "Huh, I guess it is." The sky was just starting to grow lighter. Soon, it would be time for Daria and I to head to work as well. "Do you want me to walk with you?" I asked, reaching for my own boots.

"No, I will be fine." Xen stood and shook out their winter coat before slipping it on over their suit jacket. "I am making meat pies today. Shall I bring some home for dinner?"

I smiled and nodded. "Yes, I do love your meat pies."

Daria emerged from the bedroom as Xen went to the door. "Have a good day," Xen said with a wave as they headed out.

"They're out early today," Daria observed. "And I notice you didn't come back to bed after your bathroom trip."

I shrugged and finished my affe. "Didn't want to keep you two awake."

"Is this the part where I remind you that you can talk to me about the dreams? Not just Xen?"

"I know I can but, really, it isn't anything I need to discuss. Just … Katyk memories getting stirred up."

"If it helps, she was in chains when I saw her in the premonition."

"I find that less than surprising," I responded drolly. "It was more to do with trying to remember every moment that got us here that did it. She was a part of that."

"Yes, she was. I hope to get the chance to thank her for that personally." Daria's voice was darker than it usually was.

"Are you okay?" I asked, bringing my cup back to the kitchen counter.

"I will be. Just feeling frustrated and homesick."

I could understand that, even if I had never lived anywhere long enough to get homesick for. I finished tying my boots and adjusted my somewhat rumpled clothes. I was never one to iron anything but wearing these clothes multiple days meant that by the third wear, I was wrinkled and only somewhat clean. Either I needed more clothes or to figure out how to do laundry more than once a week.

"You ready?" Daria pulled her suit jacket on. Somehow, she always looked more put together than I did.

We headed out, down the stairs, and out into a cold morning. There was fresh snow on the ground and the mud in the streets was frozen. L'âcedôm Gilder was already there, a basket full of foraged plants on the counter as she got a fire going in the big-bellied stove that heated the place. I had no idea where she'd found plants to harvest under the thick layer of snow outside.

Daria and I parted at the doorway, with me heading into my office and getting set up for the day. It was a quiet morning, probably due to the freezing temperature outside. By noon, I was considering calling it a day when I heard the bell ring over the door on the apothecary side.

I looked up from my notes as footsteps neared, standing when I saw the crimson uniforms. "Goode day, Scealcs. *Hwêne ay onðêowigan?*"

The two women wore blank expressions and didn't quite look me in the eyes. They both nodded in unison. "*L'âce, Sâcerd Mader forðý êow.*"

My heartbeat quickened at the idea that I was being called before the Sacred Mother of the church. I did my best to hide the panic. I asked if she were well, and I was told to bring my bag. I nodded and told them to give me a moment, moving back to the counter to grab various things I might need to treat whatever illness the priestess was dealing with. Almost as an afterthought, I added the bottle of sleeping gas to my canvas bag. I grabbed the equivalent of a stethoscope and nodded to my escort. They turned on their heel and I followed, lifting a hand to Daria to let her know that I was okay.

Of course, I couldn't know that I was okay. If the Sacred Mother even suspected me, this could be a trap. I followed my escort to the church, which made me feel a little calmer. I wasn't a prisoner. The sanctuary was empty but for one of the Brothers, who was cleaning. He paused and bowed his head as we passed.

The soldiers led me back to a door hidden to the left of the altar, doffing their tall hats as they passed into a hallway. At an ornately carved wooden door, one of them knocked, waited for a beat, and then opened the door, nodding to me to enter.

The priestess I had spoken with before sat behind a large desk. She looked up and nodded to the soldiers, who withdrew, drawing the door closed behind them. "*L'âce, goode day. Dances êow fer commen. Plaes.*" She stood, gesturing to a different door.

I followed her deep into the residential side of the building. As we passed doorways marked with red "Xs", I began to understand why I had been called.

The plague had found its way into the heart of the clergy.

The priestess drew me to the last of the five doors marked with an "X". The stench of death seeped through the wood toward me even before the door was opened. I wouldn't be able to save whoever lay inside. The woman stretched out on the narrow bed inside was old, her skin so pale it was nearly translucent.

I went to my knees beside the bed and made a show of my examination. Once I'd listened to her heart and lungs, I looked back up at the priestess. "*Ay canne ne fylstan hire of hê.*" The only help I could offer her was to ease her suffering, but she would be dead within hours anyway. I turned and murmured a prayer over the dying woman, hoping beyond hope that I was convincing.

I was taken to the next room where the woman was certainly ill, but much younger, and the disease hadn't yet progressed to the point of no return. I nodded in greeting before I knelt beside the bed and opened my bag. I was very aware of the priestess watching me as I started my exam.

My patient had only a few of the pustules that seemed to be the indicator that the plague was about to get worse. I nodded to myself and pulled one of the kits Daria and I had put together out of my bag. We had added a powdered form of this world's equivalent of aspirin, which would help control the fever.

I asked for hot water and soap, which they brought me. I washed my hands, then proceeded to wash my patient, explaining as I went that she needed to be kept clean and warm and that the entire room needed to be cleaned as well. I explained the medicines and how and when to take them. One of the Sisters appeared to take over the cleaning and getting my patient into new clothes before I went to the next room.

I recognized the woman on the bed as the one I had seen crossing the bridge with the Brothers who ministered to the plague victims on the other side. I repeated my exam process, but she was further along in the progression, with pustules over her face and arms. If she were going to recover, I needed to get at least some of the infection out of her. I glanced behind me nervously before lifting the bottle with the sleeping agent. I began praying, slightly louder than before, kneeling up so that my head would block the view of her face and pulling her chin down to open her mouth.

I made a show of checking inside her mouth while I unstoppered the bottle and whispered the accompanying spell to get her to a dazed state. I didn't dare get too close to her with my chaperone behind me, so I focused and did my best to drag the infection out of her from a few inches away. It took longer and I almost gave up trying when I finally tasted it. I took far less than I would have liked, but I was sure that she would live if she took the medicines.

I helped get her cleaned up and treated her pustules with the ointment before leaving the medicines in the care of a Sister who was helping. I repeated the entire thing on the remaining two Sisters, but as I turned, thinking I was done, Mader Raffa informed me that they had several Brothers on the other side of the residence that also needed to be treated. I needed more of the kits if I was to treat anymore. I scribbled a quick note into my journal and ripped out the page, asking to have someone return to the apothecary for more medicines, then I let them escort me to the rest of my patients.

At that point, the priestess left me to my work, sending two Brothers to be my helpers. Before I got to the second one, my body was starting to shed the illness. I needed to work quickly or I was going to have a problem. Two of the men would be dead in hours and I could do nothing for them. I saw another eight who had varying degrees of the plague.

I was exhausted when I was finally done. Mader Raffa met me in the sanctuary on my way out, pressing a small bag of coins into my hand. I promised to return the next day to check on everyone and headed for the door. It was late, the sun long down and the streets nearly empty but for body-boys plying their trade and rowdy women spilling out of bars and taverns. The bleeding was getting intense, hardly surprising considering how much I had done, and I knew it was going to be a problem long before I took the turn that would take me to our apartment.

A tall woman in a top hat strolled on the other side of the street, her face in shadows. I wouldn't have noticed, but she had a familiar air about her that made me look a second time. I couldn't place her or why I felt that way and as she engaged a body-boy in conversation, I turned my thoughts to the more urgent matter of getting myself home where I could tend to my needs.

It took nearly an hour in the bathroom before I could drag myself to the apartment, startling both Daria and Xen. "Thána!"

My knees buckled and I grabbed at one of the chairs to keep myself upright.

"We were very concerned for you," Xen said, slipping an arm around my waist and helping me toward the bedroom.

"Sick church people." I was having trouble keeping my eyes open and knew I would definitely sleep that night.

"Tell me you didn't perform any miracles," Daria requested solemnly.

"No, just took a little. Too many."

"You're either going to kill yourself or get yourself killed," Daria said, pacing away.

"I was careful. And they paid." I tossed her the coin purse while Xen was helping me out of my boots. "That should get us plenty of supplies to make more."

"Do you want to eat something?" Xen asked.

My mouth watered at the thought of the meat pies I knew they'd brought home, but I needed sleep more than food. I let them help me out of my pants and jacket, then crawled under my blanket. Sleep came quickly and, for once, it came without dreams.

CHAPTER 13
KATYK

"Did you hear? There's been another murder," Daria said as I joined her for lunch the next day.

"*Another* one?"

Daria cleared a place on her table for us to eat while I brought out the dinner I hadn't eaten the night before.

"A prostitute, down the street. His genitals were completely removed, and his liver and kidneys were laying in the mud."

"Any word on suspects?" I asked, cutting into my pie.

"Rumor says there was a witness this time," Daria replied. "He was drunk though, so no idea what he saw. Just said it was someone tall."

"That's not very helpful." We ate in silence for a while until the front door chimed and Daria went to see what was needed since L'âcedôm Gilder was out picking up supplies.

When she returned, I had finished eating. "I'm headed back to the church to check on my patients. I shouldn't be late."

"Be careful," Daria said. "No eating."

"I know. I promise." I grabbed my bag and headed for the church. There was a small crowd gathered and Stâlian Batorry was orating on the steps of the church. I didn't follow it all, with my attention divided, but it sounded as though she was laying the plague on the Unclean One, and that they must remain vigilant and report any suspicious behavior. Because that wasn't a sure-fire way to end up with something like what had happened in Salem.

I waited at the edge of the crowd for her to finish and took a knee with the rest of the crowd when she began a blessing. When it was over, I headed into the church.

Three bodies lay in front of the altar, surrounded by various fragrant flowers. It didn't hide the smell of the dead, however. Not to me anyway.

Three men in black robes were reciting prayers at the altar. I heard footsteps behind me and turned to find Stâlian Batorry flanked by her Scealc in their crimson uniforms. I stepped aside to let them pass as they drew near.

Instead, they stopped. Up close, she was even more impressive, standing a good six feet and several inches tall, her face square and framed by dark hair cut close to the ears. She had piercing eyes so dark I couldn't tell what color they were, and her shoulders were broad. She was solidly built, by no means a little woman.

I inclined my head deeply.

"Êower L'âce?"

Again, I inclined my head deeply. "Aye, Stâlian, L'âce Thána Alizon."

She looked me up and down. "Êow nîfara?"

I was fairly sure she was asking me if I was foreign. So, I opted for the lie we'd already been using. "Aye, intosûðweg Inkshire."

She raised one hand, her pinkie and ring fingers extended, and moved them in a small circle three times over my head while speaking a blessing over me. I bowed my head to accept the blessing and thanked her as she walked away. By the time she and her entourage had moved on, one of the Sisters I had worked with the day before was there to escort me back to check on my patients. Most were showing improvement and it was clear that even those I didn't take any disease from were responding well to the medicine.

I handed off the extra kits I had brought with me and told the Sister to send for me again if anyone else got sick or if anyone got worse. I emerged from the church to a busy square as shops began to close and people moved through the streets to go home. The sky was a dull gray with dark and foreboding clouds hanging on the horizon.

I shivered at the thought of more snow and rubbed my hands over my arms as I started back toward home. The sound of hooves on cobblestone made me look up and pull back out of the street. Scealc uniforms atop the local mounts came from the direction of the city gates, pulling a wagon with an iron cage. Inside it were three men and two women, who stared out at the people watching, their eyes wide with fear.

The prisoners shifted as the wagon passed me and a familiar face became visible. I turned away swiftly, hoping she hadn't seen my face, and bustled my way back to the apartment. My heart was racing as I climbed the stairs.

Katyk.

It wasn't so much that I was surprised to see her—Daria had warned me—but at the same time, with the whole world for her to run around in, it had seemed almost outside the realm of possibility. I shut the door behind me and leaned against it, willing my heart to cease its racing.

"Thána?"

I turned, acknowledging my sister with a nod. "Katyk," I said.

She froze, her hand holding a wooden spoon. "Where?"

"I saw soldiers escorting prisoners—she was one of them."

"Did she see you?"

I shook my head. "I don't think so, because I turned away as soon as I recognized her, and there were other prisoners between us." I exhaled slowly and pushed away from the door. "I'm going to assume she was arrested for witchcraft."

"We can hope that they take care of her for us then," Daria said, her voice cold.

I was a little surprised at the harshness, but she had lost far more than I had with Katyk's betrayal, even if she had never truly met her. "I was thinking we could go down to the Wyvern for dinner, but it looks like there's a storm rolling in. It's going to get very cold."

I took off my suit jacket and hung it on the hook on the back of the front door. "All of the Brothers and Sisters I treated yesterday are better. It's going to be a long road for some of them."

"I put up another batch of kits today after you left."

"I think we've got the right mix now. The ointment in particular is working very well. It dries up the boils almost overnight."

The door opened and Xen entered, shaking snow from their clothes, and stamping their feet. "It is frigid outside."

Daria looked at our small pile of wood. "I hope we have enough wood."

"I can get us more tomorrow," Xen said, shedding their outerwear and blowing on their hands. "Your friend was asking about you today." They touched my shoulder as they took the seat next to me.

"My friend?" I asked, momentarily confused.

"The tall one who gambles?"

"Anne?" I asked. I hadn't seen the woman since we had moved out of the tavern. "What did you tell her?"

"Only that I would let you know she asked."

Daria turned to put plates filled with eggs and meat similar to bacon on the table. "Thána saw Katyk today."

Xen looked startled. I put a hand on theirs to calm them. "She didn't see me. And she looked terrified."

"Good," Xen said, echoing Daria's sentiments earlier.

"We should be able to avoid her completely," I said. "She'd been arrested. I can't imagine they'll keep prisoners on the stockade in this weather."

We ate in silence and my thoughts wandered over what Katyk's appearance might mean for the location of the portal. It probably meant that it was within reach and not on some distant mountain or the other side of an ocean. Then it occurred to me that Katyk knew where the portal was.

"Damn it," I muttered, making Daria and Xen look up at me. I sighed. "She knows where the portal is. Our best chance of getting out of here is her."

Daria shook her head. "No."

"Would she tell us?" Xen asked.

I shrugged. "I don't know. Maybe if we save her life?"

"No," Daria said again. "She tried to kill you."

"And she'll likely try again," I conceded with a sigh. "It might be the only way though."

"I say we try to find it on our own first. It took her this long to get here; how far away could it be?"

"There are many variables," Xen said. "How long did she tarry where she landed? Did she travel on foot or a mount or a wagon?"

I pulled the kelcimite from my pocket and put it on the table. "So, our other option would be to start making targeted jumps. If we start here, and work out in circles, we can start to at least get a lay of the land."

"We still need a map," Daria said, "but yes, I say we try that first."

"I can approach the Sacred Mother Raffa and see if the church has a map," I offered. "I have earned some goodwill there. Even if just to view it so we can copy it. If any of us can draw well enough."

"Are you certain that is wise?" Xen asked.

"No, but if anyone here is going to have a map, it's going to be the church or the nobility. I haven't met any nobility, but I have helped members of the church."

"I don't like you taking all of the risks," Daria said.

"You are in as much danger as I am," I countered. "I've got this. I'll go tomorrow to speak with her."

Only, the next day, none of us went anywhere. The storm had dumped feet of snow on the city and getting out to do anything was impossible. It was two days before it warmed up enough for some of the snow to melt and make the streets passable again.

By the time I was able to return to the church, some of my patients were up and around, though they all fatigued easily. I made sure that each of them would continue with the medicine, checked on those who were still bed-bound, then went to see the priestess. I knocked at her door and waited. A Brother in black robes with a white stole opened the door and let me in. *"Goode morn, Sâcerd Mader, dances êow scêawung me."*

"Ah, L'âce, goode morn."

Now that it came to it though, I wasn't sure how to broach the subject … until a thought occurred to me. *"Beforan sê wôda, Ay snid te Scealc wið hæft. Yonder did sê læstan ûðe?"* Asking where they had arrested the prisoners might give me an in for looking at a map or at least a place to start.

"Norðdæl mæst frêoburh un–læd Alnescore. Stâlian Batorry spellian ðurhsêon ðâs."

North, from another city, was brought here for Stâlian Batorry to question and judge. Okay, so that gave me a reason to believe the portal was north of Gavelscore. *"Dos êow fêran a … um … map?"*

She frowned at me while I tried to find the word in my brain. *"Hladung?"* That wasn't exactly right, but she nodded.

"Commen."

We left her office and climbed stairs to a part of the church I hadn't seen, nodding to the Brothers and Sisters we passed. Mader Raffa stopped at a set of double doors and pushed them open, ushering me into a library worthy of any university. The walls were lined with shelves that held books and scrolls. There were study desks scattered about and the glass ceiling provided natural light. She drew me to a large tilted table near the middle of the room, upon which a hand-drawn map was waiting.

It had Gavelscore at the center of it, and I spotted Alnescore fairly easily. The capital city was north and west, a place called Evalshare, designated by a crown. The river that flowed through Gavelscore began even further north and ran south down through the border with a country named Barchdon and off to the west where it met an ocean. I estimated the distance between Gavelscore and Alnescore was too far to go in one jump unless I was amped up on xýpna or adrenaline and fear.

"Thither stêpan êow stellan?"

Mader Raffa's voice startled me for some reason. I pointed to a place south in Barchdon, close to the border with a country whose name I couldn't read. *"Hêr, bâm meate castel."*

"L'âce, Sâcerd Mader."

I turned to find Stâlian Batorry flanked by two of her Scealc. I inclined my head in respect. *"Stâlian Batorry, goode morn."*

It was clear she wanted to talk to Raffa, so I took my leave. The sun was nearly blinding as it reflected off the snow, but the air was a little warmer. I kept the image of the map in my head until I got back to the apartment so I could attempt to draw it, not that I had any illusions of being an artist. I sketched it in my journal as best I could, starting with the river, Gavelscore and Alnescore, before moving on to other cities and towns and the various borders.

"It's not perfect, because I can't draw, but there." I pushed the journal to the middle of the table. "Mader Raffa said that the prisoners came from here." I pointed to Alnescore. "So, I'm guessing that the portal is that way, but it looks too far for a single jump. And I have no idea what the land is like. Which might be problematic."

Daria bit her lip as she bent to look. "Okay, so what do we do next?"

"Thána and I can try a few jumps," Xen said. "Maybe we get lucky?"

"What if I open a portal right in front of someone?" I asked. "We'd be hung."

"Other options?" Xen asked, glancing at Daria, who had started pacing.

"There's Katyk," I said, wincing as her name crossed my lips. "Or we buy one of those horse things and a wagon."

"If we wait until after dark to try a jump, it should be safer," Daria stated. "And we should get a good look before anyone steps through."

"Sounds reasonable." I stood and went to our little window that looked down on the street. "I think it's dark enough to try." I pulled out the kelcimite and took my position.

Xen stepped in behind me, and I filled my head with the intent to take us north. The portal came easy, and Daria leaned into it to look around.

"Empty road with fields on either side."

I let the portal close. "Did you see any landmarks?"

Daria shook her head. "Maybe you should try again and we all step through, try to get a good look around?"

"Okay." I cast the portal and Daria once again stuck her head in to be sure we wouldn't be seen before she stepped through.

Xen and I followed.

We found ourselves standing on a dirt road under a vast expansive sky filled with stars. Gavelscore was behind us, its walls dark and foreboding. In front of us was a long road and off in the distance I thought I could see some trees.

"Well, that didn't get us much." I brought my arms up again and cast us back into our apartment.

"Do not be discouraged," Xen said.

"Too late." I dropped onto a chair and put the kelcimite on the table. "We're never going to get there this way."

"We just need a plan," Daria said with a forced sense of conviction.

"And a miracle." I closed my journal, frustrated.

The reality of it was that Katyk was the only one who knew where the portal was. If we were ever going to get back to Spítia, we were going to need her. Which meant risking everything because she could label both me and Daria as witches and would if it would save her skin.

CHAPTER 14
X MARKS THE SPOT

THE NUMBER OF DOORS WITH RED "X" MARKS GREW EACH DAY. THE NUMBER OF patients I could do nothing for grew as well. We could not keep up with the demand for the medicines and Daria and I were increasingly exhausted and irritable, and my body was letting me know that this pace couldn't continue.

We needed more hands, more witch hands to be precise. The medicine only worked as well as it did because of the magic involved in creating it.

I was late one night, coming from yet another long day of treating those too sick to even come to see me. It was dark, maybe close to midnight. I was dragging, my whole body heavy. I was running a fever due to the amount of disease I had eaten, bleeding heavily, and just trying to get home before I collapsed.

I took a shortcut down an alley that ran between two rundown buildings but stopped cold when I realized there were people there in the dark. At first, I thought I had interrupted a transaction of the back-alley kind but as they moved, I realized it was something else entirely. A tall dark shadow pressed a shorter shadow against the brick wall, but it wasn't for sex.

I could smell blood.

The tall one must have heard me, turning a face covered with a white mask my way before dashing off toward the street. The man who had been left behind slumped down the wall, one hand attempting to keep his intestines inside his body.

I ran toward him, dropping my bag and reaching out to help staunch the flow of blood and to get a better idea of how bad the wound was. The night air was cold, and my hands were stiff. The knife had slashed across his stomach, deep and clean. The killer hadn't gotten a chance to do more, which meant there was still a chance I could keep him alive.

I opened my bag and withdrew a small knife I kept in it for when I needed blood. I sliced my palm and pressed it down onto the wound, hoping my blood would at least kick-start the healing process. With my free hand, I pulled bandages out of my bag and pressed those down over the wound. I needed to get him into the light so I could get a better look and I was going to have to figure out how to sew him up.

The alley reeked of blood. I needed help. I stood and started yelling, bringing women from the street. *"Fultum! Sê tried ncan of hê!"* I shouted to them when they were close enough.

Two of them came running toward me.

Together, we lifted him and carried him out to the street. I pointed toward the door that would take us up to our apartment. I was calling for Xen and Daria even before I got the door open, directing the women to put the man on the table.

"I need clean water and a needle and thread," I said as Xen and Daria stumbled into the room. "And light. I need light."

Fortunately, neither of them argued nor asked questions, just jumped to the tasks I had barked at them.

"How bad is it?" Daria asked as she joined me, a large bowl of water in her hands.

"Not sure yet." I let her wash some of the blood from the skin around the wound so we could see better. Gently, I lifted the bandages and almost wished I hadn't. *Focus, Thána.* "Okay, it doesn't look like any of the organs are in distress," I said, feeling it more than seeing it. "I can't tell where all the blood is coming from—oh, there." I could feel the spurt of blood as the man's heart pumped. "She must have nicked an artery. It's a tiny cut. I have no idea how to fix this."

"Xen, get the first-aid kit," Daria called.

Xen appeared a moment later, all of our candles bundled under one arm, the first-aid kit in the other. They handed me the kit and set about lighting the candles.

Daria's hand followed mine down to where the bleeding was. "Not sure this will work but … Thána, there's a bottle marked *haut*. Unstopper it, fill the dropper, and hand it to me."

I did as she asked, and I watched her put two drops of the liquid into the wound. For a long moment, Daria didn't move, but then she nodded. "Okay good. That should hold."

Together, we eased the intestines back into place. Xen offered up a needle already threaded. Daria and I looked at each other, but as I reached to take it the floor seemed to shift, and I was falling into a deep dark pit that wanted me to die.

I wasn't out long and when I came to, I was on the kitchen floor, my head in Xen's lap. I was soaked in blood, and I was woozy. "Thána, can you hear me?"

I nodded, shifting a little so that I could see Daria stitching up our patient. "What happened?"

"I'm guessing blood loss," Daria said dryly, pointing with the needle to my groin. "You've been doing too much."

I couldn't argue the point. I needed recovery time and I hadn't been giving myself any. There was a pounding on the door and Xen got up to answer it. I was unsurprised to find the Steallere and another officer. They took in the scene while I struggled to get up. I eventually managed, though I left a bloody handprint on the wall.

"*Boda êower un–trymig?*" the Steallere asked, wanting to know if any of the blood was mine.

I exhaled and shook my head. "*Nûn, Steallere, mêdig.*" I figured I should tell the story before she had to ask. "*Ay stæpe ganot efenlang wægn selenes manslaga scrêade ðe magoðegn. Sê iernan âhwænne Ay commen.*" I had been cutting through the alley and came across an attempted murder. Sounded plausible.

I was fading again, my exhaustion pulling on my limbs almost physically. Xen moved to my side, supporting me. They explained to the Steallere that I was exhausted as I had been tending to the sick since very early in the day and that I needed to get cleaned up and get some sleep. Xen didn't wait for the cop to answer, just got me moving toward the sink to try to at least get my hands and face clean before escorting me to the bedroom and stripping me down to finish washing me. I fell asleep sitting up.

When I woke up, I felt like I had been crushed between rollers on some diabolical machine. Every muscle in my body hurt. My head was pounding, and I was feeling feverish. Xen had managed to get me into clean underclothes before they tucked me in. Both Xen and Daria were gone, and I estimated it to be around noon as I padded out to the kitchen.

The man we had patched up was gone, hopefully somewhere he could recover. The bloody mess had been cleaned, along with my clothes, which were hung on the line Xen had strung across the living space. On the table was a note in Daria's handwriting and a vile of the antibiotic. I was ordered to bed rest and medication until I was no longer bleeding.

I went out to the bathroom to deal with my bodily needs. The flow was steady, and I assumed that was because I had reached a saturation level. I had been taking too much in for far too long. I finished up and returned to the apartment to make some affe. Despite at least ten hours of sleep, I was exhausted and heavy.

For a long time, I just sat at the kitchen table cradling my cup and staring at the spot on the table where I'd watched Daria sew up the man. Flashes of the night before hit hard, the sudden realization that I could have been killed if the murderer had chosen to come at me instead of running away foremost among them.

I was still sitting there late in the afternoon when Daria came in, putting several bottles on the table before taking off her coat. "How are you feeling?" Daria asked, coming to feel my forehead.

"Tired," I answered. "A little feverish ... headache."

"I'm not surprised. Have you taken the antibiotic?"

I nodded. "What's all this?" I gestured at the bottles.

"Something I hope will help. It's a regimen of vitamins and other nutrients to help get your body's systems equaled out. I also want you to eat more meat; your iron levels have got to be nearly non-existent with all the blood loss. Which reminds me ..." She put my canvas bag on the table. "You left this in the alley last night." She opened the bag and pulled out a package wrapped in brown paper and string. "I stopped by the butcher's shop. Have you eaten?"

I shook my head. "Haven't done much but sit here and drink affe."

Daria stoked up the fire and started cooking, filling the apartment with the smell of meat. It made me salivate.

"What happened to the guy?" I asked after a few minutes.

"The Steallere and her officers took him home. He should recover as long as he keeps that wound clean."

"Good. I'm glad we could help him." I shifted uncomfortably in the chair. "I'm betting the Steallere wasn't pleased that she couldn't question me."

Daria put a plate in front of me with a healthy portion of what looked like steak before she sat with her own plate. "We told her that you would come talk to her once you were recovered."

We ate in silence for a few minutes before Daria pinned me with a stare. "What did you see?"

I replayed the moment in my head. "I was cutting through the alley, trying to get home. It was a struggle just to keep moving. At first, I thought it was just a prostitute and a john ... jane?" I shook my head. "Whatever. Then I realized what I was seeing. She was tall, maybe six feet, and she had some kind of white mask on her face. Dark suit, hat. That's about it. She heard me, looked my way, then ran."

I shivered, remembering the terror that had frozen me to the spot for that split second. "Then I just went into first-aid mode."

Daria nodded. "You could have been killed."

"I know."

"No more of these late nights. You need to set some boundaries, Thána. You are just one person, one healer. You can not expect to heal everyone in a city of this size. Not with the toll it takes on your body."

"I know that too. I promise I'll do better."

"In other news, I've started training two new techs on how to make the antibiotic. And L'âcedôm Gilder has been requested to present the technique to the guild."

"That sounds promising."

Daria shrugged a little. "I can't teach them the magic stuff, obviously, but the antibiotic and the basic treatments should work without it, just slower."

The door opened and Xen bustled in, stomping their feet free of snow before they pulled their coat off. "It's snowing again." They crossed to me and kissed my head. "You're looking a bit better than when I put you to bed."

"I'll be fine." It was a reflexive answer, but I still considered it to be true. I would be fine. I just needed to exercise a little self-control.

"There was another murder last night," Xen said, dropping into the chair beside mine. "After you scared her off that guy, she found another. It was particularly vicious too. Peeled the skin off his face and took his kidney. It was a messy scene."

"Where?" I asked.

"Down near the Wyvern. In the alley by the Dragon's Lair."

The Dragon's Lair was a sort of bordello, where body-boys entertained clients in rented rooms. They were usually a step up from the ones who worked the streets, younger, prettier. "That's a first. Up until now, she's only gone after street workers."

"You interrupting her must have upset her."

"That should convince the Steallere that I didn't have anything to do with this, I hope." I finished my food and rinsed my plate clean. "I think I'm going to go lay down again. Tomorrow, I'll go see the Steallere and answer her questions."

"And no patients tomorrow," Daria declared firmly as I headed for the bedroom.

"Yes ma'am," I replied, keeping most of my annoyance out of my voice.

She meant well but having someone dictate my actions never did sit well with me.

My fever broke and by the morning, I felt much more myself. I got dressed after Xen and Daria left for work and decided to get the meeting with the Steallere over with. The square was covered in packed snow that had been trampled and driven through so much that it was black and gray with dirt. The air was cold, but at least there were no dark clouds or wind to make it worse.

I was pretty sure that by now the Steallere knew that I was not the killer, but there was still dread as I climbed the stairs. Once inside, that dread grew with the sight of all those uniforms. There were Scealc as well as the local police and everyone seemed to be looking at me, or that's what it felt like. I got directions to a spacious office with an open door.

The Steallere's voice was tense as she spoke with someone else. I paused and waited for a break in the conversation to tap on the door and move so I could be seen.

The woman with Steallere was older, salt-and-pepper hair neatly slicked back. Her clothing spoke of wealth, as did the jewelry on her fingers. She turned to look at me and I inclined my head.

"Healdor Martin, this is Thána Alizon, our witness. L'áce Alizon, Healdor Alice Martin."

"*Good morn, Healdor*," I replied. "Steallere, I came to answer your questions about the attempted murder."

"Come in, L'áce. We were talking about these murders when you arrived. Please sit and tell us what you saw."

I took the seat opposite the Steallere and the Healdor turned to lean on the desk. "I can tell you that the woman was tall ... taller than me. Very thin. Dressed in black. She had something over her face. A mask of some kind. It was white."

"She wore a *mask*?" the Healdor asked.

I nodded. "Yes, she wore a mask."

That seemed to be new information for them. Steallere stood and went to the door, beckoning someone into the room. A young woman with a sketch pad joined us.

"Tell us how it happened, please. Be as descriptive as possible."

I exhaled and nodded. "I was cutting through the alley because I was tired and just wanted to get home. I saw movement in the shadows. I thought it was a body-boy and a client; she had him pushed up against the wall. She was taller than he was, thin. She wore a black suit and a black hat, with white fabric covering her face. I couldn't see her eyes. She had a knife. She used it to slash his stomach open. Then she ran."

The artist was sketching furiously as I spoke. "How is this?" she asked when she had a partially completed drawing.

"Gloves," I responded, suddenly remembering that she wore black gloves. "And her face was a little longer."

She made adjustments and then showed the Healdor and Steallere.

"Thank you. It isn't much, but it's more than we had before."

"My pleasure, Steallere. Please let me know if I can be of any further assistance." I stood, feeling pretty wiped out and ready to go back to the apartment. As I emerged from the office, I was suddenly face to face with Stâlian Batorry.

"Commen." She didn't wait to see if I would comply, just turned, and walked away.

I figured that ignoring her would be a bad idea, so I followed. We were joined by several Scealc as we moved down a corridor and into a small room that had a chair with straps to hold a prisoner down while they were being interrogated. The wall behind the chair was filled with implements of torture. I was familiar enough with those to know.

A Scealc officer snapped to attention as we entered. She was clearly unwell, though this wasn't the plague ravaging the city, it was something else. Her face was flushed and covered in small blisters.

"Have you seen this before?" Batorry asked with a gesture.

I shook my head almost immediately. "No, I don't think so." I knew I had to tread carefully. This could be her testing me.

I crossed to the officer, lifting her chin so I could get a look at the skin on her cheek. I'd never seen this particular disease but I was fairly sure that it was some form of virus. She was running a fever. If I had dared, I could have taken the disease and she'd be fine.

Of course, I couldn't do that, particularly not here with an audience.

"The witch cursed me," the officer said to me.

"This is not witchcraft. This is an infection." I could treat the fever and maybe the blisters but whatever this was, she had to fight it off on her own. "Is anyone else sick?"

"One of the prisoners," Stâlian Batorry said. "How certain are you that it is not a curse?"

"Why would a witch curse himself or another like him?" I smiled a little. "I can treat the fever and the blisters, but you will have to let the infection run its course. I suggest plenty of rest and warmth. It would also be good to isolate yourself, so the infection doesn't spread."

Stâlian Batorry nodded to the officer, who saluted and withdrew.

I turned to leave, just as two Scealc were escorting Katyk into the room.

"Thána?" The tremulous voice stopped me in my tracks, and I froze in place. "Thána, is that you?"

She reached out toward me, but the soldiers dragged her back. She'd lost weight and her hair was matted. She was dirty and bruised and she looked terrified.

"Do you know her?"

Do I know her? How was I supposed to even answer that question?

CHAPTER 15
QUESTIONING

Her face was a mess of dirt and tears, and there was a gash on her forehead. "Katyk." I swallowed against the need to lash out at her and instead stepped a little closer. I switched to English so only Katyk would understand. "Looks like you've got yourself in a pickle."

"Help me." I could tell she was injured; there was internal damage I was picking up. The headwound had her eyes unfocused and wobbly.

"There is nothing I can do for you, Katyk." I wondered how she'd been caught, and why she couldn't escape. Unless the injuries were impacting her magic.

"Please."

I stepped still closer. "Tell me where it is, and I will do what I can."

"What?"

"The portal, Katyk. Where is it?"

She shook her head and stepped back. "I'm not sure."

"Let me know when you are," I said, turning abruptly and heading for the door.

Stâlian Batorry followed me and asked me how I knew her prisoner. "I have met her before, yes. What is it she has done?"

"That is what we were are trying to discover with our questions, L'âce."

"You suspect her of witchcraft?"

"She appeared at the full moon, speaking a strange language, and behaving like a lunatic. I was told that she attacked a child before she was put down."

"Perhaps she was afraid. She clearly doesn't speak your language. It might be that she is no witch, only a foreigner, like me." That was the moment that I realized how I could help her. I could be her translator, and maybe in so doing I could both learn the location of the portal and keep her from being executed. "How can you question someone who does not speak the language?"

This brought Stâlian Batorry up cold and she blinked at me several times. "You understand her language?"

"We did just have a conversation, so yes, I do."

"Commen."

I shook my head. "Not today, Stâlian. I am exhausted. I have been working nonstop and let myself get sick. Tomorrow. I can come back tomorrow."

She looked like she wanted to insist but finally acquiesced. I inclined my head in thanks and left the building, aiming for the apartment to sleep for a few hours.

After a nap that lasted longer than intended, I was feeling a bit restless and hungry besides, so I got dressed to go out.

My head was filled with Katyk as I headed for the Wyvern. I nodded in greeting to Calder as I entered and paused to ask after Calina. Mastery Claudette invited me back to see her.

Calina was sitting up in her bed, reclining against the wall and her face lit up as I came in. She let me check her over and I let her chat about how she was feeling and how good it was to be able to get up and around again.

The cancer wasn't gone, but she would have a few more years to live.

I emerged into the tavern just as Anne came in from the street. "I was beginning to wonder if you'd left town," Anne said with a smile.

"I've been busy," I responded. "Lot of sick folks around needing help."

"I've heard. I also heard you were a witness to a near murder last night."

"You hear lots of things," I said wryly.

"I get around."

I took a seat at the table near the fireplace and flagged Calder over to ask for a drink and some of whatever Xen had on the menu for lunch.

Anne dropped into a chair across from me. "You any closer to going home?"

I bristled a little, unsure why she suddenly had me on edge. "Not yet. You looking to go home?"

She shrugged and kicked her feet up on the chair beside her. "I don't know. I kind of like it here."

"Even with all this death?" I asked.

"Even so."

Xen appeared with my lunch, smiling until they saw Anne. They put a plate down with one of their meat pies alongside some vegetables. "I was not expecting you."

"I got done with giving my statement to the Steallere and thought food sounded good."

"How did that go?"

I wasn't going to bring up Katyk in front of Anne, so I shrugged. "Fine. I got to meet the Healdor."

Xen could tell there was more, I could see it on their face. One eyebrow lifted and I got the strong sense that they were maybe not worried exactly, but curious.

"I should get back to the kitchen." Xen excused themselves and headed back.

"She's an odd one, isn't she?" Anne asked, making me look up from my food.

"How do you mean?"

"Oh, don't get me wrong. She's nice and all. Just odd."

I didn't like her talking about Xen at all. "Xen is Xen," I replied.

I think Anne got the hint that I was not liking the turn of the conversation. She slapped a hand down on the table and stood. "I've got a game getting started. You want in?"

Shaking my head, I turned my attention to my food. "No, thank you, but enjoy."

She moved off to another table and produced a deck of cards from a pocket. I kept an eye on her as her friends arrived. Something was bugging me, but I couldn't place it. I finished my meal and grabbed my empty plate to take back to the kitchen.

"That was a very good pie," I said to Xen as I set the plate near the sink. "Thank you."

"So, how did it really go?"

I stretched, feeling the rewarding crack of my back before I answered. "Fine, like I said."

"But? You're tense and it wasn't something you wanted to say in front of that woman."

I had to concede that point. "Batorry was there. She wanted me to look at one of her soldiers, who was sick."

Xen placed both hands on the prep table and looked at me. "Tell me you did not heal her."

"No, of course not. I promised Daria. It's a virus of some kind. I'm going to take something to relieve her fever and soothe her blisters." They looked relieved. "However, I saw Katyk."

Xen stiffened. "Did she see you?"

I nodded. "She is positively terrified. And I think her injuries have prevented her from using magic to escape."

Xen went back to wiping down the work surface. "Did she tell you anything?"

"No, but I'm pretty sure she knows where it is. With Stâlian Batorry there, I didn't want to push it."

"You know she will tell them about you and your sister if she thinks it will save her."

I didn't actually know that though. I had seen the fear in her eyes. Something had happened to her between our tumble through the portal and ending up in that cell. "She can't; she doesn't speak the language and she doesn't have a telepathic gift to sort it out. Stâlian Batorry wants me to help translate for her."

Xen stiffened and met my eyes with their own. "Is that a good idea?"

I shrugged. "They'll kill her just for not being able to understand her."

"You do remember that she tried to kill you ... repeatedly?"

I sighed. "I know, but this is different. No one deserves to die just because of who they are. Can we talk about it when you get home?"

They leaned toward me and kissed my cheek. "I can feel your resolve. I will leave the decision with you."

"Thank you. I'm going to head back. See you later." On my way out, I paid Calder for the meal and tipped my hat to Anne.

The air was bracing as I stepped onto the street, the skies gray. I shivered and pulled my coat closed. I stopped at the apothecary shop and asked L'âcedôm Gilder to send the medicines for the sick Scealc, then headed home, thinking about how I was going to tell Daria about Katyk.

I showed up at the jail early the next day, even before Stâlian Batorry arrived, and was allowed down to the cells to see Katyk and the other prisoners. She was huddled in the back of her cell, her tattered tunic pulled over her knees in an effort to keep warm. She looked like she hadn't slept, and there was a new bruise on her cheek that hadn't been there before.

I cleared my throat to get her attention and she scrambled to her feet. She moved with a limp and a quick glance at her ankle told me why. It was bruised and swollen.

"Thána! These people are crazy. Get me out of here."

"Calm down, Katyk. I convinced Stâlian Batorry to let me translate for you. If we do this right, I might be able to free you, but you've got to help me in return."

She nodded and once again I noticed that her eyes were hazy and clouded.

"Let's start with your physical condition. What are your injuries?"

"Sprained ankle, a rib I think is cracked, and a whopper of a concussion."

"Tell me everything, starting from the portal."

She sighed and shifted her weight with a grimace. "Coming through the portal, I pushed myself off of you a split second before you fell through the portal you were casting. Hit the ground hard." Her hand lifted to the back of her head. "I must have wandered for a while in a daze before I passed out. When I came to I was very confused, and I had no idea where I was. I wandered for days before I found something that resembled civilization, I was dehydrated and starving, but I didn't know how to talk to these people. I speak five languages. I've never heard anything like this."

"Yeah, I get that. It's taken me a while to get the hang of it. Go on."

She turned and limped a few feet away and then came back. "A very nice old woman gave me food and water, but it was very clear that those villagers didn't want me there. So, I left on the only road. I didn't know where I was going, but I knew staying there was not a good idea."

"When did you realize you had lost the use of your ... um ... gifts?" I asked, my voice low.

She looked at me with suspicion in her eyes. "How ... never mind. That first night. I tried to cast a fire to keep warm. Nothing happened."

"And it hasn't come back to you?"

"Would I still be in this cage if it had?"

"Stâlian Batorry said that you were arrested because you were behaving strangely."

"I finally got to a city, and I was just trying to survive. I was freezing, starving, and dealing with a concussion. These kids were taunting me, at least that's what it sounded like. I tried to scare them off, which is when I twisted the ankle, fell, and did this." She gestured at the gash on her forehead. "Which is at least the third time I've hit my head since I got here."

"L'âce, you are here early."

I looked up to find Stâlian Batorry had arrived. "Good morn, Stâlian," I said. "I wanted to examine my patient before we get started. I am concerned about her head injury."

Two Scealc guards came to unlock the cell and bring Katyk out. The Stâlian and I followed them back to the interrogation room where they strapped Katyk into the chair. The Stâlian paced around her several times before taking a leather-wrapped rod from the wall. I saw Katyk's eyes widen.

"Pardon me, Stâlian Batorry," I said. "If you don't mind, I would like to begin with prayer to the Sacred Mother for guidance and truth."

She seemed startled but nodded tightly. I moved close enough that I could touch Katyk's head, partially to calm her and partially so I could get a better sense of her injuries. She wasn't kidding about the concussion. It was pretty bad.

"Sacred Mother, please guide us in the ways of righteousness and truth that we may save the innocent and punish the guilty. See this woman's heart and show us the way."

It had the intended effect. Stâlian Batorry was now slightly off her game, and perceived me as something of an equal, at least in terms of piety. I began by asking Katyk in English for a story about where she was from, then translated a version of it. "Her name is Katyk, and she comes from a land across the ocean. She was traveling with her family when their carriage overturned on a mountain road. Her mother and sister were killed. She survived but was lost and injured."

"Why did she attack the child?"

I translated the question for Katyk and let her respond. "She says that the children were tormenting her; she only wanted to scare them away."

The Stâlian paced more, came back, and slapped the rod against her palm in a threatening way. "What about the man she is accused of killing?"

"The … what?" I looked from the Stâlian to Katyk and back again before I turned to Katyk. "Did you kill someone?"

"No. I didn't. What is she talking about?"

"Calm down." I turned to the Stâlian. "She denies this. Can you tell me about the accusation?"

"It was said that she cursed a man who saved the child. He died the next day."

"How did he die?" I asked.

"I was told he took a fever and died in his bed."

If Katyk was without her powers, she couldn't have cursed him. "It was likely the plague, Stâlian, not witchcraft."

"Thána, what are you saying?" Katyk asked through clenched teeth.

"I'm trying to save your life."

Stâlian Batorry paced more, her eyes squinted as she thought. "Perhaps we have been hasty. I will pray about this before the trial. Take her back to her cell."

"Katyk, just stay calm. Don't do anything stupid."

They took her out and Stâlian Batorry turned to me. "You have given me much to consider. I thank you, L'âce Alizon."

I took that as my dismissal and headed for the apothecary shop. Daria had not been happy that I had volunteered to translate for Katyk, but she also knew that without Katyk we would likely never get home. I was starting to wonder if we would find the portal even with Katyk after hearing her story. We certainly weren't getting anywhere trying to portal out of the apartment. There was just too much that was unknown.

CHAPTER 16
DECISIONS

I waited for the Scealc to open the door that led down a staircase into a dark corridor punctuated by iron bars and dirty yellow lanterns that barely illuminated the wall on which they hung. I had attained permission to treat Katyk while Stâlian Batorry contemplated her fate.

When the Scealc had unlocked her cell and let me in, Katyk sat up expectantly. She was dirtier than before, and she had to be freezing in the short tunic and only a ratty thin blanket against the winter chill.

She eyed me up and down before her eyes skipped to the Scealc and back. "What are you doing here?" Katyk asked, shifting so she could stand.

"I want to get a better look at your injuries, particularly that head wound." I put my bag down and reached out to position her where she was against the stone outer wall for support. "Relax."

"Easy for you to say."

"Close your eyes and center, and let me get a look."

I put one hand over her eyes, as had become my custom whenever I was going to use magic in the presence of others. It could hide a multitude of things. "I said relax, Katyk. This isn't going to hurt."

I exhaled slowly and let my awareness expand, letting my specific sense take me on a slow tour of her body. Most of her wounds were well on their way to healing, all but the concussion. I focused my attention there, the part of her brain that was bruised. A deep shadow seemed to press inward. I had never seen anything like it.

Reaching deeper, I got a sense that this spot held the control of not only her magic but something that curtailed that magic. It was not her; it was something foreign. Under my hands, Katyk shuddered, and I understood.

This was the center of Artoz's control of her. It was a near-physical thing, not merely mind control. The two things were so intertwined that her brainwashing was suppressed along with her magic.

I pulled back, blinking my way clear of the feeling of her body. "I'm going to wrap your ankle. Sit down." I went to my bag and withdrew the bandages I had brought, kneeling beside her to lift her foot into my lap. "Katyk, how do you feel?" I asked.

"Oh, fabulous, Thána, how about you?" she responded sarcastically.

"No, I mean specifically: *how do you feel about me*?"

She shrugged. "I don't understand."

"I mean, where did all the rage go? You were planning to kill me, weren't you?"

Again, she shrugged. "I'm not sure. I just … I'm not so angry, I guess."

I finished wrapping the ankle and set her foot down. "I think the same thing suppressing your magic is suppressing the brainwashing."

"What does that mean?"

I sighed as I stood. "I have no idea. For now, though, don't strain yourself. And try not to give them a reason to hurt you."

"L'âce, thank you for coming," Stâlian Batorry said, standing. The library was awash in the afternoon sunlight. The table where she sat was covered in open books and it looked like she'd been taking notes. "Please, sit."

I pulled a chair from a nearby table and sat across from her. "You seem troubled, Stâlian. How can I help?"

"I have done a good deal of soul-searching and praying since our last conversation. You opened my eyes." She paced to the next table and back. "I prayed for clarity, and the Sacred Mother reminded me of the story of Rebeka."

I nodded. Rebeka was a healer in their scripture, I had noted the story myself. "As I recall, Stâlian, Rebeka was a Hêalic who questioned the guilt of a person accused of witchcraft?"

Stâlian Batorry sat and folded her hands. "Yes, the accused was said to have cursed a woman who then died of an illness shortly after."

"And Rebeka pointed out that it was not a curse, but disease, sent by the Unclean One to tempt the people."

She reached for another book. "This is a book about Hêalics and there are no less than five stories of a Hêalic challenging a Stâlian over charges of witchery."

"I have observed that in times of plague, we look for a reason, and it is easier to lay blame on a mortal agent, such as a witch than to accept that such things are often out of our control," I said.

She was silent for a long moment. "When I was a small child, my older sister was killed by a witch. I saw the light die in her eyes. I vowed then I would hunt down all evil."

"And here you are," I said, keeping my voice neutral.

"I know that they exist. I know that because I've seen what they can do. I have always been so sure of myself." She was back up and pacing. "Now, I find myself questioning what I thought I knew."

"This is a good thing," I said. "How do you prove a person is a witch, Stâlian? Are there tests you perform, or do you only torture them until they confess?"

She stopped pacing and looked at me, her face hardening.

I held up both hands. "I only mean that without a confession or a demonstration of power, how can you be certain?"

"The Sacred Mother tells me," she replied.

I stood slowly. "Then I am certain you will make a sound judgment tomorrow, Stâlian."

The morning of Katyk's trial was bright, not a cloud to be seen. The temperatures had been steadily climbing as well, which meant that the square had thawed considerably. I had no idea which way this was going to go after the conversation the previous day with Stâlian Batorry.

The crowd was loud and raucous as the three of us arrived at the square. Stâlian Batorry had invited me to stand with her while she judged Katyk. Xen and Daria accompanied me. The prisoners were brought out as we crossed the church's steps and waited for Stâlian Batorry to speak. She appeared, resplendent in her uniform, topped with her miter and a black cloak.

Silence settled slowly over the crowd in expectation. Stâlian Batorry raised her hand and closed her eyes before opening with prayer. When she spoke to the crowd, I was surprised to hear her speak of the parable that she and I had spoken about the day before.

There was a lot of murmuring through the crowd in response, wonderment, and confusion. Stâlian Batorry moved over to the prisoners. There were five, including Katyk at the far end. She went through the same procedure as before, one by one condemning them until she came to Katyk. Her pause there was longer than the rest and I held my breath until she lifted her head and declared Katyk innocent of all charges. She raised her hand to bless Katyk, circling her head three times.

Katyk's hands were untied, and the rope removed from around her neck before the Stâlian brought her to me, very clearly placing her in my custody and keeping, and maybe subtly implying to the crowd that I too was a Hêalic. Katyk was still blinking at me in disbelief when Stâlian Batorry gave the order for the others to be hanged.

I squeezed Katyk's hand to get her to focus. "Pay attention. You need to thank her for your freedom. Say 'dances êow, Stâlian Batorry' and give her a bit of a bow."

Katyk's voice cracked as she spoke the words and I thought she was going to cry. She shivered as I drew her close, putting her between Daria and me to protect her somewhat from the very curious crowd as we made our way back to the apartment.

None of us spoke until we were through the door. "Xen, can you heat up some water? I need to get her cleaned up. Daria, bring me my bag?"

Daria's face told me she was not happy as I sat Katyk down in a chair at the table.

"I'm going to check you over, okay? Then we'll get you cleaned up and into some warmer clothes."

Daria returned from the bedroom and dropped my bag on the table before opening the door.

"Where are you going?" I asked over my shoulder.

"Out," Daria replied, the door closing firmly before she finished speaking.

I huffed but put it out of my mind. Daria had a right to her anger. I certainly wasn't going to deny it to her. I did my usual exam, easing Katyk out of the prisoner's tunic that she'd worn for who knew how long and taking stock of the injuries. "Well, by some miracle you don't have an infection of any kind, no plague or whatever virus that officer had. So, it is just a matter of keeping it that way. Not much I can do for the rib, but I can give you something for the pain."

Xen brought me the hot water with a sliver of soap and a cloth, then headed for the bedroom to get clothes. None of ours would be a perfect fit for her, but she'd make do.

Katyk said nothing as I bathed her, keeping her eyes on the floor. As I cleaned, I became intimately aware of the torture she'd been through. Her back and chest bore the scars of Artoz's artistry. I'd never noticed that night we'd been intimate because my mind was occupied with everything else about Katyk. There were fresher bruises from her mistreatment at the hands of the Scealc, but I had at least spared her worse treatment.

I helped her into my old tank top and some underwear, then sat on the floor to re-wrap her sprained ankle. She wouldn't be walking far on it for a while.

"Okay, let's get you to bed." I helped her up, one arm around her back, the other grabbing my bag. I sat her down on my bed and opened the bag, pulling out the bottle of pain potion I kept on hand, already augmented with my blood. I gave her a double dose, then followed it with the antibiotic for good measure. I didn't want to risk that head wound getting infected.

"There will be food when you wake up. I can't imagine they fed you well."

I stood to leave, but she grabbed my hand. "Thána, I don't know how to thank you."

"You can start by not trying to kill me again," I said dryly, leaving her alone.

Xen was waiting for me, their face unreadable. "Are you okay?"

I nodded once. "As long as I don't think about it. Is Daria?"

"Daria understands, even if she doesn't like it."

I rubbed my face. "I know. If I could think of any other way ... but there's just this. Whatever *this* is. She doesn't exactly know where the portal is; the concussions got her memory jumbled and she spent a couple of days wandering in that sort of woozy head that comes with it."

"But she can get us closer."

I nodded. "I hope so."

"And are you sure she will not try to kill you again?"

I shrugged. "Sure? No. But she is currently powerless, and the injury is suppressing Artoz's brainwashing too, so that's in our favor." I moved closer and took Xen's hand. "And you? How are you doing with this?"

"I am not the one she helped to torture."

"No, but she is someone I have been intimate with and I know you worry about me needing that kind of physical intimacy. I want you to know that she has no hold over me. My commitment is to you."

Xen tugged me into a hug. "I know, Thána. I can feel that."

"Okay, good." I'd never been overly good at relationships. Most of mine had been transitory or transactional, like with Cambious. I'd already been with Xen longer than anyone else in my life. The weird part was the feeling that they'd always been there with me.

Xen and I spent a few minutes in each other's arms, reveling in that feeling of oneness that had come with our bonding before we moved into the kitchen to start cooking.

Daria hadn't come home yet when Katyk shuffled into the kitchen as we were putting food on the table. She looked a little lost and still a bit dazed.

"I left you some pants on the end of the bed."

She blinked at me for a second. "Need to pee."

"For which you'll need pants. Our toilet is shared by the whole building."

Katyk nodded slowly, then shuffled back to the bedroom. When she returned, she was wearing the pants I'd left her. They were a little big on her, but Daria and Xen's would have been too small. I beckoned her to the door and walked her to the toilet, then waited for her to be sure she found her way back. Not that it was hard, but she seemed out of it enough that I worried about her mental state.

"I don't need a babysitter," Katyk advised when she opened the door.

"Your head injury says otherwise," I replied.

"And you don't want me running off."

I didn't deny it, just led her back to our apartment where we sat down to eat. The silence was almost painful. Katyk ate quickly, her eyes on her plate. Xen and I exchanged looks, and I could almost hear their thoughts.

Katyk finished her plate of food and continued to sit, staring at her plate until the door opened. Daria shed her coat and as Katyk stood, looking like she was going to say something, Daria grabbed a fistful of her tank top and shoved her against the wall.

"You are alive for one reason only. If you make any move I find questionable, I will not hesitate to put you down. Am I clear?"

"Daria—" I tried to intervene, but Daria was not having it.

"I said, *am I clear*?"

Katyk nodded, her eyes wide.

"Good." Daria released her and turned to Xen and me. "So, what exactly is our plan?"

"Haven't really gotten that far," I responded. "The only thing I know for sure is that we need to head north."

"To do that we will need a vehicle. Which will cost money," Xen said.

"Which we don't currently have," I added.

"Not a promising start," Katyk commented.

When we all turned to look at her, she lifted both hands in surrender. "Sorry."

"She isn't wrong though," Daria said.

"No, she isn't," I agreed. "And we're not going to solve this problem today. I suggest we table it for now."

CHAPTER 17
TRIAL BY FIRE

I volunteered to sleep on the floor since I was the one that brought Katyk into our space and none of the beds were big enough for two. My back wasn't too happy with that decision and by midnight, I had given up on sleeping altogether and went out to the kitchen so I wouldn't wake the others. I lit the candles on the table and sat down with my journal to document the events of the last few days.

I wasn't sure how much later something caught my attention, but there was a red glow outside the window and a flickering movement that made me turn to look. It was too early for sunrise. I stood and crossed to the window.

Fire.

It was a few streets away but growing fast in the crowded slum.

I was frozen for a moment, watching it, then realized we were probably in danger and there were going to be wounded to treat. I raced back to the bedroom.

"Everybody get up and get dressed!"

One by one they shifted and opened their eyes.

"There's a fire headed this way. We need to get our stuff and get out."

I started moving around the room, gathering anything that had been taken out of the backpacks, and left out while they got up and dressed. I shoved my feet into my boots and realized that Katyk was still barefoot. We'd have to worry about that later. For now, we just needed to get moving.

I wrapped Katyk in one of the blankets from the bed and started herding everyone toward the door. Xen shrugged into the big backpack and Daria grabbed the smaller one, while I grabbed my bag. The smell of smoke had started to permeate the air even before we opened our door. We raced down the stairs and out into a cold night, surrounded by others doing the same. People were racing around, bells clanging and over all of that, we could hear screaming.

"Where should we go?" Daria asked, looking around wildly. "This place is going to burn to the ground."

"The church?" I pointed in that direction. It had the advantage of being surrounded not by wooden structures, but by cobblestone and stone edifices, and had enough room to set up a triage. The four of us headed in that direction, jumping aside as water wagons raced toward the fire. The howling of the fire stalked us through the narrow streets, the flames staining the skies orange.

By the time we had reached the church, Mader Raffa was already setting things up to receive the injured and suddenly homeless. She saw me and waved me over. "L'âce, thank the Sacred Mother. We will need all of your gifts tonight. Our Brothers and Sisters are out directing the injured to come here."

"We're here to help, Mader. This is my sister Daria and my good friend Xen."

Katyk cleared her throat.

"And this is Katyk," I amended. "We're going to need supplies and a place to set up."

Mader Raffa nodded and beckoned one of her priestesses to us, directing her to set up a table near the altar for us, and to bring all the bandages and medicines they had. Xen, already sensing where my thoughts were, touched my arm. "The fire is far enough away for Daria and I to go to the apothecary shop and retrieve supplies."

I nodded in agreement. "Let me empty my bag for you to use." I went to the altar and opened my bag, pulling out all of my bandages, medicines, and tools before handing the bag off to Daria, who was shrugging out of the backpack. "Be quick. This is going to get very ugly."

"L'âce!"

I turned to find the first of the injured arriving, with priestesses directing them toward me.

I snagged Katyk's arm and drew her with me. "Here's where you start that thing where you thank me for saving your life," I stated. "I need you to triage. As they come in, you need to assess the injuries. Those that are life threatening, go here." I pointed to the left side of the nave, closest to the table of supplies. "Serious, but not life threatening, next. The rest can go on the other side. Got it?"

Katyk nodded, but then shook her head. "I ... I don't know how to do this."

"Just do the best you can." I sent her limping toward the door and turned to my first patient.

The man had a serious burn on his hand but was otherwise unharmed. I directed him to the Sister and told her to bathe it in cool water before I turned to the next. It wasn't long until the stream of the injured and dying was overwhelming. I stuck to the most serious patients, letting the Sisters and the other doctors who had shown up treat the ones who wouldn't need my special sort of aid.

I was sitting on the floor beside a boy who was badly burned, my hand on his head as I murmured a sleep spell to augment the gas I had already administered. I was shaking. I wasn't going to be able to save this one. I felt a hand on my shoulder and knew it was Xen.

"Here." They put a wooden cup in my hand, full of water.

"Thank you," I said, downing the whole thing. "Make sure Katyk gets some too." I looked around to find Katyk, spotting her curly head near the door as she helped an elderly woman sit.

"Where do you want us?" Daria asked.

I blinked at a rush of unexpected tears and moved away from the boy. As I stood, I realized that L'âcedôm Gilder and Stephan were with her. "Stephan with me ... I'll need you to run for supplies. L'âcedôm Gilder, if you wouldn't mind handling medicine dispensing, and Daria, I want you with me."

I moved to the next patient, an older man who was trembling with the pain of his burns. His skirt had caught fire, leaving behind blackened skin and in at least one spot, bone. "Stephan, I need clean bandages, water, and something for his pain."

As Stephan went to get those things, I brought the bottle of sleeping gas up to the man's face and unstoppered it, blowing it into his nose and mouth for extra measure.

I slipped a knife from my pocket and pierced my left palm before squatting down and holding that hand over the worst of the wounds. I met Daria's eyes as she squatted opposite me. I nodded once, hoping she understood what I was asking of her. As my blood dripped, I began to pray out loud to give cover to the healing incantation that Daria was murmuring.

When Stephan had returned with the supplies, Daria and I worked quietly to clean scorched fabric out of his burns, cleanse them as best we could, and bandage his legs to try to prevent infection. Daria helped me get a good dose of our specially-made pain potion into him before we moved on to the next, and the next, and the next.

I didn't know how many hours passed as we tried to help those we could, using our unique gifts as discreetly as possible. I couldn't tell you how many died on the floor of that church. I was achy and sore as I sank to the floor near the supply table, my hands and clothes covered in blood and soot. I did my best to wipe my palms clean on an already bloody towel.

Xen sat beside me, putting a cup of affe in my hands. I thanked them by putting my head on their shoulder. If I closed my eyes, I could fall asleep, sitting there. Instead, I sipped my affe and tried to gauge what needed to be done next. The parade of victims had slowed, but not stopped. Outside the open doors of the church, I could see that the sun was up.

"Any word on the fire?"

"It has been contained. There are still hot spots, but it is no longer spreading."

"How bad is it?"

"Devastating," Xen replied. "Much of the south side is ashes. It spread all the way to the river. They may not ever know how many died."

We sat quietly for a long time before it dawned on me that I didn't see Daria or Katyk.

"They are resting," Xen said, their hand lifting to rub my back in slow circles. "As you should be."

"How can I rest, Xen? Look at them." I gestured vaguely at the mass of bodies laying on the floor.

"You have done all that you can. And you have lost a lot of blood." They pointedly tipped my hand over to show all the puncture wounds I'd made while treating the wounded.

"L'âce, Mader Raffa asked me to give you this."

A young woman in the robes of a novitiate Sister held out a bowl of the local porridge to me, along with a hunk of bread. "Thank you, Sister."

I set aside my affe and wolfed down the porridge, suddenly starving. When I had cleaned the bowl, I went back to my affe and sipped it. I was almost ready to admit that I needed sleep when there was a cry of despair near the doors. I stood as four Scealc carried a makeshift litter into the church with a familiar figure on it.

Stâlian Batorry's face was pale except where a gash cut into the skin over and below her left eye. There was more blood than that; I could smell it.

"Bring her here!" I called, directing them to an open spot where a dead man had been moments before.

Xen moved with me as I went to her, dropping to my knees as they put the litter on the ground.

She wasn't burned. Her injuries looked more like impact trauma. She opened her eyes when I touched her, and I offered what I hoped was a kind smile. "Rest, Stâlian Batorry." I urged sleep upon her as I tried to assess her injuries. "What happened?"

"She was thrown from a fire wagon, L'âce."

"Okay, give me some space to work. Xen, I need water, bandages, and pain meds. You, Scealc, help me with this." I could see the wound that was the source of most of the blood. Her thigh was mangled.

Together, the soldier and I ripped open the pants leg to give me better access. Xen pressed a wet bandage into my hand, and I squeezed it over the wound.

The skin looked like ground beef that had started to turn. The bone was broken and had broken skin. There was trauma through the whole thigh like it had been stomped on. "We need to set the bone, but I'm not sure how," I said aside to Xen. "But she didn't rupture the artery. Let's wait for Daria. We'll control the pain and stop the bleeding for now."

Xen gave me cover for the cut I made on my right hand, which I then moved over to the worst of the injury, where I had cleaned away the most blood. I made it look like I was cleaning the wound while I let a good amount of my own blood drip into it to kickstart the healing.

I wavered as I stood, grabbing Xen's shoulder for support. My knees were made of rubber as we walked back to the altar, and as soon as I let go of Xen, they gave out. I caught myself on the altar, leaving a smear of blood behind.

Mader Raffa approached with a soft smile on her face. "Commen, L'âce. Let us care for you now."

Xen slipped an arm around my waist, and we followed the priestess to an ornately appointed stateroom. In front of a large fireplace, there was a brass tub filled with hot water and two novices awaiting me. I didn't fight Xen's hands undressing me or helping me into the tub, just sank gratefully into the embrace of the hot water.

It had been an eternity since I'd been able to soak … since California. I groaned as I lay back and the novices began to scrub my body clean. The heat penetrated my aching muscles and helped me let go of the tension my body had been clinging to for longer than I cared to consider. When they had cleaned me of blood and soot and had scrubbed my hair clean, they withdrew to allow me to soak, leaving a towel warming by the fire and Xen keeping an eye on me so that I didn't fall asleep and drown.

I didn't move until a chill began to settle into the water. "Xen." I lifted a hand for help getting up.

Xen grabbed the towel and came to me with it, helping me out of the tub before wrapping the warm cloth around me. I could have fallen asleep standing there while Xen helped me dry off, and then helped me into clean clothes.

Xen guided me to the large canopied bed and settled me into it. Compared to the beds we'd been living with, it was soft and seemed to know exactly how to cradle me. Xen hummed softly as they moved around cleaning up and the sound, along with the warmth of the bath and my exhaustion, became its own kind of magic, lulling me under.

———

I woke sometime later in the soft red glow of the fire. I was alone. I sat up slowly, stretching and feeling better than I had in a long while. I stood and found my boots before I tried to find my way back to the sanctuary.

While I slept, the last of the dead had been removed and I could smell astringent and the distinct scent of heavy rain. I hoped that meant that the last of the fire was finally out. I could see L'âcedôm Gilder moving among the patients, Stephan at her side. I didn't immediately see Daria or Xen but found Katyk organizing what was left on the supply table. She'd been given clean clothes also and someone had found her some shoes. Her hair was pulled back in a tidy knot.

"Katyk, did you get some sleep?" I asked.

She turned to look at me. "Some, yes. You?"

I nodded and turned to look for my sister again.

"They are working on food," Katyk said.

I looked for Stâlian Batorry and found that while I was asleep someone had set her bone and bandaged her thigh. I walked to her and knelt, reaching a hand to take her pulse. It was stronger than it had been. It seemed she would recover, as long as nothing got infected.

"Hêalic."

Stâlian Batorry's eyes were on me, steely and fierce. I could see the pain in them.

"Stâlian, how are you feeling?" I asked the question before it dawned on me what she had just called me.

The blood rushed to my face, and I fought to keep my expression neutral.

"You have done much good work here."

"I have only done what I can," I countered, uncomfortable with the praise. "Are you in much pain? Shall I give you something?"

She took my hand in both of hers. "Save it for the others. Pain builds strength."

In my opinion, the only thing pain built was more pain, but I didn't say that. I made it look like I was checking her bandages so I could get a better read on her injury. Whoever had set it had done a good job, but the thigh was a mess. I knew I would have been screaming for morphine or something similar if it were me.

I moved away from her and checked on the most critical of my patients. Here and there, I could sense signs that Daria had worked some small magic, but I knew that far too many had died that night.

CHAPTER 18
ANNE

The sun was just beginning to make its slide down the western skies, casting long, ghastly shadows of ruined buildings onto the cobblestone from the remnants of the nearest burned building.

From the square, I couldn't see the damage. Snake-like tendrils of smoke clung to the corners of buildings and gathered in the gutters on the streets, the scent of burnt wood and flesh hanging thick in the air. There were survivors still being pulled from the wreckage, but they were going to become fewer as time went by. Soon, it would only be bodies that they found. I walked down the street, trying to get a better idea of the destruction.

The building where we had been was still standing but had taken a good amount of damage. The apothecary shop had no roof, and the glass was all shattered, but it still had walls. I stopped in the middle of the street, watching grim-faced women shifting debris. The sense of loss was profound. I kept walking until I reached the river, where I found that most of the shantytown on the other side of the bridge had been wiped out, the surrounding trees all scorched and black.

"The upside is the fire probably saved the city from the plague."

I turned to find Anne beside me. She was filthy and she was cradling her left arm in a way that I couldn't see the injury. "Anne, are you okay?"

She grimaced and moved so I could see the burns that covered her hand and up her arm. "That looks nasty. Come with me to the church. Let me treat it." We walked slowly; the pace held because Anne was unsteady on her feet. "Is it more than the hand?" I asked as we neared the church.

"Nothing a glass of whiskey wouldn't help," Anne responded.

I didn't push but supported her as we climbed the stairs, and I took her toward the supply table where Xen had cleared one side to put a large vat of soup and stacks of wooden bowls. "Sit here."

She did as I instructed while I called Stephan over to me and asked for clean water and bandages, then retrieved what I needed from my set of tools, as well as some of the augmented pain meds. Anne had leaned back against the leg of the table, her eyes closed. I lifted her burned hand and cradled it in my lap, using it as an anchoring point to let me read her injuries.

I reached up to the table for the sleep gas, knowing that cleaning the burn wasn't going to be pleasant, and as I blew the gas into Anne's face, I murmured a spell to reinforce it. Her face went slack, and I began a more thorough examination of her body. Her left hip and ankle both had trauma, and she'd inhaled a lot of smoke.

I could feel Xen nearby, their hand settling on my shoulder. For a brief moment, our minds meshed, and they fed me energy. Just as Xen was pulling away, I got a flash of something that wasn't either me or them.

A dark alley, the sound of shuffling footsteps, the heat of blood spilled, the scent of it hanging in the cold air. Then a face emerged from the shadows. My own face.

I let go of Anne's hand and pulled back.

"Thána?" Xen looked concerned as I stood and moved away from Anne.

I drew them far enough away that I knew Anne wouldn't hear me if she woke. "Did you see what I saw?" I asked.

"Not really. Just that you were upset by it."

I nodded. "I need to see the Steallere. I think Anne is the one who's been killing those prostitutes. I think what I just saw was her memory of the night I interrupted the killer."

"How is that possible?" Xen asked.

"I don't know."

"You can't just go accusing someone. What will you tell them about why you believe this?"

I shook my head and sighed heavily. They were right. There was no way to implicate Anne without exposing myself. "No, you're right. But what are we going to do? Just let her go around killing people?"

Daria joined us, handing me a bowl of the soup Xen had made.

"Where is Katyk?" I asked.

Daria grimaced but pointed at the door. "Helping move the bodies of the dead."

"How many?" I asked.

"It may be weeks before we know for sure," Xen responded. "But thousands, at least."

The count would also probably never be accurate because countless bodies could have been reduced to ash, lost in the ruins. I glanced aside at Anne, making sure she was still out. I had no idea what to do with her. I was convinced she was the murderer, but the fire had destroyed most of the murder scenes, and likely any evidence among her possessions.

"I need a way to keep her unconscious," I said, gesturing at Anne.

"Any particular reason?" Daria asked.

"Your sister believes that she is the murderer currently at large."

Daria frowned at me. "Why?"

"I saw something." I shook my head. "I mean, I think I saw …" I pinched the bridge of my nose and let the images pass through my mind. "That night in the alley … but I was seeing it from the killer's eyes. I saw myself."

Daria frowned harder. "Since when do *you* see things?"

I shrugged a little. I never had gotten around to telling my sister about this new ability. "Just in the last few weeks. And only when touching someone. I saw Mader Raffa as a girl. And sometimes when treating patients, I see … bits and pieces of their lives."

Daria moved to Anne's side, squatting down, and putting one hand to her wrist as if checking her pulse. She closed her eyes. A moment later she was on her feet and coming back to us. "You're not wrong."

"So, what do we do?"

"I can mix something up that will keep her under, but then what?"

We looked at Anne for the longest time before I heard someone calling, "Hêalic!"

I moved around Xen to see two women carrying a woman in scorched clothing. I went toward them, directing them to an empty blanket on the floor. They eased her down and I went to my knees to start my appraisal without even looking at her face. She'd been crushed and burned. The bones in her legs were shattered and bloody, and there was internal damage and bleeding. We would be lucky if she lived.

Daria knelt opposite me, doing her own appraisal, and Xen set my bag down beside me. We worked without words, cleaning wounds, and bandaging what we could. "We need to do something about these bleeds," I said softly. "I don't know how."

Daria shook her head. "If we were somewhere else, I'd say surgery, but neither of us are qualified."

I cast about the medical knowledge I'd managed to acquire, which mostly amounted to what I'd seen on TV and basic first-aid classes, plus whatever I had learned in getting to understand my power. "I think we need to drain the blood to relieve the pressure, and then I can think of only one way to heal her inside. Xen, bring me the darkest of whatever medicines we have left and a bowl."

"What are you thinking?" Daria asked with one eyebrow raised.

I lifted the small knife that lived in my bag. Before she could object, I pointed down at the patient's chest. "We need a tube or something. I can direct you where to cut." I handed the knife to her, still thinking about the tubing.

"Hêalic, will this work?"

I looked up at the Scealc who had helped carry the women in. She was holding out a hollow rod that I'd seen some of them carry as a weapon.

I nodded and took it from her. Placing my right hand on the injured woman's stomach, I felt for the place of injury. With the rod, I pointed to the spot most likely to give us the relief we needed. "Here."

Xen's presence settled over me as they returned. Daria's hand was sure and steady as she pressed the blade into flesh, then took the rod from me and inserted it. Only seconds passed before dark red blood began to drip from the end of the rod and into the bowl.

I could sense the release of pressure and turned to Xen to take the vial of medicine. I didn't care what it was meant to treat. It was only a means to an end. Xen seemed to understand and moved to talk to the Scealc and her partner, distracting them to give me the time I needed. I took the knife back from Daria and used it to slice into the meat of my left palm. It was a deeper cut than any I'd used since the fire, but I needed far more blood for this. Squeezing my hand, I filled the vial, then closed it with a thumb to shake it up.

Daria's disapproval was tangible as she pressed a bandage against the cut and took the vial from me. "Xen, a hand?"

Xen and Daria sat the woman up and Daria pulled her mouth open, pouring the mixture in with one hand and stroking her throat with the other to make her swallow. Once that was done, I sent Xen for wood to make splints, and Daria and I set about straightening her legs as best we could. Once Xen returned, we splinted both legs and bandaged them.

She'd likely never walk again, but with a fair bit of healing blood and magic inside her, she might yet live.

Xen helped me to my feet as Katyk reappeared. She looked exhausted and dirt-smudged. She spotted us and came our way.

"So, what's with the 'Hêalic' I keep hearing?" Daria asked once we had moved out of earshot of anyone who might overhear us.

"Divine healers," Xen said, "as I understand it."

I nodded. "Apparently, Stâlian Batorry has declared me no ordinary doctor, but a healer gifted by Killi. I haven't decided if that's a good thing or not."

"Well, it's better than her deciding you're a witch," Katyk offered.

"Hêalic, Mader Raffa has asked me to escort you to her," a young novice said, bowing almost as deep as she would to Raffa or Batorry. "And your friends as well."

We fell into step behind her until we came to Raffa's office. Sitting at Raffa's desk was a woman I didn't recognize, but judging by her clothing, she was someone of importance. The purple of her suit jacket was deep and royal looking. She had a round face and deep-set eyes, with a mop of curly auburn hair cut to flatter her face. Raffa stood beside her.

"Hêalic Thána Alizon, may I present Her Grace, the Grand Duchess Marlena. Your Grace, this is the Hêalic and her friends."

Grand Duchess. I sort of bowed and the others followed my lead. "Your Grace, you honor us."

"Nonsense, it is you and your friends who honor us, Hêalic. It has been many years since we were graced with one such as yourself."

"Sacred Mader Killi sees the needs of her children," I said, hoping I didn't sound overly pious. "We are only happy to be able to serve."

"Am I to understand that your lodging was destroyed in the fire?"

"Yes, your Grace. Fortunately, we did not have much in the way of material things."

She stood, tugging at her waistcoat. "Well, now that the R'aedan has taken you up as Hêalic, I expect that to change, at least once you are officially installed that is."

"I … what?" I glanced aside at Xen, thinking I hadn't understood.

They just shrugged at me.

"I will leave Mader Raffa to explain the details. She has also agreed to give the four of you shelter until such time as the R'aedan arrives for the ceremony. Now, if you'll excuse me, there is much to be done for the city. I look forward to seeing you in a few days."

"What ceremony?" I whispered aside to Xen.

Again, they shrugged.

Mader Raffa returned from walking the Grand Duchess to the door, and I cleared my throat. "Mader, may I ask … what was she talking about?"

Raffa smiled and it lifted some of the fatigue from her face. "Several days ago, Stâlian Batorry sent a report to the R'aedan concerning all of your good work, and her belief that you were a Hêalic sent from Killi to heal this terrible plague from our city. Yesterday, word reached us that they will arrive here in three days' time to examine the evidence."

"I … guess I understood it as an honorary title sort of thing," I said.

Raffa took both of my hands. "You are a most amazing person, Hêalic. Soon, not only the poor and ill will know of you, but all of Bolnam will. But now, let me offer you what respite I can. I've already had your things taken to your rooms. I will have Novice Laney escort you."

I touched her hand lightly. "I still have patients I need to see to."

"Of course." She lifted a bell off her desk and rang it. When the door opened, she asked the novice who had brought us to escort the others and then to meet me in the sanctuary.

My mind was still racing, trying to figure out what was happening and how we were going to get out of Gavelscore now that they'd decided I was some sort of savior. All of that fled my mind, however, when I got to the sanctuary and found that the patient I most needed to see was gone.

Anne Gothfried had escaped.

CHAPTER 19
JUDGEMENT

Mader Raffa gave me free use of the library, which I took advantage of, hoping to get an idea of what to expect when the R'aedan arrived. The documentation did more to convince me of the rarity of what was about to happen than any actual information about what to expect, at least until I ventured into the liturgy.

The last Hêalic to be ordained had been over a hundred years before. Like most of the church's other liturgy and rites, the ceremony was filled with grand gestures and scripture readings, and prayers. All I had to do was know when to walk, stand and kneel, and how to respond to the formal questions. None of that concerned me.

It was what came before that. A formal declaration of my divine nature had to be affirmed by all five of the women who made up the R'aedan, who were essentially like bishops, who ruled the church. Stâlian Batorry, as my sponsor, would be the first to speak, and then she would call witnesses. After their testimony, I would stand for questioning. Then they would decide my fate.

The morning of that meeting, I distracted myself from my nerves by going out with Xen to look at the damages from the fire and see if anyone needed my help. I was also subconsciously looking for Anne. If she'd figured out that I knew about her, she might be long gone.

"She is not your responsibility," Xen said softly.

"I know," I responded. We had paused in our walk to purchase sweet fried bread and sit in the square watching the comings and goings. "She's going to do it again, though."

Xen's hand rubbed my back for comfort. "Are you prepared for this questioning?"

"As much as I can be, I think." We had debated, the three of us, on the advisability of going through with it, versus just getting the hell out of Dodge. The biggest advantage was that if I was accepted, we would have church resources to get us closer to the portal.

Unfortunately, the biggest downfall could be death.

No pressure or anything.

"How is Katyk?" Xen asked, knowing I had examined her again that morning.

"Still Katyk," I said with a sigh. "The injury keeping her magic locked down may be permanent. There's been no improvement."

"There is still a lot of anger in her, even if it is dampened," Xen said. "And you were right about the Kabeshi murdering her sister as punishment for our escape. She is very aware that you could have let them kill her and she is uncomfortable with you, or rather with the fact that you saved her after everything."

I looked at Xen, a little surprised. "Have you been reading her mind, Xen?"

Xen blushed and looked away. "I needed to assure myself that you would be safe."

"What about the rules?"

They shrugged. "We find ourselves in circumstances that the rules were never exposed to, and in case of imminent death, some grace is allowed."

"Good to know." I glanced up at the church. "I should probably head in."

We stood and Xen walked with me into the sanctuary, where we parted ways. I knocked on Mader Raffa's office door and was admitted.

Mader Raffa was dressed formally, as if prepared to lead the mass. She looked a little nervous, but I couldn't tell the exact cause. "We are nearly prepared. If you would come with me."

She led me then to a part of the church I had never seen. Plush carpeting lined hallways paneled in dark wood, lit by spherical gas lamps at even intervals. We stopped beside a set of double doors. "Wait here."

Mader Raffa went inside, only to return moments later. "They are ready for you."

She held the door open for me and I entered cautiously. The five priestesses of the R'aedan sat on a slightly raised dais, in high-backed chairs that were nearly regal. Before them was a dock where I was expected to stand. Beside that dock, Stâlian Batorry sat, her wounded leg raised on a cushioned stool. Gathered in the gallery were a host of novices and priestesses.

Stâlian Batorry grimaced a little as she stood, holding the dock's railing for stability. "Holy R'aedan, may I present to you Thána Alizon." She held out a hand, beckoning me closer.

I stepped in front of the dock and bowed deeply to the R'aedan before stepping to Stâlian Batorry's side.

The priestess in the middle stood, raising her hands before praying and blessing the proceedings. "Stâlian Batorry, you may begin."

She shifted her weight and hopped into the dock while I took the seat left to me, behind the dock.

"Holy R'aedan, I come before you today to present the case for this woman to be declared to be Hêalic, sent from our Sacred Mother to heal those afflicted by the Unclean One, he who has sent plague and disease among us."

"We recognize your claims, Stâlian Batorry. We will hear your witnesses."

"May it please, your Eminence, I call Sister Emma Baker."

The doors opened and admitted the first young priestess I had healed of the plague. She was formally attired like Mader Raffa was, perfectly pressed black pants with a crimson shirt, with a black collar under a black jacket.

Stâlian Batorry stepped down and retook her seat and Sister Emma stepped into the dock and bowed to the dais. "Welcome, Sister. Have you come today to give testimony on the matter before this court?"

"I have, Your Eminence."

"And is it your intent to speak only the truth as you understand it?"

"It is, Your Eminence."

"You may proceed."

Emma spoke about her bout with the plague and how so many were dead, but she was alive because I had saved her. Each of the surviving Sisters and Brothers I'd treated spoke in turn before Stâlian Batorry called L'âcedôm Gilder in.

"I understand that you employed L'âce Alizon in your apothecary shop?"

"Yes, your Eminence. I saw the good she was doing, her skill in understanding what the body needs, and that, combined with her sister's skill with medicine. I hoped we could help the people of Gavelscore."

"What ailments has she healed?"

"Most notably the plague in the poorest of our citizens, but also rashes and blisters, broken bones, and in the recent fire, she treated and saved many. We all bore witness to her tireless service that night and into the following days."

"Yes, Stâlian Batorry has given us her testimony of that as well."

There were several more witnesses called, some of whom I didn't even recognize, who spoke of my "heroic efforts" to save lives. More than four hours passed, and I was beginning to get a serious case of numb-butt when Stâlian Batorry stood once again to address the R'aedan.

"Holy R'aedan, these are but a small number of those who have borne witness to L'âce Alizon's divine calling. These gifts can only come from our Sacred Mader. Name her Hêalic, with all the rights and responsibilities of the title. Honor her service."

"Thank you, Stâlian Batorry. You may be seated. The R'aedan will hear from L'âce Alizon now."

I stood and offered my hand to the Stâlian to aid her back to her seat, then stepped up into the dock. I bowed to the assembly once again and looked at the ranking priestess who had been conducting the proceedings. When she nodded to me, I spoke. "I am Thána Alizon and I present myself to you."

"Welcome, L'âce. As you can imagine, there are questions to be answered about who you are and where you come from."

I inclined my head. I had spent some of my study time examining the map in the library in intimate detail to prepare for this question. "Yes, your Eminence. I understand. Most recently, I journeyed here to Gavelscore with my sister and a friend from your southern neighbor, Barchdon. Before Barchdon, we lived on an island in the eastern oceans."

One of the other R'aedon drew my attention. "Where did you study your profession?"

"To begin, with my mother. She was our town L'âce. Then a school in the Midwells."

"How is it that you possess these gifts we have heard about?"

I shook my head lightly. "I do not know, Eminence. I only know that it comes from within me, thus can only be the power of our Sacred Mother that shows me the ailments and tells me how to heal them."

There was a murmuring behind me and the R'aedan whispered amongst themselves for a few moments.

"We would see a demonstration."

"I ... what?" I hadn't been prepared for that. "I'm afraid that there isn't much to see, your Eminence. It looks much the same as any doctor examining a patient."

She gestured at the doors, and they were opened to reveal a frail-looking woman in the uniform of a Scealc commander who was aided on one side by a cane and on the other by a novice. I stepped out of the dock and went to them. As my hand met the paper-thin skin on her arm, my senses blew open. At her center, there was an angry ulcer trying to eat her stomach. The pain was intense, and she hadn't eaten properly in a long time because of it.

"Please, sit." I helped her to a chair and went down on one knee beside it to make a show of examining her, though it was without my usual tools and more cursory than I would have liked because of it. I asked her to show me her pain, then laid my hand over the spot while I asked her a few questions about her condition: how long she'd had the pain, and if it was worse after eating certain foods, and things like that. The whole time I could feel the eyes of the R'aeden on me. When I thought I'd done enough that they would believe my diagnosis, I turned to face them again.

"This is an ulcer, your Eminence."

"And you can treat it?"

I nodded. "With the right medicines, I can."

"What medicines would those be?"

That was a harder question. Normally, I told Daria what I could sense, and she would choose the medicines. "We must compound something to neutralize the acid, which is causing the pain, and reduce the swelling around the ulcer, to give it time to heal." I had no idea if an ulcer was something I could just … eat like I did the plague and other things.

"We will deliberate while you treat our sister."

Her gavel rang out as it struck the arm of her chair and the whole room stood while the R'aedan filed out. I turned my attention to the novice. "Can you help get her back to her room? I will need to fetch my tools."

I waited until the room was empty but for me and Stâlian Batorry, who was awaiting the arrival of her escort with the litter chair she'd been using to get around before I left the room myself to seek out Xen and Daria.

I found them, and Katyk, in the kitchen, assembling plague treatment kits with what must have been the last of the inventory from the shop.

"How'd it go?" Daria asked as I joined them.

"I'm still alive and not in a cell, so I guess it went well." I sighed and rested my head on Xen's shoulder. "I have a new patient, with a pretty severe stomach ulcer. I'm supposed to treat her while they deliberate. I think it's the final test."

"I think I have something that should help," Daria responded, getting up from the table and grabbing a cloth bag from the floor. She rummaged through it and came up with a jar that she shook before handing it to me. The powder inside was chalky white. "Put a pinch into tea or water to help with the acid, once in the morning and before each meal. And for the pain and inflammation, have her drink this every three hours." She handed me a small bottle. "And tell her to eat basic and bland from now on."

"Good. I'm going to grab my bag." I kissed the top of Xen's head and went to grab my doctor's bag, making sure I had the knock-out gas and some pain medicine before I went in search of my patient.

I found her with a little help from one of the novices and had little trouble getting the room emptied of anyone but the two of us. I did a more thorough exam, listening to her heartbeat and the like before I explained I needed to see her throat. I put my left hand over her eyes and used my right to open her mouth widely. I unstoppered the bottle and blew some of the fumes into her face so she'd doze off while I tried to take the ulcer right out of her.

It was a stubborn thing, and I was ready to give up the pull when I felt it give, surging up through the throat and into my mouth. It tasted like burnt coffee and dirt. I coughed a little, pulling back from her to pick up the medicines. I explained the dosage to her and set them on the small table beside her bed. "You should rest now," I said softly as I stood.

"Thank you, Hêalic."

I smiled at her, though it felt fake. "I'm not Hêalic yet, Scealc."

"You have my vote," she responded.

The sanctuary was quiet when I emerged a short time later. The smell of the dead and dying had been scrubbed clean and there was little sign left that this space had just recently been a triage center. The wounded had all been moved to temporary housing provided by the Grand Duchess.

With the large doors closed, the only light was from the candles that flickered on the altar and the small pools of colored light from the windows. The smell of incense wafted over the floors and the silence lured me into contemplation.

I'd never been a religious person, even if I had been playing one for the months that we'd been there in Gavelscore. One of my foster families had been very religious, devout Catholics that made sure all of us foster kids got a good education in their faith, but I'd never felt any sense of any god.

I stood before the altar and closed my eyes, sinking into my center to open up the senses beyond the normal five. In the quiet dark, I could feel Xen and Daria not far away. The sanctuary itself almost had a presence, one that filled me up the longer I stood there, permeated with a deep calm, love. If I hadn't known better, I might have called it god.

Something was tugging my attention, drawing me to step closer to the altar, the same way that tombstone had back at the Mauno Kort. A memory bubbled up, though it wasn't mine. No, this was one of those things tied to being a blood witch. This was *makrá vlépinta*. Another blood witch had stood here. I breathed in deeply and tried to reach the memory and bring it closer.

The sound wobbled around me, a choir singing a solemn hymn in the hush of a congregation that was witnessing the event, the soft breathing of the woman kneeling on the altar. She bowed her head to receive a blessing, rising to her feet with tears in her eyes as she was presented to the people as a newly ordained Hêalic.

The vision slipped away, and my knees buckled, landing me on the first step of the altar. I dragged in a deep breath and steadied myself. I had no idea if somehow this blood witch was a relative of some sort. I knew instinctively that she had lived well over a century before. This was not the last Hêalic, but someone before her.

CHAPTER 20
HÊALIC

My mind was spinning off in fifty different directions as I walked back to my room. There was no denying that my gifts had grown by leaps and bounds since arriving here on Gavelscore. I wasn't sure why, other than that I had been using them fairly consistently.

I got as far as my door before the fatigue crashed down on me. My vision swam a bit and I clung to the door as I opened it. It was more than fatigue though. There was a sense of urgency to it that propelled me through the door and down onto the bed, as if there was a dream demanding I give it time.

I sank into it easily, dropping into a time hundreds of years before. I knew her as soon as I saw her. She was radiant in her youth, apprenticed to a court physician, devout in her faith. I saw her in the church, kneeling on the altar stair, head bowed in prayer.

That same feeling of presence filled me and she seemed to nearly glow as the scene shifted and she was at the bedside of a woman who had severe lacerations on her stomach. The Hêalic laid her hands over the bleeding wounds and turned her face up to the heavens as she mouthed the words of some prayer or spell. When she lifted her hands, there were no wounds.

The feeling of Xen nearing woke me and I sat up as they opened my door. Instantly, they looked a little startled. "Are you okay?"

I nodded, still feeling a little strange.

"Why are you glowing?"

"What?" I looked down at myself but couldn't see any glow.

Xen rubbed their eyes and shook their head. "Must have been a trick of the light."

"I was having a weird dream," I said. "I'm not the first blood witch to have been here. She left an imprint on the altar."

"Are you sure?"

I nodded and moved closer to the fire. "I had a ... vision ... for lack of a better word, out there. She was a Hêalic, and she was ordained on that same altar." I tried to reason out the rest of it. "She wasn't just a blood witch though. I saw her do something ... impossible."

Xen grinned. "I have seen *you* do the impossible."

I rolled my eyes. "Not the same thing. She healed a woman just by touching her."

"That would be something to see."

"It was. I've never felt like that or anything close to it."

"Like someone or something beyond you was there?" Xen asked, sitting in the other chair.

I nodded, trying to reach back for that feeling. "The sanctuary itself seemed to have a presence like it was a person. Or something." I rubbed the bridge of my nose to stop myself from frowning.

"I have felt this only when visiting the birthing place. It is a sacred space where we return often in our youth. There, we are never alone."

I pondered the vision again, trying to understand what it was about, and what it was telling me about the days and weeks to come. The impending sense that *something* was coming had me on edge.

About an hour later I was called back to the hearing room. There were at least twice as many people as there had been early in the day, including Mader Raffa and the ranking Brother, whose name escaped me. Stâlian Batorry stood beside the dock, all her weight on her good leg. My mind flashed back to the way that Hêalic had healed terrible wounds and I could almost see myself doing the same for her.

The R'aedan filed in and took their seats and the room hushed in expectation of their announcement. The woman in the middle stood. "L'âce Alizon, please present yourself."

I stepped into the dock and bowed, my heart hammering against my ribs. This was the moment when they either accepted me or rejected me as a witch. "I am here, your Eminence."

"We have reviewed the evidence presented to us and confirmed the impressive deeds Stâlian Batorry has testified to. It is the decision of the R'aedan that you have met the standards of Hêalic, and in two days we will present you to the people, bestowed with the title, rights, and privileges thereof. Henceforth, you will serve our Sacred Mother and carry out the duties of the Hêalic."

I breathed a sigh of relief and bowed deeply. "I am most honored, Holy R'aedan. Thank you."

The room erupted in applause and people talking excitedly. It quickly became overwhelming as people began coming to congratulate me. I withstood it for as long as I could, but the crush of people was suffocating me, and I found myself looking for a way out.

Mader Raffa saw my distress and came to my rescue, inserting herself between me and my admirers, making space for me to leave the room. I stumbled through the door and almost directly into Xen's arms. They drew me in close and moved us down the empty hallway.

"I felt your distress," Xen said once we were safely back in my room. "I feared the worst."

I shook my head. "Just too many people."

"When will the ceremony be?" Xen asked.

"In two days."

"And then what?"

I looked up at them and realized we hadn't set any plans in motion beyond getting clear of this particular hurdle. "Well, the fire burned out a good amount of the plague here. I just need to convince the R'aedan to send me north to tackle the plague in other cities. We can use the trip to search the areas Katyk remembers."

"We will still need to be careful."

"Very. I don't know how they will react if their newly ordained Hêalic is seen running for the hills."

The church library was my refuge over the next two days. I delved deep into the religion's liturgy and commentary. It was comforting. I avoided the sanctuary but mulled over the vision and the dream and what they meant for me.

"I'm a little nervous," I said to Daria the night before the ceremony. "What if I have another vision in the middle of the ritual?"

"Maybe you need to go down to the sanctuary tonight, you know? Open all the way up, let whatever is in there when you're not in front of a crowd so that it doesn't ambush you tomorrow?"

It wasn't the worst plan we'd had since arriving there. "Yeah, I could do that."

"Do you want us to come along?" Xen asked as I put the book I had been reading back on the shelf.

I nodded slightly. "Yes, I'd like that."

Together, the three of us made our way to the empty sanctuary. It was still and calm, and I could feel that same presence I had the last time I had stood there. Xen's hand found mine and our minds slipped together so we were almost one person. Daria took my other hand, and her power and energy filled the space beside me.

Like I had before, I faced the altar and centered myself, and opened myself up to the energy in the room. Almost immediately I was surrounded by a golden wave of light, transported out of that church to stand barefoot and alone on soft grass in a vast meadow. I could still feel Daria and Xen, but they were distant now.

That presence filled the air around me, alive with an incredible energy that made me feel like I could do anything. I breathed it in, and it felt like I was being lifted off my feet. Then a rush of memories and emotions ran through me, a thousand lifetimes, a million moments, Hêalics and blood witches from a hundred different worlds.

Under all of it was a profound sense of joy and a feeling of belonging that I had never experienced before, except when Xen and I bonded. I wallowed in it.

Eventually, I felt Xen calling me back and reluctantly I let go of whatever that presence was and settled back into my body. My knees were rubber, and it took all I had to stay standing. We stood silent together for a long time before Xen lifted a hand to wipe tears from my face. I hadn't even realized I was crying.

None of us spoke until we were back in my room and even then, it was only in hushed tones.

"That was unbelievable," Daria said. "Thank you for sharing it with me."

"I do not know what that was, but it was beautiful," Xen added.

"How much of that did you guys get?" I asked as I sank into a chair by the fire.

"Mostly the emotion for me," Daria answered. "And the image of a meadow and golden light."

"There was so much more," Xen said softly. "All of those healers ..."

I nodded and rubbed a slightly trembling hand over my face. "It was like finding home, not in a place but in myself. If that makes any sense." Was that god? Is that what it felt like to believe?

I knew there would be no answers and I was suddenly exhausted. There would be an early wake-up call the next day as my preparations began with a special bath and submitting myself to the ministrations of the novices.

I did my best to submit gracefully, but I'd been taking care of myself for a long time, so it was hard not to just grab the soap and clean myself. This too was part of the ritual.

The pool was heated to a perfect body temperature and would easily seat five or six people. The novices stripped me of my clothing and walked me into the water, one on each side. In the middle of the pool, the water reached my navel, and hands on my shoulders encouraged me to dunk myself. When my head was submerged, they held me there to a count of five, then let me up. We repeated that two more times before they began the cleaning ritual.

The soap they used smelled vaguely of jasmine, or whatever passed for jasmine there, and they diligently washed my hair and body, turning me as necessary. Then we repeated the dunking ritual three times before they led me back out of the water. Two different novices took over from there, toweling me dry and wrapping me in a warm soft robe before leading me to a dressing chamber.

A vanity sat to the left as we entered, and in front of us were racks of the various religious garb of the Sisters. For the next hour, I let the novices dry and style my hair, anoint me with various oils, and rub lotion over every inch of my body.

Clothing came next and I had to appreciate the chosen garments. All black, which suited me fine, and of the finest quality I'd ever worn, the pants fit like they'd been made for me. The shirt felt like silk on my skin, the sleeves buttoned tightly at the wrist and blooming above the elbow. The boots they brought me were sturdy and comfortable, black leather that came to my knee.

I felt like a pirate if I was honest.

When they were done, Mader Raffa came into the room, her face solemn and reverent. In her hands was a long red sash. She lifted it and kissed it before approaching me.

"*Trûwa sâcred mader Killi same only in swâ êower grâdûtan duguð wann. Forlaetan hêo stician êower bærnan.*" She lifted the sash to my eyes, moving around me to tie it loosely behind my head.

It didn't block out everything; I could see a small band in front of me out of the bottom of the blindfold. Someone lifted my hands and put them on the shoulders of the novice in front of me, then there were hands on my shoulders from behind.

I was walked that way to the doors where I would enter the sanctuary and there, Mader Raffa put my hands together and buckled them lightly with a short, red leather strip. She murmured a prayer or blessing that I didn't quite catch all of before I was turned three times. The sound of choral singing leaked through the doors and washed over me as the doors opened.

When the last note faded away, a light tap on my shoulder told me it was time. I had to walk the aisle alone. Did I ever mention how I could trip over nothing, even without wearing a blindfold? Yeah, fun.

My first step was tentative as I made slight adjustments to the angle of my head so that I could get the best view of what was in front of me.

There was an expectant hush and what felt like thousands of eyes watching me progress toward the altar. My heart hammered away inside me, and I reached out to try to find that presence, that calming energy I had accessed the night before. I found Xen first, beaming joy and strength.

My toe found the altar step, telling me to stop. I bowed three times to the altar and spoke my lines. "I come to you, Sacred Mother, humbled to serve and ready to be bathed in your light."

The sounds of the congregation shuffling around as they took their seats preceded a gentle touch on my shoulder that was my cue to kneel. The choir began the next song, a hymn about the healing light of Sunna and Mônna. I couldn't see, but I knew that a procession of novices came down the aisle behind me with tall candles. Behind them came the R'aedan.

I could almost feel the increased heat as the novices spread out behind me. R'aedan Kalys would take the candle of the head novice and approach me. I sensed her movement and tried to stay still as she came in for the initial blessing. She lifted the candle and circled my head three times.

"*Menen dugud swaean of Sunna lâttêowa êower mearcpaed. Menen done as bryne un–l'aed Mônna scînan êow. Menen sê bærnan orgilde Killi behealdan êower.*" May the light of Sunna guide your path. May the light of Mônna shine on you. May the light of Killi fill you.

I shifted a little on knees that were starting to complain about the marble step as the ritual transitioned to a sermon of sorts, wherein the R'aedan took turns reading scripture and expounding upon the skills and faith of a Hêalic, and the sacred duty to which I would soon be bound.

A reverent hymn followed, during which I could almost see the movement of people in my head. The R'aedan stood across the altar and a candle was put into my bound hands, unlit. As the song ended, silence settled over the church.

CHAPTER 21
HEALING

INTO THAT REVERENT HUSH, THE R'AEDAN SPOKE. "SÊ DÂ DE FULLAN DUGUD Ûpriht Killi?" Who comes before the Upright Goddess?

To my left, Stâlian Batorry stood. I could feel the pain radiating from her leg, and smell the vague scent of infection just beginning. "*Ay forberan Thána Alizon ûser Ûpriht Killi.*"

"*Tô hwý rihtung drohtian êower streccan hiere of hê?*" What is her purpose here?

I lifted my head, hoping my voice wouldn't shake. "I come before the Upright Goddess, our Sacred Mother, to take on the mantle of Hêalic."

"Will you, Thána Alizon, accept the duties of a Hêalic?"

"Aye."

"Will you, Thána Alizon, give yourself to the people, to offer healing and comfort to all, without regard for station or wealth?"

"Aye."

"Will you, Thána Alizon, abide by the laws of Killi in all things?"

"Aye."

"Will you, Thána Alizon, forgo all alliances and ties to serve?"

"Aye."

"Will you, Thána Alizon, submit yourself to the governance of this holy body, to go where we send you for the greater good of all?"

"Aye."

Each question came from a different R'aedan, the last from the leader who now stood in front of me. Her hands were hot on my head and the feeling of that presence was swelling inside me as she prayed. I almost felt lifted off my feet.

"Mother Killi, anoint this Hêalic with your light. Guide her on your path. Spark her fire."

I heard a gasp from all around me and shifted until I could see through the small gap in the blindfold. The candle in my hands was alight, though no one was close enough to me to have lit it.

The R'aedan hesitated briefly, then her hands returned to my head, loosening the blindfold. "May you see now with the eyes of Killi." She moved behind me and wound the sash three times around my waist, tying it on my left side. Returning to her place in front of me, she unbuckled the leather around my wrists. "May your hands be guided by Killi's hands."

A gentle hand on my elbow guided me to stand, which was the cue for my knees to remind me of their hatred for marble. The leather was buckled around my upper right arm. I shifted on my feet, trying to loosen up the muscles that had tightened with all of that kneeling, while the R'aedan prayed again over me. I let the words wash over and around me, once again seeking out that presence, whether it was an actual god or just sentience or whatever.

I opened myself up to it. My chest seemed to expand, and light poured out of me, out of my pores. In that moment, I was more than just myself, I was all who had gone before me. I was vaguely aware of the congregation's awe, but my attention was pulled to Stâlian Batorry's pain. It was unbearable to me in my current open state.

Turning to her, I lifted the candle in one hand and laid my other on her leg. The wound was hot to the touch, even through the bandages. The golden light suffused me and moved through my hand, winding around the leg and as it lifted away, I felt the pain leaving as well.

Slowly, the light dissipated, and I was left standing at the altar in front of everyone who was staring in awed silence. For a long moment, no one spoke or moved.

The R'aedan leader was the first to recover, her hands circling mine around the candle. Her eyes met mine and I wasn't sure what I saw in them, but it included a fair amount of awe, not quite disbelief.

She took the candle from me and handed it off to one of her Sisters before she drew me up the last two steps to stand on the altar. She turned me to face the congregation. "Hêalic Thána Alizon."

The noise as the room exploded into applause was almost palpable. I wanted to step back, away from it, but there was nowhere to go. My eyes skipped to Xen who was wiping tears off their face, then to Stâlian Batorry who was rubbing a hand over the bandages, bewilderment on her face.

The rush of adrenaline that had accompanied me since stepping foot in the sanctuary was dissipating, leaving me fatigued and emotionally spent.

The choir began their closing hymn, which was my cue to step down and lead the R'aedan out of the sanctuary.

Outside the square was filled with thousands of people who couldn't fit inside the church. I was introduced to the crowd and subjected again to way too much noise that had me wanting to crawl into a closet with noise-canceling headphones.

Somewhere behind me Xen, Daria, and Katyk were waiting, but we would not get privacy anytime soon. Xen's thoughts were circling around what they had witnessed and filled with questions I couldn't answer. Once a blessing had been said over the crowd, I was led to a small garden that had a little pool. The walls were lined with flowers in all shades of red and there was a small gazebo with a flower-adorned chair. Here I was to hold court, essentially.

Stâlian Batorry was the first to present herself to me. Everyone else withdrew. "Hêalic, you have honored me." She went to one knee before me and lifted her hands to mine. "I wish to request reassignment to serve as your *Hierde*, if you would have me."

My brain scrambled for a translation and came back with something like a guardian. "Stâlian, it would be an honor, but are you certain? You seemed to always have a calling for other work."

"I am, Hêalic. I know my true purpose now."

I smiled and nodded. I did not want a guardian at all, let alone this one, but it would at least give me some control over her. Or so I was hoping. "Welcome then, Hierde."

She rose and came to stand to the left and slightly behind my chair. I knew she would need to go to the R'aedon for approval, but for now, she seemed content to begin her duty.

I looked up at the line forming at the garden gate and gestured for the next person to come forward. The entire clergy would come for my blessing, and I was already exhausted.

Several hours later, I stifled a yawn as the last of the brothers rose and I stretched, looking around the garden. Xen was waiting at the gate, dressed to the nines in a gorgeous brown velvet jacket and matching hat.

They smiled as they approached. "You need to come dress for the feasting," they said, sparing a glance at Batorry.

"I'd rather take a nap," I muttered, pushing myself up out of the chair.

"We might be able to let you sleep for a little while." Xen put an arm around me and drew me away toward the residential wing. "The Grand Duchess has sent you some very impressive clothing for tonight."

I rubbed a hand over my face, wanting to just crawl into bed. As we turned into the corridor where my room was, I realized Batorry was still with us. I stopped and turned to her. "I am safe enough here, *Hierde*. Please go and prepare yourself for the festivities."

She nodded tightly in acknowledgment and turned away as Xen opened my door. I followed them in and collapsed into a chair. "She's going to be a problem," I said.

"She is a true believer," Xen offered. "They are very difficult to deter."

"She has decided to cast herself as my guardian, which means we won't be able to shake her when we head north." I yawned and looked longingly at the bed. "How long do we have before we have to leave?"

"An hour, give or take."

I sighed. An hour's nap wouldn't be enough and would just leave me cranky and more tired than when I was then. "Okay, maybe a cup of affe will keep me going?"

"Or we could try something else." Xen pulled the other chair closer and sat, taking my hands in theirs. Warmth pooled between our palms and started to travel up my arms. I closed my eyes, savoring the feeling of Xen that filled my head as they passed energy through our connection.

It wasn't as good as a full night's sleep, but when they pulled back, I was suitably refreshed. "That is better, thank you. So, where is this suit I am to wear?"

A little more than an hour and a half later, decked out in an extravagant suit of black silk and velvet, with red piping at the hems and a red silk sash around my waist, I arrived in the carriage the Grand Duchess had sent for me, with Daria, Katyk, and Xen. Waiting for us was Batorry, in a new uniform. It was solid black but for white gloves and the ribbons that told her rank. She fell into step with the four of us as we climbed the steps.

I felt a bit ridiculous, but I followed the crowd into the great hall of the Duchess's manor house.

You know those scenes in movies where the poor kid gets to go into a rich person's house and stands there in slack-jawed awe? It was a little like that. I didn't think I'd ever seen a more opulent room.

The walls were the color of cream, the molding covered in gold. The art was filled with spectacular splashes of color. A chandelier that must have contained a thousand candles hung above us, lighting up the room. The people were nearly as fabulous, all of them dressed in gorgeous suits and gowns. I couldn't decide where to look, but I didn't need to worry as a trumpet rang out and a woman in livery announced to the room, "Hêalic Thána Alizon, and guests."

The whole room came to a standstill, and they were all looking at me. "Oh good. I worried there wouldn't be enough awkward tonight," I murmured aside to Xen.

The Grand Duchess, in a royal purple suit and a handsome young man on her arm, was the first to break the silence, approaching our group with a broad smile. "Hêalic, welcome, welcome. This is my husband, Arthur."

"Your Grace." I bowed slightly, the others following suit.

The Grand Duchess waived over one of the men with trays of beverages. She gave me a glass filled with a bubbly pink concoction that smelled vaguely of cherry. It was very sweet and very bubbly. I would have preferred the beer we drank at the tavern, but I smiled and thanked her.

I was uncomfortable and thinking I needed to escape, but dinner was announced, and we began filing out of the hall and into a large dining room with tables in two long rows. At the far end was a dais with a table where the R'aedan sat in high back chairs, with a space in the center for me. In front of them was a small table for the Grand Duchess and her husband.

Xen squeezed my hand briefly before they and the others were led away to find their seats. The Grand Duchess slipped her arm through mine in an almost possessive way and swept me along to deliver me to my place of honor.

The table was set with amazing china and gold-plated utensils. A golden goblet was filled with what I assumed was wine.

I was starting to sweat. All of the people in the room were staring at me, or that was the way it felt. R'aedan Kalys was on my right and R'aedan Jamis on my left, and it felt a lot like sitting between the principal and vice-principal in school. All with my Hierde standing watch behind me.

As everyone found their places and sat, the Grand Duchess remained standing and lifted her goblet. "It is my very great privilege to welcome you all here this evening to honor our Hêalic with food and wine and music." She turned to me. "I hope it is not too forward of me to ask you for a prayer before the meal?"

I was startled by the request, but the whole room was clapping, so I stood. I marshaled my facial expression into something I hoped was pious and not terrified. My eyes skipped to Xen and then I turned my face up to the ceiling. "Holy and Sacred Mother, we gather here for feast and frivolity, knowing that your love extends to each one of us and we ask a blessing upon this city and her people. May the food nourish us. May the music touch our hearts. May the company be comforting."

"Let us eat," the Grand Duchess proclaimed after a moment of silence and, on cue, men in the house livery began serving.

The bowl set in front of me was filled with a fragrant broth and a drizzle of cream. It was almost floral smelling, but the taste was more vegetal, though I couldn't name which vegetable. The room buzzed with conversation, though our table remained silent until the second course was served. The salad was colorful with leafy greens and yellows, bright orange tomato-like bulbs, a blue radish that the locals called antre, and a pleasant vinaigrette-style dressing.

Halfway through my salad, R'aedan Kalys casually said, "I never have liked this kind of salad."

"Oh?" I turned to look at her. "What do you not like?"

"The taste is too bitter for my tongue. I prefer to bite my food, not be bitten by it."

I chuckled and nodded. "I can see that." She seemed to relax beside me and lifted her wine goblet to sip at it. "The wine is quite good though," I said, also lifting mine.

"It is from very near my home village. I insisted. I can not abide bad wine."

She would probably consider my normal wine as bad wine I thought before putting my glass down. "I quite like it."

"What you did today, healing the Stâlian, was inspiring. I have read accounts of the Hêalics that came before, but never thought to see one in person."

CHAPTER 22
EXHAUSTION

WE CHATTED A BIT WHILE WE ATE, AND I TRIED TO STEER THE CONVERSATION TO mundane things, not wanting to get into theological territory. I was starting to think about excusing myself to go to the bathroom or something when dessert was served.

I glanced up at Xen, noticing that Katyk looked miserable. I raised an eyebrow in question, but Xen shrugged. I wiped my mouth with my napkin and pushed my chair back from the table. "Excuse me, R'aedan. I need to check on my friend." I put up a hand for Batorry to stay before I made my way to Katyk.

She looked up when I touched her shoulder and came away with me, stepping out into the hallway. "You okay?" I asked.

She crossed her arms, and I couldn't read the expression on her face. "Yes. No. I don't know."

"Okay, tell me what's going on."

"My head hurts. Like all the time now." She rubbed her temples.

"Have you taken anything?" I asked.

"Daria gave me something. It hasn't helped."

"Do you want me to take a look?"

"No, enjoy your party. You can do it tomorrow."

I nodded. "Okay. Do you want me to have someone take you back to the church so you can rest?"

She nodded miserably. "Wait here."

I stepped back into the dining room and hailed one of the serving men to me. "My friend is not feeling well and would like to go back to her room. Could you see to it that someone gets her there safely?"

"Of course, Hêalic."

That dealt with, I took Katyk's empty seat between Xen and Daria. "Headache. I sent her back to the church."

"They've been getting worse," Daria said softly.

"I'm going to see what I can do about it tomorrow." I took Katyk's wine goblet and drained it. "How much longer do you think I need to stay here? This is exhausting."

"I would estimate at least an hour once the dancing begins," Xen replied.

I groaned and held out the goblet for a servant to fill.

"I noticed you and the R'aedan chatting," Daria said.

"Small talk. Mostly about the food."

"She was pretty amazed this morning. When your candle lit, she almost fainted." Daria sipped her wine. "It was a nice touch."

I frowned at her. "I didn't ... it just happened."

"Oh?" Daria looked surprised. "I just assumed it was you, selling the whole miracles thing."

I shook my head. "I don't think I could explain it if I had to. I was overcome with something."

"And healing your friend?" Xen asked, glancing behind me where Batorry had once again taken her station.

"I couldn't bear the pain," I answered. "It was intense."

Music began to waft its way from the main hall where the revels would include more wine and dancing and performances. People began drifting back in that direction. We stood, waiting for the bulk of the people to go before we moved.

I was never very good at parties. Too many people in too small a space usually meant I'd be bailing out early. Now though, I let myself be cajoled into the place of honor in the room, a chair set just off the dais on which the Grand Duchess and her husband sat, and gratefully accepted the glass of wine I was offered.

My new Hierde stood to my left and Xen took up a spot to my right. The band at the far end of the room finished their song and the conductor looked to the dais. When she received the nod from the Grand Duchess, they began to play something akin to a waltz. The Duchess stood and held her hand out to her husband. Together, they glided into the center of the floor and commenced dancing.

I've never been a good judge of dancing, but they seemed to be enjoying themselves. Other couples began to join them and as if that was the release button, a river of conversation filled the room, and people began working their way to me.

Like the clergy earlier in the day, they came one by one in search of a blessing. I was there much longer than an hour, the fatigue growing. I needed sleep. I stood, a little unsteady until Xen's hand found my elbow. I turned to Batorry. "Tell anyone who did not get to see me that I will receive them in the garden tomorrow afternoon if they still wish. Right now, I need to get to bed before I drop."

"Yes, Hêalic."

My next stop was the Grand Duchess, who had just retaken her seat after a lively dance. Her face was flush, and she was fanning herself. "Thank you for a wonderful evening, Your Grace."

"Are you leaving?" She sat forward, her dark eyes on mine.

"I am. Today has been very tiring."

"I will have your carriage brought up." She gestured to a liveried man who dashed out the main doors.

Daria joined us as we made our way through the crowd. I was all but asleep as we waited on the front stairs for our ride, leaning on Xen to keep myself upright. The ride back was quiet, and Xen had to rouse me when the carriage came to a stop. I stumbled between them, down the corridors, feeling like I was eighteen again and trying to sneak into the house post-curfew after having too much to drink.

Xen helped me get undressed and into bed. I was out so fast that I never heard them leave.

Katyk had obviously been crying when I found her the next morning. Her eyes were bloodshot and puffy. She sat on the bed in her room and looked up at me. I could tell the pain was bad before I even touched her, but it wasn't just physical.

"How can you want to help me?" she asked in a small voice.

I sat beside her. "You're in pain."

"After what I did to you?" She blinked back tears. "I remember all of it, and it was awful. I was awful. I was so angry. I knew it was wrong but couldn't stop myself."

"Katyk, you know why. Artoz has his hooks in you. He sent you after me. Let me get a good look at what's going on in your head." I guided her to lay back so that I could put both hands on her forehead. Closing my eyes, I centered myself and opened up, reaching out for that golden presence before turning my attention into Katyk's body.

The dark spot that was the center of her magic and the home of Artoz's brainwashing was darker still, bigger, and now a physical thing. Like a stone that was forming and pressing into the brain matter. I attempted to feel my way into it, but it resisted. It would be difficult to remove.

I flushed the area with some of that golden light to alleviate some of the pain before I pulled out and sighed.

"That's a little better," Katyk said, sitting up.

"It won't last, I'm afraid." I paced to the door and back to the bed. "You've got a growth of some kind. That's what is suppressing your powers and Artoz's brainwashing. I have no idea what would happen if I tried to pull it out of there."

"I don't want to go back to what he made me be." Katyk rubbed her hands over her face. "I don't want to be *her*."

"I know, Katyk."

"No, you don't, Thána." She grabbed my hand and held it. "He made me do horrible things, not just to you. And the way we tortured you?" She shook her head. "I can't do that again. I will never be clean of it."

"We can't change the past, Katyk. We can only do better as we go forward."

She nodded. "What if you … could you take it all?"

"All?" I asked.

"Yes, take the magic and programming and the memories."

"You would give up your magic?" I asked, surprised.

Her eyes were wide, but she nodded, letting go of my hand. "Either that or just kill me. I can't keep living like this."

"I'm not going to kill you, Katyk. Let me talk with Daria and Xen. We'll come up with something."

I left her there and went to the kitchen where I was meeting Xen and Daria for breakfast. Xen was helping the brothers prepare food for the residents of the church while Daria was putting the finishing touches on the pain potion she was preparing for Katyk.

"You might want to make that stronger," I said as I joined them. "She's in a lot of pain."

"I doubled it," Daria responded, passing me the bottle. "Any more and it might cause other problems."

I tucked the bottle into the pocket of my new uniform pants. I hadn't bothered with the sash or the cinch but would don them before the afternoon in the garden. With a smile, Xen handed me a plate of eggs and sausage with a slab of buttered bread along with a cup of affe.

Daria swept the last of her herbs off the prep table and dumped them in the nearby bin of kitchen scraps before taking her plate. Together, the three of us found what privacy could be had in the large dining hall by sitting at the far end of one of the long tables. Soon, the room would be filled with the clergy and other church residents, but for the moment, there were only the three of us and two of the brothers I was starting to get familiar with.

"Katyk has asked me to do something that I don't know I can do, and if I can, I'm not sure I feel confident enough."

"What is it she wants?" Xen asked.

"I found out what's causing her pain, as well as suppressing her magic. She's got a growth of some kind. She wants me to ... basically take it out, all of it, including her magic."

Daria looked startled. "Can you do that?"

"Honestly? I don't know." I sipped my affe. "I think I could get the growth out. But I'm not sure about the rest."

We ate in silence for a while before I broached the subject of them helping me treat Katyk. "I'm thinking that if the three of us worked together, we might be able to do it."

"How?" Daria asked, though I could see her mind spinning over the problem already.

"I'm thinking Xen can read her to direct us and make sure we're getting it all. I can pull the growth out. You can follow behind me and clean up the mess?"

"I'm not that kind of healer, Thána," Daria said with a shake of her head.

"No, but you are a better witch than I am," I responded softly. "Taking that growth is likely to knock me over. It's ugly and resistant ... and it's more than a physical thing. It feels like ..." I couldn't think of a word dark enough. "It feels *bad*."

"What happens if you get the growth out, but not the rest?" Xen asked.

"Then we have a brainwashed part-succubus witch who wants to tear us apart," I said. "Which would be bad, yes. The question is, can we let her keep living in pain? She asked me to do this or to kill her."

"I had not realized the pain was so bad."

"It's not just the pain. It's the memories of what Artoz made her do and not wanting to become that person again."

"Guilt," Daria said with a sigh. "Let me think about it. Maybe I can come up with something."

"I am going to deliver this medicine to Katyk before I head to my meeting with the R'aedan and Mader Raffa." I stood and grabbed my empty plate and cup to return to the kitchen, then headed back to the residence wing.

Katyk was asleep when I arrived, so I left the potion for her and returned to my room to finish dressing. Once I figured out how to get the sash tied properly and the leather cinch around my arm, I went to Mader Raffa's office. The R'aedan were already there, along with Batorry and four others in the same new uniform.

"Hêalic, welcome," Mader Raffa pulled me into a hug that was both awkward and unwelcome, but I let it go.

R'aedan Kalys nodded in greeting. "Good day, Hêalic. Will you sit?"

There were more chairs than usual in the Mader's office and once I'd sat so did everyone but Batorry and those four that I assumed would also be assigned to guard me.

"You know Susanna Batorry has asked to be your Hierde," Kalys said. "We have also chosen these four to join her. They have been sworn to protect you, and your team."

"I am not sure I need so much protection, R'aedan. Xen is practically my bodyguard."

"You will find that now that you have been ordained, there will be many seeking your attention and aid. With that, there will come dangers and crowds," R'aedan Maylynn explained.

I nodded my acceptance. It wasn't worth fighting. We'd figure it out. "Very well."

"We would like to discuss your next steps," Kalys said.

"Yes, of course."

R'aedan Jamis cleared her throat. "There are many people in need of you who can not travel here."

"Yes, I am aware that the plague has hit several other cities. I was going to request supplies and vehicles to go to them."

Kalys smiled. "Good, so we are in agreement. Hierde Batorry will make the arrangements for you and your team."

"When do we leave?"

"We can be ready in a week or so, Hêalic," Batorry said.

"Good." I inhaled deeply and stood. "I should go. I promised to receive those I could not last night."

My Hierde and her team snapped to attention and together we left the office to head to the garden where I had received the clergy the day before.

CHAPTER 23
PURPOSE

By the time the flow of people trickled to a stop, the late afternoon had grown chilly in that secluded garden. I rubbed my arms as I got up and turned to go inside.

"Would this be a good time to go over protocol?" Batorry asked as we approached my room.

"Of course. Come."

Two of my new guards took up station outside my door while I lead the Hierde into my room. I offered her a chair and sat opposite her, grateful that someone had already lit the fire.

"Let me begin by thanking you for accepting me. I feel strongly that I was led here to find you."

I offered a smile. "You are a most welcome addition to my team, Hierde. You know, I think today was the first time I ever heard your first name."

"In the Scealc, it is encouraged to keep your first name private so that we don't breed familiarity, particularly with those we might have to fight with in the future. I have not heard my name spoken aloud in over ten years."

"That seems a bit excessive," I commented.

"Perhaps, but it is our way." She shifted in her chair. "As is the protocol, I am going to lay out for you. We can tweak certain portions, but not all. This is to protect you, your team, and the people."

"Of course, go ahead."

Over the next hour, she laid out what my life would look like for as long as I remained in that world. Most of it amounted to having one of them with me any time I left the church, particularly when I would be in the public eye. There would also be one of them stationed at my door at all times.

Essentially, I now had a team of five chaperones.

Which was going to make life more difficult than it needed to be. I put that thought aside after she left. I needed to focus on Katyk. The guard at my door was young, with a dark complexion and deep brown eyes. She snapped to attention as I opened the door, and fell into step beside me as I passed her.

That was going to get old right quick. I knocked lightly on Katyk's door and waited a beat to open it. Gesturing for my shadow to stay in the hall, I stepped into the room. The only light in the room was a candle by the bed. "Katyk?"

There was movement on the bed and I came closer.

"I just wanted to check in on you." Slowly, her features emerged from the shadows, her face strained. My eyes darted to the pain potion on the table with the candle. It was clear she had taken some of it.

She blinked at me blankly, almost as if she didn't recognize me.

I sat gently beside her on the bed. "How's your head?"

"Hurts."

"I know. We're working on a plan." I lay a hand on her knee, whispering a sleep spell and waiting with her until I felt it work. At least asleep she wasn't consciously aware of her pain. I yawned as I left Katyk's room. The past few days had been draining. I was thinking of calling it an early night when I heard screaming coming from the sanctuary.

My guard and I took off at a run. The sanctuary was already filling with people when I got there. The doors were wide open, and the smell of blood assaulted me before I was even close enough to see what had caused the disturbance. When I could see, I wished that I hadn't.

The front steps of the church were painted in red, puddles and rivers of it with islands of skin and hair. At the bottom of the stairs was a pile of body parts.

My guard put a hand on my arm to stop me. "There is nothing you can do, Hêalic."

"Who could do this?" I demanded of no one in particular, my eyes sweeping the square and surrounding buildings.

It wasn't bright daylight, but it wasn't completely dark either. Whoever did this took a big chance of being seen. Then I caught sight of her across the square. She was leaning casually against a building, a faint smile on her face: Anne Gothfried. She had done this, and she wanted me to know that.

I turned away as the Steallere and her officers took control of the scene, my stomach churning. There were at least two bodies in that pile.

"Are you okay, Hêalic?" my guard asked.

"I'm fine. Remind me of your name?"

"I am Dreng Rawlin, Hêalic."

There were far too many people in my life and names tended to fade in my brain. But Dreng was a title that translated roughly to soldier. "Well, Dreng, I think I'm going to retire for the evening."

"Yes, Hêalic."

She followed me dutifully back to my room and took up her station at my door. With my door shut, I stripped and went to the bed with my journal to document the last few days. When I closed my eyes, Anne's face filled my mind. I tried to push her away, but she was persistent. She had figured out that I had seen who she really was the day after the fire.

And she wanted me to know that she knew.

I tossed and turned, unable to sleep despite my fatigue. The smell of blood hounded me, dragging me through the sludge built of memories of all the times I had bled or been near blood. Toward morning, I finally drifted off but only to fall into nightmares that would chase me screaming into the day.

I sent for affe and breakfast to be brought to me, settling in by the fire to eat. I was just getting dressed when there was an urgent knocking at my door. "Hêalic, please come."

I grabbed my doctor's bag and opened the door to a novice who seemed terrified. As I stepped into the hallway, I understood why. Katyk's blood-curdling screams echoed down the hall to me. "Find Xen and my sister and bring them to me."

She nodded and took off at a run while I went to Katyk's door. I turned to my guard. "Admit no one but Xen or Daria."

Katyk's hair was matted and sweaty, and bloody I realized as I stepped closer. Her hands were digging into her head as if she could pull the pain out herself. Her eyes were glazed, and her mouth was moving, though without sound.

"Katyk, it's okay. I'm going to help." I gently pulled her hands away from her head, noticing the blood that lined her nail beds. "Lean toward me, let me see."

I pulled the candle closer, but it wasn't enough light. The door opened and I didn't even look. "I need more light."

It took a few seconds before Xen got several candles lit and brought closer. Katyk had dug her nails into the skin of her head, leaving two jagged lines of blood. Her body went rigid under me, and I ended up straddling her to keep her still.

"We have to do this now," I said. I didn't wait for either of them to speak, just pulled them in close, and feeling my connection to them snap into place at the same time I called for that golden light, letting it flush through me.

Xen's touch was light and easy to follow. She marked out everything that needed to come out so I could focus my attention. Daria was all heat and calm beside me, offering me stability. I opened Katyk's mouth and leaned in to begin trying to excavate the growth.

It resisted, even seemed to try to pull away from me and deeper into her brain. I didn't let up though. I flushed the healing light through me and used it to dig under the tumor. Katyk thrashed under me, but I didn't stop until I felt it start to give, then I sucked hard.

All the way up it fought with me, and I knew that once I had it in me, it would want out immediately. The mass of it seemed to grow as I pulled and swallowed. I fell backward as the last of it filled my mouth, tasting of charcoal and rotten meat. I rolled off the bed, letting Daria take my place and I staggered toward the door bent over.

I only made a few steps before I was vomiting up everything I had taken from her. It fell to the stone floor with a solid plop of black gunk.

"Thána, I need you."

I came back to the bed, reaching into Katyk and praying I had the strength to do what needed to be done. Daria was rapidly stitching things back together, but the damage was extensive. I breathed out and centered myself before I reached for the healing power. I whispered a prayer while I was at it, figuring it couldn't hurt.

By the time it was over and Katyk had slipped into a painless sleep, I was sweating and weak-kneed. We separated slowly and I went to squat beside the mass on the floor. "Don't touch it," I said as it appeared Xen was going to try to pick it up. "I don't know that it won't try to get inside you."

"What exactly is it?" Daria asked.

I could only shrug. "Find me something I can scoop it up with. I think we should burn it."

"And what about Katyk?"

I looked at her. "We won't know how much she lost until she wakes up. One of us should probably stay with her."

"I will stay. You should rest." Xen handed me a rag which I folded and then covered the blob with. It made a weird sucking sound as I peeled it off the floor.

"Thank you." I kissed Xen's cheek with the rag held well away. "I will relieve you when I've slept."

I was there when Katyk woke later that day, sitting in a chair near her bed, reading by candlelight. The sound of movement made me look up, to find her looking at me. "Thána?"

I set my book aside and shifted over to sit on the bed beside her. "Hey, how are you feeling?"

"Like someone ran a bulldozer through my head." She shifted a little, wincing.

"What do you remember?"

"Screeching ... in here." She pointed at her head. "And then ... quiet."

"Let me have a look." I put a hand on her forehead and centered, then examined the area where Daria and I had pulled the growth out. There was still evidence of the trauma, and Daria's magic was still working at mending up the seams, but I could sense none of the dark malignancy lurking.

"That looks much better," I said, pulling back.

"How much did you take?"

"You tell me," I said. "In the thick of it, I couldn't see clearly what all was getting yanked."

Katyk rubbed her forehead. "I remember you obviously, so I have some of those memories. And I remember when we got captured, me and Jacyk."

"Your sister?" I asked gently.

She nodded. "But there are only a few flashes of what he put me through, then meeting you ... it's all spotty there. I mean, I *know* that I did bad things, but what those were is gone."

"Let's consider that a good thing." I patted her leg and stood, stretching, and retrieving my book. "I want you on bed rest for the next two days. Then we're heading north." I went to the door, then paused. "You must be starving. I'll send someone with food for you."

I opened the door but paused when Katyk spoke. "Thána ... thank you."

I smiled and left her, sending a passing novice to bring her food before taking my book back to the library. Mentally, I was in a weird place, part of me really looking forward to the journey home and part of me feeling almost at home in my new role. It felt meaningful.

I had a purpose. It wasn't something I was used to.

CHAPTER 24
ON THE ROAD AGAIN

The morning of our departure was cold and overcast. Hierde Batorry took charge of our party, which would include the four of us, my five guards, a supply wagon, two novices, and two of the lay Brothers. It seemed a bit unwieldy to me, but I didn't argue.

Our mounts were the weird animals that looked like a cross between a greyhound and a horse. We gathered in the square in front of the church steps for the blessings of the R'aedan before we mounted up.

Our first planned stop was a village a day's ride away.

"Safe journey, Hêalic," Mader Raffa said to me, pulling me into an awkward sort of hug. "May Killi smile upon you."

I let one of the Brothers assist me up onto my mount and silently wished for a car.

Daria mounted up beside me with a wicked grin.

"What?"

"I haven't ridden in years. I'm betting we're sore tomorrow."

"I'm sore *now*," I retorted.

Xen and Katyk were mounted and ready. I nodded to Hierde Batorry and she gave the signal. We were off.

———

We stopped at midday to let the animals rest alongside the river. The mild angle of the grassy bank was the perfect place to lay back and watch the clouds move above us.

I dozed off thinking of my mother and Kota and wondering how they were fairing back in Spítia. Daria roused me when it was time to set off again and we started walking back to the others. Her hand tightened on my arm and pulled me to a stop, her eyes somewhat glazed over, and I got the sense that she was seeing something.

"Daria?"

"She's angry," Daria said breathlessly.

"Who? Who's angry?"

"The killer."

"Anne?"

Daria nodded, blinking rapidly, and then drawing in a deep breath. "She's angry that you left."

"Why?" I asked.

"No idea. Just flashes. She's going to come looking for us."

"Great. Just what we need—another psychopath who wants to murder me."

"Not sure that's what she wants. I'm sure we'll find out."

I put the thought of Anne aside and focused on making my body climb back up on my mount. I was already feeling the soreness in my thighs and butt. It was going to be a long afternoon.

Our party pulled into the town of Llevyll at just about sundown. We were met by the town's Healdor and priestess, and offered accommodations, splitting our party between the church residence and the Healdor's home.

After a light supper, Daria, Xen, and I retreated to the room we were sharing. Katyk was bunked down with the novices, which seemed like a good choice, given her fragile mental state. She'd been quiet and withdrawn the entire day.

"Okay, so tell me what you saw," I said to Daria while we prepared for bed.

She shook her head. "At first it was just her face, that day in the church. Then I saw her grinning at you over a pool of blood. She will go to the church to find you. Then all I got was a lot of anger and the sense that she would follow us." Daria sat on the bed to pull off her boots. "I don't think she wants to kill you though. I think …" She bit her lip and looked a little uneasy. "I think she *likes* you."

I rubbed my hands over my face. "Great. Jack the Ripper wants to be my girl." I dropped my pants and folded them to lay atop the sash I had already removed. "I guess we'll handle that when it happens? For now, let's get through tomorrow."

It was going to be a long day that would include a special service at the church, followed by receiving the townsfolk and, if necessary, healing what I could. Then, dinner with the Healdor and her family before a second night in these accommodations, prior to heading north.

I was already exhausted by the thought of it as I lay down to try to sleep. I dozed a little, but my brain was on walkabout, circling every encounter I had ever had with Anne Gothfried. Every circle brought me back to that night in the alley, the white mask, the smell of blood ... which in turn took me back to the nightmares of my childhood and watching my father die ... and round to the near-death experience with the brotherhood, and on to Artoz.

Realizing that I wasn't going to sleep, I got up and dressed to give Daria and Xen a chance to sleep. I tiptoed out of the room with my boots in hand and went downstairs, my guard in tow. Pausing in the sitting room, I shoved my feet into my boots and adjusted my sash and cinch before I went out into the chill of the predawn, trailed by my guard.

The moon overhead was nearly full, its silver light offering a backlight of sorts for the dark clouds overhead. I walked from the Healdor's home to the village square, soaking in the silence and solitude of the night. I found a place to sit on the church steps. The place was a great deal smaller than the church in Gavelscore, with only one priestess and a pair of lay Brothers who saw to the day-to-day running of the place.

My guardian took up station nearby, but just out of my line of sight as I closed my eyes and breathed in deep, exhaling slowly and sinking my conscious thought into my center. I'd never been great at meditation, but I kept trying, and it seemed to be easier since I had come to this place. Slowly, I opened myself up, tapping into the magic at the heart of who I was and inviting the *other* in. I still couldn't name that presence, whether it was a god or goddess or just the universe at large, but I suspected that it really didn't matter what we called it. Clearly, the people here would call it Killi.

I imagined the meadow where I had experienced it. Sitting in the grass, I called out to it, beckoned it. The warmth gathered around my head first, then down into my body, wrapping me in a cosmic hug. There was no voice but, still, I could hear it singing to me. It was a calling, and it was beautiful.

The light settled around me like a cloak as faces moved about, showing me the past and the future, healers from a hundred worlds with a hundred different traditions and knowledge. It poured into me, all that knowledge, filling me to overflowing.

When I had finally settled back into my body and opened my eyes, the sun was fully up and people had begun to gather around me, kneeling in awe. I didn't realize why at first but slowly became aware that I was faintly glowing, the golden aura clinging to my skin.

In that moment, I could feel every ailment, every illness, every disease of those before me. Silently, I beckoned one of them to me, a young mother holding a toddler who was cranky and running a fever. I took the child from her and held him, passing my free hand over his body, and calling the infection from his lungs.

It was a weird sensation. I was eating the disease without having to physically open my mouth and take it in. I handed the child back and beckoned to the next. For an hour, I sat on those steps and ministered to the townsfolk, stopping only when Xen came to find me.

"Did you sleep at all?" Xen asked as they helped me up.

"Some." I wobbled a little as the blood flow started. "Bathroom."

Xen nodded and guided me back to the Healdor's house and into her bathroom. "Hot water and a change of clothes?" Xen asked as I closed the door.

"What would I do without you, Xen?"

"I imagine you would be a mess," they replied.

I let my body drain, pondering the experience. It was almost like that spontaneous healing that had happened with Batorry, and the way I normally healed disease had fused to offer me a way to treat more than just illness.

Xen returned with a bucket of warm water, a washrag, and soap so I could clean up, then with clean clothes. When I emerged fresh and clean, we went down to breakfast.

The town was buzzing about what had happened and the church was packed for the special service. The rest of the day was something of a blur, though I know I did more healing through the day, my body expelling it readily enough. My clearest memory of dinner that evening was falling asleep against Xen's shoulder before my Hierde roused me and escorted me to bed.

Sleep came much more easily that night. I never even heard Daria or Xen come into the room. The Healdor set out a light breakfast for us the next morning before we set out. I eyed my mount uneasily. My lower body was not prepared to ride again.

I heard Katyk's voice and turned to find her with the novices, dressed in similar clothing. I watched them for a moment before turning to Xen. "She seems to be making friends."

"Yes, I heard Sister Yana and Katyk speaking last night about the life of a novice," Xen responded.

"That doesn't sound much like Katyk," I said, turning to watch them mount up.

"Consider how much has changed for her. Perhaps this is the new Katyk."

I conceded the point and let Brother Tomas boost me up into my saddle. I could think of a lot of worse ways for Katyk to reclaim her life. To find herself there, without her magic and a lot of guilt weighing on her … I couldn't imagine what I'd be thinking if it were me.

As we headed out of the village, the townsfolk lined the road to wave us off. A cold breeze followed us, whipping at our hair and cloaks.

The road to Alnescore was a long one, with one more overnight stop at a village called Shibver, where we would pay homage at a shrine dedicated to Sunna and Mônna on the site of a supposed miracle.

We would ride into Alnescore the following day, and we would minister to the plague-ridden people for an undetermined period of time.

That was the official agenda, anyway.

Xen and Katyk would spend those days scouting locations where Katyk remembered being in hopes of finding the portal while Daria and I dealt with the sick and dying.

Provided I could even move after that many days in a saddle. My butt and thighs were doing a lot of complaining as we set out. Daria seemed right at home on the beast, her body moving rhythmically with it as if they had become a single being. Katyk, as well, was looking more at home than I expected. She rode in the back with Sister Yana and Sister Lassa, the two novices with us.

As we neared the village, I dropped back beside Katyk. The novices nodded to me and moved away to afford us some privacy. "You okay?" I asked.

Katyk shrugged. "For some value of okay, yeah."

"You seem to be getting friendly with the novices." I did my best to keep my tone neutral.

She smirked a little. "Just making friends."

"Are you thinking about staying?" I asked.

She looked startled. "I … I don't know."

"You could do worse," I observed. "Have you given thought to where you will go once we return to Meerat? We plan on going directly to Spítia, but I got the impression that isn't something you wanted to do."

Katyk shook her head. "There isn't anything for me in Spítia, especially now."

"Whatever you decide, I will help in any way that I can."

"Hêalic, we are nearly to the village gates," Hierde Batorry called.

"Coming, Hierde," I responded, spurring my mount back toward the front of our convoy.

There was a small ceremony where the local Healdor welcomed us, but the town was so small that they didn't have a dedicated church building. A roaming priestess visited once a month to hold services at the shrine and the other weeks, they gathered in the town square to observe the holy day.

The shrine was not much more than a stack of stones studded with the wax remains of candles and a small statue of the twin goddesses atop it. I stretched as I dismounted, bending, and squatting in hopes that my lower body would not completely betray me.

The wind turned colder as we started the receiving line and Hierde Batorry brought me a heavy cloak against the chill, along with some gloves. It started to rain before I'd gotten to the end of the line and by the time we made it to the local tavern where we were to bed down for the night, I was drenched.

Xen and I retreated to a spot near the fire in the great room, where my guards brought us both ceramic mugs filled with warm, spiced wine. I was already yawning and ready for bed.

I watched as Katyk and Yana sat together, talking quietly.

"How is Katyk?" Xen asked.

"She's going to be okay, I think." I sipped my wine and pulled my attention back to Xen. "How are you?"

Xen smiled and rubbed their backside. "I will be better when I no longer have to ride that beast."

"Cheers to that," I said, lifting my glass. "I'm looking forward to sleeping in a bed that isn't stuffed with straw … or whatever these mattresses are stuffed with."

"And cars," Daria added as she joined us. "We'd already be there if we just had a car."

CHAPTER 25
ALNESCORE

Our arrival in Alnescore was quite the spectacle, complete with a band, jugglers, and acrobats, a welcome from the Mader of the city church, and a proclamation by the Countess Ryda. The city streets were lined with hundreds of people cheering for me as I rode in at the head of our party.

All of that despite the constant icy drizzle of rain that accompanied us into the city. I dismounted in front of the church, my four guards forming around me and my Hierde stepping to my right side, just a pace ahead to announce me.

"Sacred Mother, Countess Ryda, I present to you our Hêalic, the light of Killi, Thána Alizon." Batorry bowed deeply and moved aside so I could make my approach.

As I reached the bottom stair, my guards stopped, and I continued on alone. On the step just before the wide platform where the city's nobility and clergy waited, I dropped to one knee and bowed my head. "Sacred Mother, Countess, it is an honor to be in your company."

"Hêalic, you honor us," the Mader said, her voice soft and musical. She was tall and thin, her skin dark like the night. Her hair was gray and white, what little of it there was.

Beside her, the Countess leaned forward to take my hand and encourage me to stand. She was young, younger than me at least, her skin similar in coloring to mine. Her gloved fingers were gentle and her smile genuine. "On behalf of my cousin, the Queen, and the city of Alnescore, I welcome you, Hêalic. Our people are in sore need of the gifts you bring."

"My party and I are in sore need of hot baths, a good meal, and warm beds, my Lady. It has been a long, cold ride today."

"Yes, Hêalic, the weather has been most unagreeable," the countess concurred. "I am certain that Mader Jehan is well prepared to receive you and give you comfort. I look forward to hosting you tomorrow evening, after my cousin has arrived from Evalshare."

That startled me. "Your cousin?"

She smiled. "Aye, she wishes to meet you and did not want to wait until you made your way to Evalshare."

I bowed my head to try to hide the panic that arose unexpectedly. "She does me great honor."

"Come, Hêalic, let's get you warm and dry," Mader Jehan said, drawing me closer before snapping her fingers at her attendants who went to help the rest of my party.

I was escorted into the church residence, and into Mader Jehan's own quarters, which were beautifully appointed, if not quite as opulent as Mader Raffa's had been.

She had her own bathing quarters, however, with an enormous cast iron and enamel tub, which a novice was filling for me. "This is Sister Ela; she will be your attendant while you are with us."

Ela inclined her head, and I returned the gesture.

"Would you like dinner here in your room after your bath?"

"Yes, Mader, that would be lovely. Please have my team join me as well."

I let Ela help me out of my wet clothes and sank gratefully into the hot water. An hour later, I was comfortably ensconced in a warm robe by the fire in the main room, enjoying a hearty stew with Daria and Xen.

"So, I heard a rumor," Daria said once Ela had left us alone. "According to the novices, we are expecting the Queen?"

"That's what the Countess said." I yawned and leaned forward to take my wine goblet off the table. "Apparently, my fame precedes me."

"Is it going to complicate things?" Xen asked.

I shrugged. "I have no idea. For now, we stick to the plan."

"I also have news," Xen said. "I believe that Katyk plans to stay here and take vows."

I nodded, swallowing a mouthful of stew, and chasing it with wine. "I am not surprised. She is looking for direction now that she has lost everything she thought she once was."

"Well, at least we don't have to worry about Artoz getting his hands on her again, I guess," Daria responded. She set her empty bowl on the table and sat back with her wine. "What do we know about this Queen?"

"Not a lot. She is cousin to the countess. And she is a well-loved ruler. That's about it." I yawned widely, the warmth of the fire and a full belly dragging me toward the land of sleep. "We should probably call it a night. Tomorrow is going to be a long day."

Xen gathered our dishes and leaned in to kiss the top of my head. "Sleep well, Hêalic."

I rolled my eyes and stood. I walked them to the door, nodding to my guard. "I'm going to turn in, Dreng."

"Sleep well, Hêalic."

I stripped and blew out the candles before crawling into bed. We were one step closer to finding our way home, but it was still far off.

Somewhere near morning, my dreams turned from random replays of moments during the trip to something darker. The landscape grayed out and dark clouds seemed to chase us. I woke to someone knocking on my door and rose, grabbing the robe I'd been given and wrapping it around myself before opening the door.

Mader Jehan looked like she had just been rousted from bed as well, also wrapped in a robe and holding an oil lamp. "Hêalic, I'm sorry to wake you."

"It's okay, Mader, I was awake. What's wrong?"

"There is something you should see."

I followed her out and through the sanctuary, my bare feet padding against the cold stone floor, the youngest of my guards beside me. Outside there was a cart draped in a sheet and several uniformed officers. "Hêalic, this is our Steallere, Margret Johns."

The Steallere nodded to me and moved to the cart. "Hêalic, there was a murder." She pulled the bloody sheet back so I could see the pale and dirty face of the victim. He was young, maybe no more than sixteen or seventeen. His dress was sliced open, his chest carved with the word "Hêalic".

I swallowed and took an involuntary step backward. Arina put a hand on my shoulder to steady me. I blinked a few times, then looked at the Steallere. "Let me guess, a low-rent body-boy?"

"Yes, Hêalic. He was found in an alley near his boarding house."

"Anne Gothfried," I whispered the name, as if speaking it aloud would conjure her.

"I beg your pardon?" Mader Jehan said.

"I believe I know who did this. I think she followed us here from Gavelscore. Her name is Anne Gothfried." I rubbed my forehead, trying to wipe the image of that white mask from my mind. "Were his genitals cut?"

"Yes, Hêalic. Completely removed."

I nodded. "Yes, that's Anne."

The Steallere covered the body and gestured to her officers to remove the cart. "I take it we can expect more?"

"I'd say she's just getting started," I responded. "She killed quite a few in Gavelscore."

"What does she have to do with you?" Mader Jehan asked.

"I interrupted her one night and saved the man's life. I think that bothered her." I shivered, not entirely from the cold stone beneath my feet. "Or intrigued her. I'm not sure which. Either way, she's bad news. Steallere, I can give you a description, but first I need clothing and some affe. Shall I come by your office later?"

"That will be fine, Hêalic." She nodded tightly to us and turned on her heel to follow the cart.

I sighed and shook my head. Daria had warned me she was coming. I'd only hoped it would take longer for her to catch up. When I returned to my quarters, someone had already been in to stoke the fire and make my bed, and there was a carafe of affe steaming on my table beside a cup.

Taking the seat closest to the fire so I could warm up, I poured myself some affe and brought the cup close to my face, savoring the smell. I wanted to lock thoughts about Anne in a steamer trunk, but the lid wouldn't close. I kept seeing her the day of my ordination, across the square, smirking at me.

Once I'd downed a full cup of affe, I set about getting dressed. I chose the most casual of my Hêalic suits, plain black pants and shirt with the sash and cinch, before pulling on my combat boots. I was going to have to dress fancy for the evening festivities, so I wanted to be comfortable for the bulk of the day.

I also didn't want to go to the clergy dining hall for breakfast. My afternoon would include receiving the clergy, so for the moment, I wanted my solitude. Opening the door just a little, I asked Dreng to send for breakfast, as well as my sister and Xen.

They arrived all at the same time to find me cradling my affe by the fire. Sister Ela put a bowl of porridge on the table for me and withdrew. Once the three of us were alone, I put down my cup and picked up my spoon. "Anne Gothfried has arrived in Alnescore. There was a dead body-boy found in the early hours, genitals removed, and the word 'Hêalic' carved into his chest."

"We knew she was coming," Daria pointed out. "What do we do?"

"I'm going to give the Steallere a description of her, but beyond that, what can we do other than get out of here before she decides to move on from prostitutes?"

"Hope she is caught," Xen responded.

"Fast," Daria added.

There was a knock at the door, and I called, "Come."

Hierde Batorry opened the door and inclined her head. "If I could have a moment, Hêalic?"

I nodded and gestured for her to enter the room.

"I have spoken to Mader Jehan, and I am concerned for your safety."

"I am not in danger, Hierde," I replied.

"Yet," Daria amended.

"That you know of," Xen added.

I rolled my eyes at them, then looked at Batorry. "What do you propose?"

"Mader Jehan has offered us several of the local Scealc squadron. With permission, I would like to work them into rotation and ensure that you have two guards at all times, with all of us on duty when you are in the public eye."

That sounded like a lot of eyes watching my every move, but I nodded my acceptance, knowing she would keep hounding me about it if I didn't. She inclined her head and left to set her plan in motion.

I finished my cup of affe and pushed my breakfast away half-eaten. "I should go see the Steallere."

"I will accompany you," Xen said, standing as I did.

"I have medicine to make," Daria said. "Katyk and Sister Yana are getting supplies. So, if you need me, I'll be teaching novices how to make potions."

Mader Jehan insisted that we take her carriage to the Steallere station, if only to afford me a little privacy from a curious public. Xen and I sat across from Alina and Jalkin, the two guards Batorry had assigned.

"Alina, you look tired," I observed.

"I am fine, Hêalic. Thank you for your concern."

"I know you were on at least part of the night. When we get back, I will talk to Hierde Batorry about making sure all of you get adequate rest. I don't want any of you getting sick."

The carriage came to a stop and Alina was the first out, her eyes scanning the street before nodding to me. Xen and I got out, with Jalkin behind us. We entered the station in the same order.

It was early in the day, and the station was filled with uniforms. A murmur swept the room, and everyone slowly turned to watch us. An echo of "Hêalic" spread around the room and a woman with a nearly shaved head wearing an impeccable uniform approached us.

"I am here to see the Steallere," I said.

"Of course. We were expecting you. Follow me."

We were led to an office with dirty windows that faced a brick wall. The woman I had met earlier looked up and waved me in. My guards took up station outside the office while Xen and I went inside.

"Steallere, this is my friend Xen."

"This murder has caused quite a stir. We haven't had one in years." She gestured for us to sit.

"In a city this size?" Xen asked. "Is that not a bit unusual?"

"Perhaps. We get a fair amount of other crimes, don't get me wrong. So, Hêalic, tell me about this Anne Gothfried."

"I don't know a lot. Met her shortly after we got to Gavelscore. I know she likes to gamble, drink, and she likes men." I glanced at Xen, then back to the Steallere. "She's just shy of six feet tall, with dark red hair. Her skin is pale, with a few freckles on the nose. And she wears some kind of white mask when she kills."

She was scribbling down what I was saying, then looked up at me. "Is it only the prostitutes? Only at night?"

"As far as I know, yes. She did tell me about some other murders that happened in Gavelscore, young women killed in their own bedrooms, but I have no idea if she was hinting that it was her that killed them, or just admiration."

"And you were friends with this person?"

"I wouldn't call us friends, no. She seemed to be intrigued by me when we first met."

"Mastery Gothfried would have liked to lure Thána into her life of gambling and men," Xen added. "Working in the tavern kitchen, I was able to observe her behavior. She was looking for a partner."

I could tell Xen knew a whole lot more. She'd read Anne the day of the fire when I'd pointed out what I'd seen.

"I have sent two of my officers to Gavelscore to speak with their Steallere, and I will double the number of officers on the streets after dark. I thank you."

There was a knock at the door, followed by a young officer stepping into the room. "Sorry to interrupt, Steallere, but this was just delivered for the Hêalic."

She handed me a folded piece of paper sealed with wax and bowed before departing. I was frowning as I broke the seal and opened it.

Hêalic, I hope you liked my present this morning. He was much prettier than the last one, don't you think? I'll be seeing you soon.

I closed my eyes and passed the note to Xen to read. "It seems she is watching us," I said. "She knew I was here."

CHAPTER 26
THE QUEEN

By the time we got back to the church, the place was abuzz with rumor and my Hierde was none too pleased with me for leaving the church with only two guards. I got her placated and retreated into my room to have lunch with Xen before my afternoon of meeting and greeting.

"Are you okay?" Xen asked as they finished the soup we'd been brought.

"Can we talk about something that doesn't involve the church or Anne or this whole … mess?" I asked plaintively.

"Of course, what would you like to discuss?" Xen asked, their tone light.

I shook my head. "I don't know. Just something normal."

Xen's left eyebrow lifted along with the corners of their mouth. "Normal?"

I chuckled a little and slipped my hand across the table to take theirs, rubbing my thumb along the palm. "During our bonding, I saw a place. It was beautiful. Tell me about it?"

"That is a memory passed down during the birthing; it is of the original birthing place, on our homeworld. The island is a long-extinct volcano, lush with life. All life on that world could be found there. All the food the young will need, warm waters to swim in, giant trees to climb. When the sun sets there, the whole island gleams like a gem."

I leaned back in my chair and closed my eyes, letting their words repaint the memory in my head. It was nearly magical, drawing us closer mentally until we were again one being. I didn't even notice when we were joined by a third presence, not at first. The air in the room seemed warmer and the image Xen's words had built in my brain seemed to come to life. I could smell the salt of the ocean and the deep earth of the volcanic soil. The call of birds danced through the waving greenery and light began to puddle in the cradle of the birthing place.

It filled with golden light and drew us in. Like water, it surrounded us and bathed us, and all my fear and worry was left behind for the moment.

All too soon, however, it was time to come back to the real world. "Thank you, Xen." I squeezed their hand and stood. "I best get to the glad-handing part of my day."

At the door, two of the new guards fell into step behind me. Mader Jehan was offering us the use of her private chapel off the main sanctuary. I found a line already forming and two more of my private army waiting at the doors as I approached.

The chapel was small, and my stomach hardened into a knot. On any given day, I didn't really like groups of people, but a group of people in a small space was so much worse. "Let them in only one at a time," I said to the guard. It wasn't much, but it might keep me from a panic attack.

The small altar was ablaze with candles, the light playing over the dark paneling that lined the walls. There was a small kneeling bench and in front of that, someone had placed a high-back chair for me. I settled into my seat and nodded to the guard to admit the first person.

Most of the Sisters who came wanted nothing more than a blessing, so the line moved fairly quickly. There were a few ailments, but none requiring my particular skills.

"One more, then I need to go get ready for the evening. I will see the rest later in the week," I said to my guard. Shifting in my chair to ease my rapidly growing case of numb-butt, I didn't see the woman who entered the chapel right away and when I did, I didn't recognize her until she had knelt and turned her face up to me.

"*Katyk?*"

She looked so different as she knelt there in the clothes of a novice, her signature curls cut short. "I am taking my vows tomorrow. It would mean a lot to me if you would be there."

It wasn't just the clothes or hair; she had changed. In those eyes where I once saw nothing but rage, I saw compassion and guilt.

"Are you sure that's what you want?" I asked, reaching a hand to brush across her cheek.

"Yes, I'm sure. I can do good here."

"I would be honored, Katyk."

She smiled sadly and stood. "Have fun tonight."

"Yeah, fun." I snorted and stood too.

Together we left the little chapel and as we reached the sanctuary, she turned to go one way and I returned to the residency to get ready to party with the Queen.

"You should relax a little," Xen said as our carriage came to a stop. "You are practically vibrating."

"This is as relaxed as I'm getting," I responded.

Hierde Batorry opened the carriage door for me and I stepped out.

The party was in full swing, judging from the music and voices I could hear spilling out the door to our right. Somewhere in there, Daria was already circulating.

My guards were all decked out in dress uniforms, or at least what I imagined were their dress uniforms. We had pulled past the main entrance and Hierde pointed to a side door. Xen and I followed as she led us. We had decided to avoid the main entrance to expose me as little as possible to the crowd and any dangers it might represent.

My clothing for the evening was possibly the most decadent I had ever worn, made of silk and velvet, and adorned with gold thread weaved in a delicate braid.

A man in the Countess's livery bowed deeply to us. "Welcome, Hêalic. If you would follow me, Her Majesty has requested to meet you in private."

Xen squeezed my hand and stepped away, leaving only my Hierde and me to follow the man. I wiped my sweaty palms together and told myself to calm down. She was just a person. A person who had the power to control armies and command death sentences.

I was taken to a set of double doors where two women in military uniforms stood watch. They opened the doors and the servant who had escorted me announced me.

"Your Royal Majesty, I present Hêalic Thána Alizon."

I stepped into the room and bowed before I even got a good look at her. Plush purple carpet covered the floor under me and as I straightened up, I could see white paneling and artwork before my eyes came to the Queen.

She was dressed in white and gold, with a crown adorned with little rubies and sapphires, or at least this world's equivalent. She was smaller than I had imagined, petite even. Her silver-white hair gave away little about her age. She had a warm tan skin tone and full lips that parted to show slightly crooked teeth when she smiled.

"Your Majesty, I am honored to make your acquaintance."

"Hêalic Alizon, your fame has reached my ears and I decided that I must meet you. Please, have a seat." Her voice was high-pitched and lightly accented in a manner different from most I'd spoken with. She sat in the center of the two-seat sofa and gestured to an armchair. "It has been a long time indeed since we saw our last Hêalic."

"I am glad to be able to serve." I wasn't sure what else to say. "And to have the support of my team. One woman alone, Hêalic or no, can not stem the tide of a plague."

"Yes, this particular plague is most insidious. There is not a city in this queendom that has not been touched by it. Have you cured many?"

"As many as I can, Your Majesty. My sister is also teaching novices how to mix the medicines that we created so that the sick will still have somewhere to turn once we have moved on to our next stop."

"Ah, to be free to roam from place to place. I do miss that." She sighed and stood, pacing to look at one of the paintings on the wall. "When I was young, I traveled many places and saw many things. Weird and wonderful things. But of course when I became Queen that all ended. Now the only places I travel are for things like this, and to keep my far-flung queendom functioning."

"Life is filled with compromises," I said, still not sure where this conversation was going.

"I suppose you wonder why I asked for you?" She turned back to look at me. "I would ask a favor of you."

"Anything within my power, Your Majesty."

She smiled and came back toward me, taking one of my hands. She laid it against her stomach. "Tell me why I can not conceive."

That was not something I could have predicted. I swallowed and stood, pressing my hand a little harder. How was I supposed to know why she couldn't get pregnant? "There does not seem to be anything wrong, but it is difficult to diagnose something this way. Perhaps I can see you properly before you return to your capital?"

"Yes, of course. We have one son, but no heir, and my child-bearing days are short now."

I centered and tried to do a better reading, even though my mind was still full of thoughts about the party and Anne and the fact that I was holding a Queen's stomach. Her ovaries and uterus felt normal to me.

"Tomorrow, I will come to you with my tools, before I start visiting those suffering from the plague." I stepped back and smiled at her. "If I can help in any way, I will."

"Thank you for indulging me, Hêalic. I am aware that there are those who need you far more than I. And I am keeping you from your party. Please." She gestured to the door.

The door opened and she preceded me out. My Hierde checked in to make sure I was good before she stepped back and to my left. We were then led through halls and to a door from which we could hear the party. I had asked for my arrival to not be a spectacle. I just wanted to slip in unnoticed and find a place where I wouldn't stick out like the proverbial sore thumb.

I got the first part of my wish. The door opened and I stepped into the ballroom only moments after the Queen's arrival had set the place abuzz, so no one even looked my way as I slipped past the crowd. Hierde Batorry steered me to the spot where the rest of my entourage was waiting for us with a chair.

"Is this going to turn into another night of having to receive every damn person in the place?" I asked in a hush.

"Not if you do not wish it to," Batorry replied.

"Good. I just want to enjoy what I can. Starting with a drink." As if that request had been anticipated, I was handed a wine glass filled with a spicy red wine.

From the relative safety of that corner, I watched the floor clear, and a lively song began by the quartet tucked up in another corner. The countess and her husband appeared on the floor, and after bowing to one another, began to dance. Others soon joined them. It was like looking into a kaleidoscope, the colors all swirling.

"How was your audience with the Queen?" Xen asked when they found me.

"Interesting," I replied, sipping at my wine. "Where is Daria?"

Xen pointed to the dance floor. Sure enough, there was my sister with a handsome young man in a gorgeous blue gown. It was clear she didn't know the steps, but she was laughing and trying to follow the others.

"Who is the guy?"

Xen leaned a little closer. "The brother of the countess."

"It's good to see her laugh like that." I had never known my sister in happy times; I had never seen her truly happy, but this came pretty close.

He was the same height as Daria, with dark hair swept up off his neck. He too was laughing as they spun around and around. At least one of us was having a good time. I drained the wine in my glass and handed it off. As the song ended, Daria spotted us and headed our way.

She was flushed and smiling. "Thána, there you are. I want you to meet Phillip Ryda, brother to the countess."

I inclined my head respectfully. "You two looked like you were having fun," I commented.

"Oh, we were. Your sister, however, needs dancing lessons." Phillip's eyes sparkled with affection.

"Phillip is not kidding there. Never did learn to dance." She turned to catch a passing server and grabbed wine glasses, passing one to Phillip.

"Daria tells me you will be visiting our most ill over the next few days."

I nodded. "Yes, that's why we're here. I think tomorrow is a sick house near the city walls." Tomorrow was starting to look busy, with Katyk's vows, examining the Queen, and then actual healing work. I was already tired just thinking about it.

"What about you, Hêalic?" Phillip asked and I realized I had no idea what he meant because I'd wandered off in my head.

"Me?"

He smiled and leaned closer. "Are you a better dancer than Daria?"

I held up both hands. "The last time I danced with someone, I broke three of his toes. I'll pass, thank you."

Behind them, I saw an older woman approaching. She touched Phillip's shoulder. "You are not troubling the Hêalic are you, Phillip?"

He turned so he could guide her forward. "Of course not, Mother. We were just chatting about dancing. Hêalic, this is my mother, Princess Charolette. Mother, Hêalic Thána Alizon."

"Your Highness." I inclined my head and introduced the rest of my group. "Your daughter certainly knows how to throw a party."

"She learned from the best," Charolette said with a wicked grin. "Come, Phillip, Lady Beverly and her daughter are here."

Peter rolled his eyes, but dutifully excused himself to follow his mother.

"He seems nice," I said to Daria.

"He does," Daria agreed.

The three of us stood there observing for a while before the Countess herself came to whisk me away so that she could introduce me to people. I had no hope of remembering names or titles, but that didn't keep her from rattling them off as we moved around the room.

It was a long night.

CHAPTER 27
DEDICATION

Katyk's vow ceremony was scheduled for a ridiculously early hour of the morning, but at least that afforded me the rest of the day to see to the Queen and the sick. It was a small affair, with Katyk attended by two novices and Mader Jehan administering the oath.

She looked smaller, younger even, as she knelt there on the altar step, her head bowed. She repeated the words in a tremulous voice in the quiet of the sanctuary. For a moment, I wondered if she wasn't trading one kind of brainwashing for another, but she looked so genuine and relieved that I let it go.

I met Xen and Daria for breakfast where we strategized the day's goals. While Daria and I were working, Xen was going to make the first foray into the surrounding area to look for our missing portal under the pretense of foraging supplies for Daria, although without Katyk, who would be spending the day in contemplation.

"I need to return to the Countess's home before we start," I said to Daria as I finished my second cup of affe. "I promised the Queen a more thorough exam. I don't know that I can help her, but I can at least take the time to properly investigate."

"You said she's having trouble conceiving?" Daria asked, setting her cup down.

"That's what she said. I didn't sense any physical reasons for it though."

"It could be many things, even as simple as stress. I would imagine a woman in her position has a lot of stress. Let me check my supplies. I might have something that would help." She stood and picked up her dishes to return to the kitchen. "Meet you out front?"

"Yes. I need to go grab my bag too." I stood but lingered as Daria walked away. "Are you going to be okay out there alone today?" I asked Xen.

They nodded. "I will be fine. Go on. I'll see you at dinner."

I went back to my room for my bag, then cut through the sanctuary to find Daria already on the front steps, and our carriage and guard awaiting us. My two shadows joined the two waiting by the carriage. One held open the door, then climbed in behind us, along with her partner. The other two climbed up to ride with the driver.

The ride to the manor house was quiet, though the streets outside were busy. Upon arrival, I made two of my guards wait with the carriage. I didn't need four bodyguards to visit the Queen. At least, I hoped I didn't. We were admitted to a suite, where we found the Queen having breakfast.

"Your Majesty, pardon me for interrupting," I said with a bow.

"Hêalic, not at all, come." She was dressed casually in what looked like riding clothes.

"Your Majesty, this is my sister Daria."

"Ah yes, the Hêalic's apothecary."

Daria bowed deeply. "Your Majesty."

I set my bag on a chair and opened it to retrieve my stethoscope.

The Queen stood from her chair at the table and moved toward the low couch. "Is this okay?" she asked as she sat.

"Yes, that is fine," I replied. "I'm going to start with a few simple things to get a better idea of your health." I knelt beside her and settled the earpieces into my ears before lifting the flat piece to her chest. As I listened to her heart and lungs, I was exploring her state of being with my other senses. "Lay down for me?" I requested, guiding her back.

I moved my stethoscope down over her womb, listening, but also calling on the newest of my gifts, surrounding her ovaries and uterus with golden light. I had no idea if it would help, but it certainly couldn't hurt.

"How have your monthly cycles been, Your Majesty?" Daria asked while I was working.

"Quite normal, for the most part."

"And how many days do you have between the start of one cycle and the next?"

"Around twenty-five days."

I could almost feel Daria doing the math behind me. I helped the Queen sit back up and stood. "As I said last night, your Majesty, I do not see any physical cause of your difficulty in conceiving; however, our bodies are much more than physical. We have brought you something." I gestured to Daria who reached into her bag full of medicines for the plague to pull out a leather pouch.

"This tea will help relax the muscles around your cervix, while also stimulating the spirit, your Majesty. Use two pinches in hot water before engaging in the act. You should also concentrate your efforts on the seventh to fourteenth day of your cycle, counting from the first day of bleeding."

The Queen stood and took the bag with a smile. "How can I thank you?"

"There is no need, Your Majesty," I replied. "We wish you much success."

A knock on the door preceded a servant, who bowed. "Majesty, the royal courier has arrived."

"Send her in, James." She took my hand and held it for a long moment. "When a daughter is born, she will bear your name, Thána Alizon. You have given me hope."

The door opened again, and Daria and I took that as our cue. I shoved my stethoscope back into my bag and we departed, picking up our escort outside of the room and climbing back into the carriage for our ride to the poorer side of town.

Alnescore had decided to house the sickest together in an attempt to control the spread of the plague, and that sickhouse was our destination for the day. I had come prepared to bleed, and we not only had the bag full of medicines that Daria was carrying but also a full crate on top of the carriage.

We came to a stop and I could already smell the plague without even opening the door. It sat like a heavy fog on the ground. The sickhouse was little more than a warehouse for the dying, a drab shadow of a building on a dirt street. I let my guards get out and sweep the area while I gathered myself for the day to come. It was not going to be a good day.

When Alina gave me the all-clear, I got out with Daria beside me. The doors to the sickhouse opened and several women in lab coats appeared. They looked like they hadn't slept in a month, eyes dull and dark against sallow skin.

I approached and nodded. "I am Thána Alizon, Hêalic."

"We have been expecting you, Hêalic," the taller of the two women said. "We have heard amazing things."

"My sister and I will do our best. Could you show us around?"

They had done a decent job of triaging until they'd been overrun with victims. After touring the hall, progressing from the most ill to the least, I turned to survey the room once more. "Daria, if you want to start on the ones who will recover with just the medicine, I can start on those who need a little more."

"What of the dead?" Daria asked softly.

The stench of decaying flesh permeated the space and combined with the plague itself it was stomach-churning. I got the attention of one of the doctors. "L'âce, may I ask what is being done with the dead?"

"We wait for a relative to claim them,"

I shook my head. "No, they must be removed immediately and either buried or burned. Leaving them where they lay only endangers more people. The plague lives on even after they die."

"I will arrange a burial detail, Hêalic," Alina said from beside me.

"Very good, Alina. Thank you."

Daria moved off to the left of the room where those who would likely survive with only the medications lay on blankets. I moved toward the right, picking someone at random and settling to my knees beside her.

I could feel the eyes of the doctors on me, making it difficult to focus. I put them out of my mind and centered, offering up a silent prayer of sorts for strength before I started to read the woman's body. I ate what I could, filled them with the healing light, then administered the medicine before moving on to the next.

I'm not sure how many I treated as the day progressed. At some point in the afternoon, I took a break to give my body time to process. I was queasy with how much I had taken in, even though I was trying my best to absorb as little as possible while still saving lives. It wouldn't have been possible if I hadn't discovered whatever connection I had to whatever deity was shining through me.

I spent almost an hour shedding what I had taken in. As I returned to the sickhouse, Daria met me out front with Alina.

"We are preparing a mass grave for the dead," Alina said as she handed me a sandwich.

"Thank you, Alina."

"Hierde Batorry is overseeing the work. She said to make sure you eat and drink enough to sustain you."

"How is it going on your side of the room, Daria?" I asked after eating half the sandwich.

"Well enough, considering. You?"

I nodded and finished chewing my next bite, swallowing before speaking. "I'm wiped out, but yeah, good. I think I have a few more in me."

"I am giving the doctors the remaining medicines and explaining their use," Daria said as she turned to head back inside. "Let me know when you're ready to leave."

I finished my sandwich and took the water Alina offered, chasing down the sandwich. "Thank you. I should get back to it."

I wasn't going to save all of them. I knew that, but I was determined to do what I could.

By the time Daria insisted we leave, I was feverish and cold, my stomach churning as she hefted me to my feet. Between Daria and Alina, they got me into the carriage where I promptly passed out.

Daria took charge once we got back to the church residence, directing my guards to rouse me and get me back to my room before she disappeared to send someone for food while getting a bath ready for me. My first stop was, of course, the toilet where I dozed off while my body emptied of disease.

Sister Ela came for me a while later, helping me into the bathing room where she and Daria stripped me down and helped me into the steaming water.

"Stay with her. She's likely to fall asleep," Daria said before she left to check on the state of the food.

I dozed there in the hot water until I heard voices and felt Xen's presence settle over me. They came to help me out of the tub, wrapping me in a robe that had been warmed by the fire, before settling me into a chair and putting a bowl of stew in front of me.

"Overdid it today, I see," Xen said in a chiding tone.

"Maybe a little," I responded, my words slurring a little.

"A lot," Daria countered. "Eat so you can get to bed."

"Yes, ma'am," I replied, leaning over to get my spoon. "How 'bout you, Xen?"

"I ate already."

"Not what I meant."

Xen took the seat beside mine. "Nothing to speak of today. I believe we will need to travel further than a half day's ride to find what we seek."

I put my attention on my food, but sleep was quickly overcoming hunger. I pushed away the bowl and looked at the bed. It seemed like it was miles away. Xen's hands helped me up and guided me to the bed. Xen and Daria were still talking when I dropped into sleep.

The dreams came in stealth, easing into the memory replay of the day's work to remind me that no amount of healing could wipe me clean of the sin of murder. The faces of the sick became the faces of the people Artoz had forced me to kill, an endless parade of prisoners whose only crime was to be different. Dead eyes and slack faces, the taste of several different races on my tongue, until all that was left was Habros. Larger than life, he filled my head. His kindness. His large, but gentle hands. The forgiveness in his eyes as I bent to take his life.

I was screaming as I came awake. The door burst open, my guards ready to protect me. I held up my hand to show them I was fine. "Just nightmares. I'm fine."

I padded across the room to the pitcher of water, spilling some onto my hands and washing my face. My nightshirt was soaked with sweat and my hands were shaking. I couldn't escape his face. If I closed my eyes, he was there. When I stared into the fire, he was there.

Tears burned tracks down my face while I sat staring at the hot coals. He had been my first, at least my first since knowing what I was, but he had been by no means my last. I hadn't counted. I didn't want to know.

My trembling hands should be coated in blood. I would never get clean of it.

CHAPTER 28
NIGHTMARE

The next days were largely filled with lather, rinse, and repeat, with a rest day sandwiched between each working day so that we didn't burn out, or in my case, die.

Each night, the dreams pulled me deeper, echoing all the way back to the day my father died. Faceless voices filled my head with accusations. Thanátou, they called me. Mörderin. Death-Bringer. Murderer.

Pulling myself out of yet another nightmare, I stumbled to the toilet and emptied my stomach. It was still dark outside my window, bands of rain washing away the grime. I knew I wouldn't be sleeping so I drew my robe on and wandered out to the sanctuary, looking for some kind of peace. I placated my guards and they followed only as far as the door into the sanctuary. I would be safe enough there.

There was only one candle on the altar, the tall, red pillar that stood in for the presence of Killi. I closed my eyes and willed my tornado of accusations into silence. Tears echoed the rain outside and in that moment, I hated myself.

It was a familiar feeling, though it had been a long time since it had been this deep. I had learned to like myself once I was out of my emo teenage years, but standing there, I wasn't sure I ever would again.

Some small sound pulled my attention away from the flame. I turned to see what it was and jumped. The church doors were wide open and beyond them, lightning flashed, lighting everything up for a second. Silhouetted against that light was a figure in black with a plain white face. At its feet was a body.

Anne Gothfried.

She laughed as I started toward them, then a knife came hurtling my way, catching me in the left shoulder. "Heal that, Hêalic."

I fell over backward, yelling in pain. By the time I got back to my feet, Anne was gone, and all that was left was the body-boy she'd brought to me.

I scrambled toward him, holding my shoulder. He was still alive, but barely so. He would bleed out before I could save him. His dress was cut down the center, neck to toes. His genitals lay in one slack hand and his stomach lay open, his guts spilling out onto the floor.

My shoulder was screaming and, apparently, so was I, though I didn't really remember opening my mouth. People began to fill the sanctuary and I felt Xen's alarm as they saw me.

The man dying at my side looked like he'd lived a rough life, his face stubbled and pock-marked. I jumped when hands pressed my shoulder, gasping as Daria's voice penetrated the fog that had settled over my brain.

"I said, leave him, Thána," Daria said. Her hand pressed against my wound. "You can't save him. He's gone."

I blinked and looked around me. Clergy and novices and Brothers stood around in night garments, while my full guard, some also in sleepwear, had formed a perimeter around me. "It was Anne," I whispered.

"So I gathered," Daria said dryly. "Can you tell me how bad it is?"

I tried to feel my way around the blade from the inside. "It's in pretty deep."

"Xen, help me get her up and back to her room," Daria requested, her hands moving to help me push off the floor.

Xen was instantly on my other side and between the two of them, they got me back to my bed.

The pain was starting to register, alongside the shock that Anne had attacked like that. Daria went to my bag to pull out supplies, sending a novice scurrying to get more bandages. "Okay, Thána, I'm going to pull out the knife. It's going to hurt."

I nodded and fisted my hands in the blanket under me while Daria's hand curled around the handle and yanked. I screamed, even as Daria was pressing a bandage down to try to contain the bleeding.

"Xen, get me that pain potion. Thána, listen. I'm going to have to stitch this up." She took the bottle Xen handed her and with a glance over her shoulder, put the opened neck up to my wound and added my blood to the potion. She put a thumb over the opening and shook it, murmuring a healing spell into it before she handed the bottle to Xen.

Xen helped me lift my head and tilted the bottle into my mouth, emptying the whole thing. The sharp taste was stronger than I'd expected, and I coughed a little after swallowing.

Everything got blurry after that, with sharp points of clarity as Daria's needle bit into my skin and when she moved me away from the edge of the bed. Voices filled the space of my room and then stilled, and I drifted and eventually slept.

I woke wrapped in the warm cocoon of Xen's presence beside me. Their body was spooned against mine, one arm draped over my hip. For a long moment, I just lay there, soaking up that warmth. My bladder became rather insistent at that point, so I shimmied to the edge of the bed and stood, aborting mid-stretch as I was reminded of the gaping hole in my shoulder.

Anne-fucking-Gothfried.

I shuffled to the toilet to relieve myself, then sort of sloppily, one-handed, splashed water on my face. The rain seemed to have stopped, though it was still dark and gray outside the window that looked down over a small courtyard. I was still there, looking out at the rain-washed cobblestone when Xen's arms slid around me from behind, their head coming to rest on my good shoulder.

"How is your shoulder?" Xen asked softly, pressing a kiss to my cheek.

"Sore," I responded, returning the kiss to their cheek. "But I've had worse. Did they find her?"

"No, though the Scealc and the Steallere's forces went out looking."

"She'll be back." I knew she would. Whatever her end game, it was going to involve me. Just my luck.

"She will," Xen agreed. "And she will find you surrounded by warriors to defend you. Five more have volunteered to be a part of your guard."

I sagged against them and sighed. "That will complicate our departure."

Xen pulled away and went to the door, speaking softly to someone before coming back to stoke the fire against the damp chill. "Come sit, I promised Daria I would see to it that you rested today."

I obliged, sitting in what had become my customary chair near the fire, drawing my feet up so that I could rest my head on one knee. "Speaking of our departure, where do we stand on the whole portal location issue?"

Xen sat opposite me, nodding a little. "I think I'm getting close. Katyk and I found the last place she remembered spending a night before she got to the city. From there, we head east and north."

"Toward the capitol?" I asked, looking up when there was a knock at the door, followed by Alina with a tray loaded with affe. "Thank you, Alina."

Xen poured the affe and handed me a cup before pouring their own.

"Do you need anything else, Hêalic? Breakfast perhaps?"

"No, Alina, this will do for now. My stomach is a bit queasy."

She nodded and returned to her post outside my door. I unfolded myself to sit more properly in the chair so I didn't spill my affe. "So, our next step is to head toward the capitol then?"

"From what I can tell, Katyk followed that road once she came to it, but the portal is likely well off the road."

I nodded. That would figure. Most portals were not easily accessible, particularly the ones that were formed naturally. Meerat's ring of portals was an anomaly. "What are we going to do about Anne?"

"My suggestion would be to catch her and arrest her," Xen said dryly. "And also that you leave that to the police."

"Hard to do when she's coming at me," I responded, sipping from my cup. "Or maybe that's what we need to do."

Xen frowned. "What?"

"Bait," I replied. "Give her a chance to hang herself."

"No, we are *not* doing that."

I shrugged, then winced as pain lanced through my shoulder. "Might be the only way."

There was another knock at the door and Alina apologized. "Sorry to interrupt, Hêalic. This just came for you." She handed me a folded piece of paper sealed in blood-red wax.

I glanced at Xen before I broke the seal and opened it. *"Did you like my present, Hêalic? I didn't get to finish the work for you, so I'll try again real soon,"* I read aloud before dropping the paper on the table. "Well, she's persistent. Thank you, Alina."

"She is insane," Alina countered, bowing slightly before leaving.

"Alina is correct, you know," Xen said.

"It has crossed my mind, yes." I yawned and took another sip of affe. "What are our plans for today?"

"This looks good," Xen said, setting their cup down.

"What? Just sitting here, sucking down caffeine by the fire?"

They smiled. "Exactly."

"I've never been very good at doing nothing."

"Perhaps Mader Jehan has a book you could borrow," Xen suggested with a small smile.

I sighed, consigned to the fact that there wasn't anything I could do at the moment but sit and heal.

It was late afternoon when word came that there had indeed been another murder, only this time it wasn't some low-rent body-boy. She was the teen daughter of a local noble family, found in her bed, her body mutilated.

The Steallere came to tell me, her face ashen. "I have never seen the like, Hêalic. She was cut open like a *wildêor*, all of her internal organs removed, and set beside her on the bed."

"Like Jack the Ripper," I murmured, wondering if that was where Anne was getting her inspiration.

"Who, Hêalic?"

I shook my head. "No one you would know of, Steallere." A thought occurred to me then. "Did she take any of the organs?"

If it was possible, the Steallere blanched even more. "The heart, Hêalic."

"Well, that isn't what I expected." I glanced at Daria, then realized she had no idea who Jack the Ripper was either. I was alone on my cultural island. "I anticipate she will send the heart either to you or to me in the next day or so."

"Why would she do that?" Daria asked, her face showing her horror.

"To gloat, probably," I answered. "It might be worthwhile to have some of your officers discreetly watching who comes and goes ... though I suspect she will pay some kid to make the actual delivery."

"Already done."

I grimaced and rubbed my injured shoulder. It had already healed a lot more than it would have without magic, but I could tell it was one of those injuries that would be with me for a long time. "Hierde Batorry?"

She ducked around the Steallere, who made her farewell with a nod as she withdrew. Hierde Batorry looked harried, and I hesitated to put more on her plate, but we needed to begin moving toward the capital if we were going to find the portal.

"Hierde, I would like you to lay out a plan for our journey toward Evalshare."

"Hêalic, is it wise to leave the security of the church before they apprehend this mad-woman?"

"Perhaps not, but there are sick and dying people who need us, and that is my calling. I would like to visit all of the villages and towns along the way."

She didn't look convinced, but she nodded. "As you wish, Hêalic. When would you like to leave?"

"After the holy day. I need some recovery time."

Batorry and all the others who had followed the Steallere to my room left, closing the door behind them.

"Have you lost your mind?" Daria asked. "We will be even more vulnerable out on the road."

"Do you want to get home? We can't do that sitting here." I stood and paced, starting to feel pent up from sitting all day.

"I do, but I'd prefer all three of us get there alive."

"I am open to suggestions," I said. "Have a premonition lately?"

Daria sighed. "You know it doesn't work like that."

I turned, squinting. "Maybe it does and you just don't know it?"

"What?" Daria looked like she was getting annoyed with me.

"Well, I've been thinking a lot about how I keep doing things I'm not supposed to be able to because no one ever taught me I couldn't. Have you ever tried to specifically induce a premonition?"

CHAPTER 29
OUT OF THE CITY

"How would I even attempt to do that?" Daria asked, frowning at me.

I paced to the door and back, thinking about how I had connected to the Hêalics before me. I glanced out the window to see what time it was. Judging by the angle of the sun, we had a few hours before the Brothers would be readying the sanctuary for the night service.

"Come with me," I said, snagging Daria's hand and drawing her to the door.

She came reluctantly and huffed as I drew her toward the sanctuary, my guard in tow and Xen following behind. I led Daria to stand in front of the altar, then sit on the carpet. I sat opposite her, our knees touching and holding hands.

"Okay, we're going to start just by meditating, like we did that night I had that vision of the Hêalic, so close your eyes."

I waited to make sure she did before closing my own. Xen slid into place behind me, their hands on my shoulders, our minds slipping together with ease. I reached mentally for Daria, inviting her in as deep as my connection with Xen would allow.

Inhaling, I drew my attention down to my center before I slowly opened myself to the presence that filled the space, reveling in the warmth and comfort it offered. I felt Daria open the same way, felt her gasp at the beauty of it.

"Now, picture Anne," I said softly, doing it myself as well. "Focus on Anne. Only Anne."

I had my own image of the woman in my head, with her white mask and top hat and blood on her hands. Daria's hands tightened just a bit in mine. I took that as a signal that she was ready to continue. "Now, reach for the feeling you get when you're having a premonition."

There was a wave of frustration before she pushed it aside and tried to do as I asked. For a long time, nothing happened. Xen's hands tightened on my shoulders, alerting me to the impending presence of others. I was ready to call an end to the attempt when Daria stiffened, her body suddenly rigid. Xen moved to stand behind her in case she needed support.

As suddenly as it came over her, it was done, and Daria was left gasping for air just as the three Brothers tasked with the setup for the evening's service entered the sanctuary.

I nodded in greeting to them as Xen helped Daria up, and together we withdrew back to my room.

Daria paced while Xen and I sat and waited.

"I've never ... not like that," Daria said, rubbing her forehead. "But it was way more coherent than normal. I could follow most of it."

"Okay, so what did you see?" I asked.

She stopped pacing and turned to me, her eyes wide. "I saw you die." Daria collapsed into a chair. "Only, I know that you teach Kota how to use his magic, so you can't die here."

"What about Anne?" I pressed.

"She'll kill at least three more," Daria said, blinking back tears. "Two men and another woman."

"Did you see where for any of them? Maybe we can tip off the Steallere and intercept her."

Daria closed her eyes and seemed to think about it. "The next man will be tonight, near a tavern called the Barking Hund on the western end of Pakour Street."

"Okay." I got up and crossed to my desk, ripping paper out of my journal and scribbling down a note for the Steallere, which I took to the door. "Jalkin, please have this note sent to the Steallere, with urgency."

With any luck, it would save a life. Possibly mine.

I insisted on returning to work the next day even though it meant favoring my left arm considerably. If I wasn't going to be there for long, I wanted to make the most of it.

Daria and I were visiting another sickhouse when Hierde Batorry came to me, a box in hand. A sick feeling filled my stomach as it became clear that the box was for me. There was also a folded piece of paper sealed with red wax. I stood and moved away from the patient that I had been working with before I took the note first.

"Nice try, Hêalic, but I'm not so easily deterred. The body-boy was a real beauty and he had a wicked tongue. Now, you have it. Have a heart too. See you soon."

I took the box from Batorry with a good amount of trepidation, opening it slowly. My stomach flipped as I caught a glimpse of what was inside. A human tongue lay there, with a human heart on top of it. Blood coated the sides of the box and the smell of it was choking. I gave it back to Batorry and turned away from it to try to regain my composure.

"What of the Steallere and her officers?" I asked once I'd gotten past the urge to vomit.

"They were too late, Hêalic. They gave chase, but she escaped in the shadows."

Because, of course she did.

I needed to draw her away from the city. If she was following me into the countryside, maybe it would save lives. "Hierde, how are our travel plans coming?"

"We will be ready to leave soon, Hêalic."

"I'd like to leave tomorrow. Can we make that happen?"

"And what of this killer?"

"I think she will follow us, Hierde, and should be easier to trap where there are fewer people."

She nodded acceptance. "I will have this delivered to the Steallere and see to it our plans are in place for departure tomorrow."

"Thank you."

Daria and I finished what we could and headed back to get ourselves ready to leave the city.

Xen met me at my door, concern on their face. "You are stressed."

I kissed their cheek before opening the door. "Anne sent me a present today."

"Is that why we are leaving tomorrow?" Xen asked.

I nodded and set about getting my personal things packed into the backpack that had come with us from Meerat. There was already a trunk by the bed filled with my Hêalic clothing. "I'm hoping she will follow us, and we can prevent more killing."

"What of Daria's premonition?"

"She tells me that particular gift isn't always clear."

"But she is also never wrong," Xen countered. They took my hands and drew me to sit on the bed. "I am worried for you."

I offered Xen a soft smile. "I have no plans to die. And you heard Daria; she says I'm going to teach Kota how to heal, so even if I do die, I'll come right back. Okay?"

Xen raised an eyebrow at me. "Getting a little full of yourself, Hêalic?"

I chuckled and brushed my lips over their cheek. "Maybe. Are you packed up?"

Xen watched me get up and go back to my packing. "I am."

"Good." I put my journal into the backpack and looked around the room. "I think that's everything."

"How is your shoulder?" Xen asked as I went to the door to send someone to bring us supper.

"Sore, but better."

We ate a quiet dinner and turned in early. Unsurprisingly, my dreams were filled with blood and Anne. I woke in the small hours and knew I wouldn't sleep more, so I sent for some affe and stoked the fire.

Daria found me there an hour or so later, staring into the bright red coals and dancing flames. "Is there enough affe in that pot to share?"

I blinked and looked up at her. "Probably another cup or so. You're up early."

"Couldn't sleep." She sat and assumed a similar posture, slouched, staring at the fire while cradling her affe. "Nightmares."

"Want to talk about it?" I asked.

She didn't answer right away, just sipped her affe and watched the flames dance. "So much death," she finally said without looking up.

"Who?"

She blinked and glanced at me. "You, Habros, Xen, Mom. But I can't tell if it's real or my subconscious fear playing with my head."

At least one of those was real, but I didn't say that. I straightened up in my seat and poured the last of the affe into my cup. "I never asked, but …"

"A cliff," Daria responded. "You and Anne both."

"Note to self: avoid cliffs," I said in an attempt to lighten the mood.

She rolled her eyes at me but did sort of smile. "When do we leave?"

"At first light. There's a small village we should reach by noon, and we should be back on the road a few hours later. Hopefully to reach the next town by sundown."

"I best go get dressed in warmer clothes then. I'll see you out front in a little while."

I got up once she was gone and set about getting dressed myself. I opted for the simplest of my clothes: warm, woolen trousers with a plain black shirt under a vest. I didn't bother with the sash or cinch. I would put those on as we neared the village.

I was ready when the knock on my door heralded the arrival of my escort and the novices who would load my things onto the wagon. I grabbed my coat, because the morning was a bit nippy, and followed Hierde Batorry out into the cold.

Xen was already there, directing traffic as the supplies were loaded. Daria appeared a moment later and in under an hour we were off on the northbound road with the sun stretching its fingers across the skies to the east.

The ride was uneventful and we pulled off the road just as we could see a road that turned off toward the village. I walked off the stiffness that had accumulated while Xen and one of the novices who had come along, prepared food.

"Hêalic, may I?"

I looked up to find Sister Katyk approaching with my red sash and cinch. "I didn't see you were with us," I said.

She ducked her head, blushing slightly. "I figured I could be of help. Here," she said lifting my arms so that she could wrap the sash around my waist. Once my cinch was on my arm, we walked back to join the others for lunch.

All too soon, we once again mounted up and headed for the village. There was very little fanfare when we arrived. The village was too small to have much in the way of local officials. We were met by their visiting priestess and shown around, eventually setting up near the small town building that served as a meeting house to receive the people. Daria and I treated those with ailments or illnesses, passing out medicines more than miraculous healing.

"Hêalic, if we leave in the next hour, we should make it to the next town by nightfall," Hierde Batorry said as I stood and stretched.

I nodded acceptance and glanced around. Daria was showing a father of a young boy how to mix up something to ease the boy's cough. Xen was playing with two young kids, kicking a ball around and laughing. The rest of my entourage was readying our mounts and wagon or standing around guarding me.

It seemed strange how easily I had accepted the presence of added guards, even though I had thought that two was overkill. Now, I had four acting as bodyguards at all times and another five near enough to intervene if necessary.

I crossed to my mount, rubbing a hand along his flank, and patting his nose when he nuzzled my shoulder. Xen, flushed and breathing hard, slipped up beside me, leading their mount.

"You looked like you were having fun," I said.

"I was. I haven't played like that in a long while. Are we ready to ride?"

I looked up and around. We seemed to have everyone. "Yes, let's go."

I got a boost from one of my guards and slid into the saddle. My butt protested, but I gathered my reins and ignored my butt. It beat walking.

CHAPTER 30
BLOODY

We returned to the main northbound road and continued on, finding ourselves slowly swallowed by trees as the road entered a forest. Xen pointed to a cluster of bushes that formed a cave of sorts. "That was the spot Katyk spent a night."

"Well, at least we're going in the right direction."

The setting sun was just a strip of orange glimpsed through the trees, which made the road rather dark well before we found our turn, and by the time we had found the town it was fully dark. I let Hierde Batorry manage getting us settled while I walked off the numb butt. I was tired but strangely wired and restless.

Xen, Daria, and I were escorted to the Healdor's home, where we were served a dinner of thick stew and bread. I nibbled but didn't really eat, taking my bread to the door and watching the others moving about and getting settled for the night.

"Hêalic, do you need anything?" Alina asked.

I shook my head. "Thank you, Alina. I'm fine, just restless."

I glanced at Daria, who shrugged in answer to my unasked question. Whatever was bugging me, it wasn't something she had seen. "I think I'll turn in."

I climbed the stairs to my borrowed bedroom with two guards following. Two more stood outside the front door of the home and would all night. I stripped and left my clothes across the end of the bed. I hoped that the exhaustion would override the unnamed anxiety and let me sleep.

I tossed and turned for a while before falling into swirling dreams filled with chaos and dead bodies. Daylight woke me and I found my way to the toilet to relieve myself before I got dressed and went downstairs in search of affe and breakfast.

Not even halfway down the stairs, a blood-curdling scream brought me up short. I turned and went back up the stairs and down the hallway, shooing my guards out of my way, only to have one of them grab my shoulder and pull me back before we reached the source of the screams. The smell of blood filled the hallway as we neared the bedroom door.

My guards pushed me back so they could enter the room first. My steps faltered as I crossed the threshold and took in the scene. Two twin beds sat side by side. Blood covered the linens and the floor between the beds. It was splashed onto the light paneling and even the window sill was pooled with blood.

The Healdor's two sons lay amidst the gore, their throats slashed, their stomachs cut open, and their genitals completely removed. Their internal organs were scattered, but it didn't look like all of them were present.

I turned away just as Xen and Daria appeared. Xen drew me down the hall. My hands shook as I raised them to wipe at the tears leaking from my eyes. "She did this," I said. "I think I'm going to be sick."

I raced for the toilet and fell to my knees, retching until my sides hurt. Xen helped me up and handed me a cup of water to rinse my mouth. I knew that the scene in that bedroom had been set for maximum shock, and I knew that it wasn't over yet. There would be a note and I was pretty sure there would be a gift made of whatever organs she'd taken with her.

"Let's get out of their way," Xen said softly, guiding me toward the stairs. They sat me in the parlor on an armchair. I couldn't think past the blood. I saw it cover everything: the table, the other chair, Xen's face. It was all blood. "Thána?"

I blinked and realized Xen had been talking to me and was holding a cup of affe out to me. "Sorry, I …" I took the cup and nodded my thanks. "What were you saying?"

They smiled. "It wasn't important."

"No, really. Tell me."

"Hierde Batorry says that they found a note stuck to the front door with a bloody knife."

"Did anyone read it?"

Xen shook their head and held out a hand.

Daria put the folded paper in Xen's hand. I hadn't even realized Daria was there. The red wax seal was sticky with blood. I set my cup of affe on the table beside me and took the note.

"Hêalic, no whores here to wrap up pretty for you, so I hope you like the sweet young things I carved up. They went down easy. I took my time with them. Took

their manhood for good measure. They weren't going to need it. I'll leave them somewhere for you to find."

I dropped the paper onto the table in favor of my affe. "She's not going to stop." I sipped at my cup, my brain running in circles, trying to figure out what it was Anne wanted and why she had fixated on me like this.

Xen rubbed my shoulder for comfort.

"What I want to know is, how did she get into this house with all of these guards," Daria said.

"I would also like to know that, L'âcedôm Daria," Hierde Batorry stated from the doorway.

"Come, Hierde," I beckoned.

"Hêalic, I have examined all ways into and out of the house and can not determine how she made entry. There are no signs of force, and no one saw anything."

I nodded. I'd already determined that Anne was good at the clandestine part of what she did. That had already been in evidence. "She broke pattern as well," I said. "She's never hit a male inside their home, and never a man who wasn't working, or anyone this young."

"I will double the guards around you," Batorry said.

"No," I responded. "It isn't me she's targeting. She wants something from me."

"What do you suggest we do then?" Daria asked.

"I don't know. Anywhere we stay will be a target. We need to protect the people." I rubbed my hands over my face. "I can't stay here. Someone give my condolences to the Healdor and come find me at the church when we're ready to leave."

I stood, gathered my guards, and headed out into the chill of the morning. The ground was wet, indicating it had rained through the night. My footsteps squelched in the mud as I moved through the quiet streets. It wouldn't be quiet for long. Soon, the news of the horrific murders would spread, and the town would be abuzz.

The church was small, but it suited my need to be alone. Well, as alone as I ever was anymore. Alina swept through the church before she let me enter. Two of my guards took their place outside the door while Alina and Jalkin followed me inside. Jalkin stopped at the first row of pews. Alina stopped midway up the aisle, and I proceeded from there to the altar.

The image of those two boys filled my head. I could still taste the copper tang on the air in that room. I had never in my life seen anything even remotely like that, not for real. I'd seen movie gore, of course, but it had never been my favorite genre.

I stood before the altar and tried to clear my mind of the image. I thought about Mom and Kota, Cambious even, but the flashes still came.

Tears burned my eyes and I let them fall. The sorrow that washed through me was alive. It doubled me over and dropped me to my knees.

For a long time, I wallowed in the grief. When the door behind me opened, I straightened up, using my sleeve to wipe my face of my tears. There were soft voices, then footsteps approached.

"Hêalic, I was sent to get you."

I shifted and stood. "Are we ready to go?"

The young novice nodded. "Yes, Hêalic. The Healdor has asked for a blessing on the town before we leave."

Giving a blessing was the last thing I wanted to do, but I owed the grieving mother at least that much. I followed her out of the church, blinking at the size of the crowd that had gathered. Daria and Xen stood near the back, watching.

I cleared my throat and lifted my right hand. The crowd settled, most going to their knees. "Oh, Sacred Mother Killi," I said, my voice echoing in the stillness. "Look down upon these people and let your mercy ease their suffering. Send Sunna and Mônna to light their way and bring bounty to them." I made the customary three circles with my upraised hand and bowed my head.

A murmur swept through the crowd and as they rose, they made a path for me and my guards to pass through. No one spoke as we mounted up and started out. In fact, the only sound for nearly an hour was the sound of hooves on the packed dirt road.

That was when Hierde Batorry called us to a halt. I pulled my attention out from my internal guilt to see why. In the middle of the road, dangling on the end of a rope, was the bloody male member of one of the boys.

I blanched and averted my eyes. "Someone cut that down," I snarled, tugging on the reins to move around the offensive display and put it behind me.

But Anne wasn't done yet. We came to a place where the road split around a large boulder where Anne had artfully arranged several organs inside a blood-splashed circle, with the other boy's penis pointing east and holding down another folded and sealed piece of paper.

One of my guards brought it to me. I snapped the seal and scanned the words.

"Have you figured it out yet, Hêalic? Or should I start calling you Draca? We both know you're more like me than you would ever admit out loud. We both know what it feels like to kill."

Draca. Killer. Somehow, she had discovered me.

I closed my eyes and crumpled the paper in my fist. I should have seen it. She'd been flirting, but not in a romantic way. No, she'd been tempting me to join her killing spree.

"You okay?" Xen asked, grabbing my reins to keep me from galloping off.

"No. I am decidedly not okay," I growled. "Those boys are dead because of me. Because I haven't gotten us out of here yet."

"No, those boys are dead because Anne Gothfried killed them," Xen countered.

"I want this to be over, Xen. I just want to go home."

Xen cupped a hand to my cheek. "I know. We will soon."

I wanted to argue that they couldn't know that, or that if we couldn't find the portal we'd never get out. I didn't though. I let them think they were comforting me and tucked my guilt and despair deeper into the back of my head.

Turning to Hierde Batorry, I sighed and gestured at the horrid display. "Can we get someone to take the parts back to the family?"

"Aye, Hêalic, I will see to it."

"Good. How far are we from our next stop?"

"A few hours, Hêalic. Where the road forks, we take the east fork to a small city named Lefelscore."

"She's probably already there," I mused aloud to Xen, who nodded in agreement.

"We will not stay inside the city tonight, Hierde. We will make camp a ways away, and we will have our perimeter well-guarded."

"Is that wise, Hêalic?" she asked.

"I will not be the reason that someone else's son or daughter is found dead in the early hours of the morning. We will ride into the city after breakfast."

"Do you really think that will keep her from killing someone else?" Daria asked from beside me.

"Probably not." I took my reins back from Xen and urged my mount forward. "Let's get camped up before dark."

The only sounds for the next few miles were the sounds of hooves on the packed dirt and the jingling of various harnesses and other gear. Xen and I rode side by side behind Hierde Batorry and two of my guards.

I withdrew into the connection between us, letting it cocoon me from the mundane plodding and swirling accusations, even if they were only in my head. I was still hiding there when we came to a stop.

Bringing myself back inside my own body, I inhaled deeply and looked around. There was a small stream that rumbled over stones with a swift current that raced away from us, widening as it went. On the other side of the stream was a large meadow backed by a tree line.

Hierde Batorry was barking orders to get us across the stream and set up in the meadow. I was still getting my bearings on the meadow side of the stream when Katyk rode up beside me, her eyes sparkling.

"We're close," she said breathlessly. "I remember the stream. There's a waterfall …" She pointed downstream. "The waterfall is the first thing I remember finding after the portal."

"Good." I glanced at Xen, then looked for Hierde Batorry. "Hierde, I'm taking two guards and scouting downstream. Get us set up. We'll be back within the hour."

She started to say something, but I turned my mount and started riding, giving my two closest guards nothing to do but follow. Xen and Katyk joined me, and we followed the stream until we came to the place where it tumbled over a drop.

Dismounting, I handed my reins to Alina and walked to the edge.

Xen grabbed my shoulder. "Careful. Remember what Daria said."

I nodded, rubbing a hand across theirs. "I remember, but Anne isn't here."

Below us, the water fell maybe twenty feet, into what appeared to be a deep pool of navy blue.

"I climbed up over there." Katyk pointed to the other side of the stream. "Found the road and just picked a direction in desperation."

"Good thing you went south," I said. "We might never have found each other."

"I'd probably be dead," Katyk replied.

"Okay, at least we know where to start looking," I went back to my mount and struggled up.

We turned to go back to the camp. "And how are we to go about this looking?" Xen asked as we rode, glancing aside at our escorts.

"I haven't figured that part out yet," I admitted. "Let's start by getting through tonight without anyone dying. Tomorrow, we'll think about that."

CHAPTER 31
SNEAKING OUT

By the time we got back to the meadow, there was a white canvas tent erected and the smell of a campfire welcomed us. Two novices were preparing food by the fire and guards were pacing out a perimeter with the stream on one side and the treeline on the other.

I itched with wanting to deploy wards to keep us safe but didn't dare. I found Daria sitting inside the tent on a small stool, repacking our backpacks with supplies. She looked up as I came in and I saw it in her eyes; she'd seen the portal. Taking another stool, I raised an eyebrow at her and she nodded.

"I know how to get there."

"Tonight, once everyone's asleep?" I asked softly.

"If we can slip past your guardians," Daria replied, glancing around conspiratorially.

"I think we can manage that," I said, thinking of the spell I'd used at the Mauno Kort to keep Cambious and I hidden from the prowling manticore. "At least enough to get us to the tree line.

"What about Anne?" Xen asked from beside me.

I shook my head. "We can't let her get in our way."

"She'll find us," Daria stated. "Maybe the fall kills her, even if you survive."

"Hêalic, food is ready," a novice said from the entrance to the tent.

We got up together and went out to where the food was being served, the women gathering in groups of three or four, talking and laughing together as they ate.

We three took our food and found a spot to sit. I wasn't surprised when Katyk joined us.

"I assume you are plotting your escape," she said as she sat cross-legged in the grass. "How can I help?"

I looked her over, taking in the novice uniform and cloak, and an idea started to form. "Can you get us some clothes?"

There was a twinkle in her eye that I hadn't seen in a while. She nodded. "Yeah, I could do that."

It wasn't a solid plan, but it was a start. If we could use the novice clothes and the hiding spell to get past the perimeter, we could get a good head start on the search party that would inevitably be sent out to find us.

As the sun set, we sat around the fire chatting and watching the stars. I was nervous and tried to hide it behind exhaustion, withdrawing early to crawl into bed. Daria and Xen came shortly after, and I listened to the sounds of my entourage slowly settling in for the night.

When it had been quiet for some time, I sat up, checking on those around me and spotting Katyk, picking her way across the tent toward me, her arms filled with black cloth. Across from me, Daria was already stripping free of her clothes.

We changed as silently as we could, exchanging what we had been wearing for novice uniforms and cloaks. I frowned a little as I realized Katyk was changing clothes as well but realized her intent. She would take my place in the cot, hopefully giving us a little more time.

Daria pulled the big backpack onto her shoulders and lifted the hood of her cloak. Xen lifted the smaller backpack and nodded. I paused, looking Katyk in the eye. I didn't dare speak but I wanted her to know that I was grateful for her. She smiled and crawled into my cot, pulling the blanket up over her head. Together Xen, Daria, and I moved toward the tent door, stepping out into the silver light of a nearly full moon.

Drawing them close, I lifted my hands to my face and whispered, "*Krývo.*"

The air around us shimmered a little and we were hidden from casual observation. It wasn't foolproof but should deflect anyone not looking directly at us. Still, we tried our best to be stealthy as we picked our way toward the perimeter.

Pausing beside the wagon, we watched the pattern the guards made as they patrolled, timing it out to determine the best time to run for the trees. Xen counted under their breath and touched my back when it was time to go.

I'd never been much of a runner, but I sprinted toward the cover of the trees with everything I had. Once safely under the cover of the thick foliage, I stopped to catch my breath, leaning against a tree.

Daria was doing the same, while Xen was watching the patrols to ensure no one had seen us.

"Which way?" I asked Daria in a hushed whisper.

Daria pointed and we headed in that direction, toward where I knew the cliffs awaited us. My hand toyed with the kelcimite that I had put in my pocket as I followed Daria and kept my eyes open for Anne. Daria was never wrong when she had a premonition, so I knew that before we made it to the portal, Anne would appear and there would be a fight.

The trees began to thin as we neared the cliff. The waterfall was somewhere to our right, but we were far enough away that there was only a vague hint of noise. I peered over the drop to the craggy rocks below, some thirty feet down. That was a fall that would be deadly.

Daria joined me, pointing southward. "The portal is just there. See the big boulders?"

I could see what she was pointing at, at the foot of the next ridge. "So, how do we get down from here?" I asked, turning to look for a path or trail that would lead us to the bottom of the canyon. "We could try to portal maybe." It had been months since I'd last tried while hoping we could find the way home without Katyk. "Give me a hit of xýpna and I should be fine."

Daria clearly didn't like that idea. "Thána—"

"It's a long drop," I said, cutting her off. "And I'd rather not die if I can't hold the portal open."

She dug into a pocket and handed me the pouch.

I took half of what remained and dropped it onto my tongue, closing my eyes as the feeling of it rippled through me. I had forgotten the rush of it.

Xen stepped in behind me, their hands immediately finding my waist. Daria's hand was on my shoulder, and I picked a spot on the canyon floor that I could see fairly clearly.

Suddenly, Xen's hands left my waist, and their presence was jerked back away from me. Daria and I whirled to find Anne with a blade against Xen's throat.

"I do hope you were planning to jump," Anne said. Her hands were bloody and there was a smear of blood across the white of her featureless mask.

Xen's face was neutral, but I could sense the fear.

"I came by to give you a gift, but you were gone."

"What do you want?" I asked, my eyes on Xen and not Anne.

"I think you know," Anne said. She shifted so that she had a free hand to pull off the mask, tossing it away. "Do they know?"

"Know what?" Daria asked.

"Yes," I replied. "They know that I've killed."

"Shame, I was hoping it would shock them. Still, if they could see the stain I see on your soul, maybe they would be shocked anyway. How many?"

I frowned, taking one careful step away from the edge, my hands up and held away from my body. "How many what, Anne?"

She rolled her eyes and hitched the knife up closer to Xen's neck. "You know what I'm asking."

"I can't answer you. I was drugged for a lot of it. My memory is spotty at best. At least five. How about you?"

Her grin was predatory. "Much more than that. Do you know what a rush it was to find myself in this backward place, knowing what I do? I'd killed before I came here, liked to emulate other killers ... ah, but here? With no fingerprint or DNA tech? *Heaven.*"

"Is that why you chose Jack the Ripper to emulate here?"

"Well, only partially. The whores were good fun, but the girls ... they were all my own."

"So, I repeat my question, Anne: what is it you want from me?"

She tilted her head to one side, her eyes sliding from me to Daria and back again. "I just want to see you kill. Her."

Daria's hand squeezed my arm, but I ignored her. "I'm not going to do that, Anne."

Xen was preparing to do something. I could sense the intent, if not exactly what they were planning.

"I will kill this odd one then."

"No, you won't." I was at least partially prepared when Xen shifted their weight and stomped down on Anne's foot, bending at the same time so that Anne went off balance and Xen could step away.

I threw myself at Anne and we crashed back into the undergrowth of the forest. We tumbled to a stop, and both scrambled to get up. She had lost the knife in the chaos, but there was murder in her eyes. We circled warily. Daria and Xen were coming toward us, but I put them out of my mind and charged Anne.

We traded a few blows, but Anne was stronger than I was and knew how to throw a punch. When her fist hit my cheek, I went down, stunned.

I was holding my cheek, hot as blood rushed to the impact spot, when Xen barreled past me and into Anne.

Anne was laughing when she got clear of Xen and stood. "Oh, you're feisty. I like that. Your little pet has balls, Draca."

"Actually," Xen said, landing a kick to Anne's stomach. "I don't."

Anne fell back against a tree, the smile gone from her face. It was replaced by anger. Her voice bounced off the nearby trees, something like a growl and a howl of pain mixed together.

I backpedaled as she came at me, and Xen was close behind her. If we could trap Anne between us, we might have a chance.

Daria tried to grab Anne but was pushed away, falling back on her ass. "Come on, Draca. You know you want to kill."

"I don't, Anne. I *never* wanted to kill."

"Sure you do. You're thinking about how to kill me right now."

I landed a punch to her face, but I thought it hurt my hand more than her face. She ducked my next punch and landed one into my stomach, grabbing a fistful of hair and dragging me toward the cliff's edge. Digging my feet in against the rocky terrain, I tried to slow our movement and get back some control.

Xen's voice called Anne's name and the knife Anne had lost came hurtling at us. Anne yanked me closer, making the knife slam into my right shoulder. "Maybe you'll have matching scars," Anne growled into my ear. "Or maybe I'll just pitch us both over the edge."

We were close enough that it would take less than nothing to send us over, and it brought Daria and Xen up short. I glanced behind us, then back at Xen and Daria, slipping one hand into my pocket and pulling out the kelcimite.

Daria made a tiny nod to let me know she understood, and I pushed back against Anne enough to turn us so I could see the ground below. "You first," I growled, pushing with both feet to shove us over the cliff.

Startled, Anne lost her grip on me and hurtled toward the rocks below; I cast as fast as I could, hoping to get the portal open before I joined her. The hole opened but wasn't fully steady as I fell through it, hoping Daria and Xen had followed.

I crashed to the ground and rolled away from the spot, stopping when my body found a tree. The kelcimite fell from my hand as the breath was knocked out of me.

Xen and Daria had a better landing and I felt hands against my bleeding shoulder. My whole body was screaming obscenities at me, but my first concern was Anne. Xen pushed me back down when I tried to get up to look. "We need to control this bleeding."

"Where's Anne?"

"Dead, I'm sure," Daria responded. "Lie still." Her hands pulled the blade free and I screamed as my clavicle snapped where it had been impacted by the knife. "Xen, bandages."

Working quickly, Daria pressed down on the wound to stop the bleeding. "How bad is it?"

I blinked at her, trying to assess that myself. "The clavicle is broken, but just barely. The rest of me just hurts."

Daria raised bloodied hands and tipped the last of our pain potion into my mouth, murmuring a spell of bone healing. Xen followed that with a canteen filled with cool water. I nodded my thanks and they let me sit up.

"We need to make sure Anne is dead," I said, offering my left arm to Xen to be helped up.

"Why?" Daria responded. "Leave her to her fate. Let's go find the portal."

I cradled my right arm against my stomach, every minor movement causing searing pain in my shoulder. "I'm going to need a sling."

Daria pulled her backpack closer and rummaged around until she pulled out one of my bright red sashes, which she fashioned quickly into a sling that would support my arm while also binding it to my body. "Better?"

I nodded, glancing around, half expecting Anne to come charging at us. The skies were starting to show signs of daylight, streaks of black and navy blue punctuated with lighter gray and blue, and just at the edge of the horizon was the first hint of yellow.

"We need to move," Xen said. "They will know we are missing soon."

"This way," Daria responded, setting off through the trees.

My knees were a bit rubbery, whether from my impact with the earth or the tree, or due to the pain and blood loss, I couldn't be sure. Xen slipped up on my left side, putting an arm around my waist for support.

The ground here was damp and the canopy of trees nearly blocked any glimpse of the sky, leaving us walking a gloomy path covered in wet leaves and grass. I zoned out a little, trusting Xen to keep me moving and Daria to get us to the portal, but after maybe an hour, I had to call a halt when I saw a fallen tree I could sit on.

My shoulder was bleeding and screaming, and I was starting to think that my left knee, which was the first to hit the ground, was damaged in some way. It was swollen enough that my pants were tight around it and warm to the touch. Every step I took felt like my knee was filled with broken glass.

"Just let me rest a minute," I said, wiping sweat from my forehead.

The forest was quiet, and it felt peaceful, but Daria was on edge, pacing around us.

"Are you okay?" I asked.

She nodded. "Just anxious to get home now that we're this close."

I fumbled to try to get the xýpna powder out of my right pocket before Xen stepped in to help.

CHAPTER 32
PORTAL JUMPING

I opened the pouch and poured the last of the xýpna onto my tongue, swallowing it with a mouthful of water from the canteen. It probably wasn't wise so close on the heels of the previous dose, but it served to get me up and moving again.

Xen helped me up and supported me as we continued walking. My injuries made progress slow and my mind kept wandering. The trees began thinning and random rocks began to fill the spaces between them. Those rocks grew bigger and where the trees ended, we stopped, staring up.

"Oh, this should be fun," I muttered. "I assume the portal is somewhere up there?"

"Yep," Daria affirmed, looking around for the best way up. "From what I saw, there's a spot up there where the rock is level and that's where the portal is."

I exhaled and touched my shoulder. There was nothing to be done but to climb. We all moved around, looking for the likeliest path, or at least one that wasn't impossible with a bum knee and a dead right arm.

"This looks doable," I said as I found a dirt path between two boulders that dead-ended in a smaller boulder, one I could conceivably climb.

Daria went first, easily setting her foot to a crack and using it to leverage herself up before she leaned down to offer me her hand. I mimicked her foot placement as Xen moved in behind me for support. My left hand found Daria's and I pushed off the ground. My knee wasn't happy, but I made it up onto the boulder and stepped around Daria so Xen could follow.

The next couple of steps were easier, using various smaller rocks to get us up to the next big one. I leaned against one rock and lifted my left foot off the ground to take some of the pressure off that knee while Daria scouted our next move.

"How is that knee?" Xen asked.

"Not great," I responded. I turned to look for Daria and a rock went sailing past my cheek. If I hadn't moved, it would have hit me. I turned and scooted back to try to see where it had come from.

Xen gasped and pulled me back as Anne came into view. She was dragging one leg and even at a distance, I could tell it was broken. Her face was covered in cuts and bruises. When she grinned at me, I could see her teeth were covered with blood.

"Not done yet," Anne growled.

"I don't know; you look pretty done to me."

Xen stepped between me and Anne, ready to fight. From behind me, I felt Daria's spell building and ducked, taking Xen down with me. The *prostatévo* pushed Anne back and gave us space to climb the next boulder. Daria held the spell long enough for Xen to help me up to the largely flat top of the rock. We were close, I could feel it.

"The way I see it, you have two choices," Daria said to Anne. "Leave now and get help for your injuries; you might live. Or take one more step, and I will put you out of your misery."

"Baby sister's got bite," Anne said, wiping the blood off her face. "Do you have it in you?"

Daria's face was like stone as she lifted her hands. "Thána isn't the only one who has killed in this family."

Anne limped toward us, and Daria's hands moved while she whispered words I couldn't hear. When Daria's right hand clenched into a fist, Anne stopped cold, grabbing her throat.

Daria turned her fist, and Anne went down, dead. "And stay down this time," Daria growled.

"Daria, I—"

She held up her hand and shook her head. "Not now. Let's just get out of here."

We worked our way up until we reached the small plateau where the portal was set into the rock face. Through the portal, I could see that it was dark in Meerat, and nothing was moving. Limping closer, I scanned the part of the portal park that I could see, expecting a military presence of some kind.

"It looks quiet," Daria said, leaning in to look around. "No lights anywhere."

"What is that about?" I asked.

"One way to find out," Daria responded, stepping through.

Xen helped me follow her. There was an eerie quiet that hung over the city. The grass under my feet was charred and it seemed to disintegrate as I stepped. "Maybe they destroyed each other," I said, my voice seeming loud in the stillness.

"Maybe," Daria agreed. "There's a hospital not far from here. If the walk from the portal to Spítia is as long as I remember, you won't make it on that knee."

"Not sure I'm going to make it to the hospital," I countered.

"Stay here with Xen. I'll be back soon with what you need." Daria shrugged out of the backpack and set off jogging into the darkness.

"I need to sit," I told Xen, looking around us for some convenient place that wasn't the ground.

"There are picnic tables over there," Xen said, pointing between two portals.

They supported me as I limped to the nearest one, then ran back for Daria's backpack. Xen leaned the backpack against the table and took their backpack off as well.

"You're quiet," I said, reaching a hand to Xen's.

They nodded, letting me pull them closer. "This was my home. To see it so is painful."

From where we sat, we could see the ruined hulk of buildings and the evidence of the war that was raging here when we'd last stood on this ground. I'd never been very attached to a place, probably due to the moving around that came with being a foster kid. I'd never been in any one place long enough to form attachments.

I tried to imagine how I would feel if I walked through a door into Rochester, NY, and found it like this. It would just be something else to survive, I thought. But the melancholy rolling off Xen was incredible. We sat in silence then, our hands clasped loosely while we waited for Daria.

Xen leaned their head on my uninjured shoulder and whispered in my ear, "You are my home now."

I had never been someone's home. I didn't know that I even knew what that meant until I had met Xen. I pressed a kiss to their cheek. "And you are mine."

The sadness seemed to abate some. I looked up when I heard a noise, turning to find Daria with a tote and what I took to be a pair of crutches. She put the tote on the picnic table. Her hands were shaking.

"What happened?" I asked her.

She shook her head. "Nothing. Absolutely nothing. The whole place is empty but for the dead. I got what I could." She leaned the crutches beside the backpack and started pulling supplies out of the tote. "For starters, let's get a look at that shoulder. Xen?" She handed something to Xen, which turned out to be a flashlight.

Xen turned it on and held it so Daria could see to untie the sash that bound my arm to my stomach. I winced as she pulled it free from the bandages that had soaked with blood and dried.

"Sorry," Daria murmured. "This is going to sting." She had to pry the bandages free from the scab, ripping the wound open again and I yelled, grabbing the table. Daria ripped my shirt so she could get a better view of the wound, then grabbed a bottle and squeezed a liquid out onto the wound. It fizzed and bubbled like peroxide, cleaning away whatever might have gotten into the wound.

Daria took the flashlight back and leaned in. "How is that clavicle doing?"

"It's fine. Hurts like hell, but it should heal on its own."

"Okay, I'm going to give you something for the pain, and I'm going to numb this whole area so I can stitch this up."

"You know how to do stitches?" I asked, a little surprised. Then I remembered her stitching up the man Anne had tried to kill. Obviously, the pain was affecting my ability to think. "How do you know that?"

"I trained as a combat medic when I was still considering joining the army. I was already doing magical medicines, so I figured it was a good fit."

She held up a syringe filled with liquid that had a vaguely pink hue in the light of the flashlight, which she handed back to Xen. The smell of astringent lifted into the air and Daria swiped something cold and wet over my exposed arm before plunging the needle into me.

Daria set the needle aside and opened a small jar. "Numbing agent," she said as she scooped out a good amount of ointment and began to rub it into and around the wound.

I hissed a little as her fingers touched sensitive skin, but the numbness came on quickly, and in only moments I couldn't feel a thing.

Xen moved closer with the flashlight so Daria could see to sew up my wound. Five stitches later, she rebandaged it with fresh gauze, winding it under my arm and up over my shoulder and taping it down. She unfolded a piece of cream-colored cloth which she used to make a sling and binding so that my arm was supported. "Can you get your leg up onto the bench?"

Xen helped me shift so that my right leg was under the table and my left could stretch out. Daria dug a pair of scissors out of the tote, which she used to cut my pants from the ankle up to just above my knee. In the bright beam of the flashlight, I could see the bruising and swelling were pretty spectacular.

Daria laid one hand on each side of the knee, closing her eyes as she felt around the injury. "That's a lot of swelling. How are you even walking?" Daria asked.

"Painfully," I said, half joking. "Honestly, I think I'm just running on adrenaline and xýpna right now."

"Okay, I'm going to try to reduce some of this swelling, and then we'll brace it." She went back into the tote for another jar, opening it. The smell was pungent and strong, getting even stronger when she put a glob of the lotion on her palm before rubbing her palms together as she murmured a spell. The lotion was warm when it touched my skin and got warmer as she rubbed it in.

I imagined I could feel the swelling go down but recognized it as wishful thinking. Daria pulled something black out of the tote and, as she brought it closer, I recognized it as some kind of brace. It looked complicated.

"Xen, come down to this end and lift her foot so I can get this on." Daria pulled open several straps, then slid the brace under my knee. It fit snuggly, holding my knee in place with metal stays and those heavy-duty straps. "How does that feel?" Daria asked when she was done.

"At the moment? I feel nothing," I replied.

She chuckled. "That would be the pain meds I gave you. How about you try standing?" Daria helped me get up, grabbing one of the crutches and putting it in my left hand. I steadied myself with the crutch before I tested my weight on that leg.

"It's doable."

"Good." Daria gathered up all of the supplies back into the tote before she hefted her backpack onto her back. "Let's get out of this ghost town then."

"I hope you know which portal is the right one because they all look the same to me," I said as we made our way back inside the ring of portals.

"I do," Daria said, smiling.

She seemed more at ease than I remembered ever seeing her.

It took me a few steps to get the hang of walking with the crutch, but by the time we reached the portal, I was doing okay. Or something close to okay. We stood staring at the portal for a long moment, and it felt like a lifetime since the last time I had stood there, sending Mom and Kota away from the war.

With a deep breath, I went through to the Spítia side, moving out of the way for Xen and Daria to follow. It was late afternoon; the sun slanted against the rocks, casting deep shadows. It would be a push to get to the lake before dark, especially with my gimpy leg.

Okay, more than a push. At the two-hour mark, I was done. The pain meds had worn off and my entire body hurt. My shoulder throbbed and my knee would no longer take my weight at all. We found a clearing and Daria and Xen set about making us a camp for the night.

I eased myself to the ground near the center of the clearing, taking the wood Xen brought me to build a fire. Once Daria had deployed wards to protect us, she came to me with another filled syringe. Once she'd shot me full of the good drugs, she sat and delved into the tote, coming out with three packages that resembled MREs. She held one between her hands for a few moments, then passed it to me.

It was hot and when I tore it open, I smelled something akin to spaghetti sauce. Xen passed me a fork. I had no idea where it came from, but my stomach was telling me in very specific terms to get that food into me pronto. The taste wasn't great, but the pasta and chicken-like meat placated my grumbling stomach just the same.

We passed around a canteen and then I laid down, though I wasn't sure I'd sleep because I could not find a comfortable position. Daria moved the small backpack under my bad leg to elevate it, and that didn't help matters. I wasn't in pain, exactly, due to the drugs, but I was stiff, and I knew that come the morning that stiffness would be worse.

CHAPTER 33
COMING HOME

My waking thought was wondering if that phone Mom had given me was still with us. I thought it had at least made it out of the prison camp, but once we'd ended up in Gavelscore, I hadn't even thought about it again.

I groaned as I tried to sit up and Xen was instantly awake and alert. "You okay?" They helped me get up so that I was sitting, but that just let me know that my back and ass were very, very sore.

"I feel like I got hit by a truck," I responded. "Hand me the small backpack?"

Xen reached for it and put it beside me. I shifted uncomfortably and pulled it onto my lap, diving in, and rummaging around until my hand felt something that could be the phone. I pulled it out and turned it on.

After a moment, it pinged, and its face lit up. I punched in Merry's code and held it to my ear. Merry's voice was sleepy and low when she answered. I found myself smiling for no reason other than hearing her voice.

"Merry, it's Thána. Mom gave me her phone to call—"

Merry yelled my mother's name with excitement and I could hear her footsteps on the wood floor followed by Merry's voice saying my name.

Then Mom's voice filled my ear. "Thána? Is it really you?"

"The one and only," I responded. "We came through the portal last night."

"Daria?"

"Yes, and Xen."

"Put Daria on the phone."

I held the phone out to Daria who was awake and sitting. My hands were shaking, and my eyes were filled with tears. I think maybe I had expected I wouldn't ever see her again, never letting myself think beyond the moment so that the fear wouldn't overwhelm me.

Daria got to her feet and moved away from us, dismissing the wards. Her voice changed and softened, so I assumed she was talking to Kota. I looked away to give her some privacy and asked Xen to help me up so I could relieve my very insistent bladder. I needed help with that too because it was impossible to squat one-legged.

"Oh, my." Xen's hand ghosted over my lower back and onto my ass, and I gasped.

"Let me guess, bruises all over?" I asked once I had finished and Xen had helped me back up.

"Yes, they are impressive."

"The knee took the brunt of the fall, but my ass hit the tree pretty damn hard. I'm not surprised."

"You should have Daria look at that before we go."

"I think Daria has seen enough of my body parts. It will be fine. I'll be sore for a few days, but I'll be fine."

Daria was ready to move on by the time we got back. "Mom is heading out now; she'll be at the parking location by nightfall."

I slipped my left hand into my pocket and pulled out the kelcimite. "I can probably jump us to the lake, but that parking spot was a full day's hike when I had two good knees."

"Are you sure you want to try it?" Xen asked.

I nodded. "Yeah. Just untie this so I can move my hand."

Xen untied the binding, though I kept the sling. It hurt, but I somehow knew that the pain meds Daria had brought along would interfere with casting this particular spell. Xen stabilized me, their hands on my waist and Daria put her hand on my arm. I cast, the hole shaking and dimming before stabilizing. We stepped through, right beside the permanent fire ring where Mom and I had shared two meals.

I was sweating profusely and went down almost as soon as the portal closed. The pain crashing through my body was intense and I didn't argue when Daria dosed me up again. I drifted in and out while Xen went scavenging for food and Daria checked my shoulder.

"This looks better." She rebandaged it and re-tied the sling and binding. "But you should not have tried that."

"It's going to take us days if we don't," I argued. "I can barely walk."

She moved to remove the brace from my knee, dragging the tote bag closer and pulling out the lotion she'd used before.

"Swelling is down, but it looks nasty still." She rubbed the lotion in and again, the warmth felt nice. She redid the brace and moved to sit beside me. "I've been thinking about that."

"About what, the swelling?" I asked, frowning at her.

"No, the portal." Daria looked thoughtful. "You know when you were helping me have a premonition on purpose?"

"Yeah, what about it?"

"I think I might be able to do the same thing with the portal. It was like you pushed me past what I knew into what I never knew I *could* be."

"Okay, so you think that if you can get out of your head enough to forget that it shouldn't be possible, it *might* be?"

"Something like that. It can't hurt to try."

Xen returned then, their shirt lifted to cup a bunch of berries and a couple of the apple-looking fruits that Merry grew in her yard. Between the fruit and the last of the assorted junk food Daria had found in vending machines in the hospital, we had a decent lunch, filling if not the healthiest.

When we were done and getting up to go, I handed the kelcimite to Daria. "Xen, support her like you do me. Daria wants to try again."

They got into position. Beside Daria, I closed my eyes and reached inside, trying to connect to the light the way I had in Alnescore. When I felt it starting to fill me, I touched Daria's arm. "Close your eyes and center. Breathe in deeply, and let it out slowly. When you breathe in again, open yourself up to the light."

Everything felt serene, and I wasn't sure if it was the light, the drugs, or the idea that we were going home, but I suppose it didn't matter which it was. "When you're ready, raise your hands and aim for the tree line." It would be a short jump, but that would be okay for her first try.

It took a few attempts, and she was starting to get frustrated, which wouldn't help make it work.

"Fill yourself up with the light," I said softly. "Don't think, just do it."

I felt it hit, the power of it streaming through her hands into the stone, and then there it was. The portal wasn't huge, but it was enough, and I stepped through with Xen and Daria behind me.

Daria dropped her arms and the portal collapsed. She leaned against a tree and panted for a second. "That is harder than it looks."

"You did great!" I declared, proud. The pain pounding through my body was not as loud, and I wanted to sink into that light to try to heal my various injuries, but I knew I needed to conserve energy at this point if I was going to make it down the mountain.

The trail Mom and I had climbed was well-defined in this part of the woods, though I knew in many places the grass and undergrowth tended to encroach on the path. I pointed into the trees. "There's a place not too far ahead that has a fallen tree I can sit and rest on and just past that, you should get a clear view to jump from, if you're up to try again."

We walked in silence until we came to the tree. I sat gingerly because my ass was not happy with the idea of sitting, but my knee really didn't want me standing either. When sitting hurt more than moving, I got up and nodded. "Let's go."

The place I was thinking about was further away than I remembered, but we reached it and I pointed downhill to a clearing. Daria and Xen took their positions, and I let Daria focus on her own, leaning on my crutch so I could keep the weight off my knee. It took a while, but this time, Daria's casting was stronger and more stable.

We passed through and set to walking again, at least until I couldn't anymore. I found a rock I could sit on, and Daria gave me our last dose of the pain meds. I was probably causing myself more damage by numbing away the pain and walking on the injury, but I had to get down off that mountain somehow, and neither Xen nor Daria could carry me.

Our pace was slow and getting slower. I was drenched in sweat and leaning heavily on the crutch when Daria stopped us. "How far are we from the parking area?"

I shook my head. "I'm not sure? A few miles at least?"

She paced around us, thinking. "Tell me if I am remembering it correctly? It is a grassy area at the end of the road, big enough for maybe five cars? Circled around with fir trees and those purple bushes?"

"I don't remember purple bushes, but the rest of it sounds right; why?"

Her hand went into the tote and came out with something I couldn't see. "Because you can't keep hobbling along on that thing." She raised her hand to her nose and sniffed hard. Her eyes widened and she pinched her nose closed for a couple of seconds.

"What did you just do?" I asked, glancing at Xen, who shrugged.

"It's a mild stimulant. Not as addictive as xýpna, but it should give me enough punch to get us there." She shook her hands, then pulled out the kelcimite.

Xen grabbed her waist and this time the portal slammed open immediately.

I ducked my head through the opening. "Nice," I said, hobbling through with them behind me. She'd landed us right at the end of the pavement. "And now we wait."

I let Xen help me find a spot where I could sit and lay back against the slope of the hill. I had forgotten how exhausting it was to be injured. I closed my eyes and reached out to pull the light into my body, focusing on my shoulder and knee. The pain eased slowly, enough to let me drift close to sleep.

It was hours later that the sound of an engine pulled me out of my dozing. Beside me both Daria and Xen were asleep. I pushed myself up with my left hand just as Mom pulled in, driving what looked like an SUV. I touched Daria's hand to wake her.

Mom ran at us, her arms open wide. Daria dove into the embrace while Xen helped me get up. I hobbled a few steps, but Mom saw me struggling and came to me, pressing kisses onto both cheeks while tears streamed down hers. "You did it. You brought our family back together."

"I had help," I said.

She hugged me gently before pulling back to look me over. "What have you done to yourself?"

"Long story," I replied. "Right now, I just want a hot shower and an actual bed."

"What she needs is a doctor to help with that clavicle and that knee," Daria countered. "And then a hot shower and a bed."

"It's a lot better, Daria," I said. "I can heal it the rest of the way now that we have a long car ride ahead and I don't have to worry about wearing myself out."

Mom supported me to the vehicle while Daria and Xen took care of our things, securing them in the back. In a few minutes, we were headed down the mountain and back to civilization.

I sat in the back, my injured leg on Xen's lap, letting the flow of conversation move around me. I wasn't entirely positive I could heal myself completely, but I was determined to try. I set my left hand against my right shoulder and centered myself, opening myself up to the light. Warmth flooded through me, pooling under my hand. The bone shifted minutely, realigning and starting to mend the pieces together. My skin was warm, but in a comforting way, the edges of the wound coming together and healing over. I shifted my attention then to my knee and repeated the process.

It wasn't instant healing, like when I had healed Batorry the day of my ordination, but it was healing. A couple of sessions over the long drive would have me good as new before we got to Merry's house.

We stopped in the first sizeable town to get a hotel room for the night. Xen got me settled while Mom and Daria went to get us food. I eased the brace off to get a look at the bruising. It was so much better than it had been.

"Your new skills have served you well, it seems," Xen said. "How is the pain?"

"Better. Doesn't seem like I can do miracles on myself, but it's better."

"I am glad."

They were quiet, but discomfort rumbled through them. "Are you okay?"

Xen nodded. "I will be. The images of Meerat will stay with me for a long time."

"I'm sorry you had to see it like that."

The door opened and Mom came in with bags of food, followed by Daria with drinks. It was a quiet but pleasant evening, and we were up and out of the hotel early the next day for the rest of the drive.

Kota fairly exploded out of the house when we pulled in and Daria jumped out of the vehicle to grab him into a hug, laughing and crying. Mom came to help me out of the car while Xen carried our things into the house. When we were alone, the look on Mom's face told me that she knew what I had done to Habros. Daria had told her.

"Mom, please don't hate me."

She looked up, tears in her eyes. "I don't, Thána. I could never hate you."

"I didn't want to. He would have killed her." I was crying now and wanted the earth to swallow me.

Her hand slipped into my left hand and squeezed. "You did the right thing, Thána. You brought us back together."

My chest was tight, and the memory of that moment was pouring into my conscious brain, filling me with the same fear and guilt. Habros had looked at me with forgiveness. It was something I could not forgive.

I limped away from the car, still favoring that knee, pushing the memory down to focus on the joy that rolled off of Kota and Daria. I stepped inside the familiar home and breathed in deeply.

The place smelled of food cooking and candles burning. It smelled like Merry's house … it smelled a lot like home.

EPILOGUE

"I brought you a new batch of books from that find in Darrage," Mom said, pulling my attention from the computer where I was attempting to record all of my notes from my various journals into something resembling order. She set a box down on my desk and pulled one out. "You should find this one particularly useful."

She handed me a thick book that looked older than many of the others we had collected in the last year. The black leather cover was cracked and dry and the pages inside were thin, almost see-through, but the text was tidy and neat. I could even read most of it. My mastery of my mother's native tongue was incomplete but growing.

"*The Book of Blood*?" I paged through it, my eyes widening as I realized it was one of the texts on blood witches thought to be lost forever.

It was said to be the most thorough accounting of the specific magic of the blood witch. I stopped on a page that gave instructions for collecting blood to be used in remedies for swifter healing, complete with warnings to guard the secrets because, technically, that magic was seen as suspect at a minimum, and in some places completely illegal.

"This is great, Mom, thanks."

I glanced over to check on my students. Ciara was working on a potion recipe that Daria had given her, while Kota was reading a book on basic magic. It had taken a while to get him to agree to training, his young head still filled with a good amount of fear of showing he had gifts.

We'd been back in Spítia for almost two years and in that time, I had recovered from my injuries, reconnected with the family that at one time I hadn't even known existed, and had even taken a trip to visit Cambious at the portal to the house in California.

Together, Cambious and I went back to the house to see what was left. The place was in shambles. Walls were cracked from the force of the magic used to break the wards; shattered glass littered the floors from broken windows and mirrors. The power had been shut off due to lack of payment.

We boarded up windows and cleaned the mess before heading back to Spítia.

Daria went to work at a pharmacy, moving her and Kota into an apartment not far from the home where Mom, Xen, and I set up house. We turned the largest bedroom into an office/library, and it was there that I took on the task of teaching Kota and Ciara what I had learned about our gifts.

It had only been a few months since an archeological dig at the site of a former hospital had uncovered a treasure trove of books on all manner of lost subjects, including the largest collection of blood witch tomes, spell books, and philosophical texts to be found in the modern era.

One of my cousins, though I still wasn't sure exactly how we were related, was the director on the dig and had been forwarding me books as they found them. I'd spent a lot of my time with them, and they really helped clarify some of what I'd discovered on my own.

What I had yet to find was any understanding of the gold light I'd discovered, and how that connected me to healers from across the worlds, from many traditions.

I picked up another of the books in the box. I was startled when I opened it to find it was written in the Old English adjacent language of Gavelscore. I sat back in my chair and turned to the beginning of the book.

"Find something?" Mom asked, leaning over my shoulder.

"Maybe." I scanned through the first few pages, getting an idea that the history of Spítia, the myths, and magic, were about to be rewritten. "This posits that all magic stems from a single source," I said, my eyes tracing the words. "A place called Navita?"

Mom shook her head. "Never heard of it."

"Apparently, it is a place of infinite wonder, peopled by gods and giants who take great pleasure in the act of creation."

Mom chuckled a little and put a hand on my shoulder. "Sounds like another creation myth to me. I'll leave you to it and go get dinner started."

I nodded, but my attention was squarely on the book in front of me, fascinated. Navita. Was that the place I'd seen in my visions? Was that how I found myself remembering the lives of Hêalics and other healers?

Was it the source of that golden light that had allowed me to perform miracles?

There was only one way to find out. I would need to go and find it.

GLOSSARY OF TERMS

A

Ablissé: Drink
Acsung: Questions
Adelfí: Sister
Aderfia: Brothers
Agan: Have
Andyttan: Thank you
Anihst: Last
Ánoixe: Open
Ánoixe kleídoma aímatos: Open this lock by my blood
Apokalýpto: Reveal
Arstafa: Kindness
Âwihte: Only

B

Bâm: Am
Bêo: Be
Bluathexe: Blood Witch
Brôder: Brother

C

Canne: Can
Cniht: Boy
Commen: Come
Corse: Curse
Cran: Make

D

Dances: Thank
Dimiourgió: Break
Dohter: Daughter
Dreng: Soldier

E

Ekleípo: Disappear (used with ward stones)
Éla: Come
Elefthérosi: Release
Êow: You
Ete: Eat
Evlogim Patoras: Second Father

F

Forgefan: Forgive
Foreglêaw: Careful
Frig: Friend
Ftiáxe mia porta: Open a door

G

Gêbed: hearty

H

Haêg: Hag
Hêalic: Healer

Hîe: It
Hiexě: Witch
Hir: Her
Hierde: Guardian

I

Irémise: Quiet

K

Kapnastís: Disease eater
Kleidóste sto aíma mou: Lock to my blood
Kommer: Come
Kontá: Close
Kravu: Cow
Krývo: Hide

L

L'âce: Doctor
L'âcedôm: Apothecary/Pharmacist
Lean: Said
Lôc: Look

M

Mader: Mother
Mágissa: witch
Makrá vlépinta: Ability of a blood witch to see past/future
Mastery: Title for a woman
Menen: May
Mete: Food
Mikros: Little one
Min: My
Môdwelig: Gifted
Mörderin: Killer

N

Nân: None

O

Obersut: Colonel

P

Páfsi: Pause
Paidí: Child
Patoras: Father
Pigaíno: Go
Prostatévo: Protect
Pucian dôcincel de oon: Nosy bastard

R

Rím: May
Rostian: Cook

S

Sâcerd: Sacred
Sê: He
Sêo: See
Seke: Seek
Scead: Shelter
Slúga: Servant
Steallere: Constable
Sweostor: Sister
Sýnchysi: Confusion

T

Teíchos: Wall
Thanátou: Death bringer, angel of death
Thráfsi: Break

Til: Good
Trêowd: Faith

U

Uppan: Upon

W

Werk: Work
Wîcan: Give/Gave
Wytch: Witch
Wot: What

X

Xekleídoma: Unlock

Y

Yperaspízo: Defend
Ýpnos: Sleep

ABOUT THE AUTHOR

An avid reader since kindergarten, Natalie had read her way through the children's and young adult section of the library by nine years old, and during the summer spent most of her days scouring the library for something new to read. When the Librarian handed her The Hobbit the summer before she turned ten, thinking it would be enough to keep the girl out of the library for a few days at least, a whole new world opened up. Natalie devoured the tome and returned it to the library the very next day, wanting to know that there was more like it.

With a love of vampires and other paranormal types, Natalie infuses her fiction with magic and mythological beings, and explores the sometimes vanishing line between good and evil. Natalie makes her home in Walnut Creek, California with her two cats, Morrigan and Freya, and occasionally a stray cat she calls Artemis.

To learn more about Natalie J. Case and discover more Next Chapter authors, visit our website at www.nextchapter.pub.

Printed in Great Britain
by Amazon

36561387R10355